ANGLE OF REPOSE

Wallace Stegner (1909–1993) was the author of, among other novels, *Remembering Laughter*, 1937; *The Big Rock Candy Mountain*, 1943; *Joe Hill*, 1950; *All the Little Live Things*, 1967 (Commonwealth Club Gold Medal); *A Shooting Star*, 1961; *Angle of Repose*, 1971 (Pulitzer Prize); *The Spectator Bird*, 1976 (National Book Award, 1977); *Recapitulation*, 1979; and *Crossing to Safety*, 1987. His nonfiction includes *Beyond the Hundredth Meridian*, 1954; *Wolf Willow*, 1963; *The Sound of Mountain Water* (essays), 1969; *The Uneasy Chair: A Biography of Bernard DeVoto*, 1974; and *Where the Bluebird Sings to the Lemonade Springs: Living and Writing in the West* (1992). Three of his short stories have won O. Henry Prizes, and in 1980 he received the Robert Kirsch Award from the *Los Angeles Times* for his lifetime literary achievements. His *Collected Stories* was published in 1990.

Jackson J. Benson was born and raised in San Francisco, graduated from Stanford, and received his M.A. from San Francisco State University and his Ph.D. from the University of Southern California. From 1966 to 1997 he served as professor of English and comparative literature at San Diego State University, where he taught twentieth-century American literature. Twice a fellow of the National Endowment of the Humanities, he has published eleven books on modern American literature. Among them is the authorized biography *The True Adventures of John Steinbeck, Writer* (1984), which won the PEN West USA award for nonfiction. His latest work was the authorized biography *Wallace Stegner: His Life and Work* (1996), which won the David Woolley and Beatrice Cannon Evans Biography Award.

ANGLE OF REPOSE

WALLACE STEGNER

WITH AN INTRODUCTION BY
JACKSON J. BENSON

PENGUIN BOOKS

PENGUIN BOOKS

Published by the Penguin Group

Penguin Group (USA) Inc., 375 Hudson Street, New York, New York 10014, U.S.A.
Penguin Books Ltd, 80 Strand, London WC2R 0RL, England
Penguin Books Australia Ltd, 250 Camberwell Road, Camberwell, Victoria 3124, Australia
Penguin Books Canada Ltd, 10 Alcorn Avenue, Toronto, Ontario, Canada M4V 3B2
Penguin Books India (P) Ltd, 11 Community Centre, Panchsheel Park, New Delhi – 110 017, India
Penguin Group (NZ), cnr Airborne and Rosedale Roads, Albany, Auckland 1310, New Zealand
Penguin Books (South Africa) (Pty) Ltd, 24 Sturdee Avenue,
Rosebank, Johannesburg 2196, South Africa

Penguin Books Ltd, Registered Offices: 80 Strand, London WC2R 0RL, England

First published in the United States of America by
Doubleday & Company, Inc., 1971
Published by arrangement with Doubleday, a division of Random House, Inc.
Published in Penguin Books 1992
This edition with an introduction by Jackson J. Benson
published in Penguin Books 2000

10

PUBLISHER'S NOTE
This is a work of fiction. Names, characters, places, and incidents either
are the product of the author's imagination or are used fictitiously, and any
resemblance to actual persons, living or dead, business establishments,
events, or locales is entirely coincidental.

LIBRARY OF CONGRESS CATALOGING-IN-PUBLICATION DATA
Stegner, Wallace Earle, 1909–
Angle of repose / Wallace Stegner ; with an introduction by Jackson J. Benson.
p.   cm.—(Penguin twentieth-century classics)
Includes bibliographical references.
ISBN 0 14 11.8547 3
1. Historians—Fiction.   2. Physically handicapped—Fiction.   3. Married
people—Fiction.   4. Grandparents—Fiction.   5. Aged—Fiction.   6. California—
Fiction.   I. Title.   II. Series.
PS3537.T316A82000b
813'.52—dc21   00–062402

Printed in the United States of America
Set in Fairfield LH Light

For my son, Page.

My thanks to J.M. and her sister for the loan of their ancestors. Though I have used many details of their lives and characters, I have not hesitated to warp both personalities and events to fictional needs. This is a novel which utilizes selected facts from their real lives. It is in no sense a family history.

CONTENTS

ix

INTRODUCTION

Angle of Repose is Wallace Stegner's masterpiece, the crown jewel in a multifaceted writing career. From the time he finished his Ph.D. in 1935 to his death in 1993, he published some fifty-eight short stories, a dozen novels, two histories, two biographies, a memoir-history, and five collections of essays. He was given numerous awards for his writings, including the Pulitzer Prize for *Angle of Repose,* the National Book Award for *The Spectator Bird,* and the Lifetime Achievement Award by the *Los Angeles Times.*

From the early 1950s, he became as well known for his environmental activities and writings as for his fiction. However, it was the writing of novels that was closest to his heart, and it was as a novelist that he wanted to be remembered. In a recent poll of readers of the *San Francisco Chronicle* voting on the best one hundred novels written about the West, *Angle of Repose* was listed number one. Often mentioned by critics as one of the most important American novels of the twentieth century, it alone should ensure Stegner's reputation. (In a *Chronicle* poll of best nonfiction books, his John Wesley Powell biography, *Beyond the Hundredth Meridian,* was listed number two.)

Wallace Stegner's life almost spanned the twentieth century, from the last homestead frontier in Saskatchewan to the information age in Silicon Valley, from horse and plow to mouse and computer. The major strands of his career—his love of the land, his concern for history, his advocacy of cooperation and antagonism toward rugged individualism—and his dedication to writing can be clearly seen as products of his early life. He was born in Iowa in 1909, the younger of two sons, but the family soon moved to North Dakota, to Washington State, and then to Eastend, Saskatchewan. His father, George Stegner, was what his son later called a "boomer," a man looking to find a fortune in the West and who, not finding it in one place, went to another. His mother was what Wallace called a "nester." She wanted nothing more than a home of her own in which to raise a family.

Wallace's accounts of his growing up make it clear that a dichotomy developed early in his consciousness between the proud, tough, intolerant rugged individualism represented by his father and the friendly, tolerant, neighborly tendencies toward caring and cooperation represented by his mother. And as we can see throughout his writing, Wallace's sympathies lay with his mother and the values she represented. Although like her husband his mother never went beyond the eighth grade in school, she loved books and passed on a love of reading to her son.

Together his parents would seem to have been the archetypal western couple. In later years, as a writer, Wallace saw them as representing the exploiter, on the one hand, and the civilizer on the other. Although they are quite different in character and background, we can see Oliver and Susan Ward in their roles in *Angle of Repose* as dim reflections of Stegner's parents. (Certainly Wallace's deep love and respect for his mother contributed to his ability to create such complex and sympathetic women characters as Susan Burling Ward.) When asked by an interviewer if the life of Mary Hallock Foote, the model for the heroine of *Angle of Repose,* had reminded him of the life of Elsa Mason, the mother in the semiautobiographical *The Big Rock Candy Mountain,* Stegner said,

> Not consciously. It never occurred to me that there was any relation between *Angle of Repose* and *Big Rock Candy Mountain* till after I had finished writing it. Then I saw that there were all kinds of connections. There was the wandering husband and the nesting woman, and the whole business reproduced in many ways in somewhat more cultivated terms and in different places what *The Big Rock Candy Mountain* was about. It's perfectly clear that if every writer is born to write one story, that's my story.

Two periods in his growing up had a major influence on forming his outlook and interests. The first was his six years in childhood spent in the village of Eastend and every summer on the homestead farm in Saskatchewan near the Montana border. After the first year, his older brother, Cecil, got a summer job at the grocery store in town, and so

Wallace was alone with his parents, out on the hot prairie, living in a tarpaper shack. It was a place with "searing wind, scorching sky, tormented and heat-warped light, and not a tree." Yet, amazingly enough considering such a barren and hostile environment, he could still look back on a childhood not of suffering and boredom, but of "wild freedom, a closeness to earth and weather, a familiarity with both tame and wild animals." His summers on the homestead and winters in the frontier village during his most impressionable years marked him, as he has said, "a westerner for life." And they would eventually produce a writer determined to represent the western experience as it really was, and the relationship of its people to the land as it was, is, and should be.

Aside from the empty flatness of its 320 acres, the homestead's most prominent feature was its dryness—there was a source of water, but just barely. The Stegners' crop was wheat, which required summer rain to grow, and in four years out of five they were dusted out. During a sixth summer there was so much rain that the wheat was ruined by rust. This period in Eastend was the only time in Wallace's life that his family was together in their own home, and so having to leave Saskatchewan was for him a trauma he never forgot. Family, home, and community are valued throughout his work, and while Susan, in *Angle of Repose*, is on a much higher social level than Wallace's mother, she too is a nester who tries to create community wherever she must move in response to her husband's search. Wallace's sense of the importance of water in the West, which had been drilled into him so forcefully, eventually led him to write about John Wesley Powell—one of the few to understand the basic dryness of the West (contradicting the propaganda of the developers who promised a "new Eden"). And still later he would use as the central episode in *Angle of Repose* Oliver Ward's attempt to transport water to the near desert of southern Idaho.

His experience in Saskatchewan also led him to a consuming interest in history. *Angle of Repose*, which is about the life and thoughts of a historian and the history of his family that he uncovers, would seem to have been written as much by a historian as by a novelist, and Wallace was both. As a child, so often alone, Wallace became an omnivorous reader, reading whatever came his way, even devouring the Eaton Catalog. But neither his education in Canada, which tried to make a European of him, nor his own reading in geography or history had any relevance to the place where he lived: "Living in the Cypress Hills, I did not even know I lived there, and hadn't the faintest notion of who had lived there before me." The sense of his own lack of history grew in him as he matured, leading him to recognize the importance of knowing the history of one's own family and region. Later, in addition to writing histories and the memoir-history *Wolf Willow*, which came out of an investigation of his own roots, he would do extensive historical research as a basis for several of his novels, including, of course, *Angle of Repose*.

The second important period in Wallace's life would bring further support to his passion for history and to his interest in his roots. After leaving Saskatchewan, the family eventually ended up in Salt Lake City, where Wallace spent his teenage years. "The Mormons who built it and lived in it," he has written, "had a strong sense of family and community, something the Stegners and the people they had lived among were notably short of." Wallace never became a Mormon, but almost all of his friends were members of the church, and they brought him into its social activities. And despite the dislocations caused by his father and a dysfunctional family, he came to believe that he could belong, that he was not an outsider. In later years he considered Salt Lake his hometown, and he chronicled his returning home and rediscovering his youth in the novel *Recapitulation*. He was attracted not only by the Mormon emphasis on community and cooperation, but also by the Mormon devotion to the study of history and genealogy. He was so impressed by his experiences in Mormon culture that he later wrote his two histories, *Mormon Country* and *The Gathering of Zion*, about the development of that culture.

A sense of community and a sense of family unity were not, however, things that he had in his own immediate, personal life during those years. His father, giving up wheat farming (with which he had planned to make a fortune because of the demand during World War I), turned to bootlegging and running a "blind pig," an illegal saloon, in their home. The family moved some twenty times during Wallace's high school and college years in order to escape discovery by the police. This rootlessness, his mother's isolation, and the fact that he could not bring friends to his own home further reinforced his sense of the importance of family and community. We can see this background reflected in *Angle of Repose*'s concerns: for the effects of cultural transplantation, for the questions of what holds a family together and what drives it apart, and for having roots, in both family and place, and knowing about them.

Wallace worked his way not only through college but through graduate school as well. He had a fellowship at Iowa that kept him in school after graduating from the University of Utah. After he wrote three short stories for his M.A., his adviser, Norman Foerster, told him he should switch from creative writing and get his doctorate in an academic subject if he wanted to get a job teaching. Foerster further suggested that he investigate the writings of the western naturalist-geologist Clarence Dutton, a figure out of the late nineteenth century and early twentieth who had been largely overlooked.

By taking up this challenge, Stegner committed himself to what turned out to be a lifelong interest in nature writing. He would also develop a strong, continuing interest in that group of surveyors and geological explorers who, after the Civil War, mapped and described the West. (They included not only John Wesley Powell but Arthur De Wint Foote, the real-life counterpart of Oliver Ward in *Angle of Repose*.) And his dissertation topic led him to become an expert on the literature and history of the realistic-naturalistic period (from the Civil War to World War I)—the period that he concentrates on in the historical sections of *Angle of Repose*. Stegner would go on to teach the literature of that period—the works of Mark Twain, Henry James, Hamlin Garland, Edith Wharton, Stephen Crane, and Theodore Dreiser—throughout most of his teaching career.

He not only taught the standard fare; he spent much time in the library reading the magazines and journals of the period in order to get a better feeling for the times and to discover new material for an anthology he was editing. While doing so, he discovered Mary Hallock Foote, the real-life counterpart of Helen Burling Ward in *Angle of Repose*. In the novel Ward's true love is the most famous magazine editor of the period, Thomas Hudson, and as a result of his research, Stegner was quite familiar with the careers of nineteenth-century editors and with their magazines. Ward is seen in the novel as an illustrator and story writer (as in life was Foote), and her work, like that of her counterpart, is much in demand by the periodicals of her day.

Wallace had no plans to become a professor, but it was the Depression, and there was hardly any place for him besides school. Nor did he have any notion of becoming a writer. After writing his dissertation about Dutton, getting his doctorate, and coming back to Utah to teach, he happened to see an advertisement for a novelette competition with a prize of $2,500. He was making only $1,800 a year as a professor, and his wife, Mary, was pregnant. Almost with the desperation that leads us to bet on the lottery, he sat down and wrote a story he had heard from his wife about some of her distant relatives. The result was *Remembering Laughter*, which, much to the Stegners' surprise and delight, won the Little Brown Novelette Prize. At that point, for the first time, he thought that writing as a career might be possible.

However, two undistinguished novels followed, and he was having more success with his short stories than his novels. It wasn't until he wrote the novel that told the story of his growing up, *The Big Rock Candy Mountain* (1943), that he had another success with the longer form. Leaving Harvard, where he had been teaching writing as a Briggs-Copeland Fellow, he went to Stanford after World War II and began what became one of the most renowned creative writing programs in the country. He continued, however, to have more success with the short story (winning several O. Henry Memorial Short Story Awards) and with his nonfiction (including the Powell biography—a Pulitzer finalist) than with the novel. He was discouraged, and thought that he might give up writing novels altogether.

A breakthrough did not come until late in his career, when he wrote *All the Little Live Things* (1967). It was with this novel that he at last found his voice by inventing Joe Allston, the narrator, who is witty, sometimes wise, and often cantankerous. Allston in *All the Little Live Things* would become the pattern for the narrators in Stegner's last novels and the forerunner in several ways of Lyman Ward in *Angle of Repose*. Allston was in part a product of Stegner's own reaction—now that he himself had grown older—to the late 1960s and its radicalism, and to the blossoming of the "now" generation with its antihistoricism, intolerance, and hypocrisies. Sometimes this voice is light, even flippant, but always there is an undertone of skepticism.

With Allston, for the first time the novelist experimented with the first-person singular, which up to this point he had avoided. It seemed to him that "you couldn't deal with really strong emotions in the first person because it's simply an awkwardness for an individual to talk about his own emotions." But once he began to work with it, he found he could do things that he could hardly do by any other means:

> First-person narrative encourages you to syncopate time, to bridge from a past to a present. It also allows you to drop back and forth, almost at will, freely. When Joe Allston or Lyman Ward is working with the past, his head is working in the present.

And time, this merging of the past with the present, is not only an essential aspect of structure in these late novels; it is in itself a central theme and of particular importance in *Angle of Repose*. During this period, with the onset of the Allston type of narrator, Stegner made a conscious effort to, in his words, "interpenetrate the past and present." In several essays he has stated that his goal was to do for the West what Faulkner had done for Mississippi: discover "a usable continuity between the past and present." And he has added, "That's what western novels too frequently don't do."

With Allston in *All the Little Live Things* and *The Spectator Bird*, and the narrators descended from him, Lyman Ward in *Angle of Repose* and Larry Morgan in *Crossing to Safety*, Stegner used a first-person narrator to achieve a voice close to his own, yet fictional. It would convey a sense of truth and conviction which came not, as in his one previous major success, *The Big Rock Candy Mountain*, out of the telling of his own story, but rather out of the force of his personality and belief. These narrators fit Stegner not only because he was getting older and matched them in age and perspective, but because his character stood in strong opposition to the excesses of his times, to the nihilistic, self-indulgent, and self-centered attitudes we see expressed so often by the younger generation in *Angle of Repose*. He has said that one of the themes of *Angle of Repose* is this generation gap, especially the anithistorical pose of the young, at least the young of the 1960s. They didn't give a damn what happened up to two minutes ago and would have been totally unable to understand a Victorian lady. I could conceive students of mine confronting Mary Hallock Foote and thinking, "My God, fantastic, inhuman," because they themselves were so imprisoned in the present that they had no notion of how various humanity and human customs can be.

Early in the anti–Vietnam War movement, Stegner marched with the students, but later, when the demonstrations turned violent, he was revolted and couldn't understand how breaking all the windows on the Stanford campus could bring an end to the war. By nature Stegner was the antithesis of the in-your-face hatred and anarchy that surrounded him. He was a liberal politically, but a man of old-fashioned virtues— polite, courteous, kind—who applied a great deal of self-discipline to his life and who usually repressed the kind of witty sarcasm or outspoken opinionatedness that his first-person narrators are likely to voice. Nevertheless, he obviously enjoyed speaking his mind through his characters—to balance the penalties of aging, there can be a perverse pleasure in being candid. When asked in an interview if the voice of this narrator was close to his own, he replied, "Yes, but don't read him intact. He goes further than I would. Anybody is likely to make characters to some extent in his own image."

I.

Stegner first came across Mary Hallock Foote—the genteel nineteenth-century local-color writer and illustrator whose life became the basis for *Angle of Repose*—in 1946, when he came to Stanford. He was doing research for a chapter to be included in the *Literary History of the United States* called "Western Record and Romance." He read several of her novels and story collections, as well as uncollected stories in their original magazine publication. He judged her "one of the best, actually; she was good and hadn't been noticed." He took notes on her work, put one of her stories in his anthology *Selected American Prose: The Realistic Movement, 1841–1900,* and included one of her short novels on his reading list for his American literature class. At the time, he was probably the only professor in the country to be teaching Foote's work.

A GI student in that class, George McMurray, enthusiastically reported to Stegner that he had come across Mary Hallock Foote's illustrations and writings about New Almaden (in the Coast Range foothills near San Jose, California). He told Stegner that he had found out that Foote had a granddaughter living in Grass Valley, California (near the Empire Mine, where Foote's husband had been the superintendent). McMurray said that he was going to go up there and see if he could get Foote's papers for the Stanford library, with the idea of possibly using them as the basis for a doctoral dissertation on her life and work.

The Foote family gave McMurray the papers with the understanding that he was going to publish from them and that he would supply typed transcriptions of the letters to the family. McMurray planned to do the dissertation under Stegner's direction, but a decade went by with no progress, and he finally gave up. During the mid-1960s, Stegner borrowed the transcriptions from the library and took them with him to his summer home in Vermont to read.

> Reading her quaintly 19th century letters, I thought her interesting but certainly not the subject of a novel. She lay around in my mind an unfertilized egg. . . . What hatched, after three years, was a novel about time, about cultural transplantation and change, about the relations of a man with his ancestors and descendants.

He did not want to write a historical novel (as he commented on several occasions, western literature was too often "mired in the past"), but a contemporary one, and as he thought about the story in the Foote letters, it occurred to him that perhaps he could somehow link the two together so that the past was made part of the present. That, in turn, led him to look for the sort of narrator that had "tunnel vision," frequently focused on the past and thinking about the present in terms of the past.

The perfect model for what became his narrator, Lyman Ward, presented itself to him in the person of Norman Foerster, Stegner's dissertation adviser at the University of Iowa, who had come to the Stanford campus to retire. Foerster, unfortunately, had been struck by a disease that had paralyzed his legs. With some sorrow about what had happened to his old friend, Stegner nevertheless put himself into

Foerster's place—how would he, a largely immobile literary historian, view the world? As the novelist has said, "We all have to have in some degree what Keats called negative capability, the capacity to make ourselves at home in other skins." Here was the tunnel vision that Stegner was looking for.

Foerster did not provide a character—Stegner invented him, descended from Joe Allston—but a point of view, literally a position from which to view the world. In comparing Allston with Lyman Ward, Stegner notes that Allston and Ward are very different types. Allston is

> more emotional than Ward, less over-controlled. Lyman Ward is pretty uptight all the time. Joe Allston is likely to get drunk and disorderly and to wisecrack in the wrong places. He's another kind of character, but he has some of the same functions as a literary device.

Observer and commentator, Lyman Ward, immobile, travels through time and space via his mind's eye, which of course is precisely what a novelist does. He is not immobilized by just his disease, which does allow him to move about in his wheelchair, but also by his attachment to place, his ancestral home, and by his obsession with his family's history. Both literally and figuratively, he lives in the past. While one cannot agree with Lyman's son, Rodman, that his father's investigation of the past is a waste of time, his devotion does seem extreme—except when one realizes that his devotion is not just to the past for its own sake, but that he is also looking for guidance in his present situation. The subject of *Angle of Repose* is the life of Susan Burling Ward, but the essence of the novel is the evolving consciousness of Lyman Ward, her grandson.

The novel can be roughly divided into two parts. The first third of the novel deals largely with Lyman Ward and his experiences and thoughts about his life. Lyman's story and his character (a contemporary man who can understand and sympathize with a Victorian lady) frame the remaining two-thirds, which deals with his grandmother and whose state of mind is often conveyed to us by her letters to her eastern friend, Augusta. This Susan Burling Ward material, based on Mary Hallock Foote's papers, would bring accusations of plagiarism, charges of misuse of source materials, and even angry denunciation by feminists who claimed that a male writer had deliberately set out to destroy the reputation of an accomplished female artist. Some of the charges grew out of misunderstanding and miscommunication; some, out of spite and, no doubt, jealousy.

Stegner had gotten to know Janet Micoleau, one of Mary Hallock Foote's three granddaughters, in Grass Valley through the husband of his secretary, Alf Heller. He visited the Micoleaus on several occasions while he was thinking about using the papers, and Janet encouraged him to do something with them, since her grandmother had been largely forgotten. She hoped that through Stegner's work, interest in her grandmother's life and work would be revived. When Stegner decided to go ahead with a novel based in part on the papers, Janet told him to use the papers in whatever way he wished. Stegner assumed that she, who had had custody of the papers, spoke for the family.

There probably would not have been any trouble if the whole Foote family had been willing to become involved in dealing with the novelist and if Stegner and the Foote family had agreed on what they meant by "novel." What the Footes meant was explained by Janet's sister, Evelyn Foote Gardiner, when she stated in an interview: "I thought he would write something like Irving Stone's biographical novels. That he would invent conversations and all of that, but that he would pretty much stick to the facts of their lives." Although he changed and added in order to create a plot which gave the novel its central drama and which would bring together the past with the present, he did stick to the broad outline of their lives. However, Mrs. Gardiner and those who have taken up her cause have complained that he used too much of Mary's life and too many of her letters, accusing him of "stealing" Mary's material in order to write a prizewinning book.

The Foote family, understandably perhaps but inaccurately, has expressed the view that Mary's letters constitute a major portion of the novel. Stegner does quote (with some changes) from many of the letters (roughly thirty-five letters out of a total of five hundred). There are thirty-eight instances of letter quotation, of various lengths, for a total of approximately 61 pages in a book with 555 pages of text—that is, slightly more than 10 percent of the whole. As small as the percentage may be, however, there is no doubt that the letters are an invaluable part of the novel, borrowing the actual words of a real correspondence to give, as they do, a feeling of depth and authenticity to Susan Burling Ward's character. It was a brilliant tactic, but one that had ramifications that Stegner did not foresee.

When Janet asked him not to use real names, since he was writing a novel, Stegner used fictitious ones, and went further in protecting the identity of his sources in his acknowledgments: "My thanks to J.M. and her sister for the loan of their ancestors." In addition, in his acknowledgments he included the disclaimer "This is a novel which utilizes selected facts from their real lives. It is in no sense a family history." But Mrs. Gardiner has insisted that since he did not give specific credit to Mary Hallock Foote, as she felt he should have, what he had taken from her was an unethical act, close to plagiarism. Since he was following the family's instructions in keeping the source of his material secret, this is a very harsh and, it would seem, unfair judgment.

The situation became more complicated when Rodman Paul got in touch with Stegner, while he was working on the novel manuscript, to tell him that he had obtained backing by the Huntington Library to publish Mary Hallock Foote's reminiscences. Wallace agreed to read Paul's introduction and offered to show him the letters. But the whole idea of protecting the Foote name through anonymity was in trouble. He wrote to Janet repeating the warnings that he had given before:

> As I warned you, the process of making a novel from real people has led me to bend them where I had to, and you may not recognize your ancestors when I get through with them. On the other hand, I have availed myself of your invitation to use the letters and reminiscences as I please, so there are passages from both in my novel. . . .
>
> You suggested that I not use real names in any of my book, since what I am writing is not history or biography but fiction. I agree with that. But if the reminiscences are now to be published, it won't take much literary detective work to discover what family I am basing this story on. . . . The question arises, must I now unravel all those little threads I have so painstakingly raveled together—the real with the fiction—and replace all truth with fiction? Or does it matter to you that an occasional reader or scholar can detect a Foote behind my fictions?

He went on to offer to modify the language and change all the names, asked her to let him know what to do about changes if she thought it necessary, and, as he had before, offered to send the completed manuscript to her to read. Janet replied that she didn't think changes necessary, nor did she feel it necessary for her to read the manuscript. Stegner asked if anyone else in the family would like to read the manuscript. The answer was no, the others were too busy with their own lives to take the time.

In his letters Stegner warned Janet several times that the book would not be true to all the details of the Footes' lives. "For reasons of drama, if nothing else," he wrote, "I'm having to foreshorten, and I'm having to throw in a domestic tragedy of an entirely fictional nature, but I think I am not too far from their real characters." Despite his attempt to make sure that the Foote family had some idea of what a novel was and what he was writing, and despite his offer to make changes as dictated by Janet and to let her or other members of the family read the manuscript, part of the Foote family took great offense to the book when it was published. They blamed Janet, who suffered deeply from their upset and anger; but most of all they blamed Stegner, who they believed, despite all the evidence to the contrary, had tricked them. The irony is that the novel with its Pulitzer and its controversy has brought more attention to Mary Hallock Foote than she would ever have received otherwise.

II.

Using the Foote letters may have been a brilliant touch, but it not only caused him difficulties after the novel was published; it made the composition of the novel difficult:

> The novel got very complex on me before it was done. It gave me trouble: I had too many papers, recorded reality tied my hands. But a blessed thing happened. In the course of trying to make fiction of a historical personage I discovered, or half created, a living woman in Victorian dress. I forced her into situations untrue to her life history but not, I think, untrue to the human probabilities that do not depend on time or custom. In the end I had to elect to be true to the woman rather than to the historical personage.

The novel is certainly a complex one, probably Stegner's most complex, yet at the same time it remains a book that is not only readable, but a joy to read.

For one thing, it is a book of powerful, memorable characters. For another, it is a book with constantly building and engaging drama, dramatizing several important themes. It may seem odd on the surface that a novel that has a central character bound to his wheelchair and to his home should have such drama. That drama is built through not just one but a series of connected conflicts within Lyman Ward. While he is not a totally lovable character, he is a decent man who has had some bad breaks in life and whose thoughts engage us by both their wit and their occasional profundity. Because of his disease and because his wife has abandoned him, he has reached a major crisis point in his life. "It would be easy," he thinks at one point in the novel, "to call it quits." But he is a survivor, and as strange as it may seem, he is saved by his training as a research scholar, by his thirst for knowledge. His crisis leads him to the need to find a direction for his shattered life. That direction is provided by finding out about and trying to understand his grandparents, the events that shaped them and the conflict between them; and his curiosity as it pushes ever forward becomes ours. It becomes the medium of suspense, holding us throughout. "What really interests me," Lyman tells us, "is how two such unlike particles clung together, and under what strains, rolling downhill into their future until they reach the angle of repose where I knew them. That is where the interest is. That's where the meaning will be if I find any."

Another aspect of Lyman that leads us to empathize with him and holds us to his track of discovery is his vivid imagination. He is not only a historian; he is, in effect, a novelist, bringing his characters and their interactions to life. Joseph Conrad was by Stegner's testimony a favorite author, one that he learned much from, and it was Conrad who said,

> My task, which I am trying to achieve is, by the power of the written word to make you hear, to make you feel—it is, before all, to make you *see*. That—and no more, and it is everything.

Through the talent of Wallace Stegner, Lyman Ward has the power to make us see. And if there is any one secret to the success of this novel, this is it.

A major pattern of conflict within Lyman and hence the novel can be categorized under the past versus the present, more specifically at times, the old West versus the new. As Lyman thinks about his own situation, implicitly comparing it to that of his grandparents, we wonder how, facing so many obstacles to happiness, they are going to make it through life. As Stegner has put it, "Since [Lyman's] own marriage has collapsed he's interested in this one that didn't, even though it had all the provocations that his had to fall apart." But we also have a third pair, the contemporary marriage of the two flower children, Shelly and Larry Rasmussen. Altogether, three different kinds of marriage: each in a different time frame, running from the past to the present. " 'Progressive decline,' I would call it," the author has stated.

Certainly, as Lyman tells us in the novel, this is a book about marriage, and just as certainly it reflects Stegner's own values in that regard. We might note that he was happily married to the same woman for nearly sixty years. But one might just as well say that this is a book about forgiveness, also reflecting the author's values. While the marriage of Oliver and Susan remains intact, Oliver apparently never totally forgives his wife, doing so only insofar as he stays with her. Lyman wonders if he can even go that far in his own life and take back his wayward wife, Ellen.

One of the strengths of the novel is the complexity of its characters, the many-sidedness that convinces us of their reality. These characterizations, along with the quoted letters and Stegner's vivid descriptions, provide a depth of realism seldom found in fiction. It is like turning from the flatness of regular TV to the multidimensional picture of HDTV. After reading and rereading this novel, it is hard not to lapse into the mistake of calling the central character Mary—which may be a point in favor of the Foote family's objections. Despite the negatives attached to the two major characters, we learn to care about them and follow with concern their progress through the novel. Like our feelings about Lyman, our connection to Susan grows despite a number of flaws—her snobbery, in particular, and her treatment of her husband. But our connection grows as we come to understand her, and it is Stegner's triumph that we do come to an understanding of this woman, this genteel Victorian lady, so aloof, who would seem on first glance to be so foreign to contemporary taste.

But in so many ways she really is contemporary. Living in an age and a stratum of society in which a woman could only find the freedom to leave her family by submitting to a husband and committing herself to his life, Susan remains her own person. Outwardly a captive, she is liberated from within and makes her way to success in the larger world. What she has in common with her grandson, Lyman, is courage and a strong sense of independence. After marrying Oliver, a civil engineer, she follows him west to one mining camp after another and makes the best of each situation, experiencing a way of life so different from the society she enjoyed in the East and regrets leaving. Lyman says of her,

> Susan Ward came West not to join a new society but to endure it, not to build anything but to enjoy a temporary experience and make it yield whatever instruction it contained. . . . A modern woman in a mining camp, even if she is the wife of the Resident Engineer, lives in pants and a sweatshirt. Grandmother made not the slightest concession to the places where she lived.

Our connection to her is reinforced by Lyman's affection for her, although as the drama of her life unfolds before him, he often wishes he could take her aside and, knowing the future, warn her about apologizing for her husband and constantly comparing him unfavorably to more socially adept men.

Separated from the culture of the East, she keeps her connection by her correspondence with her friend Augusta while at the same time exercising her talents for writing and drawing, becoming the best-known woman illustrator of her time. Not being able to enjoy the liberation provided by the feminist revolution, Susan Burling Ward goes beyond the modern woman by having liberated herself. There is connected to this, of course, the theme of the conflict between traditionally male and female roles and values, here exacerbated by the strains and extremes of western life. In the Wards we have to some extent the stereotypical nineteenth-century American man and woman—the man mostly silent and devoted to making his way in the world, and the woman loquacious and socially conscious. Their complexity raises them above the stereotypes, but the basic conflict in roles and values remains.

Susan's husband, Oliver, is also a complex character, but since we see him only indirectly, he remains throughout a somewhat shadowy figure. We do know that he is quiet, competent, ambitious, and hardworking. After nearly five years of acquaintance, he proposes to Susan. He has been trying to make his way in the world to be worthy of her. He worships his wife in an old-fashioned way, but is withal a man's man. Lyman says of him,

> The silent character in this cast, he did not defend himself when he thought he was wronged, and left no novels, stories, drawings, or reminiscences to speak for him. I only assume what he felt, from knowing him as an old man. He never did less than the best he knew how. If that was not enough, if he felt criticism in the air, he put on his hat and walked out.

His complexity only comes through Susan's reflections on him, which are decidedly mixed.

Before their marriage she is attracted to him because "he had an air of quiet such as she had known in men like her father, men who worked with animals." But after their marriage she frequently compares him unfavorably to other men, particularly Thomas Hudson, the man she would have liked to have married and who marries her best friend, Augusta. But even more overtly and painfully she compares him to her husband's assistant, Frank Sargent, with whom she falls in love. In reaction to all his failures, Oliver starts drinking, much to his wife's disgust:

> "Doesn't it humiliate you to think that you can't resist that temptation when someone like Frank, living out on the railroad with the roughest sort of man, never touches a drop? Why can't you be like Frank?"
> And that was the greatest mistake of all. "Because I'm not Frank," Oliver said, staring at her reflected face. "Maybe you wish I was."

Lyman decides that Susan "must unconsciously have agreed with [her husband's] judgment that she was higher and finer than he. I wonder if there was some moment when she fully comprehended and appreciated him?" He remains somewhat mysterious to us, almost mythic in stature. He suffers the slings and arrows of many misfortunes, both personal and professional, silently. One wound that has surely grown and festered over the years is his wife's disappointment in his inability to achieve the material success that would have raised them socially. He can do his job well, but his sense of duty leads him to pass up opportunities in order to stay with his family, and he is too honest to compete in the helter-skelter western world of get-rich-quick exploitation. At heart, Lyman tells us, he was a builder, not a raider.

This is a thoughtful book with a rich panoply of characters, both major and minor, and one that explores many themes, themes that bring the novel into the center of our culture. Like *The Great Gatsby*, it helps us define who we, as a people in this new land, are. Oliver in his gallant romanticism is our Gatsby, and Susan in her own romantic snobbish world is our Daisy, and ne'er the twain shall meet until at the end they find their angle of repose. We have all, to use Fitzgerald's words, looked toward the "fresh, green breast of the New World," and we all believe, or would like to believe, in the American Dream, although we each may define that dream in our own way. We may, like Willie Loman, be defeated by the system or by our own self-delusions, but we can only live and try to go forward if we believe. Our going forward, of course, often means going west, looking for the main chance, as Stegner's own father did, or as Bo Mason, the character in *The Big Rock Candy Mountain* modeled after George Stegner, did, or as Oliver and Susan Ward did. East versus West, civilization versus opportunity, is a theme at the heart of the American experience. And as our boats beat ceaselessly into the past to find our future, we continue to ask, What have we inherited?

SUGGESTIONS FOR FURTHER READING

WORKS BY WALLACE STEGNER

All the Little Live Things. New York: Viking, 1967.

Beyond the Hundredth Meridian: John Wesley Powell and the Second Opening of the West. Boston: Houghton Mifflin, 1954.

The Big Rock Candy Mountain. New York: Duell, Sloan and Pearce, 1943.

Collected Stories of Wallace Stegner. New York: Random House, 1990.

Crossing to Safety. New York: Random House, 1987.

Marking the Sparrow's Fall: Wallace Stegner's American West. Edited by Page Stegner. New York: Henry Holt, 1999.

Where the Bluebird Sings to the Lemonade Springs: Living and Writing in the West. New York: Random House, 1992.

Wolf Willow: A History, a Story, and a Memory of the Last Plains Frontier. New York: Viking, 1962.

BIOGRAPHY AND INTERVIEWS

Benson, Jackson J. *Wallace Stegner: His Life and Work.* New York: Viking, 1996.

Etulain, Richard W., ed. *Conversations with Wallace Stegner on Western History and Literature.* Salt Lake City: University of Utah Press, 1983.

BIBLIOGRAPHY

Colberg, Nancy. *Wallace Stegner: A Descriptive Bibliography.* Lewiston, Idaho: Confluence Press, 1990.

SUGGESTIONS FOR FURTHER READING

*CRITICAL BOOKS AND ESSAY COLLECTIONS ON THE
LIFE AND WORKS OF WALLACE STEGNER*

Arthur, Anthony, ed. *Critical Essays on Wallace Stegner*. Boston: G. K. Hall, 1982.

Meine, Curt, ed. *Wallace Stegner and the Continental Vision: Essays on Literature, History, and Landscape*. Washington, D.C.: Island Press, 1997.

Rankin, Charles E., ed. *Wallace Stegner: Man and Writer*. Albuquerque: University of New Mexico Press, 1996.

Robinson, Forrest G., and Margaret G. Robinson. *Wallace Stegner*. Boston: Twayne Publishers, 1977.

I

GRASS VALLEY

1

Now I believe they will leave me alone. Obviously Rodman came up hoping to find evidence of my incompetence—though how an incompetent could have got this place renovated, moved his library up, and got himself transported to it without arousing the suspicion of his watchful children, ought to be a hard one for Rodman to answer. I take some pride in the way I managed all that. And he went away this afternoon without a scrap of what he would call data.

So tonight I can sit here with the tape recorder whirring no more noisily than electrified time, and say into the microphone the place and date of a sort of beginning and a sort of return: Zodiac Cottage, Grass Valley, California, April 12, 1970.

Right there, I might say to Rodman, who doesn't believe in time, notice something: I started to establish the present and the present moved on. What I established is already buried under layers of tape. Before I can say *I am*, I was. Heraclitus and I, prophets of flux, know that the flux is composed of parts that imitate and repeat each other. Am or was, I am cumulative, too. I am everything I ever was, whatever you and Leah may think. I am much of what my parents and especially my grandparents were—inherited stature, coloring, brains, bones (that part unfortunate), plus transmitted prejudices, culture, scruples, likings, moralities, and moral errors that I defend as if they were personal and not familial.

Even places, especially this house whose air is thick with the past. My antecedents support me here as the old wistaria at the corner supports the house. Looking at its cables wrapped two or three times around the cottage, you would swear, and you could be right, that if they were cut the place would fall down.

Rodman, like most sociologists and most of his generation, was born without the sense of history. To him it is only an aborted social science. The world has changed, Pop, he tells me. The past isn't going to teach us anything about what we've got ahead of us. Maybe it did once, or seemed to. It doesn't any more.

Probably he thinks the blood vessels of my brain are as hardened as my cervical spine. They probably discuss me in bed. *Out of his mind, going up there by himself . . . How can we, unless . . . helpless . . . roll his wheelchair off the porch who'd rescue him? Set himself afire lighting a cigar, who'd put him out? . . . Damned old independent mule-headed . . . worse than a baby. Never consider the trouble he makes for the people who have to look after him . . . House I grew up in, he says. Papers, he says, thing I've always wanted to do . . . All of Grandmother's papers, books, reminiscences, pictures, those hundreds of letters that came back from Augusta Hudson's daughter after Augusta died . . . A lot of Grandfather's relics, some of Father's, some of my own . . . Hundred year chronicle of the family. All right, fine. Why not give that stuff to the Historical Society and get a fat tax deduction? He could still work on it. Why box it all up, and himself too, in that old crooked house in the middle of twelve acres of land we could all make a good thing out of if he'd consent to sell? Why go off and play cobwebs like a character in a Southern novel, out where nobody can keep an eye on him?*

They keep thinking of my good, in their terms. I don't blame them, I only resist them. Rodman will have to report to Leah that I have rigged the place to fit my needs and am getting along well. I have had Ed shut off the whole upstairs except for my bedroom and bath and this study. Downstairs we use only the kitchen and library and the veranda. Everything tidy and shipshape and orderly. No data.

So I may anticipate regular visits of inspection and solicitude while they wait for me to get a belly full of independence. They will look sharp for signs of senility and increasing pain—will they perhaps even hope for them? Meantime they will walk softly, speak quietly, rattle the oatbag gently, murmuring and moving closer until the arm can slide the rope over the stiff old neck and I can be led away to the old folks' pasture down in Menlo Park where the care is so good and there is so much to keep the inmates busy and happy. If I remain stubborn, the decision may eventually have to be made for me, perhaps by computer. Who could argue with a computer? Rodman will punch all his data onto cards and feed them into his machine and it will tell us all it is time.

I would have them understand that I am not just killing time during my slow petrifaction. I am neither dead nor inert. My head still works. Many things are unclear to me, including myself, and I want to sit and think. Who ever had a better opportunity? What if I *can't* turn my head? I can look in any direction by turning my wheelchair, and I choose to look back. Rodman to the contrary notwithstanding, that is the only direction we can learn from.

Increasingly, after my amputation and during the long time when I lay around feeling sorry for myself, I came to feel like the contour bird. I wanted to fly around the Sierra foothills backward, just looking. If there was no longer any sense in pretending to be interested in where I was going, I could consult where I've been. And I don't mean the Ellen business. I honestly believe this isn't that personal. The Lyman Ward who married Ellen Hammond and begot Rodman Ward and taught history and wrote certain books and monographs about the Western frontier, and suffered certain personal catastrophes and perhaps deserved them and survives them after a fashion and now sits talking to himself into a microphone—he doesn't matter that much any more. I would like to put him in a frame of reference and comparison. Fooling around in the papers my grandparents, especially my grandmother, left behind, I get glimpses of lives close to mine, related to mine in ways I recognize but don't completely comprehend. I'd like to live in their clothes a while, if only so I don't have to live in my own. Actually, as I look down my nose to where my left leg bends and my right leg stops, I realize that it isn't backward I want to go, but downward. I want to touch once more the ground I have been maimed away from.

In my mind I write letters to the newspapers, saying Dear Editor, As a modern man and a one-legged man, I can tell you that the conditions are similar. We have been cut off, the past has been ended and the family has broken up and the present is adrift in its wheelchair. I had a wife who after twenty-five years of marriage took on the coloration of the 1960s. I have a son who, though we are affectionate with each other, is no more my true son than if he breathed through gills. That is no gap between the generations, that is a gulf. The elements have changed, there are whole new orders of magnitude and kind. This present of 1970 is no more an extension of my grandparents' world, this West is no more a development of the West they helped build, than the sea over Santorin is an extension of that once-island of rock and olives. My wife turns out after a quarter of a century to be someone I never knew, my son starts all fresh from his own premises.

My grandparents had to live their way out of one world and into another, or into several others, making new out of old the way corals live their reef upward. I am on my grandparents' side. I believe in Time, as they did, and in the life chronological rather than in the life existential. We live in time and through it, we build our huts in its ruins, or used to, and we cannot afford all these abandonings.

And so on. The letters fade like conversation. If I spoke to Rodman in those terms, saying that my grandparents' lives seem to me organic and ours what? hydroponic? he would ask in derision what I meant. Define my terms. How do you measure the organic residue of a man or a generation? This is all metaphor. If you can't measure it, it doesn't exist.

Rodman is a great measurer. He is interested in change, all right, but only as a process; and he is interested in values, but only as data. X people believe one way, Y people another, whereas ten years ago Y people believed the first way and X the second. The rate of change is therefore. He never goes back more than ten years.

Like other Berkeley radicals, he is convinced that the post-industrial post-Christian world is worn out, corrupt in its inheritance, helpless to create by evolution the social and political institutions, the forms of personal relations, the conventions, moralities, and systems of ethics (insofar as these are indeed necessary) appropriate to the future. Society being thus paralyzed, it must be pried loose. He, Rodman Ward, culture hero born fully armed from this history-haunted skull, will be happy to provide blueprints, or perhaps ultimatums and manifestoes, that will save us and bring on a life of true freedom. The family too. Marriage and the family as we have known them are becoming extinct. He is by Paul Goodman out of Margaret Mead. He sits in with the sitter-inners, he will reform us *malgré* our teeth, he will make his omelet and be damned to the broken eggs. Like the Vietnam commander, he will regretfully destroy our village to save it.

The truth about my son is that despite his good nature, his intelligence, his extensive education, and his bulldozer energy, he is as blunt as a kick in the shins. He is peremptory even with a doorbell button. His thumb never inquires whether one is within, and then waits to see. It pushes, and ten seconds later pushes again, and one second after that goes down on the button and stays there. That's the way he summoned me this noon.

I responded slowly, for I guessed who it was: his thumb gave him away. I had been expecting his visit, and fearing it. Also I had been working peacefully and disliked being disturbed.

I love this old studio of Grandmother's. It is full of sun in the mornings, and the casual apparatus and decorations of living, which age so swiftly in America, have here kept a worn, changeless comfortableness not too much violated by the tape recorder and the tubular desk light and other things I have had to add. When I have wheeled my chair into the cut-out bay in the long desk I can sit surrounded on three sides by books and papers. A stack of yellow pads, a mug of pens and pencils, the recorder's microphone, are at my elbow, and on the wall before my face is something my grandmother used to have hanging there all through my childhood: a broad leather belt, a wooden-handled cavalry revolver of the Civil War period, a bowie knife, and a pair of Mexican spurs with 4-inch rowels. The minute I found them in a box I put them right back where they used to be.

The Lord knows why she hung them where she would see them every time she looked up. Certainly they were not her style. Much more in her style are the trembling shadows of wistaria clusters that the morning sun throws on that wall. Did she hang them here to remind herself of her first experience in the West, the little house among the liveoaks at New Almaden where she came as a bride in 1876? From her letters I know that Grandfather had them hanging there in the arch between dining room and parlor when she arrived, and that she left them up because she felt they meant something to him. The revolver his brother had taken from a captured rebel, the bowie he himself had worn all through his early years in California, the spurs had been given to him by a Mexican packer on the Comstock. But why did she restore his primitive and masculine trophies here in Grass Valley, half a lifetime after New Almaden? Did she hang those Western objects in her sight as a reminder, as an acknowledgment of something that had happened to her? I think perhaps she did.

In any case, I was sitting here just before noon, contented in mind and as comfortable in body as I am ever likely to be. The slight activity of rising and breakfasting, which I do without Ada, and the influence of coffee and the day's first aspirin, and the warmth of the sun against my neck and left side, these are morning beneficences.

Then that thumb on the bell.

I pushed back from among the sun-dazzled papers and rotated my chair. Two years' practice has not fully accustomed me to the double sensation that accompanies wheelchair locomotion. Above, I am as rigid as a monument; below, smooth fluidity. I move like a piano on a dolly. Since I am battery-powered, there is no physical effort, and since I cannot move my head up, down, or to either side, objects appear to rotate around me, to slide across my vision from peripheral to full to opposite peripheral, rather than I to move among them. The walls revolve, bringing into view the casement windows, the window seat, the clusters of wistaria outside; then the next wall with photographs of Grandmother and Grandfather, their three children, a wash drawing of the youngest, Agnes, at the age of three, a child who looks all eyes; and still rotating, the framed letters from Whittier, Longfellow, Mark Twain, Kipling, Howells, President Grover Cleveland (I framed them, not she); and then the spin slows and I am pointed toward the door with the sunlight stretching along the worn brown boards. By the time I have rolled into the upper hall, my visitor is holding down the bell with one hand and knocking with the other.

Though I have got handier in the ten days I have been here, it took me a minute to get into position over the brace that locks my chair onto the lift, and I felt like yelling down at him to for God's sake let up, I was coming. He made me nervous. I was afraid of doing something wrong and ending up at the bottom in a mess of twisted metal and broken bones.

When I was locked in, I flipped the wall switch, and the lift's queer, weightless motion took hold of me, moved me smoothly, tipped me with the inevitable solar plexus panic over the edge. I went down like a diver submerging, the floor flowed over my head. Without haste the downstairs wall toward which my rigid head was set unrolled from top to bottom, revealing midway the print of that Pre-Raphaelite seadog and his enchanted boy listeners—a picture my grandmother might have painted herself, it is so much in her key of aspiration arising out of homely realism. Then I was level with the picture, which meant that my chair had come into view from the front door, and the ringing and pounding stopped.

The chair grounded in light as murky and green as the light of ten fathoms: the ambition of that old wistaria has been to choke off all the lower windows. I tipped up the brace with one crutch, and groped the crutch back to its cradle on the side of the chair—and carefully, too, because I knew he was watching me and I wanted to impress him with how accidentproof my habits were. A touch on the motor switch, a hand on the wheel, and I was swinging again. The wall spun until Rodman's face came into focus, framed in the door's small pane like the face of a fish staring in the visor of a diver's helmet—a bearded fish that smiled, distorted by the beveled glass, and flapped a vigorous fin.

These are the results, mainly negative from his point of view, of Rodman's visit:

(1) He did not persuade me—nor to do him justice did he try very hard—to come back and live with them or start arrangements for the retirement home in Menlo Park.

(2) He did not persuade me to stop running around alone in my wheelchair. Sure I bumped my stump, showing off how mobile I am and how cunningly I have converted all stairs to ramps. Could he tell by my face how much I hurt, sitting there smiling and smiling, and wanting to take that poor sawed-off twitching lump of bones and flesh in my two hands and rock back and forth and grit my teeth and howl? What if he could? When I am not showing off to prove my competence to people who doubt it, I can go in this chair almost anywhere he can go on his legs, and just as safely.

(3) I am not going to install a walkie-talkie on the chair so if I get in trouble I can call the Highway Patrol. He had that all worked out, and pushed it. But the only emergency I ever have is that sometimes when I am far from the bathroom and too achy to get out of my chair to perform, my urine bottle overflows. It is called the Policeman's

Friend, and the cops and I might have a pleasant time exchanging yarns about awkward times when we have been caught with it full, but I doubt that any cop would take it seriously as an emergency.

(4) I am not made anxious about "getting like my father." Clearly they are afraid these things run in the family, which is the sort of acknowledgment that under other circumstances I would like Rodman to make to history. Sure my father had a queer unhappy life, and sure he stayed on and on here after the mine closed down, and finally got so addled that Ada and Ed Hawkes had to look after him as they would have looked after a willful and irresponsible child. Rodman all but asks, What if he came up here some day and found me talking to myself like Grandpa? But I could tell him I talk to myself all the time, into this microphone, and sort of like the company. He knows as well as I do that when I quit making even approximate sense he can get the support of the law to take me away, as I had to take Father.

(5) I am not going to ask Ed and Ada to move in downstairs. They have lived all their life in the cottage down the hill, and they are as close as I need them.

(6) I am not going to give up this business of Grandmother's papers and write a book on "somebody interesting." Rodman pretends to be afraid that out of sentiment I will waste what he flatteringly calls major talents (he disparages history but was touchingly proud when I won the Bancroft Prize) on a nobody. His notion of somebody interesting is numbingly vulgar. Having no historical sense, he can only think that history's interest must be "color." How about some Technicolor personality of the Northern Mines, about which I already know so much? Lola Montez, say, that wild girl from an Irish peat bog who became the mistress of half the celebrities of Europe, including Franz Liszt and Dumas, *père* or *fils* or both, before taking up with King Ludwig I of Bavaria, who made her Countess of Landsfeld. And from there, in 1856, to San Francisco, where she danced the spider dance for miners and fortune hunters (*No, Lola, no!*) and from there to Grass Valley to live for two years with a tame bear who couldn't have been much of an improvement on Ludwig.

That's Rodman's idea of history. Every fourth-rate antiquarian in the West has panned Lola's poor little gravel. My grandparents are a deep vein that has never been dug. They were *people*.

I am sure Rodman knows nothing whatever about Grandfather, nothing about his inventiveness or his genius for having big ideas twenty years ahead of their time or his struggle to do something grand and humanly productive and be one of the builders of the West. I know that his taking the job as superintendent of the Zodiac was a kind of surrender, though I don't yet know the details. Rodman probably feels that that was the sort of job Grandfather bucked for all his life and finally made. He probably thinks of him as a lesser George Hearst, neither quite crooked enough nor quite successful enough to be interesting.

But it is interesting that, apparently in an attempt to comprehend my present aberration, Rodman should have taken the trouble to read some of Grandmother's stories and look at some magazines containing her drawings. Characteristically he saw nothing in them. All full of pious renunciations, he says, everything covered up with Victorian antimacassars. He cited me her own remark that she wrote from the protected point of view, the woman's point of view, as evidence that she went through her life from inexperience to inexperience.

Her pictures the same. If, as I assured him with quotations from the histories of American art, she was the best-known woman illustrator of her time, and the only woman who ever did anything significant about drawing the early West, how come nobody collects her? And *woman* illustrator, he repeats with good-humored condescension. Yet his name is always in the papers as a defender of disadvantaged minorities, and only last week he had his picture in the *Chronicle* in a Woman's Liberation Front picket line.

Well, Grandmother, let me back out of this desk and turn around and look at you over there in your walnut frame next to the letters of people who wrote to you as a respected contemporary. Should I take an interest in you even if you *were* historical, white, a woman, and my grandmother? Did all your talents, and Grandfather's, and all the efforts of a long strenuous life go for no more than to produce Rodman and me, a sociologist and a cripple? Nothing in your life or art to teach a modern or one-legged man something?

A Quaker lady of high principles, the wife of a not-very-successful engineer whom you supported through years of delayed hope, you lived in exile, wrote it, drew it—New Almaden, Santa Cruz, Leadville,

Michoacán, the Snake River Valley, the deep quartz mines right under this house—and you stayed a cultural snob through it all. Even when you lived in a field camp in a canyon, your children had a governess, no less, unquestionably the only one in Idaho. The dream you had for your children was a dream of Eastern cultivation.

Yet do you remember the letters you used to get from isolated miners and geologists and surveyors who had come across a copy of *Century* or *Atlantic* and seen their lives there, and wrote to ask how a lady of obvious refinement knew so much about drifts, stopes, tipples, pumps, ores, assays, mining law, claim jumpers, underground surveying, and other matters? Remember the one who wanted to know where you learned to handle so casually a technical term like "angle of repose"?

I suppose you replied, "By living with an engineer." But you were too alert to the figurative possibilities of words not to see the phrase as descriptive of human as well as detrital rest. As you said, it was too good for mere dirt; you tried to apply it to your own wandering and uneasy life. It is the angle I am aiming for myself, and I don't mean the rigid angle at which I rest in this chair. I wonder if you ever reached it. There was a time up there in Idaho when everything was wrong; your husband's career, your marriage, your sense of yourself, your confidence, all came unglued together. Did you come down out of that into some restful 30° angle and live happily ever after? When you died at ninety-one, the New York *Times* obituary spoke of you as a Western woman, a Western writer and artist. Would you have accepted the label? Or did you cling forever to the sentiment you wrote to Augusta Hudson from the bottom of failure in Boise Canyon—that not even Henry James's expatriates were so exiled as you? We shared this house all the years of my childhood, and a good many summers afterward. Was the quiet I always felt in you really repose? I wish I thought so. It is one of the questions I want the papers to answer.

If Henry Adams, whom you knew slightly, could make a theory of history by applying the second law of thermodynamics to human affairs, I ought to be entitled to base one on the angle of repose, and may yet. There is another physical law that teases me, too: the Doppler Effect. The sound of anything coming at you—a train, say, or the future —has a higher pitch than the sound of the same thing going away. If you have perfect pitch and a head for mathematics you can compute the speed of the object by the interval between its arriving and departing sounds. I have neither perfect pitch nor a head for mathematics, and anyway who wants to compute the speed of history? Like all falling bodies, it constantly accelerates. But I would like to hear your life as *you* heard it, coming at you, instead of hearing it as I do, a sober sound of expectations reduced, desires blunted, hopes deferred or abandoned, chances lost, defeats accepted, griefs borne. I don't find your life uninteresting, as Rodman does. I would like to hear it as it sounded while it was passing. Having no future of my own, why shouldn't I look forward to yours?

You yearned backward a good part of your life, and that produced another sort of Doppler Effect. Even while you paid attention to what you must do today and tomorrow, you heard the receding sound of what you had relinquished. It came to you secondhand in the letters of Augusta Hudson. You lived vicariously in her, dined with the literary great, visited La Farge at Newport, lunched at the White House, toured Italy and the Holy Land. The daily gorgeousness of Augusta's social obligations lighted your strenuous poverty in the way you liked to illuminate your drawings, with a wash of light from above and to one side. Witness this letter I was just reading, written when Augusta was moving into her Stanford White Mansion on Staten Island: "Before you put a fire in your new fireplace, gather up your children and have them stand in it, looking up, and then, with the light falling on them so, paint them and send them to me."

Where was Grandmother living when she had that sentimental whim? In a dugout in Boise Canyon.

Except for her marriage she would have been a respected part of what, marrying whom she did, she had to leave behind. I think her love for my grandfather, however real, was always somewhat unwilling. She must unconsciously have agreed with his judgment that she was higher and finer than he. I wonder if there was some moment when she fully comprehended and appreciated him? I wonder if there was a time when the East and all that Edith Wharton gentility had been lived out of her as surely as the cells of her girlhood had been replaced in her body?

Not that she made a fetish of her gifts, or held herself above anyone. She plunged into things with energy, she was never afraid of work. John Greenleaf Whittier said she was the only girl he knew who could conduct a serious discussion of the latest *North American Review* while scrubbing her mother's floor. She endured, and even enjoyed, considerable physical hardship on occasion. In Leadville she kept house in a one-room cabin, and in that one room presided over talk that she insisted (and she would have known) was as good as the best in America. All her life she loved conversation, discussion, company. When I was a child we were always being visited by people like the president of Yale College and the American Ambassador to Japan. They sat on the piazza and talked with Grandmother while Grandfather listened, working quietly among his roses.

But that was after she had reached, or appeared to have reached, the angle of repose. I can remember her as Susan Burling Ward, an old lady. It is harder to imagine her as Susan Burling, a girl, before the West and all the West implied had happened to her.

Ever since Ada left me eating supper, and went home to get supper for Ed, I have been looking through the papers covering her early years. Among them is an article that Augusta wrote, sometime after 1900, for a magazine called *The Booklover*. It is as good a thing to start with as any.

Botanists tell us that the blossom is an evolution of the leaf—but they cannot say just why that particular bud should take from the same air and sunshine a fairer substance, a deeper color, a more permanent existence, and become something at which each passerby pauses, and goes on his way happier for the sight. Why on the sturdy stem of farmers and merchants should one girl blossom into a storyteller in pencil and in words?

Susan Burling comes from a line of farmers, on the father's side, who have lived at Milton on the Hudson for many generations; on the mother's side from the Mannings, merchants; but on both sides members of the Society of Friends.

Growing up the youngest and darling of the family, always surrounded by the atmosphere of love and duty where harsh words and looks were unknown, she gained a certain discipline of independence by being sent to New York to study art. She was still a very young girl, having only gone through a high school in Poughkeepsie where she had distinguished herself in mathematics. She had from babyhood tried to draw, and the little compositions of her twelfth year have quite an idea of "placing" and story.

The School of Design for Women at the Cooper Institute was the only place, at that time, where anything approaching an art education could be had for a girl. The Academy of Design schools were hedged about by all sorts of restraints, and the Art Students' League was not yet in existence. It was here that I first saw her—very youthful in figure, delicate yet full of vigor. She rode well; an accomplishment that stood her in good stead in Mexico and the West, where indeed no one is really respected who cannot manage a horse. She skated on her little feet like a swallow flying, and danced with the same grace and lightness. She could outskate and outdance us all.

And that's enough. Skating, dancing. It tires me to think of all that young vitality, and makes me unaccountably sad to look at her there on the wall, an old woman who has given up vivacity for resignation. But still presenting the clean profile, the small neat cameo head, that her earliest pictures show, and lighted—I am sure she imposed this on the painter—by a dusky radiance from above and to one side. Despite the downcast eyes, there is something intractable about you, Grandmother, but I am too tired and sore to deal with it. I have been at this desk too long, and Rodman's visit was no help. Ada, come on, hurry up. I ache all over—neck, shoulders, back, wrists, stump. I want your key in the door, I will you to clatter my supper dishes into the sink and start laboring up the stairs.

This house creaks and shifts in the dark. It is even older than I am, and nearly as warped, and it may ache as much. Come on, Ada, before I begin to think Rodman and Leah are right. Too long a day. I must never go this long again. Tomorrow, with the sun in the room, it will be better. Mornings, and maybe an hour or two in the evening, that's enough. Ada, come on, come on. Appear in that doorway. Let me hear your gravelly Cousin Jack voice. "Eh, Mister Ward, ain't you about ready for bed?"

Mister Ward, she will say, not Lyman. Fifty years ago we used to play together, never quite with Grandmother's approval. What would she have said if she'd seen us with our pants down in the dusty loft of Attles' barn? But Ada never presumes on childhood acquaintance. None of the legendary Western democracy operated in our relations, only the democracy of childhood. Her grandfather worked for mine, and her father for my father, in this same old Zodiac whose mole holes riddle the hill under us (that's why the house has settled so crookedly). Three generations of Trevithicks and Hawkeses working for three generations of Wards. The West is not so new as some think.

Bless God, she is six feet tall and strong as a man. She is cheerful, dependable, common. She deals with my person and my problems as matter-of-factly as she would change a baby's diaper. I suppose I *am* her baby, as my father was in his last years. Does she wish all the Wards would die off and give her a rest, or would she be empty without one of us to look after? Does the sight of my nakedness trouble her when she undresses and bathes me? Is she given cold shivers by my stump? Turned to stone by my rigid Gorgon head? Does she think of me as an old friend, as poor Lyman, as that unlucky Mister Ward, as a grotesque, or simply as an object to be dealt with, like a caked saucepan?

Whatever you think, come on, Ada. I need that bath and that bed and that bedtime bourbon. Whatever you think, I have learned to think nothing. I run by routine, I accept from hired women services that I would never have accepted from my wife before I became a grotesque. When you block the doorway with your bulk, and shuffle in on your bunioned arthritic feet making comfortable noises, my soul rushes out of me with gratitude.

Already we have a comfortable rut, we go through habitual motions whose every stage is reassuring. While she starts the bath water I wheel my chair into the bedroom, just beside the bathroom door. We don't bother with the crutches. She helps her grotesque doll to stand up, and it clings to her while her gnarled hands, the end joints twisted almost at right angles, fumble with zippers and buttons. She has never complained of her arthritis to me—thinks it amounts to nothing beside mine. Grunting with effort she lifts me—she would say "hefts" me—off the chair's step, and I cling there, in pain as always, naked, helpless, while she flops a testing hand in the water. Then she returns and hefts her maimed doll bodily into the air until the last clothing falls from its foot, and lowers it with grunts and sighs into the tub.

The water is so hot that it makes the cicatriced stump prickle and smart, but it must be that hot if it is to ease the aches away enough to permit sleep. Painfully she wallows down on her knees and without diffidence soaps and rinses me all over. Her crooked fingers drag across the skin stiff as twigs. Her doll sits stiffly, pointed straight ahead at

16

the fixtures that emerge from the wall. When she is finished she bends far over and guides its arms around her neck. Then she rears upward, and up it comes, naked and pink, her hairy baby, its stump bright red. Its dripping wets the front of her dress, its rigid head glares over her shoulder.

Holding it, clucking and murmuring as she works, she towels it down as far as the knees, and then she takes it around the waist and tilts it upon her great bosom and rotates until its leg, bent to miss the tub's rim, can straighten down on the mat. Pressing it against her as intimate as husband, she towels the rest of it and eases it into the chair and wheels it to the bed. Another lift—the buttocks sink in softness. It sits there shivering in its damp towel until she comes with urine bottle and tube. When I have attached them she checks the hookup with a casual tug.

Now the pajamas, delicious to the chilling skin, and the ease backward until the body that has been upright too long is received by mattress and pillows. She sets the telephone close, she tucks up the covers. Finally she waddles over to the cabinet by the desk and gets the bottle and two glasses, and we have a comfortable nightcap together like cronies.

Oh, hurry, Ada Hawkes. I don't want to telephone. That would demonstrate something that I don't want demonstrated.

My grandfather, long before your grandfather Trevithick knew him, before he put on weight and fell in love with flowers and learned to take his consolation from a lonely bottle, was an indefatigable worker. He often rode a horse a hundred miles a day, four hundred miles in a week, accepting the testing that such journeys implied. Despite bad eyes and migraines, he used sometimes to work all night on maps and reports. When he was making an underground survey of the New Almaden mine he stayed underground for twenty hours at a stretch. He would not understand, any more than my grandmother would, this weakness that yearns for a motherly bosom and a pair of warped gentle hands.

"Best egg in the basket," he used to say of me when I was a small boy and wanted to help him plant and prune and prop and espalier his Burbank fruit freaks. I would like to be that kind of egg. I refer my actions to his standards even yet. If I were talking to anyone but myself I would have shut up long ago. Probably it's a mistake to complain even to myself. I won't do it.

But oh, Ada, Ada, get over here, it's already past nine.

And there, like a bell tardily ringing the hour, is her key in the lock downstairs.

2

Morning, the room full of sun. I wheel to the window and watch the robins digging worms in Grandfather's lawn. The grass is blue-wet in the open, green-dry under the pines. The air is so crisp it gives me a brief, delusive sense of health and youth.

Those I don't have, but I have learned not to scorn the substitutes: quiet, plenty of time, and a job to spend it on. On the long desk my grandparents' lives are spread out in files and folders, not as orderly as I would like them, and not fully understood, but waiting with a look of welcome. The loose folders I have been working on are weighted down with Grandfather's rock samples—high-grade mostly, with varicose veins of gold through it, but also other things: a piece of horn silver, carbonate ore from Leadville, a volcanic bomb sawed in two to reveal the nest of olivine inside, some jasper geodes, an assortment of flaked flint arrow and spearheads.

The solidity and weight of these relics I have several times blessed, for if my papers blow off on the floor I have a bad time retrieving them, and may have to wait until Ada comes, by which time the wind has undone all my careful order. A night or two ago, after a gust had scattered a whole day's patient sorting around the room, I dreamed I was a rodeo cowboy riding my jet-powered chair in figure eights through the place, swooping from the saddle with my vest pocket scooping dust and snatching up papers one by one like ladies' handkerchiefs. Rodman would have something to say about juvenile fantasies of self-reliance if I told him that one.

This is the best time, from eight to noon. Later I begin to hurt more, I get querulous, my mind wanders. Routine work, that best of all anodynes which the twentieth century has tried its best to deprive itself of—that is what I most want. I would not trade the daily trip it gives me for all the mind-expanders and mind-deadeners the young are hooked on.

I thank my stars that I have no such commitments to the present as

Ada was telling me about last night—a daughter at home resting up from her husband, who is apparently a head of some sort, one of the Berkeley Street People, a People's Park maker, a drop-out and a cop-out whose aim is to remake the world closer to the heart's desire. I know him, I have seen him a hundred times—his mouth is full of ecology, his mind is full of fumes. He brings his dog to classes, or did when he was attending classes. He eats organically grown vegetables and lives in communes and admires American Indians and takes his pleasure out of tribal ceremonials and loves the Earth and all its natural products. He thinks you can turn the clock back. He is not so different from me, actually, except in the matters of skepticism and a sense of history. Ada, naturally, finds him pretty repulsive. What's the matter with kids these days? she asks me. What kind of a loony bin have they got down there in Berkeley, anyway? What kind of a fellow is it that will let his wife support him for two years, living around in those pigpen places, everybody scrambled in together? Honest to John, when I look at TV and see them down there breaking windows and throwing rocks at police and getting tear-gassed, all dressed up in their kookie clothes, with their hair down to their shoulders! You were there. Did it use to be that way? When Shelly went down there to go to school she was the brightest girl in Grass Valley High. Two years later she's a drop-out, working to support that . . . She'd been better off if she'd stayed right here and gone to secretarial school and got a job here at home.

Well, I have no confused young to look after. Rodman takes care of himself, I'll give him that. My problem is to keep him from taking care of *me*. As for Rodman's mother, she no longer lies in wait for me as I go from kitchen to study and study to porch or garden. She has no associations with this house. I bypass her, somewhere on the stairs, on my way to the strenuousness, aspiration, and decorum of my grand-mother's life, and the practicality and masculine steadiness of my grandfather's.

The West began for Susan Burling on the last day of 1868, more than a century ago. It had not figured in her plans. She was in love with Art, New York, and Augusta Drake. So long as I have quoted Augusta on Susan, I may as well quote Susan on Augusta. This is from her unpublished reminiscences, written when she was in her eighties.

And then Augusta dawned on my nineteenth year like a rose-pink winter sunrise . . . sweet and cold from her walk up from the ferry: Staten Island was her home. A subsidiary aunt had taken me in that winter who lived on Long Island, and I crossed by an uptown ferry and walked down. Across the city we came together, and across the world in some respects. She was a niece of Commodore De Kay and a granddaughter of Joseph Rodman Drake. Her people belonged to the old aristocracy of New York. My people belonged to nothing except the Society of Friends and not even that any longer in good standing. She had spent her girlhood abroad and spoke three languages, I "one imperfectly." She had lived in one of the famous capitals of Europe and walked its galleries among the Old Masters while I was walking the old green hills of the Hudson and wandering the Long Pond woods, and my longest journey at that time had been to Rochester, New York.

She said she was a professional, but her friends were New York society girls and private pupils; she was in the painting class, I in Black and White, but we both stayed in the afternoons and had time for many talks, comparing our past lives and dreams for the future. We sat together in Anatomy lectures and Friday composition class and scribbled quotations and remarks to each other on the margins of our notebooks. I still keep one of those loose pages of my youth with "Let me not to the marriage of true minds admit impediments" copied in pencil in her bold and graceful hand, and on the other side in the same hand the words which began our life correspondence, not gushingly nor lightly. We wrote to each other for fifty years.

She came up to Milton that following summer and every summer after till there was no Milton for me—not that Milton! Her sharings in books and friends were the stored honey of my girlhood. The strings were tuned high for us in those years, but after we became wives and mothers, and had lost our own mothers (she loved mine and I loved hers), a settled, homely quality took the place of that first passion of my life. Salt is added to dried rose petals with the perfume and spices, when we store them away in covered jars, the summers of our past.

Several things interest me in that passage. For one thing, it tells me the source of Rodman's name. It was Grandmother's dearest wish that we give our child that label. He would never forgive me if he learned that we named him after the author of *The Culprit Fay*. Augusta's son was also named Rodman, so you might say the name has been made to run in both families.

What is more eyebrow-raising is the suggestion of lesbianism in this friendship, a suggestion that in some early letters is uncomfortably explicit. (*Good night, sweetheart. When you are here some stifling night like this we will creep out in the darkness and lave ourselves in the fountain.*) The twentieth century, by taking away the possibility of innocence, has made their sort of friendship unlikely; it gets inhibited or is forced into open sexuality. From a dozen hints, beginning with Augusta's "bold and graceful hand," we might conclude that Susan's friend was an incipient dike. Grandmother herself, outskating and outdancing them all on her little feet, could not have been more feminine. Her color was always rosy. She blushed easily, even as an old woman.

It looks like a standard case, but despite the stigmata I elect to join her in innocence. Instead of smiling at her Victorian ignorance of her own motives, I feel like emphasizing her capacity for devotion. The first passion of her life lasted *all* her life.

At the end of 1868 she was twenty-one, and had been in New York four winters. She was studying illustration with W. J. Linton, an English artist much influenced by the Pre-Raphaelites, and she was beginning to get small commissions. Her latest and most important was a farm scene for the cover of *Hearth and Home,* a new magazine sponsored by Edward Eggleston, Frank R. Stockton, and Harriet Beecher Stowe.

And observe the continuities of a life like hers, despite the years of exile. She will have a connection with Harriet Beecher Stowe—will marry Mrs. Stowe's cousin. Linton's daughter will become a governess in the shacks and tents where Grandmother will live, and will help Grandmother in the sacred task of making my father and his sisters fit to live in Augusta's world.

Now the New Year reception I have been leading up to. The place was the Moses Beach house on Columbia Street in Brooklyn Heights, then a street inhabited by great merchant families—Thayers, Merritts, Walters, Havilands "of the china Havilands." Grandmother's feckless brother Ned had married the daughter of Elwood Walter; during her first year as an art student Grandmother had lived in the Walter house down the street. She moved in this atmosphere not quite as an equal, but not quite as a poor relation, either. She was that nice young friend of Emma's from the Cooper, the pretty little one with the high coloring, the one who draws so nicely. She knew and loved the Beach house. It was all one great window on the water side, and from its bluff overlooked the whole Upper Bay with its waterbug activity of tugs and ferries and barges. Governors Island, as I imagine that last day of December, would have floated like dirty ice out in the bay; the Jersey shore would have fumed with slow smokes.

The Doppler Effect is very apparent in my imagining of that afternoon. I hear it as it was now and as it is then. Nemesis in a wheelchair, I could roll into that party and astonish and appall the company with the things I know. The future is inexorable for all of them; for some it is set like a trap.

Thanks to the prominence of the people Augusta had introduced Susan to, I can find some of them in the histories of art and others in memoirs and reminiscences. The view from Columbia Street I have seen, but much obstructed and changed. As she saw it a hundred years ago there were no grimy warehouses thrusting up from the waterfront, there was no Brooklyn Bridge, no Statue of Liberty, no New York skyline. Somewhere I have read that in 1870 the tallest building in Manhattan was ten stories. But I am like the Connecticut Yankee who has foreknowledge of an eclipse. I know that in a few years the Roeblings, who will build Brooklyn Bridge, will buy the Walter house. I could depress young Dickie Drake, Augusta's moody and poetic brother, with the story of the Statue of Liberty, for on its base will one day be inscribed a poem by a girl named Emma Lazarus, with whom Dickie will fall in love after he gets over Susan Burling, but whom he will not marry. She is Jewish. Augusta will write Grandmother all about it, and Grandmother, though she likes Emma Lazarus, will agree with the family's judgment that such a marriage would not do.

So many things I know. Young Abbott Thayer, whom I have looked up in the art histories, was at that party, monopolizing a love seat in the second parlor with Katy Bloede, one of Grandmother's Cooper friends. The Thayer painting I have here on the desk, the one called *Young Woman* from the Metropolitan collection, is undoubtedly Katy Bloede, the "typical tall, handsome, almost sexless female for which he was famous." She was not quite sexless—she had serious "female troubles"—and Thayer will marry her shortly and paint her a hundred times. As Grandmother said, "Her face was his fortune." When she dies young, Thayer will marry Emma Beach, currently playing the piano for a Portland Fancy in the other room.

Among those dancing was George Haviland, altogether the most sophisticated and charming man Susan Burling had ever seen. She admired his courtesy and his grace, though he was said to drink. She worshipped his beautiful young wife. Ah, there, George Haviland. In a few years you will blow your brains out, a bankrupt.

Or Elwood Walter, Jr., several times my grandmother's escort in those years, a man she said gave her her first lessons in flirtation. A volatile, talkative, ugly, attractive man "capable of any sacrifice that did not last too long," he will have a fate less predictable than Haviland's. He will die in the sandals and brown robe of a Franciscan monk.

Or Henry Ward Beecher, the great man of that district, pastor of Plymouth Church, late thunderer of ferocious war sermons. He was sitting with an attentive group around him in the parlor off the dining room, and the boom of his voice filled the house when Emma Beach stopped playing and the dancers paused. "Born conspicuous," Grandmother said of him, "the most naturally self-conscious man in the world." His only mode of conversation was the monologue, and his version of the monologue was declamation. Many Friends disliked him for his bloody sermons. Women on Columbia Street told each other privately that he had been seen letting himself out of the Beach house, whose library he used as a sanctuary, at late and compromising hours. Grandmother disliked him for his sermons, thought the stories of his indiscretions mere gossip, and despised his arrogance. And what a collapse is coming to that whited sepulcher of a reputation! *Mene mene tekel upharsin.* Only a little, and Theodore Tilton will bring it all down with his charge that Beecher committed adultery with Tilton's wife.

On days like this, the young ladies stayed at home and received, the young men circulated from house to house. Grandmother thought them "almost too boastful" about the number of houses they must visit before night, and found some of them almost too far gone to dance by the time they reached the Beaches'. Her own callers were few and left early. Augusta herself was receiving on Staten Island and would not be at this party. The dancing had broken up as a group of young men prepared to depart. She went into the main parlor, got herself a glass of punch, and stood by the west window watching the sun embed itself in long flat clouds. In the small parlor the Reverend Beecher was defending, against no opposition that Susan could hear, the practice of selling church pews. Through the doorway Mrs. Beach, buoyant upon her bustle, caught her eye and beckoned.

Susan, blushing pink, went in obediently and took a chair. Nods and smiles acknowledged the youthful sobriety that would rather listen to uplifting conversation than dance. Beecher's ophidian glance rested on her briefly, Mrs. Beach widened her lips in the premonition of a smile, she got an earnest, frowning regard from an unseasonably sun-blackened boy too big for the gilt chair he was perched on. She had met him, barely: one of Beecher's cousins, newly arrived from somewhere. He had a sandy mustache and fair short hair that clustered on his forehead. He looked outdoorish and uncomfortable and entrapped, and his hands were very large, brown, and fidgety.

With her own hands in her lap she sat and let Beecher's opinions reverberate around her. Her blush faded; she made herself prim. Then through the window she saw a cab draw up outside and three young men in overcoats and high hats get out. Two of them were Augusta's brothers Dickie and Waldo. Impulsively she started to rise.

Mrs. Beach said, "Susan Burling, sit down!"

The monologuist halted; all eyes were on. Burning, she said, "I saw someone coming. I thought . . ."

"Minnie will let them in." Mrs. Beach returned her attention to the great one, and Susan sat on, telling herself she would never again accept an invitation to this house. When the newcomers came in to pay their respects she barely shook hands with the Drake boys, both of whom smelled of toddy and cigars and were very willing to share her company. ("A complicated young man," she wrote to Augusta once. "I think I shall not reply to his letter after all." It isn't clear which brother she referred to; both took a considerable interest.)

"Excuse me," she said breathlessly to the room at large, and escaped.

She went up the stairs in a furious rustle of taffeta, wishing that every tread were paved with the face of Henry Ward Beecher. To do what? Read? She was too upset. Better to work at her drawing. But her room offered neither work surface nor adequate light. The library, then. Nobody would be there with the party filling the other rooms. Downstairs again, and along the hall (skating on her little feet like a swallow flying?) to the heavy oak door. A peek—no one inside. She popped in.

I see her there like one of her own drawings, or like the portrait by Mary Curtis Richardson on the wall behind me: a maiden in a window seat, flooded with gray afternoon. But where her drawings usually suggest maidenly yearning, and her portrait suggests some sort of pensive and rueful retrospection, this window-seat maiden suggests only concentration. She had the faculty of sinking herself in whatever she was doing. In five minutes the Reverend Beecher was forgotten with a thoroughness that he would have found insulting.

Some time later the door opened, letting in a wave of party noise. Hoping that whoever it was would see her working and go away, Susan did not look up. The door closed with a careful click, whereupon she did look up, and saw Mr. Beecher's cousin, young Mr. What-was-his-name, Ward. He had such an earnest, inquiring face that she felt like throwing the drawing pad at it. "I hope I'm not intruding," he said.

She laid the pad face down beside her. "No, of course not."

"You were working."

"Nothing important."

"A drawing, is it? I know you're an artist."

"Who told you that?"

"Emma."

"Emma flatters me."

He had not once smiled. Now he laid a hand on the doorknob. "No, really. If you don't go back to work I'll have to leave. I don't want to disturb you. I was just looking for a quiet corner. That much talk wears me out."

She could not help saying, fairly tartly, "Some people admire your cousin's talk."

His only answer was an odd, half-questioning, half-surprised glance. With his hand on the doorknob he waited. "Couldn't you just go ahead, without paying any attention to me?"

He had an air of quiet such as she had known in men like her father, men who worked with animals. He did not look like one who was easily upset, or talked too much, or thought he had to be entertaining. "All right," she said, "if you'll pay no attention to *me*."

"That'll be harder," he said gravely. "I'll try."

At once he turned away and began reading the spines of books in the shelves. Convinced that she could not draw a line with him in the room, she found that she could; he was simply absorbed in the library's dusk. Once she looked up and saw him standing with head bent, reading, his back to her.

Her drawing was of three girls raking the dooryard of a farm. For models she had used her sister Bessie and two Milton girls, and by their tucked-up skirts and mobcaps, and by the scrub bucket visible through the open door, she had meant to suggest that they had escaped from their tedious inside chores and fallen upon the wooden rakes in a spirit of play. I have a print of the picture, and it suggests just that. It is a gay, old-fashioned rural snapshot. The likeness of Bessie, whom Grandmother used about as often as Abbott Thayer used Katy Bloede, is one of the best.

After a time she was aware that Mr. Ward was standing behind her looking over her shoulder. Looking challengingly upward, expecting to feel irritated, she found that she did not: she wanted him to praise the drawing. But he only said, "It must be wonderful to do what you like and get paid for it."

"Why? Don't you?"

"I'm not doing anything. Not getting paid either."

"But you've *been* doing something. Somewhere in the sun."

"Florida. I was trying to grow oranges."

"And couldn't?"

"The chills and fever flourished a little better."

"Oh, do you have *that!*" Susan said. "So do I, or used to. If there's anything I utterly despise, it's malaria. The fever leaves you so stupid and depressed, and you think you've worn it out and back it comes. I feel sorry for you."

"Why that's nice," he said. She saw his face—he had quite a nice face, rugged and brown and with plenty of jaw, and his eyes were very blue—break into ripples and wrinkles of laughter, and she said foolishly, "I'm sorry about the oranges, too."

He blew through his lips, his eyes were narrowed to crescents. So he was not half as earnest and solemn as she had thought him. He said, "That was only a stop-gap. Now you get back to your drawing. I promised not to disturb you, and I did."

But she put aside her pad and said, "Stop-gap for what? What do you *want* to do?"

"I started out to be an engineer."

"And at an advanced age gave it up?"

No smile. "I was at Yale, at the Sheffield Scientific School. My eyes went bad. I was supposed to be going blind."

She was contrite, but Oliver Ward jingled the small change in his pocket, took three or four steps in a circle, and came back facing her. He pulled from the inner pocket of his coat a pair of silver-rimmed spectacles and hooked them over his ears, aging himself about a decade. "They made a mistake," he said. "I found out just the other day. There's nothing wrong with the optic nerve. I'm astigmatic, farsighted, plenty of other things, but all I needed was these."

She found him boyishly engaging. Maybe she felt motherly. She said, "So now you can go back to Yale."

"I've lost two years," said young Oliver Ward. "All my class is graduated. I'm going out West and make *myself* into an engineer."

Susan began to giggle. Ward looked dismayed. "Excuse me," Susan said. "It just struck me as funny for someone of the Beecher blood to become an engineer in the wild West."

Suspended in the act of removing his ridiculous spectacles, he stood with both hands at his ears and the glasses down on his nose. He looked annoyed. "I have no Beecher blood."

"But somebody said . . ."

Susan Burling was a pretty girl, small and cleanly made. As Augusta says in her article, "she had the dainty precision that has always seemed to me the mark of a true lady." And she had that rosy complexion and that fatal tendency to blush. I find her as attractive as Oliver Ward obviously did.

Like one patiently explaining incriminating circumstances, he said, "My father's sister married Lyman Beecher. She's the mother of that whole brood—Henry Ward, Thomas, Catherine, Mrs. Stowe, and Cousin Mary Perkins, the best of the litter." He folded his glasses and put them back in his pocket. His teeth gleamed under his mustache—

he was really quite attractive when he looked playful. "The other night she was telling me the story of her life. She said she grew up the daughter of Lyman Beecher, and then became the sister of Harriet Beecher Stowe, and finally hit rock bottom as the mother-in-law of Edward Everett Hale. She's the only one of the whole outfit that can laugh."

He demonstrated that he could laugh too, this earnest young man. They were laughing together very contentedly when the door opened and Emma Beach put her head in. "Susan? Oh, Mr. Ward. Well my goodness, aren't *you* two sly! What are you doing, studying art?"

"Discussing the Beecher blood," Oliver said.

Emma had sharp brown eyes and a nose for romance. She almost sniffed. But then the sound of the piano began again in the far rooms. "Susan, I'm sorry, but here's Dickie Drake, and he's got to go on, but he says he won't go till he dances one square with you, and Waldo swears he'll have at least as much of you, to the minute. They've been *drinking*."

Susan was already off the window seat, looking for a place to tuck her sketch pad. Said my grandfather, quite untroubled by the rush on his companion, and revealing that he could smile as well as laugh, "Leave it with me, I'll look after it."

So she passed him the pad and went off to dance with the Drake boys, who were somewhat fast but who were safe because they were Augusta's brothers. Years later, out of simple good nature or some lingering interest in his sister's friend, Waldo will help rescue Susan's husband from a bad situation by getting him a commission to inspect a Mexican silver mine; and Augusta's husband will make it possible for Susan to go along by commissioning some travel articles. I am impressed with how much of my grandparents' life depended on continuities, contacts, connections, friendships, and blood relationships. Contrary to the myth, the West was not made entirely by pioneers who had thrown everything away but an ax and a gun.

Among the belles in that house Susan went relatively unnoticed, and could escape the dancing when she chose. She chose to as soon as the Drakes left. Many years later, when she reported that evening in her reminiscences, she was hearing the Doppler Effect of time, as I am now. She was looking back more than sixty years, I am looking back more than a century, but I think I hear the same tone, or tones, that she did: the sound of the future coming on for the girl of twenty-one, the darker sound of the past receding for the woman of eighty-four.

> The parlors that New Year's Evening were filled with a large company of persons moving about and changing places, and but few were in the room by the window. Dark had fallen outside. I was sitting close to the great pane and I saw in it, as in a mirror, all the persons assembled within the rooms; we were there reflected on that background of night starred with specks and clusters of lights, but these did not obtrude. Our images were softened and mysteriously beautified—it was charming. One face in the foreground showed distinct on the darkness of the world outside. I had my drawing pad with me and I made an attempt to draw it—it was the face in line with my view—and, as it happened, it was the only one of all those mirrored in the window that has stayed with me in my own life. All the others are gone out of it years ago; most of them are out of the world.

Whose face? Oliver Ward's naturally, my grandfather's. She made him look rather like a Crusader—all he needs is a helmet, and a gorget of chain mail. His face is young, strong, resolute in profile: which is probably the way she saw it.

And why was he sitting so that his face was in line with her view? Because he was already more than half in love with Susan Burling, and after returning her sketch pad to her he had neither the social ease to make further excuses for talking to one so popular, nor the courage to tear himself away. So he sat at a little distance as if in deep thought about his coming adventure in the West, and hardened his jaw at difficulties and dangers, and hoped that he looked quietly heroic.

And why did she draw his face? Not simply because it was there, I think. He had at the least made her notice him.

On that minimum contact they came together; it is as if you should bond two whole houses together with one dab of glue. Within a week he had left for California, and for nearly five years they did not see each other again. Clearly he went with the notion of "proving himself"—that was Grandfather's character—and stayed on a long time because he had as yet no proofs. Clearly, though, he wrote to her, and she replied, for the reminiscences speak of the "understanding" that gradually established itself between them.

But not entirely of her volition, perhaps not even with her full consent. I find it interesting that in the more than one hundred surviving letters that Susan wrote Augusta Drake during those five years, there is no mention of the name or existence of Oliver Ward until more than a week after his return.

3

A bad three days, full of irritation and wasted effort. I should have my head examined for hiring that woman from the *Argus*. She couldn't bag oranges without making bonehead errors. What is worse, I let her upset me as much as I obviously upset her—it obviously made her nervous to work with a freak.

Nothing right all the time she was here—raining outside, no sun in the room, no brightness in the mornings, no warmth on my neck, no pleasure or progress in the work. Feeling with her goose-pimpled feelings, I was aware all the time of all the bare empty closed-off rooms of this house, and the Gothic strangeness of this corner where a death's-head freak fumbles around among old papers and mumbles into a microphone. She watched me with something like horror. I could feel her eyes on my back, and hear her breathing, and whenever I wheeled around in my chair and caught her eyes, they skittered away in desperate search for something they might have been looking at. I couldn't help wondering if her lamentable lacks, both secretarial and personal, were her own, or only a manifestation of the modern inability to do anything right. All the time I was trying to work with this Miss Morrow I kept imagining what a pleasure it would be to have someone like Susan Burling to sort pictures and file papers and transcribe faded and barely legible letters.

Instead of mishearing instructions, mistyping copy, losing things, dropping things, watching the clock, taking coffee breaks down in the kitchen, hitting the bathroom every half hour, and getting ready to leave before she had half arrived, Susan Burling would have been quick, neat, thorough. She would have been fascinated by the drawings instead of handling them like the kitchen silver being sorted into a drawer, the knives with the spoons and the forks among the knives. She would have been intrigued by the clothes of another period instead of finding them comical. She would have noted the humanness of faces lost in time.

In one of her letters, speaking of a family portrait she saw in the Ward house in Guilford, Grandmother exclaims that the subject has "such a charming last-century face!" Her own pictures should evoke the same comment now. But what does Miss Morrow say, bending in her miniskirt so that my peripheral vision is filled with a yard of fat thigh, her hair in a mound years out of style, her lips ghastly with colorless lipstick and her upper lids as green as shutters—what does she say, bending this mask over a row of photographs taken of Grandmother through many years, all showing her cameo profile and her indomitable elegance? She says, "Gee! Same hairdo all her life!"

Yes, Miss Morrow. Same old hairdo: classic knot and bangs. Anything good was worth sticking with. Susan disliked what she called "too much forehead." She liked two hair styles—the one that she had determined suited her own face, and the low, sweeping curve, with a deep wave, that Augusta wore. I can't even imagine what she would say at the sight of this girl's steep skull with hair piled on top of it like a packrat's nest on a cliff.

Good-bye, Miss Morrow, and thanks for your help, which I suppose I will recover from. Tomorrow I must make an effort to get started right with Ada's daughter Shelly, for if she turns out wrong I can hardly let her go. I'll be stuck with her until she settles her problem with the husband who doesn't want to be unwanted. If her hair weren't all loose down her back in the current fashion I would like her better, but having no machinery it might get caught in, I can hardly make her put it up. Also she has some of Ada in her, she might be all right.

It was an odd interview we had yesterday afternoon. I was taking my airing in the garden, the first time I've been able to go out since the rain. The apple trees are in blossom, and I thought for a while I was hearing the traffic from the freeway that has split and ruined this town, but when I listened carefully it was the sound of thousands of bees up to their thighs in pollen.

I was on my crutches, doing my eight laps up and down the path where the pines wall the garden in. It is level there, and I have had it paved. But eight laps are rough. Four are all I ever want, six I can barely manage, the last two I do with sweating hands. Every swing and peg hurts from my heel to my shoulders. When I finally crawl into the chair again it is as if all the blood in my body, at a temperature of 400° Fahrenheit, were concentrated in my miserable stump. It takes me half an hour to recover from what I am determined is going to do me good.

So I was not displeased, in the middle of the fifth lap, to see this young woman come through the gate where the path from the Hawkes cottage enters the bottom of the yard. I knew who she was, and got to my chair and watched her as she came.

She isn't big like Ada—a sort of medium person, medium good figure, and that female way of pushing backward with her open hands as she walks. Hair down her back, and the habit of throwing it with a jerk of the head. Male or female, that gesture always irritated me when I lived down where one saw a lot of longhairs. If long hair is that much of a distraction, why not cut it off, or put it up in a classic knot and bangs? But when she stopped short just at the lower line of the apple trees, and stood for a moment with her face lifted, I chalked one up in her favor. I had stopped my chair at that exact place, coming out, because right there the spice of wistaria that hung around the house was invaded by the freshness of apple blossoms in a blend that lifted the top of my head. As between those who notice such things and those who don't, I prefer those who do.

When she got within a hundred feet I could see that she has Ada's gray eyes in Ed's square face. Not pretty, not homely. A medium sort of girl, the sort who, compact in white nylon and white nurses' shoes, might take your order in a busy lunchroom in Des Moines. Why Des Moines? I don't know. She just looks that way. Not Bay Area, anyway. Not that knowing, in spite of the hair.

Her voice surprised me, though—bass-baritone. "Hello. I'm Shelly Rasmussen."

"I know. Your mother told me you were home."

I could see her wondering how much else her mother had told me. I could also see that she found holding my gorgon gaze difficult, and to spare her I turned the chair a little, casually, so that we could talk past each other instead of head on.

"She said you might need some help, the girl you had didn't work out."

"She neither worked out nor worked. Do you type?"

"Not very fast, but I'm pretty accurate."

"Ever transcribed tapes?"

34

"No. I suppose I could learn."

"Are you discreet?"

"What?"

"Are you discreet?"

A little smile, out of focus at the edge of my vision. "I think so."

"Because I'm not," I said. "I tell myself I'm writing a book about my grandmother, and I am, too, but I sit up there sometimes and let my mouth go into that tape recorder and it gets all mixed up with Grandmother's biography. I'm always saying things that would offend my relatives. Sometimes I might even say things that would offend yours. Plus a lot of stuff that would embarrass me if I played it back."

"Sounds great," she said, and laughed, a real *ho ho ho*. If I'd heard it through a wall I would have sworn it was a man's laugh.

"Great is exactly what it isn't," I said. "When I said 'discreet' I meant discreet like a machine, something with fingers and no mind."

The little smile, while she clawed the hair back over one shoulder. "A good typist is supposed to type without reading," she said. "I'm not a good typist, but I'm not a gossip either."

"Good." I wasn't very pleased with her, if the truth should be told—and I had better make sure she doesn't get *this* tape to transcribe. That little smile was more knowing than I had first thought her. But who else would I get? I said, "Have you got a file clerk's memory? Mainly what I want is somebody to learn the files and find me things when I need them. I have a little trouble working from the chair."

"Is there a lot of stuff?"

"Quite a lot."

"I'd need a little time to learn it."

"Of course. You can learn it while you put it in order."

I was looking past her, down over the apple trees into the tops of the pines, to where the old mine dump drops off into the valley, but I could see her studying me sidelong. Let her study—after all, she was going to have to get used to looking at me. Finally she said, "Didn't I see you walking up and down just now?"

"I guess you did. I *was* walking up and down."

"It's none of my business, but should you be?"

"What do you mean?"

"Shouldn't somebody be with you?"

"Somebody's with me most of the time," I said. "Now and then I like to do a little something by myself."

She heard the change in my tone, because hers changed too. As if I had rebuked her, and she had to defend herself, she said, "Mom thinks you try to do too much by yourself."

I said, "I depend on your mother as helplessly as if I were six months old. But even baby tries to crawl a little on his own."

"I'm sorry," she said. "She didn't mean it as a criticism. She thinks you're just way out. She admires you more than anybody."

"Tell her it's mutual," I said, past her. But I was surprised. Old Ada, the strong-as-a-horse family retainer? It was friendship as much as pay or inherited obligation that brought her to my house? It struck me that I had been spending too much embarrassed effort being truly a man of stone while she performed her grunting and clucking services. I was not her troublesome doll, then, her grotesque duty. I remembered her waddling to the cupboard for the bottle when I was eased into bed. Friendship, then.

"Mom's all right," Shelly said. "She wouldn't criticize."

"I know she wouldn't. She's great."

"But she'd have a lot of quiet worms if she knew you were walking around by yourself."

"Then this is your chance to practice being discreet."

Ho ho ho, a department store Santa Claus. "Does that mean I'm hired?"

There is a certain boldness about her; she strikes me as refusing to be put in any subordinate position. She gives me no odds for my age, my experience, my possible distinction, my near-helplessness. If I had been interviewing twelve girls for this job the other day, she probably wouldn't have got it, I'd have tried to find someone who disappears easier. But having no choice, I said, "I guess it does, if you want to be."

"When do you want me, mornings?"

"Not mornings, not at first anyway. That's when I feel like talking into the machine, and I can't do that with anyone around. How are the afternoons?"

"Sure. I'm not doing anything else."

"Say two to five?"

"Fine."

36

I sat still in the chair. Because I had slid back in in the middle of the fifth lap, I didn't have so much of that bloated throbbing in the stump, and the ache in my shoulders wasn't bad. But there is never any escaping—and this is especially true after exercise—the frantic, itching, lost feeling that the leg is still there. The minute I stir my stump at all, the whole leg comes back; I can feel the toes, the ankle hurts. So I wanted Shelly Rasmussen to go. I wanted to get back to the house and have my pre-dinner belt of bourbon and watch the television news and put those cut nerves back to sleep.

She stood there, making no move to leave. I could see the outline but not the expression of her face. "We didn't settle your salary," I said. "How's two fifty an hour?"

"More than I'm worth."

"Not if you're any good. But I live on annuities, it's all I can afford."

"That'll be fine. I'll try to earn it."

I squirmed in the chair to ease the stump, I put down a casual hand and rubbed, wishing the fool would go. My bladder was beginning to be insistent, too, and though I was armed with my Policeman's Friend, and would ordinarily have let fly with the secret pleasure of a bedwetter, I couldn't see myself pissing down a tube with a lady standing six feet from me. Then I thought of poor aghast Miss Morrow, who had wandered all unknowing into the freak show, and I wondered if this one was held there by a sort of fascinated aversion. If she was, I had better find out right now. So I said to the apple trees and the tops of the far pines, "Does it bother you when I talk at you without looking at you?"

"No, why?"

"Does it bother you when I do look at you?"

"No."

So I turned my chair directly toward her, and she was lying, it did bother her, though she made herself look at me steadily, pretending it didn't.

"Because I can't help it," I said. "I either have to talk past you or turn you to stone."

"I guess you wouldn't turn anybody to stone."

"Sixty seconds is usually enough." I turned the chair away again, just enough to take the heat off. "Maybe you can build up an immunity."

She had better. I don't want her either petrified or fascinated, I want her helpful and if possible interested. For it struck me after she finally went away and I headed for the house that I really would like to talk to somebody about my grandparents, their past, their part in the West's becoming, their struggle toward ambiguous ends. Of all the available people, I suppose I would most like to talk about them with Rodman, because next to me he has the largest stake in all this. But this Shelly Rasmussen with the Santa Claus laugh and the voice like the first mate of a lumber schooner—she has a little stake too. I rather like the idea that a fourth-generation Trevithick should help me organize the lives of the first-generation Wards.

4

No letters between my grandparents have been saved, and as I said, Susan's early letters to Augusta do not mention Oliver Ward. To teach me how one evening's acquaintance ripened into a tacit engagement through five years of absence, I have only the reminiscences, written in Grandmother's old age, and I don't believe in them.

She says she didn't want to be one of those girls who faded through long waiting while their young men chased fortune and excitement in the West. She says she wanted him to know she had other resources. So while he sweated on the hot mountains surveying the Southern Pacific's Tehachapi Loop, and later while he boiled alive in the Sutro Tunnel, he kept receiving these letters that talked about the commissions she was getting, the flattering things people said about her drawings, the famous and interesting people she met, the young men among whom she and Augusta pursued the life of Art. Her letters were designed to let him know how well she got on without him.

Studying her drawings in the magazines he managed to lay hands on, Oliver might have been reassured that she was still the lively little Quaker girl he had fallen for at the Beach house. Her pictures were likely to show girls in Watteau dresses hanging over a banister to see who is ringing the doorbell, or young men standing up in rowboats to part the willows that might brush their bonneted girls, or children shutting the gates at twilight on their pet lambs, or young ladies pensively reading in dusky attics. But her letters made it plain that there was already more glitter in her life than Oliver Ward could ever hope to provide.

John La Farge had spent the afternoon at Augusta's 15th Street studio, and had read them parts of a poem called *The Rubáiyat of Omar Khayyám*. Thomas Moran, encountered in the *Scribner* office, had been flattering about Susan's drawings, and had wished that he could draw, as she could, directly on the block, so as to be less at the mercy of engravers. The *Scribner* crowd had just left Milton after a weekend of picnics, boat rides, and cider parties, and the Scottish novelist George MacDonald had read from his latest book, and George Washington Cable had then been prevailed upon to read a Creole story he had just completed, and the actress Ella Clymer had bewitched them all on the midnight piazza with a song, "I Love to See Her Slipping Down a Stair." Thomas Hudson, the young *Scribner* editor, had left the company for a bare half hour and returned with a magnificent sonnet. And hardly had the *Scribner* crowd gone back down to New York than a Boston editor brought John Greenleaf Whittier around to discuss illustrations for a gift edition of *Snowbound*. They caught her scrubbing the dining room, and she had to seat them in the parlor and talk to them through the door while she finished mopping up.

She told things like that as jokes on herself, but Oliver Ward on his powder keg in his tar-papered shack could not miss the Great Name that had come to her door seeking her. She hung it up there like a jack-o'-lantern.

Snowbound fell through, but shortly she was busy on forty drawings and a dozen vignettes for Longfellow's *The Hanging of the Crane*, and a year and a half after she began that, she reported its considerable success in the Christmas trade, and a little later still she wrote that Osgood and Company had mysteriously invited her to Boston, and there surprised her with a dinner at which the whole Brahmin population of New England was present. Mr. Whittier was there, still chuckling over the floor-mopping episode. Mr. Lowell paid her a flattering amount of attention. Mr. Holmes was very witty. Mr. Longfellow held her hand quite a long time and told her he was astonished that one so talented should also be so young and charming. He made her promise to illustrate *The Skeleton in Armor*—which, it turned out, was what the publishers had brought her to Boston to discuss. Mr. Howells, the new editor of the *Atlantic*, praised her realism. Mr. Bret Harte, the celebrated California author, answered her questions about the Sierra Nevada, in which she had expressed an interest.

She was barely twenty-four, and she admits she boasted, "ungenerously." But that young man in the West was as steady as a lighthouse. He applauded her successes, he never expressed jealousy of the young men whose luck he must have envied, he accepted her ambiguous relationship with Augusta and her almost equally ambiguous relationship with Thomas Hudson, now the third of an intimate threesome.

Grandmother implies that he won her over by his cheerful confidence, so that an understanding gradually grew up between them. I doubt the understanding, and I doubt Grandfather's confidence. What did he have to be confident about? Trapped for three years in that litigated tunnel, he must have known that if it was ever finished, a junior engineer without a degree would emerge into the old barren sunlight beating on the old sterile mountains, and that if he wanted a chance at Susan Burling he would have to emerge with more than experience.

I don't think she was protecting herself from an attachment she feared might leave her on the bough. I don't think there was that much of an attachment, not on her part. He kept writing, and she didn't have the heart to shut him off. And he was a reserve possibility, a hole card that she didn't look at because she didn't want to risk breaking up the beautiful sequence of hearts face-up in her hand.

At that stage I don't see her looking for a husband. She didn't really want a fifth card any more than she wanted to look at her hole card. She had her career, she had Augusta and the marriage of true minds, and she had Thomas, whom she admired and idealized. She probably hoped their threesome could go on indefinitely. Though she was no bohemian, she was willing to be unconventional if the conventions could be broken without impropriety; and quite apart from her devotion to Augusta and Thomas, she had a tough and unswerving dedication to her art. She might even have accepted spinsterhood as the price of her career if the cards had fallen that way. And if the cards fell wrong, if Augusta should marry or move away, if art should fail, if her career should be disappointing and she should be exposed to the chilly fear that in the 1870s paled the cheek and weakened the knees of unmarried girls over twenty-four, then why wouldn't she have looked toward Thomas Hudson rather than toward an unliterary, unartistic, not-too-successful engineer, a mere pen pal a continent away?

I think she did.

A relatively poor girl making her own way—what Rodman would call "upward mobile"—she put a higher value on gentility than most who were bred to it, and a higher value on art and literature than those frail by-products of living can possibly support. She had the zeal of a convert or an aspirant. And Thomas Hudson, born as poor as herself and just as upward mobile, was gentility personified, sensibility made flesh.

Not yet thirty, he was already a reputation and an influence. He charmed both the literary and the social. Poems dropped from him as blossoms blew off the Burling apple trees in a spring breeze. He wrote a monthly department, "The Old Cupboard," in *Scribner's* magazine, that the literary waited for and discussed. Ostensibly the assistant of *Scribner's* editor, Dr. Holland, he in fact did all of Holland's work and made most of Holland's decisions and found all the livelier contributors that Holland got credit for.

Susan was his discovery, and he hers. Most of her friends she met through Augusta, but Augusta met Thomas through her. Within a few weeks they were an inseparable trio. In that Edith Wharton version of New York they ran around safe, platonic, and happy to galleries, theaters, and concerts. I have no idea whether or not the 1870s provided editors with expense accounts, but Thomas acted as if they did. I have no idea, either, whether Thomas was courting Susan, or Augusta, or both, or neither. I doubt that any of them knew. If you are genteel enough, that sort of imprecision is possible.

It is hard for me to be just to Thomas Hudson, for I had him held up to me all through my childhood, and he was an impossible ideal. But I have heard former colleagues, American literature professors who study such things, call him the greatest editor the country ever had. Recently I was looking through a file of the *Century*, which he edited after *Scribner's* closed up, and in the single issue of February 1885 I found, in addition to the Susan Burling Ward story that had led me to it, the final installment of a book by Mark Twain called *The Adventures of Huckleberry Finn*, the ninth and tenth chapters of a novel by William Dean Howells called *The Rise of Silas Lapham*, and the opening installment of a novel by Henry James called *The Bostonians*. I wouldn't be surprised if he found and published two thirds of the best literature of four decades. He was nearly as good as Grandmother thought him—a man of taste, intelligence, and integrity. He was one of the group of New York liberals who at various times cleaned up the Grant pigpen and put down Tammany Hall. A man any period could use. Thomas, thou shouldst be living at this hour. So I must curb my tendency to speak of him with condescension or amusement, simply because Grandmother used his perfection as a stick to beat me with.

In the 1870s he was gentle, thoughtful, amusing, a spirit that glowed through a frail, almost epicene body. He had come out of the war with wounds that kept him sickly, but he still managed to do the work of three. His hands were pale and attenuated, his smile was of great sweetness. He loved talk, and he assumed the stance of noble idealism as naturally as water fills a hole in beach sand. In one of her letters, Susan told him that he had a "truly feminine talent for saying lovely, sweet things, with a little pang in them." Many of her letters address him playfully as "Cousin Thomas." Over a span of several years he gave her a number of little presents—a Japanese teapot, a miniature Madonna, certain volumes of poetry—that she clung to while other things, Grandfather's letters for instance, were getting lost. The volumes of poetry and the Madonna are down in the library right now, salted away like Grandmother's rose petals.

Her editorial champion, her closest male friend, the beau ideal of genteel letters, Thomas *had* to suggest himself to Susan as a potential husband. Naturally no expression of that shows through the decorous playfulness of her letters to him. The closest thing I find is a discussion of Friendship, roughly at the level of Cicero: "When you are away from your friends, do you think of their words or of their sudden awful thrilling soul-revealing looks? There *is* something awful about a sensitive human face. What a brute that man must be who said that the finest instrument to play upon was a sensitive impressionable woman! I don't believe *he* could make that intense music and dare to boast of it afterward."

I wonder what she thought she was doing. Surely she was not subtly accusing Thomas of playing on her heartstrings, but she could well have been subtly letting him know that she vibrated. Was she a little afraid her own face might have worn, in his presence, some sudden awful thrilling soul-revealing look?

The more I study Grandmother at that age, the more complicated

43

that Quaker girl seems. She has a passion for Augusta, a crush that has lasted now for four or five years. She admires, idealizes, perhaps is in love with Thomas Hudson. She is sought by several young men, including Augusta's two brothers, who could offer her (and Dickie at least seems to have) a social position to which she is not indifferent. She is dedicated to art, and works hard at it. At the same time, if we accept what she says in the reminiscences, she has been coming to an understanding with Oliver Ward, an engineer two years her junior, whom she has known for one evening and whose existence she has never mentioned to her other friends.

Then in the summer of 1873 she began to be aware that it was on Augusta, not herself, that the uncertain needle of Thomas's affections was settling. I am guessing, but not wildly. She went back to Milton abruptly, instead of moving permanently to New York as she had been planning to do. There is a marked slackening in the flow of letters. There are no more six-page effusions—only brief notes, and those evasive. The importunity was evidently on the part of Augusta. Susan kept pleading the demands of Longfellow's Vikings. She said New York stimulated her too much. To the claim that she should not bury herself in the country she replied that if she had great genius, as Augusta had, she might think it legitimate to sacrifice parents and home to it. But her talent was humble and minor, and if it couldn't be carried on in the house of the parents who had done everything for her, it wasn't worthy of being carried on.

Such mournful dutifulness and self-depreciation. I suppose she was bruised, poor thing, for in the worst tradition of the sentimental song she saw herself losing both lover and friend. She could not have the satisfaction of charging either with treachery, and she would have reproached herself for ever dreaming of being Augusta's rival. A perfect match, an ideal couple, she would have been the first to say. Yet it left her out. In bitter moods she may have wondered if he chose Augusta because she was wealthy and well-born and could give him a social base for his career. I suppose she wept for lost gladness and the relinquishment of true friends. The letters mention bouts of sleeplessness and facial neuralgia.

Somehow she brought on a quarrel. I have no idea what about, for key letters are missing, perhaps destroyed in anger or in the passion of reconciliation. Augusta had been planning to visit Milton, and Susan with at least part of her sensibility had been anticipating a love feast. But she must have written some note that infuriated dark-browed Augusta, already pretty impatient with Susan's defection. At the last minute she wrote curtly that she must accompany her parents to Albany, and could not come, and she signed herself "Very truly your friend."

One letter of Susan's tells me all I know about it.

Fishkill Landing
Tuesday night

My dear dear girl—

Your note came this afternoon just after Bessie and I had been getting your room ready and making your bed—*our* bed where I thought I should lie tonight with my dear girl's arm under my head. It gave me a queer little sick trembly feeling that I've had only once or twice in my life—and then I thought I must see you, not to "talk things over"—I don't care about things, I only want you to love me.

So I hurried after supper and changed my dress and pulled my ruffle down low in front to please my girl [*what*, Grandmother?] and rushed into the garden for a bunch of roses—your June roses, blooming late just for you (we have been hoarding them and begging buds to wait a few days longer for your coming)—and then down to the night boat. I thought I'd either coax you to land or go with you as far as West Point. And oh! what a sick sunk feeling to see the *Mary Powell's* lights already out in the river, going every second farther away! I was distracted. I stood on this landing and wept, and then I walked, and it is only now, two hours later, that I have enough control of myself to huddle here on the bench and write you this by starlight and ask you to forgive me.

I so want to put my arms around my girl of all the girls in the world and tell her that whether I move to New York or stay home, whether she sign herself "Very truly your friend" or "Your ownest of girls," I love her as wives love their husbands, as friends who have taken each other for life. You believe that love has its tides. Well, there *was* a strong ebb tide this summer. I can't explain all that caused it—several things combined—but it only shows me how much you are to me. *Little* streams don't have tides, do you mind that?

Now please don't call yourself truly my friend again. I can stand arguments and scoldings, but—truly your friend! And then to miss you by only that widening gap of water! I should have run, dark lane or no dark lane, and next time shall. As for the chill, I'm a donkey. If I didn't love you do you suppose I'd care about anything

45

or have ridiculous notions and panics and behave like a fool, and quite break down on this landing? But I feel now as if a storm has passed. I'm going to hang onto your skirts, young woman, genius though you may be. You can't get away from the love of your faithful

SUE

Like some of Grandmother's other letters, that one makes me feel like a Peeping Tom. And I don't know whether to smile or to be obscurely shocked to think of her panting and distracted and tearing her hair on Fishkill Landing, with her ruffle pulled down low to please her girl and a rose wilting in her frantic bosom. If I had to make a guess, I should guess that neither Thomas nor my grandfather ever stirred that amount of turmoil in her breast.

But that episode marked a turning point, and that it did suggests a strength of character in Grandmother that I must admire. Right then, apparently, she put away any pre-emptive right to either Augusta or Thomas. The tide of love, as these romantic girls put it, never came full again in the same way. After her summer of unrest, she relinquished one sort of possibility; and when a month later Augusta and Thomas told her about their engagement, she took the word gamely. I have the note she wrote Thomas.

Do you know, Sir, until you came I believe she loved me almost as girls love their lovers—I *know* I loved her so. Don't you wonder that I can bear the sight of you? I don't know another man who could make it seem right. You must have been born to make her future complete, and she was born to kindle your Genius. Isn't it wonderful how it flamed up at her touch? It was there, but as unborn crystals are . . .

All right, Grandmother. Generously said. Maybe your emotions and your good-loser response were learned from novels, but they worked, and they lasted. Thenceforward you were a loving sister to Thomas, and dearest friend, without ambiguities, to Augusta. You never expressed to them or to anyone any feeling of betrayal or disappointment. I suspect that you were able to manage yourself so well because by a stroke of luck you were able just then to look at your hole card. The ace-high straight flush you had coming didn't work out, but at the last minute that buried nine filled a king-high straight.

Within two days after she heard of the engagement of Augusta and Thomas, Oliver Ward wrote that he was coming home from the West.

He arrived on a night of hard rain. She and her brother-in-law John Grant waited in the shelter of the landing and watched the three blurred lights of the ferry creep closer, separating themselves from the lights of the Poughkeepsie side. John's lantern shone back liquid yellow from the puddles, another lantern at the end of the landing threw a streak over the moving river that was roughened every minute or two by gusts. I suspect that Susan's skin was like the river, chilled by gusts of uncertainty, pebbled with the gooseflesh of anticipation. She knew his intentions; he had warned her.

What did a girl of 1873 feel, waiting for the stranger whom she had never taken quite seriously but whom she had now, in her mind, half resolved to marry? The meeting had all the dramatics of one of her more romantic drawings—shine of lantern light on the oilskins of the ferryman, a tall figure that jumped ashore carrying a carpetbag. And what was he wearing? Some great hooded cloak or ulster that made him like a figure out of a conspiratorial opera. The ferryman's lantern threw his huge shadow down the landing. She was in suspense to see his face, for she might remember him all wrong. Then he was before them throwing back the hood, shaking her hand with his big wet hand, saying some sort of greeting and in the same breath apologizing for the ulster—it was his field coat, his town coat was stolen in San Francisco.

He arrived looking suitably outlandish, a traveler from a far place, someone to be cautiously investigated. Yet intimate too, because of what had been said between the lines of letters, or what he had said and she had not denied. They jammed into the buggy and the intimacy was physically enforced. Between the two bundled men she could hardly move. They rode turning their faces away from the spitting dark, and she smelled his unfamiliar odors of pipe and wet wool, and said whatever she *would* say, while her taciturn brother-in-law listened. He had a tendency to be critical of people. She wondered how he rated this young man from the West against the writers and painters and editors he had been driving up from the landing for the last four years.

Her parents were standing in the hall to welcome him and exclaim about the wet, and after the introductions—with what shyness, with what a weight of unspoken implication—Susan guided him upstairs to his room, the one they called Grandmother's room. There he set his carpetbag inside the door and shook himself out of the ulster, and she watched him lay on the dresser, which had never seen anything rougher than a Quaker bonnet or a book of poems in limp leather, a curved pipe, and a great wooden-handled revolver.

Was he showing off? I suppose so. God knows why else a man would bring a pistol to his courting. His character and his role were already Western, he had only that way of asserting himself against the literary gentility with which her house was associated in his mind.

I don't care about that, and I don't care whether she was astonished, impressed, shocked, or amused. What I find myself held by, in imagination, is their tentativeness, their half-awkward half-willingness to admit their understanding, as they faced each other in the doorway by the light of the lamp she carried. That too is like one of her drawings —narrative, sidelighted, suffused with possibility.

She was quickly reassured that he was not impossible, at least for any society short of Augusta's. He was most admiring of her talent and respectful of her friends, he was as big and restful as she had found him in the library in Brooklyn Heights, he had a way of speaking lightly of things without persuading her that he felt them lightly. He was not talkative, but once wound up he charmed them all with his stories of life in California. Her parents sat up late to hear him, though when her New York friends visited they went early to bed. He could play chess—that promised cozy evenings. Her father said he had never seen a man pick a basket of apples faster. And when he took hold of the oars of a rowboat, the rowboat nearly jumped out of the water.

But she puzzled where to take him on some excursion. Long Pond and Black Pond, liked by New York visitors, were not enough for a man who had seen the Yosemite and ridden the length of the San Joaquin Valley through square miles of wildflowers. So she and Bessie and John took him to Big Pond, eight miles back in the woods, a wild romantic place where a waterfall poured into a marble pool and then fell through diminishing pools to the lake.

It was incorrigibly Hudson River school—brown light, ragged elms, romantic water. There they sat on the grass confronting nature. When they had eaten, they did what poets and philosophers did outdoors in the early years of the picturesque—strolled, picked early autumn leaves or late gentians. Susan sketched a little while he stood admiring by. They did not spoon, though Bessie strategically led her husband away so the two could be alone. Having no acceptable way of expressing their feelings directly, they probably vented them on nature. I can see a lot of tableaux while she is struck speechless by a view or a flaming swamp maple, and he stands there with his hat in his hand before the purity of her sensibility.

Late in the afternoon they were back at their picnic spot at the top of the fall. She had always responded strongly to storms, rain in the face, wild winds, wild waters, exciting crossings of the Hudson through floating ice. On this day she lay down and hung her face over the cliff to see down the waterfall. At about the same time, and for similar reasons, John Muir was hanging over the brink of Yosemite Falls dizzying himself with the thunder of hundreds of tons of foam and green glass going by him. Muir had a good deal farther to look down, and the rush of water was far wilder past his ear, but Susan Burling had something her fellow romantic did not. She had Oliver Ward hanging onto her ankles to make sure she didn't spill over.

Anxious? Not on your life. In these days when a girl goes to bed with anybody who will pat her in a friendly way on the rump, few will be able to imagine how Oliver Ward felt, holding those little ankles. He would not have let go if fire had swept the hilltop, if warrior ants had swarmed over him from head to foot, if Indians had sneaked from the bushes and hacked him loose from his hands. As for Susan Burling, upside down and with her world whirling, that strong grip on her ankles was more than physical contact made sweet by the fact that it came between the bars of an iron cage of propriety, touch asserting itself against a thousand conventions. It was the very hand of the protective male. When she came up out of her dizzying tête-a-tête with the waterfall she was in love.

On the long ride home they did not talk much. They jolted and rocked and smiled, intensely aware of every time their bodies were bumped together. Susan agreed without question when Oliver suggested to John Grant that there was no need of driving them clear to the Burling house. They could get off at the Grant house and walk the last half mile—there was a young moon. So they walked the last dark reach between stone walls that her great-grandfather had laid, along the lane felty with dust, through night air cool with coming fall, tannic with early cured leaves.

Somewhere along the lane they settled it. Two days later Oliver left for Connecticut to see his parents for a few days before going back West to hunt a job and prepare a place for her.

Coming emptyhanded, with nothing to support his suit but hope, he could not have timed his arrival more perfectly or found Susan in a more receptive frame of mind. If the threesome was to be split by marriage (though Augusta and Thomas swore it would not be) New York might be a less happy place, and a Western adventure looked attractive. And if Augusta, despite all her vows, found herself ready to give up art for housekeeping, perhaps her defection demonstrated that after all marriage *was* woman's highest role. And if Thomas Hudson was to be firmly given up, the eye might do worse than wander to a man of an altogether different kind, attractive in his own way but in no sense a rival of the lost paragon.

But what a confrontation when she told Augusta. I have to imagine it, but there are hints through years of letters to let me know their respective feelings. I imagine it in the studio on 15th Street where they had worked and slept together for four years in their sublimated dream of art's bachelorhood, and where Susan, looking up from her drawing, had often found Augusta's dark eyes devouring and caressing her.

No caressing in this scene now. Lovers of a kind, cats of a kind, they would have shown their claws. Augusta was incredulous, aghast, and accusatory; Susan stubborn, perhaps just a shade triumphant. You see? I am not defenseless, I am not to be left out after all. There they sat, burning under their serge and bombazine with emotions hotter than gentility could quite allow.

"Oliver Ward? Who on earth is he? Have I met him? You're joking."

"No, I'm quite serious. You haven't met him. He's been in California."

"Then where did *you* meet him?"

"At Emma's, one New Year's Eve."

"And he's been gone since? How long?"

"Four years, nearly five."

"But you've been writing to him."

"Yes, regularly."

"And now he's proposed and you've accepted, all by mail!"

"No, he's back. He's been visiting at Milton for a week."

Augusta, sitting with her head lowered, found a loose thread in the trimming of her gown and pulled it out. Her fingers smoothed the ruffled rickrack braid. Her dark angry eyes touched Susan's and looked away. "Doesn't it seem to you odd—it does to *me*—that you wouldn't ever have mentioned this man's name to me?"

"I didn't know he was going to become so important."

"But now after a week's visit you know."

"I do know, yes. I love him. I'm going to marry him."

Augusta rose and paced the room, stopped and put the heels of both palms against her temples. "I thought there were no secrets between us."

Susan could not resist sinking a claw in the carelessly exposed flesh. "Now that there's something to tell, I am telling you. Just as you told me when there was something to tell about you and Thomas."

Augusta stared with her hands to her head. "Ah, that's it!"

Her cheeks hot, Susan held her ground. "No, that's not *it*. But just as you have every right to fall in love and marry, so have I. One doesn't always know—does one?—when things are headed that way."

Augusta was shaking her head. "I never expected to see you fall in love like a shopgirl with the first handsome stranger."

"You're forgetting yourself!"

"Sue, I think you're forgetting *your*self. What does this young man do?"

"He's an engineer."

"In California."

"Yes."

"And he wants to take you out there."

"As soon as he finds the right place, with some permanence in it."

"And you'll go."

"When he sends for me, yes."

Augusta resumed her pacing, throwing her hands outward in little distracted gestures. She straightened a picture on the wall without stopping. She bent her head to gnaw on a knuckle. "What about your art? What about everything we've worked for?"

"My art isn't that important. I'll never be anything but a commercial illustrator."

"You know that's utterly wrongheaded!"

"I know I want to marry him and go where his career takes him. It won't be forever, but it may take some time. He's not flashy, he'll take a little while to establish himself. I can go on drawing. He wants me to."

"In some mining camp."

"I don't know where."

Now Augusta's agitation broke out. She stopped, she gripped her hands before her face and shook them. "Susan, Susan, you're mad! You're throwing yourself away! Ask Thomas. He'd *never* agree this is right."

"In this," said Susan, as if in a novel, "I can consult no one but myself."

"And make a mistake that will ruin your career and lead you a desolate life."

"Augusta, you've never even met him!"

"And don't want to. I loathe his very name. He can't come in and overturn your life like this. What about *us?*"

They looked, they fell into each other's arms, they even laughed at the extremity of their disagreement. But though they patched up their difference, they did not change; they were both strong-minded women. Augusta did not abate her disapproval, Susan's resolution did not weaken. Maybe she was trapped—she had given an impulsive promise, and promises with her were binding. But I think she had been stirred by Oliver Ward's masculine strength, by his stories of an adventurous life, by his evenness of disposition, by his obvious adoration. I think she was for the first time physically in love with a man, and I like her courage in going where her emotions led her.

But it was hard to know where that would be. For a while Oliver was surveying something for the Southern Pacific around Clear Lake. Then he was on the loose in San Francisco, refusing to take just anything, turning down the jobs with no future, looking for just the right place that would lead somewhere. He stayed for several months with his sister Mary, who had married a prominent mining engineer named Conrad Prager, and at last he found, through Prager's influence, a job that excited him. He wrote that he was to be Resident Engineer of the New Almaden mercury mine near San Jose, an ancient and famous mine that had furnished mercury for the reduction of the gold of the whole Gold Rush. In a few weeks he would come East and marry her and lead her West.

Then he wrote saying that he was in the midst of an underground survey and couldn't get away. He would have to finish it before he could leave.

She waited while the river broke up and the old *Mary Powell* began again to lay her plume along the high spring water. Crocuses came and went, the apple trees exploded, lilacs drenched the air, summer came with its visitors and boarders. Before long it was a year since Oliver Ward had held her by the ankles over the waterfall at Big Pond. Augusta was pregnant, they were reconciled to some new relationship, they wrote each other a good deal about the contrary pulls upon a woman who was also an artist. Augusta was very strong that Susan should not let marriage destroy her career. It was as if, having all but given up painting herself, she wanted to force Susan to be their double justification. And give her credit—perhaps she recognized in Susan Burling a capacity that she herself did not have.

But she never accepted Oliver Ward. They simply agreed not to talk about him any more than necessary.

Susan waited, not unhappily, diligent in her work, dutiful in her daughterhood, refreshing herself occasionally in the old friendships at the 15th Street studio. Counting from New Year's Eve, 1868, when she first met Oliver Ward, she had been waiting just a little longer than Jacob waited for Rachel when Oliver came back in February 1876 and they were married in her father's house.

6

No minister married them. According to the Friends' service, Oliver met her at the foot of the stair and escorted her into the parlor, where in the presence of forty-four witnesses, all of whom signed the marriage paper, they pledged themselves to each other, "she according to the custom of marriage assuming the name of the husband." There went the rising young artist Susan Burling.

And no one stood up with her. Augusta, only a month out of childbed, said she was not well enough—"and if I can't have you I won't have anyone," Susan wrote her. Faithful friendship, the old warmth. But in that same note there is a reference to "my friend whom you don't want to like." She knew very well why Augusta stayed away; she may have half-granted Augusta's reasons.

Susan Burling I historically admire, and when she was an old lady I loved her very much. But I wish I could take her by the ear and lead her aside and tell her a few things. Nemesis in a wheelchair, knowing the future, I could tell her that it is dangerous for a bride to be apologetic about her husband.

While they were honeymooning at the Brevoort House, Thomas called on them, alone. Susan watched his face and estimated his decent politeness for what it was. Later, from Oliver's home in Guilford, she wrote to Augusta:

> I haven't an anxiety in the world at present, except perhaps lest you may not like my boy when you finally meet him. They tell me stories about his boyhood which please me very much. He was such a plucky boy—hardy, enterprising, generous, and truthful. I shall have to be very weak and praise him to you, for he does not "exploit" himself . . . I am sure Thomas was a little disappointed, and so will you be at first.

In another letter—she wrote too many on her honeymoon—she expressed a confidence that to a critical ear sounds a little shrill:

I might have spared myself all my past misgivings. He has not only the will to spare me and keep me safe in every way but he knows how to do so. I ought to have had more faith in him. I knew he would do all he understood to be a man's duty to his wife, but I didn't know how far his understanding of his duty reached. I am left literally nothing to worry about except that he will work too hard. He is very ambitious and will work on his nerve more than is right. It frightens me to hear him quietly tell of the way he has lived these years past—with one object—and the devious, hard, and dangerous ways and places in which he has steadily pursued it. I know this is very weak of me and bad policy too—for you have not seen my boy and all this praise may deepen your first disappointment.

In God's name, Grandmother, I feel like saying to her, what was the matter with him? Did he have a harelip? Use bad language? Eat with his knife? You can do him harm, constantly adjusting his tie and correcting his grammar and telling him to stand up straight. Augusta has got you buffaloed.

It is all Victorian, as Rodman says, all covered up with antimacassars, all quivering with sensibility and an inordinate respect for the genteel. And not a word about that great plunge into sex, from a virginity so absolute that it probably didn't know the vocabulary, much less the physiology and the emotions. Not the faintest hint, even to Augusta, of how she felt in the room at Brevoort House, dark except for the fluttering of gaslight from the street below, when the near-stranger she was married to touched the fastenings of her gown, or laid a hand charged with 6000 volts on her breast.

If I were a modern writing about a modern young woman I would have to do her wedding night in grisly detail. The custom of the country and the times would demand a description, preferably "comic," of foreplay, lubrication, penetration, and climax, and in deference to the accepted opinions about Victorian love, I would have to abort the climax and end the wedding night in tears and desolate comfortings. But I don't know. I have a good deal of confidence in both Susan Burling and the man she married. I imagine they worked it out without the need of any scientific lubricity and with even less need to make their privacies public.

I do get some hint of her feelings from her Guilford letters, describing walks along the shore amid tempests of wind and rain, with a fire and a cup of tea and the sure affections of a sheltered house afterward. Exposure followed by sanctuary was somehow part of Grandmother's emotional need, and it turned out to be the pattern of her life.

She watched Oliver's family for signs in which she could take comfort.

> The father calls me "young lady" and holds my hand in both of his when I bid him good night. He is called all manner of affectionate and ridiculous names by his frisky children, who worship him and treat him as tenderly as if each day were his last, but always with a kind of surface playfulness. This is a family peculiarity—a reticence in expressing sentiment or deep feeling. It is all hidden under a laugh or a gay word. Kate calls her father "you permiscus old parient" with her eyes shining across the card table at him as he gathers up the odd trick and her last trump with it. Oliver calls his father "Old Dad," but follows him around the house with his chair, and listens with the most respectful attention to his views on dikes and sluices, founded on the ideas of fifty years ago.

That's better, Grandmother. No apologies or doubts there. It was nice of you to draw the old couple so that Oliver could take their picture West. And it clearly pleased you to look through the family papers and find there evidence of the sort of respectability and continuity you thought American life too often lacked: such memorabilia as a letter from George Washington to Oliver's ancestor General Ward, and a love letter to his great-great-grandmother, beginning "Honored Madame." You thought it amusing that though she rejected the suitor she kept the letter, only tearing off the signature—retaining the admiration, as it were, and obliterating the admirer.

Two weeks after Oliver arrived to be married, he was gone again to prepare their house at New Almaden. Before he left, Augusta brought herself to have the two of them to dinner. I am sure she was charming, I am sure Thomas was a friendly and assiduous host. I am equally sure that Oliver found it impossible to "exploit" himself, and sat silent, diffident, and inferior, listening to the literary and artistic jargon and the flow of public names. I am sure that Susan was a little hysterical with satisfaction and apprehension at finally getting into one room the people she most loved. She probably talked too much and made too much of Augusta's baby, who like anything of Augusta's was the most perfect on earth. Let her speak for herself.

> It seems almost impertinent to tell you that Oliver was just as impressed by you and Thomas, the house and all belonging to you, as I wished him to be . . . If he hadn't admired you I would have been very much surprised and a good deal disgusted. But it is quite different about Oliver. I should *not* be surprised if you did not like him much, or disgusted with your taste. He is not an ideal type in the sense that you and Thomas are, but nothing now can shake my utter content and faith in him. So, dear girl, don't feel *bound* to admire him for my sake. Don't *try* to like him. It will come all the easier to like him by and by when we are all together.

There she goes again, incorrigible.

Her version of the marriage was that for perhaps two years she and Oliver would live in the West while he established himself. Then they would return, and somehow or other the discrepancies between Oliver's personality and Western leanings and the social and artistic brilliance of the Hudsons' circle would all be smoothed away. They would trade evenings, their children would be inseparable. Of course it would take a little time.

Oliver wrote that he had found a cottage, once inhabited by a mine captain's family, which with renovations would make them a pleasant and secluded home. The manager had agreed to let him go ahead with the remodeling. He sent a floor plan, onto which she sketched a veranda that went three quarters around, and into whose blank rooms she inserted things she wanted, corner cupboards and such. Their letters of planning went back and forth like installments of a serial.

Help would be a problem. Oliver insisted that she look around for a servant girl to bring along, for the only local product in the servant line was Chinamen. So she found a handsome, rather sullen girl with a seven-months' baby, a girl who said she had left a brutal husband but who might never have had a husband at all. That was a chilling thought, to bring someone like that into the house. But she was quiet and respectful, and she was eager to go West. When Susan obtained a commission to illustrate a gift edition of *The Scarlet Letter,* that settled it: she would have a very adequate model for Hester Prynne in her own kitchen. But there would have to be a room for her. She wrote

Oliver asking if he would mind an infant in the house, and if it was possible to add a room. He wrote back gamely that he didn't if she didn't, and that he would put a lean-to off the kitchen. Give him another couple of weeks.

In July he wrote her to come along, the cottage would be ready as soon as she could get there. She shook the envelope, looking for a money order or a bank draft, but there was none. She waited several days, thinking he had probably put the letter in the mail without the check, and would remember and send it on shortly. No word. She contemplated wiring him and was embarrassed to think how such a telegram would look to Mr. Sanderson at the station in Poughkeepsie.

By the fourth day her agitation was extreme. Should she wait longer, and so delay the reunion for which Oliver was obviously impatient, or should she assume that somehow his money order had gone astray and that the best course was to buy the tickets herself and let Oliver straighten the situation out after she got there? Her parents advised her to wait; she could see doubt in their eyes. But after two more sleepless nights she consulted her feelings and decided not to wait. Worried and ashamed, she crossed the river and bought the tickets out of her savings, and on July 20, 1876, in the hundredth year of the republic and the seventh of the transcontinental railroad, she started West.

It was a difficult parting. Custer's cavalry had been destroyed on the Little Big Horn less than a month before, and her parents imagined Indians ambushed the length of the transcontinental rails. There was also that uncertainty about the train fare. She read their unspoken fear that she had tied herself to an unreliable man. Their silence about him she could only answer by a false cheerfulness and an artificial excitement about the journey.

How she managed to part from Augusta, God knows. I imagine them coming apart like two of the great sheets of flypaper, stuck glue to glue, that I used to separate and set out for summer flies. I know it is not a reverent way to speak of the parting of true minds, but I can't help it. Obviously I think Susan was better off in the care of Oliver Ward, train fare or no train fare, than under the influence of that glamorous and arty socialite.

Distance, of course, was not enough to keep their true minds apart.

Susan was barely to Chicago before she scribbled her first postcard, and a delay in Omaha gave her opportunity to write a five-page letter. Not a word in it about Oliver Ward, no expressed anticipations or worries about California. Those were scabs she would not pick, especially when her confidence was shaken.

But there are passages that I read as shadowy forecasts of her future. She found Omaha "Western in the worst sense of the word. There is one building—the Omaha Stock Market—*plaided*, my dear, in squares of red, white, and blue!" She was depressed by the repetitive ugly barren little towns across the sod house country, and it could be she felt a shiver of premonition as she described the "lonely little clusters of settlers' houses with the great monotonous waves of land stretching miles around them, that make my heart ache for the women who live there. They stand in the house door as the train whirls past, and I wonder if they feel the *hopelessness* of their exile?"

7

Doctor day today. Ed took me to Nevada City in the pickup. Not that I really need any medical care. I know as much about my condition as that overworked, unimaginative general practitioner does. I don't need him to tell me that aspirin is best for the pain, and that hot baths help, and that bourbon in moderation is good for body and soul. I go every month because I want it on the record that I look after myself. When Rodman feeds his data into the computer I want it to tell him, in its punch-card jargon, that I am medically motivated. It's no great bother, and it's the least I can do for Rodman's peace of mind. The whole trip takes hardly an hour, and it gives me a change of scene. Today, for a bonus, it gave me a queer little encounter with my old school acquaintance Al Sutton.

Ed left me in the doctor's office and went on to his tire shop. I said I would come down there by myself when I was through. It took me maybe twenty minutes to agree with the doctor that there was no need of further X rays until fall, and then I wheeled into the elevator and went down to the street level and out into the noon crowd.

It is not the Nevada City I knew as a boy. Towns are like people. Old ones often have character, the new ones are interchangeable. Nevada City is in process of changing from old to new. Up the hill, on the steep side streets, a lot of the old flavor remains in gabled houses and second-story balconies, and even the main street has an occasional old brick building with iron shutters, left over from the 1850s and 1860s. But mostly it is Main Street, Anywhere, a set used over and over in a hundred B movies, a stroboscopic image pulsing to reassure us by subliminal tricks that though we are nowhere, we are at home. All the clues are there, some in Gold Rush type: Chevron. General Electric. Electrolux. The all-seeing eye of the I.O.O.F. Weekend Specials. That Good Gulf. Ruth's Burgers and Steaks.

The Nevada City that I remember died quietly, along with Grass Valley, when the quartz mines closed down. The Zodiac, the Empire, the North Star, the Idaho-Maryland, the Bullion, the Spring Hill, shut off their pumps (most of which were built to a design invented by my grandfather), and let the water rise and drown all those miles of deep workings.

My father, who was superintendent of the Zodiac to the end, stayed on, and moldered away with the towns. He did not live to see their partial rejuvenation by the urbanoids who in the '50s and '60s bought up pineland and filled the hills with picture windows. I myself was away during all the years of decline and renewal, and when I came back I came not to the changed towns but to the almost unchanged house of my grandparents in these secluded twelve acres. I dislike what the towns have become, especially since the freeway, and I go through them deliberately not noticing anything, like a machine set on automatic pilot. People clear a path for me, and though their heads turn to watch the freak bore by, mine wouldn't turn if it could. Rodman would probably say that in my fixation on history and my dislike for the present I display a bad case of tunnel vision. Actually, I feel a certain anticipation every time I go to town, but the minute I get there I can't wait to get home. I don't like the smog and the crowded sidewalks, and I don't expect to see anyone I know.

Then I ran into Al Sutton, or almost did.

There was this skinny man with a little pot belly and a sagging pants' seat and glasses pushed up on his forehead, standing in front of the Peerless Laundromat looking away from me across the street. Behind him, blocking the wall side, was a crated Bendix; coming the other way, along the curb, were a woman and child. I stopped, and the skinny man heard me and turned. Unmistakable. Forty years hadn't been able to modify those nostrils that opened straight outward—we used to say if he lay down in the rain he'd drown. His little narrow-set eyes jumped to mine, apology formed all over him like instant moss, he hustled a nimble, accommodating step backward, out of my way.

"Hello, Al," I said. "Remember me? Lyman Ward."

He stared, he snapped his fingers, his brow wrinkled deeply under the pushed-up glasses and the glasses fell down astride the flat bridge of his nose. They were odd glasses that in the sunlight refracted and divided the eyes behind them so that for an instant he looked as multiple-eyed as a horsefly. His mouth opened, and sure enough, there was the old wart on the end of his tongue. It pulled in and hid behind his lower teeth, it crept out again and lay slyly between his lips.

"Thun of a bith!" he said. "Lyman!"

He pumped my hand. I was afraid he was going to pound me on the back, but I should have known Al better. Having been a freak all his life, he has a tenderness for other freaks. Even while he was still shaking my hand and thun of a bithing and saying, Thay, boy, ith nithe to thee you, those odd compound eyes were touching, and taking in, and shyly withdrawing from, the chair, the stiff neck, the crutches in their cradle, the stump under the pinned flap of trouser leg.

"Thomebody told me you were back living on the old plathe," he said. "I been thinking I might drop out and thay hello, but *you* know. Bithneth. How are you, anyway?"

"I can't complain," I said. "How are things with you? You haven't changed."

"Oh thit," Al said, "I'm indethtructible." As gently as a hand might be offered to a possibly scared or nervous dog, his eyes dropped to my stump. He said sympathetically, "They got you thort of laid up. How that happen?"

"You get careless," I said. "I was paring a corn one day."

Haw haw haw. One of the lovable things about Al Sutton was always the ease with which he could be doubled up laughing. He used laughter as a way of placating persecution in advance. Nobody ever held out for long. He could make you feel that there hadn't been anybody so funny as you since Artemus Ward (no relation). He snorted and strangled and became himself a comic figure. He got you laughing too—with him or at him, it didn't matter. Same old Al out there on the sidewalk this noon. Lyman Ward, once the town's rich kid, might have come by in a basket, or on a plank with roller skates under it, and Al would have made all the old ingratiating moves.

"God damn, you kill me. How'd it really happen? Acthident?"

"Bone disease."

His laughter had already modulated into sympathy. "Tough." He shook his head, and in the middle of a shake I saw him realize that I couldn't shake mine, that I was looking up at him under my eyebrows because I couldn't tilt my head back. He sat down quickly on the

Bendix crate to bring himself closer to my level. Few people are that understanding or that considerate.

"Howth the wife? Thee with you?"

"We're divorced."

Left for a moment uncertain whether to pursue that delicate subject or let it drop, he let it drop. Through his dizzy glasses he inspected my chair. His nostrils looked as if they had been made with an auger; I could see clear into his head. "Quite a rig you got," he said. "You get around all over in that?"

"Pretty much. I have to stay in the slow lane on the freeway."

Haw haw haw again. What a companion. A prince of good fellows.

"You thtill a profethor?"

"I've retired. Why don't you come out some Saturday and have a beer and watch the ballgame on TV?"

"Thay," Al said, "don't think I wouldn't like to. Thaturdayth are tough, though. All the working girlth do their wath."

"You own the shop?"

"Thit," Al said. "It ownth me."

He sat on the crate with his mouth open a little, his tongue protruding slightly. His nostrils were black and hairy. Behind his shifting, glittering glasses he had as many eyes as Argus. We had a real bond: one of us is about as hard to look at as the other.

"What have you got on?" I said. "What kind of glasses are those?"

"Thethe?" He took them off and dangled them by an earpiece, looking down at them as if he had just become aware of their oddity. The wart crept out between his parted lips. For fifty-odd years the poor bastard has had that thing on his tongue, filling his mouth and distorting his speech and building his character. You'd think he'd have had it off years ago. You'd think his parents would have had it off before he was three. "Thethe are my working glatheth," he said. "Quadruple focalth."

I looked at them. Four half-moons of magnification were ground into each lens. When I raised them and looked through them, the front of the building swam like hot taffy, and Al became a small crowd. "I thought I had a problem, having to look straight ahead," I said. "What do you use them for?"

Tentatively, delicately, the wart emerged, touched the upper bow of Al's smile, withdrew again. Al stood chuckling, scratching his elbow. "I don't th'pothe a profethor would ever need anything like thethe. But I'm alwayth having to fixth the mathineth. Ever try to thee with your head inthide a Bendixth?"

I get the message. Space being curved, tunnel vision and the rigid neck could leave a man focused on the back of his own head. I don't know what the effect of quadruple focals on a historian might be—nausea, maybe—but there might be virtue in trying them on.

Whose head *isn't* inside a Bendix?

II

NEW ALMADEN

1

Susan Ward came West not to join a new society but to endure it, not to build anything but to enjoy a temporary experience and make it yield whatever instruction it contained. She anticipated her life in New Almaden as she had looked forward to the train journey across the continent—as a rather strenuous outdoor excursion. The day she spent resting with Oliver's sister Mary Prager in San Francisco she understood to be the last day of the East, not the first of the West. That sort of house, full of Oriental art, and that hidden garden with its pampas grass and palms and exotic flowers, were not for her, not yet. Mary Prager was such a beauty, and Conrad Prager so formidably elegant, that she wished she could introduce them to Augusta as proof of the acceptability of Oliver's connections. Because her trunks had not yet arrived, she had to wear Mary Prager's clothes, which made her feel, in the strange garden in the strange chilly air, like someone else—Mrs. Oliver Ward, perhaps, wife of the young mining engineer who as soon as he had established himself in his profession would be able to provide such a house and life as this, preferably near Guilford, Connecticut, or Milton, New York.

Nothing on the trip to New Almaden next day modified her understanding that her lot at first would be hardship. It was intensely hot, the valley roads seen through the train windows boiled with white dust, Lizzie's usually silent baby cried and would not be comforted. In San Jose a stage with black leather curtains waited; they were the only passengers. But her anticipation of a romantic Bret Harte stage ride lasted only minutes. Dust engulfed them. She had Oliver draw the curtains, but then the heat was so great that they suffered at a slow boil. After three minutes she had Oliver open the curtains again halfway. They were thus insured both heat and dust, and were almost entirely cut off from the view.

By that time Susan cared nothing about the view, she only wanted to get there. Whenever Oliver caught her eye she made a point of smiling bravely; when he said abusive things about the weather she looked at her perspiring hands, and made mute faces of comic endurance. Now and then, as the stage rocked and threw them around among their luggage, she looked up into Lizzie's stony face and envied her patience.

It seemed a fantastically long twelve miles. Whatever conversation they attempted faded. They sat on, suffering. Susan was aware of brutal sun outside, an intolerable glare above and through their dust. Then after a long time—two hours?—she happened to glance out through the half-open curtains and saw the white trunk and pointed leaves of a sycamore going by. Their wheels were rolling quietly in sand. She thought the air felt cooler. "Trees?" she said. "I thought it would be all barren."

Oliver, sitting with his hands braced on his knees, looked altogether too vigorous and untired. He had evidently been keeping silent for her sake, not because he himself felt this jolting, dust-choked, endless ride a hardship. "Are you disappointed?" he said.

"If there are trees maybe there's a stream. Is there?"

"Not up at our place."

"Where do we get our water?"

"Why, the housewife carries it from the spring," he said. "It's only a half mile up the hill. Things are not as uncivilized out here as you think."

Lizzie's face, bent over the finally sleeping baby, showed the faintest shadow of a smile. It was not well advised of Oliver to make jokes before her. She was a jewel, tidy, competent, and thoughtful, but she should not be spoiled with familiarity. Susan watched the trees pass, dusty but authentic.

The stage leveled off into what seemed a plain or valley. She leaned to see. Ahead of them, abrupt as the precipices up which little figures toil in Chinese paintings, she saw a wild wooded mountainside that crested at a long ridge spiky with conifers. She pulled the curtains wide. "But my goodness!" she cried. "You called them *hills!*"

He laughed at her, as pleased as if he had made them by hand. "You permiscus old consort," she said, "you deceived me. Don't tell me *anything.* I'm going to watch and draw my own conclusions."

The road became a street, and no dust rose around their wheels: she saw that it had been sprinkled. On one side of them was a stream nearly lost among trees and bushes, on the other a row of ugly identical cottages, each with a patch of lawn like a shirtfront and a row of red geraniums like a necktie. At the end of the street, below the wide veranda of a white house, a Mexican was watering flowers with a garden hose. She saw water gleam from the roadside ditch, smelled wet grass. The oaks had been pruned so that they went up high, like maples in a New England village. Their shade lay across road and lawn.

"This must be the Hacienda," she said.

"Draw your own conclusions."

"I conclude it is. It's nice."

"Would you rather we were going to live down here?"

She thought that cool grass the most delicious thing she had ever seen or smelled, but she appraised his tone and said cautiously, "I haven't seen our place yet."

"No. But this looks good to you, does it?"

She considered, or pretended to. "It's lovely and cool, but it looks as if it were trying to be something it isn't. It's a little too *proper* to be picturesque, isn't it?"

Oliver took her hand and shook it. "Good girl. And too close to too many people."

"Why? Aren't the manager and the others nice?"

"They're all right. I guess I prefer the Cousin Jacks and Mexicans up at the camps."

They were going right through the Hacienda at a trot. Some children scattered, turning to stare. A woman looked out a door. "Aren't we stopping here?" she asked.

"I slipped Eugene a little extra to deliver you right to your gate."

"Ah," she said, "that'll be nicer," and leaned to the window to see as the stage tilted through dry oaks along a trail dug out of the hillside. But her mind worried a question. He though of making her arrival as pleasant as possible, and as easy for her, and he didn't hesitate to spend money to do it, but he hadn't thought to send her the fare to cross the continent—not only Lizzie's fare, which he might have forgotten, but her own, which he shouldn't have. Not the least unknown part of her unknown new life was the man beside her. From the time she had bought the tickets out of her savings she had not been entirely free of fear.

Grandmother, I feel like telling her, have a little confidence in the man you married. You're safer than you think.

The road climbed, kinked back on itself and started a sweeping curve around a nearly bare hill. Ahead she saw five parallel spurs of mountain, as alike as the ridges of a plowed field but huge and impetuous, plunging down into the canyon. The first was very dark, the next less dark, the third hazed, the fourth dim, the fifth almost gone. All day there had been no sky, but now she saw that there was one, a pale diluted blue.

At the turn a battered liveoak leaned on limbs that touched the ground on three sides. To its trunk were nailed many boxes, each with a name painted or chalked on it: Trengove, Fall, Tregoning, Tyrrell. Across a gulch on the left she saw roofs and heard the yelling of children.

"Cornish Camp?"

"Draw your own conclusions."

"What are the boxes? Is there a newspaper?"

"Oh Eastern effeteness," Oliver said. "Those are meat boxes. Every morning the meat wagon comes by and leaves Tregoning his leg of mutton and Trengove his soup bone and Mother Fall her pot roast. Tomorrow, if you want, I'll put up a box for Mother Ward."

"I don't think I should like everyone to know what I feed you," Susan said. "Doesn't anybody ever steal things?"

"Steals? This isn't the Hacienda."

"You don't *like* the Hacienda, do you?" she said. "Why not?"

He grunted.

"Well, I must say it's prettier than this."

"There I can't argue with you," he said. "It smells better, too."

The whole place had the air of having been dumped down the hillside—steep streets, houses at every angle white and incongruous or unpainted and shabby. Wash hung everywhere, the vacant lots were littered with cans and trash, dogs prowled and children screamed. At the water tank they slowed to pass through a reluctant parting, densely staring tangle of men, boys, teamsters, cows, donkeys, mules.

When Oliver leaned out and saluted some of them they waved, grinning, and stared with their hands forgotten in the air. Engineer and his new missus. She thought them coarse and cow-faced and strangely pale.

But they made sharp pictures, too: a boy hoisting a water yoke with a pail at each end, the pails sloshing silver over their rims; a teamster unyoking his mules; a donkey standing with his ears askew and his nose close to the ground, on his face a look of mournful patience that reminded her comically of Lizzie.

"Over there's Mother Fall's, where I lived," Oliver said, and pointed.

A white two-story house, square, blank, and ugly. Each window was a room, she supposed, one of them formerly his. The downstairs would smell of cabbage and grease. She could not even imagine living there. Her heart rose up and assured her that she would make him glad she had come.

"You said she was nice to you."

"Yes. A stout Cornish dame. She's been helping me get ready for you."

"I must call on her, I should think."

He looked at her a little queerly. "You sure must. If we don't have supper there tomorrow we'll never be forgiven."

Above and to the left, scattered down a long hogback ridge, the Mexican camp appeared. Its houses were propped with poles, timbers, ladders; its crooked balconies overflowed with flowers; in a doorway she saw a dark woman smoking a cigarette, on a porch a grandmother braided a child's hair. There were no white-painted cottages, but she thought this camp more attractive than the Cornish—it had a look of belonging, some gift of harmoniousness. The stage turned off to the right, below the camp, and left her craning, unsatisfied.

"Is there a Chinese Camp too?" she said.

"Around the hill and below us. We'll hear it a little, but we won't see it."

"Where's the mine?"

With his forefinger he jabbed straight down. "You don't see that either. Just a shaft house or a dump in a gulch here and there."

"You know what?" she said, holding the curtains back and watching ahead through the dusty little oaks, "I don't think you described this place very well."

"Draw your own conclusions," Oliver said. He offered a finger to Lizzie's baby, just waking up and yawning and focusing his eyes. The stage stopped.

The cottage she had imagined exposed on a bare hill among ugly mine buildings was tucked back among liveoaks at the head of a draw. In her first quick devouring look she saw the verandas she had asked for and helped Oliver sketch, a rail fence swamped under geraniums. When she hopped out slapping dust from her clothes she saw that the yard showed the even tooth-marks of raking. He had prepared for her so carefully. Both mostly what she felt in the moment of arrival was space, extension, bigness. Behind the house the mountain went up steeply to the ridge, along which now lay, as soft as a sleeping cat, a roll of fog or cloud. Below the house it fell just as steeply down spurs and canyons to tumbled hills as bright as a lion's hide. Below those was the valley's dust, a level obscurity, and rising out of it, miles away, was another long mountain as high as their own. Turning back the way she had come in, she saw those five parallel spurs, bare gold on top, darkly wooded in the gulches, receding in layers of blue haze. I know that mountain, old Loma Prieta. In nearly a hundred years it has changed less than most of California. Once you get beyond the vineyards and subdivisions along its lower slopes there is nothing but a reservoir and an Air Force radar station.

"Well," Oliver said, "come on inside."

It was as she had visualized it from his sketches, but much more finished—a house, not a picturesque shack. It smelled cleanly of paint. Its floors and wainscot were dark redwood, its walls a soft gray. The light was dim and cool, as she thought the light in a house should be. A breeze went through the rooms, bringing inside the smell of aromatic sun-soaked plants. The Franklin stove was polished like a farmer's Sunday boots, water was piped into the sink, the kitchen cooler held sacks and cans and let out a rich smell of bacon. In the arch between dining room and living room Oliver had hung his spurs, bowie, and six-shooter. "The homey touch," he said. "And wait, there are some little housewarming presents."

From the piazza he brought one of the packages that had been part of their luggage down from San Francisco. She opened it and pulled out a grass fan. "Fiji," Oliver said. Next a large mat of the same grass, as finely woven as linen, and with a sweet hay smell. "More Fiji." Next a paper parasol that opened up to a view of Fujiyama. "Japan," Oliver said. "Don't open it inside—bad luck." At the bottom of the box was something heavy which, unwrapped, turned out to be a water jar with something in Spanish written across it. "Guadalajara," Oliver said. "Now you're supposed to feel that the place is yours. You know what that Spanish means? It says, 'Help thyself, little Tomasa.'"

There it sits, over on my window sill, ninety-odd years later, without even a nick out of it. The fan and the parasol went quickly, the mat lasted until Leadville and was mourned when it passed, the olla has come through three generations of us, as have the bowie, the spurs, and the six-shooter. It wasn't the worst set of omens that attended the beginning of my grandparents' housekeeping.

She was touched. Like the raked yard, the clean paint, his absurd masculine decorations in the archway, his gifts proved him what she had believed him to be. Yet the one small doubt stuck in her mind like a burr in tweed. In a small voice she said, "You'll spoil me."

"I hope so."

Lizzie came in with luggage in one hand and the baby in her other arm. "Right through the kitchen," Oliver said. "Your bed's made up. The best I could do for Georgie was a packing box with a pillow in it."

"That will be fine, thank you," Lizzie said, and went serenely on through.

Kind. He really was. And energetic. Within a minute he was making a fire so that Susan could have warm water to wash in. Then he said that he had a little errand at Mother Fall's, and before she could ask him what he was off the piazza and gone.

Susan took off her traveling dress and washed in the basin by the kitchen door. Below her were the tops of strange bushes, the steep mountainside tufted with sparse brown grass. Looking around the corner of Lizzie's room to the upward slopes, she saw exotic red-barked trees among the woods, and smelled the herb-cupboard smells of sage and bay. Another world. Thoughtfully she poured out the water and went inside, where Lizzie was slicing a round loaf she had found in the cooler. Even the bread here was strange.

"How does it seem, Lizzie? Is your room all right?"

"It's fine."

"Is it the way you imagined it?"

"I don't know that I imagined it much."

"Oh, I did," said Susan. "All wrong."

She looked at Lizzie's room, clean and bare; went out through the dining room where her gifts lay on the table and read the inscription on the olla: Help thyself, Tomasita. Out on the piazza she sat in the hammock and looked out over the green and gold mountain and thought *how strange, how strange.*

Rocks clattered in the trail, and Oliver came in sight with a great black dog padding beside him. He made it sit down in front of the hammock. "This is Stranger. We figure he's half Labrador and half St. Bernard. He thinks he's my dog, but he's mistaken. From now on he goes walking with nobody but you. Shake hands, Stranger."

With great dignity Stranger offered a paw like a firelog, first to Oliver, who pushed it aside, and then to Susan. He submitted to having his head stroked. "Stranger?" Susan said. "Is that your name, *Stranger*? That's wrong. You're the one who lives here. *I'm* the stranger."

Oliver went inside and came out with a piece of buttered bread. "Give him something. You're to feed him, always, so he'll get attached to you."

"But it's you he likes," Susan said. "Look at the way he watches every move you make."

"Just the same, he's going to learn to like *you*. That's what we got him for, to look after you. If he doesn't, I'll make a rug of him. You hear that, you?"

The dog rolled his eyes and twisted his head back, keeping his bottom firmly on the boards. "Here, Stranger," Susan said, and broke off a piece of bread. The dog's eyes rolled down to fix on it. She tossed it, and he slupped it out of the air with a great sucking sound that made them both laugh. Over his broad black head Susan looked into Oliver's eyes. "You *will* spoil me."

"I hope so," he said for the second time.

Then she couldn't keep the question back any longer. "Oliver."

"Yes."

"Tell me something."

"Sure."

"I don't want you to be angry."

"Angry? At *you*?"

"It seems so petty. I shouldn't even mention it. I only want us to start without a single shadow between us."

"My God, what have I done?" Oliver said. Then a slow mulish look came into his face, a look like disgust or guilt or evasion. She stared at him in panic, remembering what his mother had said of him: that when he was put in the wrong he would never defend himself, he would only close up like a clam. She didn't want him to close up, she wanted to talk this out and be rid of it. Blue as blue stones in his sunburned face, his eyes touched hers and were withdrawn. Miserably she stood waiting. "I know what it is," he said. "You needn't tell me."

"You didn't just forget, then."

"No, I didn't forget."

"But *why*, then?"

He looked over her head, he was interested in the valley. She could see shrugging impatience in his shoulders. "It isn't the money," she said. "I had the money, and there was nothing I would rather have spent it for than coming to you. But your letter never even mentioned it. I thought perhaps . . . I don't know. It shamed me before Father. I hated it that he had to send me off to someone he would think didn't know . . ."

"What my duty was?" Oliver said, almost sneering. "I knew."

"Then why?"

Impatiently he turned, he looked down at her directly. "Because I didn't have it."

"But you said you had something saved."

He swung an arm. "There it is."

"The house? I thought the mine agreed to pay for that."

"Kendall did. The manager. He changed his mind."

"But he *promised!*"

"Sure," Oliver said. "But then somebody overspent on one of the Hacienda cottages and Kendall said no more renovations."

"But that's unfair!" she said. "You should have told Mr. Prager."

His laugh was incredulous. "Yes? Run crying to Conrad?"

"Well then you should just have stopped. We could have lived in it as it was."

"I could have," Oliver said. "You couldn't. I wouldn't have let you."

"Oh I'm sorry!" she said. "I didn't understand. I've been such an expense to you."

"It seems to me I've been an expense to you. How much did you spend for those tickets?"

"I won't tell you."

They stared at each other, near anger. She forgave him everything except that he hadn't explained. One word, and she would have been spared all her doubts about him. But she would certainly not let him pay her back. The hardship would not be all his. He was looking at her squarely, still mulish. She wanted to shake him. "You great . . . Why couldn't you have told me?"

She saw his eyebrows go up. His eyes, as they did when he smiled, closed into upside-down crescents. Young as he was, he had deep fans of wrinkles at the corners of his eyes that gave him a look of always being on the brink of smiling. And now he *was* smiling. He was not going to be sullen. They were past it.

"I was afraid you'd be sensible," he said. "I couldn't stand the thought of this place sitting here all ready for you and you not in it."

Supper was no more than bread and butter, tea from Augusta's samovar, and a left-over bar of chocolate. (Ah, sweet linkage! Are you thinking of me, dear friend back there in New York, as I am thinking of you? Do you comprehend how happy I am, am determined to be? Didn't I tell you he knew how to look after me?) The dog lay at their feet on the veranda. Along the ridge with its silvery comb of fog the sky faded from pale blue to steely gray, and then slowly flushed the color of a ripe peach. The trees on the crest—redwoods, Oliver said—burned for a few seconds and went black. Eastward down the plunging mountainside the valley fumed with dust that was first red, then rose, then purple, then mauve, then gray, finally soft black. Discreet and quiet, Lizzie came out and got the tray and said good night and went in again. They sat close together in the hammock, holding hands.

"I don't believe this is me," Oliver said.

"Thee mustn't doubt it."

"Theeing?" he said. "Now I know I'm one of the family."

A shiver went through her from her hips up to her shoulders. At once he was solicitous. "Cold?"

"Happy, I think."

"I'll get a blanket. Or do you want to go in?"

"No, it's beautiful out here."

He got a blanket and tucked her into the hammock as if into a steamer chair. Then he sat down on the floor beside her and smoked his pipe. Far down below, in the inverted sky of the valley, lights came on, first one, then another, then many. "It's like sitting in the warming oven and watching corn pop down on the stove," Susan said.

Sometime later she held up her hand and said, "Listen!" Fitful on the creeping wind, heard and lost and heard again, came a vanishing sound of music—someone sitting on porch or balcony up in the Mexican camp and playing the guitar for his girl or his children. Remembering nights when Ella Clymer had sung to them at Milton, Susan all but held her breath, waiting for the rush of homesickness. But it never came, nothing interrupted this sweet and resting content. She put out a hand to touch Oliver's hair, and he captured it and held the fingers against his cheek. The bone of his jaw, the rasp of his beard, sent another great shiver through her.

They sat up a good while, watching the stars swarm along the edge of the veranda roof. When they finally went to bed I hope they made love. Why wouldn't they, brought together finally after eight years, and with only a two-week taste of marriage? I am perfectly ready to count the months on Grandmother. Her first child, my father, was born toward the end of April 1877, almost precisely nine months after her arrival in New Almaden. I choose to believe that I was made possible that night, that my father was the first thing they did together in the West. The fact that he was accidental and at first unwanted did not make him any less binding upon their lives, or me any less inevitable.

In the night she may have heard the wind sighing under the eaves and creaking the stiff oaks and madrones on the hillside behind. She may have heard the stealthy feet of raccoons on the veranda, and the rumble and rush as Stranger rose and put the intruders out. She may have waked and listened to the breathing beside her, and been shaken by unfamiliar emotions and tender resolves. Being who she was, she would have reasserted to herself beliefs about marriage, female surrender, communion of the flesh and union of the spirit that would have been at home in a Longfellow poem. She could have both written and illustrated it. And if she thought of Augusta, as she probably did, she would have poulticed the bruise of abandoned and altered friendship with healing herbs gathered from all the literary gardens where she habitually walked: parted as they were, each was fulfilled in another and nobler way. When I catch Grandmother thinking in this fashion I shy away and draw the curtains, lest I smile. It does not become a historian to smile.

Her eyes popped open. Gray daylight, unfamiliar room—something was wrong. Up on her elbow, shaking the sleep from her eyes, she recognized her new bedroom, cluttered with half-unpacked belongings. She was alone in the bed. Where was Oliver? Something *was* wrong, there was crying from the other wing where Lizzie and Georgie slept, and outside now began an uproar of barking and the honking wheeze of a donkey. Then she heard Oliver shout, "Sic 'im, Stranger, take him out of here!" A growling rush, the clatter of hoofs in stones, a threshing of bushes. Oliver sent a piercing whistle after dog and donkey, and blending with it, coming in like a thin woodwind in duet with a piccolo, a queer, high voice cried, "Fis! Fis! Fis!"

Oliver's bare feet thudded down the porch. "No want fish, John. Go way."

"Fis belly flesh," said the voice.

"No want fish," Oliver said. "What for come so early, John? Go way now."

"Fis belly flesh," the voice said, receding, complaining, vanishing. Roosters were crowing both above and below. The sound of Oliver's feet crossed the living room. He opened the door upon her as she sat up in bed.

"What on earth!" she said.

He was rumbling with laughter. His blond mustache, which he had probably grown to make him look older and more authoritative, made him look about twenty. "Welcome," he said. "Everybody wants to welcome you, even a jackass and a jackass Chinaman."

At midmorning they were moving furniture around. Oliver had bought it from Mother Fall, who in her turn had acquired it from the desperate mine captain who had formerly lived in this house. He had brought his young wife here, she had had her baby here, they had laid out all they owned in furnishing the place. Then without warning he had lost his job. An ill omen, but she hardly even acknowledged that she was adapting the wreckage of an unlucky life to her own uses, for everything that she saw of the house with rested eyes pleased her. The veranda that she had drawn around three sides of Oliver's sketch, and had him spend most of his savings on, was a triumph. It took her breath to look east, it filled her heart to look west or south. The rooms themselves were good, the furniture would do for the brief time they would be here. But she gave Oliver a good deal of exercise moving it, anyway, trying it in all possible positions and combinations, and enjoying herself extremely as she stood around in a dressing sacque being a young housewife. Then he happened to glance out the window as he pushed a chair across the room. "Whsht!" he said. "Get dressed. We're being called on."

She flew into the bedroom and slammed the door, and as she fumbled into her traveling dress, all she had until the trunks came, she heard feet come up the porch and into the house, and voices, a man's and a woman's. When she came out—and she would have come out rosy and vivacious and charming as if she had not twenty seconds before been biting her lips and muttering un-Quakerish words at hooks and eyes that had disappeared in the fabric or eluded her fingers —Oliver introduced her to Mr. and Mrs. Kendall, the manager and his wife.

Mr. Kendall was not a smiler. He had gimlet eyes and a notably still, restrained manner. But he took her hand and looked into her face until she blushed, and said to Oliver, "Well, Ward, I see why you were so impatient to get readied up here." Wanting to dislike him for his broken promise, she could find no fault with his manners. His wife was ladylike, gentle, soft-spoken, and welcoming. Both of them regretted that the Wards had not chosen to live down at the Hacienda, where things were rather more civilized and where people would have had a better chance of their company. Mrs. Kendall asked if she might come by in her carriage and take Susan for a drive around on the mountain trails. She asked them to dinner the Sunday following. She was almost effusively glad to have so charming an addition to New Almaden society, she had heard that Susan was an accomplished artist and hoped to become familiar with her work, she hoped that New Almaden would offer many subjects for her pencil. They stood on the veranda and admired the view and praised what Oliver had been able to do with the old cottage. There was a lot of waving and smiling in both directions as they left.

"Well," Oliver said when the carriage had passed out of sight among the oaks. "*That's* something I never saw before."

"What? Their calling? It seems only polite."

"They've never called on anyone else."

"It's because of Conrad Prager. Mr. Kendall knows you've got an important connection."

"If he thought my connections were that important, why wouldn't he let me go East and get you?" Oliver said. "Why would he stick me for the whole price of the renovations? No, you've got them wrong. They're impressed because you're an artist. You make New Almaden look classy." He looked at her as he might have looked at a horse he was thinking of buying. "Matter of fact," he said, "you do."

In the afternoon Susan got a few minutes to herself and began a serial letter to Augusta. She got in a good deal of literary landscape painting and an impression of the manager and his wife. Mrs. Kendall, she thought, "has those qualities of surface prettiness and ladylike manners that make her at once attractive and uninteresting." Of Kendall himself she said, "It is hard to believe that this largest mine in the world—Oliver says there are twenty-seven miles of underground workings—should be under the absolute despotic control of this small, mild-mannered man, and that one's whole future should be at the mercy of his whim. Fortunately, he appears to regard Oliver highly, and Oliver, I am proud to say, bears himself in the presence of his superior as befits a man. In spite of his agreeableness I could not quite forget that he forced Oliver to spend his last cent in making over the cottage that is properly part of his compensation—the cottage moreover which he now praises for its charm."

That night they had supper with the lower echelons of New Almaden society, the crew of junior engineers, college students, and "outside captains" who boarded with Mother Fall. I don't suppose the atmosphere of a third-class boardinghouse was any more exhilarating to her than the near-gentility of the Kendalls, but at least it was honestly what it was, and Oliver was at ease in it. The talk was about evenly divided between engineering technicalities and comments an Oliver's undeserved luck. In their exaggerated joking, at once boisterous and shy, they enlisted her sympathy, because she thought them lonely, but she did not therefore think of them as potential friends or companions. When she had occasion to add a few paragraphs to her letter she told Augusta that they were "nice enough to see once in a while, but I don't think I shall care greatly for any of the people here."

A terrible snob you were, Grandmother, in spite of the Quaker background and the farm upbringing, and in spite of the fact that you would have been too warmhearted to let any of these young men see your snobbery. Thanks partly to your success in art, and more to the influence of Augusta and Thomas Hudson, you had gentility in your eye like a cinder, and there would be a lot of rubbing, reddening, and irritation before your tears flooded it out.

As they sat after supper talking and rocking on the boardinghouse porch in the chilly night air tainted with Cornish Camp smells, two miners approached and signaled Oliver down the steps. There was a good deal of snickering, some glancing up at the porch. "Now, you," Mother Fall said to them, "wot're you planning, you two?"

They shook hands with Oliver and went away, walking fast. Oliver came back and stood smiling, behind Susan's chair, pushing it so that she rocked forward and touched her toes and could spring back again against his hands. "We must go," he said.

The young men were indignant, Mother Fall was hurt. Susan stood up obediently, unsure of what was happening.

"There was some talk about a charivari," Oliver said. "I gave them money for a couple of barrels of beer. So now I'm going to take Sue home and barricade the doors."

They protested. Nobody in camp would think of pulling any

horseplay on the Resident Engineer's wife. Even if they didn't have sense enough to know that anything roughhouse would be out of keeping, they were all too scared for their jobs. Oliver should have told them to go chase themselves. Stay on here, maybe it would get lively. Get your health drunk in person.

That was just what he expected, Oliver said. He saw no reason Susan should be exposed to a bunch of beery admirers. Are you ready, Susan?

She shook their hands one by one. With some sort of inward shudder she let herself be clasped to Mother Fall's faintly onion-smelling best dress. She expressed her thanks for all they had done to make things easy and pleasant, and she went away not sure whether they would pick her to pieces as being too high toned for mining-camp life, or whether they would be groaning with envy at Oliver's luck. And what if those men did decide to play some drunken prank? She had heard of the most appalling things—kidnapped bride, imprisoned and humiliated bridegroom, Halloween destructions and practical jokes.

Walking back along the black lane, with Oliver's lantern throwing blobs of shadow ahead of them and lighting the dusty roots in the bank, she had a few minutes of near-panic. Physically it was like any other country lane at night; it might have been the lane between John Grant's and her father's. But already, back of them, she heard the loud voices of men, and she knew that in a half hour or so they would be louder yet.

"Will they come, do you think?"

He put his arm around her. "Not a chance. They just wanted an excuse to bum a treat."

"Why did we leave, then?"

"So I could have you to myself."

He had her to himself so close that they lurched and stumbled in the trail.

2

For three more mornings she awoke in her bare room, breathing air strangely scented and listening to the strange sounds that had awakened her: once the bells of the *panadero's* burro coming up the trail with loaves sticking out of the panniers on both sides, twice the distant beating of kettles and hullaballoo of voices yelling in a strange tongue—the Chinese arising in their camp under the hill. Each morning Oliver came in and kissed her fully awake and laid a wild-flower on her breast. Their breakfasts were interrupted by the seven o'clock whistle from the nearest shaft house, and they smiled because for these few days Oliver could ignore it.

Between the little jobs of getting settled, she added bits to her serial letter. Grandmother did not live in the local color period for nothing. Here, for instance, is the vegetable man:

> Lizzie does the buying and I stand around with my Jap umbrella, very much in everybody's way, and tell what we want. The man is an Italian named Costa. It is delightful to hear him say the names of common vegetables. When he asks me if I want cabbage, as he says it I feel that it must be a most tempting thing. And it is so amusing to hear him reckon up the account—'One bit carrot—two bit tomato—four bit potato—3 bit apple—2 bit blackberries.' Lizzie is washing this morning, and the baby sits in a drygoods box on the floor as happy as possible . . . Everything will be so easy that I shall grow fat and lazy. Three times a day we hear steam whistles, and here and there are columns of smoke rising. A heavily laden wagon drawn by mules passes a distant curve of the winding road, but nothing passes us. The place is as orderly as a military post, and as quiet from our remote porch as if every day were Sunday . . . How I wish you could see this place! I have taken no walks because I have no stout shoes, and no clothes until our trunks arrive except winter garments sent last spring as freight. The evenings are so cool I can be very comfortable in a serge dress, and in the daytime I wander about in a white dressing sacque which Oliver says looks "as if the feathers had been picked off the back," because the puffs and ruffles are strictly confined to the front. I never felt so free in my

life, and strange to say it does not seem far off. I feel as if you were as near as at Milton.

A Live White Woman in the Mines, she rose on the fifth morning and drank coffee with her husband before he went off to work, and gave him for the post office in Cornish Camp a letter to her parents and the fat letter to Augusta. Later that morning the trunks arrived by dray, and she spent the rest of the day unpacking. To stack the woodblocks for *The Scarlet Letter* in the corner cupboard with her sketch pads, pencils, and watercolors gave her an intense pleasurable feeling of being ready to live.

The six o'clock whistle blew while she was changing into a summer dress still warm from Lizzie's iron. Calling to Lizzie to put the kettle on, she hurried out to the hammock and spread herself there to wait.

I can see her. From here she looks terribly unlikely. She was always careful of her clothes—"Thy dress should be a background for thy face," I once heard her tell my Aunt Betsy, whose taste was not dependable—and she lived in a time when women wrapped themselves in yards of satin, serge, taffeta, bombazine, what not, with bustles and ruffles and leg-of-mutton sleeves, all of it over a foundation of whalebone. A modern woman in a mining camp, even if she is the wife of the Resident Engineer, lives in pants and a sweatshirt. Grandmother made not the slightest concession to the places where she lived. I have a photograph of her riding a horse in something that looks like a court costume, and another taken at the engineer's camp on the bank of Boise Creek in the 1880s, with a home-made rowboat at her feet and a tent pitched in the background and her third baby on her shoulder, and what is she wearing? A high-necked, pinch-waisted, triple-breasted, puff-sleeved, full-length creation of dotted swiss or something of the kind. And a picnic hat. In that baldest of their bald frontiers, at the very bottom of their fortunes, she dressed as if for a garden party. I don't suppose she had a hat on as she waited for Oliver to come back from the mine, that first real day of her housekeeping life, but she probably had everything else.

Shortly she saw him coming through the trees. Stranger lumbered up and went to meet him. Susan waved. In his mine clothes stained with red ore, his boots muddy, his face full of the light the sight of her turned on in him, he ran up the high steps and leaned against the post with his hands behind him and his face stuck out. She kissed it, and still with his hands behind him he fainted against the porch post. "Is this where the Resident Engineer lives?" he said. "You look beautiful. What happened?"

"Does something have to happen before I can look beautiful? The trunks came, so now I can be a wife greeting her husband as he returns from work."

"I like it. I guess I'll go back and come home again."

"No, you're to stay. Lizzie will be bringing tea."

"Tea, even."

She loved the way he leaned against the post. He had relaxed, graceful poses, big as he was. The mine hat with a stub of candle socketed in its front was pushed back on his head, his wool shirt was open at the neck. She probably thought him unbearably picturesque. She could have drawn the two of them just as they stood there, pretty bride and manly husband. Title, something like, "The Return from Honest Toil," or perhaps "An Outpost of Civilization." It flooded her with happiness to be there, to have him there, to be able to give him this after so many years of stale crackers and mouse cheese in tarpapered shacks.

He removed his hand from behind him, with a letter in it. "Brought you something."

She saw by the stationery whose it was, and the hand that snatched it was so greedy that she lifted a look of apology before she ripped off the end. But only one disappointing sheet, and it not even filled. Fear and its verification were all but simultaneous.

I have that piece of thin blue paper, brown along the folds and with its few lines of script faded nearly out. No bold and graceful hand here—a scrawl, and unsigned.

My darling Sue,
        This is no letter. I can't write, I can't think, and yet I must let you know. Baby died of diphtheria last night. Oh, why aren't you here! I can't bear it, everything is in pieces. I could die, I could die.

So in one stroke her picnic in the West was turned into exile. The three thousand miles that had seemed no more than the distance from

Milton to New York revealed themselves as a continent. Across that implacable distance a train carrying a message would crawl with the slowness of a beetle. Tomorrow or next day one would start across with the letter she had given to Oliver that morning. She would have given all she owned to have it back, to have back everything she had written since leaving home. For the child must have died on the first or second day of her trip, about the time she was scribbling her impressions of Omaha. All the time she had been crossing plains, mountains, and deserts, all the day she had rested in San Francisco, all the days of her getting used to Almaden, Augusta and Thomas had been suffering their sorrow. Another week, or even more, and the postman would bring to their door not comfort, not the sympathy of their dearest friend, but pages of drivel about Chinese fish peddlers and Italian vegetable men.

She took out of Oliver's hand the blue sheet, which he had gently removed from her fingers and read. By the trouble in his face she could assess her own. For a second she blazed like a burning tree. She cried out, "I must go back! I must pack at once!" But looking into his serious face she knew she couldn't. He didn't have the money to send her. Her own savings must be held for their mutual life, not for the attachments she had left behind. It wouldn't be fair, though she knew he would agree without hesitation if she asked.

Did she feel trapped in her complex feelings, caught in marriage as she was caught on the wrong side of the continent? I shouldn't be surprised. For a time, at least, while the inexorabilities of space and time ate into her. They entirely forgot tea, and when Lizzie served supper Susan sat with Oliver at the table, eating nothing herself and almost despising him for his apologetic miner's appetite. After Lizzie had cleared away, she sat on, writing a passionate hopeless letter, while Oliver smoked his pipe in the other room and watched her furtively under the spurs and pistol and bowie that hung like shy masculine mistletoe in the arch. When she stood up suddenly, he stood up too, but she gave him a quivering smile and said, "Don't come along. You're tired. I'm only going out to pick a flower."

I don't have the flower, but I have the letter.

> Oh my darling, what can I say? It seems so cruel that I did not know by instinct when the blow fell on two hearts so close to mine!

If I had only known it, there were signs everywhere as I crossed the country. The bloodred sunsets and pallid moonlight nights were full of foreboding, but I was ignorantly wrapped up in the brightness of life, and would not see that my darling was desolate.

These poor little flowers will all be crushed and withered when they reach you, but they are better than words. They grow along the roadside and keep their meek little faces white and pure in the midst of the dust . . . My heart aches with a load of sympathy for you and Thomas. I do not say much to Oliver because it grieves him to feel that it was he who separated us . . .

Poor Grandmother. She might have lived an idyll in her honeymoon cottage in the picnic West if her heart had not bled eastward. Poor Grandfather, too. Whether or not he felt guilty at having separated those two, he must have thought it almost malicious in Augusta to have her personal tragedy just when she did. Fair means having failed to hold Susan in New York and within the old threesome, she resorted to foul.

Still, who knows, perhaps Augusta's woe helped weld their incongruities into a marriage. In that remote place, where the country made a great impression on her and the people hardly any, it was as if Oliver were the only man in the world, and hers the only house. Though she followed Oliver wherever she could, to his office in Shakerag Street, to the Hacienda to dine with the Kendalls, to the post office, to the store, to the shaft house when he was going underground, she was much alone. Lizzie, though a good creature, was "not company." The Cornish wives who came to call gave Susan and themselves an awkward time, finding little to talk of except Oliver's virtues—"'e do 'ave a way with 'im"—and if they came more than once, found their way around to the kitchen door for a comfortable cup of tea with Lizzie.

None of the Cornish people, men or women, attracted her. She thought them crude, she remembered the threatened charivari and the extortion of two barrels of beer from Oliver's poor purse, she thought their accent barbarous. And when she went walking with Stranger, and met on the trails brown-faced men and women who saluted her with grave courtesy and moved aside for her to pass, watching her out of their Indian eyes, she was tempted by the pictures they made, but would no more have thought of making companions of them than of their burros. In time she came to know a good many faces, but none of them were people.

When she was tired of walking the restricted trails that Oliver's instructions permitted her—what he called her stomping ground—she worked on *The Scarlet Letter* blocks. If she got tired of drawing, she read on the veranda, mainly books that Thomas Hudson, persistently thoughtful, sent her in her exile. If she was waiting for Oliver she kept to the side facing the trail and the southward spurs of mountain, but now and then, to surprise herself, she walked to the corner and looked down on the hills that collapsed toward the valley. She wrote many letters. A new issue of *Scribner's*, with things in it by people who had once crowded the summer porch at Milton, was almost as precious as a letter from Augusta or from home.

Quiet black and white birds with rusty breasts worked among the bushes below her. Now and then one rose to an oak and blew a *cheweeel cheweeeel* into the still, dusty woods. That and the cluck and cackle of quail was the only birdsong—a starvation diet after the robins, thrushes, and white throats of Milton summers.

Oliver was gone from before seven until after six, six days a week. She lived for the evenings and for Sundays. Every night after supper they sat together in the hammock and watched the sun leave the floating crest of the San Jose Mountains eastward, and the valley's pool of dusty air thicken, darken, flare up, and fade. She felt, I imagine, both trapped with him and abjectly dependent on him. They both remarked on how much they seemed to hold hands.

I feel deeply grateful that these mountains do not close all round us. Across the valley we can look out into a vague misty distance, which is the way back to all we left behind.

In the twilight a strange fancy often comes to me that you are all there in the valley below us. Darkness broods over it, but here and there a light twinkles. I feel sure that you are all there, the Milton people and you and Thomas, all the dear ones who haunt my thoughts. It is a fancy I would not lose, for I am very near you all then.

This is a place to be very happy in—we are—we shall be—but there is a thought in common which we do not often express, but which is the undertone of our life here—that *this* is not our real home, that we do not belong here except as circumstances keep us.

Speak for yourself, Grandmother. I think you are putting into Grandfather's head attitudes that were never there. He understood well enough that a mining engineer was a Westerner by profession. He was not slopping around in that steaming mine ten hours a day, and mapping its labyrinths in his spare time, and studying engineering texts and government reports after you went to bed, just so he could give it all up and go back to an East coast barren of every mineral except maybe asbestos. You commented often enough how ambitious he was, how hard he worked to make up for the handicap of an aborted education. I think he didn't stress what your future was likely to be, because he was tender of your homesickness, but he understood it well enough. What he didn't fully understand, because he was always absorbed in his job, was how dreary long the days were for you, how lonely and how isolated and how strange.

> Don't you know how we lose the sense of our own individuality when there is nothing to reflect it back upon us? These people here have so little conception of our world that sometimes I feel myself as if I must have dreamed it.
> The few hours, comparatively, that Oliver and I spend together are like the bread of life by which I live through the rest. I have never said much to you about him, because I have already begun to take him for granted as we do all the good things. I have already forgotten to count the dreadful ways in which all this happiness might have been turned into hopeless misery. Even so little a thing as Oliver's loving this country and wishing to spend his life here, would have counted up as a serious trouble after a while. As it is, our wistful memories of home make another bond between us.

By such devices she perverted his sympathy into agreement with her fantasy that the West for them was only an excursion. Meantime, every day was the same. Morning opened like a great eye, daylight spied interminably upon her habitual activities, evening closed down. The uninterrupted sunshine made her desperate; it was like something she was doomed to.

Everything was static, in suspension, withheld. She lived a sleepwalker's life, except for the Sundays when Oliver could leave his map and his reports for a few hours and take her on picnics back into the mountain, or the afternoons when he brought home letters that bloomed for her like firelight on loved faces. Time hung unchanging, or with no more visible change than a slow reddening of poison oak leaves, an imperceptible darkening of the golden hills. It dripped like a slow percolation through limestone, so slow that she forgot it between drops. Nevertheless every drop, indistinguishable from every other, left a little deposit of sensation, experience, feeling. In thirty or forty years the accumulated deposits would turn my cultivated, ladylike, lively, talkative, talented, innocently snobbish grandmother into a Western woman in spite of herself.

Willingly or unwillingly, she collected experience and wrote it back East in letters. Perhaps she wrote so fully because she wanted to divert Augusta's depression. Perhaps she was only indulging her own starved desire for talk.

3

In the early morning the light leaned on these eastward-facing mountains. She could see it gilding the ridges southward and making a moiré of the varying leaf-faces of oak, madrone, and bay in the gulches. The fogfall that lay along the crest in a cottony roll was as white as the clouds of a fairytale.

Only the heads of the men in the skip were visible from where she stood just outside the door of the shaft house: Oliver, two of his young assistants, two timbermen, and a visiting engineer. The flat sun shone in the door and turned Oliver's sunburned face to copper, the timbermen's underground skins to pale brass. The candles on their hats burned with an almost invisible flame. Oliver was taller than the others, she could see him almost to the shoulders. Like someone leaving on a boat or train he smiled and waved. Stranger started forward, and she hung onto his collar.

There was a smell of woodsmoke and steam, the air still cringed from the whistle blast. A bell clinked; she saw Tregoning, the hoist man, reach for a lever. She stepped back a pace in the floury dust. The bell clinked again, Tregoning's shoulder shoved forward, steam hissed. With a groan as heavy and reluctant as their motion, the two great wheels that rose as high as the shaft-house roof began to revolve. Smoothly the heads sank, Oliver's last. A hand tossed upward, and she was looking through the empty shack with a black hole in its floor.

Still with her hand in Stranger's collar, she went inside, up against the plank barrier, and looked down. A gray stir of movement was receding down there. She could see shapes defined by the candles that grew brighter as the skip sank, and then went dimmer, shrank to swimming points, and went out. A damp, warm wind blew up the shaft into her face.

She turned away, she kept her composure, she smiled back at the toothless hoist man and said something cheerful, she let go of Stranger's collar and sent him wallowing up the trail ahead of her. But her heart was withered in her breast like a prune. She could not bear to think of him down there in the blackness, dropping his thousand-foot plumb lines, gluing his eye to the theodolite eyepiece while an assistant held a candle close, and while the bob, suspended in water to make its motion minimal, moved in its deep orbit hundreds of feet below and the wire which was all he had to measure by shifted its hairsbreadth left or right.

He disliked this surveying, not only because it kept him underground so much but because all work had to stop while the survey went forward. A blast, the passing of an ore car, could throw off his measurements and cause errors of many feet. When work was stopped, the men grumbled, and Oliver, who totted up their weekly production and hence their wages, might be doubly blamed. What was worse for her, if not for him, was that once he started on any leg of his survey he had to stay down till it was completed. The last time, he had been down for nearly twenty-four hours without a break.

He had sunk out of the world, or into it, and she was beached in the interminable sunshine. Ten long sunstruck hours until suppertime, and after that unpredictable further hours of dusk, dark, late reading, before he came home.

The sight of a Chinaman in a blue blouse and slippers, with a bundle of brush on his back and an ax in his hand, trotting down the trail with his pigtail jerking, made her step to one side. He passed her with one sidelong glitter of jet eyes, and left her shivering. The people here were not people. Except for Oliver, she was alone and in exile, and her heart was back where the sun rose.

Unending summer. It was hotter at the end of September than it had been in July. But the heat was more seen than felt, more hallucination than discomfort. It turned illusory even the things on which she had fixed in the attempt to make the strange world real. From her temperate veranda she now saw only void where the valley used to be— a gray, smoky void into which she peered, hunting distance and relief from the mirage of mountains that quivered around her with visible heat. The wind that breathed past her and moved the banal bright geraniums in their pots brought a phantasmal sound of bells, and expired again, tired as a sigh.

She contemplated a walk and gave up the idea at once. Out on the trails it would be too hot. Stranger was dug in like a barnyard fowl in the shady dust beside the porch. Despite all their efforts, he was still Oliver's dog, not hers. He was obedient and friendly, but his interest woke only when Oliver came home, and he lay watching the trail for hours at a time.

Down the mountain, moving beyond a curtain of quivering air, she saw the stage coming, perhaps with letters. If she started in five minutes, she would arrive at the Cornish Camp post office at about the same time as the stage. But the post office was in the company store, where there were always loiterers—teamsters, drifters, men hunting work—whom Oliver did not want her to encounter alone. And Ewing, the manager of the store, was a man she thought insolent. She must wait another two hours, till Oliver came home, to know whether there was mail. If the truth were known, these days she always looked at his hands, for the gleam of paper, before she looked at his face.

Bells again, unmistakable. She went around the corner, where the mountain fell away and the veranda stood on posts ten feet high, and looked around the corner of Lizzie's room to the hill behind. She could see the path, used only by the Mexican packers who brought wood down from the mountain, curving and disappearing among the red-barked madrones. The bells were plain and coming nearer.

Then from out of the madrones came a mule bearing an immense *carga* of split wood. His ears were down, his nose was down, he planted his small feet with reluctant, aggrieved deliberation, holding back against the weight and the steepness of the path, sliding a little, humped up behind, braced in front. The bell around his neck clunked and tunkled with every wincing step. Behind him came another, then another, then another, until there were eight in line; and behind them came an old Mexican with a sombrero on his head, a stick in his hand, and a red silk handkerchief around his neck; and behind him a younger Mexican, a helper, a Sancho, almost invisible in his nonentity.

The mules stopped. Their heads drooped, their ears waggled forward, they snuffed hopelessly at the dusty ground. The leader heaved out his sides and blew a great breath, stirring up dust. *Clunk* went his bell. The old Mexican had his hat in his hand, his brown face turned upward into the sun. He was saying something in Spanish. Since Susan's Spanish lessons with Oliver's assistant Mr. Hernandez had gone no further than four brief sessions, she caught only the word *leño,* and perhaps caught that only because of the burden the mules carried.

Pointing to her breast she said carefully, "*¿Para me?*"

"*Si, señora.*"

"Yes. Well, you may put it under the porch there, I know that's where Mr. Ward wants it."

"*¿Como?*"

By signs she made him understand. He had great theatrical gestures—swept on his sombrero, blasted Sancho with a volley of orders, fell upon one of the mules and began to loosen the hitch that held its load. The whole event suddenly acquired gaiety, it was an occasion, it so lifted the tempo of the listless afternoon that Susan ran inside and got her sketch pad and drew them as they worked. Sight of the growing pile of firewood, like the stacks her father used to stretch in October between two oaks down by the sheepfold, set her to thinking, as one might let his mind stray to the images of some secret vice, of the Franklin stove inside, polished like an art work, waiting for the time when all this sun would be quenched and Mrs. Oliver Ward could sit with her husband through long evenings by an open fire, preferably while blasts howled without. This was a girl who almost illustrated *Snowbound,* and should have.

The unloading and stacking took three quarters of an hour. When it was done, Sancho disappeared, vanished, stood on three legs among the hipshot mules. She imagined sores on his withers like the raw patches on theirs, and a stripe down his back and three or four stripes around his legs like some of them, as if there were zebras among their mutual ancestors.

The old Mexican again had his hat off. God knows how she looked to him up there on her high porch in her high-necked dress with a brooch pinned at the throat, her face rosy, her sketch pad in her hand. By that time she was well known as the lady who drew; many had met her on the trails carrying her pad and her little stool.

He said something. "*¿Como?*" she said, imitating him, and was shot to pieces by his reply, of which she understood not one word. Finally she comprehended that he wanted his pay. How much? *¿Cuanto?*

They counted it out for each other on tongues and fingers: *cinco pesos*. But when she had gone in for her purse and come outside again she could not devise a way of handing the banknote to him. He was ten feet below her, the mountain fell away steeply, the wind had begun to blow. If it blew the bill into the brush he might never find it. The old man at once understood. With a gesture out of opera he untied the handkerchief from around his neck, rolled it into a ball, and tossed it up to her.

Susan made an instinctive move to catch it, and then pulled back her hands. The handkerchief fell on the veranda floor. She stared down at the craning old man, whose brown neck, with the handkerchief removed, showed deep creases in which the sweat of his labor had deposited channels of dirt.

"Lizzie!" Susan said.

Lizzie came out through the kitchen door, and the old Mexican's admiration was doubled. Another beautiful one. This house of the engineer was full of them. With her purse open, Susan said, "Lizzie, will you pick up his handkerchief, please?"

Lizzie picked it up, Susan laid a five-dollar bill in its center, and Lizzie folded it and tied its corners and dropped it into the old man's upstretched hand. *"Gracias, much' grac',"* he said, and then something else. Expectant, he stood looking upward.

"What is it?" Susan said. "What do you want? *¿Que . . . ?*"

He held out his hand, and gazing at it with admiration he appeared to write on his extended palm. "I think he'd like to see your drawing," Lizzie said.

Reluctantly, hoping he would not take hold of it with his hands, she turned the pad down toward him so that he could see. His arm would not stretch so far, he craned and squinted with the sun in his eyes. Impulsively Susan tore the sheet off the pad, and with gestures that he was to keep it, dropped it down toward him. It planed on the wind, and he pursued it with agility, captured it in a clump of coyote brush. He admired it extravagantly, all but kissing his fingers. A masterpiece.

"Por nada," she knew enough to say in response to his multiple thanks, and she gave him her best *adios* when he roused Sancho and the other mules and they circled back up the hill and around the house

97

to the trail. The last she saw of the old man he was holding the picture against his chest as tenderly as if it had been a holy relic.

She had a warm glow at having done something gracious for one of the poor; she liked his admiration even while she smiled at it; she had the feeling of having made a friend. The fact was, she had been somewhat nettled by the comment of one of the Cornish wives, repeated to her by amused Lizzie: "Mister Ward's missus can picture anything, but what else is she able for?" She told herself that Mexicans, themselves more picturesque than the whey-faced Cornish, better understood the value of picturing.

But what would she have done if she had not had Lizzie? The thought of picking up that handkerchief gave her gooseflesh.

"Let's rest a minute, Lizzie," she said, and leaned back against the tree. Lizzie, sitting on the bulging root of a bay tree with her dark hair down and a makeshift A of red ribbon on her breast, gave up the effort to stare with an expression of guilty passion at an invisible Arthur Dimmesdale. She had a womanly body and a handsome face, with high cheekbones and a straight nose and straight, heavy, severe brows. But her expression was naturally impassive. She had trouble simulating Hester Prynne's pride and recklessness, and Susan could not instruct her too explicitly without risking reflections on Lizzie's closed past. The figure she had drawn satisfied her, and she had transformed the bay root into something appropriate to Hawthorne's dark wood, but the face wouldn't come right. In the last two hours it had been through every expression from Lizzie's native stoniness to a horrible leer, and it was now rubbed out for the fourth or fifth time.

She did not feel like drawing, but felt she must. She had signed a contract, they needed the money, she ought to keep her hands and mind occupied—there were a dozen reasons. Yet she would rather have sat torpidly and let dim thoughts coil through her head. The air was oppressive, as if it might rain, though she knew it could not rain for weeks or months yet. She drew it down to the bottom of her lungs, with its freight of dust and mold and the herb-cupboard smells of these woods, and she would have given anything for the breath of a hay meadow or the dank mossy air around the spring above Long Pond.

Even the sounds here were dry and brittle; she longed for sounds that were sponged up by green moss. She felt half sick again.

Brooding, she watched Lizzie take advantage of the rest to change Georgie's diaper. The little man-thing squirmed and rolled and gurgled, grabbing for the ribbon pinned on his mother's breast, but she took hold of his ankles and yanked his bottom into the air and efficiently shoved under it a dry flour-sack diaper with the faded word EXCELSIOR on it. With two swift motions she pinned him. She made one unsmiling tickling poke at his exposed navel and laid him back in his box. No nonsense with that fatherless mite, who already seemed to have learned some of Lizzie's stoicism. He took what life handed him and did not complain. Susan had heard him cry only five or six times.

There was something tragic about Lizzie. Was it a disastrous marriage or the betrayal of a good girl? For Lizzie *was* a good girl—Grandmother was not so genteel as to deny it, however Georgie was fathered. But once when she had asked Lizzie if it would help her to talk about her life, Lizzie had only said briefly, "Best not get into it."

Thousands of miles from friends or kin, with no husband to look after her, she bore her life patiently. When she worked she often sang to Georgie, sounding entirely happy; but once, starting to sing him to sleep, she started "Bye Baby Bunting," and stopped as if someone had knocked on the door.

She had rooms in her mind that she would not look into. Yet she was much liked by the Cornish women who came visiting, and apparently needed no other company, was less obviously lonely than Susan. Susan wondered if her own discontent was a weakness or if it was only a manifestation of greater sensibility. Was there something gnarly and tough about working-class people that kept them from feeling all that more delicately organized natures felt? If Georgie died, would Lizzie be prostrated, apathetic, and despairing, as Augusta still was, or would she rise in the morning, supported by some coarse strength, and build her fire and make breakfast and go on as before?

Susan could not imagine how it would be to know your husband for a brute, and determine to leave him. She would not even attempt to imagine being the victim of a seducer. She could not conceive the feelings of a woman who carried the child of a man she despised. But she had some inkling of how it felt to carry a child, for she had missed her last two periods. Nausea hung along the edge of her awareness like the fogfall that hung along the ridge but never rolled over.

What if she had no husband? All to go through alone, out here in this crude camp away from everything dear and safe? Like a magic-lantern slide the magnified image gleamed in her mind: Oliver's fair head, touched with the reddish early sun, sinking into the hole at the Kendall shaft to the groaning of the slow wheels. What if he never came back from one of those trips underground? A broken cable, a cave-in, an explosion, black damp, any of a dozen dangers he risked every day, could snuff him out. Then what? Oh, back home, back home! At once. Poor Susan, she went West with her husband and it was hardly three months before he was killed. No, I don't believe she'll marry again —she married rather late as it was, and she was much in love. I believe she will return to her career, live quietly at Milton in her father's house and have her old friends down from New York as before. Her dear friend Augusta, who also suffered a terrible personal loss, will have an-other baby, only a few months older than Susan's. Her sister Bessie now has two, less than a half mile down the lane. The children can grow up together, they will be inseparable.

The element of longing in her fantasy appalled her. He was too dear to her, she could never survive his loss. But how lovely it would be, all the same, to be back home, to have a woman to talk to—her mother, Bessie, best of all Augusta. She almost envied Lizzie the crude companionship of the Cornish wives.

Lizzie glanced up, and for a moment Susan saw in her face the expression she had been trying for all morning—the question that gleamed from the up-glancing eyes, the recklessness of the falling hair. "Wait," she said. "Stay just as you are." But she had barely picked up pencil and pad when Lizzie said, looking down through the woods, "Here comes Mr. Ward with somebody."

"We'll stop," Susan said, and stood up. "My goodness, I wonder what . . . ?"

Fearing emergency, she hurried, but when she met him at the gate she saw that he was relaxed and cheerful, in his mine clothes but not smeared with mud as he always was if he had been underground. The dark young man with him was Baron Starling, an Austrian engineer. They had only come to let Starling change into mine clothes.

Going up the steps, Susan gave Oliver a meaningful look. "Not in my bedroom," she meant it to say. "The spare room, even if it is full of trunks." But he led the baron straight to the bedroom door and showed him in and shut the door behind him.

"Oh, why did you take him in there!" she said to him, low-voiced. Oliver looked surprised. "Where else could I take him?"

"But my *bedroom!*"

He looked at her, frowning. The mulish look was gathering in his face, but she was too annoyed to care. "I'm sorry," he said at last. "I guess I was thinking of it as *our* bedroom."

Rebuked and angry, she was facing him on the veranda when the baron came out, ridiculous in Oliver's too-large clothes, sleeves rolled up and trouser cuffs turned up, like a girl dressed up as a man. He had thick brown hair and great brown girl's eyes, and he gave her what she supposed he supposed was a winning smile. "Thank you," he said. "Now I am better prepared."

"You're very welcome." She turned her eyes on Oliver, sulky on the veranda rail, and since she was condemned to this sort of hospitality in which her privacy was invaded and her home at the command of every stray engineer or geologist, she said, "Aren't you going to eat before you go down?"

"We'll share my lunch pail. We have to be down there when the *labor* isn't being worked in, when the men are eating." His eyes locked with hers, he smiled as if he knew his smile would be misinterpreted. "Maybe tea when we come out?"

"Of course."

They went off down the trail toward the Kendall shaft house, and she flew inside to write indignantly to Augusta. *I cannot tell you how it offended me to have a strange man taken into my bedroom. We must furnish our spare room at once if this sort of thing is to happen often.*

Oliver and the baron returned late in the afternoon, soggy from the hot mine and the hotter trail. They sat on the veranda and had a glass of ale, and she drank with them because she would not be less than polite and also because she had been told that ale was good for queasiness.

For a while the two men were talking techniques of timbering in different kinds of rock, and she was silent. But then the baron made an effort to bring her into the conversation, broke off and turned to her to praise the house and the view, and to remark respectfully that he had heard she was a splendid artist, and to apologize for being so ill-educated as not to know her work. Oliver went and got *The Skeleton in Armor* and *The Hanging of the Crane* and some old copies of *Scribner's* and *St. Nicholas* and laid them in Starling's lap. Starling was charmed. He praised the quality of sentiment she was able to convey in a mere posture, the tilt or lowering of a head. She brought out her *Scarlet Letter* blocks, and Starling was amused to find in Oliver and Lizzie the recognizable originals of Dimmesdale and Hester Prynne. Pressed for criticism, he ventured to point out a certain stiffness in one of the figures, a criticism that she accepted almost with enthusiasm.

It was Oliver's turn to sit outside the conversation. She and the baron were eagerly tracing the relations of the Düsseldorf painters to the Hudson River school, and discussing the advantages and disadvantages of studying art abroad, in the midst of cultural traditions different from and of course much richer than your own. Susan regretted never having had the opportunity, not yet; and the baron kept assuring her that the only thing an American could learn abroad was technique, that he must deal with New World subject matters if his art was to have integrity. As hers had. Those drawings could not have been made by anyone but an American artist. The understanding. The sensitivity to local character and landscape and costume and, yes, even physiognomy.

At a certain point Susan lifted her eyes to Oliver, realizing it was quite late, and asked a silent question that got a silent answer. "Won't you stay to supper—a very *simple* supper?" she asked the baron. The baron was delighted. A brief trip inside, a word to Lizzie, and she was back on the porch, talking.

Supper was a rattle and volley of opinions, reminders, acknowledgments, and discoveries of shared tastes. Starling was not only posted on art, he had read books. He was keen on Mr. James, he could quote Goethe, he had theories that the American tale was an indigenous form, quite different from the German *Novelle*. He was quick to shift the topic from Theodor Storm, whom Susan had not read, to Turgenev, whom she had. He tried to explain to her the precise meaning of the German term *Stimmung*. Listening to him, she was humiliated to see that Oliver had not properly washed his hands for supper: there was a dark smudge on one thumb.

When Lizzie had cleared away they tried the veranda again, but found it chilly. So silent Oliver lit a fire in the Franklin stove and they sat for two more hours talking about the Turco-Serbian difficulties that might involve Austria-Hungary, and hence the baron, in war; and of the reputation of Wagner, whom Starling thought overpraised by people more intent on being fashionable than in listening to music.

Oliver sat listening, nearly silent. When the baron finally, regretfully, rose to leave, he lighted a lantern and prepared to escort him down to Mother Fall's. On the veranda steps Starling took Susan's hand and kissed it. "Never," he said to her earnestly in his almost-perfect English, "never in the world would I have dreamed that an evening like this could be spent in an American mining camp."

When Oliver returned, Susan was still by the fire. She had been thinking unhappily how far out of the conversation Oliver was, just as he had been out of it during his one evening at the studio with Augusta and Thomas. How limitedly practical his talents were! His brother-in-law Conrad Prager, by contrast, would have risen gracefully to such an evening, would have been able to talk about books, art, and music, would probably have read Theodor Storm, would have quoted the baron back some Goethe. But Oliver, in such circumstances, fell silent, overmatched. No sooner had she had that treasonable thought than she was flooded with contrite affection, and determined to bring her old boy into things and not let him be shut out. But when he opened the door and stepped in and levered up the lantern's glass and blew out the flame and came to sit beside her, and she opened her mouth to say something, what did she say? She praised the baron.

"Wasn't he charming?" she said. "I don't know when I've found anyone easier to talk to."

With his legs outstretched before the fire, he seemed to ponder. Finally he said, "Kendall wants to make him my assistant."

"Oh, good!" But he did not answer, only cocked his eyebrow, and so she said, "It would be good, wouldn't it?"

"Good for supper parties. Not for the mine."

"Why, what's the matter with him?"

"He's too soft."

"Soft? He's *cultivated!*"

"I wasn't talking about his culture, I was talking about his capacities down the mine." He unlaced his fingers from across his chest and showed her the back of one hand. What in the candlelight at supper she had thought a smudge at the base of the thumb was a scraped, swollen, discolored bruise. "See that? If I didn't have that, he'd probably be dead."

It seemed all he was going to say. He looked sleepy and inert with the firelight on his face. Resentfully she waited. Finally she gave in. "Tell me."

"Just a symptom. We were in the *labor*—you know, the stope, where they're getting out ore, a sort of hollowed-out room along the vein. There's a lot of loose rock, it isn't timbered. You have to keep your eyes open. He leaned over to examine the face, and I saw dirt and pebbles fall out of the ceiling onto his shoulder. He should have felt it, too. I yelled at him, 'Back!', something like that, and what did he do? He turned around with those big deer's eyes soft and wondering, and said, 'Pardon?' When a man hollers at you down a mine and says jump, you'd better jump, not ask questions."

He sat blinking at the fire. "Then what?" Susan said. "How did you hurt yourself? I'm sorry, I never noticed."

"I pushed him. A slab fell right where he'd been leaning. Just nicked me." He put the bruise to his mouth as if kissing it.

"You saved his life. At the risk of your own!"

"Nothing quite that heroic. The point is I shouldn't have *had* to push him. You just can't work with a man who turns around and wonders why you're yelling at him."

She sat quietly. She did not doubt Oliver's judgment of Starling, not now. She was only rebellious against the conditions of their life, which excluded, except perhaps in positions of control such as Conrad Prager had, men sensitive enough to appreciate the finer things. She knew without any question, no matter what he said, that Oliver's act had been heroic; but she still wished he were more competent in cultivated conversation.

Then he hoisted his eyebrows at the fire, looking across the hands he had folded under his chin, and said through his mustache, with the edge of sullenness in his voice, "Maybe you think I'm going to recommend against him because he fell in love with you. That isn't so."

"Oh, fell in love!"

"Of course he did. At first sight. Bang." He turned his sleepy face. "Why wouldn't he? So did I."

It was precisely the right thing to say. It absolved him of jealousy and spread balm on her irritations and reassured her that she had not the slightest regret. If Thomas Hudson himself were available, she would still choose Oliver Ward. They sat up together—close together—by the open fire until the coals had fallen into ash, and all was reaffirmed and renewed. Grandmother had her identity back, having had the baron to reflect it for an evening. He was the first young man with a genteel education to encounter her in the camps and backwoods that framed much of her life. He would not be the last, nor the last to fall in love with her rosy animated face and her interest in anything that moved, especially anything that talked.

I doubt that she reopened the matter of her violated bedroom. Instead, I would guess that she took advantage of the renewed tenderness between them to tell him, with all the hesitancy demanded by her times and training, that he was going to have an heir, a fact that Augusta had known for a month.

What did he say? I am utterly unable to guess. He was not one to say much under any circumstances. He was too concerned about her safety and comfort to be very pleased that it was to happen in that mining camp, and too pinched economically to be pleased it was to happen so soon. But he was too much in love not to be awed and grateful at what she had done for him, or what they had done together.

What was there for a young husband of 1876 to say? Something ineffable, something like what William Clark wrote in his notebook when he and Meriwether Lewis saw the Pacific at the mouth of the Columbia (O! the joy!)? Certainly not what I heard my son Rodman say when Leah telephoned him from her gynecologist's office. (Shit!)

New Almaden, Dec. 2, 1876

My dear girl—

Your last letter came to us on our way from the mine to San Francisco for our Thanksgiving excursion. It is an all-day journey and only 75 miles. I enjoyed the ride on top of the stage through the fog to San Jose, and our lunch at the La Moille House was made doubly pleasant by the letters which Eugene the stage driver handed us just as we entered the hotel. There was one from you, one from home, one from Dickie. I felt as if we were all going to San Francisco by the afternoon train.

Mr. Prager met us with a carriage—I enjoyed the disgust of the disappointed hack-men—howling fiends looking and acting as if ready to devour you. Mr. Prager's name does not suggest the sort of man he is. His friend Ashburner and he should change names . . . Mr. Prager was educated at Freiburg and, pleasantly enough, two or three of his fellow students—Ashburner, Janin, etc.—are now in San Francisco. They are a very clever cosmopolitan sort of men—not easily enthusiastic—do not reveal themselves very much but draw out other people. They have been in strange countries—Japan, Mexico, South America, and those queer islands which it is so hard to remember geographically. Mr. Janin is the cynic of the trio. He is the most difficult to understand, and therefore the most fascinating. Mr. Prager is very handsome and has great harmoniousness—he never jars.

We were not in the gay set of San Francisco, but we were what seemed to me gay, after the mine. We drove on the sands below the Cliff House and through the Park. I greatly enjoyed being whirled past the long lines of spray, flashing in the sun. The water came to the horses' feet, the sea line was dark keen blue against the sky. The weather was perfect all the while we were there, the evenings very lovely, moonlight softened by fog. We were out a good deal—receptions, dinners, etc. They are very learned about cooking in San Francisco—people seem to expect as a matter of course things which we consider luxurious. Oliver and I spent all our money immediately, and only stopped because we had no more to spend.

Pray give my love to your dearest mother. She was very kind to think of me. We cannot help thinking it natural that we should be forgotten. You cannot think what a bond it was between me and the ladies I met in San Francisco—our loving remembrance of our old homes. They are all young married women who followed their husbands out here. All had a certain general line of experience—all could tell the same story of homesickness, of the return, and, alas, of the strange change which made the old seem new and unfamiliar. It made me feel like crying to hear them speak of it. *"We* do not forget," they all said, "but *they* have no place for us when we return. We must be reconciled, for what we left behind us can never be ours again. We have lost our life in the East—we must make a new life for ourselves here." They were charming women, well-bred, gentle, and very adaptable. They would go anywhere in the world where their husbands' businesses made it necessary, and make a home. But I fancied in all of them a lingering sentiment for the old home, a pathetic sense of being aliens in the new. I am determined not to share their misfortune. I should feel lost if I thought this country would see me old.

I know that you and Thomas are both growing in ways both deep and broad. It makes me tremble a little, for I am not conscious of any growth in myself, and I cannot let you grow away from me. I am so afraid when you see me again you will find me poor and common.

New Almaden, Dec. 11, 1876

Darling Augusta —

Unless your eyes trouble you, dear Augusta, please read this to yourself.

I have followed your advice in one of the two ways in which you recommended me to be anticipating the evil day that is coming —as to the hardening of the nipples—but I do not know what you mean by using oil. Is it the abdomen that is to be rubbed? I begin to have a painfully stretched feeling—would oil relieve that?

I spoke to you about the advice Mrs. Prager gave me about the future. Of course I know nothing about it practically, and it sounds dreadful—but every way is dreadful except the one which it seems cannot be relied on.

Mrs. P. said that Oliver must go to a physician and get shields of some kind. They are to be had at some druggists'. It sounds perfectly revolting, but one must face anything rather than the inevitable results of nature's methods. At all events there is nothing injurious about this. Mrs. Prager is a very fastidious woman and I hardly think would submit to anything very bad—and yet, poor thing, it is an absolute necessity for her. She is magnificently womanly and strong looking, but really very frail. These things are called "cundrums" and are made either of rubber or skin.

May I tell you of a queer thing that happened in San Francisco? I went to church with Mr. Prager on Thanksgiving morning—Oliver had an appointment with some men in town. Mrs. P. did not feel well enough to go. It was a mild, soft morning, the hill was very steep, the air very relaxing, like our first mild weather in spring, when the damp sea winds blow. We sat through the first part of the service but the organ made me feel strangely. Its throbbing seemed to stifle me and for the first time that pulse within me woke and throbbed so strongly it took away my breath. Mr. Prager sat on one side of me and Mr. Ashburner on the other. I thought I should faint and leaned against the seat. Everything grew dark and I did not know anything for a minute—I don't know how long, but I came to myself with great drops of perspiration on my lips and forehead. Mr. Ashburner was looking at me very closely.

Both Mr. Prager and Mr. Ashburner were delicate enough not to allude to it, but Mr. Hall joined us on our way home and cheerfully exclaimed, "Weren't you ill in church? You looked as if you were going to faint. Didn't you notice it, Prager?" Mr. P. said, "I thought she looked a little pale, but the church was very close," and changed the subject.

It seems absurd to talk so much about an experience common to all women—but I think it one of the *strangest* feelings—that double pulse, that life within a life. . . .

4

Now ensued a blissful time for my grandmother. Many things contributed to it, not the least of which was that double pulse. She floated listening on the placid amniotic tides. But there were other things too.

The rainy season came on and restored her to time and change. Her days had variety and excitement, the sun that had been inescapable for months was now out of sight for sometimes a week on end, wild gusts of rain beat against her house and filled her veranda with twigs and leaves, the mountain was lost and revealed and lost again in stormy roils of cloud, the hills emerged under the slashes of reasserted sun a magical fresh green. The long dry hot winter, as Oliver said, was over. The dust was laid in the trails, the smells of ripe summer garbage that had once drifted across them from the camps were replaced by clean woodsmoke. In the woods and along the trail sides marvels appeared, unexpected flowers, maidenhair. The smells of the woods were no longer dusty and aromatic, but as damp and rich as those of the Long Pond woods at home.

When it stormed, her house was the sanctuary she thought a house should be. On those days Oliver could not see to work in his dark little office past four thirty. She sat now, not on the veranda exposed to the tumble of mountains, but inside by the fire in her little redwood parlor, waiting in dreamy security for the click of the gate latch and the sound of boots on the porch. Sometimes they had a whole hour before dinner to be idle in, read *Scribner's* or Turgenev or *Daniel Deronda* aloud, fix things, talk.

In January Augusta had her child without trouble, and thereafter her letters appear to have lost their despondency as the living child began to replace the dead one. Freed from anxiety about her friend, Susan was more open to knowing her husband. She discovered in him unexpected capacities. He could make or fix anything from the broken handle of a carving knife to the sinking props under the veranda. Without their discussing reasons, he built a bed, a bench, and a bureau for the spare room, and he began on a cradle that would swing from the porch ceiling. From Mexican Camp he brought home coyote and wildcat skins, and tanned them and sewed them together into a rug for beside their bed. The baby could roll and play on it when the time came.

But Oliver was not only handy, which as an engineer he probably should have been. He revealed also the most unexpected sensibility. His suggestions about the decoration of the house astonished her, they were so often right. Without making anything of it, even being a little embarrassed by it, he could assemble a bouquet of wildflowers with a careless effectiveness that put her own most painstaking arrangements to shame. He had a touch with plants: everything he brought home from the woods grew as if it had only been awaiting the opportunity of their yard.

Even literature. She wanted to talk to him about *Daniel Deronda*, about which she and Augusta had been having a chatty and I must say tedious correspondence as they read it simultaneously. But he was impatient with George Eliot. He said she wanted to be both writer and reader—she barely got a character created before she started responding to him and judging him. Turgenev, on the other hand, stayed out of his stories, he let you do your own responding. Meekly, after that conversation, Susan adjusted her opinion in her next letter to Augusta.

They had visitors, a few, enough. Mr. Hamilton Smith, one of Conrad Prager's associates, and the consulting engineer for the mine, stopped off for dinner, sending her scurrying in panic up to Mexican Camp for a steak, for Mr. Smith was one of those formidable dining-out San Franciscans. It was "rich" day—pay day—and the whole camp was drunk. The butcher's assistant, lured from the Hosteria de los Mineros, cut her a steak with profuse assurances that this was a holiday steak, and he did not charge her for a holiday steak. Oliver, when he heard where she had been by herself, was upset, but her dinner was a success, and after dinner Mr. Smith called upon Oliver to bring out his notebooks, his maps, his drawings of pump stations, everything he had been doing, and they pored over them for two hours "much as you might show your year's work to Mr. La Farge if he were kinder and more generous." If Mr. Smith had been manager instead of Mr. Kendall, they would have gone more often to the Hacienda.

In late February, when the hillsides were patched with lupine, poppies, and blue-eyed grass, Mary Prager spent a few days. I quote from Grandmother's reminiscences: "She thought the place ideal. The valley, changing from hour to hour, battle-fronts of clouds forming along the bases of the mountains, charging, breaking, scattering in tatters and streamers wildly flying; tops of the mountains seen with ineffable colors on them at sunset and the nearer hills like changeable cut velvet. She walked the piazza smiling to herself; she laid soft hands on my housekeeping. I think our simple routine rested her after the conventional perfection she had set herself to achieve in her marriage to a man whose life demanded it; for she had been a farmer's daughter, too, and I daresay had to ask her husband what wines to serve with what courses when she gave her exquisite little dinners . . . She and Oliver sassed each other in the Ward family way; and when she saw the artist-wife in her digging hours—more really at home than in the city where she was inclined toward excess of participation under the influence of evening clothes and evening company—I think whatever misgivings she may have had were satisfied. She knew that, in the words of her father when he read that Quaker marriage contract, 'it would hold.' "

Leaving, Mary Prager held their hands and hoped they would be spared the footloose life common to the profession. Why should they ever leave New Almaden? He could be manager here one day; he had a great opportunity to succeed without making his wife into a wanderer.

As for the young men from Mother Fall's who drifted up to the Wards' veranda on chilly spring evenings, they thought Oliver Ward's clover very deep indeed. To a man they were in love with Susan, pregnant or not. One of them, a boy from the University of California with loads of undigested information in his head and a word of kindly unasked advice for anyone he talked to, stumbled off the porch one evening and blurted to Oliver that Mrs. Ward was more an angel than a woman. "Which amused both of us," Susan wrote, "but made one of us feel sad and old."

She was posing, of course. She was thirty. Oliver, whom she sometimes called Sonny, and bossed around, was twenty-eight. It was impossible that they could have been happier. Though the weekly letters still poured back to New York, the tone of them is serene, excited, amused, anything but homesick or desperate. And now and then the

East reached out a hand to her and made her realize how much she had changed in barely more than half a year.

Here came Howie Drew, a boy from Milton bent on finding his fortune in the West, and spent a weekend investigating the possibilities of New Almaden, and was advised by Oliver to move on. Because Oliver was busy, Susan took Howie around, and one morning they walked along the new road that Chinese coolies were building to the Santa Isabel tunnel. As they walked, talking about home, she looked past his red head and saw the nameless local flowers looking down at them from the bank. They passed blackened places where pig-tailed Chinese had built noon fires for their tea. The signal bells clinked from the shaft house and a tram car dumped with a rumbling roar off the platform of the Day tunnel. And here was Howie Drew from down the road, the son of the ferryman, a boy she used to look after for his mother when she was fifteen. And here was herself, Mrs. Oliver Ward, no longer Susan Burling, barrel-shaped with child, only walking at all because she had Howie to go along, only appearing with Howie because he was an old friend, almost family. Familiar and unfamiliar swam and blended into a strangeness like dreaming as she saw Howie Drew's face out of her girlhood against the mountainside of her present life. A wash of confused feeling went over her like wind across a sweating skin, for the identity that Howie took for granted and talked to and reflected back at her was not the identity it used to be, not the one that had signed all her past drawings, not the one she knew herself. Then what was it now? She didn't know.

Or here was another echo from home, a Mrs. Elliott, a friend of her Aunt Sarah's, who came up from Santa Cruz all uninvited and planted herself among them for four days. In her youth she too had had another identity: she had been Georgiana Bruce, and she was one of the Brook Farm transcendentalists. All her life she had been saving the world. She had burned for Abolition, for Woman's Suffrage, for Spiritualism, for Phrenology, for heaven knew what. She possessed, and quoted from, what Grandmother assumed to be the only copy of *Leaves of Grass* in California.

In those surroundings she was stranger than Howie Drew, for she sat in Susan's parlor and talked about Bradford, Curtis, Margaret Fuller, Hawthorne—Hawthorne, while just over in the corner cupboard ten feet from her, was a pile of blocks on which Susan had been trying for months to make Hawthorne's prose into pictures. Mrs. Elliott's talk was full of names and books and causes that Susan had been brought up to think worth reverence—and a few, such as Whitman, worth a pang of excited alarm—but in person she looked more like this careless coast than like intellectual New England. She could not have bought a new pair of shoes since Brook Farm.

Though it was Susan, in love with talk and ideas, who ought to have responded to this apparition, this gray-haired, leather-faced, shining-eyed Cassandra, it was Oliver, who liked "characters," who found her amusing. Mrs. Elliott bothered Susan because for all her ideas she was not genteel; she delighted Oliver because she was as odd as Dick's hatband.

One evening she read their heads. Susan she granted sensibility and delicacy of feeling, but Oliver who had what she called the big top, was the one with the intellectual power. She forced him to admit that he had great headaches, and she instructed Susan to pour cold water, very slowly, on a certain spot—right here, this knob—when the big top ached. Oliver hooted. Why not put a pistol to his head and be done with it?

An eccentric but not a fool, she whipped their quiet routine into a froth. Totally humorless, she made them collapse in laughter. As unkempt as a hermit, she had innumerable suggestions on dress and housekeeping. Obviously a careless mother, she dwelt on the Coming Event and irritated Susan by knowing everything that should be done in preparation and in the way of upbringing. She cast her bright enameled blue eye on Georgie, known as Buster because he busted everything within reach, and told dismayed Lizzie that he was destructive because his latent tenderness had not been appealed to. Boys should play with dolls, to teach them care for others and to stimulate their later parental responsibility—brickbats and tiles they would find for themselves.

Demanding rags, she made in a jiffy a rag baby which she laid in Buster's arms with sounds of transcendental love. Georgie took it, a wonder. Then he crawled to the edge of the veranda and threw it into the chaparral. He would come to it, Mrs. Elliott said. Give him time. He had been let to get too good a start on a wrong path. But when she left at the end of four days Buster was still throwing the rag doll into the chaparral, and Lizzie confessed to Susan that she didn't mind. It proved to her that he was all boy.

Come, come to Santa Cruz! Mrs. Elliott said as she departed. When the Great Event had happened, and Susan was rested, and wanted quiet in which to concentrate on the proper influences for that little unformed soul, she should bring him to Santa Cruz where he could wake and sleep to the sound of the sea. It would soothe his harsh masculine temperament if he was male, and reinforce her capacity for love and devotion if she was female.

Though Susan would not have called the assortment of people who passed through her house a society of a stimulating kind, she was neither lonely nor bored. Though she affected to view with dismay Mary Prager's suggestion that they plan to stay their lives in New Almaden, she took great satisfaction in how well Oliver did his job. His survey had spotted the Santa Isabel tunnel within a foot, his map grew by tiny meticulous increments and had the praise of Mr. Smith, who said there was no finer thing of its kind. Without glancing at the implications, Susan praised him to Augusta for having taken the measure of the largest and most difficult mine on the continent in a single year. She tried not to begrudge him the time he spent working at night and on Sundays, and when his eyes gave out on him or one of his headaches came on, she willingly read aloud to him the things he felt he should study—treatises on the construction of arches, reports on Colorado mining districts, technical journals full of the grimmest algebra. While she had him there helplessly listening, she generally managed to work in Thomas Hudson's latest poem of Old Cupboard essay, and she always reported him to Augusta as deeply moved.

Her own work did not satisfy her, but the closer she came to her time the harder she worked, though she could hardly sit in a chair for ten consecutive minutes. She was always one to clean her desk. Work, progress, and the inviolability of contract, three of the American gospels, met and fused in her with the doctrines of gentility and the cult of the picturesque. She was some sort of cross between a hummingbird and an earth mover. The Scarlet Letter blocks went off in March.

It would be pleasant to find that these pictures, though done in exile and against difficulties, triumphantly justify her as an artist. They don't. They are fairly routine illustrations of a kind now rendered almost obsolete by facsimile reproduction processes. However she attenuated Grandfather, who was her only male model, she couldn't make him come out looking like a guilty and remorseful preacher. As for Lizzie, she looks more propped-up than passionate.

Nevertheless, done, packed up, sent off, the contract satisfied, the money assured. Hardly had she had Oliver turn the package over to Eugene the stage driver than he brought her a letter from Thomas Hudson. He said that he and Augusta had found her Almaden letters so colorful and interesting that he thought *Scribner's* readers should share in the pleasure. Would she want to try putting them together into an article? If she could not (he was too delicate to hint *why* she perhaps could not), Augusta had said she would be glad to do the little arranging necessary. And did she have any drawings that could be used as illustrations?

"Good heavens," she said to Oliver, "I can't think Scribby is in such a bad way that it has to fall back on me for its Western correspondent. He ought to get Mr. Harte or Mark Twain or someone."

"Harte and Mark Twain don't live in New Almaden," Oliver said. "If he didn't want you to do it he wouldn't have asked you. Wait till you're rested after the baby and do it then."

"But I'm not a writer!"

"He seems to think you are."

She brooded. That night she wrote a hasty sketch and showed it to Oliver. "It's all right," he said. "But I'd take out that stuff about Olympian mountains and the Stygian caverns of the mine. That's about used up, I should think."

Meekly, astonished at herself, she took it out, rewrote the sketch as much in the spirit of discovery as possible, and sent it in. She put in Mother Fall, and her cook China Sam, who had murdered a rival and been reprieved from the rope because he was too good a cook to hang. He had a fourteen-year-old mail-order bride—sent, rumor said, by his real wife in China, who did not want to risk herself when Sam sent for her. She put in the Christmas custom of the Cornish miners, who visited the house and sang carols, those "rude uncultivated people" singing parts as if they had been born the children of choir masters. She put in every rag of local color she could think of about New Almaden, but she still mistrusted what she had done, and she still was afraid that Thomas would take it out of friendship and not for its own merits.

I have no evidence, but I think Grandmother must have been set up to be asked to write that piece. She would have loved to think it was good: It would demonstrate that marriage had not shrunk her career, but broadened it. She wanted to grow, as she imagined Thomas and Augusta growing, and as she was sure that Oliver grew, in his own way, through his work at the mine. Yet to think of herself appearing page to page with Cable or Nadal or any of the *Scribner's* writers left her cold with the fear that her sketch would show up as a lame and embarrassing thing.

She had to know. So in two evenings she wrote another little story about the fiesta on Mexican Independence Day in September, with double heroines in Mr. Hernandez's languid and beautiful sisters. This she sent off smoking hot to Mr. Howells at the *Atlantic*, submitting herself to a less partial judge than Thomas. That gave her three things to wait for.

5

Late afternoon, a soft spring day, the hills so green and soft she thought she would like to roll down them as she and Bessie used to roll down the pasture hill in Milton when they were children. Instead, she moved from the chair on the valley side of the porch to the bench on the trail side. The hammock she had given up weeks ago; she could not have got out of it if she had got in. Lizzie's noises in the kitchen, and a banging that was probably Buster among the stovewood, might have been the sounds from her mother's kitchen. The smells of damp and mold from below the porch were so familiar that it seemed her family must be just over the hill, to be visited in a ten-minute walk. Across on a blue, lupine-covered saddle two white mules were grazing, as peaceful as two white clouds in a summer sky.

Stranger scrambled out from under the porch and went off up the trail. That should mean Oliver was coming. In a minute he appeared, so much like a farmer returning from the fields in his corduroy pants and blue shirt that he might have been her father, or John Grant. He made a pass at Stranger's ears, the dog bounced around him like a playful plowhorse. She saw a letter in Oliver's shirt pocket. His forehead and nose were red from working all day Sunday in the yard. She sat still, placid and waiting, until he was clear up the steps. Then she lifted her smiling face to be kissed.

"Oh," she said, "it's been so beautiful I hated to think of you down that grim old mine."

"I came out at noon and had a good mule ride over to Guadalupe."

"Good, I'm glad. What for?"

"Remember that hoisting machinery Kendall was going to put in at the Santa Isabel, the rig he saw in the Sierra, that I didn't like the looks of?"

"I guess I don't remember."

"Oh, sure you remember. Kendall wasn't pleased when I questioned it. I told you."

"If you did it didn't penetrate. I haven't much of a head for things like that."

"I guess your head will do. Well, anyway. I knew it wouldn't work here because—never mind. He thought it would. So I proved it to him. Captain Smith and I have been redesigning it, and when Smith was down last I showed it to him. So they're going to try it out over at Guadalupe, and if it works there, which it will, they'll install it in the Santa Isabel."

For him, it was a speech. She could tell what it meant to him by the words it forced out of him. He succeeded in everything he did. She could see him broadening down, like freedom, from precedent to precedent, and because she was proud of him, and wanted his value acknowledged by his employers, she said, "Shouldn't you get something from that? Couldn't you take out a patent?"

She made him laugh. "What is it about Quakers? My time belongs to the company."

"Even Sundays? I'll bet that's not what Mr. Smith would say."

"Maybe not, but Kendall does. He also said something else today. He may not like to have me prove him wrong, but he just told me I've got a three-hundred-dollar raise."

"Which you've earned and a lot more. You're such a child anybody could take advantage of you. You've probably saved them thousands. Aren't you going to give me my letter?"

He touched his pocket. "This? It's not yours."

"Oh, pshaw. Who's it from?"

"My mother."

"Mayn't I read it?"

"It's private."

"Well, you *are* queer," she said, disappointed. Then she saw slyness in his face. "What are you up to?"

"Can't a man have private letters from his mother? You have private letters from your old beau Dickie Drake."

"Oh, Oliver, thee may read them if thee wants! Anyway he's fallen preposterously in love with a Jewish poetess named Emma Lazarus."

"Good for him, she can help raise him from the dead. After she

118

does, I'll read his letters. What I really want to talk about is you having some decent help when the baby comes."

"Yes?" she said. "Who? You know what Mrs. Kendall pays that clumsy girl she has? Her Chinamen are better servants."

"I wasn't thinking of getting you a Chinaman."

"I should think not. You're not going to get me anyone. Lizzie can manage."

"Lizzie's got all she can do to cook and keep house and look after Buster. You need somebody just for you and the baby."

"Tell me this instant," she said. "You're up to some extravagance. We can't throw away what little we've saved, just on some . . ."

Looking comfortably unpersuaded, Oliver sat on the steps scratching Stranger's ears. "It's no extravagance. I told you I wasn't going to bring you West to live in a shack, and I didn't, quite, only I spoiled it by not having the money for your fare. I didn't intend you should have a child in this camp, either, but here we are. So the least we can do is see you're looked after. Mother's found somebody who's willing to come out."

"Oliver . . ."

"Wait a minute. Not a servant, a lady. Mother guarantees her. Something happened to her man, or maybe she never had one. She's sort of aground there in New Haven. She'll come for her fare and servant's wages. If you don't turn everything upside down."

"Oliver . . ."

She labored to her feet. He handed her his mother's letter. "And we can afford it," he said. "We can afford anything you need. We could afford it before Kendall raised me and we can afford it better now."

She felt tears coming, compelled somehow out of her very physical dependency; she flung her arms around him from behind, stooping over him, and he rose awkwardly, turning to meet her. Distractedly she cried into the sweaty wool of his shirt, "Oliver Ward, thee *has* spoiled me!"

Her family and Augusta, anxiously awaiting word of Susan's lying-in, which despite her letters they probably visualized as happening on the dirt floor of a log cabin, might have saved their worry. As childbirth went in 1877, my father's was well organized and well attended.

Marian Prouse arrived on April 22, and within a day had proved herself a pleasant, soft, sensible, and helpful young woman. The day after her arrival there came a letter from Thomas Hudson enthusiastically buying the New Almaden sketch, with whatever illustrations Susan could provide. Three days after that came a letter from William D. Howells, buying Susan's Mexican fiesta piece and asking for two illustrations, on subjects to be selected by herself, as fast as she could send them. He recalled their pleasant meeting of a few years ago, and hoped that this would be the first of many contributions from her pen and pencil to the pages of the *Atlantic*. The letter is on the wall over there, framed: the beginning of Grandmother's literary career.

In the midst of general applause and admiration Susan sat down and wrote a dismayed, apologetic note to Thomas Hudson, lamely explaining how it had happened that her first published writing, and her first drawings of New Almaden, might be appearing in *Atlantic* rather than in *Scribner's*. She had been searching for reassurance and had found an embarrassment. But at least she now had confidence that if he and Augusta would help, she might make of the *Scribner's* article something that none of them need be ashamed of.

She had barely licked the envelope before she had her first pains. Oliver, who had had a mule tied outside for three days, rode over to Guadalupe and brought back Dr. McPherson, not the camp doctor but one he had known on the Comstock, and trusted. McPherson stayed the night, the next day, and part of the next night, and at long length delivered a boy who weighed a humiliating eleven pounds.

There is a whole folder of correspondence about that birth, its stages, difficulties, damages, and emotional exhaustions and satisfactions. Not even an admiring grandson can deal with it. For one thing, Susan wrote those letters with her eyes firmly closed, having been warned that use of the eyes after childbirth might damage them. For another, they are anciently, mystically, impenetrably female: their sentiments are as opaque to me as their handwriting is illegible. Among other things, she referred to my father then and for a good year afterward as "Boykins." Ugh.

So I will content myself with my grandfather's note.

April 29, 1877

My dear Thomas and Augusta,
Oliver Burling Ward sends his greetings to you this morning, or rather he did some time since and is now sleeping quietly by the side of his mother, who says she is ridiculously well and "too happy to be comfortable."

She had a little trouble from the long labor, Dr. McPherson had to make some repairs, her convalescence was somewhat extended. Though children might be born among the Cousin Jacks and the Mexicans as casually and as stoically as calves are born in pastures, the camp rallied round for this one. China Sam sent a silk Chinese flag to wrap this Baby Bunting in. A Cornish wife brought over a horrible quilt, quilted by her husband in his off hours, which Susan laughed over and nearly wept over and put firmly away where it could never be seen. But she kept it all her life—it's probably somewhere in a cupboard in this house right now. Mother Fall's young men opened so much champagne that they sent her a bouquet of corks surrounded by wild flowers, and before that joke had settled for five minutes, followed it with an armful of roses.

Lying in the parlor, which had been selected as the warmest and least drafty room in the house, Susan could look through the arch, under the pendant bowie, spurs, and revolver, and see her household going on: Miss Prouse hopping up, sitting down, hopping up again like a helpful younger sister, Lizzie serving, Oliver presiding, Buster whipping his homemade high chair. Miss Prouse was smooth and efficient and gentle with Boykins (ugh) when she bathed or changed him. She was modest, soft, and sisterly with Susan. Distracted by the test of the new hoist, Oliver was driven and divided, and away more than either of them liked, but she loved to have him stretch out beside her in the evening and talk, and not even his habit of smoking his pipe in her bed made her want to send him away. He looked upon the baby with awe, and handled him as if he might break.

Within three weeks Boykins was swinging in his cradle from the veranda ceiling—long, easy swings that they thought Mrs. Elliott would have to approve of. None of your jerky ordinary cradle motions.

Cosmic tides. Susan was resolved that he was to be the world's healthiest infant. Never so much as a cold, if care could prevent it. She bragged to her mother and Augusta that he had napped outside from the age of two weeks. (A little Western boastfulness? *You*, Grandmother?) Studying him, she decided that he was not pretty (beauty was reserved for Augusta's children), but that his face already showed character. His eyes, she reluctantly reported to ox-eyed Augusta, were fatally blue.

While she was recovering among the letters, gifts, and attentions of those who loved and looked after her, Thomas Hudson with his delicate sense of timing requested three illustrations for a ballad by the Norwegian poet Hjalmar Boyesen. He said with tongue in cheek that her experience of drawing Longfellow Vikings ought to let her do these without models, and she might find them a pleasant diversion from the duties of motherhood. She understood him perfectly: he believed in her not only as a woman, but as an artist. So there she sat, drawing burros and señoritas for the New Almaden sketch with one hand, and with the other producing the synthetic stuff that gentility thought virile. Give her credit, she laughed at herself.

She laughed even harder when she was well enough to go out sketching in the open air, hunting the local color of Mexican Camp, Cornish Camp, and the mine. Miners and miners' wives meeting her on the trails must have clutched their brows. Here came the engineer's missus in a serge walking costume and a big hat. Behind her came Miss Prouse, almost as authentically a lady, pushing Boykins in his perambulator through the cinnabar-colored dust. (He had to go along with the chuck wagon, so to speak.) Behind Miss Prouse came an urchin, Cornish or Mexican, lugging drawing materials, a stool, and an umbrella. People got clear off the trail to let them pass. Some may have laughed when it was safe to do so. But not all, and none without some sort of acknowledged respect that was less for Susan's art than for her quality.

There are several dubious assumptions about the early West. One is that it was the home of intractable self-reliance amounting to anarchy, whereas in fact large parts of it were owned by Eastern and foreign capital and run by iron-fisted bosses. Another is that it was rough, ready, and unkempt, and ribald about anything not as unkempt as itself, whereas in fact there was never a time or place where gentility, especially female gentility, was more respected. Not if it was the real thing, and no one in New Almaden doubted that Susan's was. The camps all but doffed their caps to Susan Ward, as if she had been a lady from a castle instead of from a cottage.

6

After the warm walk down the trail they stood talking at the door of the shaft house. Tregoning the hoist man sent out his window a smile from which all the upper front teeth had been extracted. Ordinarily he would have punctuated the smile with a spurt of tobacco juice from its dark center, but today he had his company manners on: bigwigs going down. Oliver went inside and leaned his elbows on the railing and talked across the machinery at him, easy and familiar.

Looking heavy, soft, and excited, Miss Prouse pushed the perambulator out of the trampled, dusty sunlight and under the shade of the nearest oak. But when Susan made some bright sound of questioning farewell and moved as if to join her, Conrad Prager said with his indulgent smile, "Susan, have you ever been down the mine?"

"Never." Her eyes went to Mr. Kendall, who was watching Oliver and Tregoning as they talked inside the shaft house. Kendall's head turned, and her eyes bounced off his impassive face like pebbles off a cliff. Mr. Kendall was the reason she had never been underground. He did not believe in women going down into mines. Mines were for the production of ore.

"Wouldn't it give you something interesting for your sketch?"

Mr. Kendall's expression was so marked that she turned to Oliver. He had quit talking to Tregoning and was listening, as impassive as the manager himself. If there was any disagreement between his manager and his brother-in-law, Oliver would have to stay out of it. She understood that. "I'd be in the road," she said. "Anyway I don't have drawing materials with me."

"How about your vocabulary?" Mr. Prager said.

"I beg your pardon?"

"I didn't mean you could draw down there. It would be too dark. I meant it might be an experience you could write into your sketch." He was wearing a canvas coat with bulging pockets, as if he were headed for a duck blind instead of toward the inspection of an ambiguously behaving ore body. He said, "Oliver, isn't it your opinion that an engineer's wife should go down at least once, just to enlarge her sympathies?"

Slightly smiling, alert to the expressions on three faces, Oliver came out of the shack. "I certainly have no objection if Mr. Kendall doesn't."

"Then that settles it," Prager said. "Domestic understanding and art both demand it. There's no objection, is there, Kendall?"

"None," said Mr. Kendall. He said it promptly and even heartily, but as Susan shudderingly let Mr. Prager fit a mine hat over her hair (*what heads have worn that hat!*) she had an impression of the manager's careful eyes and of his mouth that firmed itself into an expression too explicitly meant to be pleasant. Still, if he disapproved, he couldn't take it out on Oliver, since it was all Mr. Prager's doing, and Mr. Prager was not only a distinguished mining expert but one of Mr. Kendall's directors.

She wished she could like Mr. Kendall better, for he and his wife had gone out of their way to be friendly, and he had given Oliver every chance to prove himself. Only last week he had taken Oliver off the survey, which he was tired of, and put him on construction, where his inventiveness had a chance to show. Nothing but kindness, really, for nearly a year. Yet she couldn't quite like him, and she knew no one who did. So nearly a gentleman, Mr. Kendall was, so fatally not one.

Mr. Prager was tucking her hair up under the edges of the hat. "It wouldn't do to set you afire. You wouldn't be half so attractive bald."

Feeling with her hands around the rim of the unfamiliar headgear with its candle socket on the front, she had a dismayed thought. "The baby! How long will we be?"

"No more than an hour," Oliver said. "Unless we're going to look at more than this *labor* on the four hundred."

"That's all," Prager said. Kendall nodded without comment. "You may take him home, then," Susan said to Marian Prouse, and let Prager help her aboard the skip. It moved under her with a thin iron groan. A birdcage on a string, it hung by its cable over unimaginable depths—six hundred feet this shaft went down; there were others twice as deep.

The manager lighted his candle and replaced the hat on his head. "All right, Tregoning." The bell clinked, steam sighed, the bottom caved away, slowly the light went gray, grayer, dusky, dark. Hanging to Oliver's arm, Susan turned her face upward, staring up along the cable at the shrinking square from which daylight peered blindly down after them. She was looking for stars, knowing that stars were visible in daylight from deep wells, but she saw none. It took her a few seconds to realize that she was looking not into sky but into the roof of the shaft house.

The square of light was dim and small now, the air was warm and damp and smelled of creosote. She found herself breathing through her mouth. The candle on the manager's hat flickered along a sluggish upward flow of yellowish rock. As they sank, the shaft appeared to narrow, the walls pinched and squeezed together. If anything should slump or cave they would all be pressed into the rock like fossils.

"All right?" Oliver said. A solid shadow, he might have been looking down at her; somehow she felt he was smiling. His arm squeezed her hand against his side.

"Of course she's all right," said Prager. "This is a thoroughbred. Not one lady-like scream."

"I wouldn't dare scream," Susan said shakily. "If I started I couldn't stop."

Their laughter reassured her. They took this descent into Hades as casually as she would go down a flight of stairs.

The single candle wavered, their shadows slid on the upward-flowing rock. Then the rock became plank, the skip snagged for an instant that stopped her heart, shook free, rattled past some obstruction. A hole gaped, hollowed by dim light out of utter blackness, and in the hollow she saw a loaded ore car, a man beside it, both of them already sliding up out of sight before they had been more than half seen. "Hello, Tommy," Oliver said to the vanishing apparition. "Going down to the four hundred. You'll have a little wait."

The hole had already squeezed shut, wiping him out from the head downward. Smudged face, white eyes, yellow pocket of light, obscure body and legs and ore car, were gone. Plank was wet rock again. "There was a picture for you," said Conrad Prager.

"For Rembrandt, you mean."

Her heart was thudding from the momentary alarm of the snagging skip; she quivered from the unexpectedness of that encounter.

It was as if a shutter had opened and a wild face looked in for an awful moment and then been shut back into its blackness. It terrified her to think that the whole riddled mountain crawled with men like that one. Under her feet as she walked in sunshine, under her stool and umbrella as she sat sketching, under the piazza as she rocked the baby in his cradle, creatures like that one were swinging picks, drilling holes, shoveling, pushing ore cars, sinking in cages to ever deeper levels, groping along black tunnels with the energy of ants. It raised the gooseflesh on her arms; it was as if she had suddenly discovered that the conduits of her blood teemed with tiny, busy, visible vermin.

Another plank wall, another tunnel, empty this time, with only a pair of rails leading into it, incomplete radii cut off in darkness, disappearing long before whatever center it was they were drawn toward. The opening closed, they sank deeper, groaning. The rock that had once been yellowish now threw gleams of greenish black from its wet surfaces. "We're into the serpentine here," Oliver said to Prager.

Down, down. The air was more oppressive. With its lingering taint of creosote it reminded her of breathing tincture of benzoin from a croup kettle.

"Next level," Oliver said. "Anything wrong?"

"No. Oh no." But she was glad when the constricted shaft opened out into another tunnel. Mr. Kendall, watching the floor come up, yanked on the bell wire and the skip shuddered and rattled to a halt. The groaning died; there was a lonely sound of dripping water. When they had helped her out onto the uneven floor, Oliver scratched a lucifer match on his seat and lit her candle, Mr. Prager's, his own. In the enlarged bloom of light she could see for some distance down the timbered drift with its toy rails converging toward a vanishing point that was simultaneous with total blackness. Down this drift, with Kendall walking ahead and the others steering her by the elbows, they made their way. Inevitably she thought of Dante, Virgil, and Beatrice, and up on top Tregoning, Charon of this vertical Styx; but the thought of how silly it would sound to speak that thought made her blot it out. About used up, I should think, Oliver might say.

Their shadows climbed the walls and bent across timbers, spread, folded, disappeared, reappeared. Kendall and his shadow blotted the tunnel ahead. Her feet were already wet, she had difficulty walking on the ties, she slipped on wet wood and twisted her ankles among uneven stones.

How far? As if she had spoken aloud, Oliver said, "It's only a little way on. Listen, maybe we can hear them."

The three of them stopped, but Kendall's boots went on clattering. Then he too stopped, his candle turned back on them. "What is it?"

"Listening to the voices of the mine," Mr. Prager said. "Hold it a minute."

They stood. The candles grew almost steady, the tunnel enlarged around them. Stillness, *drip*, stillness, *drip drip*, then "Hear them?" Oliver said.

"No."

"Put your ear against the wall."

She pushed her hat askew and leaned her cheek against wet rock. "I don't . . . oh, yes! Yes, plainly!"

Tak, said the stone against her straining ear. *Tak . . . tak . . . tak . . . tak*. Then it stopped. She held her breath until the sound resumed. *Tak . . . tak . . . tak*.

"Understand their language?" Mr. Prager said.

"Is it a language? It's more like a pulse. It's like the stone heart of the mountain beating."

Mr. Kendall laughed, but Prager said, "Capital, capital. Put it in your sketch. Actually, you know, it's the Tommyknockers."

"The who?"

"Tommyknockers. Little people who go through the mine tapping at the timbering to make sure it's sound. Ask any Cornishman."

"You're teasing me. What is it really?"

Oliver leaned so that she felt his warm breath as he started her forward again. "Drillers' hammers. They're drilling blast holes."

A new sound was growing in the tunnel, a distant rumble. Through Mr. Kendall's scissoring legs she saw the rails light up as if fire were in them. A double, widening streak of red gleamed toward her and was blotted. The sound came on. Mr. Kendall turned, and Oliver and Prager pulled Susan to one side. "Car coming," Oliver said. "Stand against the wall."

The sound swelled, bounced from wall to wall, was projected down at her from the roof. She had a panicky feeling that the mere vibration of wheels on rails might shake the timbering down, and she understood instantly and completely why a race of men who lived their lives in mines would have to invent such helpful creatures as Tommy-knockers. A drop of water fell on her bare arm and she jerked, with a little bitten-off exclamation. "Plenty of room," Oliver said, misunderstanding.

Noise and light approached, the hollow mountain hummed, the light resolved itself into a candle on a hat, another on the front of the heaped square ore car. It approached, was there, rumbled past, and the leaning man pushing it turned his curious face and she recognized him: a Mexican boy she had seen numerous times, the brother of the crippled carpenter Rodriguez. Rumble, glow, glimpse, and gone, the dim luminousness moving along the roof timbers, the sound diminishing.

"So," Oliver said, and pulled at her arm. But she held back for a moment, laying her ear to the wall, half convinced that the sound she had heard there was phantasmal, that this lonely boy with his loaded car was all there was, that her vision of busy little men swarming through the dark was the product of her overheated imagination. She was oppressed and made strangely afraid by the sight of the straining boy, and by the fact that he wore a face she recognized, and she wasn't sure whether she wanted to hear the patient Morse of the drillers or whether she hoped to hear only the reassuring silence of stone.

Tak . . . the mountain said to her. *Tak . . . tak . . . tak . . . tak.* She let herself be led forward. Ahead, darkness opened to dim radiance; behind, dim radiance was swiftly overtaken by black. Shaken, dependent, nearly abject, she stumbled along thinking how for months Oliver had been surveying this honeycombed hell, how the black hole that so oppressed her was only one of dozens, a few hundred feet out of twenty-seven miles. And he knew it all, he had groped through all of it by candlelight, through parts of it scores of times. Down in this oppressive darkness and oppressive air he had stayed for fifteen, twenty, twenty-four hours at a stretch, while she sat in the cottage and felt how lonely she was. Even as she hopped and stumbled beside him, laughing a little at her own clumsiness, she felt gratitude for the big warm hand on her arm, and she knew an appalled pride in what he could do.

Then ahead the low roof lifted, the right hand wall opened into a roomlike vault, the sound of hammers came plainly through air instead of secretly through the rock. Across the opening, figures that had been bending to work on the face rose and turned; their candles stared. Behind them three fixed candles like the candles on an altar shone on a wall of living red.

While the men talked, stooping to follow something from low on one side to high on the other, looking over samples of rock that the captain picked out and handed them, Susan stood back out of the way. It seemed to her that the intent group were like priests at a ceremony. She did not try to understand what they were talking about, beyond her vague comprehension that the vein was not acting as it should, or going where it ought to, and that Mr. Kendall was ready to blame someone for something. Whether it was Oliver he blamed, she couldn't tell, and she was too fascinated by the pictures they made, the gleams and reflections that came off planes and facets of rock, the way shadows swallowed whole corners and pockets of the *labor*, to worry about it now.

How living the faces were, and how eloquent the postures, of the miners who stood or sat waiting for the bosses to get through. What things the vagrant inadequate light did to a brown cheek, a mustache, the whiteness of teeth, the shine of eyes looking out their corners at her. It was like nothing she had ever drawn, a world away from the cider presses and sheepfolds and quiet lanes and farmyard scenes and pensive maidens of her published drawings, yet this scene, lurid and dimly fearful, spoke to her. She felt it as a painting of saints in a grotto, or drinkers in a dark Dutch cellar. The curve of a shovel had the pewterish gleam of a Ten Eyck tankard, the very buttons on overalls had life.

She made an effort to see the Mexican crew as the strengthless dead flocking around visitors who had just brought word of the living world, but they did not really suggest shades. If they had been tallow-faced Cornishmen they would have served that fancy better. These dark-skinned ones could not grow pale even underground; they might be buried but they were fiercely alive. She stood memorizing them, hoping to draw them later.

"Well, why didn't you?" she heard Mr. Kendall say to the Mexican captain. "You should have come to Ward or me the minute you suspected it, instead of fooling around guessing. Now we won't know till we shoot these holes. So let's get ahead with it."

The cluster of miners stirred, one or two squatting ones stood up, a standing one reached for the hammer he had leaned against the wall. Though their eyes had kept wandering to Susan, about as common a sight down that mine as a unicorn would have been, they had obviously kept their ears tuned to the bosses. It was clear to Susan that Kendall made them uneasy. She believed that if Oliver were examining that face, and made a decision, and gave an order, they would have moved no less promptly, but with more relaxation in their muscles, and perhaps with words in their mouths, or jokes, or humorous complaints. For Mr. Kendall they said nothing, but they moved very promptly.

But now Conrad Prager was pulling something from the vast pocket of his shooting coat. "Maybe we should pour a little libation, for luck," he said.

He had a bottle in his hand. A laugh went around the miners, an alertness had come over them all. "Kendall?" Mr. Prager said, and offered the bottle.

"Not for me," Kendall said, and waved it away. Prager offered it to Oliver, who passed it to the captain. The captain took it, but before he drank he turned his dark, heavy-mustached face toward Susan and dropped his head in a grave, short bow. "*A su salud, señora,*" he said, and tipped the bottle. The next man, taking his cue, did the same, and the next. She was toasted by all of them, one after the other, seriously and without embarrassment, without even smiles. The only smiles came when the bottle had made its way back to Oliver, and he followed their example, toasting his wife. Then Prager, who bowed like a prince and put his mouth where all those mouths had been—How could he? How could Oliver?—yet it was more right than Mr. Kendall's refusing—and drained the bottle and corked it and set it on the floor.

He said something in Spanish. The men laughed. Briefly Oliver compared his watch with that of the captain. "All right," he said, "we should have the answer in the morning." He and Mr. Prager both offered her an arm. On the way back toward the hoist she paused once to lay her ear against the wall and hear the hopeless talk of hammers like the signaling of entombed men.

At the shaft Mr. Kendall yanked the signal wire twice. They

waited. "Well, Susan," said Mr. Prager, "what's your impression of life in the mines?"

"How can I say?" Susan said. "There are wonderful pictures, if one had the skill. I'm afraid they're beyond me. But I wouldn't have missed it, not for anything. Oh, those men with candlelight shining off their eyeballs, and that awful cavern of a place where they work, and that tapping through the rock as if men buried alive were trying to make others hear! I suppose I shouldn't find it so picturesque. It's awful, really—isn't it? They seem so like prisoners."

"Prisoners?" said Mr. Kendall rather sharply. "They hire out for wages, they get paid according to what they produce, they get their pay every Saturday." He laughed a short laugh. "And drink it up before Sunday."

He made her afraid that somehow, indulging her sensibility, she had put Oliver in the wrong. "I didn't mean they were enslaved," she said. "I only meant . . . working underground, in the dark . . ."

"Some of the Cousin Jacks in this mine have been underground for four generations," Kendall said. "Your husband is underground a good deal himself. We all are. Don't let your sympathies get so enlarged you tie him to the porch."

Offended, she kept still. So did Oliver and Mr. Prager, evidently unwilling to stir up Mr. Kendall when he was in a bad mood. The skip's faint groaning came down the shaft, it arrived, they stepped aboard, Mr. Kendall pulled the wire, the floor pushed against the soles of her feet. Offended or not, she told herself, she must thank him excessively for his indulgence in letting her go down. But she would work into her New Almaden sketch some of the terror of that black labyrinth, and she might even ask outright what sort of life it was, what sort of promise the New World gave, when a miner who emerged from a deep hole in Cornwall could do no better than dive down another in California, and when his children were carrying water to the mine at ten and pushing an ore car at fifteen.

The rock-walled chimney slid downward, she floated toward the surface with her head tilted back, impatient for the upper world. She felt the air grow cooler on her skin, the walls grew yellow-gray with daylight, they floated, lifted, were borne upward and rocked to a stop in the shaft house, looking out into squinting, brilliant afternoon. Tregoning's toothless smile extracted an answering smile from her; she had rarely been happier to see anyone.

She found that she was perspiring, the cool wind contracted her skin. And she had hardly put her feet on solid earth when the earth quivered, seemed to shake itself like a horse twitching off a fly. Again, and again, and again, and after a pause two more.

"The mountain is still talking to you," Prager said.

"Are they—have they set off the blasts down where we were?"

"Not till the end of this shift," Oliver said. "Those were probably in the Bush tunnel."

"And some prisoners in there are shoveling up money," said Mr. Kendall.

"You won't get much sketching done in this," Oliver said.

"If it doesn't clear I'll just take a walk."

The trail was half lost in fog, the overcast squatted on the mountain. Stranger, padding ahead, disappeared within fifteen yards. From somewhere, all around, above, below, came the tinkle of moving bells, and in a few minutes the *aguador* materialized below them—big sombrero, goatskin chaps, pinto horse. Leading his three mules, each with two kegs of water balanced on the pack saddle, he came picking uphill at an inhumane pace, his spurs digging rhythmically into the pinto's flanks. Broadly smiling, he saluted them: Susan had drawn him a few days before and made him famous. One, two, three, the hurrying mules passed, leaving the smell of dung diffused in the gray air.

There was no one at the watertank, the boxes hung crooked and empty on the meatbox tree. Across the gully Cornish Camp poked roofs and smoking chimneys into the fog, revealing a gable here, a corner there, like a quick suggestive sketch left deliberately incomplete. "You coming down?" Oliver said.

"I might as well."

Going down, they walked into a clear pocket under the fog. Main Street lay glumly exposed up the opposite slope—post office and company store, Mother Fall's, employment office, a raggle taggle of cottages set every which way, at every distance from the street. There was no one in sight, though smoke dove groundward from every stovepipe. In the gully eroded along the street side by last winter's rains, a dog backed up, dragging a bone that might have come from a mammoth, and growled at Stranger, who stood above him and watched. Not a breath stirred the dry grass, dry thistles, dry mustard stalks, scattered papers.

"She's a tough-looking place," Oliver said. "I like your pictures better than the real thing."

"Since I started to draw it I don't seem to mind it so much."

"Ready to follow Mary's advice and settle down here for life?"

She laughed. "Not quite." But then she added, "Certainly for a while, if your job was here."

"You'd starve for talk."

"Boykins is a pretty good substitute." She took his arm, climbing up the steep street in the fog, swinging the packet of drawing materials; and at the top she turned sideways and skipped beside him, watching him. "And I like having commissions," she said. "Altogether, it's not the dullest life you brought me to. I can stand it for quite a while yet."

He gave her an odd, dry look. "You may not have the chance."

"What do you mean?"

"What I said."

"Have you been talking to someone about another job?"

"No."

"What, then?"

"I don't own the mine," Oliver said. "I only work here."

They were going along the crest of the knoll, on Shakerag Street (Susan had put it in her sketch as a bit of local picturesqueness). The engineers' office stood alone in the midst of high weeds. When Oliver unlocked the door, stale indoor smells rushed out to join the taint of garbage and woodsmoke that filled the air outside. She inhaled unaired pipe smoke, dust, art gum, India ink, the neatsfoot-oil odor of boots, and stood flapping the door back and forth to freshen the place.

Oliver stood before the long drafting table and stared down at the map tacked there. Absently he filled his pipe, interrupted his hands to lean and follow with one finger a line on the map, straightened again, tamping the tobacco into the bowl with his thumb. It was as if he had become invisible the moment he entered the office. His mind had gone away and left her. In the same way, in the evening, he would lock the door behind him and turn his attention back to her, the baby, the household. She had some of that single-mindedness herself, and respected it, but it exasperated her to be totally forgotten, standing there idiotically waving up a breeze with the door. A hundred times she had tried to get him to talk about things that had happened at work, and got only grunts and monosyllables.

His match flame drew down, flared, drew down, flared, drew down, as he sucked the pipe alight, still with his eyes on the map. He flapped the match out and threw it in the wastebasket. That was when she saw the sign on the wall: No Smoking in This Office. By Order of the Manager.

"Oliver!"

He raised his eyes, noted what she was pointing at, nodded, and looked down at the map again. "Yeah, Kendall had that put up the other day."

"But why? You've always smoked in here."

"Yes."

"Is he afraid of fire?"

"No," Oliver said. "I doubt that he's very much afraid of fire."

"Well what *is* he afraid of? It seems the strangest . . ."

"Seeing how far I'll be pushed, I guess," Oliver said.

"You mean . . . ? Oliver, is he *against* you, is that what you mean?"

Now he finally faced her, shrugging, defensive, getting mulish. "It would look that way."

"What have you done? I thought everything was going so well."

"Ahhhh."

"Tell me."

"What have I done, you say."

"Yes. Why should he turn against you?"

"What have I done," he said, tapping his teeth with the pipestem, elaborately trying to remember. "Well, I made him a more accurate survey than the mine's ever had, I saved him from making a big mistake with that hoist machinery, and redesigned it so it works, I improved the pump station in Bush tunnel."

"Please!" she said. "How can he be your enemy just all of a sudden? He's been perfectly pleasant, as pleasant as he has the capacity for being. He sent his carriage around only the other day."

"I expect that was Mrs. Kendall."

"She would hardly do it if he didn't want her to."

"Look," Oliver said, "you've got enough to do without worrying about this. I'll work it out. You run along and draw some pictures and get famous."

"But I must worry about it! Good heavens, it's your job, it's our life!"

"It isn't that important. If you're afraid he'll fire me, forget it. He can't fire me as long as Smith approves of my work. Maybe he thinks if he makes life unpleasant enough I'll quit."

"I just don't understand," Susan said. "I thought you were doing just splendidly, and you are, too. But now you say he'd like to fire you if he dared."

"I was never his choice," Oliver said. "I was more or less forced on him by Smith and Conrad. We chose to live up on the hill rather than down at the Hacienda. They chose to think we thought ourselves too good for them. I know Ewing, at the store, has always felt that way, and he's Kendall's chief spy and toady. Maybe that's why I got stuck with the cost of renovating the cottage. You begin to see?"

"It's been from the beginning, then," Susan said. "Oh, it's so small!"

"Yes, I guess it is. Then I rejected his Austrian, your cultivated friend. I think Mrs. Kendall had sort of looked forward to having a tame baron around, just the way she gets some kind of satisfaction out of having an artist, even if the artist is stand-offish. And also I questioned Kendall's judgment on that hoist, and proved he was wrong."

"But he raised your salary."

"Smith told him to."

"Ah," she said, "I might have known. What a mean, petty little tyrant that man is!"

"I could hardly agree with you more completely."

"Do you think it was a mistake for me to go down in the mine last week? I knew he didn't want me to."

"I don't think he much liked your remark about the men being prisoners."

"But they *are* prisoners!"

"You bet they are," Oliver said. "I suppose that's one reason he doesn't want any sympathetic women around, especially if they write things for magazines."

"But you feel the same way."

"Yes, sure, and he knows it. He thinks I'm too chummy with the men. They talk to me and I listen. What he'd like is that whenever I hear anybody grousing or muttering I'd run to him and blab. Then he could fire the troublemakers off the mountain. He knows there's a lot of grumbling."

"You never told me. Is there? A lot?"

"All the time."

"And they talk to you but not to the others."

"That's about it. Not to the Hacienda crowd."

"Then the men didn't really blame you when you had to stop their work to run your survey."

"Not especially, no."

"I'm glad. I don't want them blaming you."

"They know who to blame. They know who the spies are, too. The whole place is wormy with fear and hate. Kendall's way of handling that is to fire anybody who opens his mouth or gets the slightest out of line. He makes examples of a few to scare the rest. Last week he fired two Mexican construction workers for walking a hundred feet off the job to hang their lunch pails in the shade. Day before yesterday he fired Tregoning, the hoist man at the Kendall shaft."

"Tregoning? That nice toothless fellow? I thought he was an absolute fixture."

"So did everybody else. Fourteen years he's worked here. Maybe he thought he was a fixture too, but nobody's a fixture with Kendall. If he's going to make an example of somebody, he doesn't care if there isn't a competent replacement in camp. There isn't, in fact. Tregoning was a good one. But he came home from San Jose on the stage the other day with some lengths of stovepipe he'd bought, and Ewing spotted him. You know the rule about buying only at the company store. Kendall gave him forty-eight hours to get off the mountain. That means by this afternoon."

"Oh," she said, "that's despicable!"

"You're damned right it's despicable."

The warning whistle blew, so harsh and peremptory it seemed some extension of Kendall himself, not simply of the company's power. Before it had stopped, doors were opening on Shakerag Street; within two minutes there were men in the street with lunch pails. Through the open door she could hear their glottal talk like a gabbling of geese. She said, "Couldn't you have done something?"

"I went to him and protested," Oliver said. "He told me my job was to keep the Santa Isabel tunnel going in, he'd take care of the men. I think he lit on poor old Tregoning so hard because he knows I like him."

"Oliver, you must expose that man to Mr. Prager and Mr. Smith!"

"Yes?" said Oliver, with a sidelong glance. "They all belong to the same clubs."

"But surely they wouldn't allow this sort of thing."

"Kendall's the manager," Oliver said. "From the point of the view of the stockholders, he's a good one. He's got the mine paying good dividends. They're not going to jeopardize their profits just because he fires a Cornish hoist man."

"But you said he'd like to fire you, too, and that *could* hurt the company. Look what you saved them on that machinery."

"He won't fire me," Oliver said. "He'll just try to make me quit. The day after I went and talked to him about Tregoning he had Hernandez hang that sign in here. He doesn't mean 'No Smoking.' He means, 'You'd better watch your step, young fellow.'"

"But you stand right in front of it and smoke!"

"Yep."

"What if he sees you?"

"I expect he will."

"But what if he calls you down?"

"He'll only do it once."

"Oliver," she said earnestly, "why do we even *try* to stay?"

"Because I'm still learning something," he said. "I'm getting a lot of good experience, and an engineer's capital is his experience. Also I haven't got any other job lined up. Also you like it here, and you've still got some drawings to do."

"I wouldn't have liked it if I'd known about all this. I can't, ever again."

"Oh, it's nothing new," he said. "There's just this sort of crisis right now."

"I hate to think of you having to submit to that man."

"Submit?" he said mildly. "Is that what I'm doing?"

The seven o'clock whistle cut loose, screaming across the gulch. Just on its dying wail Mr. Hernandez came in. Susan saw that the street outside had a woman or two in it, but not a single man. Not a straggler was hurrying to tunnel or shaft house or tramway. This morning everybody was on time. She supposed the spies would report that the object lesson taught through Tregoning and the two Mexicans had been taken to heart. When she first arrived, she had thought the place as orderly as a military post. Now she understood how it was done.

"*Buenos dias,*" she said in response to Hernandez's soft greeting. They had a pact to speak only Spanish to each other, with the result that their conversation never got beyond hello and good-bye.

Oliver laid a hand on her back. "You'd better get. No loitering in this office, eh, Chepe?"

Hernandez made a small sound with his tongue against his teeth. "Did you hear that he promised to fire anybody who bought any of Tregoning's furniture?"

For a moment Oliver said nothing, he only looked steadily at Hernandez. "What's Tregoning going to do?"

"What could he do?" Hernandez said. "He's giving it away."

For a musing time Oliver stood looking out into Shakerag Street through the dirty window. "How long have you been here, Chepe?" he said finally.

"Six years."

"Never had any run-ins with the Hacienda crowd?"

"No," said Hernandez, faintly smiling.

"Good," Oliver said. "Eight more years of faithful service and you can look forward to what Tregoning got."

"I am careful," Hernandez said. "I have a mother and two sisters."

Standing outside of this casual revelation of how deep and violent were the divisions in the camp, Susan felt as a woman running an orderly quiet household might feel if she looked out the window and saw men fighting in the street. She had been wrapped in cottonwool. Every glance between these two was loaded with meanings she had been protected from. She saw them only when they had put the mine and the manager behind them. She knew her husband not as an engineer but as a companion, lover, audience, household fixer. Her drawings of Hernandez's two sisters for Mr. Howells and the *Atlantic* had shown them languid, slim, domestic, offering figs and native wine to a visitor, herself. She had dwelt not on the harsh life at whose insecure edge they lived, but on their grace, their dark and speaking eyes, the elegance of their dancing, the attractiveness of *rebozo* or *mantilla* over their hair, the feminine gentleness of their gestures and postures. In her indignation she almost wished those blocks back, so that she could send in their place something closer to the truth of mining camp lives. Yet how would she get close to those lives to draw them? She had lived in New Almaden nearly a year and had seen only its picturesque surface.

"You run along, Susan," Oliver said. "No use to get upset. This is what you might call run of the mine."

"All right." But she laid a hand on his arm. Her eyes went to Hernandez, she smiled. "*¿Con permiso?*" she said. He lifted his eyebrows in admiration of her linguistic gifts and turned away, making himself deaf. To Oliver at the door she said, "Don't consider Boy or me for one second. Don't compromise your principles."

"Sure?"

"Absolutely."

"All right, we'll see. Maybe by now he's demonstrated his authority."

She did not linger in Cornish Camp, and she did not try to sketch, though the fog was already beginning to burn away. She went straight home past the watertank where teamsters and boys had gathered, and where the *aguador*, already down from his first trip upmountain, was refilling his kegs. It always bothered her to walk through the stares, even when she had Stranger along and had no reason to feel unsafe. Now, having had a glimpse of how rotten a string their lives were tied together with, she walked through them smiling a bright smile of fellowship and sympathy, a smile so rigid that her face hurt when she was finally past.

Tell a story like this to any twentieth-century American and he will demand to know how authority got away with that sort of arrogance. Why didn't the men strike? Try that kind of business nowadays and the UMW would tie the place up as tight as a wet knot. I remember once when they tied up the Zodiac, when my father was superintendent, because of the mine's policy of carrying the men's lunch boxes up and down, to prevent the stealing of highgrade. "No spies in the dryhouse," that sort of slogan. Fleabites, by comparison, irritations rather than injustices. Which demonstrates our need of a sense of history: we need it to know what real injustice looked like. When Kendall was running the New Almaden the United Mine Workers were a half century away, the Western Federation of Miners a generation off, the IWW wouldn't be founded until 1905.

The West of my grandparents, I have to keep reminding others and myself, is the early West, the last home of the freeborn American. It is all owned in Boston and Philadelphia and New York and London. The freeborn American who works for one of those corporations is lucky if he does not have a family, for then he has an added option: he can afford to quit if he feels like it. If you are a Tregoning, you are lucky to be fired without having your head broken as well. Beyond question, once fired, you will be blacklisted. Tregoning will never operate a hoist again, not in California. He will end up on some valley ranch doing unfamiliar labor for a few dollars a month and a shack to live in.

For buying some stovepipe outside the company store! somebody says.

Exactly. A bad mistake. He knew the rules.

When Oliver came in the gate before noon, she knew by his face what he was going to tell her. He walked with a hard, pounding haste, and he started talking, or stammering, before he was to the bottom of the steps. "Well," he said, "are you . . . I guess we . . . are you ready to move?"

"You resigned."

"I quit. Resigning would have been too polite. It was all I could do to keep from knocking him down."

"Oh, Oliver, I'm glad!" she said. She was sure she was. Her spirits surged up as if to an insult or a challenge. She would have walked off the mountain with her baby in her arms and no more possessions than the clothes on her back—but they would have been impeccable—rather than yield one inch or even acknowledge the existence of Lawrence Kendall. "I couldn't have respected you if you hadn't," she said shakily, and took hold of his arm above the elbow. It was as hard as an oak branch. He kept looking around him in an odd, furious way as if he were looking for a place to spit. "What happened?"

"Ha!" he said. "What happened! He came down and ordered me to take a construction crew up by Day tunnel and tear down Tregoning's house."

"What?"

"Can you believe it? That's exactly what he wanted. There's a crew doing it right now, poor Chepe's bossing it."

"But tear down his house? Why? What earthly good . . . He was already fired."

"Oh, sure!" he said. "Sure, sure. He was fired, he wasn't allowed to sell anything. That isn't enough, the lesson isn't rubbed in yet. Tregoning owned his own house, the manager before Kendall let him build it on company land for a dollar a year rent. That was to encourage a skilled man to stay. So now Kendall's tearing it down and scorching the earth. There are already thirty Chinamen scavenging boards and stuff, and a crowd of Cornish women just standing on the hill watching. Not a word out of them, they're like people watching a hanging. It's a wonder he *didn't* hang the whole family, or drive them off the mountain with dogs. They're off by themselves watching too. None of their neighbors dares even speak to them."

"I hope thee spoke to them. Did thee?"

"Yes," he said, and gave her a crooked, apologetic, impatient look that tightened her insides with pity and sympathy for him. She had never seen him upset. He was the laconic one who was always in command of himself. This outrage unmanned him, he shook like a dog. She could have taken his head against her breast and rocked him and told him never mind, never mind, it's not your fault, you did all you could, it's the way this brutal place is. "I hope you don't mind," Oliver said. "I gave them all the money I had, twenty dollars or so."

"Oh, Oliver, of *course* thee should have! It was generous." She hung onto his arm, huddling against his rigid body that moved in twitches and jerks. His eyes were stretched wide like those of a man trying to see in the dark, he whistled through his teeth.

"I wish I knew," he said. "Hell, I *do* know. He wouldn't go that far just to enforce a company rule or scare grumblers into line. Unless he was making an absolutely calculated move against me, he wouldn't have the gall to come to me and tell me to do his dirty work. I hate it that poor Tregoning gets it this bad just because of me."

"I almost wish thee *had* knocked him down."

"Ahhh!" He jerked and twitched; she hung on.

"At least," she said, "now thee'll explain everything to Mr. Smith and Mr. Prager."

But he made a face of disgust and distaste. "Let Kendall do the explaining."

"But you know what he'll say!"

"Sure. Insubordination, stirring up unrest among the men. I flew into a rage and quit. Too bad a promising young fellow should have dangerous opinions and a bad temper. *I* don't care what he says."

"You'd let him lie about you?"

"I'd rather let him lie about me than have to deal with him or even think about him another five minutes. If they don't know me well enough to know he's lying, that's too bad." With an eye as cold as Kendall's own he squinted along the veranda roof. "I wonder if he'll tear this house down too? Maybe I should beat him to it. I could take this porch off in an afternoon. It's ours, we paid for it."

Though she knew it was only a sour joke, it turned her cold, for it brought up the problem of their own moving. How long? Forty-eight hours, like Tregoning? But she did not dare ask until Oliver was calmer. She said, "Let him have his petty triumph. Thee can leave knowing thee has done everything thee was asked to do, and done it well, and more besides."

Oh, that was Grandmother. What though the world be lost? All is not lost. Honor is not lost.

Miss Prouse came to the door with the baby draped across a napkin on her shoulder, saw them in their intimate conversation, and discreetly withdrew. But the sight of her brought home to Susan such a tangle of responsibilities and complications that she could not keep from saying, "What about Marian? Certainly we can't afford to keep her now."

Gloomily he looked at her, saying nothing.

"And Lizzie too. Where will Lizzie go?"

"*And* Stranger," Oliver said. "Stranger's the luckiest, he can go back to Mother Fall's."

"Oh, Oliver, I'm sorry, I'm sorry!" She flew against him, in tears. She felt his lips on the top of her head.

"I'm the one who ought to be sorry," he said. "I did it. It's not the way we planned it."

She would not let him blame himself, she shook her head with her face against his chest. "Thee couldn't have done anything else."

"I could have done what Chepe's doing."

Now she reared back to look into his face. "Not you! You're too fine!" Immediately she added, in justice to poor trapped Hernandez, "And we're not that poor."

His eyes, looking down into hers, wavered almost as if in embarrassment or shame, and he broke the look by hugging her against himself again. "You're all right, Susan," he said. "You're pure gold."

Again she leaned back to look into his face. "How long will we have? Will he try to evict us?"

"He knows better. No, we'll take exactly as much time as we need. You still have a picture or two to do, and it will be at least two weeks before I can finish the map."

"The map! You aren't going to finish that!"

"Oh yes I am."

"But *why?* After all he's . . ."

"For my own satisfaction," Oliver said. She understood at once that on that point he was immovable. She could argue, he would not argue back. But he would complete the map which he owed no one, which he had done on his own time, for experience, and on the day they left New Almaden he would drop it on Kendall's desk—no, not that far, he would mail it to Mr. Smith or Mr. Prager, more likely. She could not understand that stubbornness in him which led him to punish himself. But whatever he was, he was not small, and that she took pride in.

"Where will we go?" she asked. "San Francisco?"

"Conrad and Mary, you mean? I don't think we want to embarrass them with this."

"I didn't mean to live with them."

"Even in a place of our own, they'd feel obligated. I don't want them obligated. Anyway, we couldn't afford a place of our own in San Francisco."

"Then where?"

"I'll have to go there," he said. "It's the only place I'd have a chance to find another job. For you and the baby, I was wondering if Mrs. Elliott could find you a nice room in Santa Cruz, somewhere cheap and quiet and on the shore."

"You mean—*separate?*"

"I could come down on weekends sometimes."

"Oliver," she said, "we mustn't! You forget the six hundred dollars I made from *The Scarlet Letter,* and what I'll get from Mr. Howells and from Thomas."

"Which I won't let you spend."

"But if it will keep us all together!"

"Even so."

That backed her straight out of his arm to a distance of two paces, a better arguing distance. "You'd rather have us live away from you, in some furnished room, than spend my perfectly good money for a house where we could be a family?"

That mulish, proud face. It looked as if it would take a crowbar to open his mouth. Finally it did open. "I'm afraid so," he said. "It would only be until I locate something."

She stared wildly into his clouded eyes, her voice came out of her high and stammering. "Maybe thee can keep me from spending what thee calls my money on thee," she said, "but thee can't keep me from spending it on the baby!"

He shook his head, hangdog, suffering, and immovable. "No," he admitted. "But you'd shame me if you did."

They glared like enemies. She bit her lips to stop their trembling, she felt the color leave her face, she saw him begin to melt and blur through her tears. It took a great effort, it was a wrench like renunciation of something precious, to submit to his pride. "All right," she said, and again, on an in-caught breath, "All right. If that's the way thee must have it."

In her agitation she walked up and down the veranda, head down, sucking her knuckle. One turn, two, three, while he stood watching, saying nothing; and each time, at the end of the veranda, her head lifted and her eyes swept down across the view, and each time she turned she passed the hammock. It was a bitter irony to her that now she could hardly bear to think of leaving this place where only a year ago she had sat with her hand clenched in Oliver's, fighting desolate tears, sick for home and Augusta, and torn by feelings which distance made as irrecoverable as they were incurable. Out of the corner of her eye as she passed the door she saw the black front of the Franklin stove which had been their hearthstone.

O fortunate, o happy day
When a new household finds its place
Among the myriad homes of earth

Gone, and as painful now as the thought of a stillborn child. Sentimental? Of course. Riddled with the Anglo-American mawkishness about home, quicksandy with assumptions about monogamy and Woman's Highest Role, buttery with echoes of the household poets. All that. But I find that I don't mind her emotions and her sentiments. Home is a notion that only the nations of the homeless fully appreciate and only the uprooted comprehend. What else would one plant in a wilderness or on a frontier? What loss would hurt more? So I don't snicker backward ninety years at poor Grandmother pacing her porch and biting her knuckle and hating the loss of what she had never quite got over thinking her exile. I find her moving. She is Massaccio's Eve, more desolate than Adam because he can invent the bow and arrow and the spear, but she can only try to reassemble outside Eden an imperfect copy of what she has lost. And not guiltless, either. She buries that acknowledgment under disgust and fury at Kendall and his toadies, but she makes it, then or later: she has been guilty of pride, she has held herself apart, and so has contributed to the fall.

So there she is with her two hands clenched in the front of Oliver's shirt, shaking him in her passion and her earnestness. "I'll do what thee wants, or whatever we must, but *please*, Oliver, not two weeks more here! The air is poisoned, it's all spoiled, I couldn't bear it. How long will the map take thee? A week? Two weeks? Why can't thee do it in Santa Cruz? I can finish my drawings there, there are only three more blocks, and I've done the sketches. Why not at Santa Cruz? We could work in the mornings and spend the afternoons on the shore. Thee has worked so hard, why must thee run right out and find more work? Couldn't thee go to see Mrs. Elliott tomorrow and find a place?"

He looked down at her almost absently. He blew cold into her bangs and bent his head and kissed the forehead his breath had exposed. "I could," he said. "But that wouldn't support the family."

"We have enough for a while."

"Sure. And when it's gone, then what?"

"Then there's my drawing money."

"No."

"Yes."

"Listen," he said, "I'm supposed to be the reckless one in this family."

"No, *thee* listen. Maybe Mrs. Elliott can find a place for Lizzie. She's a jewel, there's nothing so good on this coast. We won't need her if we're boarding. But we can keep Marian, so we can do things together again, and so I can work. And since she'll be freeing my hands, I'll pay her."

"No."

"Yes."

"No."

"Oh, what does it matter?" Susan cried. "Thee can pay her as long as thee has anything, and then I will. But let's go just as soon as we can."

Again he blew into her bangs and kissed where his breath was cold. "All right. For two weeks. Then I'll have to go to the City." He looked down at Stranger, sprawled on the boards with his chin on his big feet. "Eh, lad," he said, like a sad Cousin Jack. "It's back to they boardin' 'ouses for both of us. And we'll never know 'ow that 'oist works."

III

SANTA CRUZ

1

Shelly Rasmussen's shabby little soap opera is now playing at my house. I don't like being a garbage can for her kind of troubles, but considering what I owe to Ed and Ada I couldn't do anything but make the offer when the crisis blew up yesterday.

There have been better secretaries than Shelly, also worse. She isn't stupid, and she has put the files in order faster than I thought she could, and learned them in the process. Occasionally she can anticipate what I'll need, sometimes she comes up with something I've overlooked or forgotten. It doesn't matter that she's not much of a typist, because I decided very quickly not to let her transcribe my tapes—that would inhibit my mouth. If the tapes are ever transcribed I'll send them down to some steno pool in Berkeley or the City. But Shelly is good at typing off illegible letters; she is just nearsighted enough to be able to read handwriting that baffles me. Altogether, she has saved me some time and a lot of the bone-ache I used to get trying to work in the files from my chair.

A considerable improvement on Miss Morrow. But she has a ribald streak that I don't much like. She is a card-carrying member of this liberated generation, and though I am hardly one to go around clucking my tongue and asking Is nothing sacred, I find myself wondering about the state of mind that holds nothing worth the respect of un-humorous suspended judgment. Me, for instance. Once or twice I have caught her studying me as if I were somehow amusing, and that shocks me. At the very least I claim to be pitiful, grotesque, or appalling.

The interest she takes in the job we are doing is about as disconcerting as her interest in me. She is amused by the Victorian reticences and sentiments we uncover in Grandmother. That letter recording Grandmother's discovery of the "cundrum" had her in stitches—the discrepancy between decorum and vile necessity was irresistible. Until she began to guffaw, I had thought that letter a rather touching footnote to the Genteel Female's biological vulnerability, and I found it a little unseemly—I wasn't shocked, I simply found it unseemly—that a girl of twenty or so should exploit that kind of joke—about his grandmother! —to her fifty-eight-year-old employer, and a man of stone at that.

Many things that I think human and touching in Grandmother's life and character, she thinks comic. Many things that, even as a biographer, I am inclined to treat as private and essentially none of my business, she examines with that modern "frankness" which makes me nervous.

Ada has a version of Shelly's experiences in Berkeley which seems to me unduly protective of her daughter. It may be, as she has told me, that Larry Rasmussen when Shelly met him was a nice clean boy from upstate New York who came out to Berkeley to get a degree in anthropology, and fell in with the wrong companions, and learned to live on hash and guitar music and vegetables marketed by the Street People's Co-op, and left school without a degree and devoted himself, like an old-time I.W.W., to creating the new society within the shell of the old. I suggested the I.W.W. parallel to Ada, who being a miner's daughter knew about the Wobblies. She fails to see the connection. She implies, though she is not as free in such discussions as her daughter, that Rasmussen made out with every amenable chick he met in the pads and communes where they lived, and that he tried to make Shelly live as loosely as he did. To hear Ada tell it, he wanted to pimp her off for money, or utilize her as bait in wife trading, or something of the sort. Even when I taught at Berkeley there was a girl who put herself through graduate school by selling two illegitimate babies to adoption agencies. Nothing that happens at Berkeley could possibly surprise me, and so I don't necessarily doubt Ada's version of Shelly's bust-up with her husband.

Yet I don't necessarily believe it, either. In all this truth-and-freedom-seeking I doubt that Shelly was very far behind her mate. It wouldn't surprise me to hear that while he was making out with somebody, she was around the corner not doing too badly herself. She has, on considered acquaintance, a bold eye and an uninhibited tongue and a body that flops and lounges. If she didn't wear pants most of the time at work, even great stone Homer might nod and kink his neck. I cannot see her as an innocent victim of a nasty and dissolute hippie. When I was young there was a joke about the difference between dignified acquiescence and enthusiastic cooperation. I think I know where Shelly would belong. I feel sorry for Ada and Ed, who are small-town middle-class people, and not equipped to absorb these changes. Maybe Shelly rebelled against the life her husband was leading her into, maybe on the other hand, she simply got tired of supporting him.

Anyway, yesterday afternoon about four I was over by the window looking through a biography of Thomas Hudson by his daughter, checking out the references to Grandmother. Shelly was pulling out of the files all the Santa Cruz papers I was going to need for today: the letters, the illustrated article called "A Seaport on the Pacific," some maps, some local histories. The sprinkler was going down on the lawn where Ed had set it when he came back from his tire shop—one of those golf-course sprinklers with a kicker bar and a pulse like the panting of a hard-run dog, a comfortable afternoon sound. Coolness drifted in the window, and a fragrance of wet grass. Every three or four minutes the jet of water, having marched clear to the edge of the pines, would start marching back. I heard it getting closer with each *pst pst pst* of the sprinkler until a volley of drops stormed the wistaria. Then away again, *pst pst pst*.

Downstairs the door opened and closed. Ada, earlier than usual. But instead of going to the kitchen she came up the stairs. I knew she was in a hurry not only by the sound of her feet but by the fact that she didn't take the lift, which saves her legs but is pretty slow. Before she reached the top I turned my chair toward the door. At the file, Shelly turned too. We were both looking toward the door when Ada arrived there and stood, one hand spread on her bosom, getting her breath.

"He's here," she said.

For a second Shelly looked at her almost musingly, through her hair; then she put up a hand and lifted the hair over her shoulder. "Where?"

"Down at the house. Talkin' to your dad."

"Does he know I'm here?"

"He pretended he did. We swore you wasn't."

"But he didn't go away."

"Not him. He says, 'Where is she, then? I've checked out Berkeley and the City, nobody's seen her.'" Ada kept her hand spread on her chest and breathed carefully with her mouth open. She is overweight, and smokes a lot of cigarettes, and she hasn't got a lot of wind. She looked upset, angry, accusing, and her hair was half down with hurrying. "So then Dad says, 'Wherever she is, it's no business of yours unless she wants it to be. She's had about all of you she needs.'"

"Yeah," Shelly said, standing by the file. The study was quiet, like a classroom after a hard question. Outside, the sprinkler walked toward the house, *pst pst pst*, and drops hit the wistaria with a gravelly spatter. Ada's eyes jumped to the window. She touched her crooked knuckles to her lips and took them away again like someone tenderly curious about a cold sore. The sprinkler walked away.

"What'd Larry say then?" Shelly said.

"Oh, you know what he'd say! He's slick as a new cowpie. It's all a misunderstanding. He can explain. You didn't understand something. You didn't wait to talk to him before you took off. 'I know you never approved of me,' he says, 'but I want to tell you, I *love* that girl. I want to help her.' Help you, he says! Help you spend your paycheck! With that band around his head and them moccasins and some kind of purple pants. I wanted to stick a feather in his hair and make a real Indian of him. Honest to John, how you ever . . ."

"Mom, not again," Shelly said. "How was he? Was he high? Did he act drunk or crazy or anything? Wild? You know—broken connections?"

"How would I know? No, I don't suppose. He was just this slick smooth buttery same old thing like a salesman, only with all that hair and those clothes. He scares me, Shelly. He's sick. He ought to be in an asylum."

"You don't understand him," Shelly said. "He's got a thing about gentleness. He wasn't wild though? He talked straight enough?"

"I don't suppose what you'd call wild, no," Ada said.

"Did he say anything else? What was it he could explain, did he say?"

Ada shook her head.

"He didn't say anything about the night I left."

"He knows better than to try explainin' to Dad and me, I guess."

With her hip Shelly shoved the file drawer shut. Her hoarse voice had been toned down, almost hushed, while she questioned Ada. Now she said in a full bass-baritone, "Oh, Christ, I guess I might as well go down and see him and be done with it."

Ada moved her bulk dramatically across the doorway. "Shelly, don't you do it! That man's dangerous."

"Yes, Ma," Shelly said with resignation, and to me, flashing a little grin, "Mom thinks he's dangerous because he threatened to cut my throat once."

"I thought he had a thing about gentleness."

"He does. When he lets the bennies alone he's really nice. He *thinks*, you know? He isn't taken in by all the shit."

"*Look* what he's done to you!" Ada said, furious. "I wash my hands of it."

Shelly regarded her mother, started to say something, swallowed it, shrugged, said to me, "I never took the threat seriously. He was on a black crazy trip. I don't think he'd slept for three nights. He never even remembered it when he came back."

I sat thinking how little I needed any of this. I said, "I can call the police if you'd like."

Shelly was truly surprised. "What for? All he's done is come asking where I am."

"I was assuming you'd left him for some reason. It wasn't threats, then."

"I told you, I never took that seriously."

"You better," Ada said. "If you listen to me, you sure better."

"Oh, I don't know!" Shelly said violently. "Maybe I shouldn't have left him. Maybe it was just my middle-class indoctrination blowing back in my face. I just . . . Yakh. I guess I wish he'd just go away. Maybe he'll go quicker if I see him than if I don't."

"Do you think that?"

"I don't know. I guess not." To her mother she said, "Did he see you come up here?"

"He saw me go out. I went right past him, he'd have been blind if he didn't. I told him I had to go look after Mr. Ward, and I hoped he'd just swallow that you'd left him, and not make any trouble."

"He's still down there then."

"Unless Dad's run him off."

"Dad shouldn't mess with him. He might try to get even."

"That's what I said, he's dangerous."

"Oh, not by attacking anybody. He just has these really maniacal notions of what's funny. He plays they're jokes, but they draw blood. And he doesn't respect property at all, he thinks the earth ought not to be owned. He's bound to hang around if he thinks I'm here. He'll pop up from behind bushes, he'll leave these cannibal tracks in the sand for us to see, he'll get us all looking over our shoulders. I won't dare walk the Goddamned path."

I reached into the saddlebag and got out the aspirin bottle and shook two pills into my hand and washed them down with the dregs of a bottle of Coke on the window sill. "I agree with Ada," I said. "I don't think you should see him."

"But he really *isn't* the way I just said," Shelly said, and scowled at me, thinking. "I mean, he's really O.K., he's got a good head, he has these theories of a better system and he isn't afraid to live by them. And I guess he's fond of me. If he wasn't he wouldn't have come hunting me."

"But you're scared he'll hang around and leave cannibal tracks," I said. "If he does, if he practices any philosophical trespass around here, I *will* call the cops. I haven't got time to spend on cannibal tracks, and I doubt you have."

"Don't you even get mixed up in it the teeniest bit," Ada said. "We'll just have to find a way of cleanin' up our own mess."

"I was just going to say maybe she should stay up here till he goes."

"It'll bother you."

"Why should it? There are all those extra rooms, she can take her pick. If she really wants to stay out of his way."

I made that offer strictly for Ada's sake, not Shelly's. I suppose we *will* be peeking from behind the shutters every time a jaybird drops an acorn. I'll be reaching for Grandfather's horse pistol every time the house creaks. The thought of that speed freak prowling around in my woods and spying on us doesn't thrill me. Neither am I happy to have a visitor in one of my many guest rooms. I like it better when I am alone, or with nobody in the house except Ada. So I hoped I would be thanked and my offer rejected.

But all Shelly said was, "Wow. I almost hope he does stick around.

Wouldn't it bug him to find out I'm shacked up in the big house with the boss."

"Watch your mouth!" Ada said, furious.

"All right, Mom. J-o-k-e, joke."

"About as funny as one of his."

As I think it over, remembering the little incident last evening, I wonder if it *isn't* like one of his. A cannibal track for me to find and stare at. This is the ribald streak I referred to.

And what in hell could have been in her mind last night? Ada was getting me ready for bed, she had me undressed and out of the chair, standing on my one unsteady peg with my underwear around my foot and my arms around her neck, when I heard the sloppy slap of Shelly's loafers in the study, and Shelly's voice said, "Need any help, Mom?"

Help?

Ada clutched me to her bosom and turned her furious back on the door. Her blast of outrage went past my ear. "Don't you come in here!"

Once she turned, I was turned too: I stared right over Ada's shoulder, through the bathroom door and into the study, where Shelly leaned against the doorjamb in her turtle-necked sweater with the sleeves pushed up. I got a very good look at her, as she did at us. I observed that she was *ohne Büstenhalter*, and pretty opulent. I also could not help seeing very clearly what she saw—her mother in her white nurse's nylon clutching the naked freak to her breast.

"Well, I'm *sorry*," Shelly said. She looked me in the eye, she almost winked, there was a secret little smirk on her face. She pushed her shoulder away from the jamb and turned and slip-slopped across the bare study floor.

Ada said not a word, aside from her usual encouraging grunts, while she bathed me and got me to bed. When she got out the bottle for our nightcap I could see her contemplate the notion of asking me if we shouldn't ask Shelly in, and reject it. Shelly had borrowed my transistor radio right after supper, and we could hear it going, rock with a beat like a flat tire, off in the east wing where she had taken up residence. We sipped our drink and spoke of other things and ignored everything that had happened.

Finally Ada heaved to her feet and picked up the glasses and looked me over to see that I had everything I needed. She breathed through her nose and compressed her lips, wheezing. "Well, grin and bear it, I guess," she said.

"I guess."

"Get you a good sleep now."

"Thanks. You too. Don't let this business bother you. He's probably gone."

"He don't bother me as much as some other things. Well, good night now."

"Good night."

She went out, heavy and discouraged. I heard the lift's metabolism going, then it stopped. The front door opened and closed, was rattled hard in a testing of the lock. The thumping of the amplified guitars went on, deep in the house. Maybe, I thought, she keeps it on for reassurance, because she really may be scared. Maybe she came in at bath time because being alone in her empty wing spooked her.

The radio went on for a long time; it kept me awake until after midnight. For the last hour, after I had got past being annoyed at her characteristic lack of consideration, I concentrated on forgetting all about her and her speed freak and the new world he wants to create and she seems to doubt. I am not going to get sucked into this, I'll call the cops in a minute if I have to. And this is all, absolutely all, I am going to think about it. I am going back to Grandmother's nineteenth century, where the problems and the people are less messy.

One thing I did decide to do, and I did it the first thing this morning, was to go through the Idaho file and pull out a few of the letters. She hasn't got that far yet, but she'll be there soon. There is no use exposing Grandmother to the kind of scrutiny Shelly would give her.

2

Among the papers that Shelly laid out for me the other afternoon is the February 1879 issue of *Century* containing Grandmother's article on Santa Cruz, with ten woodcut illustrations by the author. It is useful to have her pictures. They make it easier to visualize that sleepy town before it was made over by a midway, and then by pious retired couples, and then by a branch of the University of California. Without the pictures I could never have imagined it as it was when they came down to it from New Almaden. Let me try out one particular morning.

They sat in a cove in the yellow cliffs, a place open to sun and sheltered from wind, their backs against a drift log. The sand was dry and pale, peppered with the charcoal of beach fires and webbed with a vine bearing perfumed purple flowers. Below where they sat, the highest reach of the tide had left a dike of kelp, whitened boards, sodden feathers of seabirds, trash; below that the beach was dark, smooth, and firm. Marian was pushing the perambulator along it, leaving a shine of crooked wheel tracks.

Left and right were promontories blackened with mussels and tide plants to high-tide mark, yellow from there to their furzy tops. Between them the sea came in from two directions, sending a constantly renewed chevron of breakers toward the beach. Out on the points where the surf broke with heavy thumps and thunders, spray flew higher than the cliffs, and above each explosion of spray burst up an explosion of black and white as the turnstones feeding on the rocks flew upward to escape being soused. Southward, toward Monterey and the sun, the sea went from white foam to heaving green glass to the mirror-like glitter of floating kelp. Far out, the bay had a glaze like celadon.

There were windows in the right-hand promontory through which, as the seas fell away, they saw glimpses of sunlit heaving sea and black rocks lashed with white. The sky was tumultuous with clearing, the world glittered. Down on the packed sand Marian was now playing sandpiper, pushing the perambulator to the lowest edge of the retreating foam, and flying up the sand ahead of the next wave. Susan could see the flash of her teeth, laughing, and the waving of the baby's legs from the buggy.

"You know what I wish?" she said.

"What do you wish?"

"I wish there were a mine in Santa Cruz that wanted an engineer with exactly your qualifications."

Sitting cross-legged and pouring sand from one hand to the other, Oliver squinted at her with what she read as irony. "What are my qualifications?"

She felt challenged. Once or twice he had dropped remarks about his "failure" at New Almaden. She would not permit it to be anything of the kind. "Honesty?" she said. "Inventiveness? Thoroughness? Ten years' experience? Didn't that cable of Conrad's and Janin's say 'entirely competent'?"

"It would be nice to think they were right."

"Of course they're right. They know you, even if you wouldn't tell what happened with Kendall."

"All right," he said, pouring sand. "Entirely competent. Plenty of people would give a lot for those two words from those two men. I wonder if they'd still think so if I turned this Bolivian thing down."

"But how can you accept it?" Susan cried. "Potosí, where on earth in Potosí? The end of the world, the highest town in the Andes, and the mine a day's mule ride out from *it!*"

He was absorbed by his stream of sand. He stopped it, let it run, stopped it, ran out of sand and scooped up more.

"Is there even a doctor?"

"I suppose there'd have to be. I can find out."

A young couple, the only people on that beach except themselves, slogged by through heavy stand, staring impertinently. When they were out of earshot she said, being reasonable, "Why would you be interested in it at all?"

A shrug, a blind blue squint. "Experience. Every mining engineer needs a chance to show what he can do on his own. Conrad's done it, Janin, Ashburner, Smith, all of them."

Silent and rebellious, she brooded about how crossed their purposes now seemed. In Augusta's life no such choices as this needed to be made. Thomas would shortly become editor of the new magazine *The Century*, and everything he had been building for years would go with him—friends, contributors, reputation, influence, wife, and family. His career was incremental, nothing needed to be stopped, there was no starting all over from the beginning. He didn't have to ask Augusta to accompany him to the top of the Andes and risk raising her children in a barefoot Indian village. She and Thomas did good in civilized ways, they had position and money, their days and nights were filled with art, literature, theater, music, good talk. Saint-Gaudens and Joseph Jefferson were their intimates, Whitman had visited their studio. Why could not her own life have taken that turn, instead of the turn that apparently led to constant uprootings and new exiles in raw unformed places, among people she tried to like but couldn't be quite interested in? She had never put permanently out of her mind Augusta's doubts about Oliver Ward.

But when she finally did speak, all she said was, "Did Conrad take Mary and the children along?"

"They weren't married till he came back."

"Mr. Janin?"

"Janin's wife is in an asylum in Delaware."

"Maybe because he did take her," she said, and immediately contrite, burst out, "I'm *sorry* we're such a millstone around your neck!"

"You're no millstone."

"But if it weren't for us you'd go. Maybe you *should* go. I did without you all that time when you were getting started. I suppose I could take Boy back to Milton." In defeat, she thought, justifying all of Augusta's doubts.

"That's not the answer."

"You know I'd go to Potosí if it weren't for the baby. I'd probably love it. I'm not afraid of roughing it, you know I'm not. But how could we take him to such a place? Even if there's a doctor he's bound to be like Dr. Furness at the Hacienda, who'd treat a caved-on miner with three broken ribs for *liver* trouble. Knowing he'd been caved on."

"I don't suppose Ollie's likely to get either broken ribs *or* liver trouble. You keep saying he's the healthiest child in the world."

"Because I take care of him!"

He had sifted some larger pebbles from the sand and was throwing them absently at the dike of drift and kelp. His eyes followed with stubborn inattention the playful swoops of the perambulator at the sea's edge. "I wasn't going to ask you to rough it. I don't think you should have to. I was thinking you could live in La Paz, where it's civilized. I could get in every few weeks."

"The way we are now?" she said with bitterness. "I've seen you once in two weeks. Have you enjoyed being apart?"

His eyes were lidded and unrevealing. "No," he said without looking at her. "Not one minute of it. Our trouble is, I picked a bad profession for a home life. I don't know what we can do about that, not till we get established." Now his eyes did meet hers. "Anyway I thought *you* might be enjoying yourself. I thought you liked this place."

"When you're here I love it. Look at it, who wouldn't? It's wonderful for Ollie. But when you're gone I go crazy with boredom and loneliness."

He threw the last pebble and brushed the sand from his hands, looking away down the beach, across the trickle of water that came from the lagoon behind them, cut through the dike of drift, and braided across the sand to meet the incoming foam. The water against the foot of the promontory was uneasy and sinking, and Susan looked past her husband to the windows in the cliff, and through them to the heaving sea beyond, pure and sunlit and brightly focused and small like a view through reversed binoculars. As she watched, the whole sea lifted, a green billow rose and drowned the cave and lashed against the rock. Over the promontory's furzy top she saw an explosion of turnstones tossed up just above the burst of spray. They were like sandpipers at the edge of the surf—they lived inches from the water and their feet were never wet.

The spray fell back, the turnstones settled out of sight, the hollow shore boomed, the green water was sucked away from the inside of the cliff, the rock streamed, the windows opened, pouring, and through them she saw again the miniature, bright, far glimpse of whitecapped sea, and a line of horizon marked in dark blue.

Oliver took his eyes off the tumultuous embrace of land and sea, and turned them on her. He smiled without showing his teeth, a rubbery lip-smile. Then, as if the attempt had generated the reality, he was really smiling. He shook his head, shrugged, banged his hands on his thighs and threw them into the air like a little explosion of spray or seabirds. "All right. I'll tell Conrad. Potosí is out."

His magnanimity nearly broke her down. In a choking voice she managed to say, "I'm sorry. I know what it costs you."

"It doesn't cost me much. Some excitement I'd probably have enjoyed. I wouldn't have enjoyed the separation. I needed to be reminded that you and Ollie can't really live in places like that."

"Something else is sure to show up."

"I suppose. But that's the only thing in a month. Every mining engineer in San Francisco is sitting in his empty office playing solitaire."

"We can hold out a long time yet."

"If I don't find something we can hold out about three more weeks."

"We haven't touched my money. I've got the commission for that Boyesen ballad, and I've been drawing Santa Cruz. I'm sure I can sell Thomas another article . . ."

"That's fine," Oliver said. "I'm proud of you. It's not your success we have to worry about. Meantime it's my job to support my family. Next time we move I want to have the train fare."

"Will you never let me forget that?" she said, and send him a smiling, pleading, puckered face. When he got that mulish look there was no talking to him. She had only herself to blame. So in a pretense of relaxation and freedom from care she leaned back against the driftwood log and sighed as if happily and tipped her face upward toward the sky scoured by the sea wind.

"You mustn't worry," she said. "Your chance will come. I didn't mean it when I said this place drove me crazy. How could it, it's so beautiful. I've missed you, that's all. Now you're back, and Ollie is so healthy and happy, and it's lovely." He did not answer, and she had to lie there stiffly relaxing until her back began to hurt. She straightened. "I gather nothing came of your experiment with cement."

"When I got through with it it was still limestone and clay. It never even made clinker."

"Couldn't you try again?"

"Sure. I'll take some more samples back tomorrow. I've got to have something to do besides walk from office to office and sit with my feet on other people's desks. But that's just an experiment, not a job."

"You say there's a big demand for hydraulic cement if anyone in this country could learn how to make it."

"Demand? Sure. It's all shipped in from England now."

"It might be profitable."

"What are you dreaming about?" Oliver said. "Suppose I did succeed in making it. To make it profitable you'd have to build a plant from scratch—land leases, buildings, machinery, cooperage, shipping, God knows what else. Money. Big money."

"You could get someone to back you."

Now she had got his full attention. He stared at her out of the corners of his eyes, suspicious and ready to laugh. "Are you suggesting I go into the cement business? I'm an engineer, not a capitalist."

"But if you could get someone to back you, couldn't you design the machinery, and do all that construction that you like so, and maybe be manager or superintendent or something?"

"You've got it all figured out."

"Why couldn't you?"

"Recipe for rabbit pie," he said. "First catch rabbit."

"Oliver, I'm absolutely *sure* thee can do it!"

"And while chasing rabbits, find some way to support family."

"The family can support itself."

"Not while head of family is healthy," Oliver said. "I'll find something, surveying or something else."

"But I want thee to experiment with cement!"

"Oh," he said, smiling. "Thee does, does thee?"

"Yes, and you know what else? I want you to discover cement, and get your capital, and build your plant and machinery, and start selling cement to everybody in this country, and then I want us to buy this laguna and this promontory and build a house that looks right straight out at Japan. We can get Lizzie back from her rancher, and bring Stranger down from Mother Fall's. Can't you see him on this beach, chasing sandpipers and getting his big feet wet? Can't you see Ollie growing up into the healthiest sort of outdoor boy and maybe learning to become a scientist or naturalist like Agassiz, studying tide pools? He can go to a good Eastern school, and then to Yale or Boston Tech, so he won't suffer from growing up in an out-of-the-way place. Oliver, thee absolutely *must* work on cement!"

Still smiling, squinting his eyes to crescents in the brightness, he said, "I intend to. In my spare time. Without any expectation of getting rich. Don't get your face fixed for that mansion right away."

"And yet it might happen. Mightn't it?"

"I don't suppose it's out of the question."

"Then that's what thee should work for. What if there aren't any jobs? Thee can do this, and it won't keep us apart as Potosí would have."

The surf boomed against the point, the air was full of turnstones, gulls, tattlers, plovers, screams and cries and the keen smells of salt and iodine. She put her hands to her cheeks, hot with sun and wind and exhortation. Oliver was watching her closely.

"Suppose I don't make it work."

"Then I'll go wherever thee must. I'll leave Ollie with Mother or Bessie if I have to, until he's old enough to come along. But thee *will* make it work, I have the most blissfully confident feeling. And we'll build our house on this promontory and watch the whales go by."

Indulgent, sleepy-eyed, he watched her. "I thought you wanted to move back East."

"Eventually. But Oliver, if thee can make this work, I'd be willing to stay here ten years. Maybe until Ollie is ready to go back to school. I could go home on visits, I wouldn't ask for more. We could lure our families and friends out for visits in our lighthouse."

His hand came out and took hold of her ankle, gave it a squeeze and a shake. He was laughing. She could see how she charmed him.

Perhaps he remembered holding her by that ankle while she hung over the waterfall above Big Pond. Perhaps he thought, though I do not believe that he did, that on that picnic afternoon of his courting he might just as well have put his hand on the pan of a bear trap.

3

In the fashion of the nineteenth-century theater, let Marian Prouse push across the stage the perambulator with a placard on its side: *TWO MONTHS LATER*. That will make it November 1877.

She awoke as if at some signal from her own flesh, a tickling or a pain. For a minute she lay listening, locating herself, identifying Oliver's warm weight beside her, strange in that stranger's bed. It made her tender to have him there, breathing softly, with a little whiffle through his mustache. Only the fear of waking him and spoiling his rest kept her from touching him.

More by memory than by sight she filled the darkness with the shapes that three and a half months had made familiar without making them dear. Mrs. Elliott's back room: there the commode, there the dresser, there the Boston rocker, there the barely outlined windows. The air was soft and stale. Would Oliver agree with Mrs. Elliott that it was unhealthy to sleep with the windows open to the night fog, or would he call that an old wives' tale, and open them up? She hoped he would. She wanted his authority asserted against Mrs. Elliott's infallibility. Three and a half months of boarding had made her want, above anything she could remember or imagine, her own house, with her husband in it instead of working himself to death in someone else's office or on someone else's survey, and running every night experiments that failed and failed.

Again the weak bleating that her ears had been tuned for. Her ghost moved in the invisible dresser mirror as she slipped out of bed. Groping, she found the doorknob. The adjoining darkness was acid with diaper odors. Bedsprings squeaked. "Yes?" said Marian's voice.

"I've got him," Susan said. "I'll have to light the lamp, I'm sorry. He's messed."

Her hands found lamp and matches by the habit of many dark mornings. In the light's bloom, there he was: wide-open blue eyes, toothless smile, kicking legs. She talked to him in fierce soft disapproval, tweaking his toes and kissing his fingers, while she cleaned and changed him. Ohhhhh, such a baby! Such a baaaad baby! All uncovered and all *messed! Icky!* Such a messy baby. Thee hasn't been a good boy at *all!*

With the dried, talcumed, wrapped, and fretful weight on her shoulder, protecting the little warm round head with her hand, she stooped and blew out the lamp. In pitch blackness hung with afterimages of the lamp's flame, a cloud of green moons the shape of ragged smiles, she found her way back to the other room. By the time she had located the rocker and sat down and opened her nightgown to let him nurse, she saw that the darkness had become dusk. The windows were gray, the furniture had acquired substance, the wallpaper all but revealed its pattern. Oliver's face, down in the pillow, had one ear, one closed eye, half a mustache.

The baby's sounds were so hungry he reminded her of some dry root in the first rains; her breast was wet and slippery with his mouthing. Creation, she thought. Emergence. Growth. Already he was a person, with his fat legs and his firm mottled flesh and his toothless smiles. He had never had a day of sickness, not so much as a cold. She was determined he never should. And he didn't weigh eleven pounds at birth, that was an insulting error of Dr. McPherson's scales. Oliver, figuring backward along his normal rate of growth, had estimated that he couldn't have weighed more than eight. *Yes,* she told him, bending to nuzzle his silky hair. *Yes, but!* You eat like that and you'll weigh as much as Mrs. Elliott's horse.

Then she raised her eyes and saw that Oliver was lying on his side, wide awake in the gray light, watching them. It made her shy to be seen so, and she turned away a little, but he lay there with his eyes full of love and said, "Stay the way you were."

So she turned back, but diffidently. She felt devoured, with his eyes on her and the baby making such animal noises at her breast. She said, "You got here so late, shouldn't you sleep some more?"

"I've already slept more than I'm used to."

"You've been working too hard. Is there anything new?"

"There isn't a job in the world, apparently."

"Well, I've got one thing to report," she said. "Thomas has definitely commissioned the Santa Cruz article. I've been drawing every day. I even drew one of Mrs. Elliott's dreadful daughters and made her look quite presentable."

"Good. They could use a little outside help." He looked at her with such shining eyes that it was all she could do not to turn her shoulder to hide her munched and kneaded breast. She made a protesting, abashed little face at him. "There's one thing," he said.

"What?"

"I made cement."

"*What!*" In her excitement she lost the baby off her nipple, and had to put him back. If she had not been so involved in her motherly functions she would have flown to the bed and kissed that sleepy, smiling face. "Oh, I knew thee could, I knew all the time thee could!"

Oliver tossed the pillow to the ceiling and caught it. "I did it three times. Even old Ashburner admits it, and he's so cautious he has to put his finger in the fire before he'll say it's still hot."

"Now we can buy our promontory."

"Now we can sit and wait. All I've done is *make* it. What would you say if some green twenty-nine-year-old engineer without a degree came into your office and said he could make hydraulic cement and needed about a hundred thousand to start a plant?"

"I'd give it to him at once."

"Yeah, but you're the engineer's wife. No San Francisco banker is going to cave in that easy. I'm not very good at the talkee-talkee."

"But thee can do it. Oh, isn't it wonderful? I'm proud of thee. I knew thee could do it. Isn't thee glad now we didn't go to Potosí?" The baby sighed and slobbered at her breast. "Wait," she whispered. "Let me get him taken care of."

He hung from her breast like a ripe fruit ready to fall. His eyes were closed, then open, then closed again. When she detached him, milk bubbled over his chin, and she wiped him off, scolding him for a piggy. He threw up so easily, not like an adult retching and covered with cold sweat. His wasn't sickness at all, things came up as easily as they went down. It was as if he were still used to the forward and backward flow of his mother's blood washing his food into him the way the sea washed food into an anemone on a rock. And her blood still remembered him: Was it perhaps his *hunger* that had awakened her this morning, and not his cry? She hated the thought that he must become a separate, uncomfortable metabolism cursed with effort and choice.

As she spread a dry diaper on her shoulder and hoisted him up, she sent toward Oliver, still watching her, a look that she meant should express her triumph and encouragement. Excelsior! But his eyes shone at her, his face was full of a not-too-patient waiting. Another hunger to be appeased. She felt a dismayed wonder at how strangely nature has made us. She thought she would prefer to remain posed there before him as the idealized figure of protective motherhood, but her skin was prickly with the touch of his eyes as she walked the baby up and down, she felt the pliancy of the uncorseted body under her nightgown, she fully understood the sensuousness of her barefoot walk.

The baby squirmed, and she leaned back to look into his eyes. Dark blue. Did they know her? Of course they did; he smiled. Or was it a gas pain? He lifted his head on its wobbling neck and tried to focus over her shoulder at where he had just been. (That early, the historical perspective.) A great belch burst out of him, his head wobbled with the recoil. "There!" she laughed softly. "Now we're comfortable." She took him to the window to show him the morning, and to delay what awaited her when she turned around.

As usual, the casement opened on fog as white and blind as sleep. Beyond the wet shingles whose edge was overflowed by the ghost of a climbing rose, there were no shapes, solidities, directions, or distances. The world as far as she could see it, which was about fifteen feet, was soaking; she breathed something halfway between water-sodden air and air-thinned water. There was a slow, dignified dripping. A geranium leaf pasted to the raised and weathered grain of the sill had condensed in its cup a tiny lens as bright as mercury, in which, moving, she saw her own face tiny as a grass seed. Another face appeared beside it, an arm came around her waist. She shivered.

"Hello, Old Timer," Oliver said to the baby. He bent to look out the window. "Thick out there."

"I love it," Susan said. "In a way, I love it. It scares me a little. It's as if every morning the world had to create itself all new. Everything's still to do, the word isn't yet spoken. It's like standing in front of a whited block that you have to make into a picture. No matter how many times I watch it happen, I'm never sure it will happen next time.

I keep thinking I'm looking into our life, and it's as vague and unclear as that. And now cement's going to change everything."

"I don't know that cement's any easier to see through than fog."

But she was too happy to be teased. They stood, she thought, the quintessential family, looking out from their sanctuary into the vague but hopeful unknown. Undoubtedly she thought of the window they stood at as a magic casement. Couldn't she hear the perilous seas? It is difficult to imagine Grandmother having to respond to the great moments of her life without all that poetry that she and Augusta had read together.

A drop as heavy as a ball bearing fell on the wet shingles. Beyond the ghostly edge of the roof there were only the faintest, tentative charcoal lines of form—suggested roses, vague mounds of shrubs down below, a tall dimness that would become a tree. From right, left, above, below, so pervasive that it seemed to tremble in the sill under her hand, she heard the Santa Cruz sound, at once laboring and indolent, a sound that both threatened and soothed, that could not make up its mind whether to become clearly what it was, or to go on muttering as formlessly as summer thunder too lazy for lightning. "Hear the sea?" she said.

"If Mrs. Elliott's right that should be good for your soul."

"Mrs. Elliott is always right. That's the trouble with Mrs. Elliott."

He was surprised. "Why, aren't you getting along?"

"Oh, of course. She's as generous and thoughtful as can be. But she helps me whether I want help or not. Her suggestions are commands."

"You don't have to take them. You're a boarder, not a guest."

"Just try not taking them! She's got a theory about everything. When I'm not looking she gives the baby pieces of raw steak to suck on."

"Does he suck on them?"

"Yes, that's what's so provoking. He loves it."

She could feel rather than hear him laughing.

"You can laugh," she said. "It's not you she's after all the time. There isn't a woman she knows that she hasn't told how to raise or wean or prevent her children. And with her own such examples. You should *hear* her in a group of women—she talks about the most impossibly intimate things. Birth control is what she's on just now. She wants to liberate women from their biological slavery. She was never in doubt about one single thing in her entire life. Don't tell me *you* like that sort of person, so good and unselfish and insufferable."

"I find her very disagreeable," Oliver said, still laughing.

"Do you think a woman ought to be contemptuous of her husband?"

"Heaven forbid. Is she?"

"Oh, she has the sharpest tongue! She tells me about the offers she had when she first came out here. It's hard to believe, she's so dowdy and blunt, but I suppose she may have, women were scarce. 'So I took the little tanner,' she says to me, as flippant as that, as if she'd been picking out a saucepan."

"What's wrong with Elliott? He looks like a perfectly good catch to me."

"He's not a New England intellectual," Susan said. "He's not enough like George William Curtis. He never washed dishes with Margaret Fuller. But wash dishes by himself, that's another matter. They have an agreement,' as she puts it. She cooks, he cleans up. The poor man is in his tan vats all day and in the dishpan all night, while those great slangy girls fool away at the piano or play whist."

Oliver's hand was moving on her stomach. "I know how the poor devil feels. I've had a lot of experience marrying women smarter than I am."

"Oh, how you . . . Who invented cement?" She let herself be pulled within his tightening arm, and said with a kind of desperation, "We've got to plan and plan and plan."

"No matter how we plan, we're in for some more of Mrs. Elliott, I'm afraid. I could be months finding backing."

"I don't care now. We can wait."

"Maybe you'd like to come up to the City with me."

"Oh dear, I wonder . . . It would be lovely, but I wonder about Ollie."

"Or find another boardinghouse here, if Mrs. Elliott gets to be more than you can stand."

"It would be a slap in the face, she's been so kind, according to her lights."

"Then all the planning we can do leaves us right where we are."

She heard the noise of Elliott shaking down the kitchen range, and in the dripping stillness that followed, distant bird cries cut through the mutter of the sea. "But not where we *were*," she said. "Because now there's a future. We can look out into fog as thick as cream and be certain it will burn away. We can hear all those lost squawks and know that as soon as Creation says the right word, they'll be birds."

"And meantime we'll all be dead of pleurisy from standing in front of the window. Let's get back to bed."

He engulfed her, but the baby was between them; his soft snore bubbled under her ear. "Don't," she whispered, "you'll wake him."

"Put him back in his crib."

"What if Marian is awake?"

"Let her take care of him."

"What if she knocks?"

"Let her knock. Lock the door."

"Then she'd think . . ."

"Let her think." His hand was lifting under the weight of her breast, his lips were on the top of her head.

"But it's so light!"

"Then you won't need a lamp to put him in his crib," Oliver said. "After that you can shut your eyes."

4

"Susan," said Mrs. Elliott, "I must give you a piece of advice."

She flapped the reins on the round haunches that worked in the shafts below. "Come on, Old Funeral Procession." Her worn shoes—she had not changed them even for Christmas dinner and Christmas calls —were propped against the dash. The hands that held the lines were freckled like tortillas. Instead of a hat she wore a bandeau or clout around her head; from under it sprouted twists of rusty wire. Her face was brown leather. She looked to Susan, setting her teeth against a headache and desperate to be home, like something put together in the harness room, like one of her own impromptu dolls.

Even the people to whom they had just delivered generous Christmas baskets—a Chinese washerman, a truck farmer with a flock of children still sun-browned in this backward Christmas weather that felt more like April, and two fishermen's families—had probably mocked her after she left. An odd, brusque, offensive sort of gift-giving. Here: this is for you. No grace in it, and no patience to wait for thanks, even ironic thanks. The town character. And she did not permit Susan to ask what the advice might be. She gave it before Susan could open her mouth.

"Let that man of yours drop this cement business. Let him find a job where he can build things. That's what he wants."

Susan took her time about replying. They were passing along the wall of the ruined mission, which she had drawn for Thomas Hudson with its climbing roses entangled among the thorny blades of a prickly pear, like the red rose 'round the briar in the old ballad. The gate opened and dressed-up children spilled into the street, bright beads from a broken string. Two nuns smiled from the archway. Old Funeral Procession pulled the dogcart past.

"You're mistaken, Mrs. Elliott," Susan said, as pleasantly as she could. "He's very interested in cement. Why else would we be staking our future on it? It's just that times are bad, and no one is willing to risk his money until he's very sure. Anyway, it's up to Oliver to decide if it has to be given up. I don't make that sort of decision."

"Oh yes you do," said Mrs. Elliott.

"But Mrs. Elliott, really!"

"Of course you make the decisions. You tell him how your life is to go. If you didn't, you'd be up in the Andes right now."

"And you think we should be?"

Mrs. Elliott laughed like a crow. "You'd be together. You keep saying you want to be."

"Not in a place that would be dangerous for Ollie."

"All right," said Mrs. Elliott. "So *you* made that decision. Let me tell you something. Any place is dangerous. Did you read about that boy and his father that were drowned at Pigeon Point the other day, after abalones at low tide? I've known children in this sleepy town who have died of eating lye, and children who have fallen down wells, and children who have been killed in runaways, and children who have died of scarlet fever. If you try to protect that boy from everything, you may wind up balking his father from ever doing what he's got it in him to do."

Susan told herself to keep her temper. The woman was well-meaning, however eccentric, and it was not Susan alone who felt her urge to dominate. She treated her husband like a hired man. She could no more keep her fingers out of other people's affairs than Ollie could help reaching for a rattle or a red ribbon. She could no more keep her opinions to herself than the gull that coasted over them just then could keep from jawing at them for not being edible. The proper response was a light laugh and a phrase that turned the advice aside. But she was too close to anger either to laugh or to find a properly light phrase. Mrs. Elliott, having said her say, drove grimly ahead.

After a minute of uncomfortable silence, Susan said, "If cement doesn't work out, of course he'll go back to mining."

"He should go back now," said Mrs. Elliott. "He hates this waiting on rich men, as if he were some swindling promoter."

Susan felt the color surging into her face. "Excuse me, Mrs. Elliott, I think he knows what he wants to do, and is doing it."

"I think he knows what you want him to do," Mrs. Elliott said.

"He *agrees* with me!"

174

"He convinces himself that he does."

"Well," said Susan, thoroughly annoyed, "what should a wife in my position do, since we're on this interesting personal subject?"

Mrs. Elliott turned on her a pair of faded, slightly bulging blue eyes that the wind had filled with tears without blurring their sharpness. "Go where your husband's work takes him. Make him feel that what he can do is worth doing. Take your child along and let him eat his peck of dirt. He'll be all the better for it, and he might have an interesting life. So might you. You won't always live like a lady, but that won't hurt you. You can help your man be somebody, and be somebody yourself. He ought to leave all this dealing and promoting to somebody like Elliott who can't do anything else."

The insufferable eye dug at Susan. Mrs. Elliott rubbed a knuckle across it, and when she took the knuckle away the eye was redder, but just as sharp.

"Thank you," said Susan furiously. "I'll think about it."

She gave her attention to a yard where some young people were playing the newly popular game called croquet. Obviously they were trying out a Christmas present. The lawn they knocked the striped balls around on had rose bushes in bloom along one side, and on the other a ten-foot pine tree hung with paper chains and strings of cranberries and popcorn that the birds were after. Her headache skewered her from temple to temple. She knew this as the worst Christmas of her life. Dinner among strangers, she and Ollie and Marian almost pensioners at the table made rowdy by the Elliotts' three romping daughters, and Oliver not there, tied up by a last-minute job he didn't think he could afford to turn down. She had been remembering all day how Christmas used to be at Milton, and how the whole week between Christmas and New Year used to be spent at receptions and house parties in New York. She had been remembering that it was now almost exactly ten years since she had met Oliver sitting on a stiff gilt chair under the controlling eye of Mrs. Beach and listening to the harangue of his unpleasant famous cousin.

"You are not to be angry with me," said the nasal New England voice at her side. "Your Aunt Sarah was my good friend. I feel an obligation to look after you."

"I'm not angry."

"Stuff. You're furious. But I'm very sure I'm right. Your husband hates promoting cement. His interest was in solving the problem of how to make it. He's got the head for doing important things."

"I believe I appreciate him almost as much as you do."

"I wonder if you do," said Mrs. Elliott, not in the least downed. "He's not a type you were trained to understand."

The horse lifted his tail and dumped a bundle on the doubletree, and for a blazing unladylike second Susan felt that he had made Mrs. Elliott the only possible answer.

A freckled hand was laid on her arm. "As long as I've already made you mad, let me tell you the rest of what I think." Susan moved her shoulders very slightly, looking straight ahead. "You're an artist and a lady," Mrs. Elliott said. "Sometimes I've wondered if you weren't maybe just a little too much of both, but my views may be peculiar. And it has nothing to do with being fond of you. I *am* fond of you, though you wouldn't believe it right now. What bothers me is that Oliver thinks you're better than he is, some sort of higher creature. He thinks what you do is more important than what he does. I don't deny you're special. You're both special. But I'd hate to see you discourage him from doing what he's special at, just so you can coddle some notions about dirt and culture. Do you follow me?"

Just for an instant Susan's eyes flared aside at the craggy, brown, long-jawed face and the blue eyes with their fuzzy eyebrows and the impossible clout bound above them. "I think so," she said. "But I can't say I understand you. One day you talk about woman's slavery and the next you talk like this. I don't mind your taking my husband's side against me—or what you think is my husband's side. Sometimes I do myself. But I want you to know, Mrs. Elliott, that I don't consider our marriage a slavery for either of us. We decide things together. You think he's slaving in the City at something he dislikes, just to keep us in comfort down here, but let me tell you, I work too. It's my money that pays our board."

"Is that so?" said Mrs. Elliott. "Then it's worse than I thought."

5

Dearest Augusta —

Christmas was such an utter failure for us that we have not quite recovered our hope for the future, which we planned in the crazy way people do 'when hope looks true and all the pulses glow.' Ten years on this coast and then home. Is ten years an eternity? Will you all be changed or dead; will we be 'Western' and brag about 'this glorious country' and the general superiority of half-civilized to civilized societies?

That sounds bitter. There are such good people here, but I simply *can't* care for them! I fear I am too old to be transplanted. The part of me which friendship and society claim must wait, or perish in waiting.

This is the way I feel when Oliver is in S.F. When he comes down, it is like high tide along the shore—all the wet muddy places sparkle with life and motion. I have discovered that I am not a serene person at all. I am fearfully down or else soaring. Perhaps I may reach a level resting-place in time. But this little bright town is a desert to me. I go about vacantly smiling upon people and feeling like a ghost. . . .

Good-bye, my darling other woman. It would not be well for one of us to be unmarried. It is better to go hand in hand, babies and all. But oh! it would be lovely to see you!

February 6, 1878

Dearest Augusta —

Miss P. has just brought in little Oliver with his bib on and a chunk of beefsteak in his fat fist—*raw* steak. Do you approve? I didn't when Mrs. Elliott first started it, but he seems to enjoy it immensely—any kind of food. His four front teeth are through and two more in the upper jaw are pressing. The gum looks clear over them and they will soon be through. He is *so* well. What a blessing it is. What should I do—what might I have done —with a sick baby and no doctor I could trust.

It is an awfully hard winter in S.F. and Oliver's negotiations continue to hang fire. Money is very tight and capitalists are holding on until better times. Oliver thought last week all was settled, but still he is obliged to wait in the most exasperating way. His patience is wonderful, it passeth my understanding. I tell him I am proud of his genius for construction, but he says he has no genius for anything, he just never knows when he is beaten. If he *is* beaten finally, I have made up my mind that I shall try to come home, for he will almost certainly have to take a place in some remote mine. I try to console myself for the injustice of what may happen with the fact that it may at least return me to where I may see you.

February 15, 1878

Dear Thomas —

I sent you yesterday the large block and the vignette for my Santa Cruz article. Others will come shortly. I am working on them as hard as I can, for the immediate future seems more and more uncertain. Things are so crazy out here—the madman Denis Kearny is shouting that the Chinese must go, and many workingmen are unemployed and surly, so that men with capital, fearing the disaster that may occur to their existing plants if a full-scale anti-Chinese riot breaks out, hesitate to erect anything new. For of course the erection of anything new would involve Chinese labor. It is cheaper.

You should be scolded for working so hard. Augusta writes that between converting old lovely Scribby into the new *Century*, and sitting on commissions, and fighting Tammany, you are seldom in your bed before two or three. You must stop this, sir. You are too valuable a citizen to be allowed to destroy your health in however good a cause.

March 4, 1878

Darling Augusta —

If nothing happens, I shall spend the apple blossom time in Milton, and the summer around generally, and not rejoin Oliver until at least the fall.

We shall have to postpone cement, and with it our lighthouse on that windy point. It is such a hard year and they all say Oliver looks so young—and when they ask him how much it will cost to make cement he hasn't the cheek to show a balance sheet with startling immediate profits, but says the plain truth, that he *don't know*. However, there are men who say they will go in on it next year. Meantime we must live. So Oliver takes up the shovel and the hoe and tells me privately that he is glad enough to lay down the fiddle and the bow. He enjoyed the wrestle with rock and clay and the triumph of finally uniting them in an insoluble marriage, but he has hated the tedious and humiliating waiting on rich men, and all the talk.

Mr. Prager has been appointed one of the commissioners to the Paris Exposition. My journey East will probably be made with them. If Oliver can only come part of the way with us it will not seem so cruel. He is at present negotiating about a place in Deadwood, Dakota Territory, the wildest of the wilds, where I cannot possibly take Ollie. But if he can come with us as far as Cheyenne, that will be four days together. I never thought that when I came back to you I would come hesitantly, but you will forgive me if I admit that coming back without Oliver will not be an unmixed blessing. But then I think of seeing *you*, and the long nights of talk. I am so restless with it all that I cannot write a decent letter. And I daren't take a walk, I dare hardly look out the window, for fear of being reminded of that windy point overlooking the sweep of the Pacific. Who would have thought that the prospect of leaving this place could make me want to weep! Oliver takes it far better than I, though the hard work and the disappointment were mainly his.

6

End of dream number one, which was her dream, not his. It came and went within six months. Others, better at the talkee-talkee, would later take his formula, which he characteristically had not patented or kept to himself, and tear down the mountains of limestone and the cliffs of clay, grind them and burn them to clinker, add gypsum, and grind and roll clinker and gypsum together into the finest powder for the making of bridges, piers, dams, highways, and all the works of Roman America that my grandfather's generation thought a part of Progress. The West would be in good part built and some think ruined by that cement. Many would grow rich out of it. Decades later, over the mountain at Permanente, not too far from New Almaden, Henry Kaiser would make a very good thing indeed out of the argillaceous and calcareous that Oliver Ward forced into an insoluble marriage in the winter of 1877.

My feelings about this are mixed, for it would have made me uneasy to be descended from Santa Cruz cement. If Grandfather had got his backing, neither he nor Grandmother would have become the people I knew. I can't imagine him a small-town millionaire, or Grandmother a prettier and more snobbish Mrs. Elliott, a local intellectual remembering her great days of contact with some equivalent of Margaret Fuller.

It makes me restless, too, to see Oliver Ward going off to Deadwood, a raw Black Hills gulch lately stolen from the Sioux. When he started for there, Custer's cavalry had been two years dead, and the Sioux were either behind reservation fences or gnawing the bones of exile in the Wood Mountain and Cypress Hills country beyond the Canadian line. So I don't fear for his scalp. I fear for his soul. His employer was to be George Hearst, then building the sort of empire that Grandfather might have built if he had been another sort of man—George Hearst who, according to Clarence King, was once bitten on the privates by a scorpion, which fell dead.

Clarence King himself, Conrad Prager's friend and superior on the Survey of the Fortieth Parallel, and later on a friend of my grand-parents, would turn out to be not untroubled by the temptations of a George Hearst. There was no reason Oliver Ward should not have been, except character. Pioneer or not, resource-raider or not, afflicted or not with the frontier faith that exploitation is development, and develop-ment is good, he was simply an honest man. His gift was not for money-making and the main chance. He was a builder, not a raider. He trusted people (Grandmother thought too much), he was loved by animals and children and liked by men, he had an uncomplicated am-bition to leave the world a little better for his passage through it, and his notion of how to better it was to develop it for human use. I feel like telling him to forget Deadwood. There never was anything there for a man like him.

But he had no options, having married a lady with a talent and having so far demonstrated his inability to keep her as he believed she should be kept. It was clear to him that, however she tried to reassure him, Susan carried his failure home in her baggage. She returned East poorer than she had come West, still homeless, and with a remoter chance of being soon settled. And she paid her own fare again, a thing that galled him.

Probably Susan consoled herself with the thought that she brought at least one good thing home: her baby. Perhaps she also had in some private corner of her mind the satisfaction of knowing that in spite of marriage, motherhood, and economic uncertainty she had not ceased to exist as an artist.

If she felt regret at having to leave Lizzie and Marian Prouse out on the edge of the half-civilized world, she shouldn't have; she could have done them no greater favor. Whatever the West of 1878 was for young mining engineers, it was the land of opportunity for unmarried women. Lizzie shortly would marry her rancher, and before she was through would give Buster five brothers and sisters. Marian Prouse, that large, soft, surprisingly adventurous young woman, would go on even farther west, to the Sandwich Islands, and there would marry a sugar planter and live on a beach more romantic than the one Grandmother coveted in Santa Cruz—a beach of silvery sand above Lahaina, on Maui, where coconut palms lean to frame the hump of Lanai across the Auau Channel.

It is odd to think, as I sit here in Grandmother's study imagining a future that is already long past, that I have walked that Lahaina beach with Marian's grandchildren, and found them, as they perhaps found me, only pleasant strangers. Irrationally, at the time, I couldn't help thinking that because their grandmother's life was briefly entangled with that of Susan and Oliver Ward, we owed each other something more than casual politeness.

No sign of failed hope showed on their trip East, for Conrad Prager had a princely way with money, food, wine, cigars, conversation, and Pullman porters, and their party included not only the Pragers and their two children, but a Scotch nurse who seemed to manage three as easily as two. It was a pleasure trip in the company of rich friends. They did not eat out of any basket; they dined largely. The talk was the kind Susan had been hungry for, the wine was picked by an expert, there were hours on the observation platform while the gentlemen smoked and the ladies watched the scenery.

Nevertheless, Susan had a spasm of utter panic, a black, blinding bolt of despair, when the train started out of the Cheyenne station leaving Oliver on the platform with his carpetbag and his rolled tent at his feet, his hat in his hand, the spring sun in his eyes. He seemed to be smiling, but he might have been only squinting against the light. She pressed her frantic face to the glass and kept her handkerchief fluttering as he walked, then trotted, beside the train. The platform ended and he stopped abruptly, began to go backward. Susan seized Ollie from his basket and held him so harshly to the window for a parting sight of his father that she made him cry. Immediately she began to cry herself, hugging him to her and straining for a last glimpse backward. He had passed from sight, the track-side ditch was full of muddy water out of which rose the stark poles of the telegraph line. It all swam and drowned in her tears. She felt the nurse taking the baby, and let him go. She heard Mary Prager say something savingly matter-of-fact, she heard Conrad murmur that he guessed he would go back on the platform and smoke a cigar.

Later it began to rain. Protected by the Pragers' consideration, she sat by herself and brooded out upon empty plains that winter had barely left and spring hardly touched. Miles of brown grass, raw cutbanks, flooded creeks coming down into the flooded bottoms of the Platte where bare cottonwoods seemed to grow out of a slough, and the benches of the flood plain, seen through rain that swept along the train and rattled on the windows, were the banks of a dreary lake. Now and then a stark, muddy little settlement—but no starker than Deadwood would be. Now and then a shack with pole corrals and livestock huddled on high ground, islanded by the floods—but better than the tent that Oliver would have to live in.

The Platte Valley slid by for a whole day before they even got to Omaha. Omaha, which less than two years before had struck her as the absolute dropping-off place, the western edge of nowhere. She remembered her bright scorn at the stockyards building, "*plaided*, my dear, in red, white, and blue!", and shrank at the image of the postman delivering that postcard to a crepe-hung door. Now here she came back, already five days on her homeward journey, and she was barely breaking over the rim of the Eastern world (how far she had been away!) bringing her excuses for her husband, her homeless baby, while Oliver fell every minute farther back among the endless plains and badlands.

She planned cunningly how she would tell her story. Deadwood was an opportunity he could not afford to give up, and so she seized the chance for a visit home. She polished phrases that would make his four-day stage ride and his leaky tent and his job for George Hearst seem an adventure. And in the process of framing the West and her husband in words, she began to leave them behind.

She was like a traveler still on the road on one of those evenings when sun and moon, one rising as the other sets, face each other across the world. Once she passed Omaha, Oliver grew steadily more remote in space and time, Milton and Augusta grew nearer. Home was more precious, and her impatience more intense, every hour. She would not let Conrad send a telegram from Chicago to announce her arrival, because she did not want to make her father or John Grant spend a night in Poughkeepsie to meet her late train. She would go to the hotel for what was left of the night, and take the ferry in the morning.

It reconstructed itself in her mind like the lines of a familiar poem: the shabby waiting room, the recognized cabman, the countrified hotel where she would be able to bathe her baby and herself properly for the first time in a week. In confidential whispers she told Ollie how she would show him the apple blossoms on the way down to the ferry, and introduce him to the ferryman, Howie Drew's father. At New Paltz Landing they would leave their luggage for John to pick up in the buggy, and they would walk up the lane that ran through her childhood, between fields familiar from the time she learned to walk. She would let him smell the dew-heavy hemlocks in the glen, and watch the birds busy in the trees, the chipmunks in the stone walls. They would stop to see how the dogwood hung outward from the woods as if to surprise a passer-by.

But their train, delayed by the universal floods, pulled into Poughkeepsie at four o'clock in the morning. Susan had insisted that the others go to bed, but had not been able to keep Conrad from staying up with her. He wanted her to come on with them to New York, take a room there, and come back rested the next day, but she would not. She motioned the porter to unload her bags, she broke away from Conrad's restraining hand and stepped down with Ollie. There was a lantern burning above the station agent's door, a lamp inside the waiting room, but not a soul in sight. Conrad was upset. "Thank you!" Susan cried brightly. "Thank you for everything, you've been so kind and good! I'll be fine, don't worry. I know this place like my own home."

The brakeman's lantern circled, down at the end of the dark train. The porter waited. More agitated than she had ever seen him, Conrad jumped up, the porter picked up his step and swung aboard, the train jerked and bumped and moved. She waved from amid her baggage, leaning back against the baby's weight, and turned, and found herself alone.

The station agent's office was dark. There was not a hack to be found. The waiting room was open, dim, empty, and the stove was cold. Susan laid the baby on a bench and tucked his blanket so that he would not roll off. Then, staggering under the weight, she carried her suitcases into the waiting room and sat down beside Ollie. The clock said fourteen minutes past four. She would have lain down except that the benches had iron arms every two feet. Her eyes smarted, her mind was numb, her feet cold. She sat shivering, dozing off: home, or nearly.

At six o'clock a waitress coming to open the lunchroom found her there and was thrown into a passion of sympathy. She lit a fire, made tea, warmed milk for the baby. At seven old Mr. Treadwell, who had driven the hack ever since Susan had been a student at the Poughkeepsie Female Academy, arrived and took her to the hotel. But she was too close now to take a room and sleep. She ate something, gave Ollie some oatmeal and softened toast, cleaned him up, washed her face and hands. At eight thirty they were on their way to the ferry, at a quarter of nine they were aboard. One disappointment—Mr. Drew had died. She had been hoping to talk to him about Howie and hence about the West. She felt cheated; she was ready to chatter about her Western experiences to fascinated listeners.

New Paltz Landing approached angling across the high spring current. At nine thirty a neighbor farmer who had brought eggs to the ferry for market dropped her at her father's door.

As in all pictures in the American Cottage tradition, there was a welcoming thread of smoke from the chimney. The crocuses and grape hyacinths were out under the porch, the trumpet vine had begun to leaf out in green as fresh as a newly discovered color. Behind it in the summer dark she had sat up late on how many evenings with the old *Scribner* crowd. Inside were the known rooms, the woodwork that loved fingers had worn and polished.

Tired to death, leg weary, her eyes full of tears, her baby a load on her arm, her back aching with carrying him, she climbed the two steps. The door opened and her mother looked out.

I find it hard to make anything of Grandmother's parents. They take me too far back, I have no landmarks in their world. They were Quaker, kind, loving, getting old, simple people but by no means simple minded. They probably thought their daughter more talented and adventurous than anyone could be. I can't see them as individuals, I can only type-cast them, a pair of character actors with white hair and Granny glasses. Leave them as a sort of standardized family welcome— tight clutch of hugs, tearful kisses, exclamations, smell of orris root from Great-grandmother's hair, scamper of Bessie's feet in from the kitchen —she here too!—calls to the barn for Father to come, Susan's home.

The April sun shone in through the net curtains, Susan thought she could smell apple blossoms even through a nose stuffy with weeping. There was so much talk, so much laughter, such an outburst of praise for her baby, so many fond minutes of watching him get acquainted with Bessie's two, that it was an hour later, and they were sitting somewhat exhausted around the kitchen table with their empty tea cups before them, before Susan thought to say, "Oh, all it lacks is Augusta! Can I invite her out, Mother? Have we room?"

"But doesn't thee know? Didn't she write thee?"

"Write me what?"

"No, I suppose she couldn't, thee would have left Santa Cruz before. That must be what the letter upstairs for thee is."

"But what's happened? Where is she?"

"Thomas has broken down," her mother said. "He's been very ill. He's been told if he wants to recover he must rest for at least a year. Augusta took him abroad last week."

May 28, I see by the calendar. The brief and furious spring of these foothills is over, summer is here before I saw it coming. The wildflowers along the fence are dried up, the wild oats are gold, not green, the pine openings no longer show the bloody purple of Judas trees, the orchard and the wistaria are in fruit and pod, not blossom. From now until the November rains, the days will be so unchanging that without the Saturday ballgame I won't be able to tell week from weekend. Who wants to? When I was a boy here, summer was narcosis. I am counting on it to be what it always was.

I am deep in my willed habits. From the outside, I suppose I look like an unoccupied house with one unconvincing night-light left on. Any burglar could look through my curtains and conclude I am empty. But he would be mistaken. Under that one light unstirred by movement or shadows there is a man at work, and as long as I am at work I am not a candidate for Menlo Park, or that terminal facility they cynically call a convalescent hospital, or a pine box. My habits and the unchanging season sustain me. Evil is what questions and disrupts.

Habit is my true, my wedded wife. Each morning, after I have stretched out the worst of the aches and taken the first aspirins, I hoist myself up by the bedpost and ease into the chair, carefully, fearful of the knock or jar that may start me out in pain. I roll to the lift and sink downstairs. On the radio news, while the percolator bubbles toward its red-light stop, I hear about the child killed by wild dogs in San Jose, the hundred pounds of marijuana seized in North Beach, the school board meeting broken up by blacks in Daly City, the wife shot by her husband after a quarrel in an Oakland bar, the latest university riot, the Vietnam score. I follow by traffic-alert helicopter the state of the traffic on the Waldo Grade, the Bay Bridge, the Bayshore, the Alemany Interchange. From the weather-alert man I learn that the day (again) will be fair, with patches of morning fog near the coast, winds from the northwest 5 to 15 miles per hour, temperatures 65 to 70 in San Francisco, 80 to 85 in Santa Rosa, 85 to 90 in San Jose. That means 90 to 95 up here. I see that as I eat it is 67 in the dark, shabby old kitchen, and I hitch over my shoulders the sweater that Ada keeps hung on the back of my chair.

Breakfast is invariable—Special K cereal and milk, a Danish roll that is less trouble than toast, a mug of coffee, and last of all, since I can't take acids on an empty stomach, a glass of orange juice.

At seven in the morning it is quiet in the house, quiet in the yard, quiet across the pine hills. The freeway is a murmur hardly louder than the chiming hum that millions of pine needles make in a little wind. I roll to the door and out onto the porch that Grandmother referred to as the piazza. Ed has brought the rose garden in the courtyard back, though it isn't what it was in my grandfather's time. It, with the mown lawn and the pines beyond, stares back at me like an old photograph caught between the ticks of time. It all looks as it looked in my boyhood, when I was back from school for the summer. My eyes have not changed, the St. Paul's boy is still there. I feel sorry for him, imprisoned in nearly sixty years of living, chained to a chair, caged in a maimed and petrified body. For an instant the familiar grounds glare and tremble, the prisoner rages at his bars. It would be easy to call it quits.

Occasionally I have these moments, not often. There is nothing to do but sit still until they pass. Tantrums and passions I don't need, endurance is what I need. I have found that it is even possible to take a certain pleasure out of submission to necessity. That have I borne, this can I bear also.

Behind the pines the sun is a shifting dazzle. It breaks through and glitters along the wet grass. Golden-crowned sparrows are hopping and pecking among the roses, a robin cocks his head to the underground noise of a worm out on the lawn, a pine top shakes to the impetuous landing of a jay. Off on the freeway I hear a diesel coming, shifting down as the hill steepens. Each gear is a lower tone, heavier and more laboring. Doppler Effect? Not quite. But I like the sound of these things better when they are shifting upward through their web of gears, not shifting down. Shifting down, they remind me too much of myself.

In the fresh air I light my first cigar of the day, and break the match before I drop it. My chair is a nest of cloth and paper at least as flammable as the California roadside. Then I wheel in, leaving the door open for Ada, and hitch onto the lift and float up into the airier, brighter upper hall. As I detach myself and turn, I can see the study door and the windows in line with it, the pines stirring beyond the windows, the desk waiting with its piles of books and folders of papers and photographs—home of a kind, life of a kind, purpose of a kind.

Do werewolves feel this sense of safety as they creep back just at dawn into some borrowed body?

My mornings are peacefully my own, except for a little conversation-break with Ada when she comes up to make my bed and do up my dishes and get my lunch. If the Giants are on the road, I eat on the porch, listening to the game on the radio. After lunch I lie down for a half hour, more for the change of position than because I need a nap. At any time between one and one thirty—she is no clock watcher —Shelly appears, and we spend an hour or two running down the answers to problems I have encountered during the morning. At three, leaving her to type whatever needs typing, and get ready whatever papers I will need the next morning, I go down into the garden for my daily Gethsemane with the crutches. And even that, because I impose it on myself, I can take a sort of Calvinist pleasure in.

Every association in this place is safe, enduring, and right. The only intrusion is the one I let in myself when I enlisted Shelly, and with Shelly all her grubby entanglements. He is gone, thank the Lord, having appeared to me only once like Peter Quint passing along the edge of the garden—outside, and looking in, but without any particular threat to me. Why should he be interested in me? If he was hanging around figuring out how to leave some cannibal tracks to scare Shelly, as I suppose he was, I would be nothing to him, just the old crip who owned the place. I looked up from my hobbling and there he was across the fence, with his thin ascetic beard and his beaded headband and his purple pants and knee-high moccasins, not sneaking, just strolling with his hands behind his back, following the fence. I went on pegging and swinging, forcing myself through the fifth or sixth or seventh lap, I don't remember, and we passed like casual walkers in a street. He looked at me pleasantly, he wagged his head in appreciation of what we shared. "Great day," he said. "Great country," and passed on, through the pines. Whose woods those were, I think I know, and they were not his.

Shelly by that time had moved back to her family's house. I assumed she thought he had gone, and so I warned her that he was still around. "I know," she said. "I've seen him."

"You've seen him?"

"Yes, twice."

"Talked to him, you mean."

"Yes."

"No problems?"

"Not really. I'm not going back, but he's all right."

"Have you told your family?"

"What for? They'd just get uptight and try to have him arrested or something."

"Why's he hanging around? Still trying to persuade you?"

"He likes it here," she said, and shook her hair back, laughing her *ho ho ho*. "Isn't it a gas? He loves the country. 'Why didn't you tell me about Grass Valley?' he asks me. 'This is a *place*, this isn't just Anywheresville. This is a place where a man could live.' He might just settle down here. Wouldn't that be great?"

"Would it?"

"No," she said. "He's just talking that way to bug me. You know, if he can't make the mountain come to Mohammed, he plays like Mohammed will come up on the mountain. It'll wear out. He'll go back to where it's at. This isn't his scene."

She read him right, he did go back. But he wasn't through laying down cannibal tracks, as witness that business yesterday afternoon.

I was on the piazza, just getting back into my chair after my nap, when this Parcel Delivery truck pulled into the drive. The driver hopped out with a clipboard in his hand and started up the steps. He saw me before he punched the doorbell.

"Rasmussen?" he said. "Care of Hawkes?"

"You should have turned off this lane at the next driveway down," I told him. "What is it? Mrs. Rasmussen works here, she'll be up in a few minutes."

"Canaries," the driver said.

"Canaries?"

"Twenty-four canaries."

Just at that moment Shelly came up behind him, around the corner. "Hi," she said. "What is it?"

"Man says he has twenty-four canaries for you."

"*What?*"

"Don't look at me," the driver said. "I'm just the delivery boy. Twenty-four canaries from the Emporium in the City. Where do you want 'em?"

"I don't want 'em at all," Shelly said. "This is some God-damned joke." She went to the idling truck and looked in. The driver opened the back doors and reached out a lightweight, paper-wrapped parcel five feet high and three feet through. He pulled off the paper and there they were. From where I watched from the top of the ramp there looked to be *more* than two dozen, in a wicker cage.

"Who sent them?" Shelly said.

"The Emporium."

"Let me see the bill."

He handed her the clipboard. The canaries were beginning to trill and chirp, now that light came into their cage.

"Oh, that son of a bitch," Shelly said. She handed the clipboard back. "Take 'em back, it's a bum joke."

"Jeez, I don't know."

"Take 'em back," she said again. "I'll call the Emporium and straighten it out."

Shrugging, the driver put the cage back into his truck and drove off. Shelly came up on the piazza to where I sat—I have to admit, laughing. I said, "It seems a shame, they might have brightened up the house. One for every room."

"Oh, man!" She flopped on the steps beside the ramp and took a strand of hair in her mouth and scowled down into the roses. She spit the hair out. "Didn't I tell you? His jokes draw blood. A present. A little gift from my loving man. Charged to me. The son of a bitch stole my charge card when I gave him my purse to get himself some cigarettes. He'll *flood* me with presents! I'll be straightening out his God-damned cute tricks from now till Christmas."

I suppose she may, at that. I wiped the smile off my face and suggested that she make her telephone call so we could go up and get to work. After an incredulous instant in which she looked as if I had suggested she bring her typewriter to somebody's funeral, so we could get off a few letters while we waited for the praying to begin, she did just that.

I wonder what Grandmother would have done with such a husband? Answer: She would never have got mixed up with him in the first place. I suppose in a way we deserve the people we marry.

IV

LEADVILLE

1

Today was Rodman day. He might as well have put a gun to my head.

He called before nine, saying that Leah was taking Jackie to her camp, and he might drop up if I was going to be home. I wonder where he thought I might be going. I'd be glad to see him, I said, not untruthfully. Ada and I plotted a lunch: avocado salad, a soufflé, garlic bread, a bottle of Green Hungarian. There is simply no sense in letting him think I subsist on canned soup and peanut butter sandwiches.

A little before noon I heard his car in the drive, then the bell. Ada let him in, and they talked a minute or two down in the hollow hall. With all the windows and doors open to let the breeze through, sounds are carried through the house with great clarity.

There is a certain endearing innocence about Rodman—he makes the world's worst conspirator or gumshoe. It has apparently never occurred to him that he has the loudest voice in the entire world, and that when he wants to be confidential he ought to retreat two miles. He reminds me of Bob Sproul, who was president of the University of California when I taught there, back in simpler times than these. There was a story they always told, that once a visitor came into his office for an appointment and heard Bob's voice booming away in the inner office. Sit down, the secretary said, he'll just be a few minutes, he's talking to New York. It seems so, says the visitor, but why doesn't he use the telephone?

That's Rodman, to the life. He bellows at Ada in a way to rattle the windows. "*Hi*, Ada. Hot enough for you? How's everything? How's Pop?"

"Doin' just fine."

"How's the pain? Any better?"

"Well, how would a person know? He don't tell you when he hurts, he just takes his aspirin. Some day he's just goin' to blow up with those aspirin, two dozen a day."

"Sleeps all right, does he?"

"He seems to sleep pretty good. I put him to bed about ten, and he's up at six."

"You work a long day."

"Oh, I don't get him up. He gets himself up. He's up and down that lift, and out in the yard every afternoon. You'd be surprised what he can do for himself."

"No I wouldn't," Rodman says. "I'm surprised he hasn't started playing golf." His voice drops a few decibels, the vase of marguerites on the desk quits trembling. "Any signs of, you know, *failing?* Still seem to have all his buttons?"

"Oh, buttons! Don't you worry about *his* buttons!" (Atta girl, Ada.)

"No problems like Grandpa's."

I can't quite hear Ada's reply. She knows, if Rodman doesn't, how sounds carry up the bare stairs, and I suppose it embarrasses her to be passing on my sanity in my hearing. I know what she thought of Father. He was such a *gloomy* man, she has said more than once. Just sat and stared at nothing for hours at a time, and got up and walked off without a word right while you were talking to him. Lived in some world off by himself. Got stingy, too, as he got worse—saved little scraps of things in the icebox, would have *lived* on scraps if she hadn't kept an eye on him. I am not like that, am I, Ada? Make a joke now and again, don't I? Show my appreciation of what you do for me? Did Father ever have a drink with you at bedtime, or sit on the porch with you and Ed drinking beer and watching the ballgame?

"Well, good," says Rodman's voice. "Great. We want him to go on just like he is, as long as he can manage. Where is he, up in his study?"

"Where else?" Ada says. "He's at that desk all hours. You go ahead on up, it'll do him good to take his eyes out of a book for a minute. I'll holler when lunch is ready."

Hard heels on the thin Beluchi rug, then on wood. He must wear leather heels, maybe with taps. I wonder if he'd begin to doubt his existence if he couldn't hear himself? He says from the bottom of the stairs, "How's this lift work? Can I ride up without a ticket?"

"Just stand on the step and push the switch," Ada says. "I ride it all the time, it's a real leg saver."

Murmur of the moving lift, the big laugh rising with it. Then the click of its stopping, the hard heels on bare boards. "Pop? Hey Pop, you there? It's Rod."

I push back from the desk, where I have been examining some F. Jay Haynes stereoscopic views of Deadwood in the 1870s, and swing my chair around. "Rodman!" I say. "What's the idea, sneaking up on me that way?"

Impervious, burly, bearded, beaming, here he comes with his hand out. Now take it easy, you oaf, my hand won't stand . . . Oh, Jesus.

Contrite, he releases me. "Whoops, sorry. Hurt your hand?"

"No, no." I let the hand down carelessly on the chair arm. Afterwhile the bones will work back into place, especially if I can catch him looking the other way and flex the fingers a little. "How's school?" I say. "Classes all over?"

"Classes all over, grades all in. I'm clean. How are you getting on with your book?"

"It keeps me out of mischief."

"I'll bet. Ninety years of Grandmother's life ought to keep you out of mischief till the twenty-first century. How far have you got her by now?"

"I've got her back to Milton, New York. Grandfather's in Deadwood."

"Deadwood? Wasn't that kind of a wild camp? Wild Bill Hickok and Calamity Jane and all that?"

"Rodman," I say, "you've been reading history."

"You never gave me proper credit. I'm not opposed to history if it's interesting." Grinning, he leans to look at the stereopticon slides spread along the desk. "Is this Deadwood? Looks like a movie set."

"It has been, plenty of times."

"I didn't know your grandfather ever got into anything like that." He picks up the stereoscope and slips a picture into the slot, takes it out and slips in another. "It really *is* like a movie set. Look at all the guns on these guys. Anything exciting happen to him there?"

"He never shot it out with Wild Bill Hickok, if that's what you mean."

Lifted viewer, ironic eye. "All right, Pop, all right. What was he doing there?"

"Building a mill ditch for George Hearst's Homestake mine. Ever hear of the Homestake?"

"I've heard of Hearst. Not the Homestake."

"Last time I looked it had produced a half billion in gold."

"And Great-grandpa built the mill ditch," Rodman says. "Good for him."

He irritates me, he always does. Nothing is interesting to him unless it's bellowing as loud as he is. I say, "Ever try living in a tent through a Dakota winter? That's excitement enough to last anybody a while. Ever see Buffalo Bill Cody and Captain Jack Crawford ride their horses onto the stage of the Bella Union Theater to re-create Buffalo Bill's single-handed killing and scalping of the Oglala chief Yellow Hand?"

He is looking into the viewer again. "The real Buffalo Bill?"

"I don't know that there were any imitations. Unfortunately Captain Jack's horse got cutting up, scared of Captain Jack's warbonnet, and he shot himself through the leg and brought down the curtain."

"You mean they were putting on an act with live ammunition?"

I say ironically, "The West was not built with blank cartridges."

"Great," Rodman says. "Now you're talking. What else?"

"So Grandfather lived in his tent in Blacktail Gulch and built George Hearst's mill ditch and George took a fancy to him and wanted him to become one of his affidavit men. That means somebody who swears to false testimony in court to get Hearst control of another claim. So Grandfather said, 'George, I guess you don't need me any more,' and got on the stage for Cheyenne, and then on the train for Denver, and on the Denver train he met a little farmerish man who said he owned a mine in Leadville that some jumpers were trying to horn in on, and he could use a mining expert who would study the mine, survey it, and testify when the case came up. That little man was Horace Tabor. Ever hear of *him*?"

He lowers the stereoscope and regards me with a smile behind which things are going on like shadows passing across a drawn blind. "You're really full of it, aren't you?"

"What's the antecedent of 'it'?"

He throws back his head and roars with laughter. I can see the strong cords in his neck where his beard thins out. "O.K., Pop, I wasn't trying to put you down. I think it's great you've got something that interests you this much. I'm glad Great-grandpa got to Deadwood, too. It'll add some zing to your book."

"I'm not going to put any of that in," I say.

"You're not? Why not? You *know* all about it. You're writing a book about Western history. Why leave out the colorful stuff?"

"I'm not writing a book of Western history," I tell him. "I've written enough history books to know this isn't one. I'm writing about something else. A marriage, I guess. Deadwood was just a blank space in the marriage. Why waste time on it?"

Rodman is surprised. So am I, actually—I have never formulated precisely what it is I have been doing, but the minute I say it I know I have said it right. What interests me in all these papers is not Susan Burling Ward the novelist and illustrator, and not Oliver Ward the engineer, and not the West they spend their lives in. What really interests me is how two such unlike particles clung together, and under what strains, rolling downhill into their future until they reached the angle of repose where I knew them. That's where the interest is. That's where the meaning will be if I find any.

In my peripheral vision I am aware that he is looking at me steadily, but I don't turn. I look a while at the gun and bowie and spurs above the desk, where Grandmother put them. Then I turn a half circle and look at Grandmother's downcast, pensive portrait. Up here in the study it is beginning to be hot.

"A marriage," I say. "A masculine and a feminine. A romantic and a realist. A woman who was more lady than woman, and a man who was more man than gentleman. I don't give a damn if he once saw Wild Bill plain. He couldn't have, anyway, because Wild Bill was killed at least a year before Grandfather blew into Deadwood. I'm much more interested in quirky little things that most people wouldn't even notice. Why, for instance, did he send the Christmas presents he did from Deadwood—a bundle of raw beaver pelts and an elk head the size of a good-sized woodshed? What would he do that for? It's as nutty as Shelly Rasmussen's nutty husband sending her twenty-four canaries."

"He did?" Rodman says, delighted.

"Yes, but that's not what I'm talking about now. I'm talking about Grandfather, who wasn't a kook, but who still sent those things, as if he was insisting on something. It's like that horse pistol up there that he brought to his courting and laid out on her Quaker dresser. He wanted to be something she resisted. She was incurably Eastern-genteel, what she really admired was a man of sensibility like Thomas Hudson."

"Who he?"

"Never mind. Augusta's husband, *you* know. Fragile and a little effeminate and *very* cultivated. Grandfather was something totally different. What held him and Grandmother together for more than sixty years? Passion? Integrity? Culture? Convention? Inviolability of contract? Notions of possession? By some standards they weren't even married, they just had a paper signed by some witnesses. The first dozen years they knew each other, they were more apart than together. These days, that marriage wouldn't have lasted any longer than one of these hippie weddings with homemade rituals. What made that union of opposites hold them?"

Too late, I realize that I have been vehement. Rodman has quietly laid the stereoscope down on the desk. My stump is twitching and my seat is numb from four or five hours in the chair. I take out the aspirin bottle and shake two into my hand.

"Want some water?" Rodman says.

"No, I can take them without."

"Works better if it's diluted and dissolved."

"O.K."

He brings a glass of water from the bathroom. There is a constraint as thick as gelatin in the air between us. A linnet looks us over from the window ledge, but when I turn my chair to face Rodman I hear the *thrrrt!* of its wings and in the corner of my eye see its dark blip disappear.

"Pop, I suppose I better tell you," Rodman says. "Mother was over yesterday."

There are certain advantages to being made of stone. I sit there, and I don't think I quiver. "She was?"

"She asked about you—where you were, what you were doing, how your health is, who's taking care of you."

"Did you give her the dope?"

His look splinters on mine. Even Rodman has difficulty with my immobility, and now he obviously suffers from embarrassment—for himself or for me I can't tell. But after that moment's cringing he holds my eye. "Yes."

"All right."

"She doesn't look good," he says. "She's shaky. She's had a bad time."

"I'm sorry."

"She's taken an apartment in Walnut Creek."

"I didn't ask."

"Pop . . ."

I take the hand that he mashed in greeting me, and work the knuckles with the fingers of my other hand. I can feel the bone hard and resistant and enlarged. Rodman is standing by the desk, so that I have to look upward at him under my eyebrows. God *damn*, it would be a pleasure to live among people four feet high, or as considerate as Al Sutton.

"I think she'd like to see you," Rodman says. "I think she feels very bad."

I do not answer. The ache which has never gone away since he shook my hand spreads up the wrist and arm, I feel it stiffening my shoulder and solidifying down my spine. Everything in me is congealing—guts, glands, blood vessels, organs, bones. My stump, as it always does when I get upset, jerks like a fish on a line. I lay the aching hand on top of it and sit, too rigid for my own comfort.

"Don't you think, maybe—" Rodman says.

"She made her bed."

He stands looking down at me; I look past him.

"Why not get us a drink?" I say. "In the cabinet, there. There's ice in the little refrigerator under the far end of the desk."

He goes away from me and I sit in the midst of my own petrefaction, hating him, hating her, hating *it*, hating myself. He brings the drinks silently and hands me a glass. Lifting my eyes upward through my eyebrows, excruciatingly conscious of the rigidity of my neck, I raise the glass an inch. "To you."

"Prosit."

But he is not going to leave it at that. He stands there bending me with his eyes, and with an expression on his bearded face that I have to read as pained, diffident, everything that Rodman normally is not.

"If I brought her up," he says, "would you see her?"

For an instant it is touch and go, the stone threatens to become weak flesh again. For the half breath that I feel that weakness, I want it, yearn for it, would willingly turn to mush if only some of the old warmth would come back. My mind darts like a boy who has stolen something and wants to get to a safe place to examine his prize. Then I am aware that throughout this instant of weakness I have been sitting there as rigid as ever. There is too much of Grandfather in me.

"You may as well understand," I say. "I don't hate her. I don't blame her. I think I understand her temptation. I'm sorry about her bad luck and her suffering. But I have nothing to say to her. Tell her so."

2

At first light she pulled her curtains aside and saw sunrise pink on distant snow peaks. Breakfasting, she sat on the left side of the dining car to watch the mountains come nearer, and she was getting her things together when the train was still racketing across empty plains. When it finally crawled between lines of side-tracked boxcars and died with a hiss at the Denver platform, she was on tiptoe behind the porter in the vestibule. But at the last moment, when he opened the door on a pandemonium of hatted heads, bearded faces, shouting mouths, blowing papers, Mexicans, Indians, frock coats, buckskins, and a ten-foot sign that said "Lunch Pails Filled 25 c. Passengers for the Mines Take Notice," she pulled back with a hollowness in her stomach and let others go first. Her eyes flew up and down, hunting him.

At once she saw him, not pushing forward but back against the station wall, using his height to see over heads. The first thing she thought was that he must not be called Sonny any more. The lines of his thinned-down face were severe, his skin looked weather-beaten except where the pink edge of a new haircut showed on his neck when he turned his head. Expressionlessly his eyes picked up and discarded one by one the passengers who descended and stood for the porter's whisking, or bolted up the windy platform. He might have been expecting a freight shipment, not a wife he had not seen for more than a year.

Had he done without her for so long he was indifferent to her coming? Did he blame her, as she blamed herself, for that empty year? Did he think she was insane to force herself on him now, just when he was getting on his feet but before he felt Leadville was prepared for her? She thought he looked closed-in, watchful, perhaps resigned.

Then the expressionless eyes found her, and she saw them change. All at once unbearably excited, she waved a black mitt. Foolishly they beamed at each other across forty feet of bedlam, and then here he came, and down she went to meet him. Folded up against him and lifted off the ground, she heard him say, "Ah, Susie, you made it! I was afraid it was another false alarm."

"I couldn't do that to you twice. You're so thin! Are you well?"

"Tiptop shape. But the altitude's not fattening. Neither is the Clarendon's food." He was holding her out to look her over. "You're a little thin yourself. How was the trip? How's Ollie?"

"I'm fine," she said, out of breath. "The trip was fine. The conductor even invited me to ride in the locomotive, but I didn't. Ollie's much better. He'll get well fast, now I'm gone. I was bad for him."

"Come on."

"Oh, I was!" She was all to pieces. In the middle of bumping shoulders and clumping boots, in all the dust that swirled around them, she wanted to confess her mistakes and get started right again. No more foolish protectiveness about Ollie, no more timorous holding-back from sharing her husband's life, no more—ever—of these meetings and partings at the steps of transcontinental trains. "I was always at him," she said. "It scared me so to see him delirious that I couldn't let the poor child rest, and the ague fits and the sweating fits were almost as bad as the fever. Mother and Bessie finally shut me out of his room. That's when I decided that even if he wasn't fully well, I was coming out to you. I won't be in your road, I promise."

"I guess you won't," he said, and laughed.

"Oh, isn't it ironic?" Susan cried. "I wouldn't take him to Deadwood because I was afraid in a rough camp like that he'd get sick and I'd be lonely. So I take him home to Milton and he gets the old Milton malaria and I'm lonelier than I've ever been anywhere. But I'm sorry about last month. I was all ready to come when he fell ill, and I was so upset I left it to Mr. Vail to telegraph you. I thought he could be trusted, since he was coming West on the same train I'd have taken."

"He could be trusted, all right," Oliver said. "He just wanted to save me a dollar, so he didn't send his telegram until Chicago. By that time I'd already left Leadville to meet you. So he saves me a dollar and costs me two hundred, and leaves me standing on this platform gnashing my teeth. I met the train for three days before Frank finally got word to me. On the way back over the range I said a few things to myself about Mr. Vail."

"Ah, but *now*," she said, and let herself be wagged back and forth between his big hands. "Now we can have a good trip in, together. It'll be like going in to New Almaden for the first time."

He was indulgent and paternal; she could see that every move she made and every word she spoke fascinated him. "Well, not exactly," he said. "Getting over there is no picnic, and you won't have my special satisfactions to compensate for the discomforts."

"What are your special satisfactions?"

"Upon arrival, I will instantly be one of the two most envied men in Leadville. Horace Tabor's got all the money and I've got the only wife."

"Really? Aren't there *any* women?"

"Some women. No wives. There are some widows, as they call themselves, and some boardinghouse keepers, and a couple of hard cases who wear pants and dig all day in prospect holes. Well, maybe one wife. Her German husband herded her over Mosquito Pass with sixty pounds on her back."

"Mercy," she said, between real and comic dismay. "It sounds like a social summer."

"You'll have to do all your talking to me."

"Poor you."

"I can put up with it." He had not let go of her arms, he waggled her shoulders with a slow, insistent motion. She had forgotten how warm a smile he had. The thinness of his face accentuated the fans of wrinkles at the corners of his eyes. The crowd thinning around them, the wind that blew dust and papers past could not interrupt their looking at each other.

Then the porter picked up her bags and carried them a few feet closer and set them down. Oliver let go of her to lay a silver dollar in the pink palm, and picked up both bags in one hand and steered her with his left arm. "Tell me about Mosquito Pass," she said. "Is it as horrible as it looked in *Leslie's Illustrated Newspaper*? Dead horses and wrecked wagons and frightful precipices?"

"Horrible," he agreed. "You'll be paralyzed with fright. But it won't be quite as bad for you as for German Hausfraus and *Leslie's* correspondents."

"Why not?"

"For one thing, I shouldn't have to put more than forty-fifty pounds on you. For another, you know all about those people who draw terrific Western pictures to scare Eastern dudes."

She had taken it for granted that they would spend the night in Denver. Even a genteel Quaker lady, after a year's separation, may dream of a second honeymoon, especially if she arrives all braced with resolves about being a model wife. But they had no time even for a proper dinner. The Denver, South Park & Pacific narrow gauge that would take them to Fairplay would leave in less than an hour. Waiting for a lunch to be put up for them, they almost missed it, and came panting aboard to find only one seat unoccupied—a broken one. Oliver spread his field coat over it and braced it from underneath with her carpetbag, and she sat eating a great sandwich of tough beef and too much mustard while the train dug into the mountain beside a torrent that Oliver said was the South Platte. The roadbed was rough, the train's grip on the rails precarious. She was thrown around, bouncing between Oliver and the window and having trouble getting the sandwich to her mouth.

"This is an adventure," she said.

"Good."

"The train's so little, after the Santa Fe. If I should draw us now, I'd take a position away behind and above, and show us as a teeny little toy disappearing into these enormous mountains."

"Hang around a while," Oliver said. "When we get to Slack's and pick up the team we'll be an even teenier speck disappearing into even bigger mountains."

"Deeper and deeper into the West. They call Leadville the Cloud City, don't they?"

"Do they?"

"That's what *Leslie's* called it."

"Good for *Leslie's*."

"You're no fun," she said. "You won't let me gush. Tell me about our cabin on the ditch. Is it really logs?"

"Really logs. A dollar a log."

"Long logs? How big is it?"

"Short logs. What do you expect for a dollar?"

"Has it got a view?"

"The only way you could avoid a view up there is to go underground."

"Are there neighbors?"

He laughed, smoothing breadcrumbs out of his mustache and brushing them off his coat and lap. He kept watching her with a delighted, sidelong smile as if she constantly astonished him. Other men in the car were watching them too, and the near ones were listening. She could not look up without encountering some gaze that immediately withdrew. The admiration of two dozen magnetized eyeballs exhilarated her. She supposed it *would* be pleasant for men deprived of the company of ladies to see one on this improbable little train, headed toward places where no lady had ever ventured. When the car hit a smooth spot and her chattering spread further than she intended, she understood that ears away out of earshot were strained to catch what she was saying.

"No neighbors unless the bird who jumped my first lot has built himself a house since last week," Oliver said.

"Jumped your lot!"

"Stood me off with a shotgun."

"But what did you do?"

"Went down to the office and picked out another."

"You just *let* him?"

"It wasn't worth much blood. I got a better lot the second time."

"I should think it would have made you mad."

"Sure."

"I should think you'd have had him arrested."

"In *Leadville*? Anyway, what for?"

"For theft. And now he'll be our neighbor."

"I doubt it. By now he's off jumping somebody else's lot or claim. He's got a kind of gift that way."

She studied him curiously. "You're queer, do you know? You let yourself be imposed on and cheated, and you don't seem to care."

"I don't like trouble, not about anything that small. I've got too ugly a temper when I do get mad, so I try not to get mad."

"Have you really got an ugly temper? I don't believe it."

"Ask my mother."

"She said you were stubborn. She said you refused to defend yourself when anybody put you in the wrong."

"I hold grudges."

"I should think you'd hold a grudge against Horace Tabor, then."

Amused, he came up from adjusting the carpetbag under their tipping seat. "That was the biggest joke in camp."

"Joke? You call it a joke? You make this gentleman's agreement, as he called it, though it doesn't sound as if he'd know what the word meant. You're to inspect his mine for the customary fee and testify about it in court, and you study that mine for three whole months, and make a glass model of the vein that everybody in Denver admired, and you win him his case—didn't his lawyer admit it was your testimony that did it?—and then he hands you a *hundred dollars!* You could have made more washing dishes."

"That was the joke. Everybody knows Horace. He may own mines worth five or six million dollars, but his hand doesn't get into his pocket very often. The moths aren't disturbed more than once a month."

"Five times that would have been too little. Ten times. That's what Conrad or Mr. Ashburner would have asked."

"All right. Next time I can ask it. Horace's payoff made me pretty famous."

"I hate to have you famous as the man who only smiles if you cheat him or jump his claim."

"I wouldn't worry about it," he said comfortably, and covered her folded hands with one of his. "It won't break us. There's no problem about making money in Leadville. Matter of fact, I'm making it hand over fist."

Slack's, at the end of the steel, was as ugly as proud flesh, a gulch of shacks and tents and derailed cars, its one street a continuous mudhole, every square foot of flat ground cluttered with piles of ties, rails, logs, rusty Fresno scrapers, wagonbeds, spare wheels, barrels, lumber, coal. Dejected mules and horses stood hipshot in corrals knee-deep in muck. The canyon walls, skinned of trees, were furrowed and gullied between the stumps. Three great ore wagons full of concentrate from the Leadville smelters were being loaded into flatcars by a gang of men.

Watched with interest by this gang, and by trainmen, teamsters, Chinamen, loafers, in fact by every eye in Slack's, Oliver carried Susan through the mud and left her treed on a pile of ties while he waded through the deeper mud up the street to get the buggy and team he had left there the day before. He kept turning to keep an eye on her; twice she saw him look out the stable door to see that she was alone, and where he had left her. The audience gave her its full attention while she waited, and during the whole operation after he came driving back in a democrat wagon, stowed her bags and parcels, lifted her to the seat, laid a buffalo robe under her feet and a gray blanket in her lap, and started her up Kenosha Pass.

"Isn't there a stage?" she asked. "Wouldn't that have been cheaper and easier?"

"There's a stage, but not a stage I'd let you ride on."

Though it was nearly five o'clock, the glare of the day blazed in their faces. The road was mud, rock, mud again, dirty snow. Then they tipped down to the creek, the horses braced back in the breeching, Oliver's hand rode the brake, and where the shadow of the wall fell across them they passed instantly into chill. The smell of water burned in Susan's nostrils, she heard the wheels clash among rocks and the water rushing through the spokes, but in the abrupt transition from glare she was as blind as if they had entered a tunnel. Hardly had she begun to see again when they tipped upward, the horses dug in, the wet wheel beside her rolled up with a felt of red mud on its tire, and the sun was in her face again like a searchlight.

After a time they passed from sun into shadow, warmth into chill, and did not come out again. The edge of sun climbed the left-hand canyon wall. From time to time they had met or passed ore wagons of every size and kind from farm wagons drawn by a pair of mules to great arks, sometimes double, pulled by six, eight, ten, a dozen animals, driven not by lines but by a rider who rode one of the leaders. Now they came upon one of these arks up to its hubs in a mudhole, and two men down in the road working on the six-horse team. There was barely passing room between the wagon and a fifty-foot dropoff to the creek.

Prompt, almost fierce, Oliver stood up in the democrat. "Hang on." She took hold of the dash and braced her feet. As they squeezed by, rattling stones over the edge, she had a long, passing look at a man's bearded face, panting and distorted, and at the same time innocent, curious, fascinated, floating the long instant between the time when he stood up from his efforts and the time when he would renew them.

His face hung like a jack-o'-lantern in the twilight of the mountains while an unlikely Eastern lady drove by. She read his face in complex ways—it was an expression she would have liked to draw. And she saw the horse, one of the leaders, that lay with its forelegs bent under it and its nose resting as if thoughtfully on the doubletree. Then they were past.

"Shouldn't we have stopped to help?" she asked.

"You can't be sure of the company."

"Would it have been dangerous?"

"I wouldn't take the chance."

"That poor horse!"

"You'll have to get used to that. In this altitude they get lung fever. Three hours after you notice they're sick, they're dead. I expect that one had it—he didn't look able to get up, much less pull."

The chilly dusk, the sight of that hopelessly mired, heavily laden wagon with its sick horse, the taciturnity with which Oliver devoted himself to his driving, made her feel small, awed, and dependent. Pulling the blanket around her, she moved as close to him as she could without interfering with his handling of the reins. He took them in his left hand and put his right around her, and they rode like lovers.

"Getting tired?"

"It seems a long time since I got up."

"I'll bet. How about another of those delicious sandwiches?"

Crawling at a walk up the darkening gulch, they ate. Right and left she saw the light orange on the peaks, the canyons almost wiped out in shadow. There was a sense—not a perception so much as an illusion or hallucination—of dark fir forests. Then there was a paleness of white trunks and bare delicate branches as they passed through aspens along a slope. Ahead, one pure star was shining through a V of dark mountains. She sagged, she almost dozed.

Then she roused up again. "Hang on again," Oliver said. "Here's the stage."

In an unearthly pink light the stage labored on the grade ahead of them. It looked like something out of Mother Goose. There were men hanging all over the top of it, at least seven or eight of them. "Always room for one more," Oliver said. "Here we go now."

He whipped up the horses, the buggy pulled abreast in a brief wide place. No more than ten feet away, faces looked down into Susan's, and she realized that the smell that enveloped the whole stage, moving with it as its own special atmosphere, was whiskey. The men above her stared, they visibly doubted their eyesight in the pink dusk, they said things, one or two, that she did not choose to hear as the horses pulled her past them.

Then she was even with the driver braced against the dash and seesawing his web of lines. He stared, he threw back his head in glad greeting and opened his mouth. For a moment she wondered if he thought he knew her, if by some miracle he could be someone from home, or Almaden. But Oliver pulled back on the lines and they bumped along side by side, and the stage driver yelled happily, "Hey there, Mister Ward! How'd you like a swim in the Old Woman Fork tonight?"

"Dennis," Oliver said. "Is that you? What're you doing on the Leadville road? You're lost."

"What's anybody doing on it?" Dennis said. "What're *you* doing on it?"

"Bringing home my wife."

"Uh?" His eyes touched Susan's in the near-dark, and she made a little smile. He was momentarily deprived of speech, and the passengers beside him, on top of him, behind him looking out the windows, were most interested spectators and listeners. Beyond them the distances between the peaks were blue, the gulfs of the canyon soft charcoal black. The buggy bumped and lurched, she hung on, Oliver lifted the whip in farewell and stung the rumps of the horses. They pulled out ahead, went over a crest, and drove hard for fifteen minutes to put the stage well behind them.

"Who was that?" Susan said, when it appeared he was not going to tell her without being asked.

"Dennis McGuire. He drove the stage from Cheyenne to Deadwood last spring, that famous thirteen-day ride over a four-day road."

"What did he mean, swim in the Old Woman Fork?"

"We got hung up by floods. Didn't I write you about that?"

"You never write me about anything. All you said was that it took a long time, you didn't say why."

"We were there two days waiting for the river to go down, but it was raining, it just got deeper. Finally a fellow named Montana and I got on the off swing and the near leader and rode them in, they wouldn't take it otherwise. All six horses were swimming in ten seconds. Cold? Oh my. I looked back and saw that old coach awash, with men swarming out onto the roof like rats out of a burning silo. Kind of lively."

"But you made it."

"No," he said. "I was drowned in the Old Woman Fork at the age of twenty-nine. Body never found."

The sky past his profiled head had gone slate blue above a jagged paleness of snow. She could not see his smile—she seemed to hear it. "It's a good thing you didn't write me about it," she said. "I'd have been frightened to death."

"I doubt you scare as easy as you make out."

With dark, or rather starlight, she stopped trying to see. Tiredness ached in her bones, she sagged and rocked, hunched in her blanket with the buffalo robe around her feet. At a washout she sat in a cold stupor while Oliver lit the lantern and looked the place over. She put herself utterly in his hands, she got out obediently and floundered behind the buggy while he led the team through. "Just as well it's too dark to see," he said. "This is a *Leslie's* sort of place. Two wrecked rigs and three dead horses down the cliff."

"How much longer?"

"No more than an hour to Fairplay."

He drove with one hand and held her with the other arm. The wind sighed and whispered like something lost. There were shapes of spruces rising to constrict a sky full of great cold stars. The horses plodded, patient and interminable.

"Remember Old Funeral Procession?" she said once.

"Who?"

"Mrs. Elliott's horse."

He laughed. "These are bad, but not that bad. Stay with it, it won't be long now."

One minute they were plodding on the dark road that wandered through the raw material of creation, and then they turned around some screening trees and were confronted by lights and sounds. There seemed to be an extraordinary number of people in the street. Every third door, it seemed, was a saloon that threw trapezoids of light across plank sidewalks raised above the mud. She heard, of all things, a piano. Open doors let out a deep commingled rumble of men's voices.

Oliver said, "Whoa." His lifted lantern shone on the rounding surface of a log wall, the edge of a hay roof. He put the reins in her hands. "Stay here." He jumped heavily down. She sat in the high seat listening to the town noise back of her in the street, the sounds of animals moving in some unseen corral. When she tipped her head and looked upward at the glowing dark blue dome pricked with its millions of lights, bigger and brighter than stars had ever been before, she felt the mountains breathe in her face their ancient, frightening cold.

A door opened on lantern light, another lantern bobbed toward her, throwing the shadows of moving legs. The sigh of one of the horses was like the breath of her own relief.

The stable boy unhooked the tugs and led the team away. Oliver helped her down, hauled the bags after her, put the lantern in her hand. "Can you carry this?"

"Of course."

"Just a little way back to the hotel."

The street was muddy and rutted, but he steered her down the middle of it, and she understood gratefully that he was avoiding contact with the men on the sidewalk. Where lamplight threw the shadow of a potted palm across the planks and revealed the hatted heads of men sitting inside, a sign said HOTEL. He led her in: a smoky room, an American flag on the wall, half a dozen men in chairs, smoking, others in the bar in the next room, brass spittoons that rounded the light. Diffident, stupid with fatigue, she stood blinking. She heard the talk pause, and felt the eyes on her. She let Oliver take the lantern out of her hand.

Behind the desk that angled across a corner a young man in striped arm garters rose and laid down a newspaper. His eyes photographed Susan in one unblinking look. He said, "Sorry, folks. Full up."

"I've got a reservation," Oliver said.

The clerk's full-lidded eyes met Oliver's in pleasant denial. Smiling his public smile, he looked first at Oliver, then at Susan, then back at Oliver. He spread his hands. "I wish I could. I filled the last room two hours ago."

With the slightest indulgence, the sagging disappointment in

Susan's muscles could become panic. Where *would* one sleep, in this wild place full of rough men? The stable? A hayloft or manger? Probably there were as few accommodations for horses as for people. She hung onto Oliver, who was looking with hard insistence at the clerk.

"If you did," he said, "you gave away the room I reserved for my wife and me two days ago. The name is Ward. I put five dollars down."

At the word "wife," Susan felt the clerk's eyes again, like the flick of a moth's wing against her face. For the first time it occurred to her what the clerk thought she was, and in a chilly passion she said, "Is there no other hotel? I think I should prefer it if there is."

"Wait," Oliver said. To the clerk he said, exaggerating the patience of his explanation, "I came through here day before yesterday and reserved a double room from a fellow with a twitch in his face. Do you recognize him?"

"Remple, yeah. But . . ."

"I put five dollars down. I signed the register. Have you got it there? Let me see it."

"Sure you can see it," the clerk said, "but I'm telling you, Mr. Ward, we haven't got a thing open. There has to be some mistake."

"You bet there has to be."

Oliver took the register and turned it around. He flipped back a page. Reading past his elbow, Susan saw his name, the familiar signature, with a pencil line drawn through it. "There it is," Oliver said. "Who crossed it out?"

"I don't know," the clerk said. "All I know is we haven't got one single solitary bed. The best I could do for anybody would be to give you bedroll space in the hall."

"That'd be fine," Oliver said. Watching him, Susan saw the fury come up so suddenly into his face that she was afraid he was going to lean over the desk and slap the clerk. The clerk thought so too—she saw his eyes widen. She said again, "Oliver, perhaps there's another hotel."

"There isn't."

"Look, I'm sorry," the clerk said. Susan thought he might really be. She did not forgive him for what he had assumed about her, but she thought he might really be sorry. "There's the boardinghouse," he said. "I could send the kid down to see if they've got a bed."

"Don't bother," Oliver said. "Where is it?"

"Next block up, on the left. Look, Mr. Ward, I can have the kid run up, you folks sit down a minute."

"Just give me back the five dollars and forget it."

Surprising her with his promptness, the clerk opened a drawer and got a five-dollar gold piece out of it. He laid it in Oliver's hand. "I'm sorry."

Outside, Oliver pushed her with angry haste to the next corner. She stumbled and tripped, holding the lantern out awkwardly to keep it from her skirts. "What do you suppose happened?" she wailed. "What can we do if there isn't something up here?"

"What happened was that somebody crossed a palm with some money," Oliver said. "Somebody needed a bed and the clerk fixed it. If you hadn't appeared, he'd have got away with bedding me down in the hall."

"But where *will* we bed down? Can we go on to Leadville?"

"Not a chance."

They reached the corner, turned left, found the boardinghouse. A man sitting in his undershirt, drinking coffee, said yes, they had a bed. It wasn't much for the lady—just curtained off. Oliver looked at her once and took it. The undershirted man picked up his lamp and led them up bare stairs and along a hall whose blue muslin walls waved and crawled with the wind of their movement, to a door that had no key. After she was inside, and sinking down on the bed, Susan saw that the room had no walls, either—only that same blue muslin, called Osnaburg, nailed to a frame that went no more than six feet above the floor. Under the one broad roof every eight-by-ten cubicle in the place shook to the same cold drafts, and glared the same sick blue in the lantern's light. She could hear the sounds of sleeping all around. It was so cold she could see her breath.

Oliver knelt at the bedside and took her in his arms. His lips were on her cold face. "I'm sorry," he whispered, echoing the clerk. "I'm sorry I'm sorry I'm sorry."

"It's all right. I think I could sleep anywhere."

"I wish we were already home."

"So do I."

"In this place we can't even talk."

"We can talk tomorrow night."

He kissed her, and she clung to him, tired and tearful. Right at her ear, it seemed, a man cleared his throat. Oliver let her go and blew out the lantern.

Too tired to be appalled at this thing called a room, but too tired to be amused by it either, she got out of her dress and crawled into bed in her shift. If she had literally carried sixty pounds all the way from Denver, and had been driven along the road with a club, she could not have ached more. Oliver's weight sagging into the other side gave her something to cling to and warm herself by. For a while they clung and whispered, then she heard that he was asleep.

But she could not sleep. After a while she rolled away and lay on her back with her scratchy eyelids stretched open. Beside her Oliver breathed evenly. The sounds of communal slumber murmured and sighed through the cloth walls. Someone had a persistent, wracking, helpless cough that went on for minutes, and quit out of pure weakness and lack of breath, and in a little while broke out again. Supporting that sound of debility and failure there were orchestrated snores. For a while a man ground his teeth horribly, only feet away. Later still a voice cried out, cracking with fear or menace, "Fred! God damn you!" She froze, expecting shots or the sounds of struggle, but the crisis tailed off into a sigh, the groaning of springs. Still later there was an unidentifiable noise like a dog biting and snorting at an inaccessible itch.

She lay tensely listening and interpreting, refusing her attention and willing herself to relax, only to find herself in ten seconds tight with alert awareness again. Phantasmal adjustments to the road lurked in her muscles.

It seemed a week since she had awakened in the berth and pulled the curtains to see dawn on the peaks of these mountains. It seemed a month since she had embraced her parents and Bessie and kissed her son's sleeping face. She felt swallowed and lost; her mind kept bending back to the room where Ollie might now be beginning another fever cycle. She tried to imagine Augusta and Thomas in this crude place, their fastidiousness cheek by jowl with all this coarse humanity, and couldn't. The very effort made her laugh. For a time she lay phrasing the day's experience in colorful and humorous fashion, as if for the pages of *Century*, and almost persuaded herself that under the rough and ridiculous circumstances of life in the Rocky Mountains there was something exciting and vital, full of rude poetry: the heartbeat of the West as it fought its way upward toward civilization.

And that made her think, with failing nerve, that whatever it was, it was to be her life. It was what she had deliberately chosen. As soon as he was well enough, she would be bringing Ollie out to grow up in it. Wanly she adjusted herself to Oliver's unresponsive warmth.

It seemed to her that she heard every noise from midnight until near morning—dogs, drunken men in the street, footsteps that came down the hall and, it seemed, stopped before her door, so that she lay listening fearfully for a long time.

Then someone in the next cubicle sat up, yawning and squeaking the bed. He lighted a lamp whose glow shone blue through the cloth wall and threw huge windmill shadows among the rafters. She heard him stamp into his boots. The light rose and moved and receded down the hall. Outside, a rooster crowed some way off, and right underneath her someone split kindling with a quick *thunk thunk thunk*. Exhausted, frazzled, wide awake, she turned in the bed, fighting for covers, and found that Oliver's eyes were open. He always woke that way, as quietly as if he had been lying there waiting.

"Can't we get up?" she whispered.

They were on the road to Mosquito Pass by seven. For the first hour she hunched within her blanket with her breath congealing on the wool held across her face. A cold wind searched out the openings in her wrapping, her feet were cold under the buffalo robe. The dropped dung of the horses smoked in the road. As they climbed through the snags of a burned spruce forest, tatters of cloud blew out of the overcast. In all the shadowed places there was snow.

Eventually they climbed through the clouds and into the sun. Looking back, Susan saw South Park filled nearly to the brim with cloud, only the saw-toothed peaks rising above it. Their crowbait horses, one black and one bay, dragged them reluctantly up a steep canyon, stopping every quarter of a mile to blow. They came out onto a plateau and passed through aspens still leafless, with drifts deep among the trunks, then through a scattering of alpine firs that grew runty and gnarled and gave way to brown grass that showed the faintest tint of green on the southward slopes and disappeared under deep snowbanks on the northward ones. The whole high upland glittered with light.

As they had need, they drew aside to let ore wagons pass with their loads of concentrate and matte. The skyline, from any part of this magical plateau, was toothed like the jaw of a shark. The road bent and dipped down through a hanging valley where mosquitoes rose in swarms from the wet grass; when it lifted them again around a corner of bare stone the mosquitoes blew away instantly, and the wind was so cold it made her teeth ache. Her eyes watered with cold and light.

"Still remind you of staging in to New Almaden?" Oliver said.

"I take it back. This is so wild and beautiful. I like it ever so much better."

"So do I. I could do without the town of Fairplay, though."

"We survived it."

"You're all right, Susie," he said. "You know that? Most women would go to bed for a week after a night like that."

"Where?" she said, and giggled. Her voice startled her, brittle as ice in that thin air. "Maybe I *will* go to bed for a week, once we get to a bed."

"I doubt it. It hasn't fazed you."

"I lay awake all last night writing it up for *Century*," she said. "I intend to be their Western correspondent. At the very least, think of the letters I can write Augusta." The thought made her laugh again; she put her black mitts to her cheeks, stinging with cold and sun. She supposed she looked as healthy as a child at a skating party. Oddly enough, she *felt* healthy too. "No," she said, "I couldn't. Can you imagine her opening a letter describing last night, and reading it aloud to Thomas at breakfast in some grand hotel dining room on Lake Leman or somewhere, with all of civilized Europe looking in the window?"

"Better spare her," Oliver said. "She thinks you're enough of a pioneer as it is." He reached the whip from its socket and touched the horses into activity. "Come on, boys, don't fall asleep."

The thin air smelled of stone and snow, the sun came through it and lay warm on her hands and face without warming the air itself. Up, up, up. There was no top to this pass. Oliver said it crested at more than thirteen thousand feet. They were long past all trees, even runted ones. The peaks were close around them, the distance heaved with stony ridges, needles, pyramids in whose shadowed cirques the snow curved smoothly. The horses stopped, pumping for air, and as they rested she saw below a slumping snowbank the shine of beginning melt, and in the very edge between thaw and freeze a clump of cream-colored flowers.

"I'd like to walk a little. Could I?"

"You won't want to walk far. We're around twelve thousand right now."

"Just a little way. I can keep up with you."

It felt good to use her legs, but she had no wind at all. With a hand-ful of the little alpine flowers in her hand and the whole broken world under her eyes, she puffed on after the democrat, and was glad when it stopped and waited. But when she caught up, Oliver was standing out in front looking closely at the bay horse. The moment she saw the closed expression of his face she knew something was wrong. She looked at the horse, spraddle-legged, dull-eyed, with pumping ribs and flaring nostrils, and heard the breath rattle in its throat.

"Is he sick?"

"I thought for a while he was just dogging it. They're not pulling any load to speak of, but look at him heave."

Tableau: tiny figures at the foot of a long rising saddle, snowpeaks north and south, another high range across the west. The road crawled upward toward the place where the saddle emptied into sky. The wind came across into her face with the taste of snow in it, and not all the glittering brightness on the snow could disguise the cold that lurked in the air. In the whole bright half-created landscape they were the only creatures except for a toy ore wagon that was just starting down the dug-way road from the summit.

It took an effort to keep her fear from shaking in her voice. "What will we do? Can we walk?"

Watching the horse with a frown, he shook his head without look-ing at her. "Don't you feel the altitude?"

"Yes, but . . ."

"Anyway, what would we do with your luggage and the buggy? They wouldn't be here when we got back to pick them up, that's a cinch. Maybe we could leave the sick one and you could ride the other

. . . No, no saddle or anything. We'll just have to drive him. He might hold out to English George's."

Once more Susan looked up at the shelf of road where the ore wagon clung. "At least I can go on walking now. I don't want that poor sick thing pulling me."

"I'll do the walking. You climb up. He'll be dead by suppertime no matter what you do."

Unwillingly she rode, while Oliver walked on the off side with the whip and kept touching up the black horse, making it pull the sick one along. The bay stumbled, hung its nose down until the collar half-choked it, wheezed and rattled for air. They had to stop every hundred yards.

"Maybe that wagon can help us," she said once.

"We'd better make it on our own."

A long, painful, halting time later, halfway up the dugway, they met the ore wagon, and Oliver scrambled into the seat to negotiate the passage. Sight of what his two hundred pounds did to the gasping bay horse was so painful to her that she barely saw the wagon driver.

"Really, I want to walk a while," she said when they were past. But she was able to struggle upward only a few hundred yards, with many rests. The thin air burned her lungs, her legs were like wood. And it did seem to make no difference to the horse whether she walked or rode. It went staggering upward a few rods and stopped, was whipped and dragged forward, stopped again. The sound of its breathing was like the sound of a saw.

"All right," Oliver said after a few minutes. "No more, now. You'll be sick yourself." He helped her up into the seat. He was panting; even in the reminding wind his face had the shine of sweat. They hung, fighting for oxygen, on a steep narrow ledge below the place where the road finally curved around out of sight. The shelf had been literally blasted out of the mountain with black powder. Beyond the curve of the road there was nothing in sight. They must be near the summit, or at it. Snow sagged against the inward cliff and around the big blocks of broken stone. The outside dropped away so steep and far she didn't dare look.

"How much farther?" she said. "Can he make it, do you think?"

"It's going to be all right. Just up this last pitch and then it's down. We could take him out and let the black pull it."

He blew out his breath, with a down-mouthed, acknowledging look of relief. Then she saw his eyes change. "Wait. Listen."

He cocked his head, with his hand raised, for only a second, long enough for her to hear something, she couldn't tell what—perhaps only the empty roaring of the sky. He dropped his hand, he threw a look right, then left. The buggy sagged and rolled a half wheel backward as he leaped onto the step. At that instant appeared around the upper bend a pair of trotting horses, then another pair, then another, then the rocking cradle of the stage. She saw sparks clash from rock under the tires. To her horrified eyes it seemed a runaway, out of control.

Oliver's whip cracked on the rump of the black horse, then the bay, the black again. Susan grabbed for the dash. They jerked wildly in toward the cliff, among the blocks of stone. And there was not room, she knew it with a certainty that froze her mind.

The sick horse, on the inside, floundered among the rocks and deep snow. Oliver lashed, lashed, lashed it—oh, how could he? She screamed and grabbed for his whip arm; he shook her off without even looking at her. The left wheels reared up, climbed, crashed down, climbed again; the buggy tilted so steeply that she hung on in frantic fear of sliding straight off under the hoofs and wheels. Oliver's hand shot out and grabbed her. She screamed again, the air was full of a sound like a high wind. There was a smoke of horse breath, a roar and rumble, a close, tense, voiceless rush, and the stage passed her so close that if she had had her arm extended it might have been torn off. Glaring up into the dangerous shadow as it thundered by, she saw a lean, hook-nosed face, a figure with feet braced against the dash, lines that hummed stiff as metal. And she saw the stage driver's queer, small, gritted smile.

Still hanging onto her arm, but leaning far inward toward the cliff like a sailor high-siding in a blow, Oliver guided the buggy up over a last rock to a bumpy landing in the road. The air still reeked with the hot smell of horse and the spark odor of iron tires on stone. The noise of the stage diminished behind and below them. They turned to watch it go.

"*God* Almighty," Oliver said, and slid back into the seat beside her. "You all right?"

"I think so."

"Too close."

She was staring in pain at the sick horse. It tottered on its legs— she could see the deep trembling that ran from pastern to knee. Its nose went clear to the ground, it shuddered and began to sink. Instantly Oliver lashed it harshly with the whip, lashed its mate, leaped to the ground and kept on lashing. The horse tottered, strained, was dragged forward, the buggy crawled painfully upward. Susan sat white and trembling, hating his cruelty, hating the pain and exhaustion of the sick beast, hating the heartless mountains, the brutal West.

Just at this point in Grandmother's reminiscences there is a somewhat high-flown paragraph:

> The mountains of the Great Divide are not, as everyone knows, born treeless, though we always think of them as above timberline with the eternal snows on their heads. They wade up through ancient forests and plunge into canyons tangled up with watercourses and pause in little gem-like valleys and march attended by loud winds across high plateaus, but all such incidents of the lower world they leave behind them when they begin to strip for the skies: like the Holy Ones of old, they go up alone and barren of all circumstance to meet their transfiguration.

I can't help reading that as more than a literary flourish; I want to read it as a perception of Western necessity, something deeper than scenery. Something must have told her, as they dragged over the summit and down to English George's, that character as well as mountains had to strip for the skies. She must have known that a Thomas Hudson, despite his urbanity, uprightness, and delicacy of feeling, would not have got that dying horse in motion fast enough to save them, or got it on over the summit to the place of help. Almost before she had stopped screaming and pulling at his hard whip arm, she felt shame. It was his physical readiness, his unflusterable way of doing what was needed in a crisis, that she most respected in him: it made him different from the men she had known. In remembering the episode years later, she makes a veiled acknowledgment of the respect that at the time, upset and sulky, she begrudged.

Even her prose strips—she does the rest of that trip to Leadville in a half dozen lines.

> I am glad I have forgotten what I said to my husband in that moment when he saved our lives, and I hope he has too. The horse died after we got to English George's, and there we hired another, or the remains of one, and he died the day after we reached Leadville. Oliver paid for both—and how much more the trip cost him (both trips) I never knew. But that is the price of Romance. To have allowed his wife to come in by stage in company with drunkenness and vice would have been realism.

That was written years after the event, and is conditioned by the Doppler Effect. That day in June 1879, they came down off Mosquito Pass silent and constrained, she scared and sulky, he worried and somewhat bruised in spirit at being thought a brute. Or I suppose that is what he felt. The fact is, I don't know. He is the silent character in this cast, he did not defend himself when he thought he was wronged, and he left no novels, stories, drawings, or reminiscences to speak for him. I only assume what he felt, from knowing him as an old man. He never did less than the best he knew how. If that was not enough, if he felt criticism in the air, he put on his hat and walked out.

3

Leadville made its appearance as a long gulch (Evans) littered with wreckage, shacks, and mine tailings. It was rutted deep by ore wagons, scalped of its timber. The smoke of smelters and charcoal kilns smudged a sky that all down the pass had been a dark, serene blue. They passed a string of corrals, then a repair yard where the bodily parts of a hundred wagons were strewn. People appeared and thickened—walkers, riders, drivers of buggies and wagons. A log cabin wore a simple sign, SALOON: it looked to be a half mile from anywhere. Farther down, a shack had scrawled in charcoal above its door "No chickens no eggs no keep folks dam." The shacks grew thicker, the road became the parody of a street. A false-fronted shack said ASSAY OFFICE.

Ahead, something seemed to be happening. People were hurrying, others stood in doorways looking toward the center of town. A young man with a flapping vest and a face pink with high-altitude exertion passed them, running hard. Still aggrieved with each other, Susan and Oliver had been traveling without much talk, but when she heard shouting up ahead Susan could not help saying, "What is it? Is it always like this?"

"Not necessarily." He stood up to look, he shrugged and sat down. The crowd sound ahead stopped as if hands had choked it off. Now Susan stood up. She could see a dense crowd from sidewalk to sidewalk in a street between false fronts, and men coming in from every direction. "What on earth! It must be something exciting."

She was jolted back into the seat, and Oliver stood up; they popped up and popped down like counterweighted jumping jacks. She heard him grunt, a hard inarticulate sound, and abruptly he cracked the whip on the haunch of their new horse, as dragging and wheezing almost as the one they had left behind, and swung the team left up a wallowed side hill between shacks.

"My goodness," Susan said. "Is this the road to our place?"

"One way."

"Could you see what was happening down there?"

"Some kind of ruckus. Nothing you need to see."

"You protect me too much," she said, disappointed and rebellious.

"No I don't."

"We agreed it was a mistake for me to stay so far out of things at New Almaden."

"This isn't New Almaden."

They bumped up the stumpy hillside. Down to the right she could see packed roofs, and beyond them smelter smokes. All across the West were the peaks she knew were the Sawatch Range. The crowd was out of sight, but she could hear it, a loud continuous uproar, then a still-ness, then a harsh, startling outcry. "*Something* is certainly going on," she said.

Oliver, with his head dropped, watched the laboring sick horse. She thought his face was stern and unloving, and she hated it that they should arrive at their new home in that spirit. Then he pointed with his whip. "There's your house."

She forgot the excitement down below, she forgot the misunderstanding that had kept them silent down the gulch. There it sat, the second house she would try to make into a Western home: a squat cabin of unpeeled logs with a pigtail of smoke from its stovepipe. "Looks as if Frank's made you a fire," Oliver said. "You'll learn to appreciate that boy."

"Frank, that's your assistant?"

"General Sargent's third son, come out West to be an engineer."

"Just like you."

"Just like me."

Her quick, upward, smiling look asked or gave forgiveness for what had been between them. "Is he going to be as good as you?"

"That's a hard standard to hold him to."

They laughed. It was better already. At the ditch bank she took his hand and teetered prettily before jumping down. The ditch was like no ditch she had ever imagined. This was as clear as water in a glass, and it shot past as if chased. When she stooped impulsively to drag her hand in it it numbed her fingers.

Two planks crossed it for a bridge. Oliver tied the team to a stump and led her across as if it were as dangerous as a high wire. At the door he stood a moment, frowning, listening to the crowd noise from below, and then with an odd, angry shrug he yanked the buckskin latchstring. "Maybe we should begin with the right omens," he said, and gravely lifted her across the sill and set her down. "In case you think you've come down in the world, let me tell you there's nothing grander in Leadville."

It was one room, perhaps fifteen by twenty-five feet. Two windows, curtainless. Five chairs, one broken, one a rocker. A Franklin stove with a fallen, ashy fire smoking in it. Two canvas cots made up with gray blankets. A table that had been knocked together out of three wide boards and two sawhorses.

"Don't look around for the kitchen or bedroom," Oliver said.

Perhaps she had been remembering the New Almaden cottage, so much better than her expectations, and so had built up expectations of this cabin that it could not support. It took an effort to conceal her disappointment. Yet as she looked around she had to admit that a log house *was* picturesque, and a house with a welcoming fire on its hearth was touching. She summoned back for her inner eye the image of the peaks rimming the world outside. "It's charming. I can hang curtains around the cots. We'll be snug. How will we cook?"

"Breakfast on the Franklin, dinner out of a sardine can, supper at the Clarendon. I'm afraid I won't be here for dinner much."

"I'm sure you'll be welcome when you can come," she said. "But I'll be busy—you'll have to keep out of my way. I brought some blocks for a novel of Louisa Alcott's."

He said seriously, "Maybe you'll want to stay at the hotel."

She pulled off her hat, she made herself at home. Feeling better all the time, she went around examining the cabin. She rocked the table —the sawhorses wobbled. She bent and tried one of the cots, and looking up to find him gravely watching her, she smiled at him with a great rush of affection and said, "I think it will do very nicely here."

"You could have a lonesome summer."

"I'll manage, I'm sure." He looked so solemn, responsible, and concerned that she skipped up to him and hugged his arm.

"It's only women we're short of. Plenty of perfectly presentable men. Plenty of other kinds too. Plenty visitors likewise. I think Conrad and Janin are coming through. Every mining man has to see Leadville once."

The thought of Oliver's elegant brother-in-law in that cabin started her giggling. "Can you imagine entertaining Conrad here? Cooking him a steak on the Franklin? Walking around that table with a bottle of wine in a napkin?"

"Do him good. He's got effete."

"Anyway, by the time he comes we'll be fixed up. Can I buy some calico for curtains?"

"I'll take you to Daniel and Fisher's tomorrow."

Just then she looked out the window and saw a man running hard up the ditch bank. Below the standing team he jumped the ditch, and his corduroy coattails flew out behind. "Someone's coming in a terrible hurry," she said, and turned in time to see the doorway filled by a very tall young man, panting, ablaze with some news.

"Frank," Oliver said, "you're just in time to meet Mrs. Ward, our civilizing influence."

She thought she had never seen a face more alive. His brown eyes snapped and glowed, he was hot from running, the smile that he produced for her, swallowing both his panting and his news, showed a mouthful of absolutely perfect teeth. "Ah, welcome to Leadville!" he said. "What kind of trip did you have? How'd you like Mosquito Pass?"

"Not as well as I like it here," Susan said. "It must have been you who had a fire going for us. That made it nice and homey to arrive."

"I hunted around for flowers," Frank said. "I wanted to put our best foot forward, but I couldn't find any feet. Nothing's out yet. I was going to be here to greet you, too, but they started . . . You almost ran into something, you know that? Did you come through town?"

She saw, or half saw, a look from Oliver that checked him. She said, "We heard a lot of shouting. What was it?"

"A town like this is full of drunks," Oliver said.

"No!" Susan said, and she may have stamped her foot. "You shan't protect me from everything! Tell us, Mr. Sargent."

"Oh, it was . . . nothing much. Little . . . business."

He looked, breathing hard still, at Oliver. Oliver looked expressionlessly back, and then moved his shoulders as if giving up.

"Tell us," she said.

He looked at Oliver one last time for confirmation or authority. "They, ah, just hanged a couple of men. Out in front of the jail."

She heard him with a surprising absence of surprise. It was more or less the sort of thing she had learned to expect in mining camps from reading Bret Harte and *Leslie's Illustrated Newspaper*. Examining herself for horror or disgust, she found only a sort of satisfaction that now she had really joined Oliver where he lived his life, some corroboration of her notions of what the wife of a mining engineer might have to expect. "Who?" she said. "What for?"

Sargent spoke directly to Oliver. "One was Jeff Oates."

Oliver took the word without expression, thought a few seconds, flattened his mouth under the mustache, lifted his blue steady eyes to hers. "Our claim-jumping neighbor. He was a little crazy, like a dog that can't stand to see another dog with a bone. It didn't call for hanging."

"If you ask me," Sargent said, "he got just what he deserved. You can't simply go around . . ."

"Who was the other one?" Oliver said.

"A road agent that shot up the stage on the grade yesterday. They had him before he got to English George's."

"And he's dead before another sundown."

"It had to happen," Frank said earnestly. "There had to be an object lesson or two. If it isn't stopped it gets worse and worse."

But Susan was looking at her husband. "You knew it, didn't you? You saw what was happening. That's why we turned up the side hill."

"It didn't look good. I couldn't tell what it was." Wry-mouthed and squinting, he held her eye. "It's not the pattern. So far as I know, it's never happened before in Leadville. If it had, I wouldn't have let you come. This fireeater here thinks it ought to be repeated, but he's wrong. If it is, I won't let you stay. So you cool down, Frank, you hear? The longer we have vigilante law, the longer it will be before we get real law."

"I suppose," Susan said, confused. Frank took the rebuke with an exaggerated cringing gesture, protecting his head with his arms as if blows were falling on him.

Oliver said, "At least now you know why that stage driver was coming hell for leather down the pass and would have run over us if we hadn't got out of his way. You know why I wouldn't stop for the boys in the bogged-down ore wagon. The way for you to live in this place is to stay out of it."

Frank took the team to the livery stable for them, waving energetically from the buggy while they stood in the door. "What a nice boy," Susan said. "And *handsome*. He looks like Quentin Durward. Do you suppose he'd let me draw him sometime?"

"I expect he'd let you do about anything you wanted. He *is* a nice boy, stays away from women and bottles, knows his business, works hard. You can depend on him. He's only got one weakness. He's a warrior, that kid. The worst thing that ever happened to him was that he missed the war. He likes excitement a little too well, he won't take anything from anybody."

"No more should he. I'm sure he's many cuts above the average here."

"I never doubted it," Oliver said drily. "Now why don't I get you a bucket of ice water from the ditch and you can take your bath and then I'll take you down to supper at the Clarendon. I can't wait to hear that pandemonium fall silent as I walk you in."

She was struck by an appalling thought. "Is it near the jail? Would they have . . . ?"

"Cleaned up?" Oliver laughed. "Oates was a Mason. They'll have him all laid out for a lodge funeral by suppertime."

She went with him to get the water. "Why do you dip with the current instead of against it?"

"Get less junk in it that way."

"You know so much."

He did not reply, only held up his hand. Down below she heard the brassy chords of a band. "Isn't that something?" he said. "A half hour after they get through the hanging they tootle out the old band and march up and down as if nothing had happened."

Standing on the ditchbank looking down over the skinned gulch where the town lay fuming, she was face to face with the Western range. The late-afternoon sun rayed out through piled white clouds. Sweetened and mellowed by distance, the music rose up toward them, suggesting order, grace, civilization, Sunday afternoons on green commons. When the music paused, she heard at first only the whisper of the ditch, and then a deeper, farther sound, compounded of boots on hollow planks, stamp mills, voices, rumbling wagons—the sounds of Leadville's furious and incessant energy. She was thinking of Oliver associated with that productive frenzy, herself as an ally of the music, the two of them together as part of something new and strong.

With the dripping pail in his hand, Oliver watched her, smiling. "Now tell me the truth. Can you manage here, or shall we take you to the Clarendon?"

"Oh, here!"

"You don't think you'll get lonesome, away from other people."

"I've got my work. And you said they aren't people I should live with."

"We can ride, it's grand country. Frank or Pricey can take you if I can't."

"Who's Pricey?"

"My clerk. Oxford, don't you know. Penniless incompetent Englishman."

"Why it sounds absolutely social. Can we have evenings?"

Squinting against the flattening sun, his eyes were crinkled at the corners like the most flexible leather. The smile hid under his mustache. "How about one tonight?"

Maybe she would have blushed, maybe they would have had a great exchange of speaking looks on the ditchbank, maybe she would have silently rebuked him for unseemly intimations, maybe she would have become giddy, and run, and got him chasing her on that wide-open bench lighted like the stage for a pageant. How would I know? The altitude does peculiar things to people. The one thing I do know is that the misunderstanding that had begun on the pass that morning was all rubbed away, and they began their Leadville life in a state of euphoria.

4

Even in a Leadville cabin she was coddled.

Those first chilly mornings, she lay in her cot and watched sleepily through her eyelashes as Oliver squatted by the Franklin stove in his undershirt, his suspenders dangling, and blew the coals into flame through a handful of shavings. His movements were quick and sure, he worked intently. Above the darkness of his forearms and below the sunburned line on his neck his skin was very fair. When he opened the outside door the fume of his breath was white and thick, and the vicarious chill made her burrow deeper in the blankets. For a moment he stood there pail in hand, a rude, unidealized figure against a rectangle of bright steel sky—fully adapted, one she could trust to take care of things, a Westerner now of a dozen years' standing.

The door slammed, she heard him running. In two minutes he was back, the door banged inward, the pail sloshed over as he stepped inside. By that time she had decided to be awake.

How would she have looked, waking up? Because I never saw her anything but immaculate, I can't imagine her with mussed hair and puffy eyes, particularly when she was young. No curlers, I assume, not in 1879. If she curled her bangs, she curled them with a thing like a soldering iron, heated over stove or lamp. A nightcap? Perhaps. I might go to *Godey's Lady's Book* and learn these intimate secrets of the boudoir, I might not. Sears, Roebuck catalogues to tell a historian how a lady was supposed to look when opening her eyes on a new day wouldn't be along for some years. I doubt that she looked more angel than woman, as the smitten boy at New Almaden had thought. Not to her husband, and at six-thirty in the morning. But maybe even to her husband she shone against the log wall like a saint in a niche. Her rosy complexion would have been rosier from sleep, I suspect; her vivacity not less on the pillow than in the parlor. And she was one who woke chirping. She talked at him as he cooked.

He made the breakfast because, as he said, there was no point in her getting out in the cold, when he was a better camp cook than she was. He was, too, she admitted it. He could broil a steak, fry bacon or eggs or flapjacks or potatoes, make mush and coffee, in half the time and with half the effort she would have expended. He had a trick of chopping up frying hash browns with the edge of an empty baking powder can. He kept insects and dirt out of an opened can of condensed milk by plugging the two holes with matches. He could flip flapjacks so that they alighted in the mathematical center of the pan.

And it *was* cold. Leadville was said to have one month of summer, but no one would say when it began or ended. It had not yet begun. She propped herself against the logs, bundling into the heartwarmer that Augusta had sent her when she was carrying Ollie, and watched with interest her husband's efficient movements, thinking that this hour of the morning was their best time together.

"You didn't tell me when Conrad is coming," she said.

"Yes I did. Next week."

"We ought to ask him to stay with us."

His look went around the cabin, and then he leaned in sideways, squinting against the heat, to turn up the brown crust of the potatoes. "Where'd we put him?"

"I don't know. I suppose we can't. It just seems so unhomelike at the Clarendon."

"He might think it was a little *too* homelike here."

"I love it," she said. "I really love it, all except having to cook and eat and sleep and dress and wash and entertain all in one room. Can we build on an ell before Ollie comes?"

The coffeepot boiled over. He tipped its lid open with the edge of his hand. "You still think you want to bring him out?"

"I'm determined to. I won't have us separated again for so long."

The cabin was full of the smells of coffee and bacon, and she shook the covers, flapping away greasy odors, while she watched Oliver fork the bacon onto a tin plate and crack eggs into the grease. He did it with one hand, cracking the shells against the edge of the pan and then opening them upward with his long limber fingers until the insides fell out. She saw them solidify in the pan like golden-hearted, frilly edged flowers.

"Can you ride today?"

"Not today, I'm afraid. I've got to go over to Big Evans."

"Might I go along?"

He considered, squatting. "Not there. I'll send Frank or Pricey to take you out."

"Can you make it Frank? Pricey is such a goose. I'm always afraid he'll fall off, and I have to poke along because he bounces so if we run."

"It's easier to get along without Pricey. Anyway you shouldn't run a horse at this altitude."

"Yes sir," she said pertly. "And how did you manage day before yesterday to ride sixty miles? Your horse must be the fastest walker in Colorado."

"I go fast because I want to get back quick."

She loved the way his eyes rested on her, she thought he had a strong, masculine, *unflighty* sort of face. He looked like a contented man. And she was a contented woman, or would be as soon as she could get Ollie out.

He was gone by seven-thirty. For an hour she lay in bed, letting the stove and the sun work on the cabin's chill. Then she got up in her dressing gown and assaulted the disorder—made up the cots, washed the dishes, swept the floor. If she didn't do that at once, her disposition remained disheveled all day. She opened the door and the two windows to let the morning sweep away the cooking odors. Only when the place was clean and fresh could she settle down contentedly to drawing, reading, sewing, or writing letters.

Here is part of one to Augusta and Thomas, then following the spring northward into the Alps.

> Do you remember, by chance, a family named Sargent on Staten Island? General Timothy Sargent? Their son Frank, who is Oliver's assistant here, believes that his family and yours are slightly acquainted. You can imagine the feast of talk we had, the first time we sat down before our fire.
>
> Frank is a splendid boy. He extravagantly admires Oliver, "the best man to work for in Colorado," and he is indispensable to me when Oliver's business keeps him in the office or sends him off on some inspection trip. Frank chops my kindling, carries in my wood, comes (at six!) to build my fire, burns my rubbish, fetches my bundles from town, runs my errands, takes me riding. It is of course quite out of the question that I should go alone.

Such a gentlemanly boy Frank is, for these circumstances. Not that he isn't capable of dealing with anything that arises—he is six feet three and as limber as a blacksnake. He is intensely excited about the West, loves the adventure of it, delights in the strange people and the queer situations. But he has been gently reared, and is not inclined to sink to the level of life in these mountains. Every month he sends a third of his salary to his widowed mother, and when I asked him what he did for entertainment in Leadville—fearing the answer—he said there was not much to tempt him. He and Pricey, with whom he shares a shack, are both readers. The other night we had quite an earnest talk. He is consciously keeping himself *pure,* both as to the awful women he might meet in this place, and as to liquor, which he has seen destroy several of his friends. Liquor is a terrible temptation to lonely men cut off from their wives, or fighting for success they cannot attain. It is exhilarating to see someone like Frank determined to stand above it. On the other hand, Oliver tells me, he is manly to a degree, and only a little while ago had to put down a bully who presumed to think Pricey, with his English accent, amusing. The bully suffered a broken jaw, and is not yet quite able to speak again. Can you imagine knowing, and liking, a man who engages in fist fights? Yet here at least they are something a man of honor cannot entirely avoid.

I sister him, and flirt with him (a little). It is amusing and harmless since I am nine years older. The devastating thing about him is that he has those darkly glowing brown eyes like yours. His devotion is so open that of course Oliver has observed it. He understands, just as he somehow understands about thee and me. *How* he understands, I don't know. He is wise for his age, my nice husband. Actually he and Frank are much alike. They have the same eagerness for Western experience, and the same coolness, and the same worshipful way of looking at your frivolous friend. But Frank is less self-contained, and more addicted to talk. I have already drawn him into Miss Alcott's novel.

Isn't it queer, at my age and in this altitude, to discover what it means to have power over men! It gives one a twinge of understanding of the sort of woman one has never met, the sort who choose to *exercise* their power. I have three men around me, almost the only society I see, and all three would walk barefoot over coals for me. Do I not strike you as a sad adventuress? But how innocent and pleasant and harmless too, to have one man to cherish and one to sister and one to mother!

The one I mother is Ian Price, Oliver's clerk, whom we call Pricey. Oliver says he is a duffer, but keeps him on because he is so helpless and lonesome. I cannot fathom why he ever came to Leadville, unless it was that he was miserably unhappy where he was before. He is as little like a Western fortune hunter as you can imagine. His flesh seems to have been put on his bones by the lumpy handful. He stammers, blushes, falls over his own feet, and when he is being teased, or when something amuses him, he has a way of coming out with a great, pained, long-drawn "hawwww!" But in his way he is good company, for he is an even greater reader than Frank, and when we are alone he sometimes talks about books in a way that quite obliterates his usual embarrassment. He loves to sit in our rocker, before our fire, and read—not taking part in the conversation but somehow taking comfort from it, with an air of great content. Seeing him thus, I can't help thinking what his alternatives would be were we not here to give him a sort of home: the Clarendon's loud lobby, or the shack he shares with Frank, where he might lie reading in his bunk by the light of a lantern hung on a nail. . . .

Try a sample Leadville evening.

The light was gentle, a mixture of firelight and the soft radiance of two Moderateur lamps bought at a frightening price at Daniel and Fisher's. The cots were curtained off, the table was shoved against the wall, which was hung with the geological maps of the King Survey. Susan had put these up, not Oliver; and they were for decoration, not study. Frank was sitting on the floor with his chin on his knees and the firelight in his eyes. Between stove and wall Pricey sat reading, and the noise of his rocking creaked in the lulls of their talk like an overindustrious cricket.

"What are you reading that's so absorbing, Pricey?" Susan said.

Pricey did not hear her. His tiny feet in their clumsy boots came down tippy-toe, pushed against the floor, and floated upward again. His nose was ten inches from the page. His hand moved, a page turned, his feet came down, pushed, floated upward. The floor squeaked. They watched him, smiling among themselves.

"I think it's a total lack of vanity," Oliver said. "Anybody else who hears his name will look up, it'll jar him a little. Not Pricey, not when he's reading. Look at him, like a kid on a rockinghorse."

"I saw him riding that old Minnie mule along the road the other day with his nose in a book," Frank said. "Mule could have stumbled and tossed him down a shaft, he'd have gone right on reading. Maybe he'd have wondered why it got dark all of a sudden."

Oliver raised his voice slightly to say, "I may have to ask him not to come over here any more. He'll rock every nail out of the floor."

They projected their joking toward Pricey and he heard nothing. *Creak* creak, *creak* creak. The little boots tapped the planks, floated upward. Pricey turned another page. Out of her suppressed laughter Susan shook her head at the other two. Don't laugh at him. Don't make fun.

Oliver said, "There's one thing the oblivious Pricey doesn't know. That rocker *creeps*. Five minutes more and he'll be in the fire."

"I doubt if it'd get his attention," Frank said.

With preposterous daintiness the boots came down, tapped the planks, rose, hung, descended. *CREAK* creak, *CREAK* creak. Wetting his thumb, Pricey turned another page.

"I swear," Oliver said, and stood up. "This is serious."

He stepped along the wall to the bookcase that stood behind Pricey's chair. Pricey hunched his shoulders aside slightly to make passage room, and a small interrogative humming issued from his nose, but he did not look up. The rockers rose and fell. Standing close behind him, Oliver took in each hand a volume of the King Survey reports—great quartos that ran six pounds to the book, the concentrated learning of King, Prager, Emmons, the Hague brothers, a dozen others who had been Oliver's guides and models.

For a moment Susan was afraid he was going to drop the books on Pricey's unconscious head, and she made a restraining motion. But Oliver only stood a moment, adjusting to Pricey's rhythm, and then stooped quickly and shoved a book under each rocker.

Pricey stopped with a jolt, his head snapped back, his jaw snapped shut. He looked up startled into their laughter. His face went pink, his pale eyes circled wildly looking for a focus. "S-s-sorry!" he said. "What?"—and then the long acceptant "*hawwwww!*" like a groan.

Yet only a day or two after that, this same Pricey showed Susan some of the incongruous possibilities of Leadville. He had been the one delegated to take her riding, and they were down on the Lake Fork of the Arkansas at a place where they must ford. It was a time of high water, the infant Arkansas was swift and curly. "Come on, Pricey!" Susan called, and quirted her horse into the water.

The creek broke against his knees, and then as he surged carefully ahead, feeling for footing, against his shoulder. His hoofs were delicate among the slippery bottom stones. Susan pulled her foot out of the stirrup of the sidesaddle and sat precariously, thrilled and dazzled by the cold rush going underneath. When the water shallowed, the horse lunged out, shedding great drops, and as she felt for the stirrup she turned to see how Pricey was making it. There he came, strangling the horn with both hands. From midstream he sent her a sweet, desperate smile.

She guided her horse through willows and alders and runted birches, leaned and weaved until the brush ended and she broke into the open. She was at the edge of a meadow miles long, not a tree in it except for the wiggling line that marked the course of the Lake Fork. Stirrup-high grass flowed and flawed in the wind, and its motion revealed and hid and revealed again streaks and splashes of flowers—rust of paintbrush, blue of pentstemon, yellow of buttercups, scarlet of gilia, blue-tinged white of columbines. All around, rimming the valley, bare peaks patched with snow looked down from above the scalloped curve of timberline.

All but holding her breath, she pushed into the field of grass. The pony's legs disappeared, his shoulders forced a passage, grass heads and flowers snagged in her stirrup and saddle skirts. The movement around and beneath her was as dizzying as the fast current of the creek had been a moment before. The air was that high blue mountain kind that fizzes in the lungs. Rising in her stirrup to get her face and chest full of it, she gave, as it were, a standing ovation to the rim cut out against the blue. From a thousand places in the grass little gems of unevaporated water winked back the sun.

She heard Pricey come up and stop just behind her. His horse blew. But she was filling her eyes, and did not turn. Then she heard Pricey say, in his fine cultivated Oxonian voice, strongly, without the trace of a stammer,

> *Oh, tenderly the haughty day*
> *Fills his blue urn with fire.*

Who but Pricey? Where but Leadville?

Mice have gnawed Grandmother's Leadville letters and created some historical lacunae. The packet is thin, moreover. That much time in New Almaden and Santa Cruz produced a bale of correspondence. Leadville's letters number only thirty.

The reminiscences don't help much, and neither do the three novels that deal with the Leadville experience, sympathetically misunderstood from the fireside. Real people and real actions may be traced in them, but they operate within plots full of the scruples of attenuated virgins of a kind that Grandmother certainly never found in Leadville. Their heroes are young engineers like Oliver Ward reduced to pasteboard, their villains are claim jumpers and crooked managers. Once the heroine is the daughter of the villain, a device that Grandmother used again in a later story. The villain has to die repentant before the young lady can marry the upright engineer.

These fictions would have been pretty much the same, with only a repainting of the background scenery, if she had been writing about Tombstone or Deadwood. She really *was* protected, somewhat by her husband and just as much by her fastidiousness. The reality in these stories is only decorative.

But a Leadville as authentic as it is unexpected lies buried in the mouse-shredded letters. It is the Leadville that found its way to her fireside.

A camp that strikes it rich in the middle of a depression speaks as urgently to the well-trained as to the untrained. In Leadville, Harvard men mucked in prospect holes, graduates of MIT and Yale Sheffield Scientific School worked as paymasters and clerks and gunguards, every mine office was approached daily by some junior engineer with a diploma and a new mustache. The Clarendon Hotel heard the accents of Boston, New York, and London; Mosquito Pass was a major flyway for migrating mining experts and capitalists.

Leadville roared toward civilization like a runaway train. Amid talk of an opera house, three mine managers, including Oliver's distant cousin W. S. Ward, were planning houses on Ditch Walk, and hoped to have wives in them before another summer. The principal boarding-house at its Younger Sons Ball drew social lines as rigid in their way as Newport's. The best saloons were gorgeous with walnut, crystal, and William Morris wallpapers. All this was just beginning to fall into place, like the bits of colored glass in a kaleidoscope, when Susan settled down to pig it in her cabin on the ditch.

One morning a knock came on the door, and Susan opened it to see a stout, bright-eyed, self-assured little lady standing there. Helen Hunt Jackson, sent to her like a valentine by their mutual friend Augusta. As a literary lady married to a mining engineer, and resident in the West, Mrs. Jackson could hardly have been more reassuring to Grandmother. If Helen Hunt of Amherst, Massachusetts, was not lost when she became Helen Hunt Jackson of Denver, then why should Susan Burling of Milton, New York, lose her identity now that she was Susan Burling Ward of Leadville? The two were intimates within fifteen minutes.

Another day several wagons, many mules, and a half dozen men set up a camp higher on the ditch, in the edge of the aspens. This was the new United States Geological Survey party, all veterans of King's Survey of the Fortieth Parallel. A little while after they arrived, a long, thin, chinless, slouching man who wore his ugliness as elegantly as his snow-white buckskins rode down and made himself known: Samuel Emmons, one of the giants, Leadville's Homer, one of Oliver's heroes and an old companion of Prager, Clarence King, and Henry Adams. He had written a book that Oliver looked upon as a bible, and he had helped make the geological maps that he was now charmed to see pinned as decorations on the log walls. It took a woman, he said, to see the aesthetic possibilities of the Silurian.

Within days, Prager and Henry Janin came over the range, and within a week Clarence King himself, a man glitteringly famous, director of the Geological Survey, author of *Mountaineering in the Sierra Nevada*, climber of Mount Whitney, exposer of the great diamond hoax. Susan didn't think of him as "the best and brightest man of his generation," because John Hay hadn't yet made that remark about him; but she knew him as a literary man and she knew Oliver's respect for him as a scientist; she had heard of him as the wittiest of talkers and a prince of story tellers. In a tone somewhere between awe and a giggle, she wrote Augusta that in his tent at the Survey camp he was served by a black valet, that he possessed an apparently inexhaustible supply of fine wines, brandy, and cigars, and that his riding clothes, like those of Emmons, were made by London tailors out of snow-white deerskins dressed by Paiute squaws in the Carson Valley of Nevada.

Except for her report of one evening, her letters contain no samples of King's celebrated conversation. Perhaps the mice got them.

With King was a large good-natured man named Thomas Donaldson, chairman of the Public Lands Commission, and in the two months that their camp was pitched there it drew a stream of celebrities. Where did they spend their evenings? Grandmother's cabin, naturally. She was a lamp for every moth that flew. In her single room whose usable space was hardly fifteen feet square there assembled every evening an extraordinary collection of education, culture, talent, eloquence, reputation, political power, and intellectual force. There was no way to keep the two cots curtained off; they were always being exposed to serve as sofas. I doubt that Grandmother was offended to have her bedroom once again invaded; she was never more stimulated in her life. Braced for dutiful and deprived exile, ready to lie in the rude Western bed she had made, she found herself presiding over a salon that (she told herself more than once) Augusta's studio itself could hardly have matched for brilliance.

If you do not believe we live gaily in Leadville, let me tell you about our July Fourth. I had Mrs. Abadie and Mrs. Jackson, whose husbands had not returned from inspection trips. Mr. Ward dropped in with his hands full of wildflowers, and then Frank Sargent on his way fishing. He helped me get lunch—Oliver has burned his leg with nitric acid and can't stoop down as one must do to cook on our open Franklin. We had fish chowder (canned) from Boston, white muscat grapes (canned) from California, tea (English breakfast, contributed by Mr. Ward), tapioca pudding with raisins à la Leadville, contributed by the Geological Survey cook who saw we were having a celebration, and toast, made and burned by Frank. Our table service was somewhat permiscus. Frank sat on a packing box, Mr. Ward rocked in our rocker and pretended he was a bad little boy bent on spilling things (he is always the wag of the party, to his own great amusement), Oliver twirled in an old screw office chair and ate his grapes out of a Budweiser tumbler left over from our last picnic. After lunch an ice cream man came mournfully crying his wares along the ditch. Oliver and Mr. Ward rushed out (or Mr. Ward rushed and Oliver hobbled), and Mr. Ward bought some oranges as well. When we went down to dinner that evening there was a foot race going on, accompanied by a brass band. Nothing can be done here, from a tightrope performance to a show by a lot of short-skirted girls at the Great Western Amphitheater, without a band. After supper Mr. Ward took us to Chittenden's to select carpets and cretonnes for his "trousseau"—he is building a house near us and next year will have a wife. You have no idea what elegant things can be bought here for money—lots of it.

Somehow we kept picking up other friends, and when we arrived home we *bulged* our little cabin. Mr. Jackson and Mr. Abadie had returned, which gave us three sedate couples, but there were in addition Mr. King, Mr. Emmons, and Mr. Wilson of the Survey, Conrad Prager and Henry Janin who have recently arrived, Mr. Donaldson of the Public Lands Commission, Oliver's clerk Pricey, who hid under the chairs, practically, but immensely enjoyed himself, and Frank, who had returned from fishing with two fish which he handsomely presented to me. He helped me do the dishes left from lunch. Mr. King went up to his camp and brought back a bottle of brandy, and we toasted the republic and sang war and jubilee songs around the fire.

Most of these people are skeptical about our determination to bring Ollie out, and my determination to stay myself. Mr. King and Mr. Jackson, in a cynical way, pretended to believe that long and frequent separations are the only basis for a sound marriage. This brought Mrs. Jackson up yipping like a little terrier, for like me she followed her husband West. Yet even she doubts Leadville as a home. She urged Denver upon us. Leadville, she said, is too high. Grass won't grow here, hens won't lay, cows won't give milk, cats can't live. Needless to say, none of them persuaded us. Oliver, who normally tests his condition by how he feels after a hundred-mile ride, says he never felt better, and I must say I feel exhilarated.

I closed the evening by getting out a note I had just had from Professor Rossiter Raymond, who had left us a little while before, after a mine inspection. He had enjoyed himself by our fire, but had caught a tremendous cold as soon as he left the mountains. He sent this humorous little roofer to express his sentiments.

> *Let princes cough and sneeze*
> *In their palaces of ease*
> *Let colds and influenzas plague the rich;*
> *But give to me instead*
> *A well-ventilated head*
> *In a little log cabin on a ditch.*

Don't you think we have pleasant times? The only single hard thing is that Oliver has to be so much away inspecting mines that, as they say here, are too poor to pay, too rich to quit. He envies the Survey men, who can ride off in the morning with a sandwich and a geological hammer and spend the whole day hunting fossils, or just looking at magnified mountains through a theodolite.

"Let me pose you a question," said Helen Hunt Jackson. "It has nothing to do with the Indian. I know how Americans respond when their interests conflict with the Indian's rights. They respond dishonorably. But I would like to know something else. How does a government scientist act when he finds himself in possession of information worth millions to some capitalist, when all his closest friends are mining experts in search of precisely that sort of information?"

Filling the rocker but not rocking, she sat with arms folded across her stomach, her shoes hanging like sash weights two inches off the floor. Imperturbably she met the smiles, murmurs, and cries of mock dismay—when she chose to, she could make every eye in the room turn her way, every mouth stop talking. All but Mr. Jackson, who looked at the ceiling and clapped a hand to his brow.

Clarence King raised his plump, animated face and laughed. "I hope you're not suggesting that any of us would have trouble telling the public interest from our own."

"I suggest nothing," said Mrs. Jackson comfortably. "I ask a question that occurs to me. Here sit you geologists charged with surveying the resources of the Public Domain, and here sit your friends whose whole business it is to get hold of such information, preferably before it's published. It seems to me to offer a nice ethical problem."

"Now," said her husband, "you see the consequences of letting women in where men are transacting business. She'll bring on a congressional investigation."

"Tell me, Mr. King," said Mrs. Jackson. "You're the head of this great new bureau. Have you never been tempted to drop a word and make a friend's fortune?"

Hoots of pained protest. King, spreading his hands, said, "Should you be asking *me*? All I have is authority. I defer to Emmons, who has information."

"There speaks a man who has been questioned by many Congressmen," said Conrad Prager.

"If Emmons refuses to answer, I can order him to," King said.

"Why should I refuse?" said Emmons. From the right-hand horn of their conversational crescent he turned his chinless, amused face to the middle, where Mrs. Jackson sat like Buddha in a bustle. "What's information for, except to inform? What higher bond is there than friendship? What virtue outranks loyalty? Of course I drop confidential words. There isn't a man here who isn't richer for my friendship. I'm a good man to know."

Protests, cries of "Judas!" W. S. Ward, the wag, pretended to take from his wallet and burn in the fire certain incriminating papers. From over against the wall, Oliver squinted through the smoke of his cigar. Frank and Pricey were crowded back on Susan's cot in the corner.

"You choose to be frivolous," said Mrs. Jackson. "What would you say if a Congressman did ask you such a question? As one sometime might."

"But Helen," said Henry Janin from the nearer cot, "none of these geologists has any information that's worth thirty cents to your husband or me. I've pumped them, I know. The Survey's function is to publish on pretty maps what's already known to everyone."

"Including the diamond-producing formations," Emmons said into his empty brandy glass.

It seemed to Susan that for a moment everybody held his breath. She thought in dismay, It's the kind of remark *duels* are fought over! But Janin only reeled from the hips, contorting his dark Creole features into an expression of anguish, and with his hand on his heart said in a high voice, "Unfair! Murder most foul!"

"Poor Henry," King said. "Deceived by unscrupulous men, he vouched for the authenticity of that wretched diamond mine. So a government scientist, whom out of modesty I forbear to name, had to expose the fraud. It very neatly demonstrates the difference you inquire about, being private interest and government principle."

Conrad Prager, consulting his long beautiful hands, said, "I've always wondered about that case, if it wasn't a put-up job. Private expert and government scientist could have planned the whole thing together, hired their accomplices, salted the mine. Janin could have gone and inspected it, all properly blindfolded and all that. Then comes King, like a knight on a white horse, to expose it—well after the accomplices have flown. Janin consoles himself for the trifling loss of his reputation with a good slice of cash—takes the cash and lets the credit go, you might say—and King gets not only cash but a great deal of credit. It's like letting thieves into the vaults of the Bank of England and then knighting them for crying 'Stop thief!' after they've stolen everything."

"Must I bear this?" Janin said.

They were all laughing, Susan not least. How characteristic, she was thinking, that these men of great capacity, captains and heroes involved in great affairs, should take their accomplishments as a light-hearted joke, and their expertness with such levity that they could joke Mr. Janin about his error, accepting the fact that they were his equals in that as in other things. Their life was the life toward which Oliver had always aspired, and she for him—a life that could provide real elegance and association with first class minds. Stopped for a moment while she watched Oliver, in shirt sleeves, sitting on the floor, reach King's brandy bottle across to Emmons, she said, "I never till now knew how unprincipled you are, Mr. King."

King said, "I call the jury's attention to the way in which speculation has become supposition, supposition certainty, and certainty accusation. It's a lesson in the workings of the expert mind, which can go from a hunch to an affidavit, and from an affidavit to a fee, within minutes. With great authority the expert says what is not necessarily so."

"I was only suggesting some of the possibilities of government science," Prager said.

"Now that you've abandoned ship and joined the enemy. Tell the people what's happened to Ross Raymond, as a possibility of private expertise."

Prager laughed and laid his hand on his thigh. "Alas."

"Alas, why?" Jackson asked.

"Alas his mine is played out. It's been high-graded to death."

"According to whom?"

"According to an upright government scientist, who just might have been tipped off by a private expert. They both got here too late to keep him from making a mistake that's going to cost somebody a lot of money."

"Oh, what a shame," Susan said. She had liked Rossiter Raymond, and he had been so uplifted by the altitude, and the prospects of the mine, and the company in her cabin. "He was such a good companion," she said.

"When he had that well-ventilated head here," Prager said. "Well, he's like Henry, he'll get over his error, unless he should make another mistake and come back to Denver and meet some of his principals. Then he'd *really* have a well-ventilated head."

"Which does not answer my original question," said Mrs. Jackson, placid in her rocker. "I know mining experts make mistakes—my heavens, I'm married to one. Mr. Janin pretends to think they are paid by investors to tell investors what investors want to hear. By that rule Mr. Raymond made no mistake at all. By any rule he hasn't been dishonest. But how does a government scientist remain honest? I read newspaper editorials saying that Mr. King and Mr. Donaldson and Major Powell and Secretary Schurz are inaugurating a period of unfamiliar integrity in the Department of the Interior. Given the temptations, how can you guarantee any such thing?"

King's lips pursed, his bright blue eyes looked at once amused and watchful. Intelligence jumped in them, words formed on his lips but did not fall. He looked a question at Donaldson, but Donaldson pushed the unspoken suggestion away with bearlike hands.

"Well," King said, "Schurz has it easy. He's a crusading Dutchman, honesty has brought him to power and there's no reason he should change. He finds it as natural to remain honest in office as Mrs. Jackson would. Donaldson has it easy, too. His report on the public lands will be the only thing of its kind ever undertaken in this country, incomparably better than anything we've had, but Western Congressmen will seize on its information and ignore its recommendations, and bury the report so efficiently that nobody will ever offer poor Tom a bribe worth taking. Powell also has it easy. Having only one hand, and having that in a dozen things, he has no other to hold out. I'm the one to pity. I'd prefer to be honest but I'd like very much to be rich. It's a precarious position."

"I shall begin to believe the *Tribune* can't be believed," said Mrs. Jackson with a smile.

"You know," said Oliver unexpectedly from his seat against the wall, "I'd kind of like to hear you *answer* that question of Mrs. Jackson's."

It was the wrong note. They were all having such fun, like skaters cutting figures on rubbery ice, and now Oliver had clumsily fallen through. His remark suggested criticism of King's playfulness. Playfulness was part of his charm. No one doubted his integrity in the least —who in the country had demonstrated more? She bent her brows very slightly at Oliver behind the semicircle of heads, but the damage was done. She could feel King, Prager, Janin, Emmons, all of them, with their impeccable social awareness, adjusting with the slightest changes of position and expression to the new tone.

"You mean you're serious," King said.

"I certainly am," said Mrs. Jackson.

"Me too," said Oliver.

She wished he had not taken off his coat, hot as the cabin was. With his brown corded forearms and his sunburned forehead he seemed one fitted for merely physical actions, like a man one might hire to get work done, not one who could devise policy and direct the actions of others. With a sad, defensive certainty she saw that he lacked some quality of elegance and ease, some fineness of perception, that these others had. It seemed to her that he sat like a boy among men, earnest and honest, but lacking in nimbleness of mind.

"How does one guarantee the probity of government science," King said,

"Exactly."

King examined his nails. Lifting his eyes from those, he threw across at Oliver a look that Susan could not read. It seemed friendly, but she detected in it some glint of appraisal or judgment. Suddenly aware of the thickness and warmth of the air, she rose quietly and opened the window above the table and sat down again. The cabin held an almost theatrical waiting silence, into which now, from the opened window, came the mournful sounds of a night wind under the eaves.

King let them wait. In her mood of critical appraisal, Susan reflected that when he was younger than Oliver—far younger, no more than twenty-five—he had been able to conceive his Survey of the Fortieth Parallel, and without money of his own, or influence beyond what he could generate by his own enthusiasm, get it funded by a skeptical Congress. He had impressed Presidents and made himself an intimate of the great. His reputation had gone around the world. But Oliver had been unable to persuade anybody in San Francisco to put money behind his demonstrated formula for hydraulic cement.

She was watching King, who now smiled at her out of the corners of his eyes. "It's quite simple," he said to Mrs. Jackson. "You pick men you would trust with your life, and you trust them with the Public Domain."

The cabin murmured with approval. Over on her cot, Frank shook an enthusiastic fist in the air toward Oliver. Susan herself clapped her hands, she couldn't help it, and she couldn't help being aware that part of her enthusiasm was for King's reply and part was relief that Oliver's insistence had not spoiled the talk, but elevated it.

Helen Jackson rocked and unclasped her arms from across her stomach. "That's very well said. Let us hope you can find enough men you would trust with your life. Now tell me, how do you manage the private experts? How do you keep their association with your men from being profitable to a few rather than to the public? How do you prevent talk?"

"Talk you can't stop," King said. "But I can tell you to their faces, Madame, that the kind of men I try to pick for the Survey can be trusted as surely with their associations as they can with the Public Domain. What is more, any mining man in this room, including that henpecked man Mr. Jackson, would be as slow to take advantage of association with the Survey as the Survey would be to permit it."

Smiling the widest of smiles, Mrs. Jackson rocked backward, then forward, and on the forward rock stood up. "I've been working too long on the Indians. That wretched history has made a cynic of me. I thought I would try you, and I'm satisfied. Mr. Jackson, we must go."

Susan felt that they had been collectively working toward a climax that they were wise to cut short. Everybody rose, Oliver's two helpers slid out the door so as not to be in the way. Such dears they were, and so right in their instincts. Shaking hands with W. S. Ward, she sent past him a warm look, first at Pricey and then at Frank, who said something elaborate and silent and then disappeared. Then Ward was gone, and Helen Jackson's plump bosom was pressed against hers, with a hard brooch watch between them.

"My dear Susan, without your house Leadville would be a desert."

She and her husband went. From the doorway, standing in the soft, buffeting, strangely warm wind, Susan saw them angle down the welted ditch in moonlight pale as milk. The mountains, luminous and romantic, lay all across the western horizon.

Emmons took her hand, then Janin—ugly chinless man, ugly crooked-faced Creole, both charming. Then Conrad Prager, whose good looks were as elegant as their ugliness: the old shooting coat hung on him like ermine. Finally Clarence King, who held her hand and gave her his full, warm, enveloping attention. She said, "If I had not heard it from Conrad's lips I would never have believed your iniquity, and if I hadn't heard it from yours, I would never have known how noble you are. We should all be grateful for you."

"Frail," King said. "Mortal and frail. I can sing my own praises until the first scandal. What we should be grateful for is you." His full-lidded, bright blue eyes fixed on hers with an easy, flattering familiarity, he kept hold of her hand in the doorway. "Let me second Mrs. Jackson. There are things about this cabin that make me gnash my teeth, one of them being that it should all belong to your undeserving husband. You hear that, Oliver? You should live on your knees. Not only do you have one of the few wives in Leadville, you have to have *such* a wife." To Susan he said, "I forgive him only on condition that my knock is never ignored."

Again he looked at Oliver, lightly smiling, as if there were some sort of understanding or question between them. Oliver said, "She'd open it even if I objected."

Their look broke off easily. Was there, Susan wondered again, a faint condescension on King's part? How much did these men know about Oliver? How much might Conrad have told them? The notion flicked into her mind that King thought Oliver Ward inferior to his wife. At once her mind began justifying and explaining, it called her attention to the injustice of a world in which Mr. King's acts of probity made him a national hero and Oliver's only lost him his job. Why hadn't she thought to turn the talk to inventiveness, so that she could have mentioned Oliver's creation of cement? Then they wouldn't all leave his house thinking of him as somehow *junior,* shaking his hand with this edged, polite condescension.

Oliver obviously did not feel it. He said, "Thank you for the brandy—again."

"A trifle," King said. "Less than Henry's reputation. Don't tell Mrs. Jackson, but I have my valet steal it from the White House cellar. It's one of the perquisites of government service."

He gave them, one after the other, the smile that melted people and made them eager to believe or serve him. Henry Adams said of him, much later, that he had something Greek in him, a touch of Alcibiades or Alexander, and Susan would have agreed. She stood hugging herself in the doorway, collecting the tossed-back good nights, watching their shadows ripple ahead of them in the windy moonlight as they turned up the ditch. When they were only an unseen grating of boots in gravel, she shut the door and turned, not entirely contented in mind.

"Well," she said. "Mrs. Jackson ended the evening with a hard question."

"And got a good answer."

"He's charming company."

"He's a great man."

"Yes," she said, somewhat surprised. "I suppose he is." She went to open both casements wide, and came back to open the door.

"Good idea," Oliver said. "We sort of smoked the place up."

She thought he watched her curiously as she turned off the lamps. They undressed in the dark, kissed lightly, and lay down, each in his separate narrow cot. The wind blew through the cabin, bellying the curtains bunched on their wire, wakening a curl of flame in the fire. Gradually the room expanded into bluish dusk. Out the open door the hillside swam in pale light, and in the visible strip of sky a cloud, dark silver with bright edges, blazed like something just out of a smelter pot. The air flowing across her felt fresh, cool, high, and late. She lay experimenting with the shadow of her hand in the slash of moonlight from the window; and still thinking rebelliously about his lacks, about his incorrigible juniorness, she said in argument against her own discontent, "It was you who got him to answer seriously."

"I wanted to hear what his answer really was."

"You ought to speak up more in company."

"That's what you're always telling me."

"It's true. If you don't, people will think you haven't anything to say."

"I don't."

"Oh, Oliver, you do too! But you just sit back."

"Like a bump on a log," Oliver said. Did his voice growl with the surliness which meant that any minute he would shut up completely and let her go on urging in the dark, getting herself more and more entangled and unhappy and exposing more and more her disappointment in him? Because that was what it was. She wanted more for him, and better, than he apparently wanted for himself.

But he didn't close up. In a moment he said, almost as if he sensed a clash coming on and wanted to avoid it as much as she did, "If I listen I might learn something. I won't learn anything listening to myself."

"Other people might."

"Not any of those people."

"You mean they're incapable of learning?"

"I mean they already know anything I could tell them."

"You could have told them something about integrity, when that subject came up. What was more to the point than your experience with Kendall or Hearst?"

He barked once, incredulously. He heaved over in the cot to face her. "What should I have said? 'Speaking of integrity, let me tell you about the time I told George Hearst where to head in?'"

"Of course you're right. I should have told them."

"If you had, I'd have died right there."

"But they ought to *know* you! You sit so silent they'll all think you're nobody, and it isn't true. You don't want to seem like Pricey."

Now surliness did roughen his voice. "You can always tell me from Pricey because I don't rock."

"Oh, Oliver," she said hopelessly, "be serious. Those are some of the most important people in the world in your field. You owe it to yourself to make a good impression."

"Did I insult anybody?"

"No, you just never *say* anything. Mr. King and Mr. Emmons won't have any idea how good you are at things, and how much you can *do*."

He said something muffled by the pillow.

"What?"

"I said, 'They know what I can do.'"

"How could they, possibly?"

"If they didn't, they wouldn't have asked me to join the Survey."

For a moment she lay completely still, with her face turned toward his shadowy shape. The room snowed slowly with flakes of luminousness. "They did? When?"

"This afternoon."

"But you didn't *say* anything!"

"No," he said with a little laugh. "I never do. Matter of fact, I never had the chance. Everybody else has been talking seventeen to the rod."

"But why didn't one of them say something tonight?"

"I suppose they're waiting till I've had a chance to talk it over with you."

"And you were going right to sleep!"

"I didn't want to keep you awake all night thinking about it."

"Oliver," she said, "they must think *very* well of you. If we can believe Mr. King, it means he'd trust you with his life."

"King's got a literary side. What it means is, he'd trust me with the Public Domain. Or with a job."

She slid out of bed and sat on the edge of his cot. His arm curled to hold her there, and she bent and said quickly into his neck, behind his ear, "Will thee forgive me?"

"Sure. What for?"

"For wanting to make thee over. I'm a foolish woman, I'm too much in love with talk and talkers. Talk isn't that important. What's important is thee. Thee is dear to me."

"I'm awful glad to hear it," he said. "Come inside, you're shivering."

Obediently she slid in beside him. The sagging narrowness of the cot jammed them together. "Will thee take it?" she asked.

"That depends on you."

"Thee'd be happier."

"Maybe. I hate all this lawing and claim jumping and swearing to false affidavits and all this playing expert in a game where both sides are crooked. It'd be nice to do a job that just expanded knowledge."

"Thee could, I know thee could." She lay still, then she said, "That's almost the first thing thee ever said to me."

"What are you talking about?"

"I was drawing in the library at the Beaches'. Thee said 'It must be nice to do what you like and get paid for it.'"

"All right, I don't take it back. Look at Emmons, as relaxed about Leadville as if he didn't give a hoot what goes on in it, or who owns what, and yet he practically made it. Everybody in the place, even the pick and shovel man at the end of a drift, consults his book. That ought to make a man feel good."

"What would Frank and Pricey do?"

"They could have the office. Frank's got a degree from MIT, which is more than I've got. He could handle it right now."

"I'd hate to see them left out, they both admire thee so."

"I'll see they're not left out."

His hands were moving on her. Often, when he was in that mood, she put them away, but now she let them come under the nightgown, all over her. She laughed a little because there was no room for his elbows, it was like making love inside a culvert. "I love thee," she said, and kissed him all over his face. "Does thee mind? I love thee even if thee isn't a talker."

"I don't mind a bit."

"Now can we bring Ollie? Can we start the ell tomorrow?"

"First things first," Oliver said through his teeth. He helped her to sit up, he stripped the nightgown over her head and exposed her in the wash of bluish light. As if she were infinitely precious and infinitely fragile, he touched her. She had the feeling that he was afraid she might pop like a soap bubble.

"King's right," he said with his lips against the parting between her breasts. "Who am I to deserve this?"

"Thee deserves everything. More than everything." Her desire to touch and be touched was so strong that she feared he might be repelled. She felt wanton and wild, she couldn't get enough of his mouth. "I love thee," she said. "Oh, darling, I do love thee, I do, I do!"

6

Shelly's stay as my house guest, or perhaps the fact that I have had a look into her private life and she has had a glimpse of me being cared for like an infant by her mother, has led her to adopt a more familiar tone with me than I quite like. She acts as if she had been employed as confidential adviser, keeper, critic, teaching assistant, and lay psychiatrist. I can see her "studying" me and drawing conclusions. I suppose my routines *are* pretty dull, and I shouldn't be surprised that she exercises herself interpreting her boss. Which is no reason she should feel free to talk to the boss about her half-assed interpretations. And I made the mistake of having her type up all the tapes that I was sure contained no personal matter. I would have been better advised to keep her from seeing any of the book.

This afternoon, after she got through typing some of the Leadville chapters, she asked me if I didn't think I was being a little inhibited about my grandparents' sex life. "Because it's a novel," she says. "It isn't history—you're making half of it up, and if you're going to make up some of it, why not go the whole way? I mean, it's tantalizing. You get close to dealing with their sex life, and blip, you turn off the light. Two or three times. Once on the honeymoon, once at Santa Cruz, now once in Leadville."

"I may look to you like a novelist, but I'm still a historian under the crust," I said. "I stick with the actual. That's what *they* would have done, turned off the light."

"I *know*, all that business about never seeing your wife naked. They were so puritan about their bodies in those days, it was bound to have screwed up their minds. Can you leave out anything that basic and still have a valid book? Modern readers might find a study of the Victorian sex life interesting and funny."

I felt like asking her, if contemporary sexual attitudes are so much healthier than Grandmother's, how Grandmother managed to get through a marriage that lasted more than sixty years, while Shelly

Rasmussen hides out in her parents' house at the age of twenty or so to escape the attentions of her liberated and natural lover. But I only said, "Interesting in what way? Funny how?"

I suppose because she has worn pants much of her student life, she feels free to sprawl on the back of her neck, with her worn loafers stretched halfway across the room. From where I sat in the dormer I could see her studying me through her hair, getting all ready for one of those open-hearted open-ended rap sessions that the young have adapted from the David Susskind show and learned to call education. They can go on for hours, and reveal all. Combined with encounter techniques they can empty the well and cleanse the soul and bore the hell out of anybody over twenty-five. The afternoon light was in her squarish face. She squinted shrewdly, she burbled with her hoarse laughter. "Well, it couldn't have been all that decorous, could it? They had sex with their eyes shut so they could pretend everything was on a high plane. Aren't hypocritical people sort of funny?"

It happens that I despise that locution "having sex," which describes something a good deal more mechanical than making love and a good deal less fun than fucking. Also I don't think anybody's sex life, Grandmother's included, very funny, unless you mean funny-peculiar, and Shelly didn't mean that. She meant funny-ha-ha, funny-hypocritical, funny-absurd. I had imagined that Leadville love scene, exceeding my license as a historian, because I felt that just then she was fighting against her ingrown gentility and snobbery, ashamed of herself for having been ashamed of her husband, and making contrite and affectionate amends. I had meant that scene to be tender. I meant it to clear away, at least for the time, all the cobwebs. I wanted it to shine the windows and polish the tarnished feelings like a good spring housecleaning. Which I have known a good love scene to do.

So I replied pretty sharply, "I wouldn't know. One of the quaint things about the Victorian sex life was that it was private. I doubt that they replayed every hand and rehashed all their honor count and playing tricks. They didn't have all these compulsions to verbalize, they didn't appear to get a sexual thrill out of words. The fact is, I haven't the slightest idea how good a lay Grandmother was. I have no idea— yes, I do too, but not from anything she said or wrote—how she looked upon *fellatio* and the other delights. Is that what you miss?"

I jarred her. She looked like a dog that had just for the hell of it barked at a stone dog on a lawn, and been barked back at. In spite of that bass-baritone and that air of amused assurance, she is definitely female. She might under some circumstances be submissive, like these dreary girls you see padding along in the moccasin tracks of hippies. Had she been one of those? For a few seconds I entertained the possibility.

She blinked, but within a second she had recovered the ironic widening smile and the ironic glance of the gray eye. She shrugged up her shoulders, obviously just *enjoying* this discussion no end. "I didn't mean, emancipate her from all her hangups. That wouldn't be historically sound, would it? I just meant, couldn't you give us a little more of the *scene*, then we'd understand all these artificial restraints for what they are."

"What are they?"

"What are they? Conventions. Restraints. Inhibitions. Hangups."

"Which of course she operated by. She had them. Her society had them."

"But you could cut through them!" Shelly said. All eager to instruct me, she sat forward. "There are hints in the letters that give her away. She tells Augusta once that 'that incorrigible shyness has passed,' and another time she says, 'Between my husband and me things are *all right*,' underlined. You could extrapolate from hints like that."

"Please," I said. "You've been taking courses in these jargon pseudo-sciences that my son teaches. If I extrapolated, as you suggest, the resulting sex scenes would be mine, not hers. She valued her privacy, she would never in this life have extrapolated. Neither would I. I would no more extrapolate in public than I would go to the bathroom on the parlor rug."

That brought out her big *ho ho ho*. She rocked forward, her hair fell over her breast and she threw it back with that irritating gesture. She was right where she wanted to be, digging up the roots of things, exposing all the shameful shams.

"That's what I was *telling* you. It's *your* inhibitions that are showing, not hers. I suppose she did have them, but that's no reason you have to, in 1970. We've learned to accept things, and the words for things, and be honest about the way we are. We don't need those purely cultural patterns of convention. Did you hear what you just said? 'Go to the bathroom.' Why?"

"Because I never learned to say shit before a lady," I said, thoroughly irritated. "Because I don't believe in progress in quite the way you seem to. You believe in it more than Grandmother did. As for those purely cultural patterns of convention you think I ought to escape from, they happen to add up to civilization, and I'd rather be civilized than tribal or uncouth."

She is not utterly insensitive. She looked at me with her head tipped to one side, and said with her mouth pulled down, "I've made you mad."

"Not personally," I said. "Just culturally."

The way I was sitting, talking at an angle, I was aimed at Grandmother's portrait, pensive and downcast in the cool light that flooded the wall covered with letters from people she had admired and been admired by. "Look at her picture," I said. "What's in that face? Hypocrisy? Dishonesty? Prudery? Timidity? Or discipline, self-control, modesty? Modesty, there's a word 1970 can't even conceive. Is that a woman I want to show making awkward love on a camp cot? Do you want to hear her erotic cries? Is that a woman to snicker at because she was a lady, and fastidious?"

"I didn't mean that, exactly. I was just thinking from the point of view of the modern reader. He might think you were ducking something essential."

"That's too bad. Hasn't the modern reader got any imagination?"

"Well, *you* know. People nowadays understand things, they can sniff out the dishonesty when somebody tries to cover something up or leave it to the imagination. How would it be if every modern novel did it like Paolo and Francesca—'That day they read no more'?"

"O.K., so I haven't fooled you with my dishonest methods," I said. "Just leave me there with old hypocritical Dante."

"Oh, you know what I mean!" she said, and slid off her chair to sit cross-legged on the floor. "Times change! Like, people have got *tired* of all that covering up. You see kids who just throw off their clothes, they want to break down that barrier and get natural again. You see it all the time, it's just . . . open. Like . . ." Earnest and pleased with herself, her bow bent against error, her lips touched with a live coal, she sat on my floor there and did her best to bring me into the twentieth century. She sat back on her braced hands and eyed me, ironic, superior, and ribald. "I don't know if I should tell you this."

"I don't either."

"Well . . ." Actually she was determined to tell me, she couldn't have been stopped from telling me any more than some of her kids could be stopped from throwing off their clothes and cleansing the world of its hypocrisy. She bowed her head on her knees so that her hair fell to the floor, she lifted her head and looked at me half smiling through the foliage. "What would you say to something like this," she said. "Suppose you were at a party where everybody knew everybody else—friends, you know?—and everybody was stoned, and it turned into a gang bang? Suppose four or five fellows banged this girl while everybody else watched. Would that seem crude to you, or dirty, or immoral, or something?"

"I'd have to say we'd come a long way from Grandma."

She laughed, this lady missionary. "You're not kidding. But how would you take something like that? It wouldn't necessarily be crude, or vicious, or anything, would it? They'd just be doing their thing, what they felt. They wanted it and so did she, so they did it. I suppose that shocks you, doesn't it?"

"Some things offend me. I'm not very easy to shock."

"But why be offended?" she said, and leaned to hug her knees and fix her wide gray eyes on me. She had quit smiling. She looked, in fact, strained. "Isn't it just an old-fashioned code that makes you feel that moral disapproval? Once you get rid of that, isn't a scene like that just as natural as two people going to bed in a dark room? Isn't watching it sort of like watching a show—Living Theater or something? Who loses anything?"

"It doesn't sound as if anybody there had much to lose," I said. "Assuming this really happened. Did it?"

She wagged her head, her chin on her knees. "It happened, yeah."

"So nobody lost anything. Maybe they even gained something—VD, for example. I understand it's making a comeback under the modernized rules."

She shook off that suggestion almost irritably. Her mood had changed within two minutes into something somber and brooding and half angry. "So you *don't* think it was natural, or like a show or a parlor game."

I began to wonder if she was talking about herself; I'm still not sure she wasn't. I said, "Would you take your parents?"

"Oh, wow!"

"Would you talk about it with them?"

"What do you think?"

"But you don't mind talking about it with me. I'm as old as they are."

"You're different. You're educated, you've been around, you're not buried in the dark ages. I feel I can talk to you. Am I wrong?"

"I hope not," I said. "But just now you were criticizing me for my dishonest treatment of Grandmother's sex life."

"Oh . . . crap," Shelly said. Clearly I inhibit her more than she admits. "I don't know. What *do* you think of a scene like that?"

"I think you're describing a kind of hell," I said. "You're talking about people who have become sub-human. Sub-mammal. Sub-worm. I wonder if even bilharzia worms, which are locked in copulation all their lives, ever sit around and watch other bilharzia worms copulate? I think our sickness has gone so far we aren't even sure it's sickness."

"Yeah," Shelly said. "I knew I shouldn't have told you. I don't know. I suppose it *is* sick. But . . . Isn't sex the business of the people having it? That's what Larry always says. Shouldn't they be able to do it as they please, in public if that's the way it suits them? The audience can walk out if it isn't entertained." Irritable and moody, she shook her hair back and leaned back on her braced hands and scowled at me. Then the scowl broke. "But that's a different thing from your book. In a book, I think sex ought to be written about just like anything else."

I twitched the chair a little further askew. I liked neither the confessional nor the evangelical aspects of that conversation. "Ah," I said, "*is* it like everything else?"

Ho ho ho. Good. We were off the confessional. "All right," she said, "it's your book. Just pretend you've had a fan letter signed 'Modern Reader' saying 'I like your book fine but why do you draw the curtain across the love scenes'?"

"I thought it was the light I turned off."

"Same thing."

She was laughing, bowed over her cross-legged Yogi squat with her hair hanging to the floor. If I had not been what I am, her mother's broken doll, a grotesque, and three times her age at that, I would have thought she had excited herself with her own talk, confessional, evangelical, or otherwise. Her eyes had a moist shine in them that a sound man would have had to make a decision about. I suppose the piquancy for her is not in the talk, which is standard fare in the crowd she has been running with, but in getting the Gorgon to discuss these emancipated matters with its stone lips.

I said, "When you come right down to it, I neither pulled the curtain nor turned off the light. If you're going to be a literary critic you're going to have to learn to read what's there. In that scene you just typed, the room is full of refracted moonlight and the door is wide open and the curtains are pulled back and the night air of the mountains is blowing through. For Victorians they weren't doing so badly. It's just unfortunate that their little love scene didn't do everything a love scene is supposed to do."

"Why? Didn't the housecleaning last?"

"Maybe a half hour. Then she found out that if he joined the Survey he'd be posted for winter field work in California, and the next summer he might be almost anywhere in the West. She'd either have to trail around boarding in the nearest town, or go back to Milton."

"So I suppose she wouldn't let him take it."

"She wouldn't have put it that way. She was worried about her child, she wondered if he'd ever have a secure home to grow up in, I suppose she wondered how she'd get along herself, without anybody artistic and intellectual to talk to. So they debated and hesitated a couple of days, and then when Grandfather was offered the managership of the Adelaide mine, he took that instead. That way, she could go on planning an expansion of the cabin, to be ready for her child and next summer's guests. It isn't quite Living Theater, I guess, but it's the sort of thing her life was made of."

She was watching me with her big gray upturned eyes and sucking on the bent knuckle of her thumb, which she now released with a slurping sound and said, "I thought she was going to quit making decisions that fouled up his career."

"So did she. In a pinch she couldn't help herself."

"He let her lead him by the nose. Was he sort of soft?"

"He was no good at the talkee-talkee," I said. "He loved his wife and child. He had just been, for a Victorian, exceptionally well loved. It wasn't an easy decision. It could have gone either way."

"I suppose," Shelly said. "I guess I don't understand this home business of hers, either. She's not only a culture hound, she's got a terrible property consciousness. What would be the matter with traveling around? When Larry and I were hitching, I loved it. That gypsy hobo life, that's it. I know a pair who hitch hiked all the way from Singapore to London. I'd like to do that. I don't dig these home bodies."

"Times change," I said, not without irony. "Why didn't you and your husband stay on the road, if it was so great?"

She was at her knuckle again. Slurp. Sidelong flash of eyes. "He's not my husband, of course. That's for the family only."

"All right," I said. "The man you travel with, then. Why aren't you still traveling?"

She threw her hands up in the air and leaned back, stretching, arching her chest upward. *Ohne Büstenhalter* again. "Yakh!" she said. "It did get a little hairy, sleeping in the washrooms of Canadian tourist parks in the rain. But I'd do it again. I mean, you're never that free again." She stood up and slapped the seat of her pants as if the floor had been a dusty roadside. "Anyway I take it back about the sex scene. Even if you'd spelled it out, I guess it wouldn't have been a climax to much of anything."

"Is it ever?" I said. "No, it was just sort of like everything else."

7

Grandmother wanted her son to grow up, as she had, knowing some loved place down to the last woodchuck hole. The rural picturesque was not only an artistic manner with her, it was a passionate conviction. She had been weaned on the Romantic poets and the Hudson River school, and what the West had so far taught her was an extension of those: beyond Bryant lay Joaquin Miller, beyond Thomas Cole spread a vast wild grandeur supervised by Bierstadtian peaks. It was never the West as landscape that she resisted, only the West as transience and social crudity. And those she might transform.

There was a real nester in that woman. When she got flirting around with a twig or piece of string in her bill she was not to be balked. In September they began the addition to the cabin—a kitchen, bedroom, and vast rock fireplace designed more for social evenings than for domestic comfort. "Ye'll have no hate in the house," said the reluctant Irish mason who laid up the stones, and delighted her with his omen in brogue.

The curtained bedroom angle that Conrad Prager had called the upstairs was decurtained and christened Pricey's Corners. It held the bookcase, the rocker, and a small table equipped with a stereopticon and two hundred frontier views, the bread and butter gift of Thomas Donaldson. I have the views here, or most of them—brown, mounted on stiff cardboard with beveled and gilded edges, the twin photographs curving in a little like weakly crossing eyes: the early West as caught in the lenses of O'Sullivan, Hillers, Savage, Haynes, Jackson—a little musty, spotted with time, but still, when I hold one of them to that binocular viewer, touched with the wonder and excitement of a new country. Along with them in their box is Donaldson's ponderous report on the Public Domain, a work as neglected by the Congress that commissioned it as King predicted it would be, but a benchmark in the nation's understanding of itself, the sort of contribution to disinterested knowledge that my grandfather would have liked to make. These things are about all that is left of the Leadville years.

Early in November, their eyes watchful of a leaden sky that dusted them with snow, a characteristic Leadville buggy-full went over the pass, accompanied by a half dozen riders. The riders were of the class of young, well-born, and well-trained men who had recently contributed twenty-seven graduates of top technical schools to the procession carrying General Vinton, son of Dr. Vinton of Trinity Church, to his Leadville grave. The buggy contained, besides Susan and Oliver, his remote cousin W. S. Ward, W.S.'s older brother Ferd, called the Wizard of Wall Street, and Ulysses S. Grant, Jr., a man who has no historical personality for me except for the somehow awful fact that as a boy of twelve or so he was posted on a hill by his father so that he could watch the slaughter at Shiloh.

If Grant had been equipped to hear the Doppler Effect of time, it might have made him as uneasy to take that ride with Ferd Ward as it had to sit through a battle. It might have made them all uneasy. Before too long, Ferd Ward as General Grant's financial adviser, would utterly ruin the ex-hero, and shred away the last rag of his dignity and reputation. He would also, as one of the syndicate that owned the Adelaide mine, put a kink in my grandparents' lives. He was not a man it was quite safe to know. But Grandmother in her innocence thought it rather splendid that Mr. Ward was going over the range with them and that he would be on the same train as herself as far as Chicago. He was a testimony to their rise, he announced the circles that by his professional competence Oliver had earned the right to move in. This time, when she left him on a station platform, she would leave him solidly established, and she would go East without the taste of failure in her mouth.

In every way this returning was different from the last. Despite the prospect of another winter apart, no tears, no dreary thoughts. In Chicago, Ferd Ward and Mr. Grant took her to a banquet honoring General Grant, and she capped her social season by shaking that conquering hand and looking into those sad, streaked eyes. She met General Sherman and a half dozen other generals of the Army of Tennessee, and she had an animated ten-minute conversation with the principal speaker, Mr. Samuel Clemens. These items are not important.

They have for me, as a historian, a sort of corroborating charm: they prove that my grandmother did indeed live in time, among people.

Through the fading autumn she came back to Milton, and after a day's dismay that her child did not know her, and after a few days of unpacking, washing, talking, and preparing, found herself ready for a winter's work. There was nothing to hinder—Augusta and Thomas were still abroad. She had finished the Louisa Alcott blocks and had no other contracts for the moment. Without planning it, she found herself beginning a novel about her grandfather, the Quaker preacher who by his abolitionism had got the whole Milton meeting set down.

Writing books about grandparents seems to run in the family.

From the parental burrow Leadville was so far away it was only half real. Unwrapping her apple-cheeked son after a sleigh ride down the lane, she had difficulty in believing that she had ever lived anywhere but here.

She felt how the placid industry of her days matched the placid industry of all the days that had passed over that farm through six generations. Present and past were less continuous than synonymous. She did not have to come at her grandparents, as I do, through a time machine. Her own life and that of the grandfather she was writing about showed her similar figures in an identical landscape. At the milldam where she had learned to skate she pulled her little boy on his sled, and they watched a weasel snow-white for winter flirt his black-tipped tail in and out of the mill's timbers. She might have been watching with her grandfather's eyes.

Watching a wintry sky die out beyond black elms, she could not make her mind restore the sight of the Sawatch at sunset from her cabin door, or the cabin itself, or the smokes of Leadville, or Oliver, or their friends. Who were those glittering people intent on raiding the continent for money or for scientific knowledge? What illusion was it that she bridged between this world and that? She tried to think whether she would possibly believe in Sam Emmons if he appeared at her Milton door in his white buckskins. She paused sometimes, cleaning the room she had always called Grandma's Room, and thought with astonishment of Oliver's great revolver lying on the dresser.

Milton was dim and gentle, molded by gentle lives, the current of change as slow through it as the seep of water through a bog. More than once she thought how wrong those women in San Francisco had been, convinced that their old homes did not welcome them on their return. Last year she would have agreed. Now, with the future assured, the comfortable past asserted itself unchanged. Even the signs of mutability that sometimes jolted her—the whiteness of her mother's hair, the worn patience of Bessie's face, the morose silences of her brother-in-law, now so long and black that the women worried about him in low voices—could not more than briefly interrupt the deep security and peace.

Need for her husband, like worry over him, was tuned low, and Augusta's continued absence aroused only an infrequent, pleasant wistfulness. They had not seen each other in nearly four years. Absorbed in her child and her book, sunk in her affection for home, she could go whole days without mentioning or thinking Augusta's name.

I wonder if ever again Americans can have that experience of returning to a home place so intimately known, profoundly felt, deeply loved, and absolutely submitted to? It is not quite true that you can't go home again. I have done it, coming back here. But it gets less likely. We have had too many divorces, we have consumed too much transportation, we have lived too shallowly in too many places. I doubt that anyone of Rodman's generation could comprehend the home feelings of someone like Susan Ward. Despite her unwillingness to live separately from her husband, she could probably have stayed on indefinitely in Milton, visited only occasionally by an asteroid husband. Or she could have picked up the old home and remade it in a new place. What she resisted was being the wife of a failure and a woman with no home.

When frontier historians theorize about the uprooted, the lawless, the purseless, and the socially cut-off who settled the West, they are not talking about people like my grandmother. So much that was cherished and loved, women like her had to give up; and the more they gave it up, the more they carried it helplessly with them. It was a process like ionization: what was subtracted from one pole was added to the other. For that sort of pioneer, the West was not a new country being created, but an old one being reproduced; in that sense our pioneer women were always more realistic than our pioneer men. The moderns, carrying little baggage of the kind that Shelly called "merely cultural," not even living in traditional air, but breathing into their space helmets a scientific mixture of synthetic gases (and polluted at that) are the true pioneers. Their circuitry seems to include no atavistic domestic sentiment, they have suffered empathectomy, their computers hum no ghostly feedback of Home, Sweet Home. How marvelously free they are! How unutterably deprived!

Oliver's letters told her little—she wondered often how she had happened to marry a man for whom words were so difficult. A few crumbs of news leaked through. Ferd Ward's son, sent out to work at the Adelaide, had been spending more time at the monte tables than at the office. He had borrowed two hundred dollars from Oliver and smaller sums from Frank. Now last payday Pricey had found the cash box short by more than a hundred, and young Ward, challenged, had admitted "borrowing" it. Oliver had written his father. Nothing else to report except that the DR&G was making progress up the valley of the Arkansas. She wouldn't have to come over Mosquito Pass when she came. Frank and Pricey sent regards.

She was provoked with him for letting himself be imposed upon, though she could not have said how he should have avoided lending money to Ferd Ward's scapegrace son. She wrote him telling him to make an immediate claim on the father, to let no time elapse. There had been rumors in the papers that the Wizard of Wall Street was shaky. She told him how well Ollie had been, how she was coming on with her novel. She reported scraps of Augusta's travels in Sicily. She walked to the post office to mail her letter, and returned to work through the afternoon. It gave her a miser's pleasure to watch the pile of manuscript grow. Her grandfather's life absorbed hers.

For a long time. She had finished the novel and sold it to *Century* as a five-part serial, and the orchards were beginning to pop their buds, by the time his letter came saying she could now get in by rail. At once, like a milldam opened, her ponded life began to flow again.

This time, conceiving herself to be leaving neither on a picnic nor on a visit, but for good, she made the hard effort to disconnect herself from the past, throwing away some things, giving away others, packing a few to take along. Not without tears, she cleared her father's attic of her stored leavings, believing that those who would go on living there deserved that space, and that she would be healthier for the finality of the move.

It was not much she took—some dresses, some linens, some silver, some hope chest items that would let her compete with the new wives on Ditch Walk. A box of books for the education of her son and the pleasure of Frank and Pricey. A few prized objects that childhood, family, friendship, and marriage had washed like chunks of amber on her beach—Thomas's Japanese teapot and the little Madonna, all of Augusta's letters, the Fiji mat and the olla with which Oliver had welcomed her to New Almaden. The rug of wildcat skins on which Ollie had learned to crawl. Two trunks full, no more.

The beaver skins that Oliver had sent her from Deadwood were a trouble. They had always been a trouble, baffling and recalcitrant. She knew no one who could work raw furs. To try to make a coat of them, as Oliver in his innocence had suggested, would have been like making a dress out of Emmons's white buckskins; she would have felt like Pocahontas in it. To take them back west would be to confuse some issue that she did not want confused. In the end, she and Bessie managed to make three of them into a muff and a little hat. The rest of them she gave to Bessie.

There was also the elk head. Like the beaver skins, it had never had a function in this domesticated place. She had never got over wondering why he had sent such a thing. Maybe he wanted to keep before her some aspect of himself that he did not want her to forget, though that is my guess, not hers. But what to do with it? Anywhere in the house it would have been grotesquely incongruous and out of scale. It would have denied the validity of her family's life. Their decision to hang it on a beam in the barn was an acknowledgment of how little it belonged. At least, there, it was out of the way. She supposed that men friends of her father's took a certain interest in it, and once she had seen John Grant standing and looking at it with an expression on his dark dissatisfied face as if he doubted its authenticity.

One purpose it had served: she had used it to impress on Ollie the idea of his father, whom he had completely forgotten. Perhaps in some way known to savages and children he thought it *was* his father. That was why she took him out to see it the afternoon before they were to start West.

In the cobwebbed dusk the great rack branched upward into shadow. The dusty muzzle was lifted, the dusty eyeballs stared into the mow's darkness. It did not acknowledge the tame-animal smells of the barn; it had an air of scorning the hay on which such animals fed. Susan, with her son held against her legs, felt how it ignored her, and she had a twinge of the shame she had felt when her father and John uncrated the box, big enough to have held a piano, and exposed this joke, or whatever it was, this inappropriate souvenir of her husband's life in the Black Hills. A boy's insensitive whim, she eventually concluded, as jarring in its way as that great horse pistol he had brought to his courting.

Under her hands she felt her little boy breathe respect in its presence.

Lightly she said, "Well, so now we'll say good-bye to Daddy's elk. Tell it, 'Good-bye, Daddy's elk, tomorrow we're going on a train to live with Daddy. Daddy will meet us where the train stops, and we'll go through the mountains to our house made out of logs, and when I'm a little bigger I'll have a pony and go riding with Daddy or Frank or Pricey, and away off in the mountains where the flowers grow higher than the stirrups we may stop to rest sometime and see an elk like you carrying his antlers into the timber, or hear an elk like you bugling from away-way up the mountain.' Can you tell him that?"

"That's too much."

"Then just say, 'Good-bye, Daddy's elk.'"

"Good-bye, Daddy's elk."

"Will you like seeing your Daddy again?"

"Yes."

She saw by his wondering stare that he did not understand what she was asking him. Not sure she understood herself, she hugged him hard and picked up the lantern, holding it high to give him a last look at the great creature on the beam.

The varnished muzzle, coated with eighteen months of dust, shone as if wet in the light. A phantasmal fire glinted in the eyeballs. It might have bugled at any moment.

"Wasn't that odd?" she said late that night when she was sitting with Bessie and John before the fire. "It simply *gleamed* at us, as if the talk about going to the mountains had wakened it from its sleep. Just hearing the word Leadville brought it to life for a second. Oh, now I feel myself coming to life, too! I can hardly wait to get back there and make a home in that wild beautiful place."

John Grant had been sitting slumped, studying the toe of his boot. His chin was against his chest, his eyes were narrowed almost shut. Now suddenly he opened his eyes wide and shot her a look that stabbed. His face was full of hatred. With the years he had grown more and more censorious, he rarely spoke except in scorn or dislike, he seemed always quarreling with something inside his head.

The black eyes blazed at her only a moment before they slitted again. For another second he brooded upon the swinging toe of his boot. Then he uncrossed his legs, stood up, and left the room. They heard his steps on the porch, then on the path that led to the lane and back to his own house.

Holding her embroidery frame in her lap, Bessie sat still. Then impatiently she shook her head and started a shining tear-track down each cheek.

"What did I say?" Susan said, bewildered. "Bessie, I'm sorry!"

"Excuse him," Bessie said. "He envies Oliver so. He's almost the only person he still speaks well of. He'd so like to be going himself. He says he's smothering here."

Susan found no reply. Her gentle sister had always had the patient role, she had never been coddled. It was Bessie who made the humble marriage, Bessie who lived as a farm wife, Bessie who was at hand to help when her parents needed her, Bessie who made the preserves that Susan's city friends carried triumphantly home as the plunder of a country visit. She had sat for hours submitting her prettiness to Susan's pencil. While Susan studied in New York and shuttled back and forth across the continent, Bessie looked after the home place. When Susan could not keep her child, Bessie kept him. Sometimes Susan had envied her the placid sweetness of her life.

She said softly, "Would thee go?"

"If it would help him. If it would make him as he used to be."

"Then!" Susan said, full of generous impulse. "Why don't I ask Oliver to look around? He can probably find him a place at the Adelaide. Thee could build a house near ours on the ditch!"

Almost with amusement, Bessie raised her eyes and looked through the ceiling. "What about them?"

"They could come too."

The delusion lasted perhaps five seconds before realism wiped it out. Busy as a Breughel, the vision filled her head: the men jostling up and down plank sidewalks that thrummed under their boots like bridges, overdressed women strolling past open doors of assay and law offices within which men in shirtsleeves argued or smoked or watched the street, wall-eyed teams plunging by, teamsters rising to lay the whip to quivering haunches, the band playing, the smoke of smelters streaming from the stacks, the earth trembling to the vibration of stamp mills, the whole place leaning as if in a strong wind, and all the corners, all the doorways, all the windows packed and staring with faces, and every face disfigured by the passion for wealth, every eye looking out its corners, alert for the main chance. At the edge of this, timid and lost between the frenzy of the crowds and the indifference of the peaks, their gentleness elbowed aside, their sweetness assaulted by every crudity, their habits outraged, their lives made nothing, that white-haired pair upstairs.

Not to be thought of. Trees transplanted do not thrive. Hence not to be thought of for Bessie and John either. What she accepted for herself and her son was impossible for her parents and unlikely for her sister. It seemed to her that she had already traveled a great distance from the still waters that had produced her. What stretched unbroken from her great-great-grandfather, who had built this house, to her father, who would die in it, was cut short in her. The book about her grandfather that she had begun in affectionate memory was really a sort of epitaph.

8

Snow blew down the Royal Gorge in a horizontal blur. With Ollie's sleeping head in her lap and a down comforter around them both, she tried now and then to get a look at that celebrated scenic wonder, but the gorge was only snow-streaked rock indistinguishable from any other rock, all its height and grandeur and pictorial organization obliterated in storm. The dark, foaming, ice-shored river was so unlike the infant Arkansas that she used to ford on her horse that she didn't believe in it. The circles that she blew and rubbed on the window healed over in secret ferns of frost.

Without knowing in what setting she would see Oliver, or what he would be wearing, she found it hard to visualize him. She knew it for a deficiency in herself that her imagination was so controlled by *things*. In her drawings, she was often unable to get expressiveness and individuality into figures and faces until she could set them in some domestic or architectural background—under a fanlight doorway, by a carved stair rail, against mantels where they could lean in costumes drawn meticulously from life. Now she kept seeing Oliver in the postures of past meetings and partings—as he had looked stepping off the rainswept ferry in his hooded field coat, or squinting into the sun as the train pulled away eastward from the Cheyenne station, or searching for her over the heads of the crowd in Denver. As if taking an oath, she assured herself that from now on she would *have* him, and so would Ollie. They would not have to imagine him any more.

The train lurched and awakened Ollie. He reared up. "Are we there?"

"Not for a long time. You'd better go back to sleep."

But he didn't want to go back to sleep. He lay and whined until she diverted him with a story about how some of her grandfather's sheep had been swept down the millrace and drowned, but she and Bessie had rescued a lamb and fed it on a bottle until it grew up to be a pet and followed them everywhere like Mary's Little Lamb.

(Years later, a frugal lady making every tiny experience count, she wrote another story about a sick lamb left behind by a Basque herder, and illustrated it, using two of her children as models, and sold it to *St. Nicholas.* I remember having it read to me in my childhood, and it sits on the desk here now, the faces entirely recognizable—Grandmother did have a gift for catching a likeness. The serious boy of ten or so with his little sister beside him, the two of them hunkered down offering a baby's bottle to the lamb, is incontrovertibly my father. For some reason the picture makes me feel old and sad.

How trivial a thing to entrap the memory of three or four generations! Three at least. Rodman's mythology contains no rescued lambs, I imagine. Perhaps I myself remember this story because it so clearly meant something to Grandmother. I can see her, when she had finished reading to me, sitting in the porch swing with her neat head bent, her lips pursed, thinking. Then, in the one eye that I could see, an abrupt round lens of water leaped out, was forced out as if under pressure. It did not run down her cheek, it literally sprang from her eye and hit the page wetly. "Oh, pshaw!" she said, and rubbed it away angrily with the heel of her hand. Her crying, so sudden and without motivation, puzzled me and made me solemn. Only later, thinking about it, I have come to realize that it was not my father's young face that made her cry, and certainly not the lamb, which died within twenty-four hours. It was the picture of Agnes, the little girl. There was a lamb that was not rescued. Grandmother wore that child like a crown of thorns.)

When stories ran out, she amused Ollie by helping him find pictures in the frosted window. A forest of ferny shapes grew upward from the bottom sash, and with her fingernail she drew into it half-revealed faces of deer and foxes, and peering from behind the thickest frost a mustached face wearing a look of astonishment. "That's Daddy," she said. "Looking for us. He thinks we're lost." They giggled together.

But at the moment of arrival at Buena Vista she did not see him as plainly as she had drawn him on the glass. She had herself and Ollie bundled up long before the train stopped, and she was the first one down the step into a whirl of steam, wind, and blowing snow. Turning, half blinded, from helping Ollie down, she saw the familiar height, the gleam of eyes and teeth from the face nearly obscured by fur hat and sheepskin collar. With a cry she threw herself into the figure's arms, and found herself kissing Frank Sargent.

"Oh, my goodness!" Aghast and laughing, she fell back, grabbing for Ollie's hand to keep him from blowing away. Frank, who had responded to her embrace with enthusiasm, was laughing harder than she was. His eyes looked at her with delight. The touch of his mustache —that was new, he didn't use to have one—prickled on her lips. "Oh, Frank, I'm glad to see you! I thought you were Oliver, that's why . . . Where is he? Isn't he here? Is something wrong?"

"You're darned right something's wrong," Oliver said out of the whirling air behind her. "Man comes to meet his wife and finds her kissing the hired man."

She was muffled in arms and cold cloth, her lips prickled with another mustache. They held hands hard while they looked at each other. She saw that he was thinner even than last year. Despite the cheerful good nature of his expression, he looked to her in his hooded coat like an El Greco ascetic. And she realized why she had made her mistake. Frank had modeled himself so completely on Oliver in dress, mannerisms, walk, mustache, everything, that they might have been brothers, a lighter and a darker.

Oliver squeezed her hands and dropped them. Very quietly he knelt down beside Ollie in the cinders and snow. She saw how unfrighteningly he moved, how reassuringly he came down to the child's size. The love in his face could not have been misunderstood or undervalued. He had always been that way with the child. Even when Ollie was an infant, he would see his father across a room and chortle and beam and kick and hold out his arms. She had been faintly jealous of that baby love affair—her child took her for granted but loved his father with a passion. Now, watching them meet gravely in the blowing snow, she saw that there was going to be no period of reacquaintance such as she had had to go through last November. After two years Ollie might not know his father, but he trusted him instantly.

"Ah, now!" Oliver said, squatting. "Here's a young fellow I want to meet. Is your name Oliver Ward?"

Not quite certain of his ground—after all, his mother had kissed the other man first—Ollie said, "Yes?"

"You know something? That's my name too. Do you suppose you're my little boy? I've got one, somewhere. Ollie Ward. You suppose you're the one?"

The child's grin wavered, his eyes moved over his father's face. "Aw, *you* know!" he said. An arm and a gust of laughter lifted him up. He perched triumphant. "I said good-bye to the elk," he said. "We rode on a train."

"You did? I'll tell you something else you're going to do. You're going to take a buggy ride all wrapped up in a buffalo robe, with a hot sadiron to keep you warm. Frank's been heating a couple on the stove in the station there for an hour."

"Ah, Frank, you haven't forgotten how to be thoughtful," Susan said. "I remember last time you had a fire burning for me."

"I had to think of something to stay even with Pricey," Frank said. "He's back there in Leadville stoking the fireplace so you can come home to a house with a lot of hate in it."

They were both pressing drivers, unsparing of the team. They said they didn't trust the weather not to get worse, and so they aimed themselves toward Leadville through the notch of a horse's ears, and whenever there was a choice between a smooth ride and a fast one, they chose the fast one. The whip was in hand more often than in its socket. Every half hour or so the one driving passed the reins across her to the other, and sat on his cold hands. Between them, sheltered by one and then by the other as the road turned them in the wind, Susan did not at first feel cold. Her feet were on the warm iron, her hands in her muff. Snuggled down behind the seat in his robe and quilt between the two lashed trunks, Ollie showed his nose like a seal at a blowhole.

It was such a day as she had left the mountains on months before. The wind was pebbled with dry snow, the valley was black and white, without a rumor of spring, the peaks were blotted out. Milton and its opening apple blossoms were part of another, gentler creation.

The questions she asked got laconic answers.

The winter had been bad, one blizzard after another.

No ladies back yet.

The town not so much on the boom as last year—troubles underground, the price of silver down to $1.15. Some mines had been stripping highgrade to boost the price of their stock. As a stunt, the Robert E. Lee had produced $118,000 in silver in one seventeen-hour day. The principal stockholders of the Little Pittsburgh, who had paid themselves $100,000 in dividends every month for half a year, had just unloaded 85,000 shares at an enormous price and left the new owners with a gutted mine. The Chrysolite had labor trouble, had locked out its miners and was standing twenty-four-hour armed guard against possible dynamiters.

"Did Ferd Ward pay back what his son stole?"

"What he took from the payroll. Not what he borrowed from Frank and me."

"Did you make a claim?"

"I mentioned it twice."

"But he never paid you."

"Not yet."

"He never will!" she cried into the wind. "Oh, Oliver, why must it always be you who gets cheated?"

He seemed amused. "Your guess is as good as mine. You have any idea, Frank?"

"Can't imagine."

"You're as bad as he is," Susan said.

"Worse," Oliver said. "Sneaks up and kisses the boss's wife."

"I thought it was nice," Susan said. "There! At least he doesn't borrow money and not pay it back, or rob the payroll."

"Just waiting my chance," Frank said.

"Matter of fact," Oliver said, "if it wasn't for the Staten Island Kid we wouldn't have a mine."

"Who?"

"The hired man there."

"Really? What did you do, Frank?"

"Foiled the wicked claim jumpers. Just like Diamond Dick."

"No, tell me."

"I told you about the trouble we were having with the Argentina," Oliver said. "Also the Highland Chief."

"You never tell me about anything. Honestly, if I had to depend on your letters to know anything, I'd be . . . uninformed."

"Well, that sure wouldn't do." He heaved back, creaking with clothes, and pulled aside the buffalo robe and looked down in. "Asleep," he said. "We'll have to keep an eye on him so he doesn't smother, down in that hotbox. You warm enough?"

For answer she raised her hands in their muff above the blanket. He touched the fur with a gloved finger. "Beaver?"

"Yes, those you sent me from Deadwood."

"Good," he said, pleased. He looked across her at Frank, who was driving. "Aren't you going to tell her?"

"Not much to tell. They tried to come in, we shut 'em out."

"He's modest," Oliver said. His nose was leaking, his eyes were ice blue and teary, he touched the back of his glove under his nose. "They've been claiming for months we're running over the line. I made that survey, I know we're not. But our best ore body is close to the Argentina's claim. While I was in Denver a couple weeks ago they thought they could sneak in and take over our drift. They had a tunnel driven right up close to ours, and one Sunday they broke through."

"But what . . . ?"

"Possession. Nine points. Especially when it takes a year to get anything into court. They could have cleaned it out before we could get a judgment. But the Kid there got a tip, and he and Jack Hill were waiting for them with rifles. So now there's a door on their tunnel, barred on our side, and we've still got possession."

Their tone left Susan uncertain whether to be appalled or amused. They acted like boys playing robbers. Frank, a self-conscious juvenile, flapped the reins on the horses' rumps. "Why Frank," she said, "that sounds *heroic*. How many men?"

"Five."

"And they had guns?"

"We've got 'em now."

"Ugh," she said, shivering her shoulders. "Weren't you frightened?"

"Scared to death. But as Jack says, a Winchester is mighty comprehensive."

"I don't like it," she said. "It sounds *grim*, it sounds like war. What are they doing now? Did they give up?"

"They're the ones who have to take it to court," Oliver said. "Right now, all they can do is sit on the porch at the Highland Chief boardinghouse and give us hard looks as we ride past. So we carry six shooters and carbines. They're so scared of the Kid they don't dare do anything."

"Don't you believe him," Frank said. "He's the one they're scared of. The boss is a very good shot, did you know? Under all that trusting good nature is a very tough hombre. Every day or so we hold target practice outside the shaft house at noon, so Oliver can knock off a few cans at fifty yards. The word gets around."

Laughing, baring his perfect teeth into the wind, he pounded a hand on his thigh. "Here," Oliver said, reaching. "Let me spell you."

Studying her husband's face curiously, Susan decided that he did not look like a tough hombre. He looked like a man without either meanness or impatience. But he did look tired. She supposed the strain of being constantly on guard had worn on him. It all sounded unpleasant and dangerous, but there was always the possibility that they were playing an old Western game, telling bear stories to the tenderfoot. "Goodness," she said lightly, "and all the time I thought I was married to a mine manager, not a gunman."

The hooded head turned slightly, the wind-reddened, tear-glassy blue eyes looked at her sidelong. A strange, almost unpleasant smile lurked under the soup-strainer mustache. "Well," he said, holding her eyes, "that's Leadville. That's what we chose."

Shocked, she stared back at him while her mind translated for her: That's what *you* chose. Was that what he meant? He looked embarrassed, and heaved around to check on Ollie. On the way back from adjusting the buffalo robe, his right arm hugged her briefly. "Hi-up, there!" he said, and plucked the whip from its socket and laid it on one haunch, then the other.

Susan, huddled into herself, kept still. It had stopped snowing. The meadow they were crossing was as bleak as midwinter, scratched like an etching with gray and black trees. The shore boulders of the black, swift creek they forded were shelled in ice. The wind searched out the cracks in her covering and froze up her will to talk. Her mind was as torpid as her limbs. She would be worrying as soon as she thawed out, but she couldn't worry when she was so cold. Perhaps she had imagined that look of blame, that unpleasant smile. After a while she pulled the blanket clear over her head, and took her dismay into the dark.

Brief words passed above her, separated by long silences. Several times Oliver's arm braced her shoulders when the road got rough; she wondered if he were being especially protective because of what he had let slip. From the careful quiet with which he occasionally leaned back to check on Ollie, she knew that her son still slept.

A long time of stupefying cold. The wind came through her blanket as if through cheesecloth. She hunched her shoulders and clenched her jaws and endured.

Then she realized that the lurch for which she was braced had no returning lurch. The buggy had stopped. Oliver's weight left the springed seat, she heard him grunt as he hit the ground. Her hands lifted at the blanket, and working her cold cheeks she emerged into gray late afternoon. There was her cabin, above it W. S. Ward's house, above that another only half completed. The ditch rushed by, edged with ice into which brown grass was bent. The sky was dull pewter, smudged to the south by smelter smoke. The wind blew her a tremble of Leadville's incessant sound, and blew it away again.

"Ooooh!" she said, moving her stiff shoulders and icy hands. Then she looked again, and said, "I thought Pricey was going to have the house full of hate. There's no smoke."

"Boy, he'd better have a fire," Oliver said. "I'll lift his scalp. Maybe he got to rocking."

"Don't you joke about Pricey." She gave him her hand to be helped down. "If he said he'd be here, he's here."

Her buckling legs would hardly hold her. It seemed to her that Oliver was especially solicitous, with his arm around her. To Frank he said, "Don't try to muscle those trunks. I'll help you in a minute."

Frank handed him down mummied Ollie, still sleeping. "Some April weather," he said. Oliver steered Susan toward the door. The latchstring was out, and she pulled it for him so that he could kick the door open. "Pricey?"

Empty room. The change that she felt in the air was not from cold to warmth, not the lovely prickling and burning of a chilled skin in a hot room, but only a change from wind to stillness. The cabin was stone cold. Carrying Ollie, Oliver went to bedroom door, kitchen door. "Pricey?" No answer.

He gave Susan one look. Then he set Ollie into the rocker and said, "Stay under the covers for a couple of minutes, Old Timer. It's cold. I've got to start a fire."

While Susan stood close, stamping her feet, he crumpled newspaper and pyramided kindling. The outside door opened and Frank walked a trunk through it on his thighs. Surprised, he said, "Isn't he here?"

"Hasn't been here," Oliver said. "The fire's dead out."

He scratched a match, flame jumped upward, a wind blew down the chimney and puffed out into the room a smell of shaving smoke. He leaned split lengths of pine above the flame. The kindling began to crackle with such a sound of comfort that Susan edged closer, though there was yet no heat, only light. "It just isn't like Pricey."

"No."

"Why don't I run down to the office and see if he's there?" Frank said. "I'll just get that other trunk in. You stay here and get warm."

Oliver stood up. "I'll give you a hand."

They were outside longer than she thought it should take them. Ollie started to fight his way out of the comforter and she pulled it back over his head. "Stay in a little longer, you'd better. It's *icy*."

But he wanted to see. With only his fair curly head exposed, he looked wonderingly around. He watched his father and Frank carry in the second trunk and put it in the bedroom. He watched his father come out with the gun belt and six shooter and buckle it around him. So did Susan. "Oh my dear!" she said. "Where is thee going?"

"No reason to worry. We're just going to check up on Pricey. Probably something came up and he couldn't leave."

"But the gun!"

He laughed, not infectiously. "Part of the act."

He would not look at her as he piled more wood on the fire. She could feel the heat growing against her legs and at the same time smell the cold outdoor air in his clothes as he moved. When he stood up again she forced him to meet her eyes. She felt a kind of splintering, and told herself bitterly, "It's Leadville. It's what I chose."

"We'll only be a little while," Oliver said. "Better pull in the latchstring."

"Oliver . . ."

"Don't worry," he said, and closed the door and shut her in. She pulled in the latchstring.

The firelight on her son's face made him look like so domestic a cherub, so much like one of her own drawings of Bessie's children at bedtime, that she felt mocked.

"Where did Daddy and the other one go?"

"The other one is Mr. Sargent. They'll be back afterwhile."

"Why did Daddy take his gun?"

"I guess he's afraid something might have happened to Pricey."

"Who's Pricey?"

"A friend of Daddy's—of mine."

"Is this Leadville?"

"This is Leadville. How do you like it?"

His round, browless, white-lashed eyes went around. "They have logs on the walls in Leadville."

She had to laugh and hug him, and she felt better. While he hung in front of the growing heat of the fireplace she started a fire in the kitchen stove and put on the kettle, propped open the bedroom door to let a little heat into that mausoleum, set the table hopefully for five, found canned soup and crackers, cheese, canned peaches. When after a very long time the kettle began to sing, she made tea, doctoring Ollie's with sugar and canned milk, and they sat on the hearth and sipped it and ate from a tin of English biscuits. Through the log walls she could hear nothing outside; when she went to the window she saw only that it had grown dark. She looked several times at the locket watch pinned to her breast. They had been gone more than an hour, then an hour and a half. She stoked the fire.

Now that it began to grow warm enough in the room so that they could move a little distance from the fire, she let Ollie try the hammock that Oliver had slung in the corner, and she told him how she had swung him in it in New Almaden when he was brand new. He was passionate to sleep in it; she said he could. But the hammock aroused such homesickness in her, and the ticking away of time made her so nervous and worried, that she opened one of the trunks and rummaged until she had found some of the household goods. The olla she set on the mantel. The Fiji grass mat, its hay smell obscured by two years of storage camphor, she spread on the table and reset the dishes on top of it. The rug of wildcat skins she spread before the fire and invited Ollie to roll on it.

"Let's see if Daddy notices," she said. "We won't tell him, we'll just wait and see if he notices how *homey* it is."

The thumping on the door made her leap to her feet. A kicking, not a knocking—the sound came from low down. "Sit still!" she said to Ollie, and swiftly crossed the room to stand with pounding heart a foot from the rough-hewn planks. The kicking continued, violent and loud. "Yes?" she said. "Who is it?"

"Open up, Sue. Hurry."

She shoved up the wooden latch, the door burst inward, brushing her aside. Oliver backed in, followed by Frank walking forward. They were carrying a man's body between them. She got one look at the face, and screamed.

9

Grandmother draws the curtain on those months. The letters all but stop, the reminiscences skip over that time with a distracted brevity.

For weeks she was Pricey's nurse, after that his keeper. His cut mouth and broken nose and crushed cheekbone and cracked skull healed, but his mind and his eyes ducked and hid. The weather was unrelievedly bad, the trouble at the mine went unresolved. She was filled with anxiety for Oliver, Ollie, herself, Frank. Men who had broken into the office to steal or destroy papers, and who had done what they had to harmless Pricey, would do anything. She hated the weather that kept Ollie cooped up inside with the smell of carbolic acid and the sight of Pricey's face. What dreams the child must have! What a parody of all she had promised him when she took him to join his father in the mountains!

Their carefree sociability was gone like last year's leaves. Few experts passed through Leadville: they had made their investigations, written their reports, taken their fees, and gone. Even if there had been anything like last summer's visitors she could not have welcomed them freely to her fire. Over in his corner like the family's imbecile child Pricey was always rocking and reading. If visitors did come, he grabbed up the stereopticon and hid behind it, and peeked. Did he fear all strangers, or was he sensitive about his disfigurement, or did he periodically need to bewitch himself with three-dimensional photographs of the West to which he had come hunting . . . what? It sickened her to see him maimed, body and mind. She wept over him, unable to forget that he had been beaten because he was one of theirs. Yet she sometimes felt him around their necks like an albatross, and she grew frantic at the effect he might have on Ollie.

They were a family that, simply because they could hire, acquired the direction of other lives. Like the climate and the altitude, they were an arm of destiny. To bring a Lizzie or a Marian Prouse out West was one thing; women were in demand. But a Pricey was not, in the West or anywhere else. His English family, notified of his condition, wrote back with what Susan felt was a mean, self-saving caution. They did not, they said, have either the health or the money to come for him. His brothers were both married and tied down by jobs and families. They thought it might be best, if Ian did not show improvement, to try to find some good woman, widow perhaps, or someone whose children were grown and gone, to look after him for a fee, which they would try to help pay. They did not like to think of him in an institution.

"You know who that good woman is likely to be," Susan said. "Me! Fond as I am of him, I can't see us saddled with him indefinitely. It will do horrible things to Ollie. They ought to be *made* to bring him home."

"How?" Oliver said.

"If there were only someone we know who's going abroad. He's so gentle and quiet he wouldn't be a trouble."

"But we don't know anybody who's going abroad. Anyway, he'd be scared to go anywhere except with one of us."

"But it can't go on as it is!"

There was a bitten furrow between Oliver's eyes, he moved as if the slightest step jarred him to his heels. She could literally see one of his headaches coming on. Before night he would be lying in the darkened bedroom with a wet cloth over his eyes. His voice was already roughened by the pain in his head.

"Do you want me to put a tag on him and ship him across like a trunk?"

"Of course not. He'd die."

"Then I can't see any way but going on as we are, at least for a while."

Pain or frustration made him spread his hands before her with a tenseness that she saw as dangerous. He looked at her frowning, his voice shook. He was as worn out and frazzled as she was herself. "I'm sorry, Sue. That's just the way it is."

"I know. It's Leadville. It's what I chose."

For a second they confronted each other like enemies. Then she made a contrite, inarticulate sound and grabbed his hand and held it against her cheek. "Don't pay any attention to me. I wouldn't think of abandoning him. It's just—I watch Ollie getting pale and mopey and losing his funny little sense of humor, and I . . ."

"Yeah," he said, and looked away, over her head. "If we could get the Argentina thing settled, or really hit it so Ferd and the others would give us the money to get into big production, we could work it out. I've got some cousins in Guilford, girls, eighteen or so. Maybe we could bring one of those out."

"Where would we put her?"

"Yeah."

"That mine is a *prison* for you!" she said. "Oliver, I admit it was a mistake! I take the blame, I made you decide wrong. Could you still get on the Survey?"

"I doubt it. That's all changed, you know."

"Changed how?"

"Powell's not likely to need me. He's hiring topographers and geologists where King hired mining men. King's quit as director, did I tell you?"

So her fingers were hammered off that gunwale too. "He has? Why?"

It bothered her to see such scorn, disgust, and sour amusement in his face; his face was made for other expressions than those.

"To get rich as a mining expert," he said.

"Oh my goodness!"

"Yeah," Oliver said. "Doesn't it kind of shake you?"

Then late in June there was an afternoon after a morning shower. The sky boiled with big clearing clouds. When the sun swam into a pool of blue it blazed down with midsummer warmth, and the earth steamed. Standing in the doorway smelling that freshness, soaking up the sun deep down to her moldy and softened bones, Susan said to the cabin behind her, "Ollie, Pricey, let's all take a walk along the ditch and pick some wildflowers."

In the strong light outside, Pricey looked more disfigured than in the dark house. His nose, which had once been lumpy and somehow touching, was flattened like a prize fighter's. He had a permanent bluish bump on his left cheekbone, a dent in the bone above one eye as if he had been hit with a hammer. Maybe he had. They would never know, for he remembered nothing about it, unless his fear of strangers was a memory. He hung close to her as they walked, and his mouth was a blackness empty of all the front teeth.

"Go ahead, look around," she said. "See how many kinds we can find."

Tipped head, questioning look half timid and half trusting. He went a little way out from the path, he stooped seriously and picked something, looked back at her and held it up. His mouth opened in a smile that was infantile and pathetic. "Good," she said. "Get some more. Get a lot. We'll have whole glasses full on the table for supper."

Ollie brought her a sweaty little handful, mainly without stems, and went for more. Pricey worked away earnestly, going farther away from her than he had done since he was hurt. Eventually he came back with a fat bouquet. There was so much trust in his battered face, and so much eagerness to be praised, that she was effusive in her admiration, and hugged him as she would have hugged a good child. Whatever they had done to him, they had not beaten out of him that shy desire to please. She accepted his fistful of wildflowers as an offering in payment for two wretched months.

He stood at her shoulder, peeking, while she examined the varieties. Paintbrush, yes, and the pink ones are primroses. The blue one is a pentstemon, those are nice, and the white one a columbine, lovely. The creamy one with the five petals is some kind of cinquefoil, I knew something very like it back home in New York. But this little yellow one with the gray leaves, that's something new."

"Puc-puc-puccoon!" Pricey said. "Lithospermum multiflorum."

"*What?*" She stared at him, jolted into laughter that was half hysterical. "How did you know that?"

Pricey was confused. He stammered and shrugged, searching her face as if the answer might be there.

"Never mind," she said, and patted his arm. "Pricey, you're getting well, do you know that? That's *wonderful* that you remembered."

A cold shadow fled along the slope faster than a horse could run, the sky winked like a great eye, winked again and flooded them with renewed warmth. Beside them the crystalline ditch rushed to run the mills and gather the rubbish of Leadville. Beyond the piled whiteness of the clouds the sky was so hurtfully blue that she could not help saying, "Pricey, remember that day last summer when we were riding on the Lake Fork? 'How tenderly the haughty day fills his blue urn with fire'?"

"Hawwww!" Doubtful, filled with dismayed uncertainty, narrowing his eyes to think, he stared at her out of sandy-lashed pale blue eyes. His tongue was between his lips, the lips moved in and out, puckered and rubbery. In pity she tapped his arm again, releasing him, and put his bouquet to her nose and inhaled its faint wild fragrance. But she felt better about him. For a moment there, when that fragment of a Linnaean botany book had burst out of him, the dimmed mind had brightened. She gathered her two charges, one on each side, and walked again, thinking.

If Pricey got well he could go back to live with Frank—just come over evenings and tuck into his corner and read or listen. Now and then she and Oliver would be free to dine at the Clarendon; it seemed the height of gaiety. Now that Leadville's summer had finally arrived, there would be more ladies—they might have a picnic at Twin Lakes for the Fourth. She could ride again, assuming that Oliver or Frank would dare leave the mine to go with her—most surely they would not let her go alone. She might sleep again, instead of going around wound up ready to snap, or prowling the dark cabin in her dressing gown from Ollie's hammock to Pricey's cot, or staring out the window into barren starlight. Maybe, maybe. Maybe the Adelaide would finally hit that rich carbonate that Oliver was sure was there, and the skinflint owners in New York would give him some support (how wry that one of them was Waldo Drake!) and the court would rule against the thieves and roughnecks at the Argentina and Highland Chief, and Oliver could go off to work without that hateful pistol and that scabbarded carbine. Maybe her house would at last cease to be a hospital and a prison, and begin to be the home she had hoped to make it.

The moment the wish expressed itself, she felt that it was fulfilled. Between the morning's rain and the bursting out of the sun, something had changed. Leaving Ollie and Pricey to play in the yard—that was how she thought of Pricey now, as a second and more difficult child—she put their flowers in glasses of water, and then she got out her drawing materials and stool, and idly, but with an extraordinary sense of well-being and release, sketched her little boy digging happily in the ground.

As if to add his testimony to the evidence of change, Pricey lugged a couple of pails of water from the ditch. He had hardly staggered the second one into the kitchen when she saw Oliver coming up the bank with his coat over his shoulder. She stood up, afraid. "Is something wrong?"

"Naw," he said. "I just got fed up. I dumped the office on Frank and came home to loaf."

For more than an hour he sat on the ground making Ollie a little threshing machine out of a spool, some shingle nails, and a cheese box. With this the two of them threshed out four or five tablespoonfuls of early weed seeds. They ate supper with the door wide open and the sun shining in, and afterward, when they were sitting on blankets against the warm west wall and watching the sun sink into a fat cloud with fiery edges, Frank came up from town carrying a mandolin. He said he had bought it from a broke miner for three dollars. The time of the singing of birds was come, he said, and as soon as he limbered up his fingers and rediscovered how to play the thing, the voice of the turtle was going to be heard in the land.

"Turtles can't sing," Ollie said. Languid after his afternoon in the sun, he leaned inside his father's knees and picked at the broad gold wedding ring on the hand that loosely held him there. The sun in that one afternoon had turned him pink.

"Only snapping turtles," Frank said. "Wait."

His dark head bent over the mandolin while he tuned it, he seemed to Susan a dear friend, a brother, a handsome and carefree boy rather than an assistant engineer who stood off claim jumpers with a Winchester. The way his eyes touched her, the way he smiled, made her tender. Everything had in one day grown gentler and more endurable. Oliver, sitting against the log wall with Ollie between his knees, looked domestic enough to be drawn for *Hearth and Home*. Just beyond him, Pricey hugged his knees. He had that habit of edging as close as he could, and then making himself silent and invisible. Even the roofs of town, the torn-up hills and ugly shaft houses of Leadville, looked picturesque in that light, and the evening noise of the streets below was no more than a tremble on the air. The plink of Frank's tuning was thinly musical, tunelessly incessant, like the fiddling of a cricket.

When he was ready, Frank plinked out a minstrel tune. He played well enough; Susan declared happily that he was a master. "Good enough for those turtles, maybe," he said. "What'll we sing? Name something, Ollie."

But Ollie lay back against his father with his thumb in his mouth and had no ideas.

"Come on, Ollie," Susan said. "Take that old thumb out of your mouth, that's a good boy. What do you want to sing? What do you like?"

He still had no ideas. The thumb that his father had pulled out of his mouth slipped back in. "He's tired," Oliver said. "Want to hit the hammock, old boy?"

The answer was small, querulous, muffled by thumb, negative.

"Too much sun, perhaps," Susan said. "He'd better go soon. But he has to hear the turtle first. Start something, Frank."

Frank started "Sewanee River." After a quavery bar or two he got his confidence and sang out. He had a good baritone voice; the mandolin shivered against it like a girl in white backed against a dark tree. Susan came in with the alto part, Oliver with a growling bass. To Susan's ear they sounded quite good. Then high and sweet, a tree-toad sound, here came Pricey's tenor and made them whole. They rounded their eyes at one another, pleased; they rounded their tones and leaned together. After two bleak months they sang like mockingbirds on a May Sunday, and loved every sound they made. At the end, which they drew out long, they broke up in laughter, clapping, praising themselves.

"Aren't we *good!*" Susan cried. "We sounded absolutely professional. We could hire out in bar rooms or give concerts at the Great Western. Pricey, you're *wonderful!* I didn't know you could sing. You too, Frank. You've got a very nice voice. You're so *true.*"

Friendly and full of laughter, their eyes touched. She saw that he wanted to take her remark in more ways than she had meant it. Why not? He *was* true. Neither she nor Oliver could have done without him. But there was even more in his brief, laughing look, and she acknowledged that too. His adoration made her feel excited and flirtatious, the way she was often made to feel by agreeable company and dress-up clothes. She could feel her color come up.

"More!" she said. "What do you know the words to, Pricey? Hymns? 'Abide with Me'? 'Ein Feste Burg'? 'Turn Ye to Me'? 'Drink to Me Only with Thine Eyes'? Let's sing them all, let's sing all night!"

They filled the dooryard with harmonies while the sun set and the west died out and the bats began to stitch through the darkening air. It was like an hour of thanksgiving for their emergence from trouble. And there sat Pricey, singing away with never a stammer, knowing the words to everything, even songs that she had thought of as strictly American. The day had brought him out like a flower. Surely, now, they were past their bad time. Above the Western range Venus was large, white, and steady.

"Sing, Ollie," she said. "You know some of these songs. Sing 'em out. Or are you still sucking that old thumb?"

"He's a little cold, I guess," Oliver said. "He's shivering."

"Why didn't you get him a blanket?"

"And interrupt a song?" He laughed and bent over the top of Ollie's head to look at him. "You cold, boy? Want a blanket, or are you ready for bed?" Ollie made no answer. "Hey," his father said, "you *are* shivering. It's not that cold."

Tense with premonition, Susan was on her knees. "Maybe he got too much sun, he looked quite pink."

"I think he's playing jokes. Come on, Old Timer, you don't have to shake as if it was thirty below."

He lifted the boy to his feet and turned him around, peering at him in the dusk. He shuddered and shook in his father's hands, his teeth clacked. Even before Susan could scramble across to feel his cold face, before she got him inside and lighted the lamp and saw his fingers fishwhite, his nails blue, she knew. The ague fit, the return of the old Milton curse. In a few hours he would be burning with fever, in another few soaked with sweat. It would go on that way for weeks, ague fit, fever fit, sweating fit, a few days of delusive well-being, and again the ague fit, the whole cycle, every cycle leaving either the disease or the patient weaker, until one or the other wore out. And nobody to take him to in Leadville except the drunken doctor from whom she had rescued Pricey.

10

I can remember from my childhood how uneasy Grandmother could make a sickroom. "Let the child alone," Grandfather would growl at her. "Let him sleep it off." That was his way—turn his face to the wall and turn down his metabolism until something inside told him he was well enough to get up. But Grandmother treated illness the way she treated her insomnia. She could never simply lie still until she fell asleep. There was always some last-minute adjustment, some final arrangement for relaxation—a glass of water, a little bicarbonate to settle her stomach, a fresh pillowcase, a pulling-down of the blinds to shut out a crack of light, the checking of the front door lock or the drafts of the stove. By the time she got fully ready to sleep it was time to get up.

So with illness. Her chilly hand was always being laid on the hot forehead of suffering. She woke you to see if you didn't need something to make you more comfortable. She listened to your breathing, studied your clouded eyes and coated tongue, sighed and clucked and murmured, went away reluctantly and left you alone and was back before your eyes could close. The Chinese farmer who kept pulling up his rice to see how it was growing was a relaxed man beside Grandmother. It was a wonder Father survived his measles and chickenpox, much less his malaria. It was a wonder *she* did. After a week of crisis she was as attenuated as wire sculpture, with eyes that she would describe, looking with distaste into the mirror, as two burned holes in a blanket.

This time Ollie's sickness was so violent, his chills so wracking, his fever so high, his sweats so profuse, that she slept only in catnaps, dozing in her wakeful chair a half hour now and a half hour then when Ollie seemed well enough to be left to Oliver or Frank. She didn't trust them to detect danger signs. The very fact that she must leave them to do what she herself, exhausted and muddle-headed as she was, was the only person capable of doing—that woke her from uneasy sleep and set her on her feet toward the bed before she knew where she was.

She hardly noticed the routines of her house. Someone did most of the cooking, but whether she or Oliver or Frank she could not have said. Someone took furtive Pricey away, and in a lucid moment she noted that he was gone, but forgot again before she could ask what arrangement had been made for him. Someone brought the German woman around to do up washings every two or three days, for with wet sheets for the fever, and towels for the sweats, and changes of night-clothes daily, there was a linen crisis, but she hardly noticed the woman's presence or the copper boiler steaming on the stove. She only snatched whatever she needed off the line as soon as the wind had dried it.

Like a burning glass she focused on her big-eyed child with his terrifying pallor and his pitiful thin neck and his terrible gentleness. She sat watching by his bed for hours on end, and when he woke to himself, and neither shook nor burned nor sweated, she would coax Oliver, against his judgment, to carry him out to the hammock where he could lie and see things going on and be part of the family again and delude her with the hope that he was past the crisis; and in a few hours, or a day, she would have to have him carried back to the bedroom frozen-jawed and blue-fingered.

Six weeks of that. Everything in her life stopped but nursing. She saw few friends—even when they called she hardly saw them—and there were no evenings by the fire, not even with Frank and Pricey. In all that time she apparently wrote no letters except a note to Osgood and Company refusing a contract to illustrate a novel by Mr. Howells. She rejected Oliver's suggestion that they telegraph one of his Guilford cousins to come out and help. Where would they put her? She would only be in the way. She herself was sleeping in the hammock, Oliver in Pricey's cot.

Since there was no way to go but forward, that was the way she went. She never thought to inquire how things went at the mine, she forgot the apprehension that had tightened the pit of her stomach every time Oliver went to work armed like a bandit or a sheriff. All her concern now was to know when he would return to spell her or help her in the sickroom.

It was August before she was sure Ollie would get well. He had gone three days without a symptom, he was sitting up and taking an interest, he ate the custards and gruels she spooned into him, each morning he was stronger. Still she could not trust herself to sleep, for while she lay senseless, what if the chills returned, what if no one noticed and wrapped him in blankets and the wildcat-skin rug warmed before the fire?

Then one afternoon Oliver came home with a sleeping draught obtained from the polite drunken doctor whose services she had rejected. She would not take it. She considered sleeping draughts immoral. What if she got the habit? She preferred insomnia to its alarming remedy. If Oliver would promise to wake her in four hours, she would lie down now and sleep, really sleep. If all was well when he woke her, she would go back to sleep for another four hours. That was all she needed. She didn't trust him to watch for more than four hours at a time. He slept *too* well, that was the trouble.

"Drink this," he told her, "and no more palaver. Ollie's all right, he's sleeping now. Have at least as much sense as a four-year-old."

Finally, hesitating, fluttering, dreading, changing her mind and having to be persuaded all over again, she drank it and stared at him over the cup as if it had been the arsenic of a death pact. She kissed Ollie's sleeping face with the emotions of one going on a long journey, and tucked him into his hammock and touched his cool forehead and let herself be led away and put to bed. Within minutes she was up again to lay out the makings of the eggnog laced with brandy that he was to have, to strengthen him, as soon as he awoke. She extracted promises, she took a half-irritable scolding and a kiss, she lay back and braided her hair into pigtails and felt her weakness flow into the bed as if the sleeping potion had begun to liquefy her body. She blinked a tear, and talked a little while Oliver sat at the bedside and watched her. Sometime in the midst of her talking, the potion snuffed her like a candle.

She awoke to find Oliver sitting just where he had been when she had dropped off, and thought she had only drowsed. Her mouth was fuzzy and her mind felt numb. Then she saw that the blind was up and the window opened on broad daylight. It had been dusk when she went to bed. Morning, then. Oh, good! A bumblebee buzzed in, crawled around on the cretonne flowers of the curtains, and buzzed out again. Oliver was watching her with a slow, amused, memorizing look; she knew that he had been watching her sleep. Rigid with readiness, she sat up. "How is he?"

"Asleep."

"Have you felt his head?"

"I've about worn his skull out, feeling his head. He's cool, he's fine."

"Did you give him his eggnog?"

"Three times."

"*Three times!* What time is it?"

"A little after two."

"Oh my goodness! How long have I slept?"

He consulted his watch. "About sixteen hours."

She was awed. "What on earth did that doctor give me?"

"Just what you needed. What you ought to take every time you get wound up like that."

"Oh no," she said, "no, I couldn't." Groggily she turned her head to look at the brightness outside, the brown hill sloping up to aspens that wavered as unstable as water. "You should have waked me up. I've kept you from going to the mine."

"Frank's there. There's nothing to do but wait anyway."

"Ah," she said sympathetically, "I haven't been paying enough attention to my husband. Is everything still all snarled up?"

"Still snarled up."

"I keep hoping you'll run into a rich ore body."

"We won't do that unless they give us some money to operate with."

"And they won't do that till the suit is settled."

"Maybe it'll be settled by 1883 or so."

She put out a hand. "I'm sorry it's so hard for you. How's Frank? He's been such a lamb about helping out, and I've hardly said good morning or good evening. We've got to have him up for supper. Tonight. Let's get the Wards and some others and have an evening again."

"That'd be good. Frank would like that."

"And Pricey. How *is* Pricey?"

He had opened his knife and was working at the horny callus on his palm. His eyes lifted, without any movement of his head, he looked up at her over half-moons of white, so apologetic, ashamed, angry, or embarrassed that he scared her. "Pricey's gone."

"Gone? Gone where?"

"England."

"Did they send for him?"

"No. I sent him."

The tears that welled weakly to her eyes made him swim and flow, fluid and out of focus in his faded blue shirt and blue jeans. "Oh, Oliver, *why?*"

"Why?" He sat with his jaw bulging. His knife clicked shut, he stretched his leg to slide it into the tight pocket of his jeans. "Why," he said, thinking. His eyes came up again, the pupils coldly furious. Every gentle and good-natured line in his face was hardened and coarsened. "Why!" he said a third time. "Because we couldn't look after him. Because he was in the road."

As if the expression on her face maddened him, he moved his shoulders and flattened his mouth. She stared at him through her tears. "If you're going to ask why we didn't take him to the mine with us," he said, "we did. He remembered, he shook like a dog, he was scared to death. I tried taking him along when I had to ride anywhere, but he held me back. Frank tried setting him up in their shack with all the books he could borrow. You'd think that would be Pricey's dish, but Frank would come home and find him gone, and then he'd have to hunt all over Leadville for him. Once he was in jail—where else would Leadville put a fellow that can't look after himself? He kept wanting to come up here. I told him Ollie was sick and you were swamped and there wasn't any room, he'd have to stay with Frank. Where do I find him— not once, three or four times? Hiding behind W.S.'s privy, just hanging around and looking down here like a mongrel dog waiting for scraps to be thrown out the door." He brushed nothing off the tight thighs of his jeans. "Do you think I *liked* sending him home?"

"No. Of course not." She could not help the weak tears that kept welling to her eyes. They broke through her lashes and ran down both cheeks and she did not wipe them away. "It's just—he was so helpless. It's like kittens being put in a bag to be taken to the river. How could he travel?"

"Frank took him as far as Denver and put him on the Santa Fe and paid the porter to look after him to New York. I wired the Syndicate to have somebody meet him and put him on the boat, and cabled his father to meet him at Southampton."

"I wish you'd told me so I could at least have said good-bye."

The fiery cold eye touched her, held a moment, looked out the window. "I didn't think you needed anything else."

"Oh, I know. You were being thoughtful. How did . . . When Frank left him in Denver, how was it? What did Pricey say?"

"He cried," Oliver said.

He would not look at her, he stared stubbornly out the window. She let her own wet glance go the same way. Out there the dry hillside shimmered with tears and summer, the aspens flashed light off their incessant leaves, the grasshoppers whirred and arched. A mourning dove was who-whoing off in the timber. In the blinking of a tear it would be fall. She had missed the spring and half the summer, the home that they had bragged they would make at the edge of timberline was a disaster.

The dove's long mournful throaty cooing was a dirge for the failed and disappointed, for the innocent and incompetent, themselves not excepted, who wandered out to this harsh place and were destroyed.

As if he had read her mind, Oliver said, "He never did belong. He never could have made it even if he hadn't been hurt."

"Just the same," she said. "Just the same! If that Syndicate had any heart it would have done something for him. It didn't, did it? Who paid his fare?"

"I did."

"And will never get it back."

"Do you care?"

"No. But I hate that heartless mine, all those people so many safe miles away who let people get hurt or killed and never care, so long as they get their dividends."

"Which they're not getting."

"They're too callous to deserve anything. Too timid and too callous. Why don't we quit?"

A little laugh was jolted out of him. He looked first out the window and then into his hands, as if in search of something that would catch his eye. "Frank would feel terrible, for one thing. He'd stay here ten years without pay, and trade buckshot with those people every afternoon, just to beat them."

"Are you talking about Frank or yourself?"

"All right," he said. "I'm not exactly friendly with them. And I don't like to lose."

"You need a vacation, that's what you need."

"So do you."

"So does Ollie. We all do. It *hasn't* been good here, Oliver. Helen was right. Grass won't grow, cats can't live, chickens won't lay. We were mistaken to think we could make a home on this mountain. We ought to get out."

He had out his knife again, digging at his horny palm. She saw the V between thumb and forefinger thick and yellow with callus. In the absence of money to hire a crew, he and Frank and Jack Hill had been mucking in the mine like common laborers, hoping to turn up something that would persuade the New York office to commit itself and its money. Carefully, without looking up, he said, "Would you consider Mexico?"

"Consider it?" she said suspiciously. "Why? Have you had an offer?"

"Not exactly. But I could, I think."

"Where is it? Off on some mountaintop, like Leadville or Potosí?"

She saw his forehead pucker. His eyes returned from outdoors and met hers steadily. His head was up so that the pupils sat in the middle, not up against the upper lids, and there was not that sinister half-moon of white below them. "Sue," he said, "it's my *profession*."

She was contrite. She hadn't meant to sneer. "I know. Tell me."

"Letter came a week or so ago—ten days, two weeks, I don't know. The Syndicate's given up on the Adelaide until the suit's settled. We're just sitting here. They've got an option on a mine in Michoacán. There was this sort of question, if it worked out that way would I be interested in inspecting it."

"And then what?"

"Then we'd come back here, assuming the Adelaide wins its suit."

"What about Ollie?"

"He couldn't go, not on this inspection trip."

"Back to Milton?"

"Milton or Guilford. Milton's more his home than anywhere else."

"How long?"

"How long?"

"You say you'd have to inspect it. How long would that take?"

"I don't know. Two months, maybe more."

"Could I go along?"

"I wouldn't go otherwise."

Absently her hand came out and settled on top of his. He was being scrupulous not to influence her, he simply laid out possibilities. "I hate to think of Ollie," she said. "Just barely well, if he *is*."

He said nothing. He watched her.

"I wonder if I could get Thomas to commission an article," she said. "Mexico might be exciting to draw."

He sat inert.

"If we didn't go there, we'd just mildew here," she said. "When will that suit come up, do you think?"

"Not before winter. Maybe spring."

"And Frank could hold the fort here, if we went."

"Why not?"

"If Thomas would commission an article, we might make more by going there than by staying here. We could leave Ollie with Mother and Bessie, I *know* they're better for him than I am."

"You mean *you* could make more," Oliver said, steadily watching her.

"Oh, Oliver, please!"

"Two questions. Will you leave him? And would you like to go? If the answer is yes to both, I'll write Ferd. He has to pay me whether I stay here or go there. I imagine he'd just as soon get some work out of me."

The dove cooed again, distant and sorrowful, and was answered from a great distance by another. She laughed shakily and stretched the salt-stiffened skin of her cheeks. "Oliver, let's! I keep thinking it's morning. I keep thinking it's a fine sunny morning after a spell of bad weather. I feel like popping out of bed and being energetic and cheerful."

"All right," Oliver said. "You pop out of bed and be energetic and cheerful. I'll go down to the office and see how Frank's doing, and maybe write a letter."

"What if I wrote Waldo Drake too? Would that help?"

"I don't know. Would it?"

"It might. I've known him a long time."

He looked at her. He shrugged. "O.K., if you want."
"Would it seem like . . . taking advantage of a connection?"
"I suppose it might."
"Even if it does!" she said. "I don't care."

V

MICHOACÁN

1

My mother died when I was two, my father was a silent and difficult man: I grew up my grandparents' child. As those things went in Grass Valley, I also grew up privileged, son of the superintendent of the Zodiac and grandson of the general manager. Every child I played with came from a family that worked for mine.

Grandmother deferred to my father, seemed almost to fear him. Certainly she assumed the blame for the taciturnity that made him formidable to deal with, and certainly she saw in me a second chance to raise up an ideal gentleman. Rough and dangerous play, adventures into old mine shafts, long hikes and rides, those her life in the West had led her to accept and even encourage: Let me be tried in manliness. But honesty, uprightness, courtesy, consideration for others, cleanliness of body and mouth, sensibility to poetry and nature—those she took as her personal obligation. Never severe, she was often intense. She instructed me as if out of bitter personal experience, she brooded along the edges of my childhood like someone living out a long Tennysonian regret. My lapses from uprightness troubled her, I thought, out of all proportion to the offense.

Once in a while, when she had a visitor she liked, some old tottering friend such as Conrad Prager, I might hear her chattering on the porch or in the pergola, long since torn down, that used to be a part of Grandfather's prize rose garden. On those occasions I sometimes heard her laugh aloud, a clear, giggly laugh like a flirting girl's; and I was surprised, for around my father, my grandfather, and me she seldom laughed. Instructing me, especially in moral matters, she used to shake me by the shoulders, slowly and earnestly, looking into my eyes. It was as if she were trying to yearn me into virtue, like Davy Crockett grinning a coon out of a tree. I was never never *never* to behave *beneath* myself. She had known people who did, and the results were calamitous. The way to develop and deserve self-respect, which was the thing most worth seeking in life, was to guide myself always by the noblest ideals that the race had evolved through the ages.

Somewhere back in her mind lurked the figure of Thomas Hudson, in shining mail. His example dictated my training as it had dictated my father's. In some ways, Grandmother hadn't learned a thing since the time when she sent my poor scared twelve-year-old father out of Boise to attend St. Paul's School and become an Eastern gentleman. When my time came around she sent me too to St. Paul's, my father silently consenting. Gentility is inherited through the female line like hemophilia, and is all but incurable.

The children of Grass Valley, who were far from genteel, might have made things difficult for a little gentleman except for two things. One was the affection the town felt for my grandfather and the respect it had to pay my father. Any boy who picked on me would have been whaled, out of policy or principle or both. The other reason was that I opened up special opportunities.

For example, my grandfather might take a bunch of us down the mine, or he might let us pile into the Hupmobile, driven by Ed Hawkes's father, and ride through town like blackbirds in an open pie. He might let us help him in the orchard where he fooled with Burbank hybrids and developed hybrids of his own, and when fruits were ripe he was not stingy with them. Many a taste bud in Grass Valley and Nevada City, blunted by sixty years of greasy french fries, ketchup, and bourbon, must remember as mine do the taste of sun-warmed nectarines and Satsuma plums up there in the end of the orchard where I now take my eight hard laps on crutches.

Likewise many a fat or tired or sick or otherwise diminished man and woman in this town must remember afternoons when Lyman Ward, the rich kid, had them over to the big house, where they played run-sheep-run among the pines on Grandfather's three acres of lawn, or hide-and-seek through the servants' wing, by that time unused, with its dozen dark closets and cupboards, its twisty back stairs, and its narrow hall whose floorboards betrayed hider and seeker alike. Afterward, the Chinese cook would prepare and the Irish maid serve sandwiches and lemonade and ice cream and cake; and the little barbarians, sweating from their games and abruptly quelled, would sit like little ladies and gentlemen, and cast slant eyes at my grandmother, in long gown and choker collar (she was sensitive about what age did to a lady's throat), her thinning hair in its bangs and Grecian knot, moving up the polished hall or across the library's bearskins, or standing in the doorway coercing from them the handshake and muttered thanks–good-bye that were their first instruction in manners.

My father, despite his Idaho governess, had gone to St. Paul's badly prepared, an inferior Western child. Grandmother was determined that I should not, and being past her working years, and with time to spare, she saw to my education personally. She read me poetry, she read me Scott and Kipling and Cooper, she read me Emerson, she read me Thomas Hudson. She listened to my practise recitations and helped me write my themes and do my numbers. My homework went in bound in neat blue legal covers, moreover, and a lot of it was illustrated by Susan Burling Ward. The quick little vignettes that ornamented the margins of themes and arithmetic papers looked as if they had been made by the brush of a bird's wing. They delighted my teachers, who pinned them up on blackboards and told the class how fortunate Lyman was to have so talented a grandmother.

I accepted her help willingly, because it brought me praise, but I had no clear idea of who she was or what she had done. The bindings of her books in the library were not inviting, and I can't recall ever reading one of her novels when I was young. I didn't know her writings, apart from a few children's stories, until years after her death, nor much of her art either, since most of that is buried in the magazines that published her. I would have been surprised to hear that some people considered her famous.

But I remember a day when I came home from school and told her I had to write a report on Mexico—how Mexicans live, or something about Mexican heroes, or some incident from Cortez and Montezuma or the Mexican War.

She put aside the letter she was writing and turned in her chair. "Mexico! Is thee studying Mexico?"

Yes, and I had to write this report. I was thinking Chapultepec, maybe, where all the young cadets held off the U. S. Army. Where were all those old *National Geographics?*

"I had Alice take them up to the attic." Her hand reached up and unhooked her spectacles, disentangling the earpieces from her side hair.

I thought her eyes swam oddly; she smiled and smiled. "Did thee know thee might have *been* Mexican?"

It didn't seem likely. What did she mean?

"Long ago we thought of living there. In Michoacán. If we had, thee's father would probably have grown up and married a Mexican girl, and thee would be Mexican, or half."

I had trouble interpreting her smile; I could feel her yearning toward some instructive conclusion. She took her eyes off me and looked out into the hall, where the light lay clean and elegant across the shining dark floor.

"How different it would all be!" she said, and closed her light-sensitive eyes a moment, and opened them again, still smiling. "I would have stayed. I loved it, I was crazy to stay. I had been married five years and lived most of that time in mining camps. Mexico was my Paris and my Rome."

I asked why she hadn't stayed, then, and got a vague answer. Things hadn't worked out. But she continued to look at me as if I had suddenly become of great interest. "And now *thee* is studying Mexico. Would thee like to see what I wrote, and the pictures I drew, when I was studying it? It started out to be one article, but became three."

So she led me up here to this room, and from her old wooden file brought out three issues of *Century* from the year 1881. There they are on the desk. I have just been rereading them.

As a boy I never came into this studio without the respectful sense of being among things that were old, precious, and very personal to Grandmother. She flavored her room the way her rose-petal sachet bags flavored her handkerchiefs. The room has not changed much. The revolver, spurs, and bowie hung then where they hang now, the light wavered through the dormer, broken by pines and wistaria, in the same way. Then, there was usually an easel with a watercolor clothespinned to it, and the pensive, downcast oil portrait of Susan Burling Ward that I have moved up from the library is no proper substitute for Grandmother's living face; but reading her articles this morning I might have been back there, aged twelve or so, conspiring with her to write a paper called "My Grandmother's Trip to Mexico in 1880," illustrated with her woodcuts scissored from old copies of *Century Magazine*.

Her traveler's prose is better than I expected—lively, perceptive, full of pictures. The wood engravings are really fine, as good as anything she ever did. Our scissors left holes in both text and pictures, but from what remains I get a strong impression of the excitement with which she did them.

I remember excitement in her face, too, or think I do, and in her leaning figure, and her fine old hands, when we resurrected those drawings forty years after she had drawn them. She chattered to me, explaining things. She excited herself just by talking, she remembered Spanish words forgotten for decades, she laughed the giggly laugh she usually reserved for safe old friends. Her agitation was too violent for her, it was close to hysteria and not far from pain. She got the giggles; she ended by bursting into tears.

Her Paris and her Rome, her best time, the lost opportunity that she may have regretted more than any of the other lost opportunities of her life. She would never have admitted it, she would have denied it with vehemence, she kept up all her life the pretense that Augusta was a superior Genius, but Grandmother was a much better artist than her friend, and she would have profited from, and certainly couldn't help envying a little, Augusta's opportunities for travel and study. Probably she nursed a secret conviction, which she would have suppressed as Unworthy, that in marrying Oliver Ward she had given up her chance to be anything more than the commercial illustrator she pretended she was. That sort of feeling would have grown as she felt her powers growing.

She came before the emancipation of women, and she herself was emancipated only partly. There were plenty of women who could have provided her the models for a literary career, but hardly a one, unless Mary Cassatt, whom she apparently never met, who could have shown her how to be a woman artist. The impulse and the talent were there, without either inspiring models or full opportunity. A sort of Isabel Archer existed half-acknowledged in Grandmother, a spirit fresh, independent, adventurous, not really prudish in spite of the gentility. There was an ambitious woman under the Quaker modesty and the genteel conventions. The light foot was for more than dancing, the bright eye for more than flirtations, the womanliness for more than mute submission to husband and hearth.

The conventions of her time and place never inhibited her, I think, because it never occurred to her to rebel against them. The penalties, the neurasthenia and breakdowns of the genteel female, she never experienced either. But the ambitions that gave her purpose and the talents that helped fill a life not otherwise satisfying, she never fully realized or developed. That she never got off the North American continent, and lived most of her life in the back corners of that, was a handicap she couldn't help feeling. Once she turned down a commission to illustrate a novel of F. Marion Crawford's because, as she said, she didn't even know the kind of *chairs* they sat on in the great European houses and *palazzi* where the story took place. She could infuse with her own special emotion anything she could draw, but she could draw only what she had seen.

Mexico was indeed her Paris and her Rome, her Grand Tour, her only glimpse of the ancient and exotic civilizations that in her innocent nineteenth-century local-colorish way she craved to know. Now for once she traveled not away from civilization but toward it, and thanks to the Syndicate's desire to present a confidently prosperous front she traveled first class. Among her baggage were twenty-four whited blocks hastily prepared at the *Century* office, and in her portmanteau was a cabled commission from Thomas in Geneva—a commission that had arrived along with two dozen long-stemmed roses.

To Susan's eye, the island ports they touched at on the way down were unbearably picturesque. They wore the patina of romantic time, their fortresses had been guarding the approaches to the Américas when her own home on the Hudson knew nothing but wild men dancing feast dances. She begrudged sleep, stayed up late to watch the lights and listen to the sounds from shore, and to see the moon set behind palms, got up before dawn to see the light grow across the perfumed open sea. As if on a honeymoon cruise, she and Oliver danced, dined, drank champagne at the captain's table, listened to Spanish lovesongs from the Cubans down in steerage, sat up half one moonlit night to hear a fantastic recitation of the *Frithjof Saga* in the original by a young Swedish engineer on his way to build a Mexican railroad.

He reminded her of themselves; she liked the way he took his tradition with him into cultural strangeness. She herself, who thought herself an especially understanding audience because of all the Vikings she had drawn for Thomas, Longfellow, and Boyesen, went to bed that night and reassembled her own somewhat dispersed inheritance, resolved not to let it be weakened by whatever Mexico should provide. One of the charming things about nineteenth-century America was its cultural patriotism—not jingoism, just patriotism, the feeling that no matter how colorful, exotic, and cultivated other countries might be, there was no place so ultimately *right*, so morally sound, so in tune with the hopeful future, as the U.S.A.

Then after five days they went on deck one morning and saw a rosy snow-peak floating high on a white bed of cloud: Orizaba. A little later they steamed into the harbor of Veracruz, and Mexico rose before Susan Ward like something rubbed up out of a lamp, as different from the false fronts, cowhide boots, flapping vests, and harsh disappointments of Leadville as anything could possibly have been. Mexico was an interlude of magic between a chapter of defeats and an unturned page.

My grandfather, operating on his belief that ladies were to be protected, conspired with the Swedish engineer to fill all the seats in the first-class carriage to Mexico City with the more desirable passengers, but he had no such control over the diligence that took them from Mexico City to Morelia. For four days they sat jammed into an old Concord coach with six other people, none of whom spoke English but all of whom turned out to be of an excruciating politeness. Grandmother's first article drily remarks that their intimacy ripened rapidly from their being thrown much together. Their driver, ancestor of all modern Mexican bus drivers, was one of those who put on speed for towns, arrivals, departures, turns, steep down grades, and stretches of rough road. Beside him on the box a *mozo* with a leather sack of stones encouraged the lead mules when they needed encouragement. Beside and before and behind, a protection against bandits, rode a detachment of *guardia civil* in gray uniforms, with carbines and swords, and in the intervals between their bursts of speed, to which they responded as hunting dogs respond to sight and smell of a gun, they dozed in their saddles or eyed the ladies in the diligence or sang to themselves endless *corridos*, those improvised songs that are part ballad, part newspaper, part wish-fulfillment.

If they eyed the ladies, so did one lady eye them. She saw everything and drew much of it; her sketchbooks, if they had been preserved, are something I would have cherished. All I know of them is that Thomas Hudson thought them superb and that Winslow Homer and Joseph Pennell both praised them. Even the two dozen woodcuts that were developed from the sketchbooks have great variety and spirit: Toluca with its sixteenth-century profile of bell towers, terraced roofs, tiled domes, and cypresses; Indian huts where women set out on cloths weighted with stones the pulque, tortillas, and fruit of roadside refreshment; packmules and burros, old subjects from New Almaden; bullock carts with solid wooden wheels; sandaled Indians bent under hundred-pound bundles of *camotes*, or towers of pottery woven together with cords, or bales of matting; swineherds driving herds of black pigs and wearing capes made of dry corn leaves so that they looked and sounded like walking corn shocks. Somehow, staggering after dark to one of the bare rooms that inns provided, she managed to pause long enough to get sketches of arcades and courtyards. Rising at three, in total darkness, she stood in the *corredor* long enough to catch the scene below, where men brought out and harnessed the mules by torches of agave rope dipped in pitch.

She had a heart as well as an eye, and they were sometimes at war. Patient Indian women with their babies slung in *rebozos*, men bowed under their burdens, looked to her like people waiting for their souls. A cathedral rising out of a huddle of huts, a ranch whose stone waterworks seemed to her to rival those of Seville, made her ashamed of the delight she took in a picturesqueness created out of so much driven human labor. She saw a bullfight in Maravatio and was sickened by it, but got her sketches just the same.

At two o'clock in the morning, after twenty-three hours on the road, they crashed through the silent streets of Morelia, past what her fellow passengers murmured was San Pedro Park, and into the courtyard of the Hotel Michoacán. A sleepy *mozo* came out and took the mules, a sleepy maid smiled at them from the doorway, a tall man dressed in American business clothes met them in the lobby and presented his card: Don Gustavo Walkenhorst. Speaking English with a German accent and Spanish turns of phrase, and with a look in his pale pop eyes that asked them to observe how well he played the role of international grandee, at home anywhere and with anyone, he said that he had waited only to welcome them, not to dismay them with his company when they were—especially the señora—so tired. He had taken the liberty of ordering beds for them, and a light supper. Tomorrow, when they were rested, he begged permission to call on them. He and his dear dead wife's sister, who kept his house, would be honored if Señor and Señora Ward would be their guests at Casa Walkenhorst during their stay. And now, with permission, he would take his leave. Until tomorrow. Sleep well. He hoped the room would be satisfactory. He had particularly specified that they were to have this poor hotel's best.

He put his hat on his pomatumed hair and left them. The maid led them, Susan reeling and lightheaded with fatigue, to a vast room with a tile floor and a four-poster bed carved like an altar piece. The *mozo* brought their bags, the maid brought Don Gustavo's light supper, which proved to contain cold chicken, cold ham, bread, cheese, strawberries, tacos filled with guacamole, oranges, tiny bananas, Puebla beer, and a bottle of cold white Graves. They sat and ate hungrily, smiling foolishly into each other's faces as they gobbled, craning their necks to search the corners of their great room. Night blew in on them in soft gusts from the balcony's open french doors.

"Well, Señora Ward," Oliver said. "You look just a *leetle* done in."

"I'm dead." She had taken off her shoes, and her stockinged feet slid voluptuously on the cool tiles. The room, the food, the secret soft air from the balcony, were so coolly opulent after the wracking, jolting, dusty, baking diligence that she felt tearfully happy. One glass of wine had gone to her head. Half undressed, she lay down on the bed, propped with bolster and pillow, and let Oliver peel her an orange and fill her glass. The stem in her fingers was as fragile as a straw; the candles winked in the wine. "But oh, how different from Leadville!" she said.

"It is, at that. Want to stay on here, or accept the invitation of our pompous friend Don Gustavo?"

"How can we refuse? He may be pompous, but he's so courteous— *wasn't* he courteous? They all are. Even the way an Indian woman hands you a tortilla on her flat palm is like a movement in a dance. And their voices are so soft. They seem to be born with good manners."

A little later they stepped out onto the balcony and looked over the silent city. Two street lamps, lemon yellow, pooled their light and shadow on the rough stones of the street. Across dark trees there was a ghostly intimation of bell towers. From one of them a great bell spoke once, a sound as single and heavy as the sound of a drop falling from an overburdened leaf. It gathered itself and spoke again, gathered again and spoke a third time.

Shivering, Susan crawled in under Oliver's arm. "Oh!" she said. "I have never been *anywhere* till now!"

2

In her dream she moved with some great procession bearing banners and saints' images through streets that hummed with the bronze of bells, and woke, and felt the last vibrations from the church tower in the Plaza of the Martyrs quiver through the room and break in soft shock waves against the inner court of the Casa Walkenhorst. As if summoned, the two young bloodhounds chained in the court woke and bayed, a sound that went down her spine. Instantly, harsh and challenging, Don Gustavo's gamecocks crowed from their gallery above the rear court, and when they left off she heard the voices of doves, soft and heavy as droppings, falling from the high window ledges. On the other side, through the shutters, the growing, shut-out, disregarded sounds of day were beginning out in the square.

Beside her, Oliver slept with his face deep in the coarse linen of the pillowcase. She slipped out of bed and put on her dressing gown and carefully, not to creak the hinges, went out into the *corredor* to watch the Casa Walkenhorst come awake.

The *corredor* was an open arcade that went around all four sides of the court, one story up. Twenty rooms opened off it, but of all those doors only hers was open. Through vine-wreathed arches she looked down into the court pillared like a church crypt, clean and empty in the gray light except for the hounds that surged against their chains in frenzied greeting of something underneath Susan, where the stables were. The gateway into the rear court framed the corner of a sunny corral, a stone watertank, bamboos from whose arrowy leaves shadows shook across the pavement. The sun intruded in a sharp, early triangle four or five feet into the main court.

Now Ysabel, the coachman, came into view below her, leading a string of two white mules and three horses. Their shoes clashed on the paving stones, the hounds stood up on their hind legs and leaned choking against their collars. Their ears hung down beside their sad faces, their tails went wild. Ysabel led his string past them through the gate and into the sharp new sunshine, and they crowded to dip their noses and suck up water from the tank. While they drank, Ysabel came back and released the dogs, which went around with their noses to the ground and now and then anointed a pillar or corner. Then Ysabel sat down on the coping of the tank and smoked a cigarette with the shadows of bamboo leaves flickering over him, but by the time she thought of her sketch pad he had risen and was leading the horses and mules back through the court and under her, out of sight.

Then the air was full of wings, the doves came down out of the sunny blue like angels in a painting, and she saw old Ascención, in black trousers and white jacket and scarlet sash, scattering grain down in the kitchen corner of the court. He left the doves pecking and labored up the stairs with a heavy water jar on his shoulder; and, sandals shuffling, went along the *corredor* tilting a quart or two of water into each flower pot. When he came to the corner opposite Susan he lifted the hood off the parrot's cage, and the parrot, as if being electrocuted, shrieked, *"Enrique, mi alma! Enrique, mi alma!"* Ascención watered the last pot, set down his jar, picked up from the corner a short broom like a bundle of twigs, and backed away down the opposite *corredor*, sweeping.

Down in the court a white poodle had joined the bloodhounds. A maid, Soledad, came out of the kitchen and sloshed water around on the stones. The dogs walked wet-footed, lapping at little puddles. Now out of another door burst Don Gustavo's ten-year-old daughter Enriqueta, and embraced the poodle, crying *"Enrique, mi alma!"* From over her head the parrot took her up in a voice demoralizingly like her own. *"Enrique, mi alma! Enrique, mi alma!"*, and then, in a conspiratorial mutter, *"Buenos días. Buenos días."*

Unseen, Susan stood in her arch and watched life gather in the court—bloodhounds, poodle, Soledad, Enriqueta, old Ascención, now the cook, thin as a snake, with a peevish, bitten censoriousness between her eyes and fierce peremptory gestures. Across from Susan a door opened and Emelita, Don Gustavo's sister-in-law and housekeeper, came out adjusting a shawl over her unfinished hair. She clapped sharply twice. Down in the court Enriqueta popped out of sight and young Soledad quit fooling with the dogs and craned upward. A soft flow of Spanish poured on her; she nodded and went inside. Turning to go back to her room, Emelita saw Susan watching from her place under the vines. A sweet, startled smile passed across her face and left her looking guilty. Her fingers fluttered in the incomparably Mexican, secretive, feminine greeting that Susan had seen flash from carriages and balconies at the time of the *paseo*. Then she too was gone. One of the bloodhounds rushed at the feeding pigeons and sent them flapping. Susan retreated into the dimness of the shuttered bedroom and found Oliver stretching widely in the wide bed.

"I love the way the Casa Walkenhorst wakes up," she said.

"Prussian efficiency or Spanish order?" Oliver said. "Who calls the tune, Don Gustavo or Emelita?"

"Oh, Emelita! She's an absolutely *perfect* housekeeper. Why she let herself get enslaved to that German, just because he took a vow when his wife died. He prides himself so on that vow, but it's Emelita who makes it possible."

"I thought you thought he was so courteous."

"He *watches* himself being courteous. With admiration."

"I can take you back to the hotel."

"You just try! I love Emelita. She has the kind of face you can only get by devoting yourself to others. She reminds me of Bessie. And really, what a housekeeper! She showed me her linen room yesterday. Dozens and dozens and *dozens* of linen sheets and pillowcases and bolster covers like this, as coarse as canvas but just like velvet from so many washings. *Shelves* of everything. If I'd been a true housewife myself I'd have gone down on my knees. It's a shrine."

"You ought to see the saddle room. Museum pieces. Enough silver on every one to break down a horse in five miles."

"That part I don't like," Susan said, and sat down on the bed. "It's too showy. And their spade bits, and those big cruel spurs. But the house is another thing, it's so graceful and civilized. And they wake up every morning to the sound of bells."

Oliver was yawning, smiling, and indulgent. "Once the Syndicate gets its hand on the throttle we'll change all that. Whistles, we'll have. Run the place the way Larry Kendall would run it. Plenty whistles, no siestas, no buying *pulque* outside the company store."

"You make me hope the mine will turn out worthless. How *does* it look? What were you talking about so late? Who was there?"

"I'll answer your questions in order. It looks all right on paper and in the samples. A fellow named Kreps came down here six months ago and studied the faulting, and he thinks he knows where the vein went when it petered out on the Spaniards. Walkenhorst and Gutierrez have sunk a shaft on the basis of his map. I'm supposed to tell them if they've hit what they think they've hit. Question two, we were talking about that, about the mine. Question three, Don Gustavo, Don Pedro Gutierrez, and our mortal enemy Simpson were there."

"Why our mortal enemy?"

"His principals sent him down to make an independent report, to check on mine."

"That's insulting."

He was amused. "Why? I'm the Syndicate's man. Naturally I'm going to make a Syndicate report. So Simpson's people have sent him down to report the truth."

"You sound as cynical as Henry Janin. They both want to hear it's a rich mine, don't they?"

"They sure do. But Walkenhorst and Gutierrez want it to be rich right now, unmistakably, so the Syndicate will take up its option and start paying royalties. The Syndicate wants it to look rich, whether it's really rich or not, so it can sell its option for a pile to Simpson's people. If it's *really* rich, Ferd will take up the option and work the mine himself. Simpson's crowd would prefer if Simpson could detect riches that aren't apparent to Walkenhorst, Gutierrez, or me, so they can buy cheap and get rich later."

"What are you going to report?"

"I haven't even seen the mine yet."

"What does Simpson think?"

"I don't suppose he'd tell me, would he?"

"Would you tell him what you think?"

"I don't suppose."

She got up and went to the window. Through the shutters she looked down on the Plaza of the Martyrs. The beggars who sat all day in the niches of the Morelos monument were already there. Women were hurrying toward the cathedral, and now its bell began to boom again across the sunny square. A girl with a wide flat basket of flowers on her head crossed the street, herself a flower, a nodding sunflower on a graceful stem, and stopped, swaying and topheavy, while a customer selected a blossom from her tray.

When Susan turned, she found Oliver watching her with his amused, relaxed, speculative expression. His hands were locked behind his head, his chest was hairy through the neck of his undershirt. He had gained back the flesh that Leadville had taken off him: he looked rested and confident. Here in Mexico she kept being surprised at how blond he was. Much more than Don Gustavo, who was dark and thin, he looked the part of the invading Nordic capitalist.

"Are we in for more litigation and fighting?" she said.

"Why?" he said, surprised. "My only job is to inspect and report."

"It sounds as if there might be disputes, and testifying in court, and all that."

"Then I misled you. It's all very agreeable."

"I'm glad. I hate all that. It scares me." She listened to Ascención's broom scratch down the *corredor* and past their door. "All that greedy fighting for rights and boundaries and ownership. I want this trip to go on being perfect."

"To go *on* being."

"Yes. Don't you think it has been, up to now?"

"I guess."

"You guess! You know."

"I guess I know."

His hand caught the hem of her chemise as she went past, and he pulled her close to kiss her bare back above the corset laces. "In case the mine does turn out all right, how'd it be if we came back here to run it?"

With her hands in her hair she turned. "Is that a possibility?"

"Simpson suggested it last night."

"Our mortal enemy?"

"He's no enemy. We think pretty much the same way. He'd recommend me, he said."

"Would you take it if it was offered?"

"Would *you?*"

"Oh my goodness, that's something I never even thought of."

"You could keep house in a palace like the Casa Walkenhorst."

"I'd have to think. What about Ollie?"

"He'd grow up a *charro*. I suppose he'd have to have a tutor like Enriqueta. My guess is he'd like it here."

"You want to do it."

"I don't know. It may not work out that way at all. But if it did, it would be a way out of the Leadville box. It's also a long way out of the world, almost as far out as Potosí."

"But the railroad's coming."

"Two years away, at least. Meantime your only company would be Don Gustavo reciting his Spanish poems entitled 'Yo,' and a few families like the Gutierrez', and maybe an American or Scotch or Swedish engineer now and then. Remember New Almaden?"

"But here you'd be in charge. There wouldn't be any Kendall. You could run a humane mine. And it's civilized, it isn't crude at all. There was nobody at New Almaden like Emelita, either."

Again she went to the window. This time she saw the carriage with the white mules, driven by Ysabel, come out the gate and head down toward the cathedral. Through the closed windows she could make out two crow-like forms that had to be Emelita and Enriqueta. She thought, washed by a shiver of strangeness, *What if I too . . . ?*

"It's only a possibility," Oliver said to her turned back. "It wouldn't do to bet on it. But if there's a mine there, Simpson's crowd will buy it, or the Syndicate will decide to work it. Either way I might be offered the job. It's likelier than that—I'm nearly a cinch to be. So you be looking it over while I'm gone. See if you think you'd want to live here."

3

The stone of the Moorish arches around the courtyard of the Casa Gutierrez was twisted like rope, and looked as soft. The stairway was the finest in Morelia. The ladies posed for her at the head of the steps, black against the pink stone, docile, smiling, their faces pale and soft like the faces of nuns. But when the *mozos* led out into the court a great clatter of horses and mules, the artist turned the page of her sketchbook and crowded to the balustrade with the others.

Again she was struck by the contrast with Leadville. There, when Oliver and Frank went out on a mine inspection, they wore buckskin and corduroy and battered felt hats. They creaked up into fifty-dollar Whitman saddles and yanked the lead rope of a packhorse carrying a pair of bedrolls, a few cans of beans and a slab of bacon and a frying pan, a loaf or two of bread, a pick and shovel and geologist's hammer. The tarp that covered the load by day would cover their beds at night.

Down below her, Oliver was the only familiar thing, and he, wearing what he would have worn in Colorado, looked very shabby to her critical eye. Don Pedro Gutierrez, supplying mules and horses and servants for the expedition, was clearly bent on upholding the prestige of his family and impressing the engineers of two syndicates. He stood just at the gate, with all the seethe and clatter of twenty-five mules, a half dozen saddle horses, and eight servants under his eye, and coerced it into ceremonious order.

No corduroy or stained buckskins for him. His tight leather trousers, belled at the bottom, were embroidered down the seams. His leather jacket was gorgeous with togs and silver buttons and embroidered frogs. His white beaver hat had a brim like a halo, and around it for a band was wound a silver cord. His boots looked as soft as gloves, his silver spurs were wheels. A serape of great price was folded narrow and tossed over one shoulder. He might have been ridiculous; instead he was close to magnificent. Susan, seeing him at breakfast the morning before, had thought him the sort of little dark man of fifty who might have sold dry goods on Sixth Avenue, but she revised her opinion as she labored to catch his likeness from the *corredor*. His family went back to the Conquest, he owned great ranches and historic mines, he would have scorned to measure the extent of his lands. Standing by the gateway he moved the sweating servants with an eyebrow, directed them with half-inch movements of his head.

In her quick sketch, Don Pedro's small, quiet, ornate figure came forward, larger than life, dominating all that swarming activity and the other figures who might have competed for attention. Oliver, Simpson, Don Gustavo, grown men capable of decision and authority, stood back against the wall smoking cigars and leaving everything to Don Pedro. Trying to catch in some expression or posture the authority that flowed from him, she thought of other kinds of authority she had observed in other men—Ferd Ward's utterly confident money power, Thomas Hudson's mixture of sensibility and probity, Lawrence Kendall's tight-mouthed rigor, Conrad Prager's *savoir faire*, Oliver's promptness in a crisis. Don Pedro, gaudy as a ringmaster in his noisy courtyard, was more impressive than any of them.

Like the shaped stone, the fully formed architecture, the household with its routines as fixed as holy offices, he represented a civilized continuity unbroken even by transplantation to a new country. He expressed a security of habit such as that which made Milton dear to her, but older, more cultivated, and with more power to shape the individual to the group image. The Inquisition spoke through him, Ferdinand and Isabella, the conquistadors. The black-clad, soft-faced, subservient women on the balcony confirmed his potency. If he had raised his voice or his hand it would have had an effect like another man's fury.

How did one draw that? She couldn't, not to her satisfaction. But she looked at Don Pedro long enough and hard enough to comprehend him as one aspect of what life would be like in Morelia: around a man like that, life stayed within traditional bounds. His perfection as a type made Don Gustavo look like a pretender, Simpson an outlander, Oliver all but uncouth. Unwilling to accept the implications of what her drawing was leading her to, she gave it up and simply watched.

They were going out for three weeks into the mountains, up trails as steep as ladders, and would be camping in country dozens of miles from any town—justification, she would have thought, for taking every necessity and eliminating every luxury. But she saw go onto those twenty-five mules iron pots and Dutch ovens, bundles of silver knives and forks and spoons wrapped in soft deerskin, china that from the *corredor* she thought she recognized as Limoges. There were crates of chickens, hampers of fresh fruits and vegetables, hampers of canned goods and vintage wines that had already traveled from Europe by ship, and from Veracruz and Mexico City by train, diligence, and packhorse. There were down pillows in silk covers, linen fit for the trousseau of a duchess. She saw what the Señora Gutierrez y Salarzano said was a camp bed—solid brass, complete with springs and mattress—taken apart and lashed onto two mules.

One by one, as the pack animals were loaded, Don Pedro's eyes inspected them and gave some signal invisible to Susan. One by one the *mozos* led them out into the street. The courtyard thinned, the piles of boxes, crates, hampers, and leather *maletones* were gone. Only the horses remained, in their enormous silver-mounted saddles and their bridles and martingales whose leather was a crust of filigree and rosettes. They stood mouthing their bits and rubbing their noses against the pink pillars, each one held by a *mozo* in a scarlet sash. Don Pedro looked deliberately around the court, then at the three men standing against the wall. They threw away their cigars and came to him as obediently as acolytes attending a priest.

The ladies were already drifting into line as the men started up the stairs. As in a court ceremony, the gentlemen bent one by one over transparent hands. The ladies gave them murmured adjurations to go with God. But Oliver, at the end of the line, came to a stubborn uncourtly decision that Susan saw take form in his face and manner. Here came Don Pedro bowing, here came Don Gustavo imitating him, here came Simpson, sandy-haired and amused, imitating them both. And here came Oliver shaking, not kissing, each extended hand, and giving each lady in turn a wholly inadequate friendly nod.

Susan was embarrassed for him. In matters such as this he hadn't the least grace. Then when Don Pedro stood before her, grave and deferential, she put out her hand, saw how brown it was, and lost her own poise. "It is not a hand fit to kiss," she said in English. "I've been too much in the sun."

Interrupted in his bow, Don Pedro slid his eyes sideward toward Don Gustavo, seeking translation. Don Gustavo translated. Don Pedro returned his gaze to Susan, wagged his head ever so slightly, smiled with a look like mild reproof, and brushed, or did not quite brush, her knuckles with his lips.

Don Gustavo, coming after him, had prepared a compliment: "It is a privilege to salute a hand at once so shapely and so gifted." He gave her hand a wet smack that she instantly wanted to rub off. Because she felt like kicking him, she smiled with extra warmth.

"Please," said Don Gustavo. "While we are gone, my poor house is your own. Whateffer you wish, command." His pale pop eyes crawled on her like slugs. She smelled the pomatum on his hair.

"Thank you," she said. "You're very kind," and moved her eyes to Simpson, coming up.

Grinning, he bent over her hand, which she felt dangled out there like a hurt paw or the hand of a statue on a newel post. "I'm not very graceful about all this," Simpson said, "but you can't blame me if I enjoy it."

"More than Oliver does." She looked for a moment or two into his shrewd light-lashed eyes. She liked him. Perhaps one day he would be Oliver's collaborator. She might be entertaining him at dinners when he came down to consult, or to make periodic inspections. By then would they all be wearing Mexican clothes and taking all this Mexican courtliness for granted, acting like Don Gustavo, who had been in Mexico twenty years and wished it to appear that he had been there two hundred? The worst thing she knew about Don Gustavo had to do with blue eyes: despite his Mexican pretensions, he took pains to make it clear that the blue eyes of his wife and daughter and Emelita derived from a superior strain related to his own. They might be Spanish, but they were really Visigoths. By such means he excused himself for having married into an inferior race.

"It could become a bad habit," Susan said drily. "Good-bye, Mr. Simpson. I hope you find what you came looking for."

"What we all came looking for," Simpson said. "Next time I kiss your hand on a balcony I'll be loaded down with silver like one of Don Pedro's horses."

Now Oliver. Not only did he not feel his own awkwardness, she saw, but he was enormously tickled by the whole circus. He took her hand with formality, as if just being introduced, and shook it up and down. Out of the corner of his mouth he said, "And I thought we were going camping."

"You're a little underdressed for the parade," she couldn't help saying.

In surprise he looked down at himself: corduroy pants, leather shirt, revolver, bowie, big iron spurs. "Why, it's authentic Colorado. And the spurs are authentic Chihuahua."

"Iron, though. Not silver."

Laughing, he hugged an arm around her shoulders, making her self-conscious. "Isn't it nice that *something* isn't silver? Would you like me to look like Don Pedro? He makes Clarence King look like a piker, doesn't he?" In front of them all he leaned and kissed her lightly, and when she pulled back, frowning, he looked at her with his smile hanging on his lips as if he had just made a joke. "Just be yourself," he said softly. "Don't let all the grandeur buffalo you."

His good sense released her from some inhibition or pretense that had been trying to establish itself. Looking from him to Don Gustavo she comprehended how foolish she had been about to be. She did not want Oliver to be a pretender, she didn't want to be one herself.

"I'll try."

"Get a lot of sketches."

"I've already made three times more than I can use. I'll have to see if Thomas won't print more than one article."

"Write it so he has to. Get rich."

"You too. Find a mine richer than the Little Pittsburgh."

"Or the Adelaide," he said, and pulled his mouth down. "You keep your eyes open, eh? Maybe we could do worse than Michoacán."

"I'll know by the time you get back. I'm pretty sure already."

"Good-bye."

"Good-bye, darling. Be careful."

The laugh bubbled out of him again. "The worst that could happen to me would be that I'd fall out of that brass bed."

"Do you get to use that?"

"I don't know. I can't wait to find out. Certainly it's not for Don Pedro. He wouldn't put a guest on the ground and sleep in splendor himself. So who is it for? Don Gustavo? Simpson? Me? It's a protocol problem."

The others were standing, men in one group, women in another, waiting. Susan kissed him quickly again, impropriety or no impropriety. The men clanked and jingled down the stairs, mounted, rode single file to the gate. Don Pedro looked an imperceptible message to the *mozo* there, and the gate opened. The ladies were fluttering handkerchiefs from the balustrade. Don Pedro bowed from the saddle, Don Gustavo bowed from the saddle, Simpson bowed from the saddle, not without being amused at himself. Oliver touched his hatbrim, looking upward specifically at her.

He was tall, fair, sober, shabby in his worn field clothes, and he slouched as he rode. He could not have been pompous like Don Gustavo without laughing. He had to be himself—nothing spectacular, nothing gorgeous or picturesque. Just, as she had more than once said in her letters to Augusta, her plain boy. But it was on his skill and judgment that everything hung. Having doubted him through the picturesque hour of departure, she now saw him go with a quick, strong rush of love and pride.

Casa Walkenhorst
Morelia, Michoacán
September 12, 1880

Dearest Augusta —

It is now over a week since Oliver went off with the owners and
the engineer of the prospective buyers to inspect the mine. They departed
like a Crusade—but I shall save that for when I see you. It seems too good
to be true that this letter can be mailed to the dear old studio address,
and that when we return next month you and Thomas will be back in
New York. After how many?—four long years when I have been deprived
of the sight of you! My darling, we shall have more than Oliver's Crusade
to talk about.

I am settled as happy as a worm in an apple at the Casa Walkenhorst, the home of Morelia's Prussian banker. With my *norteamericana*
habits I am probably almost as disconcerting as a worm, or half a worm
as Bessie would say, giggling—to Emelita, the sister-in-law who keeps Don
Gustavo's house. But she is such a sweet and gentle nature, and such a
model of consideration, that she would never let me know, no matter
how much I disrupted her household. I could go around on stilts, and
wearing a bearskin, and she would keep her countenance and her sweetness, convinced that these were the whims and eccentricities, or perhaps
the native customs, of an American woman artist. For I am an artist here
—my reputation is greatly enlarged by their inability to consult any of my
work. But once when I made my own bed (having been brought up my
mother's helper and having been maid of all work in a log cabin on a
ditch) I heard her afterward scolding the maid for not being prompt, and
so I have subsided not unwillingly into luxury, laziness, and daily
drawing.

I have a double reason for soaking myself in this walled, protected
domestic life. It provides me many sketches, and it gives me a model for
what may become my own future. Oliver told me before he left that
there is a good chance, providing the mine turns out well, that he will be
asked to come back and run it. I will then have the problem of making a
home here that we can live in according to our own habits, but that will
not offend against Mexican conventions, which have little *give* in them.

You can imagine how such a house as Emelita's, beautifully run and
hypnotically comfortable, affects my thwarted home-making instincts. I

love the peace of this house, which was once a priests' college and retains its cloistered air. In the mornings there is a most satisfying sense of women's work going on, the hum of voices in far rooms, the chuckling of doves on their high ledges, old Ascención's broom scratching down the *corredor*, and from the rear court the slap and flop of clothes being washed, and whiffs of woodsmoke, strong soap, and steam. The other morning, coming past the work room off the kitchen, I stopped still, smitten by such a lovely smell of fresh ironing that I was instantly melted into a housewife. I make Emelita write me out the receipt for every unusual dish we eat—whether we stay or go, such things are beyond price.

I am as intimate here as a sister, as privileged as a guest, and I tag around after Emelita on her morning rounds, carrying my sketch pad and stool. The *salas* are uninteresting—overdecorated, with too much crystal and heavy furniture, but the kitchen is a treasure, hung with copper pots above its charcoal fires, and a thin, peevish cook who would be dismissed in a minute if she were not capable of such mouth-watering food. So we all praise and placate her instead, and she takes our praise and turns it instantly sour, and I draw her in her sourness and get a picture that I think Thomas and even you will like.

I draw everything—Ascención watering his flower pots, Soledad making up one of the great *lit du roi* beds, Concepción sweeping, crouching over her short-handled broom, the Indian women sousing their washing in the copper tubs that are sunk in stone furnaces in the back court, across from a fountain that plays with a cool tinkle into a stone horse trough under bamboos. I envy those washerwomen the place in which they labor, but my *norteamericana* instincts led me to suggest to Emelita that scrub boards might ease their backs, as a longer-handled broom might ease Concepción's. Ah no, she said. It would confuse them. They are used to doing it the old way.

I am having to learn a good deal of Spanish, for you know how I love to get together with others through the tongue, and there is now no English-speaker in the house, with the men gone, except little Enriqueta's Austrian governess, a rather desperate, solitary woman who rarely leaves her room and who focusses all her feelings upon Enriqueta's poodle, Enrique. So one side of my sketch pad acquires pictures and the other side acquires Spanish verbs and nouns. And at the same time I learn some of the mysteries of Mexican housekeeping.

How many servants, I asked Emelita the other day, for a house just big enough for the three Wards?

But you will need a large house, she said. Your eminence (!). Your husband's position!

I couldn't run one, I said. Not as you do. A middle-sized house at most. How many servants?

So she thought them off on her fingers. A coachman. A cook. A chambermaid. A nurse or governess. A *mozo* for general sweeping and to mind the gate. Five at least.

I told her that the last servant I had, that wonderful and never properly appreciated Lizzie, was cook, washerwoman, chambermaid, *mozo*, sometimes nursemaid, and also artist's model.

She said there are no such people here.

I said suppose I could find one to bring down.

But she said it wouldn't do. Look at Fräulein Eberl. She was very lonely, that one, unable to associate with the family and unwilling to associate with the servants, and with no one of her class in all Morelia.

If Don Gustavo had not taken a vow, on which he greatly prides himself, never to marry again, I suppose that Emelita would have married him long since. I can't make up my mind whether I wish she had, or whether I'm happy she hasn't and he won't. She is at least entitled to the dignity of her position. It irritates my republican and suffragist sentiments to see such feminine perfection tied like a servant to that Prussian self-satisfaction. She is not pretty, except for her dark blue eyes, and like the other respectable women of Morelia she dresses richly without dressing well. But I have learned to love her in less than two weeks, and she makes the thought of living here very attractive.

You see the things that my mind plays with, mostly at siesta time when everything hushes and even the city outside shuts its doors and stills its bells. I am no better sleeper than I ever was, and so I lie and let the exciting and troubling possibilities buzz around in my head. Or I write you, which is more profitable.

Things are beginning to stir in the house. That means it will soon be time for our afternoon drive, our "airing" as it is called, though we never open the carriage windows. It is during this hour of freedom, such as it is, that I realize how close to imprisonment is the life of a Mexican woman. I watch Emelita and learn discretion. She being the head of a household and I being married, we may acknowledge the bows of gentlemen, but only of *certain* gentlemen. The young men riding their English thoroughbreds so proudly around the *zocolo* stare at all the ladies, but the ladies do not stare back, or bow. If they are marriageable, they may hardly acknowledge the existence of anyone male, or even of the female relative of a possible suitor. Inferences would instantly be drawn. So we go around the park every afternoon, getting neither exercise nor air, fluttering our fingers at balconies and carriages, while all around us the gentlemen are walking or riding and getting their blood flowing in the cool of the afternoon, and Indian girls in embroidered chemises—they look as if they had gone happily out of doors without putting on their dresses—swing up and down, and use their *rebozos* not to hide their faces but to enhance their eyes, and giggle and hug one another and cast slant eyes at passing boys.

Respectability is a burden perhaps greater than I want to bear. Unless I can be forgiven my habitual freedoms I shall find it hard to be a Morelia wife!

This afternoon I shall know more about the possibilities. Emelita tells me of the house of the town advocate—I believe there is only one— who is in Germany seeking relief for his gout. It is a small house, only twelve rooms! She will have Ysabel drive us past when we take our airing.

I can't tell you whether I hope it will suit or not, whether I want to stay or not. But I believe I do. I miss my little Ollie, of whom we have not heard since we sailed. I know he is safer with Mother and Bessie than he would be with me, but I wish we had him here just the same. After all that sickness in Leadville, and all the moving he has done in his short life, he deserves a safe home.

More later. I hear Ysabel bringing out the mules.

Next day. I have seen the house—white stucco around a central patio, with a white wall around it all, and a bougainvillea swarming over the wall. Very definitely it will do. The rooms are good, and the arrangement of square within square, a wall around the house and the house around a court, will let us live as we please. It is very near the park, so that the three of us could ride there together, assuming that I can ride without shocking the citizens. Oliver will not mind, I know. He has a way of walking through conventions of that kind as if they did not exist, and being so much himself that pretty soon people begin adapting themselves to *him*.

Even when he is at the mine, which he will surely have to be half the time, Ollie and I might ride, accompanied by some Rubio or Bonifacio, once we had accustomed people to our irregularities. It gives me a delightful sense of wickedness to contemplate it, though I wouldn't think of being so cavalier with the proprieties at home.

I think it will do, I honestly think it will. You and Thomas can visit us here, instead of at that lighthouse on the Pacific to which I once confidently invited you. Morelia isn't Paris, but it is gorgeously picturesque. Much of it is made of a soft pink stone that in certain lights, or when wetted by a shower, glows almost rose. I think you would find subjects for your brush, as I find them for my pencil, on every corner.

Today, as we were returning from looking at the house, we passed the market, which I had never seen. It was thronging with Indians, the men in white pyjamas, the women with their heads and infants wrapped in *rebozos*, the children often in nothing at all except a little shirt. And the things spread out there on the ground, under the matting roofs! Oranges, lemons, watermelons, little baby bananas, *camotes* (sweet potatoes), ears of their funny particolored corn, strange fruits, strange vegetables, chickens hanging by the legs like so many bouquets of Everlasting drying in an attic. Turkeys, pigs, beans, onions, vast fields of pottery and baskets, booths where were sold tortillas and pulque and mysterious sweets and coarse sugar like cracked corn. Such a colorful jumble, such a hum of life, such bright hand-woven cottons and embroidered chemises! Over one side soared the arches of the aqueduct, and in the center was a fountain from which girls were drawing water, gathered around its bright splashing as bright as flowers. (In this place, the poor look like flowers, the rich like mourners—at least the women.)

I cried out at once that I must come and draw it in the morning, when the sun would be on the other side of the aqueduct and would throw its looped shadow across the market, and give me a chance to hold down the boil of all that human activity with some architectural weight. I asked Emelita if I could be spared Soledad or Concepción, to accompany me for a couple of hours. She never quivered. Of course. ¿Como no?

To her, I am sure it seemed a reckless and dangerous and improper request, for in the streets of this fascinating city no respectable woman walks, even accompanied by a maid. My stilts and bearskins were showing, but no one would have known from Emelita's face that I had asked anything at all out of the ordinary.

Later. What day? I lose track of time. I have been keeping back this letter for the post that leaves tomorrow for Mexico City. Every day is like the day before, but every day there is something that to me is new, too.

When I spoke to you last, I was planning to go and draw the market. I went. In the morning Emelita came to me, dressed in her black silk, while I was drawing Enriqueta at her lessons with Fräulein Eberl, and said that Soledad was free to go with me whenever I was ready. I was ready very soon, for I didn't want to miss the proper light, and went into the courtyard to find an expedition prepared that rivaled Oliver's Crusade. There was Ysabel with the carriage and the white mules. There was Soledad with a French gilt chair and a black umbrella. There was Emelita in her black silk. I had come down in my usual morning dress, and for once Emelita's resolution to notice none of my improprieties was not up to the occasion. Her look told me that I would embarrass her. Of course I made an excuse and went back and changed. But even when I was in proper costume, you cannot possibly imagine the consternation I caused—I on my gilt chair with pad and pencil, Soledad standing and holding the umbrella over me, Emelita bravely out of the carriage, but not *too* far, and looking as if every moment were not only mortal sin, but its punishment. It was all Ysabel could do to keep back the curious.

I could not bear to stay more than twenty minutes, keeping Emelita there in the sun scorning even to lift her hem from the dust, and my sketch was very sketchy. But the morning taught me two things. One is that it is perfectly *safe* to do most of the things that propriety frowns on,

327

the other is that I won't again embarrass my Mexican friends by making them share my indiscretions.

Today one of the *mozos* returned from the Crusade, reporting that all were well and that they would be back as scheduled. He came for a fresh supply of wine, one of the mules having fallen and crushed his hamper. Don Pedro is not the sort to make his guests do without their luxuries, though it means sending a servant on a two-hundred-mile round trip.

In a week, therefore, I shall be seeing Oliver, and we shall be planning the shape of our future. My darling, I wish I could tell you now, but I must await Oliver's news. I shall have to tell you in New York— and how can we get around to the future, with all that past to catch up on?

Good night, darling Augusta. I have just been out in the *corredor* prowling up and down. The house is black and still. The starlight doesn't penetrate the shadows under the arcade, and does only a little to lighten the sunken court. It seemed profoundly peaceful and undangerous, strange but at the same time familiar, and I thought of summer nights at Milton, everyone else asleep, when we used to creep out in our night dresses and run barefoot on the wet grass. I fear I am a strange creature, my two great loves are of such different kinds. When Oliver is away from me I miss him and am restless until he returns, but isn't it strange, his absence makes me think so much more acutely of *you*.

Will you visit us in our white house with the bougainvillea, away down here in Michoacán? I mean to keep tempting you with my little exotic sweetmeats until you fall. But first I shall see you in that loved studio where we were girls and art students together a thousand years ago. Even if we are to stay here, as I now truly hope we will, we shall have to be in New York for a considerable time getting prepared.

Good night, good night. The church bells are solemn across the Plaza of the Martyrs. I feel smothered, lonely, eager, I don't know what. The future is as dark as the *corredor* out there, but might be every bit as charming once light comes on it. One thing I do know—it must have you in it, somehow, somewhere.

Your own
SUE

5

Propped by bolster and pillows, shoeless, stockingless, corsetless, clothed only in her shift, she was asleep in the big carved bed. She had been looking through her journal, rewriting incidents and observations into coherent paragraphs for her article, but the siesta hour, the shuttered dusk, the trance of quiet that held room and house and city, had been seductive. The notebook was flat on her stomach, the pencil had fallen from her slack hand.

She was in a quandary, for the guests she had been expecting, the poet and editor Thomas Hudson and his brilliant wife, had arrived simultaneously with an appalling dozen of others. Her entrance hall and *sala* were like a hotel lobby at convention time. The American ambassador was there with his wife and several aides. She saw Ferd Ward with a bowler hat in his hand, Clarence King in white buckskin, her sister Bessie trying to calm her daughter Sarah Birnie, who cried and cried. She saw a famous general with gray, sad, streaked eyes, whom she recognized but could not place. Pricey and Frank looked hopefully smiling in the door. They all waited to be taken to their rooms, but there were not rooms for all of them, there was only one pitiful room, the one she had prepared for the Hudsons. The house was too small, as Emelita had warned her—fatally small. She saw signs of exasperation and impatience in every face. Augusta, as always when angry, had grown regal and cool.

Out of her desperate dilemma her eyes popped open. A tapping on her door.

"*¿Quien es?*"

A servant voice, a male servant voice, whined, "*Con permi-i-i-so.*" The door handle rattled, the door began to open.

"No, no!" she cried, or screamed, and snatched at the trailing spread to cover herself. The door swung on open and Oliver put his head in.

"Uh huh. Caught you napping."

"Oh, Oliver, you *idiot!* You scared me to death." She bounded off the bed, he hugged her hard, kicking the door shut behind him. His clothes smelled of horse, leather, sweat, dust. "Did you just get in?"

"Foolish question number one. Did you think I might have got in yesterday and stopped at the hotel?"

"I didn't hear any noise."

"We left the caravan at Don Pedro's and walked over."

"I was dreaming," Susan said. "A dreadful dream. We had a dozen guests and only one room. I suppose it may have been something that brass bed suggested. Who slept in it?"

"Nobody. We were all too polite."

"Isn't that ridiculous. So was my dream, because, you know, I've *found* us a house, and it doesn't have just one spare bedroom, it has five, nice big ones. There's an enclosed court, and stabling for six horses . . ." She was stopped by the look on his face. "What's the matter? Isn't the mine any good?"

The horseplay of his entrance had meant nothing. She saw now that he was tired, disappointed, and grouchy. He moved his shoulders as if shrugging off a persistent insect.

"It may be some good, it may not. More likely not. At least I know Kreps wasn't right. What he thought was the lost vein *isn't.* You could work it, but it wouldn't make you rich."

For the moment, all her disappointment was frozen into quiet. Almost carelessly she said, "So you'll have to turn in a bad report."

"I don't see how it can be very enthusiastic."

What a moment before she had taken quietly now hit her like a slap. It was the corroboration, not the news, that weakened her legs and stiffened the muscles of her mouth. Her eyes were stretched, glaring at him, and as she stared she was blinded with sudden water, she could not control her breath, which gulped and caught in her throat. "Oh . . . *damn!*" she cried, and hid her face in his chest.

He laughed. She could feel the laughter in his chest and it infuriated her. "What?" he said with callous lightness. "Cussing? You?"

She reared back against his arm and knuckled at her wet eyes. "I don't care, that's just the way I feel! Thee can think me a fishwife if thee wants."

"Sue, I'm sorry. I had no idea you were that set on it."

"I don't think I've ever . . . wanted anything . . . more!"

He was frowning down into her face as if she were written in Sanskrit. "I'm astonished. Why?"

"Why! Because! A million reasons. Because I work so well here. Because it's beautiful. Because we could all be together in a pleasant house. Because it would have given thee a chance to show what thee can do."

"I suppose it might have been good, in a way," he said. "But look, it isn't quite the paradise you make out. Once you get under the surface a little . . ."

She barked at him, wanting no sour grapes comfort, and pulled away to sit down violently on the bed. "Does Simpson agree with you?"

"More or less. He's a little more bullish. He might even recommend that his people take a chance, if they can get the option cheap enough. He knows they haven't found the old rich vein, but he's half inclined to think they might break even with this one, and hit the old one later."

"What you've been doing in the Adelaide."

"More or less."

"Why would you do it there and recommend not doing it here?"

"The Syndicate didn't send me down here to find another Adelaide."

"But if Mr. Simpson is willing! Isn't it just what his people were hoping for? It looks better to them than to you? So they can buy cheap?"

"I don't know he's willing, I'm only guessing." He frowned, and a sort of slow meanness came into his face. "What are you suggesting? That I sweeten the report? Make it more encouraging? Tell 'em what they want to hear?"

They stared at each other almost in anger, until she rose and touched his arm. "I know thee can't. But if Mr. Simpson reports favorably his people will want to buy, won't they?"

"Depending on what the Syndicate wants for its option."

"And if they bought, wouldn't they ask thee to run it?"

Sulky, resistant to what she was edging toward, he grunted. "After I've said I don't really believe in the mine?"

"But why do they have to see your report at all? You won't be reporting to them. Why do Mr. Simpson's people even have to know what you said?"

"Because I've talked it over with Simpson."

"You just . . . blurted it out?"

He watched her with his head slightly turned. Almost absently he unbuckled the belt and tossed it, heavy with revolver and bowie, onto the bed. His eyes were on hers as if he were concentratedly bending something. "I just blurted it out," he said. "I'm just a big green boy too honest for his own good. I'm not smart enough to play these poker games with grown men. I don't know when to keep my mouth shut profitably."

"Oliver, I didn't mean . . . !"

He was stooping, unbuckling the spurs. One after the other they lit on the bed beside the revolver belt. He pulled over his head the buckskin shirt, releasing a stronger odor of sweat and dust, but when his face and rumpled hair emerged he would not look at her. She felt like shaking that closed, mulish expression off his face.

Tightly she said, "Won't it look odd if the Syndicate's engineer turns in a negative report and the other people's engineer is more favorable?"

Blue and cold, his eyes touched hers and went indifferently away. She felt that somehow he blamed *her* for this. And he would refuse to talk about it, he would retreat into wooden silence. "Yeah," he said. "I expect Ferd may think it's kind of odd."

"So it's certain that *he* at least isn't going to ask you to do any more in Mexico."

"I guess you've got it about right."

He sat on the bed, pulled the bootjack from under it, fitted a heel into the jack, and pulled. The boot came off. He wiggled his stockinged toes. Everything about him, from his sulky face to his animal odor, was offensive to her. Under his eyebrows he looked up, groping absently with the other foot for the jack. "I'll tell you something else. If the Adelaide ever settles its troubles with the Argentina and the Highland Chief and gets to be a working mine again, I'm not likely to be running that, either."

For a moment she took that in. "You mean we not only can't stay here, we can't go back to Leadville either."

"That'd be my guess."

"Then where *do* we go?"

"Honey, I don't know."

He pulled loose the handkerchief knotted around his throat. He concentrated on the bootjack until the second boot slid off. In her bare feet Susan went quietly around the room. She touched with her fingertips the cool carved wood of the footboard, the embossed leather of the chest, the tipped edges of the shutters, the mantel's cold stone. "I wonder," she said.

She turned and saw him sitting on the bed, still feeling criticized. And he would not bend, that was what made her so resentful. He would not defend himself or justify himself. When she questioned him, wanting to be on his side, wanting to help work out a future for them both, he acted as if she were accusing him of deliberately, out of some stupid notion of honesty, throwing away their chance. His honesty was not stupid, that was not what she meant at all. Only . . .

"Is it fate?" she said, more bitterly than she intended. "Is it just bad luck? What is it? Why are you always having to take a stand that hurts us or loses you your job? Doesn't honesty ever get rewarded?"

Her tone, she recognized, was the intimate tone that would normally have brought the Quaker "thee" to her tongue. Yet she called him "you." Perhaps he noticed, perhaps he didn't.

He shrugged, sitting there in his undershirt and stockinged feet (and I in my shift, she thought. Like a pair of quarreling shopkeepers).

"I have to do what I have to do," he said.

She stood at the mantel, and after a moment she said, "Yes. And all of us have to take the consequences."

Now she touched him. His head came up, his stare was full of disbelief and resentment. He heard, registered, acknowledged, what had come out of her mouth, but he would not answer. She would have liked to be comforted for hurting him, but he would not bend, and they spent the evening in bruised silence, one-word questions, monosyllabic answers.

It did not occur to her, apparently, though it occurs to me, that he was more frustrated and sore than she was, and mainly for her sake. *She* thought he was unfeeling.

6

The Casa Walkenhorst had overnight become a different place. The air was full of tension, Don Gustavo's looks were full of barely controlled dislike, as if, in coming to an unfavorable conclusion about the mine, Oliver had abused his hospitality. From the *corredor*, Susan witnessed a little episode in the courtyard in which Don Gustavo lashed the gate *mozo* across the back with his quirt. Emelita, every time Susan tried to talk with her, escaped with timid, hurried smiles that begged understanding. Time they were gone, taking with them their private breakage.

With Don Pedro there was no such chill; he was a grandee to the end. Just before they were to leave, he sent over for the use of Señora Ward one of his personal horses, a *rosillo*, a strawberry roan with a light mane and tail, which he hoped she would find easier-gaited than any of the broncos they might hire.

Not to be outdone in courtesy, Susan sent back the sketch she had made of the Señora Gutierrez y Salarzano at the head of her splendid stairway. It was one of her best, one she had counted on transferring to a block for the *Century*, but she did not hesitate. If Don Gustavo had made any friendly gesture, she would have felt obligated by her dislike to respond threefold. She atoned for accepting his hospitality by giving Emelita drawings of herself, of Enriqueta, of the poodle Enrique, and of the parrot Pajarito.

The evening before they were to leave they went early to their room, where Oliver worked at his field notes and his geological map that corrected the map of Kreps; Susan got out their bags for packing, and dumped them onto the bed. At the bottom of one carpetbag were her Colorado riding clothes, never used since she had packed them in Leadville. As she shook them out, there rose out of their wrinkles the smells of horse and woodsmoke, the styptic odors of spruce and bitter cottonwood, the witch hazel smell of willows. She stood holding the divided skirt to her nose, caught by recollection as strong as pain.

Her best rides were in that complex smell—mountain water, the sky whose light hurt the eyes. Pricey was in it—not the beaten disfigured Pricey but the diminutive rocker with his nose in a book, the smiler from the saddle he sat so uncomfortably. Ah, Pricey, how tenderly the haughty day! The circle around her Franklin stove was in it—Helen Jackson, King and Janin and Prager and Emmons, the laughter and the talk and the sense of empires being hewn out of raw creation, all the hope and excitement of that new country. Frank Sargent was in it, his tall limberness rising to anticipate some wish of hers, his eyes across the room as brown and glowing as the eyes of an adoring dog.

She saw him on the morning of their departure, when the two of them stood among the boxes and bags in the cabin whose door stood open on the fume of Leadville and the front-lighted Sawatch. Oliver had taken Ollie into town on a last minute errand. In the litter of departure Susan and Frank looked at one another, and Susan made a wincing, regretful face. She was close to tears.

"You won't be back," Frank said somberly. "I feel it in my bones."

"I think so. I hope so. Who could know for sure?"

"I suppose you're glad to be getting away."

"In a way. Not altogether." She laid her hand on his wrist. "We'll miss you, Frank. You've been a dear, true friend."

As if a butterfly had alighted on his wrist and might be scared away by a movement, Frank stood still. She knew precisely what froze him there. His eyes on her face, his strained smile, made her want to hug him and rock his head against her breast.

"You know how I feel about you," he said. "Always, from the minute I came in here and saw you in your little traveling hat. The day they hanged Jeff Oates."

"I know," she said. "But you mustn't."

"Easier said than done. You know how I feel about Oliver, too."

"He feels the same. There's nobody he trusts more."

The laugh that came out of him struck her ear unpleasantly. "He should read Artemus Ward: 'Trust everybody, but *cut the cards.*'"

"I don't understand." Troubled, she started to take her hand away, but he caught it with his right hand and held it down on his left wrist.

"Nothing. Forget it. I'm just . . ." Smiling, he studied her; he shook his head and laughed. "You're beautiful, you know? *And* kind. *And* talented. *And* intelligent. You're a thoroughbred."

"Frank . . ."

"You're everything good I can possibly imagine in a woman."

She tugged at her anchored hand. "You're forgetting."

"I'm not forgetting anything," Frank said. "I know who you are, and who I am, and who Oliver is, and what a gentleman does in the circumstances. I know all about it, I've thought about it enough. But I can't get up on my hind legs and cheer about it."

What could she do but smile, an affectionate, shaky smile.

"Once you kissed me, by mistake," he said. "Would you kiss me good-bye, *not* by mistake?"

Only for a second she hesitated. "Do you think . . . ? Yes. Yes, I will."

She stood on tiptoe to brush his cheek with her lips, but while she was still coming up, with puckered lips, she saw something happen in his eyes, and she was grabbed hard and he was kissing her, not on the cheek, but hard and hungry on the mouth. It was a long blind time before he let her pull away.

"That wasn't . . . fair," she said.

"It's little enough. I'm not made of wood." He would not meet her eyes. He began carrying the luggage outside to be ready for the buggy.

With the skirt still against her face, Susan looked across at Oliver, his fair hair rumpled, his neck and arms burned dark, working at the table under the ornate oil lamp. She felt she owed him something, she wanted to say something that would restore them. Crossing behind him, she slipped one hand over his eyes and with the other held the skirt under his nose. "Smell. What does that smell like?"

Obediently he sniffed. "Mold?"

"Oh, mold!" She yanked it away. "It smells like Leadville, that's what it smells like. Can you imagine? It makes me homesick. In spite of everything, I want to go back."

Half turned in his chair, he took her outburst with complete seriousness. When he was very tanned, as now, his eyes were as blue as blue turquoise. "Sue, I wouldn't count on it."

One last time she sniffed at the skirt—sniffed and couldn't be sure she had really smelled in it that intoxicating essence of the mountains. She gave it up. "I suppose not. It just came over me like a gust. For a second I knew exactly who I was: Mrs. Ward from Ditch Walk. I guess I'd better get ready to be the Wandering Jew again."

"He's immortal, isn't he?" Oliver said. "He *never* gets to settle down. We'll make it, sooner or later."

"In Heaven, I expect."

"Oh ye of little faith. Come on, Sue, we'll make it. We'll get that right job and that house and that yard and that attic. We really will."

"It's hard to see how, or when."

"*Mañana*," Oliver said. He gave her a pat on the hip and turned back to his notes and map. "Hadn't you better get packing? We've got forty miles to ride tomorrow."

She had to laugh. No sooner did the talk get around to settling down than it was time to go somewhere.

End of dream number three, which like the Santa Cruz dream was more hers than his. A short dream, but intense, it had briefly enchanted the artist as well as the wife. She put it aside, and did not mope, and made the most of the trip back. It is a commentary both on her personally and on the Genteel Female that she rode the two hundred and fifty miles to Mexico City in a little over five days, and on the way, literally writing and drawing in the saddle, made all the notes and some of the sketches for a third *Century* article.

She had the terrier temperament, and she was interested in everything that moved. Through the black silk face mask that Emelita had given her as protection against the *muy fuerte* Mexican sun, her eyes were very busy. Her pencil was always out.

They were four—she and Oliver, Simpson, and a villainous-looking colonel of cavalry, one of Diaz's colonels, who rode a horse he called Napoleon Tercero and whom they suspected of having been a bandit before patriotism ennobled him. They accepted his company because there were many of his kind, un-ennobled, along the roads they must travel.

Behind the riders came the little train of two pack mules, two lead mules, and two spare horses, managed by six servants, the last of whom rode his mule very close to the tail, at the very end of the procession, and so far as they could see, did nothing but adjust the angle of his sombrero according to the angle of the sun.

Ahead of them by six hours rode a trusted servant of the house of Gutierrez who prepared their way at the great *estancias* where they rested in the afternoons or slept at night. Nothing could have appealed to Grandmother's romantic medievalism more than those houses. They arrived like knights errant, a seneschal swung open the gates, at the inner gate the lord met them and made them welcome. Vassals led away the lady's palfrey and unbuckled the knights' spurs, demoiselles led the lady to her room. They dined at feudal boards with retainers clustered below the salt, while outside in courts lighted by torches there was minstrelsy on the guitar.

Fairyland, a storybook country of antique courtesy and feudal grandeur, with a passionate concentration of the picturesque on which Susan Ward throve. She left every great house with reluctance. As they jingled and shuffled along a road through some sun-baked high valley, their shoulders keeping the same motion, the cartridges clunking in the men's carbines to the same rhythm, she may have thought that they owed it all to Don Pedro Gutierrez, and that if Oliver's report were only going to be different, they might still become part of that world. I catch her, in the reminiscences, wondering wistfully if those *estancias* have managed to survive within sound of the train whistle, if there are still houses like Querendero and Tepitongo and Tepititlan, where their whole cavalcade of ten people, twelve horses, and four mules could be taken in on an hour's notice and cause not a ripple except the friendly, grave stir of hospitality.

There is only one passage in her third *Century* article to indicate that she sometimes forgot the romantic color of what she was seeing, and let her mind brood on the fact that this picturesque road led nowhere but *back*, and back to what? Not even the meager stability of Leadville.

"We met no one but Indians," she writes. "Once it was a young man who had given his straw hat to the woman behind him and went bareheaded himself, his coarse thatch of hair shining like shoe blacking in the sun. She carried a sleeping child swaying heavily in the folds of her *rebozo*. With one hand, which also carried her shoes of light-colored sheepskin, she held the end of the *rebozo* across her face. In the other hand she carried a rude guitar. Over the blue cotton cloth held across her face she stared at us fixedly out of her great black eyes.

"I wondered at her look of awed curiosity, until I realized that I was riding with my hands clasped behind me, to rest them from holding in my *rosillo*, while Oliver had taken my bridle and was leading me along. I was wearing the black silk mask that Emelita had given me. To that Indian woman I must have looked like a captive, bound and masked, being led away to the mountains."

I hear you, Grandmother. *Entiendo.*

VI

ON THE BOUGH

1

"Susan," said Thomas Hudson from his William Morris chair, looking at her over his tented fingers, "do you have any idea how remarkable you are?"

"Oh my goodness!" Susan said. "Here we sit, just the three of us, the perfect leftovers of a perfect evening. Don't spoil the best part with flattery."

"Look at her, Augusta," Thomas said. "Isn't she beautiful? As rosy as one of her father's apples. You absolutely charmed Godkin, you know. It's a pity Mr. James was indisposed, he'd have found a new model for the American girl."

"Girl! Anyway I'm not sure I could stand being attenuated in Mr. James's fashion. I was half glad he didn't appear, isn't it awful? I'd have been terrified to find myself talking to him. And he would have distracted my attention from you two."

She felt warm, tired, cherished. Before the fire's warmth she positively blinked. It had been the kind of evening that heightened her color and loosened her tongue. First dinner at the house of E. L. Godkin, the editor of *The Nation*, to meet his houseguest Henry James, who didn't appear—sent down his apologies because of an earlier indiscretion with coffee. So she had to put up with being seated between Mr. Godkin and Joseph Jefferson. Then *Patience*, with Godkin on one side of her and Thomas on the other, laughing themselves weak. Then oysters and champagne for eight here at the studio, and praise for her Mexican sketchbooks, spread out on display. Now this sweet and intimate late half hour of low fire and warm eyes. She would have to go back to Milton and work hard for a week to take the bubbles out of her blood.

Thomas's smiling, narrow face watched her from the shadowy chair. All around, on walls, mantel, whatnot, highboy, were mementoes of the Hudsons' rich life—the sort of life she had shared all evening: photographs of the famous, a drawing of Augusta by Homer, a pair of

343

china lions, the gift of Raphael Pumpelly, a whole wall of Japanese prints, a Malay *kris* with a wavy blade, an Australian boomerang, a lugubrious wooden saint from a Burgundian church. They gathered objects as they gathered friends; the richness of their accumulations was an index of the open-handedness of their giving. They made the wildest incongruities harmonious. They took Susan Ward, a country cousin, and blended her with Jefferson, Godkin, themselves—could even have blended her with Henry James if he had appeared. Now they sat and looked at her with such love and approval that her warm face grew warmer. It was joy to hear them praise her; she could not resist.

"All right," she said, "you may tell me in what way I'm remarkable."

Augusta from her hassock—soft face, dark hair, shining brown eyes, said, "As if you didn't know."

Thomas slid farther into his chair with his elbows propped and his fingers tented before his mouth and talked to the weathered saint on his pedestal behind Susan.

"How art thou remarkable? Let me count the ways. Hmm? She's been out in the unhistoried vacuum of the West for nearly five years, as far from any cultivated center as possible. What does she do? She histories it, she arts it, she illuminates its rough society. With a house to keep and a child to rear, she does more and better work than most of us could do with all our time free. She goes to Mexico for two months and returns with a hundred magnificent drawings and what amounts to a short book—she writes as well as Cable and draws better than Moran. She has been over Mosquito Pass in a buckboard and across Mexico by stage coach and saddle horse, she has been down mines and among bandits, places where no lady ever was before, and been absolutely unspoiled by it. There isn't a roughened hair on her head. To cap it, she is so vivacious and charming that she makes an old political warhorse like Godkin beg for sugar lumps, and draws a hundred pairs of glasses to our box."

"Of course I don't believe in this woman at all," Susan said. "Those glasses were on Augusta."

Thomas ignored her, with a sidling smiling look at his wife. "Her husband is away," he said. "She has to deal with all the routines of life.

344

So what is she doing? I know of at least three commissions for drawings that she is working on, and I would bet a year's salary that she is also writing something."

"Something ridiculously beyond her powers," Susan said.

"What?" Augusta said. "Tell us."

"Ah!" Susan said, "what do you care what I'm doing? You're both doing things so much better and more important."

"Of course we're important," said Thomas. "I would be the last to deny it. But I call your attention to the almost diseased modesty of this young woman we're speaking of. To hear her tell it, she is a clumsy illustrator and a writer of amateur sketches. The fact is, any editor in the country would jump at the chance to sew up everything she does. I live in daily fear that she'll be lured away from the *Century* by gold and flattery."

"What *are* you writing?" Augusta said. Where she sat by the fire, the light touched one side of her face, which glowed with dark warmth. Her skin had always been Susan's despair, it was as flawless as wax fruit. "You have to tell us—we're your first public. Did you know I've kept every single letter from you, ever since you went out to New Almaden?"

"And made up my first sketch for me out of them. If I *am* anything, you two made me."

"Nobody made you but yourself," Thomas said. "I also suspect the hand of God—no other hand could be quite that sure of itself. Now tell us what you're writing, in those hours when lesser people sleep."

He was one who could make her believe in herself. Close friend, once a sort of suitor, he was also the most respected editor in the United States. Merely to be his contributor made one's reputation. She said, "Something beyond me. I'm constantly being stopped by ignorance. I have always to write from outside, from the protected woman's point of view, when I ought to be writing from within. I'm doing a novel about Leadville."

"Will it serialize? Never mind. We must have it. I'll top all other bids."

"There won't be any. Nobody but a friend like you would publish it."

"If it were something by Mr. James I wouldn't guarantee to take it with more confidence. You're sure fire, Leadville is sure fire. Howells will gnash his teeth."

That beautiful, reassuring smile! "Ah, isn't it nice to be loved by you two!" Susan said. "Yes, it's about Leadville, and the Adelaide's trouble with the Highland Chief and the Argentina. Pricey is in it— do you remember Pricey? I'm sure I wrote you about him, the little Englishman who stood up in his stirrups one day and quoted Emerson to me on the banks of the Arkansas. He was terribly beaten by the Highland Chief thugs when they came in to steal or destroy records in Oliver's office. There's a girl in it whom I've made the daughter of the villain, and a young engineer who's in love with her but at war with her father."

"They sound like people I know," Thomas said, slumped and attentive.

Susan laughed and felt herself coloring. "Oh, she's much more attractive than her author, and the hero isn't Oliver Ward. Actually he's more like Frank Sargent, your old Staten Island neighbor. He's a perfectly beautiful young man."

"In love with you, like everyone else," Augusta said.

The color would not go down in Susan's cheeks, though she willed it down. She laughed again. "Frank? Why do you say that? Well, yes, I suppose he was, in a harmless way. I sistered him. It was Oliver he worshipped, and he hated the Highland Chief crowd so, because of Pricey, that he'd have stayed there for years just to beat them. But of course as soon as Oliver won the Adelaide's case for it, the wretched Syndicate let them both go. Frank's down in Tombstone, the last I heard."

"I never can keep Western places straight," Augusta said. "Tombstone—really, what a name! Is that where Oliver is, too?"

Her interest was false; she did not care where Oliver was. Susan read in her half-flippant exclamation every sort of half-contemptuous dismissal: anyone who was associated with the West, and in particular Oliver Ward, brought a new tone to Augusta's voice, the tone she used for troublesome tradesmen, tedious women, boring men. Her brother Waldo was a member of the Syndicate to which Oliver had made his disappointing report: there was ill opinion confirmed. Susan understood that her husband's name was to be mentioned and passed by, not dwelt upon; he was to be walked around like something repulsive on a sidewalk.

She shot Augusta a hot look and said, "Not Tombstone. After he sold the cabin in Leadville he went up to look into a gold strike in the Coeur d'Alene country of Idaho. Now that winter has shut things down, he's in Boise, the territorial capital."

"My dear," said Augusta, and bent her glowing glance on Susan and seemed to forget for a moment, in that searching, half-smiling, meaningful look, what it was she had started to say. "Coeur d'Alene," she said after a moment. "He was well advised to choose that over Tombstone. Coeur d'Alene, that's charming."

"The mine he's interested in is called the Wolf Tooth," Susan said.

Lovers and antagonists, they stared at each other. "My friend whom you do not intend to like" was between them as solidly as if he stood warming his coattails at Augusta's fire. Susan read in Augusta's face her opinion of men who followed gold strikes and wound up wintering among the seedy politics of territorial capitals. Her own chest was tight, she felt overcorseted and smothered. She might in a moment jump up and leave the room, or fly to Augusta and throw her arms about her and cry that it made no difference, no matter what direction her life had taken, no matter whom she was married to, Augusta would always have her place. But he's not what you think him, he's not! she felt like saying. Why must you always pull back from touching even his name? Why must you act as if I had married a leper or a cad or a ne'er-do-well?

Because the silence was growing tense, she withdrew her eyes from Augusta's and looked at Thomas. Sleepy-eyed, without untenting his fingers, he said, "How does your story end?"

"Not the way ours did," Susan said, and made a face and laughed. "The villain has to die, I think. I think he has his men set a powder charge in the hero's drift, to blow up that entrance to the mine and shut the right people out. The men beat up Pricey when he stumbles on them setting the charge. Then the hero finds Pricey, and goes hunting them with a Winchester. He finds the dynamite and carries it into the enemy's tunnel before it explodes, and the villain, coming down to check on his villainy, is killed by it."

Again she made a face, threw a look at Thomas and then, for a flickering instant, at Augusta, and then looked down at her hands. She felt embarrassed, all her pleasure in the evening was gone. In this room hung with the trophies of culture, her story sounded melodramatic and rough. She felt like a squaw explaining how you tanned a deerskin by working brains into the bloody hide and then chewing it all over until it was soft. Augusta was sitting with her head bent, frowning at the jeweled hands on her knees.

"I know nothing about explosives," Susan said. "I know nothing about the motives of criminal, drunken, brutal men, nothing about the working of mines, nothing about how it feels to be beaten up or to hold off a gang of thugs with a Winchester. Oliver keeps all that to himself, he thinks I should be protected from it."

Another quick clash with the dark eyes. Augusta's mouth was pursed, her brows raised as if she asked a question. You see? Susan meant to tell her. I'll defend him. I declare his right to be.

"But I nursed poor Pricey," she said to Thomas. "They broke his nose and his cheekbone and kicked out his front teeth and hurt his head so that he was never right afterward."

"I believe your qualifications are adequate," Thomas said with his slow smile. "How about the engineer and the young lady? Wedding bells?"

"I . . . don't know. I don't think so. She has been raised in the East, she is altogether above her father, though he was once a gentleman. I think, don't you, that a girl with any delicacy of feeling couldn't bring herself to marry a man indirectly responsible for her father's death. No matter how much she was in love with him."

"An unhappy ending?" Augusta said. "Oh, Sue, why?"

Susan's oppression had grown until she felt she would shrink away to nothing under the weight of it. Her story, barbarous to begin with, and hence open to Augusta's unspoken scorn, was silly when told from the woman's point of view, and hence open to her own. It was as if Mr. James should write a dime novel. And Thomas's imperturbable consideration could not warm away the chill. She knew that with Oliver in New York an evening like this would simply not have happened. The one time they had gone together to dine, the studio had been full of dark spaces, uncomfortable silences, too much trying on both sides.

"Isn't that the way things do end?" she said—she threw it at Augusta like a stone.

Again Thomas rescued them; his tact was clairvoyant. "However it ends, we must have it," he said, and yawned and sat up straight. His smile was of a steady, incomparable sweetness. Susan had tried many times to draw it; she thought it the friendliest and gentlest and most understanding expression she had ever seen on a human face. "Isn't anyone else tired? It's nearly two."

"I am," Susan said. "Terribly, all of a sudden."

Promptly, with a queenly rustling of taffeta, Augusta rose from her hassock, and in an instant, in a look, everything was right again, all the love that had radiated through the familiar room until five minutes ago was restored. It was like coming out of chilly woods into sunlight. "We've kept you up too long," Augusta said. "It was utterly stupid of us. You shouldn't be allowed to overdo."

Through a danger of tears, with lips gone suddenly trembly, Susan said, "How could either of you two ever be thoughtless? It's beyond your capacity."

They went with their arms around one another to Susan's bedroom door, and there they stopped. Augusta was inches taller than Susan, and her bearing made her taller than she was. Her dark eyebrows were bent in a slight frown; her hair came in a dark wave across her forehead. The moment of her breathing woke a diamond like a blue-green firefly in the hollow of her throat. She took Susan by the arms. "Sue, are you happy?"

"Happy? It's been one of the happiest evenings of my life."

"I don't mean tonight."

"Of course," Susan said steadily. "I'm very happy."

"This young man, Frank Sargent, does he mean anything to you?"

"He's a friend," Susan said, and steadied her eyes on Augusta's face, conscious of a faint astonishment. "He's ten years younger than I am. Anyway I'll probably never see him again."

"You wanted this child that's coming?"

"Yes."

"Does Oliver know about it?"

"Not yet."

349

The dark head bent toward her, the dark eyes narrowed, glowing with a question, the jewel winked in the hollow throat. "Why not?"

"Why not? Well, first he was in Denver and Leadville, back and forth, and much too busy to be bothered with that sort of news. Then he was off in the mountains where mail was very uncertain. I didn't want my letters falling into other hands. Sometimes people in places like that get so hungry for news of any kind that they literally read other people's letters."

Steadily the dark eyes watched her. "Is that a real reason?"

"No."

"What, then?"

"Why do you ask?" Susan said with a flash of returning resentment. "You're not really interested in him."

"I'm interested in him because I'm interested in you. Why haven't you told him?"

"Because I'm afraid he'll think that with two babies he'll have to take any job that comes up. I want him to find just the right place, where he'll be happy and have a chance to prove what he can do."

"Will he come home for the birth?"

"I don't want him to unless he's found what he wants."

"But when he does find it, he'll send for you and you'll go."

Susan took a breath. She found it hard to bear up under the weight of eyes. "Augusta, if your husband's profession took him a long way away, and he sent for you, wouldn't *you* go?"

"With a four-year-old and a new baby? To a wilderness?"

"I wish you liked him."

Augusta looked for a moment at the ceiling. Her hands shook at Susan's shoulders. "Of course I like him! I couldn't dislike anyone so close to you. But I love you, my darling, do you see? He's kept you from us for five years, he's taken you out of the world you belong in. Thomas is right, you *are* remarkable. You're more remarkable even than you were."

"Then he can't have been bad for me," Susan said, and shrugged her shoulders free while Augusta with bent head watched her, frowning. "Anyway you don't have to worry that he'll send for me soon. Things haven't gone well for him, poor fellow. The Wolf Tooth doesn't seem to be much of a mine, and Heaven knows if he'll find anything around Boise."

"Isn't there anything an engineer can do in the East?"

"Only if he's established and in demand, like Mr. Prager. And, I don't know, he's addicted to the West, he's happier there."

"At your expense."

"You don't like him," Susan said. "He has great capacities, you've never seen him at anything like his best. When he finds something he wants to do, I'll go to him, infant or no infant."

She pinched her lids tight on the throb of a growing headache. The dim hall swam when she opened them. She would lie sleepless half the night.

"But I know it won't be soon," she said, "and oh, Augusta, I'm only half sorry!"

Her arms went out, she flung herself on her friend and buried her face in stiff silk. After a moment she pulled back her head and spoke to the diamond that winked and went out and winked again in Augusta's throat. "You pretended to think there was something between me and Frank Sargent. There isn't—but I'm guilty, just the same. What kind of wife is it who half wants her husband's bad luck to continue so that she can stay longer near someone else? You."

2

She was on her way to the kitchen when she saw him coming up the path with his carpetbag in his hand and his coat slung over his shoulder. His eyes searched the porch, he stooped to see in the kitchen window. Then she had the door open and was onto the porch and he leaped up the three steps and engulfed her. He rocked her back and forth, his lips were jammed under her ear. Eventually he held her away and looked her over as if for symptoms of disease.

"Susie, are you all right?"

"I'm fine, there wasn't a bit of trouble. But how are *you*? Oh, it's been so long!"

"Don't ever do anything like that to me again," he said.

"I didn't want to worry you."

"Worry me. *Worry* me! Where is she? Can I see her?"

"She's upstairs, asleep."

"Where's everybody else? Where's Ollie?"

"Down in the orchard with Father. Mother and Bessie and the children have gone over to Poughkeepsie shopping."

"It's just us, then. Good." His hand was feeling along her shoulder and neck; it took her by the nape and held her, the big warm hand going nearly all the way around. "Ah, Susie, how are you, really?"

"I'm fine, honestly I am. I've been up and around for days. I've even worked some on the galleys of my story."

"You're crazy. You ought to be in bed."

"After nearly three weeks? I'm perfectly well."

But she went up the stairs slowly, helping herself by the rail, stepping up one step and bringing the other foot after. Coming behind her, he was not persuaded by the bright smile she threw over her shoulder. "Should you be climbing stairs?"

"As long as I take them slowly."

"Let me carry you."

"My goodness, you'd *really* put me back to bed!"

"You don't look after yourself."

"I've got better advice than yours, Mr. Ward. Mother and Bessie would have me in bed if they thought I belonged there."

Up in her room he stood above the basket, lifting the corner of the pink blanket to get a look. He studied his daughter quietly. Susan had the conviction that if the baby awoke and found his strange face looking down on her, she would not cry.

"You've named her Elizabeth."

"After Father's mother and Bessie. But it isn't final, if you'd prefer something else."

"Elizabeth's fine. Only we'll have to call her Lizzie or Betsy or something to keep her sorted out." Softly he let the blanket down. His eyes, very blue, came up to meet hers. "*Hecho en Mejico*," he said.

"Yes. She's one thing we got out of that."

Wind rattled through the maple outside, and the curtains blew inward from the open window and snagged on the basket. Susan lifted them off and pushed down the window a few inches. When she looked up again, Oliver was still watching her. "Susie, didn't I deserve to know?"

"What could you have done? It would only have upset you."

"Don't you think it upsets a man to get a letter saying his wife has had a baby he never even knew was coming?"

"I'm sorry. I suppose I was wrong. I just . . ."

Her mind was darting into corners, her feelings were confused. She both granted his right to blame her, and resented his doing so. She knew perfectly well why she had more than once stopped herself in the act of writing him. He was a threat to Milton's placid domesticity, to her restored intimacy with Augusta and Thomas, to her position as an artist and writer known and acknowledged by a public. The demands he might make on her were demands she wanted to postpone. For months he had been hardly more than the photograph of someone loved and absent and not miserably missed; she could take him out when she chose, and cry over him, and put him back. And then when she might have told him, when she had fully intended to tell him in time for him to come home if he could, then had come his letter, with his own news. Her mouth, opened to apologize, stiffened in resentment and anger; from being pliable and loving, she found herself throwing his blame back at him with a stammering tongue.

"I'm at fault, yes. I should have written. Thee has a r-right to be upset. But haven't I too? D-doesn't it upset a wife who is staying home and working and h-holding things together to hear that her h-husband isn't doing at all what she—what she thought he was doing, what they'd agreed he'd do, but is out, is off in some *wild* impossible scheme to bring water to two, three, what is it, three hundred thousand? acres of desert. Didn't *I* deserve to know?"

"That wasn't quite the same thing."

"But it concerned us all, just as much."

"Sue, I just had to be sure, first."

"Sure!" she cried. "What kind of word is that? *Sure!* I didn't write you about the baby because I thought you were hunting up just the right place, some deep mine where there would be a future and we could all live. I didn't want you to be diverted. And all the time you . . ."

"I doubt there is any such place," Oliver said. "You and the children couldn't have lived in any of the camps I was in, and none of them have a future."

"Then you should have written and told me. How long have you been—fooling around with this irrigation scheme? Months, apparently. And not a word to me. Were you afraid, or ashamed, or what?"

"I told you. I had to be sure."

Angrily she stared at him. He stood before her filled with an idiotic confidence, a county-fair Moses with his sleeves rolled up, ready to smite the rock. If he didn't throw away his foolish staff and quit dreaming, he would humiliate her and himself, and justify every doubt her friends had ever had of him.

"I wrote you the minute I was sure we could pull it off," he said.

He made her shake her head, he jarred out of her some hard laughter. "How can you say such a thing? How can you be sure you can pull it off, as you say? It would take millions of dollars."

"Not right away. We'll do it in stages."

"Each stage taking only half a million."

"Listen," he said, and took her by the wrist, scowling down on her. Then he smoothed out the scowl and made it into a smile, he coaxed her with his eyes. "Come here." He led her to the foot of the basket. The breeze from the window stirred the baby's fine pale hair, and Susan reached to pull the sash clear down. Outside, though the August sunshine was full and hot, weather was building up. She caught a glimpse of thunderheads off beyond the river, and a far flicker of lightning, too far away for thunder. Oliver held her by the wrist, looking down at the sleeping baby.

"Do you think you can bring her up?" he said. "Can you make a woman of that baby?"

"What kind of mother would I be if I didn't think so?"

"You're confident."

"I hope so. I think so. Yes, why?"

"Will you believe me when I tell you I'm just as confident I can carry water to that desert?"

She saw in his face that he had contracted the incurable Western disease. He had set his cross-hairs on the snowpeak of a vision, and there he would go, triangulating his way across a bone-dry future, dragging her and the children with him, until they all died of thirst. "I believe you're confident," she said. "I know I'm not."

He led her to the bed and made her sit down; he drew from the pocket of his coat, hanging on the bedpost, a brochure in a green cover. I have a copy of it here. "The Idaho Mining and Irrigation Company," it says. Inside, on the title page, fellaheen in loincloths are carrying water in pots slung on a pole, and underneath the woodcut is a quotation which with great difficulty I have determined comes from Psalms: "I have removed his shoulder from the burden; his hands were delivered from the pots."

"I showed that to Clarence King," Oliver said. "Did I tell you I met him on the train, coming East? He says that quotation alone insures us success."

She was appalled: he was a child. "Mr. King is a great joker."

"Maybe, but he wasn't joking about this. Neither am I. Go ahead, read."

Shakily she laughed. "I thought I was the only writer of fiction in this family."

"Fiction, is it?" He flipped the page. "See who the president of this company is? General Tompkins, who is also president of American

Diamond Drill. He's not used to backing fictions. Look at the figures. Look at the facts."

Unwillingly she read about damsites, weather, rainfall, storage capacities, topography, soil analyses, placer production from the Snake River sands. She read two interviews with settlers already irrigating out of Boise Creek, and thought them enthusiasts of the same stripe as her husband. He *was* a child. It took some tough financial pirate, some Gould or Vanderbilt, to do what he in his innocence thought he could do.

His thumb came down and dented the map spread before her, made a deep crease at a point where the contour lines crowded together and the wiggle of a stream flowed away. "There's the principal damsite. We won't do anything about it yet. At first we'll just throw a diversion dike across the creek lower down, and turn the creek into our canal system. That alone will take water to thousands of acres."

"I don't see how you make money," she said helplessly. "The land isn't yours to sell."

"We don't sell land, we sell water rights and water. The more settlers come in, the greater the need. That's when we'll build the dam and lengthen the canal line clear to the Snake. Here goes the canal, along the edge of the mountain here, right across the drainage. The whole valley's under the ditch."

"I never could read contour maps," she said.

"Never mind," he said, and took the brochure from her lap. "Can you imagine one enormous sage plain that drops in benches—a big nearly level plateau for a mile or two, and then a fifty-foot drop, and then another bench? Can you visualize it? That canal will eventually run seventy-five miles and not cross any man's land. Do you know what that means?"

"I know what it sounds like."

He waited.

"It sounds like a country without life, people, schools, anything."

"It sounds to me like a country with a future."

"And no present."

The impatience she created in him troubled her, and yet she had to resist his enthusiasm. For her own sake and the children's sake and for his sake she had to be sensible. But she smiled, trying to express love even while she blocked his way; she felt that she begged, that he could not insist if she made it clear how much the prospect appalled her.

He flapped the brochure against his knuckles, thinking. "Boise's not a village, it's a little city, the territorial capital. The Oregon Shortline will go through it and put it on the main line to Oregon. There's a cavalry post, there're balls even. The mountains rise up right behind town, the riding's wonderful. You can have a horse, so can Ollie."

With her hands in her lap she sat, not wanting to look up at him. "And he can go to a one-room school. He'll be starting, you know. This fall."

"You were going to take a tutor along to Morelia. Why not to Boise?" But she remained silent, and he exclaimed in exasperation, "Don't you see it? Any of it? Doesn't it challenge you at all? Do you even see the significance of those seventy-five miles of canal across the public domain?"

"I'm afraid I don't."

"No right of way problems. Not one old coot who can make you divert your ditch around his land. No lawsuits. Just one big simple engineering problem."

"And one big money problem."

"That's not a problem."

"What?" Now she did look up.

"General Tompkins has already lined up backing from Pope and Cole. We're talking to them in New York tomorrow."

Slowly she rose. Her shoulder twitched, she felt weak and tired, aggrieved that he kept her talking and resisting him instead of letting her go to bed. "You mean you've already committed yourself. Without ever talking to me."

Beyond his head the maple leaves outside hung without movement, as still as his face. The air was brassy. "Everything moved so fast," he said. "I hoped I could persuade you."

"But how can I decide so suddenly! It's so different from anything I was prepared for. I'm not strong yet, you really can't expect . . ."

Women's tactics, unfair. She saw them take effect. Moodily he turned his eyes out the window.

"It's not only me," she said. "Baby's too small. I wouldn't dare, with winter ahead."

"Winters there are a whole lot milder and healthier than they are here."

"But there's no safe job. There's only this . . . speculation."

"Do you think superintending a mine is safe?" he said, and laughed so unpleasantly that she wanted to cry. "Didn't Almaden or the Adelaide teach you anything?"

"Yes," she said, looking down. "So did Mexico. How easily something can go wrong—*always* goes wrong!"

"Sue, I *know* this scheme. I made it up, I surveyed it, I laid out the plans. It'll work."

Wearily she looked up, let her eyes meet his stubborn blue ones. "Well, go in to your meeting tomorrow and see what they say. We can't settle it now."

"There's no point in talking to Pope and Cole if you aren't willing."

The flick of their eyes meeting and breaking apart again. "Suppose I wasn't," she said. "What would you do?"

It took him a few seconds. Then he answered steadily, "Stay here, I suppose. Get some sort of job. Pick apples. Hire out to John."

The ghost of Mrs. Elliott was whispering to her. She took her throat in her hand and swallowed against the pressure of her fingers. "You know I wouldn't stand in your way or make you . . . give up what you want. Could you run it from out there and come back here for —between whiles? Like Conrad and Mary?"

"That's the sort of arrangement you didn't want when we were talking about Potosí."

"It would be different, here at home."

Another silence, while the baby stirred and sighed and turned half over. "No," Oliver said at last. "Now *I* won't have it. I've lived away from you all I want to."

"Oh, Oliver!" she cried. "Don't think I don't love thee! Don't think I want thee living apart from us! It's only that I feel safe here. Thee is asking me to give up what I love almost as much as thee. That little mite there has taken all the recklessness out of me. Let me think. Go to the meeting, but let me think a while."

For a while he held her there, saying nothing. Then he walked her to the window, where a wind was thrashing the maple outside and stirring the curtains through the cracks of the closed sash. She stood with his arm around her, leaning on him and looking down to where the ferns along the edge of the lane bent limberly in the gust. She heard him say, "Look at her. She's nursing in her sleep." His arm squeezed her, shook her, let her go. "All right. You get used to my news and I'll get used to yours. Maybe they'll turn out to be compatible."

"Maybe."

But she had already given in. She knew that sooner or later, this fall or next spring, she would be packing up her children and her depleted collection of household goods and going West again—not, as at first, on an adventurous picnic, and not with a solemn intention of making a home in her husband's chosen country, but into exile.

VII

THE CANYON

1

Darling Augusta —

I am sitting, or lying, in our old hammock—the same old hammock that hung on the piazza in New Almaden, and later served as a bed for Ollie in Leadville. It hangs now between two cottonwood trees in the ragged yard that surrounds this house, built by a missionary Jesuit since called to other fields. On hot afternoons it is my favorite spot, if I can be said to have a favorite spot in this drab new town where ladies say ma'am and servants don't, and Irish miners still calloused from pick and shovel are erecting their millionaire houses with porte cocheres and stone turrets. Oliver is out at the engineering camp in the canyon much of the week. With the help—it isn't really that—of a good-natured clumsy town girl, I have been able to establish a routine of work in the mornings. I am writing another Leadville novel, being poor in experience and having to make do with what is at hand. In the afternoon when baby is fed and put down, and Ollie has gone up for his nap, I come out here to read, and write letters, and listen to the dry lonely rattle of wind through the cottonwood leaves.

It is a life without much stimulation or excitement. The bugles from the cavalry post just above us mark off the days as inexorably as the whistles of New Almaden or the church bells of Morelia. I open my eyes to First Call, rise to Reveille, nurse my baby to Mess Call. When I am working at my desk I am often spurred on by the thrilling notes of the Charge from the drill field beyond our pasture fence. When I hear To the Colors, as they lower the flag in the evening, I know it is time to bestir myself about supper. I go to bed to Taps, and drift off to sleep as Lights Out blows eastward across the mesa, a long, fading, musical relinquishment as sweet and sad as the call of a mourning dove.

The house is comfortable, the children are very well, Oliver's work goes ahead steadily, I have my own work to keep me from thinking too much about all I left behind, and so I have no right to belittle this place where we shall spend our lives until Oliver gives up being a field engineer. There are one or two Army wives, Eastern ladies, who are good company. The town ladies I can say less for. You never saw such attention to dress and manners, and to so little purpose. They have been eager about paying calls, but most of their calls I shall not return. They may think me snobbish if they wish.

Oliver hoped that I would find the Governor and his wife attractive. We dined with them a few nights ago, and alas, I am afraid I thought him pretentious, his house tasteless, and his wife common. For O's sake I do not admit this, for the Governor is his supporter, and of much use to him in cutting red tape.

It is strange to find ourselves people of consequence. My old boy has sold them all on his dream. I am sure they all hope to get rich out of him, or richer—some shareholders in the company are the Irish millionaires I mentioned. There has been a considerable land boom already, and the land office is doing—I just realized where the phrase comes from—a land-office business. Oh, couldn't you and Thomas homestead a claim and lay the foundations for a western place of visitation? Quite seriously, it would be a profitable thing to do, and on "desert" or "timber-culture" claims there is no residence requirement as there is for a homestead. You need only have someone make minimal "improvements," as they are called, and wait. Don't you want to join us in the making of a new country? Have you no impulse to see the banks of the Snake? Or is that one of those horrid Western names that put you off?

The country, as distinguished from its improvements and its people, is beautiful—a vast sage plain that falls in great steps from the mountains to the canyon of the Snake, and then rises gradually on the other side to other mountains. It is one of the compensations of being a pioneer that one may see it wild and unbroken. Coming out, we had to leave the Union Pacific at Granger, in Wyoming Territory, and board the single passenger car attached to a construction train on the Oregon Shortline, which is not yet completed. Oliver met us with a democrat wagon at Kuna, the end of the line.

I wish I could make you feel a place like Kuna. It is a place where silence closes about you after the bustle of the train, where a soft, dry wind from great distances hums through the telephone wires and a stage road goes out of sight in one direction and a new railroad track in another. There is not a tree, nothing but sage. As moonlight unto sunlight is that desert sage to other greens. The wind has magic in it, and the air is full of birds and birdsong. Meadowlarks pipe all around us, something else—pipits? true skylarks?—rains down brief sweet showers of notes from the sky. Hawks sail far up in the blue, magpies fly along ahead, coming back now and then like ranging dogs to make sure you are not lost. Not a house, windmill, hill, only that jade-gray plain with lilac mountains on every distant horizon. The mountains companionably move along with you as the dirt road flows behind. The plain, like a great Lazy Susan, turns gravely, and as it turns it brings into view primroses blooming in the sand, and cactus pads with great red and yellow blooms as showy as hibiscus.

We had miles of that, while Betsy slept and Ollie got to drive the team, seated between his father's knees. It was touching to see how he responded to the wild empty country—touching and a little alarming. I would not be fully easy in my mind if I thought he might grow into a Western child, limited by his limited world.

And yet how beautiful it is! For the first time I understood Oliver's enthusiasm. We went softly on that sandy trail among the sage, and that dry magical wind from the west blew across us, until at last we came out on a long bench above a river valley, with mountains close behind patched with snow and forest. To our right, the stream broke out of a canyon cut through the sagebrush foothills. To the left, across a bridge, was Boise City climbing up its stepped benches. Below town the crooked line of cottonwoods marking Boise Creek groped across the plain until in the distance trees and river sank below the benches and the plains healed over. From a mile or two away, unless one is on a high place, neither the Boise nor the Snake can be seen at all, sunken in their canyons.

Canyon gate and creek and city were no more than a scribble on the great empty page across which Oliver hopes to write a history of human occupation. He stopped the team and we looked at it a considerable while. It was good for me to see it as he first saw it when he came down from the Coeur d'Alene and was struck by his great idea. Oliver knew, in that quiet way he has of knowing, that if I once saw it I would feel about it as he does. It *is* a great idea, difficult of accomplishment but not impossible. I have become half a believer, and though I cannot say I am fully reconciled to the life it will lead us, I am no longer fearful of failure.

Now that we are here and the work is going forward, there are even indications that the West which so lightly and cruelly separates and scatters people can bring them together again—that the binding force of civilization and human association is as strong, perhaps, as the West's bigness and impersonality. I allude to the fact that Oliver has managed to locate his old assistant, Frank Sargent, and has arranged for him to join us here. I am glad—but not because, as you once or twice playfully suggested, Frank is romantically attached to a woman ten years older than himself. I have been concerned about him, a well-born and educated young man from the East, thrown among rough men in the rough camps where he has worked the past several years. He used to talk to me in Leadville about his mother and sisters, and about the temptations that assail any young man in the West, and his determination to resist them. But if rumor is correct, he has not been able to evade them entirely in Tombstone, as dreadful a camp as the West ever spawned. Oliver tells me that in Arizona Frank participated in the hunt for a man who had murdered a friend, and that the hunt ended, down across the line in Mexico, with the murderer swinging from a tree. It is hard to believe this of the Frank I know, so ardently gentle—and yet there was always a young warrior in him. When Pricey was beaten in Leadville, only Oliver's restraint kept Frank from going after his assailants with a gun.

To us, he is a dear and loyal friend, and to boot, as they say out here, a beautiful and patient model. He would try all day to balance on a toadstool while I drew him as Oberon, if only I asked it. He will add much to Boise. He arrives next week.

How gossipy this sounds, like chattering with you and Katy and Emma in the halls of Cooper!

Oliver's other young assistant is a Boston Tech man named Wiley, as sunny and good natured as some cheerful bird. You must know, having had it from the beginning, what a happiness it is to have one's husband completely contented in his work. O. has always handled his jobs conscientiously and well, but I think his heart was never in a job until now. He works all day, and at night buries himself in the history of irrigation, and reports on systems in Persia, India, China, everywhere. Reading aloud to him the other night when he had a headache, I came across a quotation from Confucius that made us both laugh, it so perfectly expressed Oliver Ward. Confucius said, "I find no fault with the character of Yu. He lived in a mean low house and expended all his strength on the ditches and water channels." Oliver at once painted the whole quotation on a board and nailed it above the door of the canyon shack, like an epigraph at the beginning of a chapter.

I must end this. Ollie has just come out and asked if he can go up to the post, where a sergeant—one of the men who hunted down Chief Joseph—has promised to teach him and some of his playmates to ride like cavalrymen. I suppose it is safe, but at least I must go up and take a look at this sergeant. At *five*, to ride like a cavalryman!

Good-bye, dear Augusta. It eases me to talk to you through half an afternoon this way. You will have many miles of my illegible hand to decipher, I fear, before we have brought this valley into the civilized world.

Your own
S.B.W.

I have heard publishers, lamenting their hard life over Scotch and soda, complain that they must read a hundred bad manuscripts to find one good one. Having practiced the trade of history, I feel no stir of sympathy. A historian scans a thousand documents to find one fact that he can use. If he is working with correspondence, as I am, and with the correspondence of a woman to boot, he will wade toward his little islands of information through a dismal swamp of recipes, housekeeping details, children's diseases, insignificant visitors, inconclusive conversations with people unknown to the historian, and recitations of what the writer did yesterday.

Susan Ward, a devoted correspondent and sometimes a very interesting one, had her dry spells like other mortals. She also had her reticences and her pride: having made up her mind to follow her husband into that sagebrush desert, she would not complain more than humorously; she would have to adopt the attitudes of a tourist confronted by the picturesque. Result: she chatters a good deal during her first year or so in Boise. Her only companions are Army wives who never come back into her life—are transferred away, or dropped, or forgotten about.

Nothing there that I want to know about, neither events nor feelings. I have to keep turning the pages of those chatty, empty letters for a long time before I find any that are worth stopping at. The first of these comes eleven months, one novel, one miscarriage, some anxious cases of measles and whooping cough, and some miles of her hasty illegible scrawl after the one I have just quoted.

> P.O. Box 311
> Boise City
> May 17, 1883

Dearest Augusta —
    Please note the change of address, which was effected last week. For the summer, we shall get our mail only when someone rides

into town, ten miles. We have given up Father Mespie's house and moved bag and baggage into the canyon. Pope and Cole, our Eastern backers, have suffered reverses, and tell General Tompkins that they are unable to go on with us.

Oliver takes the blow with a lightness I could never manage. He says he never did expect to sail right through without delays and troubles, but I am sure it must be maddening to him to have to stop, for he drove himself very hard through the winter to complete the topographical work, and had just arranged with a contractor for the digging of the first eight miles of ditch—a unit which will be called (it makes me want to laugh at the intended compliment and shed a tear for the bad luck!) the Susan Canal. Now we must postpone everything while General Tompkins finds new backers. The likeliest prospects seem to be the Keysers of Baltimore, who are connected with the Baltimore and Ohio Railroad.

In the circumstances, the canyon camp is a godsend. Oliver is on standby salary. Frank and Wiley are sticking with us on no salary at all beyond the privilege of putting their legs under our camp table. We shall keep John, the handyman, to do the minimal work required to keep our claims and permits clear, and the Chinese cook, named Charley Wan—doesn't he sound *faded*? He isn't at all. He is a little grinning idol of old ivory, and a great dandy. On Saturday he rode into Boise, spent the night, and came back barbered and shining and smelling of lotions, in time to get Sunday breakfast. Betsy calls him the "pitty Chinaman."

The failure of our money frightens me—it is what I feared, or half feared, all along—but for the summer I like the canyon much better than Boise. I would rather be picturesquely uncomfortable than comfortably dull. The camp consists of a shack, a cook tent with a "fly" over our table, Wiley's and Frank's tent on the beach, and an abandoned miner's cabin downriver, where John sleeps. The shack used to be the office, but as Oliver says, you don't need an office to mark time in, and so now it houses the four Wards and Nellie Linton. "A mean low house," etc—and don't we *wish* we could expend all our strength on the ditches and water channels!

It was Nellie more than myself that I worried about when it became plain that we must move out here. You remember I wrote you about her—my old teacher's daughter who once expressed an interest in sometime coming West. But oh, my, to come West, not to a civilized house, but to a shack in a canyon! There was no way to stop her, she was already on her way from London, where she had been teaching the children of an American diplomat. So Oliver and the juniors hastily built on a bare, pine-board room, I all the time sure that, being a gentlewoman, and fastidious, she would look once and turn around and go back.

But she is an absolute *brick*. Coming in day before yesterday, Oliver had to stop the team and kill a rattlesnake in the trail. She watched without aversion or screams or hysterics; only her lips pulled back a little from her teeth. She admires the scenery in a really Wordsworthian way, and she says her room will do splendidly. She has already fixed it up with pictures and china hens and bits of Paisley and her mother's inlaid workbox. Her dressing table is a box set on end and curtained with muslin, her bed is a home-made bunk. And this for a girl who was brought up in an English country house (it now belongs to Ruskin!), whose father is a famous artist and whose stepmother recently published a book called *The Girl of the Period!*

Nothing like her has ever been seen in Idaho. Before she came, I confess I had some notion that she and one of the juniors, perhaps Wiley, might find their situation romantic, but Nellie is a somewhat homely little body, with rather too many teeth and too little chin, and I am afraid all her gifts, wonderful as they are, are sisterly . . .

More later. We are very busy, as you can imagine, getting established in our primitive camp.

> Your own
> Sue

3

Among my grandfather's few papers, along with offprints of his articles in *Irrigation News* and *Transactions of the American Society of Civil Engineers,* is a government publication on the Arrow Rock Dam, at the time of its completion the highest in the world. The bulletin lists, in addition to the politicians who took credit for the dam, the engineers who built it. Oliver Ward's name is not among them, but A. J. Wiley's is. It was Wiley, by that time a great name in reclamation circles, who sent the book to Grandfather, with a scrawl across the flyleaf: "It's your dam, boss, whatever it says here—the same one we talked about on the river beach twenty years before the Bureau of Reclamation was ever heard of."

As a practitioner of hindsight I know that Grandfather was trying to do, by personal initiative and with the financial resources of a small and struggling corporation, what only the immense power of the federal government ultimately proved able to do. That does not mean he was foolish or mistaken. He was premature. His clock was set on pioneer time. He met trains that had not yet arrived, he waited on platforms that hadn't yet been built, beside tracks that might never be laid. Like many another Western pioneer, he had heard the clock of history strike, and counted the strokes wrong. Hope was always out ahead of fact, possibility obscured the outlines of reality.

When they moved to the canyon camp, for example, they expected to stay only through the summer. They stayed five years.

Naturally I never saw the camp in Boise Canyon. Before I was old enough to hear about it, it was three hundred feet under water. Just as well. Abandoned in its gulch, its garden gone to weeds, its fences down, its ditches drifted full, its windows out, its bridge no more than broken cables trailing in the creek, every nail and fencepost tufted with the wool of passing sheep bands, it would look like failure and lost cause.

But while they lived there it was hopeful struggle, not lost cause, and for a while it was a little corner of Eden.

Eden had three stories. The upper one ran from the canyon rim up high sage slopes toward the aspen groves, pines, mountain meadows, and cold lakes and streams of the high country. The middle story was the rounding flat in the side gulch where a spring broke out and where their buildings and garden were. The lowest story was the river beach.

Just below the mouth of their gulch the cliffs pinched in, and the pinnacle called Arrow Rock, into whose slot Indians were supposed to have shot arrows to appease or subdue the spirits, stood up close against one wall. Rock slides had partially dammed the river and created a rapid below, a pool above. Except in very high water the pool was smooth, with a gravel beach which was their front yard. Into the natural reservoir that was a forecast of the much larger one they intended some day to build there, logs came down on the spring run-off, followed by loggers in sharp-prowed boats. If they needed fence posts or timbers they could sail out in their own black boat, called the Parson, and harpoon what they wanted with picks, and drag it ashore. They pulled breakfast from the pool, the children waded its edges and caught crayfish under its stones, the juniors took icy swims in it before the ladies were up or after they had gone to bed. Through the nights of five years their campfires threw red light on the lava cliffs and touched the moving river with the mystery of transitoriness, and framed the triangle of the tent against the dark in an assertion of human purpose. Even in low water, the rapid below was a steady rush and mutter on the air.

On the beach, while they were still all together, they held their conferences and sang and talked in the evenings. Much planning went on around their fires, much hope went downriver and was renewed from upstream. This was the place where for a while Grandfather had everything he had come West looking for—the freedom, the active outdoor life, the excitement of something mighty to be built.

In Grandmother's old photograph album with the Yellowstone bear on its cover there is a snapshot of Grandfather, the juniors, and the Keyser son who came out to inspect the irrigation scheme his family was considering. They are standing on the beach with saddle horses and a laden packhorse droop-headed behind them, and an edge of river and the black pillar of Arrow Rock in the background. Across the bottom, evidently at some later time, Grandmother has printed in white ink, in the neat print that is so different from her hasty script, "*How Hope looked. Aug. 1883.*"

Hope looks very young, young enough to seem dubious to less cautious men than the Keysers. Young Keyser himself, the man upon whose word their future hangs, is a bare-faced boy. Wiley is even younger, only twenty-three, but he is important to them because it turns out that he attended St. Paul's School with young Keyser, and they have become in this slot in the Western mountains instant friends. Sargent with his dark sideburns and mustache looks like a young actor impersonating middle age, and he bends upon the camera, or upon the person holding it, who was Grandmother, a smile like the smile of a man watching the play of children who are dear to him. And the Chief, in a pith helmet that he must have dug out to impress visiting capitalism, looks nearly as young as the rest of them, so young that I have trouble recognizing my grandfather in him. His skin is burned dark, his eyes look very light. He too is smiling into the camera—a young athlete with a powerful long body and a candid face. But also pukka sahib of the Sawtooths, on his way to prove to careful money men that his scheme is sound and that its creator, young as he looks, is a man of skill, judgment, and experience.

It makes me melancholy to see him so youthful and girded with determination, ready to mount and ride off into the future more than eighty years ago.

I skip over that summer, in which nothing much happened but the passage of time, and jump to a chilly night in September 1883. The four of them sat around a big fire on the beach. Under a wide river of sky the river of water went with wet splashings, sunk in the rock, and above and along the river of water, down the beaches and around corners of worn stone, flowed a river of cold air that was sucked into the draft of the fire and spewed upward as sparks that multiplied the stars.

Susan felt it numb on the back of her neck, and pulled up the collar of Oliver's sheepskin coat and tightened the *rebozo* around her hair.

Reddened with firelight, its weeds casting black shadows, their path started up the gulch, up toward where Wan's cooktent was pasted orange on the darkness. On the other side of the fire, lapped with shining, unseen wetness, the beach pebbles gleamed like the scales of a fish. Against the creep of the downcanyon wind the sound of the rapid was only a mutter. They sat hugging their knees, low-spirited, frowning into the flames.

I can visualize them pretty exactly, because a little later Grandmother drew her three men in that posture for a series called *Far Western Life*—the best things she ever did, I believe, better even than the Mexican drawings. I saw them described in an art history the other day as "beautiful examples from the golden age of woodcut illustration." This picture she titled *Prospectors*, and she captioned it with a verse from Bret Harte:

> *The glowing campfire with rude humor painted*
> *The ruddy tints of health*
> *On haggard face, and form that drooped and fainted*
> *In the fierce race for wealth*

In their hour of disspiritedness, the haggard face and form that drooped and fainted were authentic enough. They had worked hard and hoped hard, and their disappointment was as great as their expectations had been. But the money motive demeans them. They were in no race for wealth—that was precisely what disgusted Grandfather with the mining business. They were makers and doers, they wanted to take a piece of wilderness and turn it into a home for a civilization. I suppose they were wrong—their whole civilization was wrong—but they were the antithesis of mean or greedy. Given the choice, any one of them would have chosen poverty, with the success of their project, over wealth and its failure. It was some such perception that made Susan raise her voice above the lonely night sounds of fire and wind. "Ah, *well!* The Keysers aren't the only people with money."

No, they said. Of course not. Sure.

"General Tompkins is working. You might get a telegram to-morrow."

"If we did it wouldn't do us any good this year," Oliver said. "Our construction season's gone."

"Isn't there anything you can do in the winter?"

Frank Sargent slapped his dusty boots, a sound loud and impatient. "Why don't we just start digging that ditch ourselves, the four of us?"

"Because it wouldn't do to get people laughing," Oliver said. "If we'd got started we could have gone on till Christmas. Now it isn't worth starting. Not with four men, one team, and one Fresno scraper."

"At least you can use the winter for more planning," Susan said.

Across the fire he sent her a slow, narrow-eyed smile. "We're already oversupplied with that. There's one thing we can do through the winter, though."

"What?"

"Wait."

They laughed. They threw sticks and pebbles at the fire. Huddled in the coat whose sleeves came four inches below her fingertips, listening to the secret noises of the river, watching the light flutter on the cliff behind Frank Sargent's profiled head, Susan tasted the word and did not like its flavor. Wait. They had done little else since he came East to convert her to his scheme. She remembered him standing above the basket of his three-week-old daughter and declaring himself as confident of success as she was that the baby could be brought up to be a woman. Betsy was now a month past her second birthday. Their home was this wild canyon, their hearth this river beach, their hope as far off as ever. Farther, for then they had Pope and Cole behind them, and now they had no one.

"Waiting's got its problems, though," Oliver said.

"I thought we were getting pretty good at it," Wiley said, and laughed again.

Oliver did not laugh. He looked at Susan and then into the fire. "We can't go back to town—can't afford it. We can't keep Wan—no money, no room. We can't ask Frank and Wiley to go on working for nothing. They've been doing it since the first of May."

Wiley looked up once, quickly, and then began to dig in the coarse sand with a stick. Frank arched his back against the log and relaxed again. It occurred to Susan that though she had drawn him in many poses, she had never tried him as an Indian. He had a high-nosed, proud, touchy look. She imagined a blanket around his shoulders, his hair in braids with bits of feather and bone plugs. Yes.

She heard him say humorously, "What are you doing, firing us?"

"I'm giving you the chance to do something besides wait."

"What if we'd rather wait than do something else?"

Oliver threw a stick at the fire. He had the ground around him cleaned down to the gravel. His hand went on absently feeling for other scraps of things to pick up and throw. "These are the years you should be establishing yourself, instead of bogging down in a stalled project."

"Shoot," Wiley said, "don't you believe in this project? I do."

"So do I," Frank said.

Oliver said patiently, "There's no place for you to *live*, Frank. Even if you two were crazy enough to go on working for nothing."

"Crazy?" Susan said. "Oh no, loyal!"

She embarrassed them. They sent her way wags of the head and depreciatory smiles. "What's the matter with the tent?" Frank said.

"Through the winter?"

"Don't think you'll be much better off in the shack. Would you say, Art?"

"She gets a little fresh," Wiley said.

"We'll have to fix it up. Tarpaper it, something."

"Look," Frank said, and sat up straight against the log, "I don't think Mrs. Ward is going to enjoy that shack whatever we do to it. That's just not good enough for her and the children and Nellie. Why don't we build her a house? We won't be doing anything else."

Oliver looked amused. "Out of what?"

"Logs?"

"Sure," Wiley said.

"Too late to get 'em cut," Oliver said. "No water to float 'em down."

"Rock? There's plenty of that."

"What do we do for roof, floors, framing, windows, all the rest of it? I'm telling you, the company's broke and so am I. You'd better line up something else. If we ever start again, and you want to come back, you're hired, at a good raise."

It seemed to Susan that he dealt callously with their loyalty and their faith. They had been in it together too long to break up now like casual travelers after a train ride. She said impulsively, "But Oliver, we *will* have some money. I'll be getting a check from Thomas for *The Witness*."

Right back to their old argument. She saw his face go wooden. His hand groped for something to pick up, found a piece of stick. His fingers broke it absently, broke it again. "Which is not for building houses," he said, and warned her with his eyes.

But she threw back the sheepskin collar and leaned forward into the fire's heat, pulling the *rebozo* tighter around her head. Mexico had taught her what such a shawl could do for a pretty face. As I imagine her, bright-eyed and intense, she might be by Murillo.

Lightly she said, "I'll tell you what. I'll put up the money to build a house, and I'll retain title, and when the time comes I'll sell it back to the company for a construction headquarters. And I'll charge you twice what it costs."

She made him laugh, which was much. His stubbornness seldom lasted through his laughter. To the juniors he said, "Boys, when you get married, marry a Quaker. They can buy from a Scotchman and sell to a Jew and make money."

"Is it a bargain?" Susan said. "Then we can stay together. We *must* stay together! Isn't that what you want, Frank? Mr. Wiley?"

She saw her enthusiasm light them, but they wouldn't come out with the resounding word she wanted. They hemmed and hawed like embarrassed bumpkins, their eyes slid toward Oliver, estimating their place in an argument that was none of their business. "Is it a bargain?" she said again. "Please!"

Oliver sat a minute or two looking into the fire. Without speaking he leaned and reached the lantern close, levered up the glass, snapped his flint and steel at the wick, and waited while the flame spread from a point to a line. The wind sighed and crept and cowered along the cliff. Up above, Wan's tent had gone dark, and if there was a light in the shack she could not see it for the bulge of the hill. She watched her husband's face, intent on the lantern's flame. Was he going to condemn them to a breakup none of them wanted, simply to gratify his masculine notion that a man did not make use of his wife's money?

The lantern, held close, threw the shadow of his mustache across the side of his face. Then he lowered it. His eyebrows were cocked, the wrinkles had deepened at the corners of his eyes.

"Strictly business, eh? How's it sound to you, Frank?"

"I have no opinion," Frank said. "But I'd like to stay on."

"Wiley?"

"Me too."

"All right," Oliver said. He sat a moment with his lips compressed and his eyes on the fire. "Frank and Wiley to stay on and get their reward in Heaven, or some time in the future. Susan to make her pound of flesh out of the company. All of us to be in the same boat— the canal boat. Maybe we can even keep Wan. Is that what we all want? All right, we'll build the best damned house in Idaho. I get to be architect and chief engineer." He stood up and swung the lantern around his head. They cheered.

The Canyon
Jan. 8, 1884

Dear Thomas —

I send you with this the first two blocks in the "Far Western Life" series, together with a thousand-word sketch to accompany each. Please, *please* throw these last away if they fail to come up to your standards, and have some competent writer do something in substitution. The pictures I am surer of—at the very least they are authentic. "The Last Trip In" I was fortunate to catch just as that great double freight wagon drawn by ten mules passed along the bench above us on its way to a mountain ranche where we spent two days last summer fishing. You may recognize members of our little band: Frank Sargent is the man in gaiters who stands by the stirrup in "Cinching Up." I have drawn him many times—indeed, if it were not for my family and our little group of last-ditchers I should be starved for models. He is a hard person to change or disguise, being proudly and rather fiercely himself. I hope it will not be construed as a weakness that he has already appeared in *Century* as a Leadville engineer, a ne'er-do-well, a packer, a stage driver, and a mucker in a mine, and that Osgood and Company have known him as the young man next door in a Louisa Alcott novel.

Mr. Wiley I find harder to draw, though he patiently submits himself to whatever I demand. He is constantly cheerful, endlessly kind. He reads to the children by the hour. And all three of my engineers are so clever with their hands that I have only to express a wish and some invention is created to make it come true.

As I write you, I am sitting in the very prow of our latest accomplishment. It is a house, but from a little distance could hardly be told from a ledge of rock. Our joint hands, brains, and enthusiasm built it. Oliver designed it and supervised its construction, I made certain suggestions from the point of view of the housewife, all of us helped build it, even Wan and Nellie, even the children. It is made of rock hauled by stoneboat from the rockslide just back of us, held together with cement that Oliver made of the earth beneath our feet—that experiment with cement in Santa Cruz has finally proved useful after all. The word was throw in the rock and spare the hammer. Mud was cheaper than labor, and time was short.

Have you ever built a house with your own hands, out of the materials that Nature left lying around? Everyone should have that experience once. It is the most satisfying experience I know. We have been as fascinated as children who build forts or snowhouses, and it has made us the tightest little society in all the West. We are not the kind of ideal society that gathers around you and Augusta in the studio, yet we are not without our ideal aspects. A Brook Farm without a social theory, and a melting pot Brook Farm at that: a Chinese cook, a Swedish handyman, an English governess, three Eastern-American engineers, two children, and a lady artist. I have watched with admiration how you two first created a place for yourselves in New York and then molded and shaped it within a world of art and ideas. Let me tell you how it is done in primitive Idaho.

Having determined the proportions of your temple, which Oliver said should be 21 by 35 feet—multiples of seven, the proportions of the Parthenon!—and your site, which we agreed should be the knoll behind the cooktent, you dig a trench three feet deep and nearly as wide all around the circumference of your foundations. Into this you pour wheelbarrow after wheelbarrow of cement, or "mud" as

Oliver calls it, and tons and tons and *tons* of rocks. When the walls have reached ground level you erect forms on top of them, between four and five feet high and sloping inward at the top to a width of 18 inches. Then, standing on stagings and running your wheelbarrow up and down planks, you pour in more mud and more rocks, "puddling" as you go. I forgot to say that you frame off openings for doors and windows.

It was a scene of the most fascinating activity—Oliver and Frank and John wheeling and hauling, Wiley mixing cement, Wan puddling, all of us throwing in such rocks as we could lift, even little toddler Betsy contributing her pebbles. Ollie had a heavenly time and worked like a stevedore, "proving" himself to the men. He is like his father in that. I tried to draw all this, but could not find a focus. It was like trying to draw a colony of ants.

While the walls "cured," the men hauled lumber, windows, etc., from town, and also scooped out the whole interior down to the base of the walls, using John's scraper when they could, and picks and shovels when they had to. Then they built a great central chimney with four flues, and fireplaces on all four sides, and laid on a low-browed roof, and installed windows, and built a door out of planks like the door on our Leadville cabin, with a buckskin thong for a latchstring which we have sworn will never be pulled in. Oh, for the day when you and Augusta pull that thong! It is a low door, at which both Oliver and Frank must stoop. They say it teaches them humility.

By frantic effort, we were able to move in for Christmas Eve, and oh, the snugness, despite the unfinished nature of everything, and what a chimney for the children to hang their stockings by! Our great window looks out at ground level into trampled snow, but inside it is snug as a bear's den. The windowsills are deep, as I love them— even near the top our walls are two feet thick. The woodwork is unpainted, the walls are the natural warm tan of the cement. The chimney spreads its warmth in every direction, and even the three small bedrooms all along one side benefit from it. Nellie's is at one end, ours at the other; the children's, with a fireplace of its own, in between. The chimney partly divides the long narrow main room so that we can separate if we wish, I to work, the men to study or read, Nellie to teach the children. Or we can gather together in commons. We have no kitchen—that has been left in the tent.

In summer, the men assure me, we shall be as cool as in winter we are warm. You never saw such a trio. They work hard and long and enjoy it all. They cackle like geese over every completed job and solved problem. Their ingenuity is now exercising itself in creating a multitude of little cupboards and storage nooks and seats, and in the rehabilitation of the shack as winter quarters for Frank, Mr. Wiley, and Wan. The shack's loft is already designated the drafting room.

The shut-in time of winter does not dismay us. The engineers have laid in books, reports, journals, and much else. Oliver has in mind a couple of little inventions and has already started on an automatic waste-weir that he calls the "flop-gate." And thanks to you and Augusta there is that whole Christmas box of books—in our canyon, such riches! They are already going from hand to hand through our little community of saints. Moreover, Nellie, who is constantly astonishing me with the way she adapts herself to our crude border life, turns out to have studied bookbinding under her father, and to have brought her presses, stamps, and other tools along. She has offered to teach us all, and Frank and Mr. Wiley have already set up her machinery in the drafting room. Oliver understands tanning—the children still use between their beds a rug of wildcat skins that he tanned and sewed in New Almaden—and with plenty of cattle and sheep hides available for a song, he promises that our entire library will be in leather by spring.

Did you ever see an engineering report in limp leather with gold stamping? I believe you will. My engineers are capable of panning the gold dust and making their own gold leaf, if necessary.

As if these projects were not enough to occupy them, along with constant wood chopping, water hauling, care of the animals, trips to town, and all the chores of a frontier ranche, they plan to swing a cable footbridge across the river, between the cliffs where we dare hope that one day a dam will back up the waters. On this side a horse trail goes upriver along the foot of the cliff, but the wagon road to the mountains must go around, over the bluffs where I drew the freight wagon of "The Last Trip In." We must haul our supplies roundabout and bring them down into our gulch by a steep trail, or haul them on the shorter road across the river and trans-ship them by the Parson, which is so lopsided it can hardly be rowed in calm water, much less when the river is high or clogged with ice. It is too cold and dangerous to try anchoring cables to the cliffs now, but at the first sign of spring I expect to see my men crawling around there like spiders.

Isn't life strange? Where it takes us? As you know, I didn't come out here with entire willingness, and I can't be anything but anxious over the delays and uncertainties that we face now. And yet of all our wild nesting places this is the wildest and sweetest, and made up of the most extravagant incongruities.

Above our lava rock mantel hangs a print of Titian's virgin, alone in the clouds in her amazement and wonder. On the walls, besides one or two watercolors of mine that the men insisted must be hung, are a half dozen watercolors contributed by Nellie, who has more of her father's paintings and more of his lithographs of English wildflowers than her own walls will hold. And so she enriches us all with the delicacy of her father's art, here where every other impression is of strong, rough Nature. From my desk, now that the working light has begun to fail, I can look into the other end of the room and see the children at tea and Nellie finishing, aloud, something she has been reading to them. Her voice is sweet and soft, but can ring on the sterner passages. Her English profile is sharp against the deep-toned West. The long window behind the three heads gives the whole of the canyon, like those detailed backgrounds in miniature which the early Italian painters liked to put in behind their saints and virgins. There comes a moment in these short winter days—it is at hand just now—when the light suddenly changes and becomes like the light during an eclipse. It is very strange—a pause before the passionate moment of the afterglow which will follow.

Wan, having prepared the children's tea, is out in the cooktent preparing supper, probably singing through his nose some outlandish Chinese tune. When I was first at New Almaden the sight of a Chinese made me positively shudder, and yet I think we all love this smiling little ivory man. He is one of us; I believe he looks upon us as his family. Is it not queer, and both desolating and comforting, how, with all associations broken, one forms new ones, as a broken bone thickens in healing.

I shall be as quiet this winter as my men are active. I am expecting again, as Augusta must have told you—a consequence of the optimism that flooded us all when it seemed that young Mr. Keyser took such a glowing report eastward. After my bad luck last winter in Boise, the doctor says that this baby will make me or break me. I am forbidden to take more than the most gentle exercise, and in particular am forbidden to ride any conveyance, either wheeled or footed, that we possess. You can imagine how much this house means to me. We call it The House That *Century* Built, for it was your check for *The Witness* that made it possible.

Our Christmas to you two was small and mean by necessity, not through any lessening of our love. Yours to us was rich and warm, and will touch our minds and hearts through the whole winter. God bless you, Thomas Hudson, and your lovely wife. Think of us—continue to think of us—in this far canyon. But do not think of us as unhappy. Do you remember Bishop Ripley, or whoever it was— "By God's grace, we shall light such a fire . . . ?"

Your own
SBW

4

I have made no chronology of their years in Boise Canyon. Except for a flurry during 1887, when for a while it seemed as if Henry Villard might find a place for them in his empire-building schemes, most of Grandmother's letters are dated only by month and day, and could have been written any time between 1883 and 1888. Whoever sorted them when they were returned to Grandmother after Augusta's death has made numerous mistakes that I can detect from internal evidence, but Shelly and I have done only the roughest reordering. It doesn't much matter what year they were written in; those years were cyclic, not chronological.

Imprisoned in reiterative seasons, vacillating between hope and disappointment, they were kept from being the vigorous doers that their nature and their culture instructed them to be. Their waiting blurred the calendar. The days rolled across from canyon wall to canyon wall, the seasons crept northward until at summer solstice the sun set directly behind what they called Midsummer Mountain, and hung there a little while, and started creeping southward again toward the canyon mouth that gulped December sunsets. Summer or winter or in between, the sky out over the valley was filled with light for a long time after their gulch lay in shadow. Sometimes Susan felt as if evening were a blight that lay on them.

They were ten miles from town, and town was only a little territorial capital twenty-five hundred miles from the springs of civilization and amenity. Their visits and their visitors were few. They all preferred the high pastures, the canyon, and the mountains to the town, whose fluctuations among mining boom, railroad boom, irrigation boom, and statehood boom were too much like their own recurrent fevers of hope.

No life goes past so swiftly as an eventless one, no clock spins like a clock whose days are all alike. It is a law I take advantage of, and bless, but then I am not young, ambitious, and balked.

Grandmother was luckier than Grandfather, because she could work steadily at writing and drawing, and he could occupy his hands and his empty hours only with puttering. There was a period in the spring of 1885 when they were building the suspension bridge and the construction frenzy restored them to an exuberant cheerfulness. Then that was finished, and became a part of their routine. No word came from General Tompkins, no backers appeared to rescue the coming construction season. Susan's pregnancy prevented her making any of the expeditions to the mountains that had once been their standard entertainment, and because she could not go, the men went less often too.

High spring made them restless. On Oliver's urging, Frank and Wiley were looking around for jobs. Wiley's came first—an irrigation project on the South Platte, in Colorado. He left them, swearing it would take only a telegram to pry him loose from any job in the world and return him to the canyon. He kissed the children and shook hands with Nellie and stood before Susan like an embarrassed youngster, obviously thinking that a handshake couldn't express all he meant, and obviously uncertain that he was permitted more. Susan stooped her heavy body forward and kissed him. It was the end of April, the poppies they had sown all over their knoll were blooming, the rose bushes on each side of the door were in bud, great fair-weather clouds marched eastward along the mountain. A bursting spring day. Wiley's departure left it feeling hollow and false.

A week later Frank Sargent came back from town and announced that he had an offer from the Oregon Short Line. "Take it," Oliver said.

Almost sullenly, Frank looked at Susan where she stood, seven months along, bracing her hand on the drafting table from which she had just risen. She thought his look flared with some troubling resentment or blame. "I've already taken it," he said. "I'm leaving tomorrow."

They stood awkwardly, each one a point of a triangle that they all understood and were determined to ignore. "You'll be back," Oliver said. "What about your stuff? Want to leave it here with Wiley's?"

"I guess. I'd better tear the tent down."

"I'll help you." His eyes touched Susan's, steady and uninsistent. It was as if he were reassuring her about something. "Where's Ollie?"

"Down in the drafting room, I think."

"He'll want to give us a hand, I expect."

He ducked his head to the low door and went out. They heard him calling, his voice receding toward the shack. How understanding he was, and how decent, Susan thought; how characteristic of him to make an excuse to give them a minute alone. She was standing by the table where she had been drawing; Frank was by the door. He was looking at her very steadily.

"Well, Frank," she said.

"Well, Mrs. Ward."

"We'll miss you."

"Will you?"

"Must you ask? It will be poor and shabby without you. The children are going to be lonesome."

"Only the children?"

"We too—I too." She laughed, a mere catch of the breath. "I'll miss the sound of your mandolin down by the river."

"Well, if that's all you'll miss."

She tried to coax his sullen unhappiness with a smile. "I'll miss our talks—who else is there around here I can talk books with? I'll miss our drawing sessions. Oh, we have had fun, haven't we? We've had happy times. We will again."

He took a step toward her, and in some sort of panic at what his feelings—his only, or hers too?—might lead to, she snatched up from the table the half-finished drawing she had been working on. It was a picture of Frank and Ollie watering horses at the river. Frank's limber length was bent a little as he listened to the boy, who with face upturned was telling or asking him something. There was an intimation of trust and confidence between the two figures. Their horses stretched their necks to suck water from the stream. It might have been any casual moment from more than two years. Interposing the pad between herself and Frank, ready to—what? Divert him with it? Ask his judgment? Give it to him as a parting gift? Hold him away with it?—she stared at him in confusion that was almost fear.

He stopped at long arm's length. She had drawn him so often that she could have drawn him blindfold. Dozens of times she had labored to communicate in a drawing the peculiar warm intensity of his eyes. Now they literally burned at her. She expected him to kiss her; she expected to kiss him back in some sort of affectionate, half-gratifying relinquishment.

His hands were at his sides. He said, "It's time I was getting out. Past time."

"Don't say that. You'll be back."

"I wonder."

"Oh, Frank, of course you will! You must! When it finally works out you'll be back and you'll all build the canal and we'll be a happy family again."

"Happy family," Frank said. His eyes shifted, and she became aware, with acute embarrassment, that he was looking directly at her swollen belly. "Increased by one," he said.

The blood spread quick and hot into her face. She had taken him—Wiley too—so much as a part of the family that she had not tried, as a modest woman would do in town, to hide her pregnancy from him. How could she have, anyway, seeing him constantly, eating three meals a day with him, drawing him? She lowered her head and said to his booted feet, "That's the only ungentlemanly thing you ever said to me."

It took him a while to answer. "Then I'm sorry," he said finally. "Only—do you think it's easy for a man—a man with an incurable disease, to . . ."

Her eyes came up. His glance burned and withered her, but she could not help saying, "To what?"

"To see you," Frank said. "To see this . . . evidence . . . of how much you belong to someone else."

"I have other children."

"I didn't have to watch them born!"

She put one hand to her flaming face, she turned her back, as it were snatching her bulging belly from the brutality of his eyes. In a few seconds his steps went toward the door. She did not turn or speak, but stood with her head bent, her teeth sunk hard into her lip.

Later she looked out the broad window to the river, and saw him, Oliver, and Ollie, with Nellie and Betsy for audience—the whole family except herself—working over the dismantled tent. His cot, table, camp stool, and trunk sat in the smoothed and bleached rectangle that had been his floor. His life was turned out like an exposed mouse nest at the foot of the lava cliff.

Later still she gave him her hand and a sober word of good-bye. If Oliver noticed that she did not kiss him as she had kissed Wiley, he made no sign.

Jump to midsummer 1885. She was bloated, breathless, near her time. If she had been a cow she would have headed off, heavy with premonition, into the brush. If she had been a dog she would have dug under some shed. Being Susan Ward, she tried to work. By now, after three years of the Idaho Mining and Irrigation Company, she was providing more than half of what they lived on. She mined and irrigated every slightest incident, she wrote and drew her life instead of living it.

It was quiet in the stone dugout curtained against the heat. Mrs. Briscoe, that disaster who passed for a practical nurse, had gone somewhere. Oliver was out tinkering with the miniature irrigation system he had developed for the garden, Wan was taking his regular Saturday off in town. She felt abandoned, left behind; she thought with motherly affection of Wiley, who kept in touch with them by letters, and with uneasiness of Frank, who had disappeared without trace where out the Oregon Short Line toward the coast.

From Nellie's room came a brief light gabble of talk or lessons. In her muddleheaded condition she at first confused it with the buzzing of a fly caught between curtains and window.

Working was impossible. Her eyes kept drifting out of focus, her head throbbed. Every few seconds the life inside her rolled over or kicked. She took it into the bedroom and lay down on her back to give it all the room there was, but even then it was restless. And there was a fly in the bedroom too, a big irritating blow fly with a buzz like a bumblebee.

She lay still, arms flung wide, eyes on the rough-sawn rafters and roof boards above her. There were footprints and wheelbarrow tracks on them, left from the time when with mud on their feet they had swarmed from mixing trough to lumber pile. She might have thought of them as a record of the good time before waiting had become the hopeless pattern of their lives. She might have responded sentimentally to the small eternal footprints of her children. Instead, she felt a spasm of disgust at how raw, untidy, and unfinished everything was, and she wondered if Oliver with a brush and pail couldn't scrub her ceiling clean.

Her legs twitched with the spastic jerking that her generation called growing pains. I can tell her, having learned it while investigating the sickness of my own skeleton, that they indicate a calcium deficiency—something I would willingly put up with, being cursed with altogether too much calcium in places where I don't need it. She thought the twitching was nervousness, part of the impatience she shared with the unborn child. She would not be able to contain that irritable life much longer.

It kicked her hard, and with a curious deadness of feeling she smoothed the shift across her bulging stomach and craned her neck, watching until she felt the soft blow and saw the swift slight upward denting of the cloth. She did not want this baby. It made her desolate to think what it would be born into.

It kicked her again, the twitching in her legs was intolerable. She sat up and went heavily to the door. "Mrs. Briscoe?"

The woman was still out somewhere. Susan went through the living room, pausing to look into the children's room that opened by a very narrow door next to the chimney. Empty. Her mind made the note that Betsy and Ollie must soon be separated. Betsy was getting too old to share a room with her brother. And how would they manage that? Build another room? And where would they put the new one when it outgrew a basket?

"Mrs. Briscoe?"

The mutter of voices had stopped in Nellie's room. She tapped and looked in. Nellie's thin, gopher-toothed face looked up inquiringly, her hands stopped crocheting, her rocking chair paused. The lace at her throat and wrists was as crisp as lace in a Dutch painting—she was always crocheting, or washing, or ironing cuffs and collars. How uncomplicated, undemanding a life!

On the floor was her workbox, a thing of marquetry inlaid with ivory and ebony and mother of pearl, fitted inside with exquisite little drawers and lidded boxes crammed with papers of pins, reels of cotton and silk, yards of linen tape and braid, bobbins, buttons, hooks and eyes. Betsy had dumped one drawer between her legs and was sorting buttons. She did not even look up.

"Have you seen Mrs. Briscoe, Nellie?"

"She said she was going for a walk."

"She? On a day as hot as this?" Vexed by the unpleasantness of her own laugh as much as by Mrs. Briscoe's absence, she looked over her shoulder, afraid that meeching pig-like presence might be behind her.

Nellie laid aside the crocheting and stood. "Can I do something?"

"No. No thank you, Nellie. I thought I might like a cup of tea. But she shall fix it, when I find her. She has to be good for *something*." Looking down on the tow head of her daughter, studiously bent over the buttons, she said, "You've spilled Nellie's workbox all over."

"I told her she could," Nellie said. "She loves buttons. She's a little housewife, *very* neat. She puts everything back, don't you, duck?"

"I hope she does. Where's Ollie? I thought he was in here at his lessons."

"He went out to help his father at the windmill."

"His father knew he was supposed to put in extra time at his reading. Has he been doing any better?"

"He tries, he truly does."

"But still isn't doing well."

"He loves to be read *to*. It isn't that he doesn't like reading. He just has difficulty recognizing words, even when he's had them over and over. It's as if he'd never seen them before."

Dyslexia, says my 1969 overview. The poor kid was a dyslectic eighty years before the condition will be discovered and named. Word-blind, and the son of my grandmother.

"He *must* learn," Susan said. "If he really tries, he can. You must be strict when his mind wanders. He'd so much rather be out playing engineer with his father."

"It's not that he's a dull boy," Nellie said. "At maths he's very good. He's learned things from his father and Mr. Sargent and Mr. Wiley that are quite beyond me. It's only the reading."

"Nevertheless," Susan said. "Right now he was told to stay in and work at what he's weak in, and he's out irrigating. At this rate he'll *never* get into a good Eastern school. And where on earth is that Mrs. Briscoe?"

She turned from Nellie's door and went to the back window that looked down the knoll to the spring. Passing sheep bands had trampled and half ruined it, and now there was a dug well with a windmill mounted on it which was supposed, when the wind blew, to pump water onto a home-made waterwheel which poured it down a sluice into a hydraulic ram which boosted it into a higher sluice which ran into a ditch high enough to irrigate the garden. Beside the motionless wheel she saw Oliver, alone, bent over some problem. The sun all but obliterated him. The bare ground, cocoa-brown in ordinary light, glittered like snow. Oliver spun the windmill fan by hand until a little water gushed into the upper cup of the waterwheel. The wheel moved a few inches, the water splashed into the hat he held under it, he put the dripping hat back on his head. Alone, puttering, absorbed, he looked like some frontier farmer.

When she opened the casement, dust sifted from the deep sill. The outside air, hot even on the shaded north side, surged into her face. She called, and Oliver straightened, turning. "Where's Ollie? Isn't he with you? Where's Mrs. Briscoe?"

He laid down the wrench he held and came up the slope as far as the garden fence. "What?"

"Where are Ollie and Mrs. Briscoe?"

"Down by the creek."

"He was supposed to be working on his reading."

"I know. I let him off."

"I wish you wouldn't do things like that. He needs to study."

"I suppose." He squinted up at her, blind in the sun. "I thought it was pretty hot."

"It isn't half as hot inside as it is out there. Don't you stay out working, you'll get sunstroke."

For answer he lifted the dripping hat off his head and clapped it back on. "How you feeling?"

"All right. But I don't want Ollie going down to the river with nobody more sensible than Mrs. Briscoe. What if they should run into a snake?"

"I expect Ollie'd kill it."

"Did you remind him not to go swimming or wading?"

"Oh come on," he said. "He's dependable. Old Briscoe wanted him along, I expect she's nervous without somebody. They're just down in the canyon where it's cooler." Across fifty yards of sun-blasted gravel he squinted up at her. "You want me to go get 'em?"

"Oh, no. Just don't let him stay too long."

"You want La Briscoe?"

"Oh, what for!" she said, and shut the window. Through the dusty pane she saw Oliver stand for a minute, looking up at the house. Then he went back to the windmill, spun up another splash of water, and soused his hat again.

Her skin tingled as if that coolness had touched her own warm face and neck. She thought enviously of how chill the river would be to wading feet, and how tendrils of cool air would wander along the river as erratic and constant as the sounds of flowing. The canyon narrows would be dark and cool. Could she, with Oliver's help, get down the hill and back? No. Unwise. After months of the most finicky caution she would be insane to risk her baby within a week of its birth.

But she crossed the room, wanting a sight of the river, and drew the curtains and looked down the sun-whitened slope. Under her eyes lay their life, with its constriction, its improvisations, its beauty and its transience. From the narrows the river poured white and broken into the mineral green of the pool, which smoothed it within fifty feet. At the bottom of the pool the water visibly bulged, walling against the rockslide, and twisted right to find a way through. Narrowing, slick as glass, it went under the bridge and into the slot below Arrow Rock and out of sight. Like something alive, wild, and shy, it burst from shadow into sun and slid snakelike into shadow again, ignoring the intrusions they had made on it: the Parson pulled up on the shingle, and on the far bank, in the little round flat over there, shed and haystack surrounded by pole corral. Their path led from the corral across the bottom, disappeared behind a jut of cliff, and reappeared just at the far end of the bridge.

Of all Oliver's engineering ingenuities she liked the bridge least. It had frightened her pale to watch them build it, suspended above a furious spring runoff. When the wind blew, as it always did morning and evening on days as hot as this, the spider-webby thing kinked and swayed underfoot. Even on calm days it gave way alarmingly to a foot placed on it, and the water shot underneath at a dizzying speed. The single rope handrail struck her as too frail a support when she had to cross alone, and she had forbidden the children to go near it without an adult. The fact that Oliver, and before they left, Frank and Wiley too, slammed across it without touching the rope, and wheeled supplies across it on the wheelbarrow, did not persuade her it was safe. It always stopped her heart to see Betsy carried across on Oliver's shoulders. Two days before, it had taken all of Oliver's strength and patience to push and pull and drag fat gasping Mrs. Briscoe across, every thirty seconds prying loose her death-grip on the rope.

As still as a curve in a drawing, the bridge hung from cliff to cliff. Its image, complete even to hand-rope, floated on the smooth water above the tongue of the rapid. To her tranced eyes it seemed to sweep downstream, and yet it remained where it was. Her eyes went up and down the beach. Ollie and Mrs. Briscoe must be up in the narrows. In exasperation she thought, I could be having it right now, how would she know? What good would she be? Stuffs herself and makes herself sick the very first night, so that Nellie and I end up taking care of *her*. And now wanders off. Oh, how am I ever going to let that woman touch me or my baby?

Well, you must. There's no one else to be had.

Something moved just inside the corner of the cliff, beyond where the juniors' tent used to stand. Moving to the extreme left of the window, she could see half of Mrs. Briscoe, sitting on half a rock inside the edge of shade. As she watched, the left hand lifted a flat bottle, bottle and lips met in a long kiss, the hand lowered the bottle and tucked it under the edge of the long skirt.

Oh my goodness.

In a fury she craned and peered. For a time Mrs. Briscoe leaned almost out of sight, as assuredly she thought she was. Then she leaned back, her face turned down and across the river. Her left hand rose in a hoo-hoo sort of wave. Susan's eyes followed the gesture, and there was Ollie coming out onto the far end of the bridge.

She made a moaning sound and put her hands flat on the windowsill, watching as he edged out, testing the sway of the span. It seemed to her he filled his lungs with air. Paralyzed, cut off from him by glass and distance, she may or may not have screamed at him to stop, not to come on. But he came on, carefully inching along the planks, carrying a package of some sort under one arm. He stopped to get a better hold on the rail-rope; he shot an estimating glance across the hundred feet he still had to cross; he shoved the package more firmly under his arm. Below him his shadow paused, buglike, on the shadow bridge. Then it moved. And as it moved, shadow and bridge, bug and boy, began to sway.

Susan's held breath was choking her. She forced it, clogged with harsh sound, out of her lungs. She saw the shaking sway of the cables communicate itself to Ollie's knees. He grabbed for the rope with his left hand, the package fell straight down into the river, the lurch of the boy's falling against the rope kicked the planks sideward, and there he hung across the rail rope with his legs desperately rigid to keep his feet against the planks.

Susan screamed, and screamed again, and was at the rear window tearing at the catch, screaming down toward the windmill, "The bridge! Ollie! The bridge!"

Oliver's face turned, hung in the heat-shriveled air for half a breath. Then his wrench went flying and he was lunging down the slope in great leaps. She was back at the front window without knowing how she got there. Ollie, still hanging by his elbows across the rope, was just lifting his feet to let the walk swing back under him. He caught it with a knee, both knees. His face turned upward toward her. "Don't move!" she cried to the glass. "Hold on!" and was outside.

Heat exploded in her face, the small bright terrible image her retina carried dissolved in a red blur. She put her hand against the wall, steadying herself, and felt a bright, distant pain. Someone's arm—Nellie's—was supporting her. Something small was whimpering and clamoring down on the ground. Her sight cleared and she saw Betsy. She moved her stinging hand and found that she had thrust it into the rosebush beside the door. "What is it?" Nellie was saying, and then her head snapped around as Oliver appeared, thundering down toward the river, and she saw it all. Oliver was shouting as he ran. On his knees, Ollie clung, patient and small above the curve of swift water.

Susan started down the path, was held back. "Let me go, Nellie!" Clumsily she braced and slid and stepped. The rocks she touched were as hot as stoves, the sun beating off the hillside blinded her, the little flowers of mallow stared up at her like coals. She had to watch the ground, for fear of slipping, but she stopped every few steps to watch Oliver and her son. Nellie, protesting and trying to hold her back, she shook off. Somehow she found herself holding Betsy by the hand.

Oliver plowed through the gravel and leaped up the path to the bridge head. He stooped, steadying the vibration out of the cables while he shouted something at Ollie. Then he started out onto the planks. He moved smoothly and swiftly. His weight sagged the walk, his motion shook Ollie where he clung. Down to the deepest part of the sag, then up. His arm went out, he had the boy hooked tight. For a second they were very still, as if resting.

"Oh, thank God!" Nellie said. She was crying and laughing, and she still clung to Susan's arm. Susan pried loose her hand, and holding Betsy's small wet paw she went on down the path. By the time she reached the shingle, they were off the bridge. Evaporating tears were very cold on her cheekbones. She said something gentle to Betsy, transferred her hand to Nellie's, and held out her arms to Ollie. With one white look upward at his father, he came into them. She could not hold him against her naturally because of her great belly; she had to hold him against her hip. One hand was on his whitey-brown hair. Over the top of his head she looked at Oliver, red with exertion, his shirt wet, his eyes like blue stones. As if restoring the circulation of his hands, he hung them at his sides and shivered the arms from the shoulders.

"Oh, Ollie," Susan said, "*why* did you do such a thing? Why did you cross by yourself? You know you're forbidden to."

He said nothing.

"He's safe," Oliver said. "That's what matters."

But she was all to pieces, and her agitation came out as blame.

"Have you learned a lesson?" she said to Ollie's double crown. "Has it *taught* you something? Next time I might not be looking out the window . . ."

Then she remembered what else she had seen out the window. Her head turned, and there was Mrs. Briscoe, who must have stood in her tracks during the whole excitement, just starting toward them. Susan took Ollie by his thin shoulders and shook him. "What was it she sent you for? She did send you, didn't she?"

He looked away, he said nothing. She shook him hard enough to rattle his teeth, furious at the stubborn wordlessness that was so exactly like his father's. "Didn't she!"

Held away and forced to glance up, he said, "Yes ma'am."

"Why? What for?"

"Sue . . ." Oliver said.

She ignored him. "What for?"

"She'd left something on the other side. She was afraid to go get it herself."

"That package you were carrying."

"Yes. I . . . It *slipped*, Mother! When the bridge wobbled it just slipped and fell in the river, I couldn't hang onto it. I could have come across easy except for the package. It kept slipping."

"No you couldn't. Don't even begin to think you could. What was in the package?"

"Sue, can't this wait?" Oliver said. "Let's get you out of the sun."

"*What was it?*" Susan said. "Was it a bottle?"

She cut her eyes aside to watch Mrs. Briscoe plowing through the gravel. She had sweated half-moons under her gingham arms, and her face, at a hundred yards away, was already fixing itself in an expression she obviously hoped was agitated concern.

"What kind of a bottle?" Ollie said. He was staring at her. So was Oliver. Nellie held Betsy off to one side.

"A whiskey bottle?"

"I don't know," Ollie said. "It wasn't big. I could carry it easy, only it kept slipping."

"Where was it? Where did she tell you to look for it?"

"On the poles over the shed door."

"Yes," Susan said, and straightened up. "Not exactly left by accident." She pressed down on Ollie's shoulders. "You shouldn't have gone. You knew better. But it isn't really your fault. It's that . . ."

Bunion footed, wearing her look of a supposedly house-broken dog which is called upon to explain a puddle on the floor, Mrs. Briscoe labored toward them. Susan turned her back squarely and met Oliver's eyes.

"Is that it?" he said. "How'd you get onto it?"

"I saw her. She's got another bottle buried down there on the beach. I saw her drinking from it." She turned Ollie toward the house. "Come along. I don't want to speak to her. You'll have to take her back, Oliver."

"Then who do we get?"

"I'd rather have nobody."

"You can't have nobody. It might take five or six hours to get the doctor out here."

"Mrs. Olpen will come in an emergency."

"She couldn't stay. She's got five of her own to look after."

"Please!" she said, and pushed Ollie ahead of her up the path. The sun was like thunder on her head. Her hair, when she put up her hand, felt hot enough to smoke.

Oliver had her by the arm. "Nellie," he said, "could I ask you . . . No, I'll tell her myself as soon as we get Mrs. Ward to bed."

"Don't waste ten minutes," Susan said. "I want you to clear the canyon of her."

She shut her lips, she turned herself inward. All the way up the hill she was thinking of the difference between this coming childbirth and the first, in the comfortable cottage at New Almaden, with Lizzie and Marian Prouse and Oliver all building a protective cushion around her and the doctor only an hour away at Guadalupe; and the second, in her old room in Milton, where she could hear Bessie's step in the hall and see her mother's face look in the door every time she sighed or coughed. That time Oliver had been missing, already chasing his dream. Each child marked a decline in the security of their life. Now she would have her third child in a canyon cave, unattended, or attended by a rough-handed settler's wife. Meanwhile, her children ran daily through dangers that turned her cold even on that flaming hillside, and were only kept from becoming as crude as their background by the constant efforts of Nellie and herself.

Before she would lie down, she made Ollie go in and finish the reading he had skipped. How else, she asked him, would he ever get into a good Eastern school?

An hour after she heard the buggy grating up the hill on the bluffs road, taking Mrs. Briscoe back to Boise, she had her first pain.

I have no intention of writing an account of how a pioneer woman, gently reared, had a child in a canyon camp with no help but that of an old maid governess. I am not going to heat up all those pails of water, or listen for the first weak bleat from the bedroom. Neither am I going to let Susan get up the day after her lying-in, to churn the butter or put out a washing or finish her story. This is not a story of frontier hardships, though my grandparents went through a few; nor of pioneer hardihood, though they both had it. It is only Lyman Ward, Coe Professor of History, Emeritus, living a day in his grandparents' life to avoid paying too much attention to his own.

She was no novice, had had two children and a miscarriage, and she did not panic. She thought she had a few hours. Depending on whether he took the bluffs road back, or the canyon road, it would take Oliver three to four hours to return. When he got back he could ride down to the Olpen ranch, send Mrs. Olpen up, and go back into Boise for the doctor. Perhaps Wan would come home early, or John might come up from his cabin, and one of them could be sent. She lay in her darkened room with a wet cloth over her eyes and waited for her body to do what it must.

But Nellie Linton, gentle spinster, Victorian virgin, was more agitated. To quiet Betsy, she turned her recklessly loose with the total contents of her workbox, and she let Ollie off, without comment, from his reading and conferred with him outside. In a way flattering to his eight-year-old judgment, she asked him if he could ride to the Olpen place and fetch Mrs. Olpen.

But his father had the mules, and there were no horses on this side of the river.

Could he walk it? Would he be afraid?

He wasn't afraid, but it was a long away around on this side.

Perhaps he could walk down to John's cabin and have him go for help.

But John's cabin was also on the other side, and you couldn't shout loud enough to be heard across the river there. There were rapids.

Nellie wrung her hands. If his father had just waited one hour!

Was his mother sick? Ollie wanted to know. Did she need the doctor?

Yes, and some good woman. Mrs. Olpen would be of *enormous* help, if only they could reach her.

They fell silent. The sun had dropped far enough so that the house laid a precise triangle of shade across the bare ground. Any minute now Mrs. Ward would call out, in there.

Miss Linton?

Yes Ollie.

I could get there quick across the bridge. I could zip across and ride my pony down.

Oh my goodness, no!

But if she's sick. That's the quickest.

Right after you had to be *rescued* from that bridge? No no. Oh no.

I went across easy. It was the package, coming back.

No. Your mother would die at the thought.

Then it came, the harsh, grunting cry that Miss Linton had been dreading. She saw Ollie's eyes widen, she saw the blood leave his face.

Wait here. I must go and see . . .

But when she came back, having been able to do nothing but hold Mrs. Ward's hand until the spasm passed, she made a small sound of her own, a sound of horror. Ollie was already halfway across the bridge, moving along crabwise with both hands on the rope. The farther he went the more rapidly he moved, until he jumped off onto solid rock. He looked back and saw her, his arm waved, he bolted around the corner of the cliff. In two seconds he appeared at a dead run, headed for the corral.

Shading her eyes, caught between two fears and a hope, Miss

Linton watched him come out of the shed with the oat can and bait his brown pony out of the pasture to the corral bars. He poured the oats on the ground, and when she dropped her head to them he got the halter rope around her neck, stretching with both arms in a sort of embrace. He climbed the corral poles to haul her head up and get the bit into her mouth, the headstall over her ears. Inside, Miss Linton heard Susan say something, not in the tone of pain, but conversationally, which meant that Betsy had wandered in and must be dealt with. But she hung in the sunken entrance watching until Ollie had pulled the mare close and flung himself in a bellyflop across her back. He kicked, straightened, his hands shook out the reins, his heels drummed at her ribs. Riding like a cavalryman, as his mother sometimes said with pride and dismay, he bolted across the little flat toward the canyon gate. Like a cavalryman? More like an Indian. His spidery shape clung to the mare's withers, his tow head was down. He lashed the mare with the ends of the reins and fled out of sight behind the cliff.

It is an effort for me to imagine my way backward from the silent father I knew to the boy in Boise Canyon. Like my grandfather, he was not a man of words, and it is an easy mistake to think that non-talkers are non-feelers. Grandmother herself may have made that mistake. I have heard her say, in her rueful voice with its overtone of regret, what a brave, manly little boy he was, but I never heard her say how sensitive he was. Yet I think he must have been. But though it is from her letters that I get that impression, I think she herself never understood how deep he ran, any more than she understood his difficulty with reading.

It was his capacity for feeling that she should have attended to: by failing to comprehend it, she probably contributed to his silence.

Feeling, more than manliness, drove him across the bridge against the warnings of his conscience—a horrified sympathy for his mother's pain, a sense of fatal responsibility in his father's absence. He was not a disobedient child. He simply overflowed obedience on a flood of emotion, and he had some of his father's readiness in a crisis.

I see him going down that rough canyon pushing his mare as his father always pushed a horse. He was wound up as tight as a ball of wet rawhide. The last two or three hundred yards before John's cabin the trail was soft silt, and he lashed the mare into a run, and so excited her that he could hardly pull her in before the door. She danced and cartwheeled, and he shouted, fighting her hard mouth. No one came out. He let the mare stiff-leg him around the corner to where he could see John's corral. Empty. Before he had had time to frame a thought he was galloping down the canal line that followed the contour around the foot of the sagebrush hills.

He found John sitting on his stoneboat in the shade of a cottonwood, resting himself and his mules. He had been moving testimonial dirt off the right of way. Before Ollie had panted out three sentences John was on his feet stripping the harness from the jenny, letting it fall into the cottonwood fluff that covered the ground like feathers or light snow. He tied the other mule, he looped a halter rope around the jenny's nose and bellied up across her back. He was a big heavy man, not excitable. He sang when he talked, and he could not say the sound *oo*, it always came out *iu*.

"Yiu go back," he said. "If Ay don't run into your pa Ay bring the doc myself."

"I've got to get Mrs. Olpen."

The mare side-stepped, pulling at his arms. From the jenny John gave Ollie a long appraising squinting look, the look of an adult asked permission for something dubious. "Ya," he said finally. "O.K. That's gude idea. But yiu be careful."

He turned the jenny and kicked her into a trot down the partly graded canal line. He rode loose and heavy, his toes pointed out. His relaxed weight made the jenny's trot look smooth. He did not look back. Ollie watched him, feeling hollow and relieved, his burden divided. But then he thought how long it would be before John, or his father, or the doctor, or anyone, could get out from town, and he remembered the animal sound of his mother's pain. In a moment he was galloping back along the canal line toward the river trail.

He had the Olpen place in sight from a good way off—log cabin and stable, hay-roofed shed, pole corrals, a gnawed and tattered haystack, tall cottonwoods. As he got closer he saw Mrs. Olpen come out into the yard, and chickens running stretch-necked in every direction, scattering the cottonwood fluff. He came in at a trot, with his arm across his face to hold out the dust. When he could see, there was Mrs. Olpen, leathery, slab-sided, standing by the chopping block with a Plymouth Rock hen by the legs in one hand and a kindling ax in the other. Rough men's boots poked out from under her skirt. With her ax hand she held back a string of hair from her eyes, squinting upward.

"Havin' it, is she? Needs me?"

"Yes, she's sick, she was crying. Miss Linton said . . ."

"Just a second."

She laid the chicken sideways on the block—round eye, leathery lid, open beak—and with one short blow chopped off its head. The ax remained stuck in the block beside the small, perfect, very dead head; the headless chicken flopped and bounced around them, scattering blood and stirring up cottonwood fluff. Ollie held the hard-mouthed mare in tight. Mrs. Olpen wiped her hands on her apron and then reached back to yank the strings. "Sally!" she bawled. "*You*, Sal!"

Wading through dust, feathers, and cotton, she hung the apron on a post, hoisted her skirts, and climbed through the corral fence. Ollie, looking at the horse inside, felt desperate. It was a Roman-nosed plow horse of the kind his mother always called Old Funeral Procession.

Impulsively he slid off, pulling the reins over the mare's ears. "You can take mine. I can walk."

But Mrs. Olpen glanced once at the mare's slick wet back and shook her head, just one complete wag, over and back. The plow horse resisted the bit and got a crack across the nose. Ollie, reins in hand, felt the insides of his legs go cold in the evaporating wind. Down on the river bank the two youngest Olpen boys came out of the willows carrying fishpoles, and the sun glinted off the silvery side of the fish they carried between them. "Sal!" yelled Mrs. Olpen, cramming the plow horse's ears into the headstall.

Someone yawned loudly from the house. Ollie turned, and Sally Olpen was in the door, gaping and stretching. She started deliberately down the yard, stopped and scraped her bare foot disgustedly against the ground, and came on again. On the side of her face was printed the pattern of a doily or cushion cover. Her black eyes glittered sideways at Ollie; she leaned on the corral poles and yawned, shuddering and shaking her head.

"Git that chicken plucked and drawed," her mother said. "If I ain't back tonight, you and Herm are to help Pa milk, hear? You git supper, too. You're It."

"What's the matter? Where you goin'?"

Mrs. Olpen, not answering, laid on the plow horse a blanket crusted with sweat and hair. She moved slower than anybody Ollie had ever seen. He resented the wise look that Sally Olpen was bending on him, but to hurry things up he said, "My mother's sick."

"Ah, yeah, I know," Sally said. "Havin' a baby."

"Oh she is not!" He was furious. What did she know, with her raggedy hair and her face all dinted and her dirty feet? He hopped up and down. He said, "Hurry, Mrs. Olpen!"

The woman hauled off the top bar a saddle with one stirrup broken down to the iron, and skirts that were curled and dry. She heaved it onto the Roman nose and settled it by shaking the horn. "You git at that chicken," she said to Sal. "Don't leave it lay out in the sun. And don't you pluck and draw it right by the door, where feathers and guts gits tracked around."

Sal smiled a secret smile at Ollie, picked up the chicken, and held it up thoughtfully by the legs, watching its neck drip. Mrs. Olpen grunted, heaving at the latigo, and kicked old Roman nose briskly in the belly to make him quit holding his breath. She was so *slow!* The two boys had started to run up the river path. Ollie stood on the corral bar and remounted, so as to be above them when they arrived. His mother had never encouraged him to make friends with the Olpens. They were another tribe, potential enemies. But then from the mare's back he saw the dust of a rig coming fast up the river road, and recognized the black and tan mules and the tall man on the seat.

"It's all right!" he cried. "Never mind, Mrs. Olpen. Here's my father! It's all right now!"

In front of them all—leather-faced Mrs. Olpen, that girl with the bloody chicken in her hand, the panting boys dangling their dust-patched fish on a forked stick and bursting with questions—he started to cry. Blindly he yanked the mare around and kicked and lashed her out of the yard to meet the buggy.

His father had met John on the road; there was no need to tell him anything. He didn't let Mrs. Olpen linger even to unsaddle the plow horse, but had her in the buggy almost before the wheels had stopped rolling. To Ollie, biting his lips and stretching the stiffness of tears off his cheeks, he said, "You want to ride with us, Ollie? We can lead your pony."

Ollie shook his head. For a second his father studied him, unsmiling. Then he turned, said a word to Mrs. Olpen, and laid the whip to the mules. They burst off and left Ollie standing, so that he rode furiously after them, not only to catch up but to leave behind with the Olpens a vision of his reckless horsemanship.

It was raining in the mountains. Black clouds covered the peaks, and above those, white thunderheads with bright silver edges were piled high into a sky still blue. Lightning licked and flickered across the storm front, thunder rumbled like rockslides down the canyon. Just where the trail entered the canyon gateway Ollie turned his head and saw the broad sagebrush basin behind him still in dust-thickened sunlight. The canyon was a sudden coolness, his sweating skin shrank, his shirt was cold on his back. He wound his hand in the mare's mane and hung on as she lunged and labored on a steep pitch.

Ahead of him the buggy's wheels grated and ground on the rocks. His father looked back, but made no sign. Mrs. Olpen rode with her face aimed straight ahead out of the tunnel of a sunbonnet. Between their two heads Ollie could see the corner beyond which the canyon widened into their little flat where their corral and haystack were, and to whose right, across the swinging bridge, the stone house hardly more noticeable than a ledge of rock looked down on the river. He wondered if the mother he adored and thought himself unworthy of was still crying for pain.

The buggy rolled through the pasture gate, and Ollie slid off to fight the wire loop over the post. Running, dragging at the mare's holding-back weight, he led her to the corral, where his father and Mrs. Olpen had already alighted. On the hill across the canyon Nellie Linton was waving a dishtowel, either in jubilation or in urgency, from the doorway.

"Take care of the horses, Ollie," his father said. "I'll be back for you."

"Yes, sir."

They hurried up the path toward the unseen bridgehead. Ollie pulled the bridle and turned his mare loose, unhooked the tugs from the curled iron ends of the singletrees, unbuckled the harnesses and dragged them through the dust and boosted them, all he could lift, onto their pegs in the shed. When he came out, his father and Nellie were just disappearing inside the house. Mrs. Olpen was resting halfway up the hill, with her head down and her hand on her knee. Ollie took the oat pail and poured three equal heaps onto the ground. The mules and the mare bent their heads to the piles, nudging him out of the way. He watched Mrs. Olpen make it to the door and go in. The lightning cut a jagged gash in the clouds upriver, and after several seconds the thunder went rumbling away. A wind whirling down the opposite slope hit the river and roughened the slick water of the pool.

He felt lonely, small, and scared. He wished he could cross the bridge before the storm came on. What if his father should forget, and not come back for him? What if his mother was so sick he couldn't leave? Or dying? Abandoned on the wrong side, he could not cross because he had already been disobedient twice and knew he must be punished.

He had been waiting at the end of the bridge for a long time before his father came down the path and out onto the span without touching the rope, and pounded across as if the swaying planks were bedrock. Ollie stood up. "Is she all right?"

His father, in a hurry, took his hand. "I think so. I hope so."

"Is she crying?"

Now his father looked at him in a searching way, and the hurry went out of him. He let go Ollie's hand, leaned against the cliff, and filled his pipe. "She'll have to cry some more before it's over. But she'll be all right if that doctor will only get here."

There was a swarming smell of rain in the air, the sweet smell of tobacco, then the sulphur smell of a lucifer match, then smoke.

"Mrs. Olpen's dirty," Ollie said.

"She's a whole lot better than nothing. She's kind-hearted, at least."

They stood silent, Ollie as close to his father as he could stand without bumping into him. The north winked brightly, winked again before the first flash had been wiped from his eyeballs. Thunder crashed loud, then louder, then began to roll. Full of his feelings, which included a sense of sin, Ollie stood in the drift of pipe smoke and instead of looking at his father, looked at the river, where heavy drops, unfelt in the shadow of the cliff, were dimpling the water.

His father's hand came heavily down on his shoulder. He froze. Now it was coming. He accepted it, he knew it was deserved. The fingers squeezed hard on the bones. His father said, "Ollie, you did something."

"Yes, sir."

"You did something very grown up. Nobody could have done better."

Ollie's eyes flew up to his father's face. The face looked down at him seriously. The hand was so heavy on his shoulder that he had to brace himself to stand straight under it. As if testing the resistance it invoked, the hand left the shoulder and fitted itself around the back of Ollie's neck. The fingers closed clear around his throat under his chin. "You're all right, my friend," his father said. "You know that?"

As if impatiently, he let go, though Ollie would willingly have stood there all evening with that hand on him. "We'd better get back before we get wet."

Uncertainly Ollie offered his hand, to be led across, but his father looked down at him with his eyes narrowed and said, "You came across by yourself when you went for John and Mrs. Olpen, is that right?"

Was it coming now? First praise and then punishment? "Yes, sir."

"Have any trouble?"

"No, sir."

"Scare you, after this afternoon?"

"No, sir. A little."

"Did you think about this afternoon? Did you think you might be punished?"

"Yes, sir."

"If you'd done it for any reason than getting help for Mother, I'd have to punish you. You know that, don't you?"

"Yes, sir."

"All right. Your mother doesn't know, and we won't tell her. It would only worry her when she shouldn't be worried. Now do you want to go back by yourself?"

The look they exchanged was like a promise. "Yes, sir."

His father motioned him onto the bridge, stepped out of the way to let him by, let him get twenty feet out onto the planks before he himself started. He stayed that distance behind, all the way across the bridge.

The doctor came just before sunset. Ollie and his father, closed out of the house, had played three games of horseshoes and then been driven inside by a flurry of rain. But the flurry had come to nothing. Out the door Ollie could see that the yard's dust was pocked with the dried craters of single drops, though lightning still flared on the sky. Above the sound of Nellie Linton's voice reading to Betsy up in the drafting room he heard nearly continuous thunder.

His father knocked out his pipe impatiently against the doorjamb. "Quite an evening to be born." They stood together in the south-facing door and looked out over the canyon and the falling mountains to where the sky over the valley was rosy in the last reflected light. Above the rosy haze of valley dust the sky over there was still blue.

The doorway beside him emptied, his father's quick steps took him along the front of the shack as if he had suddenly remembered something he should have done long ago. But at the corner he stopped. "Good Lord," he said. "Look at that."

Ollie went to the corner. In the northwest the sun had broken around the lower slope of Midsummer Mountain and was sending a last long wink across the Sawtooths, straight into the black mass of rain cloud. Clear across the stone house, bridging from mountains to river bluffs, curved two rainbows, one above the other, even the upper one as bright as colored glass, sharp-edged, perfect from horizon to horizon.

"By George, your mother ought to see that. It's an omen, no less."

They ran up past the cooktent with the wetted dust adhering to their shoes. Ollie's father knocked, listened, opened the door. Ollie, behind him, saw past him to the closed door of the bedroom. He waited while his father crossed the room and tapped with his fingernails.

"Sue? Sue, if you're able, look outside. There's an absolute sign, the most perfect double rainbow you ever saw."

The door opened, the doctor stood in it, wide, shirt-sleeved, his hands held fingers-upward in the air. Every lamp in the house seemed to have been lighted behind him; his shadow fell clear to the front door. Ollie's horrified eyes made out that the stiffly upheld hands were enameled with blood.

"Your wife isn't interested in rainbows," the doctor said. "You've got a daughter three minutes old."

Let two years pass—and they literally pass, like birds flying by someone sitting at a window. Seven hundred and thirty risings of the sun, seven hundred and thirty settings. Twenty-four waxings and wanings of the moon. For the woman, six short stories, one three-part serial, fifty-eight drawings. For the man, an automatic waste weir and a box for measuring the flow of water in miner's inches—both described in technical journals, neither patented. For both of them, for all of them, three times of rising hope and three times of disappointment, the latest of each attributable to Henry Villard's abortive move to expand his empire.

And now midsummer again, 1887.

In that latitude the midsummer days were long, midsummer nights only a short darkness between the long twilight that postponed the stars and the green dawn clarity that sponged them up. All across the top of the world the sun dragged its feet, but as soon as it was hidden behind Midsummer Mountain it raced like a child in a game to surprise you in the east before you were quite aware it was gone from the west. One summer week out of four, when the moon was nearing or at or just past the full, there was hardly anything that could be called night at all.

Whatever it was called, she was alone in it. Oliver was in town, trying to rescue something out of the Villard debacle, raise a little money by borrowing on the sale of some of his own stock. He thought that if prospective backers could only see a mile of completed ditch, they would believe, and he would build that mile at his own expense if he had the money.

It was now nearly eleven; his long stay might be good omen or bad. The children had been long in bed, John had gone to his cabin immediately after supper, Wan had swatted the last flies and miller moths gathered around the lamps and gone out to his tent, Nellie had closed her book an hour ago and said good night and retreated to her room.

There sat Susan Burling Ward, tired-eyed after a day's drawing, dragged-out after a day's heat, and tightened her drowning-woman's grip on culture, literature, civilization, by trying to read *War and Peace*.

But her eyes were too scratchy. When she closed them and pressed her fingers to the lids, thick tears squeezed out. Sitting so, looking into the red darkness of her closed lids, she heard the stillness. Not a sound inside her cave-like house, not a sigh from the room behind the chimney where Betsy and Agnes slept. Not a fly or moth left to flutter around the light. She opened her eyes. The ragged flame along the wick trembled without sound.

And outside the silent house, the silent moon-whited mountains, the vacant moon-faded sky. No cry of bird or animal, no rattle of hoofs among stones, no movement except the ghostly flash along the surface of the river, no noise except the mutter of water as muted as rumination. Her mind was still moving with the turmoil of Tolstoy, and the contrast between that crowded human world and her moonlit emptiness was so great that she said aloud, "Oh, it's like trying to communicate from beyond the *grave!*"

1970 knows nothing about isolation and nothing about silence. In our quietest and loneliest hour the automatic ice-maker in the refrigerator will cluck and drop an ice cube, the automatic dishwasher will sigh through its changes, a plane will drone over, the nearest freeway will vibrate the air. Red and white lights will pass in the sky, lights will shine along highways and glance off windows. There is always a radio that can be turned to some all-night station, or a television set to turn artificial moonlight into the flickering images of the late show. We can put on a turntable whatever consolation we most respond to, Mozart or Copland or the Grateful Dead.

But Susan Ward in her canyon was pre-refrigerator, pre-dishwasher, pre-airplane, pre-automobile, pre-electric light, pre-radio, pre-television, pre-record player. Eyes too tired to read had no alternative diversions, ears that craved music or the sound of voices could crave in vain, or listen to Sister Lips whistle or talk to herself.

Restlessly she stood up, waited for her roiled sight to clear, and went to the door. It let in the pale wash of moonlight and the sunken mutter of the river. The moon was directly above her in the southern sky, with only a small irregularity to mar its roundness. It was not flat like some moons, but visibly globular; she could see it roll in space. Its light fell like pallid dust on bare knoll and cooktent and lay in drifts along the roof-planes of the shack. It might have been a snow scene except for the shadows, which were not blue and luminous but soft and black.

Below, to her right, the canyon was impenetrable, without even a flash from the water, but the little flat across the river, with its haystack, shed, and corral, was a drawing in charcoal and Chinese white, a precise, focused miniature in the streak of moonlight across the shoulder of Arrow Rock. Out of their flat shadows the poles of the corral and the trunks of the cottonwoods bulged with a magical roundness like the moon's. As she watched, charmed, the trees below must have been touched by the canyon wind, for flakes of light glittered up at her and then were gone. But there was no sound of wind, and where she stood there was not the slightest stir in the air. The glitter of soundless light from that little picture lighted in the midst of darkness was like a shiver of the earth.

But where was Oliver? He had never stayed this long on any of his prowling, unsatisfactory trips to town. The momentary fear that he might have been thrown off his horse, or in some way hurt, she dismissed. He was not one to whom accidents happened. She had never worried about him in that way even in Leadville after Pricey's beating, when he rode to work armed, through enemies who would have drygulched him if they dared.

Some delay, somebody he had to wait a long time to see. Perhaps even some success. He had more than earned it. He had turned down four different offers, one in the governor's office, to stick to his great scheme, and she had been loyal, had she not? She had supported him and encouraged him and believed in him and put up with what her support cost her.

As if cupping her hands to catch falling water, she extended her arms. She turned her face upward again to the moon.

> *Rose-bloom fell on her hands, together prest*
> *And on her silver cross soft amethyst*
> *And on her hair a glory, like a saint . . .*

Her image of herself held her breathless. She was aware of how she would look to someone—Oliver? No, he was not likely to notice. Frank? Perhaps. Augusta best of all. As she stood reaching for the soft fall of light she studied the ethereal pallor the moonlight gave her hands, and she thought, with Augusta's mind, *Unchanged. Still Susan.*

The upper half of the path to the river was deceptive and without depth in the wash of moonlight; once she passed into the shadow cast by Arrow Rock the blackness stretched her eyes and put caution in her feet. Feeling her way, she made the loud gravel of the beach. The hollow hole, whenever her feet were still, plashed and guggled with river sounds; it was cool with river chill. By now her eyes had adjusted. She could make out the dividing line between opaque shingle and faintly shining water, with a flutter of white like a ruffle where it tumbled out of the narrows into the upper pool. From where she was, the shed and corral across the river were characterless, lost in a paleness without dimensions. When she tipped her head back and stared for a good while at the glowing sky and the light-paled stars, the luminousness changed her eyes again, so that when she looked back down she could not at first see her own body.

The lighted opposite bank lured her. Dared she cross the bridge in the dark, and be waiting at the corral when Oliver rode up? She walked to the bridgehead and stood in the dark there until things swam obscurely into visibility: pale planks, the blackness of the cliffs against the sky. From below, the river noise came up strongly, and a damp chill flowed around her feet. She could not see the water, only a darker, inverted sky down there, with nearly lost stars in it. For all her eyes could tell her, the bridge might lie on black bedrock glinting with mica, or it might span bottomless space opening under the bottom of the world.

Tentatively she moved out a yard or two, and stood. It seemed remarkably steady. The damp water-breath excited her. With one hand she lifted her skirts above her shoe tops, and with the other she laid hold of the rope's weather-softened twist. Steadily, holding her breath but not hesitating, she walked the sway downward, then upward. Then she was on rock. Then she emerged from the cliff's darkness into cool moonlight, and the river smell was replaced by the smells of dust, sage, horses, dry hay. Exhilarated, feeling no bigger than a doll, she crossed to the corral and went around it to the shed side. She spread her forearms on the top bar and put her chin on her stacked hands, a white figure flooded by the moon, rounded and highlighted against the rounding white poles, with her shadow stretched on a rack of fence-shadow behind her.

A trance was on her eyes, she saw up, down, ahead, and to both sides without moving head or eyeballs. Before her, reaching to her feet, was the pocked, silvered dust of the corral, across which the shadow of the opposite fence was drawn like a musical staff. High across the river her window glowed orange; straight ahead, and up, Arrow Rock jutted black beside the moon. All her right hand was a blackness of cliff. Upward the sky opened, a broad strip of silver gilt with the moon burning through it and stars like fading sparks flung down toward the world's rim.

She stared with eyes stretched to their widest, and as she stared, the firmament rolled one dizzying half turn, so that she was looking not up, but down, into a canyon filled with brightness, on whose bottom the moon lay among silver pebbles, a penny flung for luck into a cosmic Serpentine.

"I wish . . ." she said, not knowing what she wished.

Her neck stiffened, her chin came up off her hands. She listened, caught by some sound. Then she heard it again, a musical, drawn-out howling downriver. It paused, broke into a kind of barking, lifted again into the howl.

The hair prickled on the back of her neck. She was familiar with the usual animals of their mountains and deserts, and she knew this was no mountain lion—a mountain lion mewled and complained like a distressed child. It was deeper and more thrilling than the yap and quaver of a coyote. A wolf, then. Even the sheepherders, who liked to dramatize the dangers of their life, admitted that wolves were getting scarce. Yet what else could this be? And if there was ever a night on which a wolf would want to tilt his muzzle to the moon and let out the sound of his wild heart, this was the night.

The sound was gone, diffused in sky, lost among canyon walls. Her straining ears picked up only a sort of ringing in the air, and that, she was sure, was not in the air at all, but in her own head. She put her chin back on her laced hands and brooded into the patterned shadows of the corral.

In a minute she heard the sound again, this time definitely closer. It had come around some obscuring corner; it was moving her way. In quick fear she took a step backward, estimating with her eye the distance to the hidden end of the bridge. But then she stopped and turned her head sideward to listen once more.

There was something un-wolfish about this wolf, something too human. He howled something too close to a tune, he barked something too reminiscent of words. In double relief she laughed aloud. It was Oliver, riding home in the midnight quiet, picking his way from shadow into moonlight and into shadow again, his hat off, maybe, his shirt open to the softness of night, and singing like a boy on a hayride.

Perception and inference were all but simultaneous. If he rode home singing, his long day must have had results. Someone must have put up the few thousand dollars he needed to dig his mile of the Susan Canal. Any potential investors sent out by General Tompkins in the spring might see water flowing around the contour at the canyon's mouth, and a wheatfield on the sagebrush bench above the Olpens'.

Another corner; the sound came suddenly louder, enlarged by echoes.

> How the old folks would enjo-o-o-o-oy it,
> They would sit all ni-i-i-ght and lis-ten,
> As we sa-a-a-a-ang
> I-i-i-innnn the e-e-e-ev'-ning
> By-y-y-y the moo-oo-oo-oonlight.

Alone, contented with himself and the world, he bellowed in a way to make her smile. As soon as he had sung the melody through, he instantly sang the same verse in the bass, as if trying to sing harmony with himself, and she was reminded of the guides Augusta had told her about, who sang two notes up into the ceiling of the baptistry at Pisa, and let the roof fuse them into a fat round chord.

He was as moon-mad as she was. She heard hoof-irons ring on stone —he was getting close. In a few seconds he would ride into the flat and into visibility. Impulsively she skipped into the shadow of the shed, and there, pressing her back against the rounding logs, she waited to surprise him.

The hoofs passed from rock to dust, came close, closer, stopped.

"Hoo, boy," Oliver said. The saddle creaked. She peeked around the corner of the shed and saw his long leg swing over the cantle and around, his body with its back to her jackknifed in the act of dismounting. Then there was a hard, angry grunt, and he was flat on his back in the dust.

She cried out, and sprang from her hiding place to help him. The mule shied sideways, dragging Oliver by the foot still in the stirrup. "Whoa, whoa!" he was saying, and his body convulsed itself upward and his hand caught the stirrup, or his foot. For another few feet he went bumping, and then he and the mule separated. The mule skittered to the far fence and stood wall-eyed in the moonlight. Oliver sat still.

"Oh my dear!" Susan said.

"Great God, what were you trying to do, get me killed?"

"Oh, when you fell I couldn't help . . . Are you all right? Are you hurt?"

He stood up and beat the dust out of his pants until the moonlight was a palpable haze around him. "No," he said in a voice thick with disgust. He went to the mule and picked up the trailing reins, wrapped them once around the corral bar, hooked the near stirrup up onto the horn, and fumbled for the latigo on the mule's dark side. "What are *you* doing, still up? What're you doing over here?"

"Just looking at the moon." When she came and stood close behind him he went on loosening the cinch and did not turn his head. "I heard you singing. I knew something good must have happened. I was going to surprise you. I'm sorry, I should have known better than to jump out like that when you fell."

"Ugh," Oliver said. The cinch swung loose under the mule's belly, the saddle went up on the rail.

"What did happen? They agreed, didn't they—somebody did. You got some help."

Now he turned, but not the whole way. His face was shadowed by his hat, he looked off down the canyon. "No," he said. "They didn't agree. Nothing happened. I got no help."

"Oh, *Oliver!*"

"So far as they're concerned, the canal's dead. I'm a good fellow, they like me fine, but they've all been burned. They wanted to sell *me* some stock."

He sounded like a boy from whom something has been expected, and who has disappointed himself and everybody else. She moved to put her hand on him in comfort, but he turned away and pulled the head-stall over the mule's bending ears. His hand spatted haunch, he walked around Susan as if she had a diameter of ten feet and took the bridle into the shed and brought out the oat can. She heard the disgusted breath whistle through his teeth as he bent to pour the oats on the ground.

"But you were singing so happily!" she said, and now she did come close and lay a hand on his arm. She stopped short, she leaned fiercely to see his face. "You've been *drinking!*"

For the first time, he faced her; she realized that until now he had been trying to breathe around or past her. Their look was long. She saw that he was uncertain, unable to think of anything to say. "Yeah," he said finally, and turned and reached to set the oat pail upside down on a post. He missed, the pail fell clattering, he stooped and got it and crammed it hard on the post's top with both hands.

"You're drunk," she said. "You can barely stand up. Oh, how *could* you!"

He stood before her and said nothing.

"To come home like a common drunkard!"

He stood there. He did not reply.

"Are you even sorry? Are you ashamed?"

He stood there.

"Are you even going to explain?"

Her maneuvering had brought her around so that in facing her he had to look into the light. His face was stubborn and hangdog. "Sorry?" he said. "Sure I'm sorry. But what is there to explain? We talked a long time, got nowhere. I had a few too many."

"Where were you? Where did you do this talking?"

"The back room of the Coarse Gold."

"That saloon!"

"I guess you'd call it that."

She put her fingers to her eyes and pinched out the sight of his stubborn face. When she took her hands away, his shape weaved and staggered in her sight. His tongue was thick, he couldn't even speak clearly, after a ten-mile ride home. What must he have been when he left Boise?

"I'm ashamed, if you're not," she said. "We'll get nowhere trying to talk when you're in this condition. I'm going up to bed."

Going up the path she felt that she was crying silently inside, drowning in desolate unshed tears. Behind her his feet stumbled, and she hated his clumsiness.

At the bridge he caught up with her and took her arm; she stopped without turning. "Wait," he said. "You can't go across there without a hand."

Her eyes were fixed on the gray planks that hung wireless and unsupported between the two darknesses of cliff. The chill from the water pebbled her skin, the sound of the river was like sobbing. "Do you think *you* can?" she said. "I think I'd better help *you*."

Oliver dropped his hand. She went on across, seeing nothing but the planks under her feet, feeling nothing but the uneasy shifting under her soles and the rope's roughness in her hand. His weight twice lurched the bridge so that she had to pause and cling before going on. Falling off his mule! she thought. A rider as good as he is, falling off a mule!

All the way up the hill she did not look back. When she rested, his feet stopped behind her. When she went on, they followed. With vindicated vindictiveness she heard the unsteadiness of his steps.

Out of the shadow, into the light. She turned her head then and saw the moon float free from behind Arrow Rock. The whitened knoll rounded off around her. Her house, dug into the hill, would hardly have been visible without its lighted window, but cooktent and shack were braced with charcoal shadows and drifted with pale light.

When they came to the place where the path forked between house and shack, she heard Oliver say, "I guess maybe you'd like me to sleep in the shack."

"That might be best."

The promptness with which he turned down toward the shack made her want to scream after him. What are *you* upset about? Why should *you* act as if you're angry with *me*? She felt as empty as the mountains. After eleven years, she wanted to say after him. After eleven years you finally prove to me that Augusta was right.

She found that she had followed him, unintending. They stood before the door of the shack. Oliver would not look at her, he stood obstinately silent. After a long wordless minute he opened the door. "Good night," he said.

He went in, the door closed, she stood alone before the shack whose unpainted front in the moonlight was as white as the gable of a New England farmhouse. Above the door she saw the quotation from Confucius Oliver had nailed up there five years before. Its bottom half had split off, but the rest of it, faded by weather, was clearly readable in the midnight radiance.

> *I find no fault with the character of Yu.*
> *He lives in a mean low house*

6

About this time I need some Mister Bones to say to me, "Doesn't this story have anything in it but hard luck and waiting? Isn't the man ever going to get that ditch dug?" Then I can reply in summary fashion, and get by this dead time.

For I find that it bothers me to wait it out with them. I don't want to follow Grandfather on his trips to the post office, where there is nothing but a letter for Grandmother from Augusta Hudson that rubs into his raw conscience the realization of his wife's exile, or a check from Thomas Hudson that reminds him, with barbs, how he is supported. I don't want to drift with him up to the territorial offices or the Coarse Gold. I don't want to watch him accept drinks from men who offer them half out of personal liking and half out of alertness to evade what he may ask of them.

Neither do I want to take any of those long train rides to New York, where General Tompkins periodically got a fire going in some handful of damp financial shavings. I don't want to watch them blow hopefully into one little smudge after another until it went out. I don't want those depressed rides home, six days long, carrying each time a bigger accumulation of failure. No wonder he spent most of his time in the club car.

At home, after those episodes, he could go out and work off his disappointment helping John grub sagebrush out of the right of way. He was past believing that the skinned line around the corner of the hills would fool anyone into thinking that the canal was making progress; he was simply one who did his worrying with his muscles. I, having no muscles left, cannot share even that minimal relief. It makes me nervous and restless to imagine his condition, I think too much, I lie awake, I lose confidence in what I myself am doing, I even find myself bending toward the notion of an inane tranquilized existence in Rodman's Menlo Park pasture. Maybe I would have been smart to devote my hermit years to some silly untroubling subject such as Lola Montez.

What bothers me most is to watch the slow corrosion of the affection and loyalty that have held Oliver and Susan Ward together. I am ashamed that he hits the bottle when he gets low, I hate the picture of Grandmother sitting in the canyon house, a sulky, sullen dame, worrying half spitefully that he may fall off the bridge coming home, or show himself sodden and sottish before the children. And feeling, too, the profoundest, most hopeless pity, wanting to help and having no notion how. She knew that drink must be an almost irresistible temptation, even while she expected him, if he was a man, to resist it.

Less and less a companion, more and more a grind, she was bolted to her desk by her desperate sense that the family depended entirely on her; and the more she drove herself to work, the more she resented the separation that her work enforced between her and her children and husband. I can visualize her coming out in the still early morning and looking down across the lonely desolation where she lived, and shuddering for what had happened to her; and if she caught sight of her own face in the water bucket's dark pane, she was appalled.

If he said—and I'm sure he did, more than once—"Let's get out of here before the place caves in under us, let's go up the mountain for a few days and do some fishing," she refused because of her work, suggesting that he and Ollie go. Then when they did go, she felt deserted, one who had to work while others played, and all the time they were gone she fretted over Ollie's missed lessons. How was he ever going to learn to read properly if he was always out fishing?

Yet when jobs were offered Oliver—a mine in Kellogg, a bureau in the Governor's office—she closed her mouth on the impulse to influence him, and accepted his decision when he made it against, as she had to think, all the best interests of his family. There was always a clearing of the air when they had considered and he had rejected some alternative to their bondage. Yet within days of such a decision she had added it to her cumulative grudge.

Her children ran barefoot through Rattlesnakeville. She nagged them for growing up like savages and taking too lightly their lessontimes with Nellie. Even if there had been places she wanted to go, she would not have left the canyon: she had no clothes she considered decent, and she would not appear in Boise visibly shabby-genteel. And every time Oliver returned from town she managed, bent on busy errands, to pass close to him and sniff. I discovered in my childhood that she had a nose like a hound. If I had eaten some forbidden poison such as licorice within two hours, she knew. So I know how a guilty party might have felt in 1888, how resentful of her infallible powers of detection.

Miserable, both of them, everything hopeful in them run down, everything joyous smothered under poverty and failure. My impulse, and I hereby yield to it, is to skip it all, to document not one single miserable hour until a day in November 1888. That day the post office finally produced a letter with the seed of change in it.

It was not the letter Oliver waited for, guaranteeing funds for the completion of his project. It was from Major John Wesley Powell, who had succeeded Clarence King as director of the United States Geological Survey. It said that the Survey, recently charged by Congress with surveying all the rivers of the West, designating irrigable lands and spotting reservoir sites, could use his help. Captain Clarence Dutton, who would be in charge of the hydrographic survey, had recommended him warmly (there was an echo of one of those evenings in Leadville). Major Powell understood that Mr. Ward's own project was temporarily inactive. Would he be willing to take leave from it for perhaps two years and sign on as regional assistant to Captain Dutton, taking as his province the Snake River Basin on which he had already done much work? If Mr. Ward decided to accept the position, he should plan to come to Washington for a week in January, and be prepared to take the field as early in the spring as the weather would allow.

Oliver and Susan, talking it over, understood perfectly that taking a two-year leave from the Idaho Mining and Irrigation Company meant giving it up forever. They also understood that if Oliver signed with the Survey their life would drastically change. Susan and the children and Nellie could not stay alone in the canyon. She would not move into Boise, which she despised.

"Maybe you could make a visit home," Oliver said. But she folded her arms across her breast and stood frowning at the floor. Her parents were both dead. The old house was up for sale. There were only Bessie, who hadn't room for them in her little house, and Augusta, before whom she would be ashamed. When she lifted her eyes and said something, it came out as something cheap that she didn't really mean—a thing near the surface that she seized on as an excuse. "In the same old dress I left in?" she said. "Eight years out of style, with darns in the elbows?"

She saw him consider, and understand, and forgive what she had said. He didn't even suggest that it was now not impossible to get a new dress. He only said, "Well, then, what do you do if I take it?"

"I don't know," she said, "but you *must* take it."

"Give up."

"You wouldn't be giving up everything. All your work would be useful for this government survey. Maybe when that's done, irrigation will be better understood and you'll get your backing and can go on."

"Do you believe that?"

"I don't know. Don't you?"

"No."

"Still . . . !"

"Still I ought to take it."

"I think so, yes."

"And what do you and the children do?"

"It doesn't *matter* what we do! I'd be happy anywhere if I thought you were working and . . . satisfied with yourself. I can support the children. Haven't I been doing it?"

It was not the thing to say. She knew it, but could not help saying it. The steady, heavy stare of his eyes told her that he resented her and hardened himself against her, and the moment she saw his reaction, she resented *him*.

"It will do you good to get away from those people and that town," she said. "You'll be out in the mountains doing what you like to do. I want you to take this job and I want you to promise me you'll stop drinking. If you're working, there's no *excuse*, is there?"

"No," Oliver said.

At his tone she flared up. "Is there? *Is* there? I've tried to understand, I've excused you, because I know how . . . But now if you're working again there *isn't* any excuse. You've got to promise me!"

"You'd better let me work that out for myself," he said. "I do better when nobody is pushing or pulling."

"You think I'm pushing and pulling?"

He looked at her and said nothing.

"If that's what it is," she said, close to crying, "if you think I'm a bossy managing woman, it might be better if I took the children away somewhere and never came back."

He was exactly like a balky mule. She could see his hind quarters settle and his ears lie back. Aghast at what she had said, more than half afraid she meant it, she stared into his frowning face.

"That's what I mean by pushing and pulling," he said. He walked away from her and sat on the table, looking out the window down toward the bridge and Arrow Rock. He talked to the window, or to her reflection in it. "You're a lot better than I am," he said. "You think I don't know that?" In the glass his eyes found and held hers. "You think I don't know what I've put you through? Or that I don't care? But I tell you, Sue, I'm not going to do any better because anybody, even you, is hauling at me. I'm doing my best right now."

Wordless, hugging herself, letting the tears run down her cheeks, she watched his angled face ghostly on the glass, with the opposite rim and the sky beyond it.

"If a promise means anything, I have to make it to myself," Oliver said. "Then if I break it I'll be harder on myself than you'd ever be. But I can imagine breaking it. If I'm out somewhere by myself, thinking how you're all God knows where and the canal's shut down and the company broke and all these years blown away like trash, I'm going to feel low a lot of the time. I haven't felt any other way since I can remember, practically. I don't feel any different now, just because of a letter from Major Powell. If somebody comes by when I'm feeling that way, and takes a bottle out of a saddlebag, I might help him kill it. If I did, I'd probably ride straight into the nearest town and get some more. I know myself that well."

She shook her head, letting the tears run down. In the glass she saw his shoulders move with impatience.

"I suppose I'll take this job," he said. "What else can we do? We're licked. But you can't make me like it."

"I can't understand," Susan said. "I try, but I can't. Doesn't it *shame* you to be . . . enslaved that way? Doesn't it humiliate you to think that you can't resist that temptation when someone like Frank, living out on the railroad with the roughest sort of men, never touches a drop? Why can't you be like Frank?"

And that was the greatest mistake of all. "Because I'm not Frank," Oliver said, staring at her reflected face. "Maybe you wish I was."

In confusion and distress she broke off their reflected look, turned away. "No," she said, away from him. "I just don't see why you won't promise."

In his voice, to which she listened keenly, trying to hear in it all she had turned away from in his face, she heard no tenderness or compassion or love, nothing but the grate of resistance. "Don't push me," he said. "It won't do any good to fog it all up with words. But I'll tell you one thing. I'm not taking anything along. I won't be Clarence King with a mule load of brandy. I won't be Mrs. Briscoe, and lay in a supply."

That was the best she got out of him. That was where they left it.

7

"If you're still in need of an end man," Shelly said yesterday when I came in from the garden just about five, "I've got all sorts of questions for Uncle Remus."

She wasn't exactly opportune. I was hot, exhausted, and hurting, and I needed no end man. That was a purely rhetorical need. Shelly's interest bothers me, moreover, because it isn't really interest in Grandmother. It is a sort of speculative interest in me, and some of it is mere boredom and desire to talk. Her husband has been after her again by telephone; probably she wonders why I haven't asked about him. Or maybe she feels sorry for me, locked up in myself as she conceives me to be. She's like an idle adult who is willing to squat down and help a child make a sand castle on a beach.

It's a mistake to give her these tapes to type off, but I can't seem to resist. I've worked by eye so long that I can't believe in what is done by ear. I doubt that I've done anything until I can see a typescript.

"Questions such as what?" I said.

"Such as, Was she really thinking of leaving him, or are you guessing?"

"I'm extrapolating."

"Ah," she said, "right on the rug. Shame on you."

I was really in no mood for one of her discussion periods. My wrists were stiff and sore, my stump jerked, I ached from footboard to neckrest. But as I turned my chair to go back down to the porch where Ada would bring me a drink and let me be quiet, Shelly said, "I know he was a juicehead when they lived here, so I guess she never did get him to take the pledge."

"How did you know that?"

"Dad. He said your grandfather owned this underground placer up on the Yuba, and Dad's father used to drive him up there every once in a while to inspect. They were cheating him blind, Dad says. They'd give him the sand and keep the gold."

"He was easy to cheat. That was one of Grandmother's exasperations."

"But nice?" Shelly said. "Everybody respected him? Dad says the miners all thought he was the fairest man they ever worked for. He'd give anybody a second chance."

"And a third," I said. "Not a fourth. When he was abused beyond his toleration he could be implacable."

"He didn't sound implacable the way Dad talks about him. He doesn't seem implacable in your book, either. That's why it seems so funny he'd have to take these three-day trips up Yuba Canyon and put on these big drunks with his driver. Just drink till he went to sleep, and then sleep it off and come home again."

"He had a chronic drouth of the soul," I said. "Every now and then I guess he had to irrigate."

"Did you ever see him drunk?"

"How would I know? I was a boy. He was never noisy, or sloppy, or anything like that. He never drank on the job, and I'm sure he never drank around Grandmother. He was a restful sort of man, as I knew him. I sort of felt he held the world up and kept it running. I can remember times when he took me down the mine."

"Yes?"

"Nothing. Just . . . He had a big warm hand. You know how the pump shaft of the Zodiac runs right alongside the main shaft, just some timbering between?"

"I never was down the Zodiac. It closed up before I was born."

"Really?" I was surprised. The Zodiac is very real to me. To her it is not even a memory, it is only some decaying buildings and a boarded-up entrance and a lot of rusting cable and iron overgrown with weeds.

"It's a sloping shaft," I said. "The pump rod goes down nearly a mile. Grandfather designed the pumps—it was his first job when Conrad Prager brought him here to open the Zodiac up again after the lower levels flooded. Twelve pumps worked off the same rod. Going down, you walked down the track, but every once in a while you'd have to step back into the timbering to let a car pass, and then you'd feel that great rod working in the dark right behind the back of your neck. It would crawl up to its top pitch, and strain there for a second and then ram down. The shaft was always full of gulps and sobs way down in the dark where the pumps sucked water. They went twenty-four hours a day, seven strokes to the minute, like a slow, heavy pulse. The old Cousin Jack who tended them always spoke of them as "she," but I never stood there between the timbers hanging onto Grand-father's hand without thinking of them as somehow part of *him*. They had his sort of dependability. It was as if I could feel them beating in his hand."

Shelly was looking at me with her head on one side. Her eyes, which are normally a cool skeptical gray, warmed nearly to brown. "You liked him a lot."

"I suppose I liked him—*trusted* him—more than I've ever trusted anyone."

"I think he must have been a lot like you," she said, still with her head on one side and that smiling look of speculation on her face. "He understood human weakness, wasn't that it? He didn't *blame* people. He had this kind of magnanimity you've got."

"Oh my dear Shelly," I said. "My dear Shelly."

I think that her impulses are mainly confessional. She would love it if every afternoon we could start up one of these truth parties. It must puzzle her that since my one look at her private life I have not explored it further. It may annoy her that I don't solicit her opinions on the problems of human conduct (she would call it behavior). She has her little drama, poor thing, and she would like to play it to a packed house. She would also not mind being the audience for my confessional moments. Her discussions of Oliver and Susan Ward have this torque in them, they twist toward Lyman Ward too often.

I could tell her, and may have to, that if there is one thing above all others that I despise, it is fingers, especially female fingers, messing around in my guts. My guts, like Victorian marriage, are private.

So I fumbled a couple of aspirin out of the bottle in my saddlebag, and eased my good leg out to a full stretch, and rubbed a little on my twitching stump, and said, "Would you bring me a glass of water, Shelly, please?"

She brought it, but she didn't get the message. When I had downed the pills she took the glass and said, "How do you know he was a drunk away back in 1887?"

"Not a drunk. A drinker. Don't make the mistake Grandmother did."

"A drinker, then."

"From some of Grandmother's letters."

"Where she says she's upset about his drinking."

"That and some other things."

"That's funny. I don't remember any letters like that, and I've been through nearly everything up to the time they came down here."

"Those letters aren't in the files."

"Really? Why not? Where are they?"

"Because they're the most private things I know about her," I said. "All of a sudden that poor Victorian lady is stripped bare, and it's kind of awful. She found herself having to deal with emotions that a genteel education hadn't prepared her for."

"Why? What happened?"

"I don't know, exactly. That's why we wrote a while back to the Idaho Historical Society, to see if someone could search the Boise papers for us."

Shelly studied me with a frown. She was sitting on one foot, and her corduroy pants were stretched tight on her thighs. The loose loafer flapped up and down as she wiggled her toes inside it. "It seems to me she made an awful lot of fuss because her husband took a few drinks."

"I didn't say that was all."

Finally she began to feel the chill. "Well, you're very mysterious. What was it? Did she really get mixed up with Frank Sargent? Do I get to see those letters?"

I didn't answer. I swung the chair and looked over her head to where Grandmother sat in her gilt frame, looking down in a sidelong wash of light. Somehow I don't want anybody messing around in her guts any more than I want anybody messing in mine.

Why then am I spending all this effort trying to understand my grandparents' lives? What am I talking and organizing all this for? Why do I hire this girl to make my talking real by typing it off the tapes? Why do I drive my drifts and tunnels toward the hidden lode of Susan Ward's woe? Is it love and sympathy that makes me think myself capable of reconstructing these lives, or am I, Nemesis in a wheelchair, bent on proving something—perhaps that not even gentility and integrity are proof against the corrosions of human weakness, human treachery, human disappointment, human inability to forget?

My stump was twitching, I felt upset, cornered, and angry. "Maybe sometime," I said. "I'll have to hunt them up."

Time is not on my side. I am distressed by the slow progress I have made. Here it is nearly September. I have used up the spring and summer getting Susan Ward to the age of forty, and she doesn't die until she is ninety-one. If Shelly goes back to Berkeley next month, as she makes noises about doing, I shall have more privacy and probably make even slower progress.

Furthermore, my little general practitioner in Nevada City now wonders if I should risk staying through the winter without a proper nurse. What he means is two shifts of nurses, and he knows as well as I do that I can't afford them and don't want them. Like Grandfather, I do a little better without any pushing and pulling. Ada is all the nurse I want. She will come when I holler, but not try to run me. Dr. Hines, when I suggested this, said she had troubles of her own, bad arthritis in the winter, a lot of respiratory trouble, and might not be dependable. I will face that problem when it arises. Meantime all his concern is unconvincing. I smell an Afro in the woodpile, and his name is Rodman Ward. Behind him is another Afro whose name is Ellen Hammond Ward. My son, I believe, has given me all the playtime he thinks is reasonable, and in his growing conviction that something must be done, he has become an ally of his mother, the woman I was married to for twenty-six years.

How would I explain, if I were susceptible to Shelly's truth parties, or even if I were writing a book about myself instead of about my grandmother, my relations with Ellen Ward? All that long history of intense couple-ship during graduate school in Cambridge, was that all falsehood and waste? I can't think so. Did she harbor all those years a resentment at giving up her own degree and her own career? It was not I who persuaded her. She said herself that if she wasn't going to have a professional career there was no point in preparing for one; and she had no interest in being a faculty-wife amateur trusted with the details of teas in the art museum.

Those five years at Wisconsin, fighting for a promotion which in the Depression years was about as likely as male parturition—were those arid and empty years for her? Oh no. Rodman was born there, we had firm close friends, we had money enough to get along and so were spared the attic apartments and the peanut butter sandwiches of many of our contemporaries. Of the friends we had then, some are dead, a few are famous, some are lost sight of, hardly any are rich; but all were once close in ways that only Ellen Ward and I, almost secretly, as a couple, understand.

Does all that, and the years afterward at Dartmouth and Berkeley —does it stick in her head? Mean anything? A wasted life? Does she remember as I do the years right after the war when I was beginning to get noticed, when all the saturation in books began to pay off for us? Does her mind's eye ever get caught by the image of me coming out of the study after a good four-hour morning? Does she ever set up in her mind the iron table out in the garden on Arch Street where we lunched nearly every day the sun shone? Sentimental images like that? I suppose not. I suppose all the time the life that I thought sane and quiet and good was *too* quiet for her. It must have made her restless to see me with endless things to do, a lifetime full, and herself with only household routines. She was never one for the Faculty Dames, or bridge, or the PTA, or causes, or playing store at the Co-op. A reader, a walker, a rather *still* woman. I thought we had a good life.

I will never understand it. Maybe toward the end I might have noticed something if I hadn't been preoccupied with my stiffening skeleton. What might I have noticed? I don't know, unless that she simply wasn't happy. But she looked after me with anxiety. I know she worried. She soaked her pillow the night after they told me I'd have to have the leg off.

Yet only a few months after that, she a woman of fifty, and a quiet woman at that, and I a new amputee immobilized in the hospital, she leaves that note on my bedtable saying she is leaving me. And whom does she pick? The surgeon who has just removed my leg, a man with a reputation maybe a little bigger than mine, not much, and no youngster himself, at least as old as she, once divorced, with grown children. Give him credit, he had the consideration to turn my case over to a colleague and go on a long leave. It might have embarrassed both of us to have him taking care of me while he was living with my wife. Though I suppose they could have arranged to call on me separately.

Why? How? By what dissatisfied whim or out of what smolder of long dislike? Hanging onto her youth? Trying to pretend it wasn't already gone? She never gave any sign of that sort of vanity. A belated ambition to be something in her own right? But what greater freedom did she have as the wife of a surgeon than she had had as the wife of a scholar? A lot fewer evenings at home together, for sure. Perhaps the menopause frightened her, perhaps it unsettled her. They can write on my tombstone that I was undone by female bodily chemistry. But if that was it, why did she stay away? That sort of upset lasts only a little while, and anyway can be taken care of with pills.

Whatever brought it on, her romance couldn't have been unluckier. And now I, Ahab, dismasted and with tunnel vision, seeing the back of my own head through the curved lens of space-time, had better watch out. Conspiracy begins to hatch. Her desperation fertilizes Rodman's decision-making capacity. More data for the punch cards. I would bet plenty that Rodman has put up Dr. Hines to scaring me with the possibilities of winter difficulties and accidents.

What does winter weather matter to me? I can live inside. I will take my walks around the empty downstairs rooms. I will install a gymnasium, with a whirlpool bath and a sauna, and spend my principal on a battery of nurses and an athletic director, before I let them persuade or force me off my mountain into some place where they can back me against the wall and thumbscrew Christian forgiveness out of me.

I notice that so long as Ellen had her surgical playmate there were no suggestions of forgiveness or reconciliation. How unfortunate for her that he took a walk out from their cabin on Huntington Lake and never came back. What anxiety, what uncertainty, not unlike mine. Had he left her? Committed suicide? Run off with someone else? Lost his mind? Chosen to disappear like those quiet thousands of men who every year walk out on obligations they can't support? I suppose she was frantic. With some interest I followed the search in the newspapers. Posses, Boy Scouts, forest rangers, helicopters, combed the area for two weeks, until the first storm dumped two feet of snow on the Sierra and made them give up. It wasn't until the following summer that some fisherman found his bones in a ravine. By that time I was in the convalescent hospital, the only one there who was going to convalesce.

Now, after all her woe, Ellen comes back and lets her haggard face be seen, she takes an apartment in Walnut Creek and renews acquaintance with the son she probably hasn't written to in two years. (Or would she have? I haven't any idea. We have never discussed her except on that one visit of his up here.) She perhaps gives him to understand—he no great believer in orthodox marriage anyway—that she is willing to forgive and forget, and naturally take care of poor old Dad if only he will make an attempt to understand, and put the past behind him.

Those two poor old crocks *need* each other, Rodman is probably telling Leah and himself. They're better *off* together. Why not? It's the most reasonable solution for them and all of us.

I have thought about all this. How could I help it? Forgiving I have considered, though like my father and grandfather before me, I am a justice man, not a mercy man. I can't help feeling that if justice is observed, mercy is forever unnecessary. I don't want her punished, I want no eye for an eye, I hope I don't gloat over her misfortunes. I just can't feel about her as I once did. She broke something. I know no way of discounting the doctrine that when you take something you want, and damn the consequences, then you had better be ready to accept whatever consequences ensue. Also I remember the terms of the bond: *in sickness and in health, for richer or for poorer, till death do us part.*

Death, the word is, something not quite a matter of whim or choice. It could be she thought I was going to be permanently disabled, and she had better make alternative arrangements. (No matter how I try, I can't believe that, though I can believe that her medical adviser may have given her that prognosis.) My family have all been notably long-lived; maybe she foresaw thirty fading years as nurse of a hopeless case. Or maybe she was simply victimized by an unseemly post-menopausal itch. I'd rather think it was that, not calculation.

It is even possible she couldn't bear to see me day after day, a gargoyle that was once a man. Does a woman ever leave a man out of intolerable pity? Or because she fears what pity may do to her and him?

If she had left me when I *was* still a man, with two legs to stand on and a head that could turn aside in shame or sorrow, I would have hunted among my own acts and in my own personality for her justifications, and would have found them. I did take her for granted, I did neglect her for history, I did bend her life to fit the curve of mine, we did have our share of quarrels. But she didn't leave me after a quarrel. She left me when I was helpless, and she knew she cut such a shameful figure that she didn't dare tell me to my face, but left that note by me as I slept my two-Nembutal sleep. She laid no charges against me, and so I have to conclude that what finally led her to break away from me was my misfortunes—missing leg, rigid neck, solidifying skeleton.

The hell with her. She earned my contempt, and contempt doesn't yield to Rodman's social antibiotics or the doctrine of King's X.

Grandmother, I want to say to Susan Ward as she nurses her grudge through the winter of 1887 and into the spring of 1888, and finally decides to take Nellie and the children off to Vancouver Island while Oliver leads a party into Jackson Hole—Grandmother, take it easy. Don't act like a stricken Victorian prude. Don't lose your sense of proportion. Ask yourself whether his unhappy drinking has really hurt you, or your children, or him. Don't get impatient with the man's bad luck. You risk too much.

Naturally Grandmother didn't hear my warning blowing backward out of the fog of consequences that is her future and my past. She was not a brooder, but she had had her disappointments and her grievances and her anxieties, and she believed in the aspirations, refinements, and pretenses of gentility. She had watched her hopes recede, had had her pride humiliated. Her ambitions for her children seemed certain to be frustrated. The life she had given up lay far off and far back in time, unbelievable as a mirage. She had a reputation and enjoyed a certain fame, but all by mail, all from a distance, or else among the ladies of Boise whose opinion she did not choose to value.

By then her parents were both dead; one of the bitterest results of their poverty was that she had been unable to go back, either time, to help Bessie lay Father or Mother in loved Milton ground. If she dreamed of going back to renew however briefly her intimacy with Augusta and Thomas, she had to remind herself that her friends were now close to the very great indeed. Stanford White had recently built them a grand house on Staten Island. Their casual guests were cabinet ministers and political leaders and ambassadors and millionaires and internationally famous artists. Their closest friends, the couple with whom they slipped away for quiet weekends at their cottage on the Jersey shore, were President Grover Cleveland and his wife.

Imagine her feelings. The First Lady of the Land had stolen her place in her friend's heart, a place she might still occupy if she had not married exile and failure. If it gave her a mournful pride to know her dear ones valued in such high places, it only made all the more insufferable the worry she felt every time Oliver went moodily into town.

Her reminiscences are not quite candid about the breakup; they reduce what was complicatedly personal to simple economics. "Since I could not march with my beaten man," she wrote, "I preferred to march alone somewhere down to sea level and have my children to myself for a little while and learn to know my silent boy of eleven, who if I could possibly arrange it would be leaving us for an eastern school in the fall."

Closing up the canyon camp was like closing up a house after a death. ("It is easier to die than to move," she wrote Augusta once; "at least for the Other Side you don't need trunks.") She went about the long packing with a tight face and a knot in her solar plexus and a sense of disaster in her mind. Wan was mutely expressing his distress by washing everything—blankets, linen, dishes, clothes—before it was put away. Everything he hung on the line, every article she packed or threw away, every object that met her eye, every meal they ate at the trestle table the juniors had built under the cooktent fly, assaulted her sensibilities with its testimony of lost felicity and abandoned hope.

After one day of it, as they sat eating their noon soup and sandwiches, she burst out, "Oh, why must we pack everything? Can't we just lock it up and leave?"

The way he chewed, thoughtfully, with his head down, struck her as wary; he seemed to be sorting possible replies. Finally he said, "You have to expect to be back if you do that."

"Don't you?"

Tough of eyes, the sort of look a man under orders might have given his superior, a look in which there was acquiescence but no agreement. "Yes," he said, "but I didn't think you did."

She in turn meant her own look to be plain as day to him. She meant it to mean *Yes, if.*

He held his sandwich in both hands and looked at her over it. "You don't have to leave at all, really. John can move up to the shack and look after you. I can get back once or twice during the summer. In the winter we can rent the place to the Survey as an office, and stay on."

Susan thought about it. If she stayed on, what would her staying imply? What would she be staying *for*? How long could her children go on living in an isolated canyon without growing up eccentric or barbarian? How long could she herself give up contact with all culture without loss of herself? Anyway, it was hope that had held them there, and that was gone. She gave a simple answer to a complicated question. "No. It wouldn't do."

"Then we've got to clear it out. If we locked it up and left it, the first sheepherder that passed through would be sleeping in your bed and lighting fires with pages of your books."

"I suppose," she said. "What *about* the books? What about Frank's and Wiley's?"

"I wrote and told them last week where their stuff would be."

"There are dozens," she said. "And all those leather bindings they worked so hard over. They wouldn't want to lose those."

A little later, Oliver and Ollie took a load of things to town for storage. Betsy helped Nellie clear her room. Agnes, who was sick with summer complaint and some form of the bronchial trouble she seemed to be susceptible to, lay in a window seat while her mother put books in a box. She was pale, big-eyed, and languid. Nellie, passing by, smiled and shook her head at her and said in her North Country voice, "Little wist-faced baby!"

"This climate isn't good for her," Susan said. "I hope the sea air will be better. She's never well."

Nellie went back to her room, and Agnes lay and watched her mother stow in the box their *Household Poets,* the cover read completely off and replaced with calf; and *War and Peace,* and *Fathers and Sons,* and some Dickens and Thackeray and Howells and James, and some Constance Fenimore Woolson, and some Kate Chopin, and some Cable. She insisted on having each one pass through her hands, so that she could pat it and brush it neat, before it was put away.

Then a volume in limp leather, tooled and stamped in gold: Tennyson's *Idyls of the King*, bound for her by Frank Sargent as a gift on her thirty-eighth birthday. She let it fall open, and of course what did it open to? "The old order changes, yielding place to new." She flipped to the title page and read the inscription. *"To Susan Ward, on her birthday."* But she knew it came with love. Nellie had told her he had worked on it for a month, and spoiled two other books, before he got one he was willing to give her.

She rubbed her palm across the rough, inside-out leather, thinking about that devoted young man. Young man? He was thirty-two; she was forty-one. In a story written that spring, in desperation for money and out of the voiceless longing of the canyon April, she had made him into a Lochinvar who rode in to an isolated ranch and carried off the daughter of an embittered solitary—once a gentleman—and rescued her for society, the world, fulfillment. But the maiden of that story had been twenty.

In forlorn amazement at herself she laughed aloud, a sound so harsh that Agnes looked at her curiously, reaching for the book to give it her housekeeper's pats. Wist-faced baby indeed, and more in need of rescue than any fictitious maiden designed for the pages of *Century*. Susan let her have the book, and lifted a hand to the little girl's forehead, feeling for fever or the clamminess of debility. As she did so she glanced out the window, down across the hill and the river with its parabola of bridge, and by one of those coincidences that happen all the time in Victorian novels, but that nevertheless sometimes happen in life too, there was Frank Sargent unsaddling his sorrel horse Dan at the corral gate.

It was as if she had thought him into existence again, as if her mind were a flask into which had been poured a measure of longing, a measure of discontent, a measure of fatigue, a dash of bitterness, and *pouf*, there he stood. Gladness and guilt hit her like waves meeting at an angle on a beach. She hung a moment, half inclined to slip out the back and not be findable when he came up the hill. But only a moment. Then she was at the door, waving and calling from the top step. He could not have heard her for the river, but he must have been unsaddling with his eye on the house. She saw his teeth flash in his dark face, he waved exuberantly, flapping a long arm; he spatted the horse into the corral, rammed the gate poles home, and came running. The bridge slowed him no more than if it had been a rigid sidewalk; he came up the hill in great long-legged strides. She met him with both hands outstretched.

"Frank, Frank! Oh, how wonderful! What are you doing here? You're almost too late—we're leaving."

His long brown hands, with a turquoise ring from Arizona on the ring finger of the left, held hers tightly. He was panting from his rush up the hill, he laughed and talked and smiled all at once. She had told him once he was the only man she knew who could talk while smiling.

"Oliver . . . wrote me. I came to get my stuff."

"Ah, is that all?"

"No. To see you, mostly. How are you? Let me look at you."

Still holding her hands, he turned her into the bald sunlight, and she shrank a little, remembering the last time he had looked at her steadily. It seemed to her that what he saw was wan, weathered, and rebellious, and her good sense told her that at forty-one a woman should neither be looked at in that way by a man not her husband, nor should accept such a look with so much willingness.

Then his eyes left her and saw Agnes, round-eyed and hostile in the doorway. "And this is . . . ?"

"Agnes."

Out of my body. What you saw as an ugly swelling, and an ugly reminder of the secrets of marriage, the last time you spoke to me. Before she was born she was more than you could stand. My poor unwanted child, my poor excluded lover!

"I don't like you," Agnes said.

"Agnes, child! What are you saying?"

Frank's smile faded but did not go entirely away. His hands hung onto Susan's. His glowing brown eyes looked at Agnes for a long quiet time; he made no attempt to win her, he only looked. "She's like you," he said without taking his eyes off her scowling face. "She's like what you must have been."

"Heavens, I hope not, with that face!" But some sort of elation came over her; in one remark he wiped away the bitterness in which they had parted. Having accepted the fruit of her womb—even when it looked at him with suspicion—he moved in some way closer to her, awkwardness was lifted off her as a cover might be lifted off a parrot's cage, releasing all that pent-up garrulity. Belatedly, with a laugh that was half embarrassed and half playful, she looked down at her imprisoned hands until he let them go.

What would Susan Ward and Frank Sargent have said to each other in the two hours before Oliver and Ollie returned from town? Having brought them together, I find it difficult to put words in their mouths. Their words, like their actions, would have been hedged by a hundred restraints. She was incorrigibly a lady, he was self-consciously honorable. The novels of their time, to which they were both addicted, were full of hopeless and enduring loves too lofty for treacherous thoughts or acts. Their training urged them toward self control, not toward "naturalness" or "self-expression." Those contemporaries of Shelly's, those young men hot as he-dogs, those antic maidens who yank off their blouses and dance around maypoles in the People's Park, or couple with a series of partners on somebody's parlor rug, would find Susan and Frank as amusing as all the other Victorians. What a hangup about bare skin! What a hypocritical refusal to acknowledge the animal facts of life! The Victorians were a race without biology.

Horsefeathers. Grandmother grew up on a farm and lived much of her life on crude frontiers. She knew the animal facts of life as few of us are likely to again. Without embarrassment she accepted the animal functions of, say, buggy horses that would bring giggles and hooraws from emancipated moderns. Until she and Grandfather built Zodiac Cottage in 1906, she habitually used a privy, and no gussied-up WPA privy either. She could kill a chicken, and dress it, and eat it afterward, with as little repugnance as her neighbor Mrs. Olpen, and that is something most of us couldn't. We have been conditioned to think of chickens as neatly sorted cellophane packages of breasts, wings, legs, thighs, and necks, without guts or mess, without death. Death and life were everyday matters to Grandmother. The breeding of horses, mules, cattle, the parturition of dogs, the smug and polygamous fornications of chickens, raised no eyebrows. When animals died, the family had to deal with their bodies; when people died, the family's women laid them out. In the 1880s you suffered animal pain to a degree no modern would submit to. You bore your children, more likely than not, without anesthetic.

We have only switched prohibitions and hypocrisies with them. We blink pain and death, they blinked nudity and human sex, or rather, *talk* about sex. They deplored violations of the marriage bond and believed in the responsibilities of the unitary family and thought female virginity before marriage a guarantee of these, or at least a proper start. But wild boys and young bachelors they winked at because they must, and both wandering husbands and unfaithful wives they understood, and girls who "got in trouble" they pitied as much as they censured. They could tell a good woman from a bad one, which is more than I can do any more. And they managed to be fertile in times when fertility meant inevitable sorrow, when women had six or eight children in order to be sure of three or four.

So what happened when base desires and unworthy passions troubled the flesh of men and women inhibited from the casual promiscuity, adultery, and divorce that keep us so healthy? One thing that happened was platonic friendship, another was breakage. The first always risked the second.

Frank Sargent was deeply in love. He had to be, to have hung around as he did for eight or nine years. He would have thought it the act of a cad to take advantage of her friendship or betray the confidence of Oliver, but in those nine years he would have learned to mistrust his own self control. The thing he most prided himself on, his hopeless faithfulness, was precisely his greatest danger. As for Susan, though she knew that danger, she was disappointed in her husband and her hopes, bruised in her domestic sentiments, distraught with uncertainties and with the sense of how much she had lost and might still lose. She had always made a companion of Frank. He loved books, loved talk, was altogether readier and more romantic and more enthusiastic than the man she was married to.

What might have happened? I guess they would have found plenty to talk about, after nearly three years. I guess I think it would not have taken Frank long to discover that the object of his hopeless devotion— *Noli me tangere, for Caesar's I am*—was in a mood of serious disillusionment with Caesar. I guess I think that after greeting Nellie, and kissing Betsy, and shaking hands with Wan, he would have looked around the hill spotted with spring flowers, and sniffed the wind that blew down the canyon, and listened to the river heavy and incessant with the spring runoff, and suggested a walk up on the bluffs.

And now I can't avoid it any longer, I *have* to put words in their mouths. Not very personal words at first. Questions and answers. Probes. Time-fillers.

They were climbing up the gulch road, steep and full of loose stones. He helped her along by the hand. When the pitch leveled off he said, "I gather the canal boat is really on the rocks."

"Who told you that? Somebody in town?"

"Yes."

"I despise those people!" she cried. "They're so eager to write our obituary."

"Why? Aren't they right?"

"That's the trouble. But if one or two or three of them had had enough faith at the right time, we'd have . . ."

He sprang up a boulder that the trail had straddled, and reaching down a hand, helped her up. He said, "Must be hard on Oliver."

"Terribly."

"You too."

Shrug. "All of us."

They rested, getting their breath. He said, "I'm anxious to see Ollie. He must be a big boy by now."

"Big and silent. It hasn't been good for him to grow up in the canyon. He hasn't seen enough boys and girls his own age."

"I always thought he loved it."

"He does, but it hasn't been good for him. He ought to be sent East to school."

"Don't you plan to?"

"With what? What would we use for money?"

They started again, pulled up through the shallowing gulch until it flattened out onto the sagebrush plateau. The wind, blowing erratically from the west, moved in the sage and chilled their warm skins. She burst out, "And yet he *must* be exposed to cultivated people somehow, he *must* see plays and hear operas and go to galleries and listen to good talk! He mustn't grow up as silent as his father!"

Brief and questioning, his glance touched her, and then went far off over the valley to the southern mountains, very high-looking from

439

up there, their slopes hazy jade, their peaks hazy lavender crowned with hazy white. He said, "His father's the best man in Idaho, with the biggest ideas."

"All of which have failed."

"Oh, now, Susan, where's the faith?"

"Gone. Withered away. Dried up."

"I can't believe it." Again he took her hands, and bent down on her a look that was puzzled, frowning, and intent. She felt like someone trying to hold down blowing papers in a wind; everything was flying away in confusion. "That just won't do," Frank said. "You've got to have faith in the Chief and in the canal."

Her eyes would not lift to his. They fixed themselves on the tops of the blowing sage behind him. She felt her mouth twist with bitterness. "Faith in the canal I might manage, even yet," she said.

For a long time he stood facing her, holding her hands, not answering; and she, appalled at what she had said, stole a swift glance upward, a moment's flick of the eyes. His face was thoughtful and closed. Finally he said, "Tell me about it?" and started her walking along the bluff trail. But he retained one of her hands.

Later they were sitting on the lava rim where more than once he had sat for her as a model. She had his Norfolk corduroy jacket folded under her to save her dress. Before them opened the gulf of air, with swallows swimming in it. Below them the river was busy digging itself deeper in the lava. They could see how the lava had capped the foothills, or created them, and how the river, coming from the big mountain valley above, had cut down through the dam. (The big valley above would one day all be under water, her engineers had assured her.) They could look down into the top of the slot where the river had cut through (a potential damsite, but not so good as the Arrow Rock site below) but their first sight of the river was where it boiled out, white as a ruffled shirt front, into their pool. On the knoll above the side gulch, Wan's wash, hung on two lines, waved like a double line of prayer flags.

She sat so close to Frank that their arms brushed when they moved, and she was acutely conscious of every slightest contact. Looking down that steep perspective to the little drawing at the bottom, she said, still in the tone of bitterness, "There lie the most wasted years of our lives."

Frank, braced back on the hand farthest from her, did not answer. The little scene on which her eyes were fixed had the clarity of a miniature imprisoned in a lens. The cottonwoods in the hole across the river were bright and twinkling, the gulch was thinly washed with green. The wind gusted from the west, and the swallows tilted in it. Under her dangling feet they were either building or serving nests in crannies and pockets of the cliff. She could hear the river, or the wind, or both, a steady murmuring; and now in a momentary hush the long, sad *wheeoooo hoo hoo hoo* of a dove.

"Yes," she said. "Mourn!"

Frank moved, bumping her shoulder. He muttered an apology, but she did not reply, or look at him. Her eyes were fixed on the shrunken image of their communal life, her heart was sick with the dove's calling.

"Sue," Frank said.

Her mournful preoccupation was both compulsive and somewhat theatrical, half false, for through it she took alert notice of the name he called her by. He had always called her Susan; before strangers, Mrs. Ward. But she did not turn. "Sue, it's not for me to tell you this, but he's had to sit through six years of nothing but disappointment."

"So have we all," she said into the wind. "So have you. Have *you* taken to drink?"

"I haven't staked my whole life on that canal the way he has."

Now she did turn. "Haven't you? I thought you'd staked a good bit of it."

"You know what I've staked my life on. And how much good it'll do me."

He moved, straightened, picked up the hand on which he had been bracing himself, and brushed off the lava pebbles and showed her with a laugh, in explanation of his suddenness, the dented and bruised palm. Somehow the sight of his punished hand broke her quite down. She said to the bulge of her knees under the long white dress, "Frank, what am I going to do? I can't trust the children's future to him. He'll go on trying and trying, and failing and failing, and the more he fails the more his . . . weakness . . . will control him. The children will grow up like Willa Olpen's, they'll be savages! I've tried, you know I've tried."

"I know."

"But what are we going to do?"

"I don't know."

Without his propping hand, he was leaning awkwardly ahead and away. He leaned back, tensed against the awkward position and the wind, and their eyes met. Hers were full of tears. Her teeth bit down on the trembling of her lips. His left hand went behind her, to brace him. With an exclamation he circled it clear around her and pulled her into his arms.

Tears, kisses, passionate and despairing words. Hands? Perhaps. I find it hard to conceive in relation to my grandmother, and to judge by her photographs from that period, there were an awful lot of clothes. Nevertheless. She had been bottled up a long time.

But in the end she pulled herself free and stood up from the sweet and fatal embrace—stood up with her hands to her streaming eyes, and flung her hands, wet with her tears, groundward in a gesture of utter woe—Massaccio's Eve, I have called her that before—and walked away from him, fighting for composure, and stood with her back to him on the trail.

For some time he sat where she had left him. Then he stood up and followed, touched her on the shoulder. She did not turn.

"Don't," she said.

"I'm sorry."

"It's all right."

The wind pushed them, flattening his shirt against his back, shaping her legs under her skirts and petticoats. There was wild pink phlox spreading in a mat from near her feet into a bay of the sage.

"I don't know what we can do," she said, speaking away from him, down the wind. "But I know one thing we mustn't do."

He waited.

"Any more of this."

He did not speak.

"Any more of this!" she said violently, and turned and faced him. Her cheeks were wet, her eyes were reddened, but she was calmer. She stared into his eyes, she put out a hand in love and pity to touch his. "I must take the children and go away just as soon as I can. Tomorrow. Next day at the latest."

"And that leaves me . . . ?" Frank said.

She bent her head and bit down hard on her quivering lip; she turned and looked away from him across the blowing sage.

They would have looked very small, to anyone on a high place, as they walked the trail back to the gulch road. From the photographs in her old album, I should judge she was probably wearing one of those dresses with a half bustle, several years out of style by then; but it would cost me more research than it is worth to know for sure. I know that her skirts would have brushed the dust, that her throat was choked in a high collar, that her arms were covered in leg-of-mutton sleeves that came to the wrist. Only her woeful face and her hands were exposed. The face looked straight ahead. One of the hands was clenched at her side. The other was wound tightly—oh, tightly, with spasmodic squeezings and convulsions of feeling—in Frank Sargent's.

That was the way they were walking when they came to the gulch road and quite suddenly—the wind was blowing sounds away from them—met Oliver and Ollie in the buggy, just turning off the mountain road into the gulch.

She wrenched her hand free of Frank's, she swerved to put space between them. Almost without hesitation she waved a greeting, and she heard the whish of Frank's coat as he swung it around his head. Oliver pulled in the team and waited. They came on down the trail shouting and accepting shouts: *Look who's here! Look who came back for a look-see! Hey, you old rascal! Hi, Ollie! What's the idea, abandoning the old ranch? We've just been up taking a last look at it.*

There was handshaking and arm-punching, some exuberant expressions of friendship and reunion. It had all the outward signs of warmth. But Susan, climbing into the seat while Ollie and Frank piled into the back, rocked and bumped down the canyon in silence, wondering if her tears had marked her face, if they had seen her pull her hand free from Frank's, if Oliver's friendliness was forced, if the expression on Ollie's face was illusory, part of her own guilt, or if it expressed what he felt, or sensed, when he looked up and saw his mother and Frank Sargent walking close together with locked hands, coming down the trail with guilty distress written all over them.

VIII

THE MESA

1

Grandmother says she submitted to that separation; I think she created it. My only evidence is the letters to Augusta, and those are careful. They mention Oliver only in the most matter-of-fact way, and they mention Frank Sargent not at all. She was absorbed in her children and herself, like a widow mending a torn life.

> . . . struck me how often in the past dozen years I have had this feeling of suspension and unreality. Each move leaves me less myself. One can grow used to the security even of a wild canyon, and feel uneasy and afraid outside it. Here in this quiet very respectable very English place I am not Susan Ward at all, or at best I am Susan Ward bewildered and fuzzy-headed, as if after a bout of malaria.
>
> Yet it is charming, and people are kind. We have taken a cottage out by the strait, in the James Bay district, on a lane called Bird Cage Walk. The weather is beautifully mild and soft after our sunstruck gulch. I have a girl who comes by the day, and Nellie is as always perfection—her life would look as beautiful hung on the wall as one of her father's watercolors. She is more the mother of my children than I can afford to be, for I must work long hours, and can only lift my head at evening for a brief walk. I renew myself religiously every Sunday by taking the children for a picnic on the shore.
>
> They are such good children! I am blessed. Ollie is growing into a manly boy, quiet and steady, not handsome as his pictures show Rodman to be, but my own good boy, and a strength to me. He misses his pony and the canyon more than I anticipated, but as he makes more acquaintances here, and grows used to the place, I expect him to enjoy it as the rest of us do. It will do him no harm to hear accents more cultivated than those of Idaho, where they speak of "airigation," and call a closet a "cubby," and "wrench" the soap out of their wash, or "worsh."
>
> Betsy at seven is a little mother, a little housekeeper in love with brooms and silverware and dishwashing. It is touching to see what jealous care both she and Ollie take of their little sister, who is another kind altogether.
>
> She charms us, makes us laugh, awes us, *frightens* us almost.

How she came among us on our crude frontier I shall never know. It is that double rainbow she was born under. She comes from a better world than this, and she has moments of remembering it. She speaks with the fairies. Sometimes I sit and watch her playing quietly in my workroom when the other two are at their lessons, and I see pass over her sweet little face reflections of some pure life she lives within herself. She conducts conversations with invisible playmates, sings songs that she makes up herself, draws pictures with a confidence and imagination that her mother, at least thinks utterly remarkable for a three-year-old. There is no doubt which of my children will be the artist of the family. When she looks up at me and laughs it is as if someone had thrown open the windows of a stuffy house and let the clean sea air rush in. And the sea air is making her bloom. She has a rosy color, and none of the bronchial troubles that Idaho's dust and wind induced.

I am ashamed to bother you, knowing how full your days are, but I am so far from everything, and can think of no other way. Could you somehow get me the addresses of several of the best schools—St. Paul's, Kent, Phillips-Exeter, Deerfield—what others are there?—together with the names of their headmasters if possible? I wish to write and see what I can do for Ollie. He is not a brilliant boy, and I am afraid his difficulty with reading will be a handicap, though Nellie works with him constantly. But he is very steady, and in most subjects sound. Before long he shall have gone beyond that Nellie can give him, and I am determined he shall have his chance.

No hint in these Victoria letters of her marital difficulties. The implication is always that as soon as Oliver finishes the field work of his survey they will be reunited. Yet she stayed on through the summer and fall of 1888, when Oliver was locating damsites on the Snake and its tributaries, and through the winter, when he was working out of a Boise hotel room, classifying irrigable lands in the Snake River Valley, and through the spring of 1889, when he was off to the mountains again. Ollie did not go East to school. She was unsuccessful in getting him any scholarship aid, and she hadn't the money to send him herself.

Like a widow, she was, grim and diligent to support her brood. She does not sound unhappy, but in two separate letters she refers to herself as one "who wants above all to be alone." She did for Vancouver Island the sort of illustrated travel sketch she had previously done for New Almaden, Santa Cruz, Mexico, and the canyon, but except for that impersonal geography her work did not reflect her life closely. The confessional mode was no more common in genteel fiction than in genteel lives.

What she wrote was a version of her old story of the upright engineer torn between love for a young lady and opposition to her wicked father; and a story about a dissolute but charming cavalryman who came to a bad end; and a story about romance that blossomed during two days when a transcontinental train was snowbound in Wyoming. Only one thing she wrote in Victoria seems to me revealing, in the way the Lochinvar-Frank story was revealing. It is the story of a young and promising singer, married to an engineer in the West, who finds that in the harsh Western climate her voice is cracked and destroyed, so that she must reconcile herself, nobly, to live within her deprivations.

She was a factory—a lonely factory, depressed, bravely industrious, afflicted with worry and insomnia, perhaps a little poisoned with self pity. Yet she stayed away. She neither went back to visit Bessie and the Hudsons (money? pride?) nor did she return at once when Oliver's telegram arrived. I don't have the telegram, only the letter in which Susan reported it to Augusta.

Victoria, May 14, 1889

Dearest Augusta —
  Wonder of wonders, the irrigation scheme is not dead after all! I have had a telegram from Oliver, who had barely begun his summer's work in the Salmon River Mountains when word followed him that General Tompkins has at last succeeded in finding new backers. The canal has been named the *London* and Idaho Canal, in deference to the source of the funds, which is English. The Syndicate's representative, a Mr. Harvey, was out more than a year and a half ago, but he moved so quietly and seemed so little excited by what he saw that we gave him up almost as soon as he arrived. Now it appears that he was greatly impressed, thought Oliver's surveys and plans superb, liked the country, liked the prospects, liked everything about us, in short.

  And of course, having waited so long to make up its mind, the Syndicate now wants water flowing within weeks, and wheat ripening by fall. Oliver feels he cannot leave the Survey until he has completed the field work and written his report, which will take the rest of the

449

year, perhaps longer. Isn't it provoking that having held himself ready for so long, he should now be prevented from plunging into the canal as he wants to! But he has arranged a short leave while he goes back to Denver to arrange construction contracts, and he has brought Wiley from Colorado and put him in charge of digging the "Susan" Canal, the first element of what will eventually be a network of ditches. He himself, though on leave to the Survey, will continue to be Chief.

Oh, Augusta, how I wept when I read that telegram with all its enthusiasm instantly renewed and all its hope as intact as if we had not spent these six years—seven, nearly—pursuing disappointment. I wept for joy that Oliver's hope is revived, and for bitterness that it was so long frustrated, and for grief that years of failure have left scars we may never be able to forget. Do you understand me? I hope you do—completely. I should not like to be understood only partially, and yet that is the way I understand myself. And I wept for fear, too —fear that hope may be dashed again as it has been dashed so many times.

These contradictory feelings have led me to postpone my return for now, though my impulse was to catch the first train. Oliver will be incontinently busy, as he likes to be, and away much of the time. We will have no firm place to stay, since the canyon buildings are already converted into engineering headquarters, with their windows gloriously unwashed and their floors pocked with boot nails. Boise itself does not appeal to me, especially with Oliver much away. So it is Victoria for another while longer.

Let me urge you—how ridiculous this is, and yet nothing would make me happier than to have my suggestion taken—that if you want to file on land in the Boise Valley you should empower Oliver to do the preliminary filing for you at once. I shall write him to do so; you can let me know if you want him thereafter to go ahead. Presently, all government lands are withdrawn from entry pending their classification as irrigable or nonirrigable, and the land offices are packed with angry speculators denouncing Major Powell, Captain Dutton, and my poor husband. But all the lands under our ditches have been certified, and await only the President's proclamation to be re-opened to entry. (And how I wish your dear friend Mr. Cleveland were still in office to make that proclamation, and complete the great land reform that was begun in his term!) With the constitutional convention due to convene in Boise this summer, and the Susan going forward as fast as Wiley can drive it, there will be such a land boom as Idaho and perhaps the West has never seen.

Do you see the effect on me of the first good news in years?

Already I am infected with optimism, and am almost willing to expose myself and the children yet again to the uncertainties of life in the Boise Valley, and to those other uncertainties that I dread.

Uncertainties about Grandfather or about her treacherous feeling for Frank Sargent? Since Frank had gone up to Kellogg to the gold mines, I have to assume it was Grandfather whom she doubted. I suppose her letters must have suggested that now, with the canal going forward and his anxieties removed, he might promise her never to give in to his weakness again. I suppose he would have ignored any such suggestion. Love her and admire her and respect her he did; let her manage him he would not. He was as stubborn as a post, and in his way as word-blind as my dyslectic father.

So I assume that he neither stooped to beg her to come home, nor made any promises. Nor, understanding the Frank Sargent situation, would he have asked any of her. He probably reported on the progress of the ditch and ignored the state of his feelings, while he waited for her true feelings to reassert themselves. At last, in August 1889, after fifteen months away, she came back.

Once more they met at the steps of a transcontinental train. They were both watchful and restrained; the presence of Nellie and the children kept their reunion from being too personal; any diffidence in his greeting of her could be covered up in the exuberance of greeting his children. Then they gathered up their suspended life and carried it off once more in a democrat wagon.

Driving, they had no chance to talk. Her critical eye found the streets of Boise as swarming as the streets of Leadville, and not half so picturesque. They had to halt and pick and kink their way through a morning crowd of buggies, wagons, dogcarts, buckboards. The plank sidewalks were full of men, women, children, soldiers, settlers in overalls, politicians in derbies. Two men in frock coats, two of that political crowd that had led Oliver to debase himself in barrooms, raised their hats to her with impertinent smiles. She gave them back a smile as dishonest as their own, and a good deal chillier. Oliver greeted them casually, steering past their stares. For Susan, it was like having to walk through a room where she had just been humiliated.

"The convention's burst the town's seams," Oliver said. "That and the reopening of the public domain."

"And the canal. I suppose they're all on your side now."

His look was surprised and questioning. "I don't know that they were ever against me."

Susan did not reply. Nellie was having trouble keeping the children quiet in the back. Ollie kept leaping up to point out landmarks to his sisters: it seemed he had forgotten nothing. Finally his father turned full around, put his nose right against the boy's nose, and said, scowling, "Sit you down, friend."

Ollie was not cowed. He looked as if he had a secret pact with his father. And he looked, Susan thought, as excited as if coming home to Boise were the greatest event of his life. "Can I drive?" he said.

"May I," Susan said.

"Later," Oliver said.

They turned off the main street, and within a block were heading out of town on a bench road that Susan did not remember. "This is new," she said. "Yeah," Oliver said.

The mountains were familiar on the left, the remembered sage plain dropped down its terraces, the southern horizon crawled with overheated peaks. Her traveling dress was too warm. "Are we going to the canyon? I thought Wiley and his crew were out there."

"They are."

She waited, but he offered no more. The old impatience at his wordlessness twitched in her mouth. She would not ask him another thing—where he was taking them, where they were to live. Within a half hour of seeing him again after more than a year's separation, she felt imprisoned in his life, dragged along after his warped buggy wheels.

The following wind blew their dust over them, the air was heavy with dust clear to the canyon's mouth. After the green gentle earth and the soft sea air of Victoria she found the country of her exile arid, barren, and hateful. The dry wind roughened her lips and parched her nostrils. When Oliver whipped up the team to outrun the dust, she was thrown roughly around.

They slowed. Ollie, standing again, hanging onto his father's shoulders, said, "Can I drive now?"

His father reached an arm and dragged him over the front seat. His knees and shoes scuffed Susan as he went through. Along a track where the sage had been crushed and the ground pulverized by wagons, they plodded and creaked. After a half mile or so a less worn track forked off southward. Oliver touched the right rein and had Ollie guide them down it. Susan sat silent, watching the sage flow by, her nose full of dust and her eyes full of the desolate country and her mind full of desolate thoughts.

A lane opened to the left, grubbed out of the level sage, and at its end, a half mile or so away, she saw one of the dreary ranches that she supposed would now crop up, sprouting on the promise of water, to make the benches even more forlorn than when they had been empty of everything but wind. A house the color of earth, a windmill that winked—some Olpen family with a slattern wife and a tobacco-chewing husband and a flock of unlicked children wilder than coyotes, a clutter of slovenly corrals, a yard made filthy by scrub hens. She could see it, it burned into her mind like a raw, unrealized drawing.

Oliver's hand again touched Ollie's, this time on the left rein, and they turned down the lane.

Susan's head snapped around, she stared at him with a terrible question, but he rode slumped, looking ahead over Ollie's cap. Trying to get her bearings, she half stood. The odor of crushed sage filled her nostrils like sal volatile. The grubbed-out bushes had been stacked in windrows along both sides of the lane, and inside the windrows of gray brush she saw the lines of little trees on each side, each tree staked in its bowl of dug earth, each basin damp, watered that day. Hanging to the back of the seat, she stared ahead at the house and windmill. They had a certain air of confidence, closing off the lane as if someone with imagination had set them there. The house, now that she saw it clearly, was large, much more than a settler's shack. A veranda like a promenade stretched all along its front.

"Oliver Ward," she said, "where are you taking us? Is this our land? Is that *our* place?"

"Mesa Ranch," Oliver said. "Model farm. Thought you might like to see it."

She thought his eyes asked something of her, warned her, said "Wait." But she couldn't wait, too much was dawning on her all at once.

"When did you build it? You've even planted your half mile of Lombardies!"

His eyes warmed, narrowed, held hers with an expression she could not read, a kind of urgent, knowing look not far from mockery. "Best foot forward," he said. "With only the well to irrigate from, I couldn't swing the lawn and the orchard and the wheatfield and the alfalfa patch. They'll have to wait till water comes down the Big Ditch."

"Oliver . . ."

"I *had* to start the trees," he said, watching her. "Four hundred and fifty for the lane alone. A hundred locusts and box elders around the house. I didn't want you to wait any longer than you had to for your grove."

"The way you planned it."

"The way we planned it."

She made note of his pronoun.

"I was too late to start the rose garden. That'll have to wait till next spring. But I did move the yellow climber down from the canyon. Never even set it back. It's blooming right now, not quite over."

She looked ahead, while Ollie with his eyes looking out the corners at them and his ears obviously wide open, steered the team toward the barren house squatting on the bench. She saw that the veranda was deep, with square pillars every ten feet or so supporting a broad low roof. Wherever he had planted the rose, it didn't show. Neither did the hundred trees of his grove—well, yes, a few, staked-up, spindling saplings, hardly higher than the sagebrush. In something like despair, she cried, "When did you do all this?"

For the first time since they had met at the station she saw her old Oliver in him, loose-shouldered, humorously apologetic. "I didn't do much of it. The crews have been working since a week after we got the go-ahead on the ditch. This'll be the demonstration farm. The Governor loaned me the Territory's well-drilling rig, and the boys from the canal crew scraped out the road."

She closed her stinging eyes, held them painfully shut, opened them, said, "The Lord hates busybodies and people who do too much." Then she burst out, "But the *money!* How will we pay for it?"

The children in the back were clamoring, "Is this ours? Is this our place?" and Ollie, twisting to look into his father's face, was saying,

454

"Aren't we going to live in the canyon?" Both she and Oliver ignored them. He said over Ollie's head, holding her eyes, "For a start I used the money the company paid you for the canyon place. It was the first check I signed."

"You sold it!"

"For twice what it cost. That was the bargain. I took a chance you'd agree it ought to go into this."

"Dad, don't we own the canyon any more?"

"Not exactly. But you can go there. All you want."

"Even twice what the canyon house cost wouldn't pay for this," Susan said.

"I sold some of our canal stock to John and Bessie."

She was appalled. "Oh, Oliver, you haven't led *them* into this! You haven't tied *them* to our canal boat?"

"They wanted in," Oliver said. "They had the money from your family's house. I've filed a timber claim and a desert claim for them, down under the Susan." His stare was level and steady. "Wouldn't you like Bessie living out here?"

"Oh," she said, distracted, "they shouldn't risk their poor little money! And you never said a word. Neither did Bessie. Why?"

"I asked her not to," he said, with his sidelong, ambiguous, searching smile. "I wanted to spring it on you that they'd be moving out. Along with the house, you know. A bouquet of surprises."

"Well, of course, it'll be wonderful to . . . but . . ."

"So now you have to make up your mind whether you want to camp out here in the dirt or stay in a boardinghouse in town. Because I didn't get it done in time."

The wheels ground in sand, dust hung over them, she saw the wind whip a whirl of dust around the bare corner of the house, and turn it into a half-formed dust devil that spun eastward past a lumber pile and a stark privy.

"Here, I should think," she managed to say. "There's no sense in spending money on a boardinghouse when we have our own place."

"It's pretty primitive yet."

"Is that anything new for us?" she said.

Her tone was sharper than she intended. But he did not reply—

only studied her a moment and then heaved around to say, "Nellie? How does it strike you?"

"Why it seems nice," Nellie said comfortably. "With all of us to help it shouldn't take long."

"Is Patch here?" Ollie said, and Betsy, hammering on her father's shoulders, said, "May I have a pony too, Father? I'm nearly eight," and Agnes stood up in Nellie's grasp and said, "Me too! I'm four!"

"You'll all have ponies," Oliver said, and took the reins out of Ollie's hands and stopped them in the raw yard.

Susan sat with her hands tight in her lap, knowing she should force some enthusiasm, however false. While she held herself apart in Victoria he had driven himself every spare hour to prepare this place for her—the place they had sketched and erased and redrawn through dozens of shut-in evenings in the canyon. She knew with precision, to a decimal point, what he hoped to make it, and she could have wept for the premature trees and the transplanted yellow rose that had put out its first blooms the summer Agnes was born. Yet the exposed yard, a scab on the sagebrush mesa, made her feel like weeping in another key. In homesick hours she had dreamed of the soft dry wind of this valley, but she had dreamed it clean, not with these dust devils that whipped across skinned land, and the haze of dust that she supposed arose from the ditch construction along the edge of the mountain. She had dreamed the valley clean and wild, not made ugly with such raw beginnings as this. So many years must pass before it could be made into anything beautiful or civilized, so much of their lives would have to be spent in the hard preparations to live. The canyon house had been one thing, a temporary camp. This house was where she would spend the rest of her life.

Oliver hopped down. Over the wheel, a little grimly, he said, "You might as well see the worst. She'll be dirty in the dry and muddy in the wet, and there's nothing to break the wind. But I call your attention to the view."

She did not look at the view; she looked into his eyes. "Yes," she said, almost under her breath. She was aware of the children, still sitting uncertainly as if unwilling to get down in this totally strange place.

Then a ranch dog came wagging out from a shed, and after her four fat puppies. The children piled out and went to her and squatted down where she cowered and wagged in the dust. The puppies attacked their fingers and rolled on their backs, exposing naked bellies to be tickled.

Tentatively, Agnes put out a hand to one of the pups. It seized her fingers in its mouth, and she yanked her hand back, frowning. The pup got hold of her shoe buckle and tugged, backing, with fierce growls. Agnes let him tug, her face breaking up into smiles, and then suddenly, squeezing her eyes gleefully shut, her arms stuck out from her shoulders, her skirts lifting to expose her nimble black-stockinged legs, she twirled away. The pup pursued her, fat and ferocious, as gleeful as she. Her sailor hat came off and flew behind her, held by the elastic under her chin. Across the yard, around the lumber pile, around the shed, she went like a baby dust devil, spinning with some happiness as privately her own as her silvery hair. The pup, near-sighted, got lost and stopped, looking and sniffing around him until here she came spinning back, and wound herself into a tangle as she neared him, and fell in the dust. The pup dove for her exposed ears and she shrieked, covering them. Dust rose.

"Oh my goodness," Susan said. "She'll be *filthy!*"

Ollie and Betsy were rescuing Agnes and diverting the pup. Oliver stood by the wheel laughing. Many summers of sun and wind had roughened and seamed his skin. His jaw seemed to have grown heavier, his mustache hid his mouth. To Susan he looked as impenetrable as a rock, and older than his thirty-nine years.

"She seems to be in great shape," he said.

"Yes. All of them."

Nellie got down and went to dust Agnes off. For the moment the two were alone, with nothing to divert them from looking at each other straight. She looked for signs of dissipation in his face—How had he been living with her not there to save him from his weaker self?—and could see only a rude outdoor strength. He had the kind of face, she realized, that John had. Put him on a frontier ranch and he could not be distinguished from the cowboys. But she thought she was entitled to some sort of assurance that she had not come home to a repetition of their old quarrel. "Oliver . . ."

457

His look, bright blue, direct, fully comprehending, warned her off. He refused to be put in the position of defending himself or justifying himself or taking any oath. He did the best he knew how, his look said. He was himself, for better or worse. He did not grant her the supervision of his habits. "You married *me*," his look said. "Maybe that was a mistake. But you didn't marry what you could make out of me. I wouldn't be much good remodeled."

Something in her that had been trembling to open, closed again.

"Aren't you coming down?" he said, with his hand up.

"Yes."

His big calloused hand closed on hers, she stepped from the step to the ground. Nodding, he said, "I put that veranda all along the west side to keep the sun out of our eyes till the trees grow up."

"That was thoughtful," she said. "I hate a room full of glaring sun."

The back door had opened, and Wan stood in it, wildly flapping a dishtowel. She stood on tiptoe to wave, calling, "Oh, Wan, hello, hello! I didn't know you were here! This is wonderful! Just a minute . . ."

Betsy and Ollie left the puppies and bolted to greet him. Agnes, dusted off, hung back, not quite sure who he was.

"She doesn't remember him," Susan said. "But how wonderful you could get him back. It broke my heart to see him go. It'll be almost like old times, with Wiley and Wan and all of us. And John? Is John with us?"

"He's filling the water wagon down at the windmill. I saw him as we drove in."

"Oh, *really* like old times!"

There was another name that hung between them unspoken. She saw it in Oliver's eyes as plainly as if it had been spelled there. Unsmiling, dry, calculatedly expressionless, he stood by her in the dusty yard. Then he moved his head, indicating something to the north, up toward the canyon. "The whole tribe," he said. "Here comes Frank, I expect, to say hello."

She turned, as much to hide her face as to look, and saw a small moving dust midway between her and the hazed mountain front. The appropriate words, the appropriate feelings, tangled in her throat and

458

breast. Anything less than gladness would be noticed, too much gladness would be marked. She was not sure, anyway, whether what she felt, what had made her heart jump at that name, was gladness or panic.

In a voice that to her own ears was brittle and false she said, "Frank? He too? Oh, good. I didn't know he'd come back." She continued to look at the moving dust, since that kept her from having to look at Oliver.

"After he invested three years in this ditch?" Oliver said. "I brought him back first thing. He's bossing the diversion dam and the Big Ditch, while Wiley bosses the Susan." He took her arm. "Come on, don't you want to see your house?"

She came along, feeling obscurely rebuked. Old friends to greet, the whole canyon family restored as a surprise for her, everything as it was. She heard the children shrieking inside as they explored the house, and she shook Wan's hand with both her own in fierce, overdone enthusiasm. She hurt her face with smiling, she examined the rooms with the eagerness of a housekeeper.

But her mind went steadily on something else, bubbling along like dark water under sunlit ice. Just now she had searched Oliver's face for signs of drink, prying at him to discover if she had made a mistake to return, all but asking him outright what he had done and what he intended to do. Had he, when he mentioned Frank, been searching her face for an answer to a question of his own? Had he seen an answer? For her heart had leaped at the name, the gladness had come before the fear, and before the furtive, alert sense of how dangerous it was to show what she really felt. Had he seen that?

She almost wished he would ask, so that they could have it out, so that she could promise and therefore demand a promise from him: she thought of it as a sort of trade, in which each must give up something. She was shaken and in danger; she was also determined to lie in the bed she had made when she married him.

As she walked from room to unfinished room making pleased or judgmental noises, she was resenting her husband's wordlessness, she smoldered with grievance that he would not submit to talking their problems out. It was harder to get words from him than it was to get gold from rock. He tortured her with his silence. What did he mean, bringing Frank back on the project? Was he testing her? Tempting her? Was he so dense that he did not feel the undercurrent in his house?

Why don't you come out with it? she felt like saying to him in anger. I'm sure you think there's something. Why don't you say it, so I can tell you there isn't?

2

I am going to have to ask myself a question not too different from the one Grandmother wanted to ask Grandfather. What does it mean for my future, such as it is, that I sit at my desk at ten-thirty in the morning with a half-emptied bourbon and water at my elbow? For quite a while it has been getting easier to put down the old aching bones by a little roll over to the liquor cupboard. What am I to infer from the fact that every day for the past two weeks I have been half stoned before lunch?

I know perfectly well what I am to infer. I'm close, I'm maybe over the line. Pain, is that the reason? Am I a pathetic broken creature becoming a juicehead, as Shelly puts it, to dull my agonies? Nothing so dramatic. My kind of pain isn't the screaming kind, it's only the tooth-gritting kind.

Am I beginning to draw the dividends on my investment in isolation? Stir crazy? Rodman might think so. Sit out on that mountain doing nothing but read his grandmother's letters, it'd drive anybody to drink.

Or am I feeling my isolation threatened? Do I hear Rodman and Ellen and that cat's-paw of a doctor conspiring to move in and capture me? Am I some Kafka creature sweating in its hole?

Maybe all of those reasons, maybe none of them. I have never been a very social type: age and infirmity only confirm what youth and health used to crave. For years I have spent every morning in the study, just as I do now. It is true I used to be pulled out by classes, meetings, examinations, visitors, trips to the library, and a lot else. My afternoons used to have more in them than eight laps on the crutches and a little conversation with Shelly or her mother. My evenings used to go, as they do now, to reading, but very often they went to dinners, friends, concerts, shows. I used to think I lived a good old-fashioned scholarly life. What I don't have now that I had then is friends. Some of those dropped away, out of embarrassment, when Ellen left and I became a gargoyle; the others

461

I simply moved away from when I came up here. I don't think their absence is enough to explain that glass there.

I was always one whose arm twisted easily. I have always felt better and talked better when I was a little high. My grandfather in me? Why not? What begins as safety-valve binges and gestures toward social ease ends as habit. I have no reason to be surprised if I have by now picked up a physiological craving that has nothing to do with pain, boredom, reticence, tension, lack of friends, or anything else.

But it's too risky. If I let myself go that way I give them a handle, I lose it all. Suppose I do have pain? I can put up with it, or go back to cortisone; and if cortisone blows me up with water retention and gives me insomnia, why then I have taken what I want and paid for it. I'd rather be sleepless, and even more a Gorgon than I am, than turn into a helpless old stewbum that Rodman can handle as he pleases.

So for the sake of my independence, here goes my felicity. As of this minute I'm on the wagon.

What about the half-emptied glass? Dump it in the sink? Why? My backbone is rigid enough, I don't have to stiffen it with symbolic gestures. Now then. One smooth brown swallow sluiced around in the mouth, cool among the teeth, and put it down. That's the end of it.

Now do I feel better? Think. Try to be exact.

No, I don't feel better. I feel aggrieved, picked-on, and pursued. I want to know why a bunged-up old scholar can't have his drink in peace. I want to know why I must be wary of the uncertain future. What future? Not Lyman Ward's. He has converted back to kerosene and is living his grandparents' life. His own future ought not bother him or anyone else. His grandfather's horse pistol three feet from his forehead tells him that there is always a solution if things get unbearable. The fact that he isn't tempted seems to prove that they aren't unbearable yet. But they are going to be a lot less pleasant without Old Grand-Dad.

So right on, as the activists say. Right on, Lyman. Fifty whole years of Grandmother's life to go. Make them last.

Of course it's impossible. I'll never finish. Autumn is already nearly here, Shelly has had about all the country quiet her physiology can stand, and will be leaving soon. Ada has been having trouble with her breathing. She smokes too much, there is always a cigarette dribbling ashes down her front and into her dishwater and onto her ironing, and

I hear her wheeze like an old dog when she makes my bed. Emphysema, I shouldn't be surprised, her breathing apparatus gone as slack as an old garter. Hyperventilation, pains in her chest and left arm, maybe heart involved too. Good Christ, what would I do if she collapsed?

The very thought of it brings an element of desperation into my delusions of independence. I will not kid myself that this summer of quiet routine and country air have left me much better off than when I came. I have had six aspirins and a bourbon since I got up, and still I ache.

What the hell, my right is in retreat, my center is giving way, my left is crumbling, I have just sent my bottled support to the rear. I shall attack. I shall go on writing the personal history of my grandmother, following Bancroft's advice to historians: present your subject in his own terms, judge him in yours.

Actually, I'd just as soon leave out the judgment entirely. I don't feel at ease judging people. And I'd just as soon let her present herself: her letters from the Mesa are among the longest and fullest she wrote during that long half century of correspondence.

3

The Mesa
August 16, 1889

Darling Augusta—

We have slept five nights in our house in the sagebrush. Like everything here, it is large and raw. It is for the future, it sacrifices the present for what is to come. In time it may be charming, but now it seems hopeless. We need *everything*—awnings, more chairs, boardwalks around the premises, lawn, shrubs, flowers, trees, *shade*. The sun beats on us from sunup to sundown. We are like a seashore place, with dust instead of sand. Dust lies drifted two inches deep in the piazza, dust blows in our faces if we attempt to sit there and read or work, dust whirls about the yard, dust is tracked in by every pair of feet, dust hangs above the canyon mouth and hazes the whole valley, especially at sunset.

I used to write you from Almaden how strangely transformed the dust clouds were after the sun went down. It is the same here. In some ways this mesa is a return. We look off, just as we did at Almaden, into a vast stretch of valley, with the moon at our back. Not a single tree in sight as far as we can see south, east, and west. To the north lie the irrigated lowlands along the river. The noble shape of the country lies bare under the sky as if just made, and ready for the birth of trees and crops.

It is a vision that absorbs Oliver. He follows it like a man panting after a mirage, and he works, works, works. He manages his survey, he supervises the ditch construction, he confers with politicians and contractors and shareholders, he takes visiting representatives of the Syndicate over the works—we have been visited twice since I arrived—and in the hours between dusk and dark, and even after dark, he is out with John doing something to the land or the buildings or the well. He is full of excitement and energy. But my heart whispers to me that all he dreams of is still years away, and that meantime we grow old, we diminish, we lose touch with all that used to make life rich and wonderful. I have just counted on my fingers how long it has been since I saw you. More than seven years.

But I began to speak of our house, before dust and the years obscured it. We have again the mud-plastered walls of the canyon house. The adobe is not as tough as that of the canyon, but a better color—a greenish-yellow gray, like beach sand. We are going to paint the wainscot and woodwork in one of the rooms old ivory—I think it will bring out the color of the walls. Even one finished room would cheer me. I must think in those terms —one room, then another, and another, till all are done, and then grass outside instead of dust, and hammocks on the veranda for the watching of sunsets.

Then if you could only come we could give you a peaceful, roomy sleeping chamber, and a house in which your serene beauty would feel at home. How solitary and strange this great sweep of country would look to you! Yet I can fancy you would like to lie on the hill slope by a clump of sage, and gaze down over the valley and into the bosom of the mountain range opposite, almost as we used to lie on Orchard Hill and look across at the farms of Dutchess County.

Wiley has driven the Susan Canal more than eight miles. It will go twenty before water is turned into it, to water claims that lie below ours. That is for next summer. Meantime the "Big Ditch" is alive with teams and scrapers, and the canyon resounds with blasting. It awes me to see how big this scheme is. In all the years I thought I was helping dream it, I hadn't the imagination to understand what I was dreaming. The Big Ditch will be immense, a man-made river, and eventually will water nearly three hundred thousand acres—nearly five hundred square *miles*. There are countries in the world no bigger than that. There will have to be several storage dams, but those will come later. Even without the dams, this will be one of the grandest things in the West.

The finished section, so far hardly more than a half mile, sweeps in a great curve around the shoulder of the mountain, eighty feet wide at the top, fifty at the bottom. The twelve-foot banks slope back at the "angle of repose," which means the angle at which dirt and pebbles stop rolling. Down the bottom of the ditch fifteen horsemen could ride abreast, without crowding. It was good for me to see it all the other day, in company with the gentlemen from the London syndicate, and to be reminded how all of it is owing to my old boy's imagination and his refusal to be beaten.

He works far too hard; he always has. It is a thing I have sometimes held against him, that his family must come second to his job. Now he has to make one last trip to the mountains to complete some field work for the Irrigation Survey, and that means Ollie must start East without seeing his father again. It is a great pity, for they are very close. But what can I do? Ollie can't afford to pass up the chance that St. Paul's has given him. He will be lonely, and will miss his pony and the excitement of the construction, to which he attends all day, riding the line with Wiley or his father. He *lives* on his pony.

All through our stay in Victoria he talked about the canyon as if it were the Paradise from which we had been evicted, and from the moment of our return he wanted to go out there. Yesterday I threw up my hands over everything that needs doing here, and rode out with him. Wiley was there, and showed us the changes. He and Frank share our old bedroom, two draftsmen use the others, the shack overflows with men. It seemed a very different place from the quiet canyon where we lived on hope. But it pleased me to see that the trees we planted are doing well, and that the poppies have seeded themselves around the knoll and bloom without human encouragement.

It was strange, that return to Eden. There went the river below, there went the clouds overhead, just as before. The sun beat down as I remembered—sometimes I have thought I could *smell* the scorched gravel of that gulch! There was everything as we had left it, but changed, too. The sleepiness of our seclusion was replaced by a great busy-ness, and strange faces kept looking out of doors where I was used to seeing only the faces of our local community of saints. It made me melancholy, rather, and I am sure it bothered Ollie too: his memories were thrown out of line. But of course I could not get him to talk about it. He folds things in, and thinks about them, and does not give them outlet, and that worries me for his future. He can be easily hurt.

On the way back we rode past John's old cabin, and found its little flat obliterated by a great construction camp of eighty men and two hundred horses. There Frank is supervising the tearing down of a whole hill to make the diversion dam that will throw the river into the Susan and later into the Big Ditch. Frank has lost, I am afraid, some of his freshness and exuberance, and has grown almost somber. Like Oliver, he drives himself into the work with a relentlessness that I fear will break him down.

Oh, Augusta, you know my hopes! You know my anxiety, though being the ideal creature you are, married to that ideal man who completes and supports you, you cannot comprehend the unworthy contradictions of someone less sure of herself. You were of course right, years ago, about Frank's feelings. But he is a thorough gentleman, he understands. So it does not alarm me that Oliver is to be gone for two weeks. I am quite safe, on this mesa and in myself, and I find the same satisfaction in work that Oliver and Frank seem to. This morning, amid all the disorder, I blew the dust from my table and wrote for two hours. Tomorrow I want to go up to the Big Ditch and sketch the teams pulling their scraper-loads of dirt up the banks. My "Life in the Far West" series must include the preparations for the future, for that is what life in the Far West is about.

The Mesa
August 30, 1889

Darling Augusta —

This morning I sent my little boy away, and I know his heart broke as mine did. Nellie and I have been trying to keep up his courage and determination with our tales of what wonders he will see, and what fine things he will learn, and what fine men he will study with and what fine boys he will come to know as friends. But this morning after breakfast I sent him to his room to get dressed and ready—he was to catch the ten-thirty train—and when he didn't appear for a long time I went in and found him ready dressed in his new school clothes, just sitting on the bed with his eyes big and dark and his face as pale as if no Idaho sun had burned it for the last three weeks. "Why, Ollie," I said, "what is it?" and he looked at me, nearly crying, and said, "Mother, do I *have* to go?"

Oh, oh, it was all I could do to keep from huddling him against me and drowning him in my tears. Only twelve! Think what it must be to travel all the way from Idaho to New Hampshire by yourself at that age, going toward something new and strange, where you don't know a soul, and where you are afraid you will be an ugly duckling from the West, ignorant and unable to learn! I know he feels that way—he told Nellie, though he would not tell me.

It is just as well Oliver is not here. He has never been as sure as I am that the boy must go East. "Why send him away?" he said to me only last week. "I'm just getting to know him again. Why not let him go to the high school in Boise?"

Of course it would not have done. He knows hardly more people in Boise than he will at St. Paul's, actually; and from the local school he would emerge a barbarian, prepared for nothing and untouched by culture, believing in the beauties of Idaho civilization! I had to harden my heart to a stone, and in the end he got over his panic. But when the train pulled away, and I saw his young scared face pressed against the window, and his hand making brave half-hearted desolate waves at Nellie, his sisters, Frank, and me, I quite broke down, and I have been crying off and on all afternoon.

I can't bear to think of him, by now off in Wyoming somewhere, huddled in the seat and watching the country pass and thinking—what? That his mother sent him away. What choices we are offered in this life, if we live in Idaho. Yet in the long run he will have to realize that it is worth any amount of unhappiness to be given the opportunity to learn and grow and become something good and true, perhaps even noble. I confess it is one of the things I hug to my heart, a thing I envy my poor little boy for—his opportunity to see you and Thomas. He has heard about you all his life, but of course doesn't remember you. Now he can at last know what I have been talking about. But if having him down for Thanksgiving will be the slightest bother, if he will interfere with the great things that fill your life now, do not hesitate to tell him not to come. I would rather he were a little lonely and unhappy than that he should ever become a burden or duty to you.

His sisters and Nellie will miss him as much as I do. The girls depend on their big brother for all sorts of things from mending a toy to saddling their ponies. As for Nellie, poor thing, she cried as if it were her own boy she was sending off.

The Mesa
November 10, 1889

Dearest Augusta—

After such a summer of heat, dust, and wind you can imagine how gladly I accept winter, which is at least fairly clean, and with what passion I long for spring. It has been build, build, build, all through the fall, and since we are more than two miles from town, the workmen have had to be boarded. Wan has cooked for the family, many visitors, and an average of seven additional men, though that will now be reduced.

With paint, carpets, and curtains we have done something toward making the house habitable, and in addition have built an icehouse, shop, blacksmith shed, and office, all under one roof, making quite a picturesque little building, with outside stairs leading to a storage loft.

The Big Ditch, after progressing well for a time, has run into infuriating delays, and cannot reach us for perhaps another year. We shall have to depend on the well for one more season, and its forty barrels a day will not stretch to everything we would like to spread them on. The Susan Canal is now nearly twelve miles long. By next summer, water from it will be soaking into many hundreds of acres, and the demonstration of Oliver's original scheme will have reached the end of its first step.

Two claims on our lower line have been "jumped"—which means that someone has detected some deficiency in the filing, or some failure to complete the "improvements," and so has "pre-empted" the lands. The original filers in these cases were trying to evade the letter of the law, but they are both poor men, and worked hard, and we feel sorry for them. They have consulted Oliver constantly on their plans, and counted on the Susan Canal, and he feels in a way responsible. Yet there is nothing we can do. One of them lost his claim because his wife would not come and live there six months, but when I think of *my* months here—only three, and with everything done to make me comfortable—and look at the shanty where she was supposed to live, I hardly wonder she objected. Almost every claim around us has now been jumped except John's and Bessie's. On timber-culture and desert claims such as theirs, no residence is required, only "improvements," which they will take care of when they come out.

We have a poor-white family camped at the well. The husband has taken a contract to plow a hundred acres of our desert at so much per acre, and do such other jobs as will make Mesa Ranch into the showplace of the district. Oliver's next task is to get them a cabin built near the windmill where presently they live in two sheep wagons—father, mother, daughter, son-in-law, and two children.

They are all the color of gypsies. They have two sons "up on Camas, lookin' after the stock," and a full-blooded bull pup worth more than any team they own. Each morning, while the weather holds, the teams are driven afield, four horses hitched to a sulky plow. The double shares rip up the ground in great swaths, sage brush and all, and leave it in a chaotic mess, roots and branches sticking up out of the raw earth. It looks as if the land had been plowed for the sowing of dragons' teeth instead of the first peaceful wheat crop. Before snow flies, I want to get out and try to sketch that scene of crude ugly power out of which (we hope) this new civilization will rise.

After I had taken down some late squash the other day, the ladies from the plow camp came and called on me. "How comfortable you look, out of the wind," they said as they walked in. It was an interesting visit in a way. They are Southern, and they have that remarkable command of language that we see in Miss Murfree's stories, and an equanimity equal to that of a duchess. For all that I was out of the wind, I am sure they would not willingly have changed places. They *belong* in this crude place. I live here on sufferance, a permanent exile, awaiting the day when all of Oliver's efforts will have produced in this valley a civilization in which any woman but one of these plowing Malletts would feel at home.

I cannot bring myself to do as Oliver urges me to—go into Boise oftener, make calls, cultivate women friends, attend the "functions" of the place. For one thing, we have put everything we own and everything we can borrow into this ranch, and I have no desire to be known as the engineer's wife with the darned elbows. For another—how shall I specify that other? I am not of Boise and do not wish to be.

And so I live an interim or preparatory life. Oliver is bent upon making these thousand acres of ours into something that all men can look at and be inspired by, a sort of pledge of what the country can do when it has water. His goal, he told me the other day, is to make something as near as possible to Querendero, one of those grand Mexican *estancias* at which we stayed when we rode back from Morelia. He will fence our thousand acres and push his improvements clear to the fences—wheat, lucerne, timothy, wild pasture, orchards, berry patches and gardens. He swears he will have a rose garden that will make me forget Milton. He will make father's roses look like a posy bed! He frightens me, he is so willing to stake everything we have. But when I raise objections, he tells me I can see only what is in front of my nose.

Faith! Faith! he tells me. Faith can reclaim deserts as well as move mountains. When this pioneering enthusiasm takes hold of him, he is not my wordless husband at all. A few days ago, in the last of the Indian summer weather, we rode around the whole place so that he could show me what he wants to do with each part of it. We have kept most of the poplar lane alive, with great effort, by means of the windmill and hose cart, but some of our "grove" has perished. Until we get water from the Big Ditch we must get our results mainly out of native, resistant things, Oliver says. The slope of the mesa will be our wild garden, planted to wild syringa, wild clematis, and buck sage, which has a yellow flower that Nellie admits is almost as handsome as furze. This will cover, some day in the future for which we live, the "upright" of the great step. The "tread" will be covered with grass.

I grew almost hysterical, sitting my horse there on Pisgah's top and being shown the Promised Land, which consisted of a sweep of sage and our barren house and the dots of three distant settlers' shacks, with off to our right the desolation that Hi Mallett has created with his sulky plow. "Remember Querendero?" Oliver kept saying to me. "Have you forgotten the grace and romance you found in Tepitongo? Well just look at this with the eye of faith. This can be as good."

In truth, he half convinced me. Let the water project be completed, and it can be splendid; there is literally no limit to what one might do. I rode home feeling almost exhilarated, and I have been very cheerful since. Maybe, maybe. I cling to that possibility as a child clutches a piece of sea-worn magic glass on the beach.

This, you see, is one of my hopeful days, all because I have been given a glimpse of what lights up Oliver's mind even when he seems taciturn and silent. All because the windmill has pumped us past the dry season with only modest casualties. All because we have had a rain to settle the summer dust cloud. With his hand on his heart, Oliver swears that next spring we shall have a lawn all along the front of the house to hold down all the Idaho dirt that wants to blow inside.

This must sound incredible, read on Staten Island.

The Mesa
January 10, 1890

Dearest Augusta —

It was so good of you to have Ollie for Christmas. It was out of the question that he should come home, for we hadn't the money for his fare. Without you, he would have had to go to Milton, sadly reduced now that father and mother are gone and the old house sold, or stay over with two or three other waifs at school. Dr. Rhinelander and his wife are kindness itself, but it wouldn't have been Christmas.

He wrote me after returning—one of his characteristic twenty-word letters—and said that "he had fun with Rodman," and that "Mrs. Hudson was nice to me and asked a lot of questions." I hope he had the manners to write to you.

Just today I heard from Oliver, who has taken his Irrigation Survey report east (Major Powell is in difficulties with a certain clique of Senators, and wants all possible ammunition for this session of Congress).

Before going to Washington, Oliver found time to run up to Concord. All is not quite as I had hoped. Ollie is struggling, keeping afloat in his studies but only barely. He is somewhat lonesome and isolated, Oliver says. He feels his difference, and resents the allusions of his schoolmates to it. Shortly after he arrived last fall, he appears to have got into an actual fist fight with a boy who sneered at the place he came from. "Idaho is my *home!*" he told Dr. Rhinelander, as if that justified everything. And he wears a sprig of sage in his jacket buttonhole, as a Scotch lassie might wear a sprig of heather!

I am miserable at the thought of his homesickness and his fighting— he is not a rude or brawling boy. It makes me doubt the wisdom of my plans for him. Yet he has come to know you and Thomas and your children, he has traveled by himself like a grown man, he is studying with the finest teachers, among the finest Eastern boys. I know he will thank me in the end for forcing this on him.

In his letter he asks for a photograph of his sisters to put up in his room, and also one of his pony. Evidently the information that he has a pony has helped gain him prestige among his schoolmates, and he has always been very manly and protective about his sisters, especially Agnes. I have asked Wiley, who owns a camera, to bring it next time he rides this way, so that we may send Ollie what he wants.

One thing in Oliver's letter made me feel like crying with an odd mixture of feelings. It seems that after talking with Dr. Rhinelander and saying good-bye to Ollie, Oliver slipped up into the balcony of the chapel and watched unseen during the chapel service, which he says was impressive, and the boys well behaved. Oh, I would give anything I own to do that same thing, only for ten minutes—to look down from my hiding place in that dim, scholarly light, with solemn noble words on the air, and see my own boy's brown head down there among the others, absorbing it and gathering in wisdom and the sense of what it means to be civilized!

Instead, I look out my window and see thin, rippled snow, and sagebrush that bends stiffly in a bitter northwest wind. Our hope of restoring our old community of saints here has not quite been gratified. The men have been frantically busy, Frank and Wiley have been up in the canyon most of the time. Now Oliver is away and Frank is about to go East and visit his parents for the first time in five years. I shall give him a letter to you, for I want you to know each other. If he expresses himself freely to you, please listen, and do not judge him or me too harshly. It will be the next best thing to talking to you myself. We are all right—life continues, the old bonds hold—and if there is a certain unhappiness, a real regret, why that is what man, and even more woman, is born to. I repeat, I am *all right.*

471

The Mesa
March 1, 1890

Darling Augusta —

You have been much with me for the past two or three days. The other evening I was rereading *The Freshening Day,* that first book of Thomas's poems, and our wedding-present copy from you, with the date of my wedding day fourteen years ago. You remember you painted a rose spray across the silk-lined fly leaf, and daisies in the back. Two of the sonnets Thomas wrote in Milton, on one of those summer weekends that seem more and more wonderful as time tries to efface them. I felt strangely, miraculously preserved as I read, and yet oh! so melancholy and sad! The book of life turned back in my hands to that time of maidenhood and expectation.

Who could have foreseen for the bride of that day the picture that is and has been—the *shall be* is still to be unfolded. Sometimes it chills my heart to think about the future almost as much as it warms it to think about the past. I believe that I can foresee my life to come much better than I could, and I feel that I have the strength to bear it, whatever it may be. And yet, *bear* it! What of a future of which it can even be thought, it might have to be *borne!*

It is a sort of insanity not to be happy, when one has reasonable health and good children and a true, energetic husband who is doing something extraordinary, drawing in the outlines of civilization on the blank page of a desert. I tell myself it is true happiness to be still the friend of the most blessed of women. And yet I cannot boast that I am *very* happy, or even encourage you to think that some day I might be. I feel as stiff and frozen and ungainly as the sagebrush out there in the wind. But I suppose that, like the sagebrush, I shall at least endure—unless some Hi Mallett should come with a sulky plow and plow me quite up.

That, without your intending it, was nearly the effect of your letter reporting your visit with Frank. I knew you would like him at once. He is truly noble, with the loftiest ideals and the most sensitive understanding. I know he must have found it a relief to talk with you, for among us, in our entangled and encumbered situation, there are no opportunities to speak out. And yet how it shook me to have you report his words about his "incurable disease"! How wretched, how wretched, for him, for me, for Oliver, for all of us, that a boy so clean and fine should be torn between loyalty to the friend he most values in the world, and this incurable disease! And yet his dilemma and his torment cannot be worse than mine.

I must say no more of this. I beg you to think no more of it.

Oliver, having just returned from New York, has had to turn around and start back, to confer with General Tompkins and two members of the London syndicate who have just arrived. It seems there is dissatisfaction with the progress of the Susan Canal, which these gentlemen believe should have been completed to its full twenty miles last fall, so as to be ready for use this spring; and someone seems to have raised a question as to Oliver's judgment in pressing ahead with the Big Ditch at the same time. It makes me worse than cross to think of people who have only the dimmest idea about this project, questioning the man who conceived it and has pushed it through against every sort of odds. To him, the Susan is only a sop to the skeptics. It means little by comparison with the Big Ditch—is only a secondary canal to that great one, and even if completed now would not put any large acreage under irrigation.

Still, he has had to go and justify himself. He hates it. More talkee-talkee. At least, he told me as he left, he can now bring back a lot of bare-root roses. The varieties available here are somewhat common. I know he is bent upon that rose garden for my sake. He hopes it may help repay me for all the dust and discomfort of last summer, and persuade me that the waiting is not in vain, and that life in the Boise Valley can be given grace and beauty, and that we will not have to wait until Agnes is a woman before our surroundings are fit for civilized living.

He is so good a man I want to weep, and what makes me want to weep most of all is my failure of faith in him. For I cannot help it. Though there has been, ever since my return, a blessed absence of that trouble you know of, I have seen that weakness among all his strengths, and I cannot forget it. I fear the strain of uncertainty, I am frightened by these long wearing trips and the influence of the kinds of people they throw him among. I *watch* him, I wonder if he watches *me*. We are polite to each other.

We do not speak of any of this. It is impossible for Oliver to discuss such personal matters, he is made voiceless by them. We pretend that by not speaking of them we have made them not exist. Yet it is not the marriage I dreamed of, not the marriage it was. It is a bruised and careful truce; we walk in bandages and try not to bump our wounds. After fourteen years, that bride whose judgment you questioned finds herself unable fully to trust either the man she married, or herself. Without you and Thomas shining so steadily there on your rock, this darkness would be darkness indeed.

The Mesa
June 17, 1890

Dearest Augusta —

Yesterday the water was turned into the first fifteen miles of the Susan Canal. This much, at least, is done after eight years. Oliver and the juniors are only half happy about it, for the diversion of effort has stopped the Big Ditch, and since even the Susan is being put to work before it is ready, the money return to the Syndicate will be small. Nevertheless, with Idaho due to become a state on July 4, and all here convinced that the eyes of the nation and the world are upon them, Oliver thought it as well to make an occasion. The Governor and his wife and many dignitaries (who would not be dignitaries anywhere but Idaho) assembled on the mesa to watch the first water come down. Frank and Wiley were disappointed that I was not asked to break a bottle of champagne against something, perhaps a clump of sagebrush, inasmuch as the canal is named for me, but I decided that the Governor should have the limelight, he craves it so, and so he was given the principal role, with a shovel instead of with a bottle.

Frank and Wiley were stationed up at the diversion dam at the canyon mouth, to open the gates at a specified time. Ollie, who had not been home from school three days before he begged, and got, permission to live in the canyon with the engineers, came flying down the line on his pony as soon as the gates were opened. He rode so fast that he beat the water to us by several minutes. It was dreadfully hot and unprotected. The dignitaries had removed their coats, and the ladies were melting under their parasols and surrey canopies as we waited by the raw ditch.

Then, around the gentle curve of the canal, there it came, a low, rolling, muddy tide that actually kicked up dust ahead of itself, and rolled over the dust and absorbed it in its thick wave. Twigs and weeds and grass and dirty foam rode the surface. The crowd raised a cheer—and indeed it was exciting to see the result of all our work actually flowing toward the dry earth. The Governor dug a hole beside the ditch and one of his aides set a Lombardy poplar in it, which another aid then watered with a bucket of mud dipped from the ditch. Eventually (it is all part of Oliver's dream) willows and Lombardies will line the Susan from the canyon mouth to its lower end, and bind its banks together with their roots, and drop their leaves on its current to spin in its slow whirlpools and snag on weeds and roots and make a resting place for darning needles and dragonflies. By their living green presence along the line of the ditch they will be, he says, the truest testimony to the desert's fertility, and the beacon of hope to settlers and their families. This is all in that future when our grove will be tall and cool around our house, and when we will leave that coolness for a different coolness on the banks of the Big Ditch, under *its* line of sheltering trees, and watch the sunsets reflected in our man-made river sixty feet wide.

Within a few minutes the first dirt and trash was swept away, and the water came more cleanly, filling the ditch within eighteen inches of the top. There was much laughter and congratulations, and the Governor made a speech in which he particularly praised Oliver, and aired visions of the future far more grandiose (and based on far less knowledge of the limiting facts) than those of my engineers, who pride themselves on being *realists* with vision.

Later the party came to the Mesa for cakes and champagne, and some of the gentlemen, playing their game of the visionary future, made a pretense of walking the ladies in the *grove*. The sun soon ended their charade, for the trees are no higher than a lady's bonnet. But the Mesa did serve its function as show piece, and drew much admiration, especially our new lawn on the west side, which we keep green with the hose cart, and the rose garden, which is now beginning to bloom. What a joy those roses are, more than two dozen varieties, including everything from exotic hybrids such as the immaculately white Blanc Double de Coubert and the black-crimson Deuil de Paul Fontaine to such old favorites as the General Jacqueminot, which you remember from Milton, and the Maréschal Niel. And on the piazza pillar our old Harison's yellow from the canyon, a hardy pioneer if there ever was one, a rose we have seen in every mining camp in the West.

It might have been a pleasant affair, for everyone was in high spirits, and it was a triumph for Oliver, and a fitting preliminary to the coming statehood celebration. But it was spoiled for me by the misery of my Belgian girl Sidonie, whom I hired this spring because of the floods of people we have had to feed and entertain. She was to have been married this summer, to a lawyer named Bradford Burns. He has been associated with the canal company as their "connection" man to the Land Office, was a delegate to the state convention, and has been appointed County Surveyor of this county. He is considerably above her in education and position.

Well, she went to town two weeks ago to see about the final arrangements, and met Burns accidentally in the street. They went to the house of a friend, and there on the piazza, the friend being away, he told her that he had changed his mind, that she wouldn't be up to her position as his wife. Imagine the poor thing coming home with this to be known by everybody! I had already arranged for another Chinese, a friend of Wan's, but Sidonie was so crushed I could not possibly let her go. She declares she will work for me all her life, and I more than half wish this cup would pass from me, for though she is good-natured and good, she is not a good servant.

Now imagine that on the day of the celebration, with Sidonie in her white apron passing cakes on the piazza and through the rooms, this man Burns was one of the guests. Poor Sidonie could not bring herself to pass near him, and I hope he got no cakes at all. Yet there was no way he could have been excluded, short of his own realization of the delicacy of her position, for he is one of the political crowd, and a "coming" man. He, of course, brazened it out and chatted and laughed, while that poor clumsy girl, who might have been attending the affair as his wife, went red and numb among the guests with her tray of cakes!

Oh, you must come to Idaho! It is the only place I know where your servants' problems and your guests' problems turn out to be the same.

At least, Idaho being what it is, some other young man is likely to come to my relief, for Sidonie is a handsome creature, however untrained.

My little girls, whose first "big party" it was, were allowed to dress themselves in their best frocks, and attend for a time, and help serve. They ate too many cakes and thoroughly enjoyed themselves. As usual, the gentlemen all fell in love with Agnes, who was a shameless flirt and quite irresistible. But I am glad to say the ladies found Betsy what I know her to be. More and more I am thankful that we named her what we did. She is Bessie all over again, in sweetness if not in beauty—and who can tell what nine will become by nineteen?

Now that the opening of the Susan has made water available for their claims, Bessie and John plan to order the requisite "improvements" made, and in the fall will sell the last of the old Milton place and move out here. I hate the thought of Milton's being entirely gone, and I confess that when I heard they had gambled their little savings on the ditch I felt the blackest premonitions. I felt like the scapegoat that had led them to their destruction. But now I think my greatest happiness will be to have Bessie living only a little more than two miles away. John has always ached to come west, and Bessie is the most loyal of wives. What a joy it will be (and how tired I get of writing "will be" rather than "is"!) to have her come calling in the afternoons when her work is done, and to have her to sit with through whole evenings, and talk with, and read with, and remember with, and lend things to, and borrow from! I live in a busy but lonely house. Next to you, Bessie is the only person who could redeem it for me, and to see her Eastern children thundering with my Western ones up the lane on their ponies will be—*will be!*—pure heaven.

Meantime, the Big Ditch is stalled until the Syndicate decides to provide this summer's construction money, and all salaries are in arrears. The engineers occupy themselves with finishing and improving the embankment of the diversion dam, and riding the length of the Susan to detect and repair leaks.

The Mesa
July 2, 1890

My darling Augusta—

I can hardly bear to write you this letter, and would not if it could possibly arrive in time to spoil your pleasure in the medal a grateful city will be giving Thomas day after tomorrow. Believe me when I say I would be thinking of nothing but his deserved honor, and doing nothing but read and memorize the magnificent poem you sent me that he has composed for the occasion, if we had not had poured upon us enough trouble, deserved and undeserved, to unhinge my mind and break down all my defenses. Will you listen, and give me your silent sympathy? I cannot write to Bessie—not yet, not until every hope is exhausted, as I fear it will be.

First, the Big Ditch is dead again. The Syndicate are quarreling among themselves and accusing General Tompkins and Oliver of Heaven knows what. Mr. Harvey, our friend and supporter, is cruelly dead, by the most brutally unpredictable accident. An absent-minded, enthusiastic, childlike man, he walked one morning, reading his London *Times,* and stepped in front of a train. If he were alive, I should have more hope. Now funds are cut off, the contractors are unpaid and angry, Oliver and the juniors are unpaid and apprehensive, the ditch is stopped at the three-mile mark—the ditch which was to extend for seventy-five miles. All chance is gone for the massive effort that Oliver hoped to put out this summer. What faces us is either a painful reorganization, with the originator of the scheme perhaps squeezed out and his authority assumed by men eight or ten thousand miles away, or the total collapse of everything.

And that is but the beginning.

I must have written you about the claims that Oliver filed on for Bessie and John, nearly a year ago. In his eagerness to come West, John also invested in canal company stock to a considerable extent. A month before, he might have bought a wagon load of it for very little, but by the time he came in, the news of the reformed syndicate had gone around, and there was none for sale except at very inflated prices. So Oliver, thinking he was doing John a favor, and needing money for the building of this house, sold him some of ours—two thousand dollars' worth, at what was then a bargain.

That stock now stands a good chance of being worthless. When I think of what that much money means to John and Bessie, when I think that it represents my mother's and father's lives, and my grandparents' lives, and great-grandparents' lives, all the loving labor that went into the Milton orchards and fields, now poured out into a dusty ditch in Idaho! It is bad enough for our money to go that way, but theirs!

And that is not the worst.

The worst is the work of our slippery acquaintance Bradford Burns, the man who so cruelly jilted poor Sidonie. He is one of those who came west looking for the main chance, a lawyer who would do any sort of little job, and was particularly active in land claims. Because he was always an energetic believer in irrigation, the company used him as its representative; and Oliver, when he was frantically busy completing his Irrigation Survey, and organizing the beginning of the canal work, and getting this house built, and the well drilled, and the road graded, and the trees planted, left a good many details to him.

The other day, just one day after the bad news had come from General Tompkins, Oliver was in Burns's office and happened to mention the Grant claims.

"The Grant claims?" says Mr. Burns. "What are they?"

"The ones I left with you for preliminary filing," Oliver said. "A year ago."

"I guess I don't remember them," says Burns. "I file so many I forget. If you left them for filing, I must have filed them. Where are they located? Show me on the map."

He got the map out and Oliver showed him, two half-sections side by side under the Susan Canal.

"But those are *my* claims!" exclaims this Mr. Burns. "You told me your relatives weren't interested, so I filed on them myself."

"Weren't interested?" said Oliver. "When did I say anything like that? I left the completed papers with you to be executed."

"You must have forgotten," says Burns. "I remember now. You put them on the desk and said they were one thing, at least, you didn't have to take care of now. You recall telling me that."

"No," Oliver said. "I remember nothing of the kind. I said nothing of the kind. What did you *do* with those papers?"

"Lord," Burns says, "I suppose I probably threw them away. I wouldn't have kept them. You said your relatives had decided against filing."

Augusta, it was *your* claims he was speaking of, or pretending to speak of—the ones I had urged you to file on simply as a speculation, in the hope that I might by that means lure you and Thomas out to Idaho for a visit. I had written Oliver from Victoria, asking him to start the formalities. And Oliver *had* told Burns to discard those, after he heard that you weren't interested. So he couldn't entirely deny the possibility of a misunderstanding. He made Burns search all his files and drawers, and he checked the Land Office, but of course no papers were found, and the claims were discovered in Burns's name. It is one man's memory, and one man's word, against another's, and Burns is smooth and persuasive, and Oliver is not. Unless we can somehow manage to shame or force them out of him, that man now owns Bessie's and John's claims, with water from the Susan to make them valuable, and he can show the proper papers and receipts, and we can show nothing. He has jumped those claims, in short.

Oliver, who never mistrusts anyone unless the evidence is overwhelming, is inclined to take the blame. He says that Burns could have made an honest mistake. I say he did not. He had access to the company's maps and plans, he knew exactly where the Susan would go, he knew that water would reach those claims before it could reach any of the lands higher up. And he will make no gesture toward redeeming his "mistake." He says he has made his first payment on that land, has little money, can't be asked to give up what he has staked his future on. In some desperation Oliver offered to buy the claims, but Burns says he is making plans to build. He already has another wife in mind, the daughter of one of the pick and shovel millionaires. Wouldn't you think he might be sure enough of his future to sacrifice those acres of desert? Tomorrow I shall send Oliver back to town to see if Burns won't sell one of the claims, at least. I know the answer in advance. And if he should say yes, where would we get the money? We are in debt up to our necks.

So I shall not see my sister this fall, and my children will not have cousins to ride with or do lessons with (Nellie was prepared to enlarge her school to take in Bessie's three). Poor John will not realize his dream of coming West. We may or may not have money to send Ollie back to St. Paul's. We may not even have a job, we may have not a leftover crumb of hope. But we do have a great deal of dry land, unless when we weren't looking someone has jumped ours too.

Forgive me, I should not be bitter. Yet I cannot see one ray of light. Perhaps we can sell this house to someone who can afford it, Burns perhaps, and move down into the Mallett cabin and herd people's sheep or plow their sagebrush. It seems the logical conclusion of our effort to reclaim and civilize the West.

4

From the wide doorway where she perched on her stool with the drawing pad in her lap, she looked out into and through the piazza, past the hammock where Betsy was reading to Agnes, past the heavy pillars and the balustrade on which sat the old Guadalajara olla with its inscription half visible—*asita*—and on across the lawn and the spreading sagebrush to the far line of the mountains. The indoor light was tea-colored, sepia; the lawn was whitened under the sun like an overexposed photographic negative, the sagebrush went palely, growing dimmer and paler with distance, until it ended at the foot of the mountains that were pale, dusty blue against a sky even paler and dustier. She thought it was like being inside a cool cave and seeing out into an allegorical desert plain, the sort of place where wayfarers are bewildered and creatures die of thirst.

She looked from the hammock to her drawing and back to the hammock, estimating the grace of the young bodies curved in the netting, heavy as carried cats. The sweet treble of Betsy's voice was the only sound. She was reading *The Birds' Christmas Carol.* The two lay facing different ways, their feet entangled. Agnes, with her wide eyes open and glazed with imagining, kept pulling out strands of silvery hair to arm's length as if measuring them.

Susan worked with her lips pressed together, her brows tightened a little under the mouse-colored bangs. There was a fist of hair at the back of her head, a little too tightly knotted to be becoming; but the head itself was small and shapely, the neck delicate, the profiled face cut like a cameo. In her high-necked dress with its leg-of-mutton sleeves, its pinched-in waist, its overskirt and bustle, she was antiquely attractive, the portrait of a lady, a tidy, fastidious lady who looked younger than she was.

Nevertheless, as I reconstruct her there, there was in her figure some quality of tension, a certain stiffness suggesting strain or anxiety too pervasive to be forgotten even in the absorption of work. She sat frowning down on her drawing, which reproduced in small space the things that filled her eye—the girls in the curve of hammock, the heavy pillars, the misty desert suggested beyond. Across the bottom of the sheet, as if to keep herself reminded of her subject, she had scrawled in a hurried, untidy hand, *A Hot Day on a Western Ranche.*

Her head turned slightly, she listened. Sounds of a trotting horse. She laid her pencil on the pad and the pad on the table, and stood up. "All right, children. That's enough for this morning. Thank you for being good."

But they looked up, her two very different daughters, with identical looks of protest on their faces and an identical question in their mouths. "Can't we finish it?"

"So sad a story?"

"Yes, Mother!"

"Ollie's been at his lessons for an hour. Nellie will be wondering what's happened to you."

"Just this chapter!"

"All right. Then off you go."

Boots came in from the back, loud on the tile floors, then soundless on a rug, then loud again. She turned, her face full of an intense question, to confront Oliver coming across the dining room. His face was weathered, rugged, and hot. He had pushed back his rancher's hat on his head, above the red line that circled his forehead. His mustache hid his mouth, the squint wrinkles fanning out from the corners of his eyes gave him a look of smiling, but the look he sent ahead of him through the doorway was not a smiling one. The light treble of Betsy's reading voice went on as the two of them looked at each other. He moved his mouth and lifted his shoulders.

"Ah!" she said—a harsh, angry exclamation. "He won't."

Again the delicate lift of the shoulders.

Behind her she heard Betsy's voice round off to a theatrical conclusion. The book clapped shut. She turned. "Now off to your lessons."

Betsy rose, but Agnes lolled and hung in the hammock. "Do we have to now? Can't I go down to the windmill and see Hallie?"

"And miss your lessons?"

"Just for a *minute?*"

"No, it's too hot," Susan said. "Anyway, the last time you went down to the windmill you had to have your mouth washed out."

"I won't *listen!*"

"Come on, you little whortleberry," her father said. "You go tell Nellie she wants you. Tomorrow you can ask Hallie up for the fireworks. I brought back a whole saddlebag full."

"Goodie!" Betsy said. "Can I shoot off a rocket?"

"Maybe. Depending on how good you are all day."

"Oh, I'll be very good," Betsy said. "I'll be the best. Can I shoot off *more* than one?"

"You wouldn't want to be a pig."

"Yes I would."

She hung onto his hand and swung by it. "Not you," he said. "There's less pig in you than in anybody around. Now how about those lessons?"

She swung a last swing all around him and ran out, but she had barely let go before Agnes had wrapped herself around his leg and put her two feet on his boot. He carried her around a few steps that way. Her upturned face was a baby replica of the strained face of her mother. "I'm not a whortleberry," she said.

"Well it's news to me. How would anybody know? You *look* like a whortleberry."

"I look like a girl!"

"You look like a blue-eyed whortleberry to me. Or a whortle-eyed blueberry?"

He lifted her, kissed her, set her down, turned her three times, and spanked her off toward Nellie's schoolroom, but she swerved, looking provocatively over her shoulder, and began hopping on one foot from tile to tile down the piazza. At each post she put out her flat hand and touched the side face, the inside face, then the other side face. Along the balustrade she patted the adobe every third hop. She did not put her left foot to the ground, but turned the end in three quick hops, three pats, and came back hopping, still with her left foot withered upward, carefully patting wall, window sill, doorframe, and made it back to him and patted his hip, home free, and fell around his leg again. She tried to climb aboard his instep but he lifted her off.

"You're a witch," he said, "but I'm the head wizard. Shall I put you under a spell? Shall I fix you so you can't come to the fireworks until you spell *imbrication*? Or should I make it *trapezoidal*?"

"Not *either!*"

"Then you'd better get on to Nellie."

She fled, screaming with laughter, and he looked up to find the older, tenser version of her face waiting for him. He made a smile, he gestured with his head at the drawing pad. "Working. I guess if the world was going to end tomorrow you'd be hurrying to finish something before Gabriel blew."

"I must!" she said. "How else will we live? Tell me what happened."

"He won't sell."

"Not even the one."

"No."

"And there's nothing we can do."

"We could sue. I doubt it'd do any good. I've got no proofs."

"Your word ought to be proof enough against the word of that . . ."

"You don't get far suing a lawyer in a town like this."

"Then we must buy someone else's claim!"

"Any claim with water is going to cost plenty. We haven't got it."

"Isn't there any land not filed on?"

"Not under the Susan."

"There must be *something* we can do!"

Oliver laughed through his nose. "I can keep my eyes open and when somebody fails to complete his improvements I can pre-empt him."

"It's hardly a thing to joke about."

"I wasn't joking. It's about the only thing I could do."

"What if we gave them a farm out of our land? What do we need a thousand acres for?"

His eyes were steady and—she thought—pitying. "I'd do it in a minute. But what good is land under the Big Ditch if the Big Ditch is dry? What can John do with three hundred and twenty acres of sage-brush?"

"What can *we?*" she said, and turned away bitterly, not wanting him to see her face. "Oh, I had set my heart on having Bessie here! I wanted the children to have some companions whose mouths weren't filthy with barnyard talk."

"I was thinking some of letting the Malletts go. We'll probably have to anyway. Bessie and John could have their cabin, and maybe my office for an extra room, till the company gets straightened out and we can finish the Big Ditch. Then they could take their pick of our land."

"Finish the Big Ditch," she said, and bent her head to stare at the red tile floor. Her hands were tucked up in her armpits as if they were cold. Her feet took her down the piazza, along the balustrade where Agnes had hopped a few minutes before, and across the end and up along the wall. Her hands were tight in her armpits, her head down, her face set and flushed. She was not one who easily went pale, even during great stress; it was her rosy complexion, as much as anything, that made her look ten years younger than she was. Stopping at the table where her drawing lay, she raised her head and gave him a glance of scorn and misery. "Of course," she said, "when the Big Ditch is finished, then the stock will be valuable, too."

"Sue . . ."

"Oh, I can't *bear* it!"

"Sue, that stock's still got a chance to be worth thirty times what they paid for it. General Tompkins hasn't given up. Neither have I. We've got assets to burn. The Susan's producing a little revenue, the Big Ditch is well started. They're crazy if they pull out now. They'll reorganize, buy out the ones that want to quit. If they stick a little longer they're in clover. The project's just as good as it ever was."

"Yes," she said on an indrawn breath. "Just about."

In anger he took her by the shoulders. "Susie, you too?"

Unyielding, stiff in his hands, she cried into his face, "Oh, how could I help it! Eight years of exile, eight years of living on hope. For what? Till now it's been all right, I could put up with it, I had faith in it. . . ."

Her voice gave out, she was hung up on his eyes. He let go of her arms. "Did you?" he said.

"What? What do you . . ."

Very still, he stood before her. His face was weathered like a cowhand's, his fingers hung half closed at his sides, constricted by their calluses. Almost whispering, he said, "Did you? Did you have faith in it? Did you have faith in *me*?"

As if he had slapped her, she stepped back. "That's not fair!"

"Isn't it? Sometimes I've wondered." He stared into her eyes, he smiled a bleak smile, he shrugged. "Not that I've deserved much faith."

"Ohhh!" she said, wagging her head back and forth, her eyes on the floor. "You speak of faith and trust. How much better off we'd all be if you hadn't trusted that Burns. Then at least Bessie and John would have their land. We wouldn't have dragged them completely under with us."

Abstractedly his eyes went to the drawing on the table. He studied it, read its caption: *A Hot Day on a Western Ranche*. His eyes lifted, went outward through the door between the piazza pillars, across the sunstruck lawn, past the withering poplars, across the sage, to the mountains. The sage pressed in upon them from every side, they looked out upon it as people on a raft would look out on the sea.

His eyes came inside again, he regarded her soberly. The fans at the corners of his eyes tightened, he seemed to smile. But he was not smiling. "The fault's mine," he said. "I should have taken those papers down myself, I knew how important they were to all of us. I just let myself get too busy, I was going too many ways at once. I've got no excuse. But this general business of trusting people, I don't know. I doubt if I can change. I *believe* in trusting people, do you see? At least till they prove they can't be trusted. What kind of life is it when you can't?"

There was a heavy, questioning, underlined meaning in his words. She stared up at him wordlessly, her face as set and hard as so pretty a face could be. Her mouth, which was usually firm in a precise, pleasant expression tilting always toward a smile, was twisted. Their eyes met, held, wavered, held again. The rosy color drained very slowly from her face.

It was July 4, evening, the end of a long hot day. The piazza was still thick with heat, the pillars and balustrade were as warm as banked stoves. Wait, she told herself bitterly. In ten years the trees will have grown up enough to shade the house in the late afternoon.

But the air, warm or not, was fresher than inside, and there were tendrils of coolness wandering in off the lawn, where Oliver had set the hose cart to irrigate the grass. Suspiciously, as if expecting to smell some sort of incriminating evidence, she sniffed at the mixed odors of hot day and cooling evening—sage, dust, firecrackers, the wet wood of the waterwagon like the smell of an old rowboat, and among these a freshness of wet grass and a drift of fragrance from the yellow climber at the corner. The northwest had cooled from its hot gold, the hills were black against it. But she looked at their silhouette without pleasure, hardly seeing it, intent on the shapes of trouble in her mind.

It was so quiet that she could hear the creak of buggy wheels receding far down the lane toward the road, and the voices of the girls surprisingly clear and close-seeming, though they must have been almost a half mile away. Her first act after waving them good-bye had been to rush into her stuffy bedroom and get out of dress, corset, shoes, everything confining, and into a dressing gown. In her bare feet, shaking the loose gown to get air to her released body, she stood in the doorway and listened to her receding family until she could hear their sounds no more. There was a secret small gurgle of water from the hose, and then in a moment like a sigh the last of the water ran out and that sound too ceased. She listened for the windmill, whose clanging and creaking were as much a part of their days and nights as the wind itself, but could not hear it. The blades must be hanging like a great open flower in the twilight.

She let her weight down, heavy and tired, into the hammock. Bats wove back and forth, utterly soundless, across the openings between the piazza pillars. At first she could see them against the sky, erratic and flickering and swift; then she couldn't be sure whether she still saw them or whether she only sensed them as movement across the dusk. The house behind her was as dark and empty as herself. Her eyes were fixed on the framed view of mesa, black hills, saffron sky. The last brightness of already-gone day burned darkly on a cloud that went slate-color as she watched. She saw a star, then another.

Utterly cut off, sunk into the West, cut off behind arid hills, she lay thinking backward to another piazza and the smell of other roses. It was hard to believe that they no longer existed, not for her—the old house of her great-grandfather sold to a surly farmhand grown up, the vines of the porch now screening his evening relaxation, the kitchen "fixed up" by his vulgar and ambitious wife. No home there any longer, parents dead, Bessie wronged and ruined, herself adrift in the hopeless West, Thomas and Augusta farther from her in fame and associations even than they were in miles. To sit with them just one evening, an evening such as this! To sit with them even here, on this barren piazza! She acknowledged that all her preparations in this house had had them in mind. When it was ready, when they could be induced, she would offer herself to their love all over again, in her new setting, and prove to them that her years of exile had changed her not at all.

Noiseless as a flower opening, a rocket burst above the hills. She sat up, watching the white stars curve and fall. Then *BOOM!* All the night air between her and the town, two and a half miles of it, trembled with the delayed report.

Pshaw! she started to think. *They won't be in time, the children will miss it,* and then remembered that from out on the mesa they would be able to see the whole thing as if from a balcony. They would do better to stay out, rather than try to find a place among the crowds drunk on statehood and spread-eagle oratory and worse. The thought of that vulgar little city, and all its sharpers, trimmers, and hopeful naïfs seething with the importance of their moment in history, crawled on her skin like a spider. She heard herself saying to Oliver's waiting, sober, questioning face, "You go, take Nellie and the children. It means nothing to me."

What she had meant—and after what they had said to one another in the past two days he could hardly have misunderstood her—was "None of it means anything to me any more. I'm sick and disspirited and without hope. We have bled our lives away in this desert like that watercart draining into the sand."

"You ought to come," he had said. "It'll take your mind off things."

"I'm tired. I'd rather stay here."

She could see in his eyes, in the tasting movement of his lips under the mustache, that he felt the blame she could not help laying on him. But she could not make herself smile, or lay a hand on his arm, or send him away with an injunction to enjoy himself.

There was a long, probing meeting of eyes. "No quarter," he said.

"I don't know what you mean."

He let it go. "I'd stay here with you, but the children are counting on it, and there's nobody else to take them."

"You mustn't think of not going."

"I'm sorry."

Sorry, of course. And what good did it do? He could not be sorrier than she.

Another rocket seared across the sky at an angle and bloomed with hanging green balls. Another went up through the green shower and burst into an umbrella of red. Then three together, all white. Then one that winked hotly but did not flower. *BOOM!* went the cushioning air. *BOOM! BOOM BOOM BOOM! BOOM!*

It was hot and close in the hammock. She left it and sat on the warm adobe of the balustrade. Above the town, streaks of smoke were lighted by the rocket bursts. Under the sodden booming she heard a continuous musketry of firecrackers, big and little. She could imagine the boys and drunken men who would be darting around through the crowds on the Capitol grounds throwing cannon crackers under the feet of tied horses and dressed-up girls, and into the buggies of the dignified. Pandemonium, a foolishness costing thousands of dollars. Before morning there would be runaways, clothes and buildings set on fire, fingers blown off, eyes put out. Her family were infinitely better off watching from the mesa.

And yet from a distance how beautiful! There was a colored mist all above the unseen city, as if the smoke of the explosions were now lighted by fires from below. The torchlight parade. The so-called Governor's Guard, including that wretched Burns, would be parading in their uniforms. She stood up, trying to see better, bracing herself against the warm pillar, and from up there heard, faint and far off, sweetened by distance, carrying wonderfully on the still air, the sound of the band.

And something else: the sound of footsteps coming around the house, solid and heavy on the board walk.

In one motion she snatched the dressing gown around her, crouched and jumped, soft-barefooted, and put herself back into the deeper dark of the hammock. The footsteps ceased, either because the walker had paused or because he had stepped off onto the lawn.

"Anybody home?" his voice said.

Tension flowed down her wrists and away. She breathed once, deeply. "Oh Frank! Come in, I'm on the piazza."

He stood above her, a troubling shadow, saying, "I thought everybody must have gone in for the celebration."

"Everybody else has. Wan and Sidonie and John left right after breakfast. Oliver celebrated the Fourth by doing John's irrigating and I celebrated by cooking two meals."

He sniffed. "Smells like firecrackers."

"Can you still smell them? My nose is numb with gunpowder. We've been slapping out smoldering clothes and smearing lard on burned fingers all day. The children looked like the children of a charcoal burner."

"Wiley and I meant to come down, but his mare got cut up in the barbed wire, and we had to doctor her."

"You only missed a lot of noise and a headache. But the children were happy, and so they were good."

"I guess that's what it takes."

"I guess."

"And now they're all gone in to watch the pyrotechnics."

"They just left twenty minutes ago, they won't have made it in time. I suppose they're watching from the road."

His tall outline lounged across the opening, with the fountains of light playing on the sky behind it. She could barely see his face—couldn't see it really, only the outline of his head and shoulders. Then he moved abruptly, pulling back against the pillar. "Excuse me, I'm cutting off your view."

"It's all right. I'm not child enough to want to watch fireworks long."

"I was watching as I rode down the bench. Quite a show."

"Yes."

The distance rumbled and crackled with the bombardment, the lights flared and hung and died and flared again. "Did you want to see Oliver?" she said. "I'm afraid he won't be back till quite late."

"I can see him tomorrow."

"How are things in the canyon?"

"Glum."

"They're no different here. Did you hear about that Burns?"

"Oliver told me. He ought to be lynched."

From her darkness she studied his shape jackknifed against the sky frantic with bursting lights, and thought of the day she had entered Leadville, the day the man Oates who had jumped Oliver's lot there had ended his life at the end of a rope in front of the jail. Frank had seen that—it had been an excitement that bulged his eyes and stammered on his lips when she first saw him. She thought also about the story they had heard from Tombstone—the murdered friend, the hard ride after the killer, the body swinging from a tree somewhere down in the Mexican desert. Frank had not only seen that, he had been one of the avengers. Perhaps his hand had knotted the rope or lashed the horse from under or cut the body down. It chilled her to think of. And yet in her present mood she was half inclined to think manly rage a better response to wrong than the self-blame of a man who trusted too much and then refused to condemn.

"At the very least he should be taken to court," she said. "Oliver won't. He says it was his own carelessness."

"Everybody knows what Burns is. Court's too good for him. A horsewhip might serve."

"But he'll neither be horsewhipped nor sued," Susan said. "He'll be allowed to get away with it."

"Would you like me to horsewhip him? I'd love to."

"Ah," she said, "you're a loyal friend, Frank." Then, because the feeling in her was like a boil that could have no relief except to burst, she burst. "Oh, when I think of Bessie and John I could simply *die!* To think that it's our fault, and no cure for it!"

Among the fountains of light that arched and showered down, intense green, red, yellow, and blue balls now burned in the air. Because he said nothing, and because she was ashamed of her outburst and afraid of silence, she said, shrugging out a little laugh, "How do they make all those colors?"

"Colors?" Frank said. "Metallic salts. The yellow's sodium, the white's magnesium. Red's calcium, I think, and the green may be copper salts, maybe barium. I don't really know. I'm no fireworks expert."

"You're an expert in so many things." She felt almost as if she were going to vomit; she had to keep swallowing her Adam's apple to keep it down. "I can't imagine how a woman could have lived all those years in the canyon without her Corps of Engineers. That was the best time of all the West. I loved those years."

He made a small indeterminate noise, *hm* or *mm* or *ha*. The light of a rocket two and a half miles away brushed his face with ghastly green. She saw it shine and fade in his eyes. "I didn't come down here to see Oliver, you know."

Almost to herself she said, "I know."

"I came down hoping they'd all be gone to town but you."

"Yes," she said, though she felt she should not.

"I never see you any more."

"But Frank, you see me all the time!"

"In a crowd. With the family. Always managing a houseful."

"There's been so much to do."

"Well *that* will be changed, at least."

His laugh was so short and unpleasant that it wrung her heart. The wretched ditch had changed him as it had changed them all.

Beyond his lean profile the lights were coming less thickly, as if both enthusiasm and ammunition had run out. The booming and crackling were dying down, but the reddish mist still hung above the town. Speaking away from her, indifferently watching the dying-down of the fire fountains, he said, "I miss the rides, do you? I miss sitting while you draw me. I miss talking to you. I could stand it if I could just be alone with you once in a while, the way it used to be."

"But there were three whole years when you didn't see me at all, and then more than a year when I was in Victoria."

"Yes. And I'm a dead pigeon the minute I see you again, no matter how long it's been. Remember that day in the canyon, just when you were getting ready to leave? I had myself all persuaded. You were a friend, no more. Then I looked up from that corral and saw you waving from the doorway and I blew down like an old shed. The whole place was abandoned, there was nothing but failure in sight, and there you were in your white dress looking as cool and immaculate as if you were just about to call on somebody. Going down with all flags flying, the way you would. I don't know, you looked so brave and untouched up there on the hill, I . . ."

"Brave?" she said in a weak voice. "Untouched? Oh no!"

"Oh yes. You're one thing I *am* an expert on."

"There are no flags flying now."

"Plenty in Boise. Hip hip hurrah. Statehood."

She had to laugh. "Isn't it ridiculous? Isn't it ironic? Isn't it *pitiful*, even. Years ago, when we left you in Leadville and went to Mexico, I fell in love with Mexican civilization, and the grace of their housekeeping, and the romantic medieval way they lived . . ."

"I know. I read your articles. Down in Tombstone."

"Did you? Oh, that makes me feel good. I was talking to you without knowing it. Then you remember those great houses we stopped at coming home, Queréndaro, Tepetongo, Tepetitlán, and the others. That's what Oliver's dreamed of making here. He wanted to build me such a place. Even the tile floors—those are Mexican. The stone and adobe house, and the way it nearly encloses a courtyard. It was going to enclose it completely some day—well, you remember from the canyon, when we used to plan it so carefully—so from the outside rooms we could look outward on this reclaimed desert, and from the inner rooms we'd see only the protected center—flowers, and stillness, and the dripping of water, and the sound of Wan singing through his nose."

"Maybe yet," Frank said.

"No. Never."

"You don't think so?" he said, and then, "Maybe not," and then, after a second, "I suppose not," and then after quite a long pause, "So I'll be on my way again."

She was silent for longer than he had been; she could find no answer except to deny what she knew was true, to quote him Oliver's hope in which she had no faith at all. "It might . . . maybe they can reorganize. Oliver thinks . . . He can surely find some way to keep us all together."

"How?" Frank said. He sat against the pillar with his legs drawn up and softly slapped his gloves into the palm of one hand. His profiled silhouette remained still, near, and troubling against the sky restless with light. "Even if he could," he said.

"Please don't," she said to his indifferent profile. "Please try to find a way to stay. If you go, where will I get my comfort?"

"If I stay, where will I get mine?"

Bowed in the hammock, pressing with her right-hand fingers against the ache above her eyes, she closed her eyes as if to do so would be to shut off the pain. "Poor Frank," she said. "I'm sorry. It's the way it must be."

"Is it?"

The two words hissed out of the darkness, so bitter and challenging that she opened her eyes and pressed even harder against the ache that lay above them. Her muscles were tense; she had to take charge of both her muscles and her breathing. Relax, inhale, exhale, smooth away the engraved trouble from her forehead. Kinked like a carved bookend against the pillar, Frank sat still, looking away from her with an apparent indifference utterly at odds with the harshness of his tone. Above the fiery mist of the torchlight procession the sky was now empty of everything except its own shabby stars.

"Thee knows it is," Susan said.

His silhouette changed; his face had turned toward her. "That's the first time you ever thee'd me."

"It's the way I often think of thee."

"Is it?"

"Does thee doubt it?"

"Then you renounce too easily," he said through his teeth.

A wandering dog of a night wind came in off the sagebrush mesa carrying a bar of band music, and laid it on her doorstep like a bone. Her skin was pebbled with gooseflesh. "Not easily," she said with a catch of the breath. "Not easily."

"Then come with me!"

"Come with you?" she said in a tiny strangled voice. "Where?"

"Anywhere. Tepetitlán, if you like. There are always jobs for an

493

engineer in Mexico. I know people, I could get something. I'll get you an *estancia* where you can have the things you ought to have. You can be the lady you ought to be. In another country, nobody's going to . . ."

"Frank, Frank, what are you asking? Some sort of disgraceful elopement?"

"Disgraceful? Is that what you'd call it?"

"The world would."

"Who cares about the world? Do you? Do you care about Boise?"

"That's different," she said. "What about the children?"

"Ollie's set. The girls are young."

Her laugh was wire-edged. In her own ears it sounded like a screech. "So they wouldn't understand about their change of fathers?"

In his silence there was something tense and sullen and explosive.

"What *about* their father?" Susan said. "Would you do that to your best friend?"

"For you I'd do it to anybody. Not because I'd like it. Because I can't help myself."

"Oh, oh," she said, and took her face in her hands, and laughed through her fingers. "Even if I were that reckless, what would the world say to a woman who would leave a bankrupt promoter for his unemployed assistant, and jump with her children from poverty to pure uncertainty?"

"Is it money that holds you back?" he said. She heard the sneer, and then the soft spat of the gloves being slapped into his palm. "I'll go out and get some. Give me three months. I'll come back for you, or send for you."

"And meantime I should live with Oliver, planning all the time to leave him? I live enough of a lie as it is. It isn't money, you know it isn't. I only said that to . . ."

"To what?"

"Frank . . ."

"Susan."

His shadow moved, his boot hit the tiles, he reached a long arm. His fingers closed around her bare foot.

Touch. It is touch that is the deadliest enemy of chastity, loyalty, monogamy, gentility with its codes and conventions and restraints. By touch we are betrayed, and betray others. It was probably touch, in some office or hallway, or in my own hospital room while I snored away the anesthetic and dreamed of manglings and dismemberments, that betrayed Ellen Ward—an accidental brushing of shoulders or touching of hands, those surgeon's hands laid on her shoulders in a gesture of comfort that lied like a thief, that took, not gave, that wanted, not offered, and that awoke, not pacified. When one flesh is waiting, there is electricity in the merest contact. And maybe pure accident, maybe she didn't know she had been waiting. Or had that all been going on behind my back for a long time? So far as I knew, or know, she had no more than met him at a couple of dinner parties before I was referred to him for the amputation.

Perhaps pure accident, perhaps an opportunity or willingness that both recognized at the first touch, and I absolutely unaware. There is a Japanese story called *Insects of Various Kinds* in which a spider trapped between the sliding panes of a window lies there inert, motionless, apparently lifeless, for many months, and then in spring, when a maid moves the window for a few seconds to clean it, springs once and is gone. Did Ellen Ward live that sort of trapped life? Released by the first inadvertent opportunity, was she? Seduced because she was waiting for the chance to be?

It is easier these days than it was in Grandmother's time, faster, more direct. Ellen Ward's seduction took only weeks, and was total. Susan Ward's, if it was really seduction, took eleven years, and may never have translated impulse into act. I know none of the intimate circumstances; I only guess backward from the consequences.

But when Frank's hand closed around her foot hanging over the taut edge of the hammock, her body was not encased in its usual armor; it was free and soft in a dressing gown. She was in no danger of swooning, as many genteel ladies did swoon, from being simply too tightly laced for deep-breathing emotions. She was aware of night air, darkness, the dangerous scent of roses, the tension of importunate demand and imminent opportunity. Come into the garden, Maud. If one were a young woman entertaining her betrothed, it would be easy: only hold onto propriety and restraint until marriage let down the barriers. If one were a bad woman, it would be equally easy: ten minutes, who would know?

She was neither a young woman entertaining her betrothed nor a bad woman. She was a decent married woman forty-two years old—a lady, moreover, fastidious, virtuous, intelligent, talented. But also romantic, also unhappy, also caught suddenly by the foot in intimate darkness.

What went on on that piazza? I don't know. I don't even know they were there, I just made up the scene to fit other facts that I do know. But the ghosts of Tepetongo and Queréndaro and Tepetitlán, of the Casa Walkenhorst and the Casa Gutierrez haunted that dark porch, both as achieved grace and as failed imitation, and perhaps as offered possibility as well. I wouldn't be surprised if the perfumed darkness of her barren piazza flooded her with memories of the equally perfumed darkness of Morelia, and if the dangerous impossible possibility Frank suggested brought back the solemnity of bells, the grace and order of a way of life as longed-for as the nostalgias of Milton, and as far as possible from the pioneering strains of Idaho. I wouldn't be surprised, that is, if she was tempted. To flee failure, abandon hopelessness, disengage herself from the stubborn inarticulate man she was married to, and the scheme *he* was married to, would have been a real temptation. And of course, in 1890, for Susan Burling Ward, utterly unthinkable.

What went on? I don't know. I gravely doubt that they "had sex," in Shelly's charming phrase. Some, even in the age of gentility, did make a mockery of the faithfulness pledged in marriage. The rich often did, she knew some who did; and the poor probably did, out of the sheer brutishness of their condition. Grandmother's middle class kind did not, or did so with awful convictions of sin and a shameful sense of having lowered and dirtied themselves. I cannot imagine such a complete breakdown in my grandmother, who believed that a woman's highest role was to be wife and mother, who conceived the female body to be a holy vessel, and its union with a man's—the single, chosen man's—woman's highest joy and fulfillment.

I cannot imagine it, I say. I do not believe it. Yet I have seen the similar breakdown of one whose breakdown I couldn't possibly have imagined until it happened, whose temptations I was not even aware of.

So I don't know what happened. I only know that passion and guilt happened, in some form. In their world, their time, their circumstances, and given their respective characters, there could have been no passion without guilt, no kisses without tears, no embrace without despair. I suppose they clung to one another on the dark veranda in a convulsion of love and woe, their passion no sooner ignited by touch than it was put out by conscience.

And I approve. For all my trying, I can only find Victorian solutions to these Victorian problems. I can't look upon marriage as anything but serious, or upon sex as casual or comic. I feel contempt for those who do so look upon it. Shelly would say I've got a hangup on sex. It seems to me of an almost demoralizing importance; I guess I really think that it is either holy or unholy, and that the assurances of marriage are not unrelated to its holiness. I even respect Victorian rebels and fornicators more than the casual screwers and fornicators of our time, because they *risked* something, because they understood the seriousness of what they did. Well. Whatever Grandmother did, I take it seriously, because I know she did.

When Frank had gone, already furtive, already thinking how to evade or avoid his returning friend and boss, slipping out back to his tied saddlehorse before the sounds of the buggy should be heard in the lane, I can imagine her walking barefooted and distracted around the sopping lawn and along the border of the rose garden, smelling that heavy night-distilled fragrance and torturing herself with the thought of how Oliver had searched through half of Connecticut for some of those new hybrids, and transported them twenty-five hundred miles, to try to make her feel at home in her exile. She was assaulted alternately by anger at his presumption that she could make her home in this place, and by gusts of pity for him, and love, and the will to heal and comfort, and by exasperation over his trustingness and his lapses of judgment, and by despair over the future, and by misery over what she must write Bessie, and by loathing of her own lack of control—a woman of forty-two, with three children, swept off her feet like a seminary girl. And intruding into all that web of complicated and contradictory feeling, the tense memory of straining kisses only minutes ago, and the hands to which she had lifted and tightened her breast, and guilt, guilt, guilt for just those treacherous kisses, and something like awe at what she had been proved capable of.

But when she heard the creak and rattle of dried-out buggy wheels coming down the lane through the starlit dark, she pressed her palms upward along her cheeks to rub and stretch away the stiffness of tears, and ran soft-footed to the door, and slipped in. She was in bed, with a cloth over her eyes to signify headache, when she heard her door open softly, and then after a listening time close, just as softly. She could hear Nellie's exaggerated North Country voice croaking, "Coom, children, to bed, to bed!"

The house settled, the noises went behind thick adobe walls. Through the open window she heard the hose cart groan as Oliver dragged it off the grass; he never left it overnight because its wheels would dent the new lawn. Then for a time she heard him walking up and down the veranda, slow and steady on the tiles, thinking the bleakest thoughts, no doubt, looking into the lightless future. Poor fellow, poor fellow! to see everything come down, every hope and ambition destroyed. She half sat up, impulsively ready to go out to him and hook her arm in his and walk out his failure with him.

And lay back down, thinking of the failure he had brought about for her, and staring blankly into the failure she had made for herself, her teeth set in her lower lip, her ears spying on him. When his pacing paused, the house was intensely quiet; it rang with silence. Outside, the great western night had closed in, with only distant, widely spaced pops of gun or firecracker from the town.

After a long time he came in—carrying his shoes, evidently, so as not to waken her. He undressed in the dark, his careful weight sagged the bed; she moved as if in restless sleep to give him all the room there was. He lay on his back, and she could hear, or feel, the faint rustle and movement of his breathing, slow and steady. Finally, without turning his head, he said softly up into the dark, "Asleep?"

The impulse to go on pretending was only momentary. "No. How were the fireworks?"

"Fine. The kids enjoyed them. We didn't go clear in, we watched from the road."

"I was hoping you would."

"Couldn't you see them from here?"

"Pretty well."

"What did Frank want?"

"What? Frank?" She thought the bound of her heart must have shaken the bed; she lay breathing shallowly through her mouth.

"He was here, wasn't he?"

"Yes," she managed to say, giving up another possible lie. But her heart was now beating against her chest wall like a bird caught in a room. It was unbearably hot, she could not stand his warmth so close, and shifted her body and flung the light blanket impatiently off. "I guess he wanted to talk to you," she said. "His life is all torn up too. He didn't stay. We sat on the piazza and watched the fireworks for a little while. He said he'd see you tomorrow."

"Ugh," Oliver said, unmoving.

Half uncovered, she lay on her back. The night air moving sluggishly from the window tightened her damp skin. She tried to speak casually, and heard how badly she failed—what a bright falseness was in her voice. "How did you know he'd been here?"

"He left his gloves on the railing."

He reared up and leaned and found her cheek with his lips. She did not turn her head, or respond. Quietly he lay back.

"Good night."

"Good night."

Her cheek burned as if he had kissed her with sulphuric on his lips.

6

For several weeks now I have had the sense of something about to come to an end—that old September feeling, left over from school days, of summer passing, vacation nearly done, obligations gathering, books and football in the air. But different now. Then, during prep school and college, and even afterward when teaching tied my life to the known patterns of the school year, there was both regret and anticipation in it. Another fall, another turned page: there was something of jubilee in that annual autumnal beginning, as if last year's mistakes and failures had been wiped clean by summer. But now it is not an ending and a beginning I can look forward to, but only an ending; and I feel that change in the air without exhilaration, with only a heaviness and un-willingness of spirit. With a little effort I could get profoundly depressed.

Part of my uneasiness comes as a direct result of living my grand-mother's life for her. For the last few days I have been studying the Xeroxed newspaper stories that finally arrived from the Idaho Historical Society, and though they do straighten out for me some facts that I have never until now understood, they also raise some questions that are dis-turbing. There is some history that I want not to have happened. I resist the consequences of being Nemesis.

But another part of what obscurely bothers me is the probability that Shelly will be leaving very soon, with consequences to me and to my routines that I can only contemplate with anxiety. And yet there is a sort of comic relief in Shelly, too. One result of throwing away all the maps of human experience and the guides to conduct that a tradition offers, and flying by the seat of your moral or social pants, is that you fly into situations that are absurd or pitiful, depending on how indul-gently one looks at them. My own indulgence is wildly variable. Witness this afternoon.

Through most of the summer Shelly has worked seven days a week, the way I like to work, but the last two weekends she has taken off. I supposed she was getting organized to go back to college, but Ada tells me she has been seeing Rasmussen. "She don't tell me, but I know. Ed saw him over in Nevada City last week, purple pants and all. Honest to John, what she sees in that . . . What's he hanging around for? What's he want?"

"Maybe he's really fond of her."

But that only got a glare from Ada. She doesn't *want* him to be fond of her.

Nevertheless, neither Ada nor I should expect a girl of twenty to sit in this quiet place very long, working seven days a week for the Hermit of Zodiac Cottage. For reasons best known to herself, she chose to cut away from the Berkeley scene and rusticate herself here. But here she is a stranger to everybody she used to know, including her old schoolmates. They have nothing to offer her, she has nothing to give them except an occasion for a lot of lurid gossip. Probably she *was* the brightest student in Nevada City High, as Ada resentfully says. Somewhere, sometime, somebody taught her to question everything—though it might have been a good thing if he'd also taught her to question the act of questioning. Carried far enough, as far as Shelly's crowd carries it, that can dissolve the ground you stand on. I suppose wisdom could be defined as knowing what you have to accept, and I suppose by that definition she's a long way from wise.

Anyway, this afternoon when I was sitting on the porch after lunch she came in and without a word, with only a prying, challenging sort of look, puckering up her mouth into a rosebud, handed me a sheet of paper. It was mimeographed on both sides, with stick figures and drawings of flowers scattered down its margins—a sheet that might have announced the Memorial Day picnic-and-cleanup of some neighborhood improvement association. I've got it here. It says

MANIFESTO

WE HOLD THESE TRUTHS TO BE SELF EVIDENT TO EVERYBODY EXCEPT GENERALS, INDUSTRIALISTS, POLITICIANS, PROFESSORS, AND OTHER DINOSAURS:

1) That the excretions of the mass media and the obscenities of school education are forms of mind-pollution.

We believe in meditation, discussion, communion, nature.

2) That possessions, the "my and mine" of this corrupt society, stand between us and a true, clean, liberated vision of the world and ourselves.

We believe in communality, sharing, giving, using without using up. He is wealthiest who owns nothing and needs nothing.

3) That the acquisitive society acquires and uses women as it acquires and uses other natural resources, turning them into slaves, second-class citizens, and biological factories.

We believe in the full equality of men and women. Proprietorship has no place in love or in any good thing of the earth.

4) That the acquisitive society begins to pollute and enslave the minds of children in infancy, turning them into dreadful replicas of their parents and thus perpetuating obscenities.

We believe that children are natural creatures close to the earth, and that they should grow up as part of the wild life.

5) That this society with its wars, waste, poisons, ugliness, and hatred of the natural and innocent must be abandoned or destroyed. To cop out is the first act in the cleansing of the spirit.

We believe in free and voluntary communities of the joyous and generous, male and female, either as garden communities in rural places or as garden enclaves in urban centers, the two working together and circulating freely back and forth—a two-way flow of experience, people, money, gentleness, love, and homegrown vegetables.

NOW THEREFORE

We have leased twenty acres of land from the Massachusetts Mining Corporation in North San Juan, California, four miles north of Nevada City on Route 49. We invite there all who believe in people and the earth, to live, study, meditate, flourish, and shed the hangups of corrupted America. We invite men, women, and children to come and begin creating the new sane healthy world within the shell of the old.

What to bring: What you have.
What to do: What you want.
What to pay: What you can.

FREEDOM MEDITATION LOVE SHARING YOGA

Address: Box 716, Nevada City, California

When I finished the front side and looked up, Shelly was watching me, moodily running a rubber band through her front teeth like dental floss. She said nothing, so I turned the sheet over. On the back were three quotations:

> *Let the paper remain on the desk*
> *Unwritten, and the book on the shelf unopen'd!*
> *Let the tools remain in the workshop!*
> *Let the money remain unearn'd!*
> *Let the school stand!*
>
> *My call is the call of battle, I nourish active rebellion.*
> *He going with me must go well arm'd,*
> *He going with me goes often with spare diet, poverty,*
> *   angry enemies, desertions.*

WHITMAN

The practice of meditation, for which one needs' only the ground beneath one's feet, wipes out mountains of junk being pumped into the mind by the mass media and supermarket universities. The belief in a serene and generous fulfillment of natural desires destroys ideologies which blind, maim, and repress—and points the way to a kind of community which would amaze 'moralists' and eliminate armies of men who are fighters because they cannot be lovers.

The traditional cultures are in any case doomed, and rather than cling to their good aspects hopelessly it should be remembered that whatever is or ever was in any other culture can be reconstructed from the unconscious, through meditation. In fact, it is my own view that the coming revolution will close the circle and link us in many ways with the most creative aspects of our archaic past. If we are lucky we may eventually arrive at a totally integrated world culture with matrilineal descent, free-form marriage, natural-credit Communist economy, less industry, far less population, and lots more national parks.

GARY SNYDER

Let these be encouraged: Gnostics, hip Marxists, Teilhard de Chardin Catholics, Taoists, Biologists, Witches, Yogins, Bhikkus, Quakers, Sufis, Tibetans, Zens, Shamans, Bushmen, American Indians, Polynesians, Anarchists, Alchemists . . . All primitive cultures, all communal and ashram movements . . . Ultimately cities will exist only as joyous tribal gatherings and fairs.

BERKELEY ECOLOGY CENTRE

I passed the sheet back.

"Keep it," Shelly said. "I've got more. What do you think?"

"I like the part about the home-grown vegetables."

"Come on!"

"What do you want me to say? OM?"

"Whether it makes *sense* or not."

"It's got plenty of historical precedents."

"What do you mean?"

"Plato," I said. "In his fashion. Sir Thomas More, in his way. Coleridge, Melville, Samuel Butler, D. H. Lawrence, in their ways. Brook Farm and all the other Fourierist phalansteries. New Harmony, whether under the Rappites or the Owenites. The Icarians. Amana. Homestead. The Mennonites. The Amish. The Hutterites. The Shakers. The United Order of Zion. The Oneida Colony. Especially the Oneida Colony."

"You don't think there's anything in it."

"I didn't say that. I said it had a lot of historical precedents."

"But it makes you smile."

"That was a grimace," I said. "A historical rictus. One aspect of the precedents is that the natural tribal societies are so commonly superstition-ridden, ritual-bound, and warlike, and the utopian ones always fail. Where'd you get this?"

"It was handed to me."

"By whom? Your husband?"

"So to speak." She scowled at me, pulling her lower lip.

"Are you being asked to bring what you have to this joyous tribal gathering?"

Letting go of her lip, she smiled with a look of superiority and penetration, as if she understood my captious skepticism and made allowances for it. "I didn't say." But then the smile faded into a discontented pucker, and she burst out, "If something's wrong with it, tell me what. I've been trying to make up my mind if anything is. It's idealistic, it's for love and gentleness, it's close to nature, it hurts nobody, it's voluntary. I can't see anything wrong with any of that."

"Neither can I. The only trouble is, this commune will be inhabited by and surrounded by members of the human race."

"That sounds pretty cynical."

"Well, I wouldn't want to corrupt you with my cynicism," I said, and shut up.

But she kept after me; she was serious.

"All right," I said, "I'll tell you why I'm dubious. These will be young people in this garden commune, I assume. That means they'll be stoned half the time—one of the things you can grow in gardens is *Cannabis*. That won't go down well with the neighbors. Neither will free-form marriage or the natural-credit Communist economy. They'll be visited by the cops every week. They'll be lucky if the American Legion doesn't burn them out, or sic the dog catcher on their wild life children."

"None of that has anything to do with *them*. It only has to do with people outside."

"Sure," I said, "but those people aren't going to go away. If they won't leave the colony alone I'll give it six months. If it isn't molested it might last a year or two. By that time half the people will have drifted away in search of bigger kicks, and the rest will be quarreling about some communal woman, or who got the worst corner of the garden patch, or who ate up all the sweet corn. Satisfying natural desires is fine, but natural desires have a way of being both competitive and consequential. And women may be equal to men, but they aren't equal in attractiveness any more than men are. Affections have a way of fixing on individuals, which breeds jealousy, which breeds possessiveness, which breeds bad feeling. Q.E.D."

"You're judging by past history."

"All history is past history."

"All right. *Touché*. But it doesn't have to repeat itself."

"Doesn't it?"

She sat regarding me in a troubled way, puckering up her mouth and making fishlike, *pup-pup-pupping* noises with it. "I don't see why you're *opposed*," she said. "It's one thing to think it's sure to fail, but you sound as if you thought it was *wrong*. I suppose you think it's lunatic fringe, but why? You can't think the society we've got is so hot. I *know* you don't. Haven't you sort of copped out yourself? What's this but a rural commune, only you own it and hire the Hawkes family to run it for you?"

"Do you resent that?" I said.

"What? No. No, of course not. I was just asking something. Take

marriage, say. Is that such a success story? Why not try a new way? O
look at your grandfather. Is this manifesto so different from the come-or
he wrote for the Idaho Mining and Irrigation Company, except tha
he was doing it for profit? He was trying something that was pretty sur
to fail, wasn't he? Maybe it wasn't even sound, maybe that sagebrush
desert might better have been left in sagebrush, isn't that what you
think? All that big dream of his was dubious ecology, and sort of greedy
when you look at it, just another piece of American continent-busting
But you admire your grandfather more than anybody, even though the
civilization he was trying to build was this cruddy one we've got. Here's
a bunch of people willing to put their lives on the line to try to make
a better one. Why put them down?"

"Look, Shelly," I said, "I didn't start this discussion. It doesn't make
that much difference to me what they do. You asked me what I thought."

"I'd really like to know."

"Is that it?" I said. "I thought you were trying to convert me. That'd
be hopeless. I wouldn't live in a colony like that, myself, for a thousand
dollars an hour. I wouldn't want it next door. I'm not too happy it's
within ten miles."

"*Why?*"

"Why? Because their soft-headedness irritates me. Because their
beautiful thinking ignores both history and human nature. Because
they'd spoil my thing with their thing. Because I don't think any of them
is wise enough to play God and create a human society. Look. I like
privacy, I don't like crowds, I don't like noise, I don't like anarchy, I
don't even like discussion all that much. I prefer study, which is very
different from meditation—not better, different. I don't like children
who are part of the wild life. So are polecats and rats and other sorts
of hostile and untrained vermin. I want to make a distinction between
civilization and the wild life. I want a society that will protect the wild
life without confusing itself with it."

"Now you're talking," Shelly said. "Tell me."

"All right. I have no faith in free-form marriage. It isn't marriage,
it's promiscuity, and there's no call for civilization to encourage promiscuity. I cite you the VD statistics for California as one small piece of
evidence. I'm very skeptical about the natural-credit Communist economy: how does it fare when it meets a really high-powered and ruthless

economy such as ours? You can't retire to weakness—you've got to learn to control strength. As for gentleness and love, I think they're harder to come by than this sheet suggests. I think they can become as coercive a conformity as anything Mr. Hershey or Mr. Hoover ever thought up. Furthermore, I'm put off by the aggressively unfeminine and the aggressively female women that would be found in a commune like this. I'm put off by long hair, I'm put off by irresponsibility, I never liked Whitman, I can't help remembering that good old wild Thoreau wound up a tame surveyor of Concord house lots."

It was quite a harangue. About the middle of it she began to grin, I think to cover up embarrassment and anger. "Well," she said when I ran down, "I stirred up the lions. What's that supposed to mean, that about Thoreau?"

As long as I had gone that far, I thought I might as well go the rest of the way. "How would I know what it means?" I said. "I don't know what anything means. What it *suggests* to me is that the civilization he was contemptuous of—that civilization of men who lived lives of quiet desperation—was stronger than he was, and maybe righter. It outvoted him. It swallowed him, in fact, and used the nourishment he provided to alter a few cells in its corporate body. It grew richer by him, but it was bigger than he was. Civilizations grow by agreements and accommodations and accretions, not by repudiations. The rebels and the revolutionaries are only eddies, they keep the stream from getting stagnant but they get swept down and absorbed, they're a side issue. Quiet desperation is another name for the human condition. If revolutionaries would learn that they can't remodel society by day after tomorrow—haven't the wisdom to and shouldn't be permitted to—I'd have more respect for them. Revolutionaries and sociologists. God, those sociologists! They're always trying to reclaim a tropical jungle with a sprinkling can full of weed killer. Civilizations grow and change and decline—they aren't remade."

She was watching me steadily, discreetly and indulgently smiling. "But your grandfather needed the bottle."

"What does that . . . ?" I started to say. Then, "Quiet desperation, you mean? It may be the best available alternative."

I have not had a drink for a week, Ada is upset and confused when in the evening after my bath I make her take a drink but won't take one myself. Her generosity makes her uneasy. And I don't need her daughter to remind me of the strength, maybe even the necessity, of human weakness, and the harshness of the pressures civilized living can put on a man. In the land of heart's desire, up in North San Juan, these things don't apply.

The rubber band that Shelly was running through her teeth broke, and snapped her on the lip. Wincing, she put her fingers to her mouth, but her frown didn't leave her face. Through her fingers she said, "You think Larry is a kook."

"I never met him," I said. "Sight unseen, I'd say he bites off more than I think he can chew."

"He's very bright, you know."

"I haven't the slightest doubt. So was Bronson Alcott."

"Who was he, Brook Farm?"

"Fruitlands. One I forgot to mention."

"Oh."

Probably she didn't hear what I said. She was thinking about her husband, boy friend, mate, whatever he was—the man she used to travel with—and her words came out of her thinking, not as a reply to me. "He can be so damned convincing. He could convince even you."

"I doubt that. But he seems to have convinced you."

"I don't know. He's got me all up in the air."

I had myself turned askance, as usual, and my eyes fell onto the pile of papers I'd brought down when I came to lunch. One was a letter from Rudyard Kipling, another a letter from Kipling's father. I couldn't see the dates, but I knew they were both from July 1890. Right in that time of disintegration and collapse Grandmother had finished the illustrations for something of Kipling's, and had those warm letters of thanks. How many lines an alert life has its hands on at once, even in exile! Grandmother sat like a spider with her web all around her, spun out of her insides. Probably she read those Kipling letters hastily, with a brief pleasurable surprise, while the rest of her attention went out on trembling threads to the Big Ditch, or Frank Sargent, or Agnes, or Oliver, or Ollie in his far-off school, or Bessie, or Augusta, or the odious Burns. I had left her in a disturbed state of mind, and I wanted to get back, the old werewolf craved cool historical flesh to live in and refrigerated troubles to deal with. I felt a certain irritation at Shelly Rasmussen, very brown from lying in her family's back yard, sitting in Grandmother's old wicker chair and littering my porch with her foolish young life. I thought it would serve her right to go to that nut-farm and become a den mother, head of a matrilineal line in a natural-credit Communist economy.

"I gather you've patched things up," I said.

She shrugged, a gesture at once loose and irritable. "Maybe. If I could be sure he'd stay the way he is now. He's a lot better off when he's got something to be enthusiastic about. Then he doesn't sit around and think up ways to take your skin off."

"Have you been seeing him?"

"Couple times."

"Been up to San Juan?"

"I was up this last weekend."

"And you like it."

Her gray eyes met mine, she closed them deliberately, puckered up her rosebud mouth. "Oh, you know me. I'm soft headed, I ignore history and human nature. But it was sort of nice, you know? I mean—pine woods and a clearing. Off from everything. Part of it's just a gravel pile, they worked all that country with monitors. But there are some old mine buildings they're fixing up. Eight people so far, two kids. Later, as more come in, they'll build geodesic domes. What's the matter?"

I had only made the sign of the cross. How many times lately has the future perfect been framed in geodesic domes?

"They've got chickens that roost in the trees and lay eggs under the porch," Shelly said. "None of this scientific egg culture that never lets a hen set foot to ground in her whole life. It's *obscene*, the way they keep them on chicken wire. They got there too late to plant a garden, but they're putting in berry bushes, and they're going to plow a patch for winter wheat. They'll grind their own wheat and corn. Can you see me with a *metate* between my knees?"

She laughed her hoarse laugh, rocking back and forth. *Ohne Büstenhalter*. Her breasts were very live under her thin pullover, her erect nipples made dents and dimples, appeared and disappeared again as flesh met cloth. Every now and then, in her careless unconscious (is it?) way, she makes me aware that I am only fifty-eight years old, not as old as I look, not old enough to have lost everything else when I lost my leg. I felt a hot erection rising from my mutilated lap, and fumbled my sweater over myself, though it was not cool on the porch. Maybe she noticed, maybe she understood. She stretched in her wicker chair and reached her arms over her head, yawning, with her eyes shut. The other eyes looked at me boldly from her expanded chest.

Her arms fell, she flopped back. "I don't know," she said almost crossly. "You're skeptical. But it was sort of good—no poisons, no chemicals, no gadgets. Healthy, sort of. Fun. All the time I was up there I kept thinking it was the way it must have felt to your grandmother in Boise Canyon, when they were doing everything for themselves and making something new."

"Not new," I said. "Ancient. But fun, I believe it."

Shelly threw the broken rubber band in the wastebasket by the wall. "Well, what do I do? Should I try it up there—I know what you'll say—or should I tell him no dice and go back and finish my stupid degree and enter a teaching intern program and start grinding wild life through the education machine?"

"There's another alternative," I said. "You could go on doing what you've been doing. Thousands of letters still to go, years and years of them. Don't miss tomorrow's exciting episode."

At certain times her eyes, wide and gray, get smoky and warm. They went that way then. She said, smiling, "Would you keep me on?"

"I'd like it very much."

"I'd like it too. I've really enjoyed working for you. Only . . ."

"Only," I said. I had subsided, that fleeting foolish dream was gone. "O.K. You know what you want to do."

"I wish to hell I did." She got up and walked, pushing chairs, adjusting things on tables. "I don't know—I think I've got to get out. There's nothing here, this is only a pause, sort of. The only lively times I have are at work, talking to you. You know—" She stopped, looking at me with her head bent. "Why couldn't I come down from San Juan—" She looked at me again. "No. You wouldn't like that."

"No," I said, "I guess I wouldn't."

She sighed, she looked at me with those wide gray smoky eyes overflowing with female, troubling warmth. "What'll you do?"

"What I'm doing now. Not so pleasantly, not so fast."

"Can you manage?"

"Of course."

"I know you don't think I should go live with Larry in his commune."

Live with half a dozen fellows in their commune, I felt like saying. Be on service to the community. No, I don't think you should. Aloud I said, "You'll have to excuse me, Shelly. All I said was that *I* wouldn't want to. How do I know what you should do? You'll do what you think you want to do, or what you think you ought to do. If you're very lucky, luckier than anybody I know, the two will coincide."

"Yeah," she said vaguely. "I suppose." Her smile erupted, her spread hand clawed back the hanging hair. "Tell me something."

"If I know the answer."

"You said this kind of commune will be full of aggressively un-feminine and aggressively female women. Which am I?"

But I evaded that one. "I haven't heard of you joining the Women's Liberation Front," I said.

She came up behind my chair, she bent over me and put her arms around me and hugged my rigid head against her uninhibited bosom. She loudly kissed the top of my head. "You're a gas, Mister Ward," she said. "You're O.K." She went on upstairs to work and left me there, looking out into the rose garden and across Grandfather's acres of lawn, and feeling bleak, bleak, bleak.

Up to now, reconstructing Grandmother's life has been an easy game. Her letters and reminiscences have provided both event and interpretation. But now I am at a place where she hasn't done the work for me, and where it isn't any longer a game. I not only don't want this history to happen, I have to make it up, or part of it. All I know is the *what*, and not all of that; the *how* and the *why* are all speculation.

For one thing, there is a three-month blank in Grandmother's correspondence with Augusta. From July 2 until the end of September 1890 there is only one brief note mailed between trains in the Chicago station. If other letters from that period ever existed, they have been destroyed, either by Augusta or by Grandmother herself after the correspondence was sent back to her. As for the reminiscences, they pass over those months of disaster and desolation in one sentence, and not a revealing sentence either.

As one who loved her, I am just as glad not to have to watch her writhe. As her biographer, and a biographer moreover with a personal motive, probing toward the center of a woe that I always knew about but never understood, I am frustrated. Just where there should be illumination, there is ambiguous dusk. Right at Susan Ward's core, behind the reticence and the stoicism, where I hoped to see her plain and learn from her, there is nothing but a manila envelope of Xeroxed newspaper clippings that raise more questions than they answer. I fight my way through all the giants and wizards, I cross to her castle on the sword-edge bridge, I let myself down hand over hand into her dungeon well, and instead of my reward, a living woman, there is a skeleton with a riddle between its ribs.

"Don't tell me too much," Henry James is supposed to have said, when some anecdote vibrated his web and alerted him to the prospect of a story. "Don't tell me too much!" But he was not writing biography, and he had no personal stake in what he did. He could invent within the logic of a situation. I have to invent within a body of inhibiting facts that I wish were otherwise. If I had had Shelly put them in chronological order I might be able to start in on those clippings in some business-like way, but I have not shown them to Shelly. I ran through them with the avidity of a thief counting his loot when they first came, and then I stuffed them back into their envelope, unwilling to do the peephole detective work they seemed to demand.

But if I don't do it, what do I do? Stop? She has kept me alive all summer, that woman. I have been her private werewolf. I know, furthermore, that my reluctance to expose her trouble is calculated to spare myself, not her. What point is there in sparing a woman who has been dead more than thirty years? So I will do it like fortune telling. I will start at the top of that little stack of clippings and read down through them and see what they tell me.

The first one is a very brief notice, a pencil-encircled paragraph from the "Of Local Interest" column for July 22, 1890. It says that Mrs. Oliver Ward, accompanied by her son Oliver junior and her daughter Elizabeth, left on that day to visit relatives at the East, and to put young Oliver in school in New Hampshire.

Either because his readers would all have been full of the affairs of the Oliver Wards and the London and Idaho Canal Company, or out of some feeling of charity or compassion, the editor says no more than that—nothing about the events that for two weeks have been the sensation of the town. And at once, with his bare notice of Susan's departure, he presents me with a question that is unanswerable by reference to any of the known facts.

From later letters, I know that Grandmother delivered my father to St. Paul's sometime around the first of August, a good month before school opened. Since they left Boise on July 22, and would have taken the best part of a week crossing the continent, she could have paused in Milton only two or three days before taking him on to Concord.

Why that haste? They were all stunned, distracted, grieving, shot to bits. Why wouldn't that mother have kept the remains of her family around her? Wouldn't her silent manly boy have been a comfort to her, wouldn't she have felt that she should be near to comfort *him*? I suppose she may have felt uncomfortable about throwing herself on the mercy of Bessie and John, after the loss and disappointment those two had had on account of her and hers. But Bessie was the warmest and most affectionate of sisters; in the circumstances she would have opened every door and room and heart in her house to Susan and her children. And even if Susan felt that she herself shouldn't or couldn't stay, why wouldn't she have left Ollie to have a healthy and healing time with his cousins on the farm? He was big enough and handy enough to be a help to John, and he would certainly have been happier there than moping around in a deserted school with his loneliness and misery. Yet his mother snatched him away from Milton after barely forty-eight hours, and took him up to Concord and unloaded him on Dr. Rhinelander as she might have sped an unwelcome visitor.

Why?

All her life she spoke of Dr. Rhinelander with gratitude, because that summer and two summers thereafter he took Ollie in with his own family, carried him along to a Maine island, found scholarship money to support him through St. Paul's, and when he graduated, got him a scholarship to MIT. Reasons enough for gratitude. But put that kindness of Dr. Rhinelander's against the fact that my father did not come home again for ten years. Until he graduated from St. Paul's, he spent every summer vacation with the Rhinelanders; after he started at MIT he took summer jobs. One of them brought him out on a surveying crew to the Idaho mountains where his father had worked years before. By then his family were living here in Grass Valley, but their son did not come the rest of the way west to see them. He saw his father once or twice a year in New York. His mother he saw not at all. When he graduated from MIT he found a job in Korea—and sailed from Seattle without a visit home—and he stayed in Korea until the Russo-Japanese War drove him out. Then, and only then, he accepted Grandfather's offer to become superintendent of the Zodiac when Grandfather became general manager.

Ten years. What am I to make of that? Especially when I remember the lifelong taciturnity that was more like a disease than a mere quality of his temperament? Especially when I remember how Grandmother deferred to him, and feared his silences? Especially when I remember her frantic haste to get rid of him in the summer of 1890? I have to conclude that he knew something, or suspected something, or had seen something, or thought her to blame for the catastrophes that within three or four days had shaken down his world. I have to believe that in her distraction and self-loathing—he could not have blamed her more than she blamed herself—she could not bear the look in her son's eyes. And though I could probably make up some episode to corroborate what I suspect, I think I shall not. Let it go at the fact that from that time on he had an aversion, all but incurable, against his mother; and that she read his mind before they left Idaho, and could not stand what she saw.

So there they go again on a transcontinental train, this time not merely in defeat but in utter rout—a sullen white-faced boy, a scared little girl not quite ten, a mother strung up like a piano string, turning a white blank smile toward people who came up to her or called from the platform—Boise was a town that met the through trains. But it all came apart when Nellie broke down into terrible weeping, grabbed the children and hugged them and wet them with her tears, clung to Susan with sobs that shook and shattered them both. They were all crying. With streaming eyes Nellie stood back, tried to say something, strangled, looked at them all piteously for a moment with her weak English chin trembling, and pressed her handkerchief to her mouth and put her head down and fled. Susan herded the children aboard, a sympathetic porter found their seats and brought their bags and left them, they huddled in the high Pullman plush and hid from the eyes of the curious. It was like coming into a room full of people with all their desolation plain upon them. They could hear the rustling of newspapers. For some reason the man across the aisle chose that moment to pick up the orange skins and litter on the seat and floor around him. They turned their faces away from his peeping. Susan took Betsy's head in her lap and bent into the corner, stroking the child's trembling back. Ollie put his forehead against the window and stared out, blind as a daytime owl. Eventually the train jerked and started.

Five days of it—a day of Idaho, a night of Wyoming, a day of Wyoming and Nebraska, a night of Nebraska, a whole morning of sitting at the platform in Omaha. An afternoon of Iowa, a night of undistinguishable dark prairies, another whole morning of sitting in the station in Chicago. An afternoon of Illinois and Indiana before they burrowed under the dense night heat. Their windows were open, their car was littered with papers and the remains of food, they were grimed with cinders, their hands came black off the plush, their beds, made up crisp and white in the evening, were wrinkled, damp, tossed nests by morning.

And not a change in that boy all the way across. In the daytime he sat with his forehead against the glass, indifferent and slack. He would not meet her eyes—and for that she was half thankful, for when by accident her glance brushed across his reflected eyes in the glass it was as if she had been lashed by thorns.

She did what she thought she should, or what she could. She called the children's attention to things they passed, she got out a sketch pad and let Betsy draw, she asked them when the news butcher came through if they wanted candy, wanted magazines, wanted oranges. Betsy sometimes did, Ollie never did. When lunchtime or dinnertime came he ate, dutifully, and came back and sagged into his corner and put his forehead against the glass. He sat facing her all those five days, and she could not meet his eyes without grief and panic; and at night he crawled up into his upper berth with a word of good night and lay there silent and unreachable through all the dark rocking hours, while she hugged Betsy to herself down below, and once or twice had to waken her from a screaming nightmare and, her own face wet and anguished, soothe away the fear.

The boy was wordless, he was his father all over again; and she felt that there was no forgiveness in him. Her own numb grief, her sluggish guilt, could be held down in the daytime, when the eyes could be fixed on something outside, when blind words could be read out of books or magazines, when the details of washing and eating could be clung to like rafts. But at night she lay and heard her daughter's breathing beside her, and thought, and remembered, and wept, and contorted her face and buried it in the pillow and clenched her arms over it to shut out things that came. And in the morning when she came out through the green curtains, there was the ladder already placed for Ollie, and there was Ollie coming in from the washroom with his great burned-out eyes in which she read everything, everything, she had thought during the night.

So (I think) she made up her mind during that trip that if she was to survive at all she must unload him, for his sake and her own. She was the sort that survives—how else do you live to be ninety-one?—and by the time they reached Poughkeepsie she had had nearly three weeks to bring herself to accept total calamity. Very well, she would have to bear what she had to bear—her life was destroyed, but it was not over. Being who she was, she knew it would not be over until she had somehow expiated her weakness, guilt, sin, whatever it was she charged herself with.

Apparently, after delivering my father to Dr. Rhinelander, she returned to Milton, where that saintly Bessie was looking after Betsy, her namesake. She intended to go into New York, take rooms, put Betsy in a school, and turn herself in grim earnest—and grim is the right word—to the career that she had tried to combine with marriage to a Western pioneer.

One thing, the year before, she had told Augusta she would give anything to experience for ten minutes: the sight of her boy's browny head down among the other heads in the St. Paul's chapel, listening to grave wise words, soaking up wisdom. She never had that experience. Her last experience, and her only one, at St. Paul's was to part with her son there in the headmaster's study, to stoop and hug his unresponsive stiff body, to cry at him to learn, to study, to love her, to write. He stared at her with his great burned-out eyes and said a reluctant word or two, and watched her go.

She intended to go into New York and take rooms and go to work at her writing and drawing; this much is clear from some of her later letters. But she never did. She started. She took poor forlorn little Betsy away from the Milton farm and steered her toward that new, meager life; but something happened in her head and in her feelings. She winced aside, she refused the jump. With Augusta and Thomas waiting for her in there, with the whole life that she had given up to marry Oliver Ward open again to her ambition, and she not old—at her very top, actually, in imagination and skill—she could not do it. She got on a train, but it was not a train headed downriver to New York. It was another transcontinental train headed West. At ten the next morning, August 6, "near Chicago," she scribbled the note which is the only correspondence surviving out of those three months.

> My own darling —
> Forgive me if you can. At the last minute I could not come, I lacked the courage. To visualize myself knocking at your door and waiting for the sight of your face turned me faint with panic. Too much has happened, I am too deep in another life. *It would not have been me!*
> I am going back. Behind all this anguish, I believe, has been my refusal to *submit*. I do not mean to my husband only. I have held myself above my chosen life, with results that I must repent and grieve for the rest of my days. I have not been loyal. If there is ever a chance that our lives may be patched together, it must be in the West, since that is where I failed.
> I will write you when I am in control of myself. Good-bye, dearest Augusta, my ideal woman. I am not worth your sympathy or your tears, and yet I am weak enough to hope that not all the love you once had for me is effaced. I am not likely to see you, ever again. It is one of the saddest of my many sad thoughts. Good-bye, my dearest.
>
> SBW

That's it, that's all. When the letters begin again at the end of September, she is in control of herself, stoically making headway toward a patched-up life. None of her subsequent letters bothers to explain to Augusta, who presumably knows anyway, exactly what happened in July. She puts that behind her. Almost as if she were a bystander—and her letters repeat some of the things reported in that stack of Xeroxed clippings—she records through the next six months the death throes of the canal company, the lawsuits, the receivership. Matter-of-factly she reports her efforts to keep Mesa Ranch alive through a dry fall with no man to help except John on Sundays. I find it hard to imagine my grandmother and Nellie Linton, a pair of Victorian gentlewomen, hitching a team to the hose cart, filling the cart at the windmill, and creeping, stopping, creeping, stopping again, along the lane of dying Lombardies in the brass of a desert evening. Whether I can imagine them or not, it is what they did. Not even the Malletts were left them— gone back to the Camas to raise horses.

Most of her hours were filled with the literary and artistic drudgery by which she supported them. Till mid-afternoon she wrote or drew. At three she gave herself over to drawing lessons for Nellie's six pupils, most of them daughters of the pick-and-shovel millionaires she had despised. They came in a surrey every morning and were called for every afternoon. Some of the parents grumbled at the driving, and suggested to Nellie that she move her school into town, where it could easily double its size, but she would not leave Susan or Mesa Ranch.

Even in her own house, Susan humbled herself to teach those girls. She knew well enough that some of their mothers sent them not so much to make them into ladies as to patronize the lady who had failed to return their calls. One or two, she thought, craved the pleasure of pitying her, but she was impenetrable, she turned on them the bright face of self-sufficiency.

Yet she allowed Betsy to make friends with them (for who else was available to poor Betsy now?), and she did her best to help Nellie teach that buggyload of shaggy dogs to modulate their voices, to pronounce words properly, to sit with their knees together, to walk as if they were women and not muckers in a mine. She gave them the rudiments of drawing and perspective, the beginnings of a taste in literature.

I am bothered by the thought of her reading aloud to those children. It is a measure of her humbling, for household reading had been one of their chief pleasures when they were all a company of saints out in the canyon, and Frank, Wiley, the children one by one, herself, Nellie, even Grandfather, picked a favorite poem and read it. Everyone knew everyone else's favorites by heart; they chanted them aloud like a Greek chorus pronouncing wisdom or doom. And I feel that scene, both in its warm family shape and in its colder, reduced shape as a schoolroom exercise for unlicked Boise. I could probably come in off the bench cold and substitute for any one of them, for Grandmother imprinted me with those same household poets a quarter of a century later.

Her letters through the fall and winter keep assuring Augusta that she is well and safe. People drop by—John, Sidonie, Wan, even near-strangers, for not even Boise, which Grandmother had scorned, would leave two women and a child unlooked-after in an isolated house. She speaks of having ice hauled and stored in sawdust against the coming summer. She speaks of her intention to replace the trees that have died, as soon as frost is out of the ground. She discusses what she is drawing or writing. She reports that she has moved her work out to Oliver's office to avoid competition with Nellie's pupils.

But one part of her life has been abruptly cut off. It lies on the other side of a stern silence, as a severed head lies beyond the guillotine knife.

Only four letters in more than six months mention my grandfather at all, apart from that reference to her use of his office. The first one, in November, says only, "Oliver continues to send a money order on the first of each month. I am grateful from the bottom of my heart for this sign that he has not forgotten us, though as to the money, we could make do without." The second, dated December 10, says, "Oliver's draft which came today was mailed at Merced, California, whereas the others have come from Salt Lake City. I must wait as patiently as I can, to know what this may mean."

The third, dated February 12, 1891, says, "A money order from Oliver yesterday, this one from Mazatlán, Mexico, and today a letter from Bessie which explains it. He has written to her, and has sent John two hundred dollars on the debt he says he owes him for the collapse of the canal stock. Bessie is uncertain about accepting it—she suggests sending it to me! Of course she must keep it, it is a debt of honor. But oh, it warms my heart that he should take it so! It dispels the gloom of this long cold snowless winter. And I am glad he is now in a position where he can *build*—he is always happiest when he is building something. Our dear old Sam Emmons is responsible. He and some others own an onyx mine down there, and they have brought Oliver down to construct a short-line railroad and a port facility for the shipment of the stone. I feel it as the beginning of better times. There is hope in this news, as in the first crocus."

The fourth of these letters, though, has sunk back; it is neither stoical nor hopeful, but depressed and sad. It is a long letter and a gloomy one. The snowfall has been very light, it will be another dry year, Boise is dead and hostile, as if, being the only remaining representative of the London and Idaho Canal, she caught all the blame for the collapse that disappointed so many.

I wait for spring, and fear it, [she says]. Exactly what I am waiting for I do not know, or whether I am waiting for anything real. Sometimes I go rigid with the thought, *All the rest of life may be this way!* With the drafts from Oliver, and the too-generous checks that Thomas sends me for the poor things I am able to do, and with Nellie's school for a "grocery account," we are not in need. But I shall have to get John, or some other hired man, once the weather breaks, to keep Mesa Ranch from burning out. I want to keep it alive—that is the thing I cling to. *I do not want it to die!* I don't want to lose so much as one more Lombardy or locust. I am determined, if possible, to get a crop of winter wheat sowed next fall in the acres that Hi Mallett broke. I want the lawn as green as Ireland, however dry the summer. If I dared, I would even restore the rose garden. But I daren't. That would be to question or resist my punishment. He meant that to be before my eyes from day to day as a reminder, and I accept that as only justice.

Oh, there are times when this place opens before me as if I saw it for the first time, and saw it all—all its possibilities, all its bad luck and failure and tragic mistakes, and then I want to turn my back on it and run away beyond *any* reminder. But I know I must stay here. It is poor Ollie's only inheritance, and in spite of what happened to him here, I know he loves it.

I said I waited for spring, and feared it. The blasted rose garden is one reason for my fear, for every time my eye lights on it I will remember everything. Yet the one rose that remains, the old Harison's yellow on the piazza corner, has the power to disturb me more with its promise of life than all the others with their reminder of death. I can hardly wait for it to bloom again, though I know that when it does I shall cry myself sick. As you know, it came into its first blooming in the canyon the summer Agnes was born. When I came out into the sun for the first time, and she lay in her cradle in the entry, that golden profuseness yellowed the air all above her face, and scented the whole yard.

My God, Augusta, how could I ever, what blindness of discontent could have made me responsible for so much bitterness in those I most love! In punishment I have lost three of them—four, for Ollie writes only the letters the school compels him to, and they are as cold, as cold, as a stone at the bottom of a river.

Do you ever think how death may be? I do. I think of it as dusky and cool, a room with a door open to the outside, and a soft wind coming in as cool as if it blew off the stars. In the doorway, which faces *away*—in these visions I am never looking back—may at any moment appear the faces that one has wholly loved, and the dear voices that one remembers will be saying softly, like a blessing, *We love you, we forgive you.*

I have already turned away from what I started to do, which was to look at those newspaper stories and discover what they can tell me beyond the raw happenings. I must remember who I am. I am a historical pseudo-Fate, I hold the abhorréd shears. I have set myself the task of making choral comment on a woman who was a perfect lady, and a lady who was a feeling, eager, talented, proud, snobbish, and exiled woman. And fallible. And responsible, willing to accept the blame for her actions even when her actions were, as I suppose all actions are, acts of collaboration. For her, conduct was like marriage—private. She held herself to account, and she was terribly punished. And now I really must get down to it. No more of this picking a random card. Let me find the crucial one—the first crucial one. Here it is.

It says that on the evening of July 7 Agnes Ward, daughter of the chief engineer of the London and Idaho Canal, drowned in the Susan ditch after becoming separated from her mother while taking a walk. There is a lot more, but that is the essential part. *Who what where,* and to the extent that people were able to piece it out, *how.* The *why* is more difficult.

That's the first one. It is accompanied by three or four lesser items— funeral and all that—which tell me nothing I really want to know. But now comes the second crucial one, front page and two-column like the first, which reports that on July 11 (the day after Agnes's funeral, though the story does not say so) Frank Sargent, thirty-three, son of General Daniel M. Sargent of New York City, was found dead in his bed at the London and Idaho's engineering camp in Boise Canyon. He had put the muzzle of a .30-.30 saddle gun in his mouth and pulled the trigger with his thumb. Associates said he had been despondent over the financial difficulties of the canal company, of which he was assistant chief engineer.

The reporter made no connection between the drowning of Agnes Ward and the suicide of Frank Sargent, except to remark that for the unlucky London and Idaho people tragedy came in bunches. But Susan

Ward and Oliver Ward, and probably Ollie Ward too, made such a connection, and so must I.

I know that Frank Sargent was out of a job and intending to go away. I know that his long, smoldering, "incurable disease" of love for my grandmother had burst out like a spontaneous-combustion fire in the airless loft of their failure. I know that Grandmother would have had to see him—or at least I am morally certain she would, either because her own feelings were dangerously inflamed or because she felt it necessary to break off for good. It would not be easy to see him at her house, where Nellie, the children, John, Wan, the Malletts, Oliver himself, were always coming and going. It would have been awkward to ride up to the canyon camp to see him because Wiley was there, and because after the July 4 visit she felt that Oliver was suspicious. But Frank still rode the Susan Canal nearly every day: two months before, she had written a story about a young engineer patrolling just such a ditch in just such a valley, trying to discover who kept creating little breaks in the bank that rapidly widened to let the whole ditch run dry. He had found a girl doing it, the daughter of a local rancher who felt that the ditch was robbing him of water rightfully his, and their little drama was worked out just at twilight, with the last of a red sunset reflected on the slow, spinning current of the ditch and the mountains going cool and black all around the horizon.

Life copying art? Not improbably; her mind worked that way. Suppose she was truly afraid to meet Frank Sargent alone, and didn't dare give him her good-bye with others around? Who might she take along, as camouflage or protection? A child, maybe? A child of five, too young to understand speaking looks or the hidden emphasis of words? Young enough to be sent off to pick flowers or catch polliwogs while two adults held their tense, nearly silent interview? On that bench the sagebrush was four feet tall, tall enough for seated people to be hidden from sight, tall enough for a child to disappear in it within fifty feet.

There is nothing in the newspaper story either to corroborate or deny such speculation. The mother, the paper says, was too distracted with grief to give a coherent account of the accident, but according to the father, they had become separated while searching for wildflowers among the sage. When Mrs. Ward became aware that she was alone, and began to call, there was no answer. She ran calling through the tall sage and along the ditch bank. Her cries attracted Mr. Ward and his son, who happened to be riding the ditch trail, and they joined the search on horseback. It was the boy who found his sister's body a quarter mile downstream, kept afloat by the air inside her dress. Efforts by the father and by Mr. Frank Sargent to revive the little girl by artificial respiration proved unavailing.

Efforts by the father *and by Mr. Frank Sargent.* Where did he come from? Did he just pop into the action as he pops into the newspaper story, out of nowhere? Had he been riding down the ditch with Oliver and Ollie? The paper does not say so. Did he come along later? We don't know. Was he there all the time—had he been sitting hidden in that tall sage with his arm around Susan Ward, or with Susan Ward's two hands in his, pleading his urgent, ardent, reckless, hopeless cause? Were those two so absorbed in themselves that they forgot for a while to wonder where Agnes had got to? Did Susan, pushing away the misery of their parting, or whatever it was, stand up at some point, looking anxiously around in the growing dusk, on that bench like a great empty stage, under that sky beginning to show the first weak stars, and call out, and have no answer? Did the two of them go through the sage and along the trail and down the ditch, calling? And is that when Oliver and Ollie, attracted by the voices, came riding down?

If so, it is not what Grandfather reported to the Boise *Sentinel.* It is only by a seeming inadvertence that Frank Sargent is in the story at all. But there he is, ambiguous, having to be dealt with. And four days later, after hanging around the edges of their grief for four days, after standing helpless and excluded, probably hated, through the service and the burying, blaming himself not unjustly for everything that had happened—he took the same view of individual responsibility that Grandmother did—he went back to the canyon in his funeral suit and lay down on the bed that had once been Susan Ward's and blew the top of his head off.

And that would have confirmed everything that Oliver Ward thought he knew. As surely as that slug went through Frank Sargent's head, it went through Susan and Oliver and Ollie Ward.

There is also that business of the rose garden.

Once a long time ago, forty years—oh, more, more than forty-five—I was helping my grandfather in the rose garden here at Zodiac Cottage. He paid me a dollar or two a week to help him, more for the company, I think, than for any actual work I did. I brought peat moss or manure in the wheelbarrow when he wanted them, and wheeled potted cuttings into the greenhouse and set them up on tables, carefully labeled, when he was through slipping or grafting them. Mostly I sat around and watched his big, clumsy-looking, clever hands work with those frail shoots and frailer grafts. He rarely said more than ten words an hour. Sometimes he sat down by me and smoked a pipe and played me a game of mumbly-peg on the lawn.

I remember this special afternoon because of my Aunt Betsy, by then married and living in Massachusetts, who was in Grass Valley for a month's visit. She was a nice woman, gentle, rather sallow, anxious about small things. She came walking alone through the yard from the orchard, strolling in and out of the shade on a bright afternoon—June, probably, since all the roses were loaded with blooms. She strolled along the cross path to the greenhouse, stooping to sniff, snapping off a blossom, walking with it under her nose, her eyes searching and abstract.

"Having fun?" she asked when she reached us.

Grandfather looked at her over the tops of his glasses, wiped a big hand across his face, smiled, and said nothing. His fingers pressed and tamped soil and moss around a little plant, he set it aside and picked up another pot.

"The roses are simply gorgeous," Aunt Betsy said. "So many kinds, and all out at once."

"Mmm," Grandfather said around his pipe.

"You've been working on them. They weren't like this when I lived here."

"No. I suppose not."

"You've got a real knack."

He straightened, smiled, laid his pipe aside, took out his pocket knife, and honed it on a little stone he kept lying on the bench. Aunt Betsy sprawled in a broken-backed lawn chair made of wooden slats, and sniffed her rosebud, a talisman, one of the sweetest smelling kind. "Daddy," she said.

Grandfather answered only with his eyebrows, holding them up in a welcoming sort of way, testing the knife's edge against his thumb.

"You remember the rose garden on the Mesa."

Now his old eyes were on her, the whites faded and a little coffee-colored, the blue bright and watery. He said nothing, he only waited.

"You pulled it up," Betsy said. "One after the other. I saw you."

Pleasantly inquiring, his eyes rested on her. She seemed upset by his silence. Her eyes came up and fell again, her face reddened. "Why?" she said. "It was years ago, but I've never forgotten it. I couldn't imagine why you'd do it. I loved those roses, they were so opulent in that desert-y place. I never got over wondering why you did it."

Grandfather squinted across the bench at her. His heavy face was without any particular expression, the wrinkles fanned out from the corners of his eyes. In the V of his open shirt I could see the softened flaps of his neck.

Absently he clicked his knife shut and put it in his pocket. His heavy body squeezed past the end of the bench and came around into the path past where she sat with her legs stretched out and her face flushed and her eyes searching his face for some sort of answer. He had his pipe in one hand. Now he put it in his mouth, reached a hand to touch her shoulder briefly, and went heavily on past her, out through the orchard toward the back lot, shambling along aimlessly as if he had forgotten where he was going or what he was going for.

"Why *did* he pull up all the roses?" I said to my Aunt Betsy. But she only shook her head at me, hurriedly, as if embarrassed or annoyed, and bent her nose to her talisman bud and went on into the house. I thought she was a little crazy. Why should Grandfather, who would putter all afternoon on one rose bush, pull up a whole garden?

But now I think he did. "A reminder," Grandmother said in that miserable letter while she waited for spring in the first year of her widowhood on the Mesa.

I see it as very early morning. The windows, screened with cheese-cloth, are wide open. The cheesecloth stirs in no wind. There is a sense of suspended time, suspended heat, as if the whole night has been used up radiating away the heat of yesterday, and now it is all to start over again, the heat of today is ready to burst over the horizon and dry up this interval of cool twilight.

Susan Ward lies in the double brass bed, flat on her back, wide awake, staring straight upward with eyes that are dark and cried-out.

In a week she seems to have aged years; she is a worn, tense woman. The pillow beside hers has not been slept on.

Her head lifts slightly, she listens. In a moment she slips out of her bed in her nightgown and goes quickly to the window. Things outside, seen through the cheesecloth, look like an illustration, cool black and white and gray, patterned with the cheesecloth web like a fine-screen half tone.

Central in the picture is a horse, Oliver's blood bay gelding, standing with trailing reins in the middle of the lawn—that tender lawn on which even the children have been told to walk barefoot or not at all. Oliver himself is standing farther on, at the edge of the rose garden. He looms above the blooming bushes, he looks taller than the Lombardies along the western edge of the yard. The sky behind him is clear pale green; the sage that begins just outside the line of Lombardies sweeps away clear to the mountains, up the slopes and over them, spilling over the edge of the world.

Oliver stands with bent head, as if thinking. Then he leans, and with his bare hand takes hold of the white rose called the Blanc Double de Coubert. He pulls, and with a slow tough resistance the bush comes up by the roots. He drops it, takes two steps, and leans to take hold of the Mareschal Niel.

"Mother!"

Susan whirls around, and there is Betsy in the doorway. She has seen, she is already crying. It is all they have done for a week, cry.

"What's he *doing?*"

"Shh." Susan puts out her arm and takes the thin little nightgowned figure against her. Together they stand behind the cheesecloth screen and watch him go heavily, impassively, expressionlessly, up the row. One by one he tears the bushes from the ground and leaves them lying— Jacqueminot, American Beauty, Paul Fontaine—rose-pink, black-crimson, rich red. One by one, not yanking in a fury but tugging thoughtfully, almost absent-mindedly, he destroys one row and comes back along the other, down the long narrow bed. At the end, when it is all done, he stands inspecting his bloody hand, and then steps across the lawn and picks up the reins of the standing horse.

"Mother . . ."

"Shhh!" says Susan harshly, and sets her teeth in her lip.

The left hand gathers the reins over the neck, the bloody right hand turns the stirrup, the worn boot slips in, the weight swings up. The horse leaves deep hoofprints in the tender lawn. Not hurrying, he rides across through the sage and into the lane. He diminishes, not hurrying. His right hand is cradled against his stomach. He has not once looked at the house.

That was when she bundled her family together, or what was left of it, and fled eastward. That was about July 21, 1890. She thought then that her marriage, her hope, and her exile had all ended together, but in less than a month she was back in the ruins, trying to hold things together while she waited for something she didn't dare name.

She never blamed her husband for abandoning her in her grief and guilt, she never questioned the harshness of his judgment, she did not turn away from those dead roses that he left her for a sign. She thought he had suffered as much as she, and she knew that for his suffering she was to blame.

Nevertheless I, who looked up to him all his life as the fairest of men, have difficulty justifying that bleak and wordless break; and that ripping-up of the rose garden, that was vindictive and pitiless. I wish he had not done that. I think he never got over being ashamed, and never found the words to say so.

IX

THE ZODIAC COTTAGE

1

I didn't hear any car, I didn't hear footsteps on the gravel or up the ramp, I caught sight of no movement through the wistaria. Just, suddenly she opened the screen and was standing there, white-skinned in a green summer dress, behind our half circle of Grandmother's old wicker chairs drawn up in front of the television.

I was on the extreme right, she materialized on the left. It was all under my eye. In our abrupt immobility, the kinetic nervousness of our small arrested movements, we were like something out of an art movie, the camera focusing on mouths, hands, heads stopped in the motion of turning—successive images made portentous by the obsessiveness with which they were seen and the persistence with which they were returned to. Squashed scorpions on a white wall, two people talking, intensely unaware of being watched, in a parked car—Robbe-Grillet, that sort of thing. *Last Year at Marienbad*, revolving views around statues, moving views down halls, frozen and hypnotic and with held breath, and all the time the television screen jittering with meaningless motion as the Giant pitcher took his warmup throws for a new inning, and the catcher pegged down to second and the infielders peppered it around.

Ada, next to me, had twisted around and was sending out a squinted glare through the smoke of the cigarette that dangled between her lips. She knew who the woman was. So did Ed, in the next chair with a beer can between his feet. His eyes canted upward and sideward, he leaned and dropped his butt with a hiss into the can—a steady man getting his hands free in anticipation of trouble. Shelly had been interrupted in the act of clawing her hair back—a gesture which does not cease to trouble me, it is so like a deliberate provocation. Her liberation from the bra, which earlier in the summer was an occasional thing, seems now to be complete, an insistence, part of a life style that says take it or leave it. I have seen Ada eying her, disapproving, fascinated, and puzzled. I thought the visitor might note and misinterpret her costume; her arrogant nipples poked at the thin jersey, and her arm was raised as if to accentuate them. On her face the realization of who the visitor was came like a wind that turns up the underside of leaves in a tree.

Al Sutton, behind whom the woman had appeared, had leaped nimbly to his feet to offer his chair, and remained with his hand on the wicker back, while ten complicated responses went visibly through his computer, neutralizing each other. For a moment the only sound was the breath in his flat nostrils and the crowd noise of the ballgame. The wart flickered tentatively between his lips.

As for Lyman Ward, he twitched his chair around to face her, thinking furiously, above the pounding of his heart, *She's been sneaking around, spying.*

"Hello, Ellen," I said.

"Hello, Lyman."

Her skin was pale and pure. There was no gray in her hair—though that means nothing. Her eyes were still her best feature—dark blue, large, inquiring, like the eyes of a rather solemn child. They flashed around us once, she smiled and slipped into the chair that Al pushed toward her, sitting with her knees together and her hands holding her white summer handbag in her lap. Her skirt was short enough to be fashionable but not so short it looked frivolous. The exposed thigh looked firm. I saw it—I saw all of her—with the eyes of these curious, cautious others, and I observed that Mr. Ward's ex-wife, while not a beauty exactly, was an attractive older woman, well-preserved, well-dressed, citified in our slovenly country circle. How old? I am fifty-eight. That makes her fifty-three.

"You remember Ed and Ada Hawkes."

"Yes, of course. I think we met once, years ago. How do you do?"

Ada did not stand up or take the cigarette out of her mouth, but when Ellen stood and leaned and reached out her hand, Ada gave her three reluctant crooked fingers like Grendel's claw. She has never discussed my former wife with me, but I know what she thinks. She thinks I was callously abandoned when I was sick and helpless. With certain qualifications, that is what I think myself. I watched her in her city clothes, her face carefully friendly, that middle-aged well-kept composed American woman, break up and dominate our comfortable Saturday afternoon, and I was filled with hatred and terror. And curiosity. I looked for the signs in her of what Rodman had suggested—*She doesn't look good, she's shaky, she's had a bad time*—and couldn't see them, any more than I had seen, before her treachery, the signs of her growing intention.

Ed was politer than Ada. He stood up to shake hands, his face as creased and imperturbable as an old boot. One of the blessed things about Ed is his quietness. He is unflappable. He does not doubt, question, judge, or blame. He knows what he can do and lets others do what they can do. He deals with what is. It must have been that quality in his father that led Oliver Ward to make a driver and companion of him.

"This is Shelly," I said. "She's helping me with the book."

"Ah, yes!" Nothing that I could have specified changed in her face, fixed for friendliness, and yet as she leaned and shook Shelly's hand I saw her take in the revealing jersey pullover, the hair, the sprawl, the sloppy loafers, the shorts, the exposure of brown legs. She snapped that girl up as a bird snatches an insect on a lawn, and settled back with the expression of careful goodwill on her face and her mind made up that Shelly was wrong, impossible, would not do. "I've heard how you all look after him," she said. "My son says it's like a summer camp with one camper and three counselors."

It was a remark that we all resented; we let it fall without an answer. I gloried in the solidarity with which my gang met her—they were as stony as cliffs. But then I saw Al still standing, bereft of chair and ease, and I said, "This is Al Sutton, an old friend from away back in junior high school."

He wagged like a dog, he showed her his wart, he let her look up his nostrils clear to the back of his head. She was considerably shaken by what she saw, and turned away as soon as she politely could, and found herself facing me. When she first came in, she had taken me in stride. Now I saw her eyes widen. An expression of pain and revulsion grew in her face, and I became aware that my stump was flipping and flopping as if someone had just landed a salmon in my lap.

Protective and angry, I put both hands on it. "It does that sometimes," I said. I felt like saying, *It recognizes you.*

Everyone was watching and trying not to. Ellen sent me a beseeching urgent message with her eyebrows. I grew more and more confused, the stump twitched and jerked. Oh, do something! my ex-wife's face was saying. It's horrible!

Eventually I grabbed the newspaper from the side pocket of my chair and fumbled and flattened it out in my lap. The paper leaped and rustled. I put both hands on it, and through it took hold of that anguished stub of meat and bone and choked it down. When I dared, I took one hand away and shook two aspirins from the bottle into my palm, and threw them into my mouth and swallowed them without water. Immediately I was sorry I had done it. They had all watched every move, my gang protectively, she with a narrow-eyed, flinching interest. I sat there before her a hopeless case, twitched by spastic reflexes, pouring down pills. They made a hard, pebbly obstruction in my throat that I could not swallow.

And of course my two handmaidens, seeing me choked and watery-eyed from those dry pills, put on an act to prove that indeed they did take care of me. Ada grabbed off the cover of the Styrofoam cooler and reached out a beer and was about to pull the aluminum tab, but I waved my hands and stopped her, unable yet to speak.

"Ah, yeah," Ada said disgustedly, "I forgot you was on the wagon."

Shelly was on her feet. "Glass of water?"

I got the pills past the obstructing place and said, "Oh, sit down, quit fussing! Watch the ballgame."

We watched the ballgame.

Matty Alou walked on four straight pitches. Roberto Clemente on a 3–1 count hit one of Gaylord Perry's spitters to the base of the flagpole in centerfield, and Alou came all the way around. Out on the lawn the sprinkler kicked out its traveling arc of water. Our eyes were careful not to stray from the television screen. Under my hands I felt the leap and tension of the stump like the physical embodiment of my panic at seeing her there, a threat or a premonition.

I watched Willie Stargell come to the plate, reverse his bat, and knock dirt out of his spikes with the little end (baseball is like ballet, it is full of traditional movements). The camera was on Perry, pitching from the stretch. He leaned, got the signal, straightened, stretched his arms over his head, brought them down. His head turned; he glared at second base. Then his gloved right hand went wide, his long left arm went back, he threw. Stargell hit it over the right centerfield fence, and the television roared at us with a sound like a bathtub filling. Ed held his nose, Al Sutton laid the wart between his lips as if he were spitting out a seed. I sat there alert to my once-wife, intensely, acutely aware of her body, her feet, her knees, her white summer handbag like a white kitten in her lap, and wondered why she was there, what I could do, how I could escape, and with both hands I pressed on my stump the way a boy might hold onto his tumescent organ, gritting his teeth with emotions he is not prepared for and cannot cope with.

Quite suddenly Ed stood up. "It ain't our day. I might as well go take down those dead pines. You want 'em sawed into fireplace lengths?"

He is a remarkable man, Ed Hawkes. He understands a lot without having to be told. In one simple question he made up for the over-protectiveness of our women; he let me recover from my uncontrollable stump and the nervousness of those pills; he gave me the chance to say casually, "Sure, we can use a good woodpile this winter."

With a working of the eyebrows at me, a pleasant little nod at El-len, he went out. Ellen hardly noticed his going. Her eyes were on me, so that I turned myself a little away, absorbed in the ballgame. Outside I heard Ed moving the sprinkler and then running hard to get away from its moving arc. After a couple of minutes his pickup started and went out the drive.

I moved my body, for pain was working up the sawed-off bone clear into my hip joint, and as I turned, there was Ellen still watching me like the lady that's known as Lou, like a leopard in a tree, like a gun on the wall.

"You're staying on through the winter, then," she said.

"Of course."

"I understood there was some . . ."

"Question?" I said. "None that I ever heard of."

But of course I don't talk to Rodman, or that doctor, as you do. And don't drop your eyes to poor old Ada's crippled claws, or listen to her wheeze. She's as strong as a horse, she's good for a lot longer than I am.

My attention had wandered. I saw that my adherents and pro-tectors were on their feet, the whole bunch of them—Shelly with a decisive bounce, Al nimbly, not to be caught seated while a lady stood, Ada groaning up onto her bunion-bulged carpet slippers. She looked at Ellen Ward with dislike and resentment. "I guess them dishes won't do themselves. Shelly, you want to help?"

"I was thinking I'd better go sort out letters."

"What letters?" I said. "What dishes? Sit down, both of you. It's Saturday afternoon. Stick around."

"I've got fifteen years of Grass Valley letters still to put in order, and there isn't a lot of time," Shelly said.

"Isn't a lot of time before what?" I said.

"School starts in ten days."

"I thought you weren't . . ."

Smiling, she frowned a warning: not in front of Mom. I shut up, but she made me mad, talking about breakups just when all our conversation should emphasize the comfort and security of routine.

"Don't let all those Grass Valley things weigh on you," I said. "They're not important. All that is after."

"After what?"

"After everything's happened," I said crossly. "After I've lost interest."

"Didn't they put up a lot of refugees from the San Francisco fire and earthquake up here? I've just glanced through them, I thought I saw something about that."

"Yes," I said. "Who cares? Sit down. Watch the ballgame."

But she ignored my desperation, that insolent wench. She looked at me with her head on one side and said that if I didn't need her to work she guessed she'd go wash her hair. Brown-legged in her shorts, filling her cotton jersey, she smiled at Ellen, murmured a good-bye, and left.

Ada had already hoisted the beer cooler up onto her stomach. Her arms squeezed the top so that it popped off. She put it back on. Her fingers slipped and scrabbled on the Styrofoam, the last joints turned at excruciating angles. Her ankles sagged inward on her overweighted arches, her slippers with holes in them to ease the swollen big toe joints shuffled like crippled animals across the floor. None of this was lost on Ellen Ward.

Grunting, Ada got over the sill and inside. That left Al Sutton alone with the two of us, and he couldn't wait to be gone, though I begged him to stay and have another beer and help generate a Giant rally.

"Fat chanth," Al said. He was painfully embarrassed, laughed uneasily, shrugged, pulled out his quadruple focals from his shirt pocket and put them on and looked at the television through them, flinched back, said "Jethuth!", yanked the glasses off, laughed guiltily, put them in his pocket, took them out and put them on again, looked at me and then at Ellen through them, gave another hollow laugh like a groan. He pulled the glasses down on his nose, and the eyes which had been rolling and changing back of the lenses like the eyes of nigger baby dolls you used to throw baseballs at in county fairs looked at us with anguished kindness and apologetic goodwill. He stepped back into a chair. "Woopth, pardon," he said, and set it back where it had been before he bumped it. The wart appeared between his lips and was sucked back into a sweet imbecilic smile. "Boy, I better get out of here before I butht thomething," he said. "Nithe to meet you, Mitheth Ward. Lyman, you take care, now." He managed to get hold of the screendoor handle, let it slip, banged the door, yanked it open, walked into its edge, got by it, and clowning his own clumsiness, the back of his neck red, pulled his head between his shoulders, tightened his neck muscles and widened his mouth, picked up his feet very high and tiptoed away laughing hollowly, leaving me with the ballgame and my ex-wife.

The withered, whittled, hopelessly alive stump twitched and jerked under my down-pressing hands. Out on the lawn the sprinkler called attention to itself like a conspirator in a melodrama, *pst! pst! pst!*

Now! my fear and anger said to me, and I turned my chair to face her head on. She was not ready to meet me; she frowned down on her hands and handbag as if on the verge of some decision. I cried at her silently, You dare to come here and sit on my porch and drive away my friends! You dare to sit there as if you were welcome, or had a right? Do you remember at all what you did to me? Have you no shame? What do you want here? What have I got left that you'd like to take away from me?

She said to her pale hands, "This business of staying through the winter, of course you can't be serious."

537

"Oh yes I can," I said, and up came her eyes, one swift open look, dark blue, familiar, shocking. I find it hard to describe what it is like to look fully into eyes that one has known that well—known better than one knows the look of one's own eyes, actually—and then put away, deliberately forgotten. That instantly reasserted intimacy, that resumption of what looks like friendly concern, is like nakedness, like exposure. Right then it was as if a woman whom I despised and feared had opened her dress and revealed herself and smiled, asking something that made me rage and grit my teeth. One flicking look, no more. I held onto my stump and told myself oh, be careful!

"Who'll look after you?" said Ellen Ward in the reasonable tone she had used to use on adolescent Rodman when he wanted a motorcycle or demanded to go hitch hiking with a mixed crowd of high school students and spend Easter weekend on the beach at Carpinteria or La Jolla. "It's just not sensible. The young one's going—and you're well rid of her, if you ask me—and the old one's so crippled up she can't even hold a cigarette. She'll drop you and break your hip or something. You can't stand anything *else* wrong with you, darling."

"I can stand anything I have to stand!"

Her eyes came up again, she eyed me speculatively where I sat trapped in my chair. I was pressing down hard with my hands, but the newspaper in my lap shook and rustled. She smiled, to reassure me; then her eyes left me and went to the television. She half rose. "Do you want this on?"

I did not answer, glaring at her in defiance and despair. She shut off my ally, inconsequent motion and irrelevant noise. "Well, we can discuss it later." (Later?) "Now that I'm here, won't you show me the place?"

"I don't know that you'd like it."

"Not like it? It's lovely, so quiet and old fashioned. I was noticing the roses as I came in." She smiled; her teeth were pointed. "I'm sure it's been very good for you. It's only that once the weather gets bad, and with only that old woman, you can't . . ."

"She's about four years older than you," I said. But it was a boy's defeated bleat. She smiled with her filed teeth, ignoring my hostility.

"Come on, show me around. I want to see the yard and the house and all of it. Where you work, where you sleep." The way she smiled and smiled made me frantic with apprehension. Coaxingly she said, "Can't I be allowed a *little* curiosity about you?"

The *monster*.

I spun the chair and started for the screen door, either intending to escape or to hold it open while she passed through—who can say for sure?—but she was alert, she got there first and held it for *me*.

I saw that I had no choice but to take her around, and I resolved cunningly that the sooner she saw everything, the sooner she would leave. On the way up through the orchard I gave the chair full throttle, trying to outrun her, but my batteries were low and she easily kept up. The fruit was reddening among the leaves of Grandfather's old apple trees, the wasps were busy in the windfalls, the air smelled of cider and incipient fall.

At the top I wheeled into the flat path along the fence, and stopped. "This is where I do my daily dozen," I said. I lifted the crutches out of their cradle, laid them across the chair arms, and with my hands pushed myself up until I stood on my one leg.

"What are you going to do?" she said.

"Take my exercise. Do you mind waiting a few minutes?"

"Must you, now?"

"This is the time."

I took pleasure in the anxiety on her face. Now let's see who's helpless, I said to her, or thought at her. Let's see who needs looking after. I had the crutches in my armpits, my one foot was on the footboard, my hands felt the weight as it came on them. First one crutch on the ground, then the other. Now the part that called for concentration. Lean, hop. There. Smooth as glass. Furious, pumping like three-legged racers at a picnic, I swung off up the path, out from under the hand she put anxiously out to steady me. Steady yourself, I thought. A bit late, there. Always a bit late.

Turning and pumping back, I enjoyed the consternation in her face. I swung, I pegged, I flew, I turned with the precision of a guardsman in front of Buckingham Palace and went pounding up the path again. Let her stand there and get an eyeful of my independence and my manual skill and the endurance left in the old carcass she pretended to be so concerned about. Lost your boy friend, did you? I said as I dug and swung. Like to be asked in out of the cold? Well the hell with you. I don't need you. I've got a life I'm content with. Every afternoon I run up and down this course—my version of jogging. One legged or not, I'm in shape. Jumping stump or not, pains and pills or not, it isn't an utter has-been you're dealing with. Get an eyeful.

I intended the full eight laps, or maybe more, but at the end of six I knew I had to stop it. My heart was bursting my chest, my stump was red hot, I had to swallow my breathing so that she wouldn't hear it. All casually, ready to pop, I swung my foot up onto the footboard and started to turn, ready to let myself down. But the chair rolled a few inches, I was thrown off balance, I dropped the left crutch and grabbed for the arm. And she was right there, bracing me. I was half leaning on her. I could smell her.

Trembling, I eased myself down into the seat. She kept hold of my arm until I was down, and then stooped and retrieved the fallen crutch. She said nothing; her face wore an erased, concealing look.

"Thank you," I said, and put the crutch in its cradle. Raging with humiliation, my stump making tired, convulsive jerks, I started back down toward the rose garden.

She came along, but she stayed back so that I could not see her. I had the sense that she watched me, and her silence worked on me like a poultice. I babbled, telling her how Grandfather had started this rose garden even before Zodiac Cottage was built, back when he and Grandmother and Betsy lived in the little house where Ed and Ada Hawkes lived now. How he spent all his evenings and weekends puttering, developing his own hybrids. I showed her some of them, or the descendants of some of them, cuttings made by my father, or by Ed Hawkes after Father began to lose his buttons. A real family rose garden, three generations old, some of the varieties unique. I took pride in it, more than I had all summer. It seemed to me then that my own position was more secure if that rose garden was important to me. I told her that until Father got so eccentric that he drove people away, rose fanciers used to come from all over to see that garden, and beg or buy plants or cuttings.

To all of my babble she made no response except an occasional murmur. I couldn't tell whether I was boring her, or whether she was using the rose garden tour as an excuse to study me from behind. I hoped I bored her stiff, I hoped she could make not one thing out of the unmoving back of my head. I wanted her to go away, I wanted to wear her out. Purposely I led her around the paths that were still in the sun, where it was baking hot. But she came along, murmuring, invisible, and I went before her like a man with a gun in his back, scared to turn around, until we came to the old arched arbor at the far end, covered with the small dark glossy foliage of a climber rose. There I stopped.

"That's one of his hybrids," I said. "He never sold or gave away that one. Privately he called it the Agnes Ward, for my aunt who died in childhood. He crossed some sort of moss rose with the old Harison yellow climber they used to have in Idaho, and got this climber with red blooms tipped with yellow. In certain lights they're like flames."

I sat aimed through the arbor like a key about to enter a keyhole. From behind me she said, "I wish it was in bloom," and then a moment later, "What a lovely idea, to make a rose in memory of someone!"

"It was about the only way he had," I said. "As far as I know, he and Grandmother never mentioned her name. You know the old Cockney ballad—'Now 'er picture's turned fyce to the wall'. That sort of thing."

"Really? My goodness, what did she do?"

"Nothing," I said. "She was a sort of fairy child, and she died. Isn't that enough?"

"No. It isn't enough to explain why they'd just—wipe her out."

"They didn't wipe her out. They just never spoke of her. But they didn't wipe her out. After all, Grandfather made a rose. He made a dozen roses, in fact, trying for just the right one. You know how long it takes to cross and fix a hybrid rose? Two or three years. He could never get just what he wanted. He liked these blooms, but he couldn't get them in a repeater. If he got one that would go on blooming, something was wrong with the color, or it didn't have any odor. If he hung onto the color he wanted, it bloomed in May and was done for the season. Eventually he had to give up and accept a brief, early blooming."

She stood behind me, silent. I had the unpleasant sensation that her hand was resting on the back of my chair, as if she were my keeper or nurse ready to push me further around on my dull afternoon airing. I gave the chair some power and moved two feet, but felt no drag from a hand. Under the arbor the air was dense and warm, and came thickly into my lungs. I heard the woman say, "How do you know all this about the rose, if he never talked about her?"

"Oh, he talked to *me*."

"But not to your grandmother?"

"No."

"Why?"

It was a moment I had been half-consciously maneuvering for. "Because my grandfather was a man who couldn't forget," I said. "Forget or forgive."

Her feet stirred in the gravel. In a voice that I listened to intently —it sounded small and swallowed—she said, "He sounds like a hard man."

"On the contrary, he was soft. People imposed on him. Grandmother always said he was too trusting. Actually he never expected much of people, and so he wasn't upset if they turned out to be shysters or chiselers or crooks. But a few people he trusted absolutely. It was when *they* betrayed him that he turned to rock. Come on, I'll show you the vegetable garden."

I started the chair, talking straight out ahead of myself, through the arbor and around the corner of the house. Hurrying, almost running, her feet caught up with me and came close along behind.

Maybe I addled my brains, running around out there in the late sun. I felt confused, and also I felt a wicked compulsion to show that woman every leaf of every pole bean, every cluster of green and ripe on the tomato plants, every ear on every cornstalk. Show me the place, she said. All right, she would see it. I led her around in every corner, I lost track of time, and when, worn out myself, I brought her back up the ramp and onto the veranda, it seemed so late and dusky that I called to Ada, expecting her to be in the kitchen. No one answered. I called again. In the hollow house my voice hummed as if I had shouted into a cello. As I listened for some reply I became aware that the porch screen had not slammed shut behind me. Ellen must still be in the doorway, half in, half out, the screen door held by her hand or caught on her thrust-back heel. Reluctantly, more to break the listening stillness of the house than to make her welcome, I moved ahead. In a moment I heard the screen click shut. She was in there with me, absolutely alone.

"May I see the house?" she said. "I'd like to see where you live and do your work."

Still looking away from her into the shadowy house—who dares look behind him, what child walking under dark trees has the courage to do anything but look straight ahead and put one foot after another and try to keep from breaking into a panicky run?—I said, "I live and work upstairs. We don't use any of the downstairs at all except the kitchen and once in a while the library."

"Show me the upstairs, then."

She was implacable. She stood behind me and insisted on wedging herself back into my life. But the thought of her upstairs in my intimate rooms filled me with dread. I listened. I called once more for Ada, and the house gulped that one little living word as a big fish gulps a minnow; I could hear it, or feel it, quivering after it was down. The thought that they had all gone and left me, given me up to this woman, blackened my sight with terror. I needed to get a look at her, I wanted to know what her face showed as she stood behind me, hooked as close to me as my shadow, but I did not dare turn my chair around. And so I said, "Well, you might as well see it down here. It used to be quite a place," and rolled over the ramped sill and into the hall.

As we rolled or floated through the rooms and I turned through doorways I got a glimpse or two of her coming along, serious, pale, wearing a slight knitted frown. She was carrying her shoes in her hand, and in her stockinged feet she followed me without a sound. It infuriated me all afresh to see her take that liberty, as if she belonged. Holding the pantry door open for her, I watched her pass briefly in front of me, blank as some Blessed Damozel, moving as if some wind blew her; and nothing would serve but that I should put myself again in front of her before she would move on.

I fled her along the bare redwood walls dark with age, past the bare fieldstone fireplaces, under the high beamed ceilings, through doorways where the plank floors gathered light in dim long pools. Any ordinary passage through those rooms reverberated, but I on my rubber wheels and she in her stockinged feet passed through as silently as spiders spin their webs, or dust settles. In the library the pale square on the wall where Grandmother's portrait used to hang stared at us. The books were dead in their shelves.

In that stagnant air the oppression of her soundless inescapable unspeaking presence grew on me, and by the time we were back in the front hall I was sweating; my hands stuck to the arms of the chair as I turned it, at bay, at the bottom of the lift.

"Well," I said, "that's it." I was facing her full on, doing my best to be Gorgon but feeling cornered rat. "This is where I live. I live very comfortably, as you can see. I've got good help. Now if you'll excuse me, I have some things to do."

But she did not go away like a dismissed student. She stood in front of me, her eyes questioning and her mouth faintly smiling, and I heard my ridiculous speech die out in the hall. There was not a sound anywhere in the house—no pans or dishes or running water in the kitchen, no typing or footsteps upstairs. Sometime while we were inspecting the grounds, Ed must have returned and shut off the sprinkler. I wiped a hand across my greasy face. "Ada?" I called into the stillness. "Shelly?"

Whimpers, made all the worse by the fact that I was holding my Gorgon gaze on her and she was unaffected. It splintered against hers, which was, so far as I could see, only soft and sad and thoughtful. I couldn't talk past or around her, I had to talk at her.

"Good-bye," I said. "I'd be lying if I said I'd enjoyed your visit, but I don't wish you any harm. Go with God."

I actually used that phrase. *Vaya con Dios, mi alma, vaya con Dios mi amor.* Go with *God?* Go with my curse, go with my spittle on your face and dress, I surely meant to say. In my confusion I fumbled the chair around and backed it onto the lift and finally locked it on and pressed the switch.

To my horror she came along beside me, floating up the stairs in her stockinged feet as if she had been filled with helium: she had stepped onto the lift beside the locked wheel of the chair. For the first time I began to fear that I would never get rid of her at all; her beak would never be out of my heart or her form off my door. Helpless, backward, unable to draw ahead or fall behind, helpless even to turn my head and look at my succubus, I was dragged upward.

And yet when we reached the top, and I found myself intact, untouched, and was able to unlock myself and roll free into the broad hall, my sweating fear was eased. I could look at her, and she looked harmless, even humble. I felt exhilarated; I could hardly wait to show off my arrangements, I *wanted* her to see the private center of my independent life. Rolling down toward the study's open door, I ran my hand along the satiny redwood wainscot. I pointed out the beauty of the rubbed plank floors, such floors as you couldn't find short of Japan. One of the earliest Maybeck houses, this—a landmark. A pity if they should ever tear it down. It ought to be turned over, and I would see that it was, to the National Trust.

I stopped and made her go into the study ahead of me. She went willingly, and I had to wonder if I had imagined all that implacable pursuit that had seemed to follow me around the garden and through the downstairs. Inside, she looked over my desk, the pictures and framed letters on the walls, the files, the folders of still-unordered letters, the dormer with its squared glimpse of pine tops and evening sky. She stood before Susan Ward's portrait a good while.

"Is this your grandmother?"

"Susan Burling Ward. You ought to remember her, from pictures."

"I guess I never paid much attention. But she looks the way I sort of imagined her."

"Good."

"Sensitive and high-minded."

"She was all of that."

"But not happy."

"Well, that was painted when she was close to sixty."

She turned, and there they were side by side, my ex-grandmother and my ex-wife, two women upon whom I have expended a lot of thought and feeling, the one pensive, with downcast eyes, in a wash of side lighting, the other pale, dark-haired, sober, with a pucker in her brows and the eyes of a hurt and wondering child. Female animals, wives, mothers, civilized women. Ellen said, "Can't a woman of sixty be happy?"

"Why ask me?" I said. "As Grandmother's biographer, I'd have to guess she was never really happy after, say, her thirty-seventh year, the last year when she lived an idyll in Boise Canyon."

Her eyes troubled me. Why should the *Gorgon* have to drop his lids?

"But she lived a long time after that," Ellen said.

"She lived to be ninety-one. My grandfather lived to be eighty-nine. She had practically no time to be senile and alone."

"But she wasn't happy."

"She wasn't unhappy, either. Do you have to be one or the other?"

I focused into the middle of her dark blue, wondering glance. I focused, actually, between her eyes, and I was thinking as I appeared to look at her, Why does an unblinking, wide-eyed, questioning look always strike me as *unintelligent*? Is it? Or is it possible it is only open, *willing*?

My brief exhilaration had passed. Out the window, the sky was losing its light, there was no sun on the pines. Where on earth was Ada? It was away past the time she should have come to start my dinner. The dread came back and squatted like a toad on my heart. Suddenly, before the woman could question or stop me, I had wheeled to the side of the bed and was dialing the telephone. On the fourth ring it was answered: Shelly, sounding as usual like a longshoreman.

"Hello," I said. "Is your mother there?"

"I was just going to call you," she said. "We've had a kind of time. She's sick—some sort of seizure. Dad's taking her in to the hospital right now. I probably ought to go along. Do you think you could wait supper till I get back? Maybe an hour?"

Heavy and coarse as a man's, her voice boomed and crackled in my ear. She sounded excited and hurried and breathless, as if she had had to run to the phone.

"Of course," I said. "My Lord, yes. You do whatever she needs, don't worry about me. I can make a sandwich. Give her my love."

"O.K.," said her breathless baritone. "I guess that's . . . I'll be over later, then. Don't try to fix your own, I'll be there. O.K.?"

"What?"

"Horizontal. Permanently."

"Ah!" She moved her shoulders, half turned, looked at me and away. Talking to Grandmother's portrait she said, "Death? Living death? Fifty years of it? No rest till they lay down? There must be something . . . short of that. She couldn't have been doing penance for fifty years."

I shrugged.

Skating in her stockings, the nylon faintly hissing on the floor, she carried her drink over near the desk, where she stood a while inspecting the piles of letter folders, the books, the tape recorder, the manila envelope of Xeroxed news stories from Boise. I was afraid she might open that and read, but instead she opened a folder of letters. With her mouth ruefully pursed, she read a while, folded the folder shut. Then she lifted her chin and looked closely at the spurs, the bowie, and the revolver hanging in their broad leather on the wall.

"What's this? Local color?"

I thought her manner veiled and unconvincing; it seemed to me that since my outburst I was in charge, not she; she had lost the initiative.

"Grandmother had them hanging there when I was a boy," I said. "I found them and put them back."

"I didn't know she was the cowgirl type."

Too flippant; patter words. I nailed her down.

"They were to remind her of whom she was married to."

Her back was toward me, the shoulderblades showing through the thin green cotton. She did not turn even part way, but spoke to the wall. "You make it sound like such punishment. Didn't they get along at all?"

"They got along," I said. "They respected each other. They treated one another with a sort of grave infallible kindness."

I saw her thin shoulders shrink and shiver. Still without turning, she said, "It sounds just . . . awful. And yet he must have been a warm and decent man, to think of making a rose in memory of his daughter. And he had been—you say—treated badly, and still he was big enough to take her back."

"O.K." I hung up.

"What is it?" Ellen said, though I was sure she had heard it all—Shelly's voice came out of the earpiece as if out of a megaphone. What luck! Ellen's face said. Just what we were hoping for! It was bound to happen sooner or later, she was really *too* decrepit.

Her shoes were still in her hand, her head was on one side. "You need a drink," she said. "You look sunk." Bending, she slipped on her pumps, one, then the other. "Where's there a bottle? You don't want to go on with that nonsense about being on the wagon. This is an emergency. I'll fix you a drink and then I'll go see what I can find for you to eat."

"I can wait. Shelly'll be over in an hour."

"No, no. Why should you?"

She came in like a reserve quarterback hot to prove the injustice of his being kept out of the game. Helpless and troubled, I stared at her, unable to find the words that would stop her. I let her fix the drink, popping two aspirins into my mouth while her back was turned. I put out a cold and sweating hand and took the cold, sweating glass.

"Would you like the television up here, for news or anything?"

I felt like something stiff and rigid propped in the corner. "No thank you."

"Anything else you need? Any pills or anything?"

"Nothing. I'm fine."

"Well, you just sit and enjoy your drink. I'll be back in a jiffy."

Her heels on the planks were brisk, she went down the stairs in a clatter—nimble, well-preserved, and vigorous. I sat by the window and let the bourbon wash around in my mouth—and why in hell had I let her subvert me, after a week of will power?—and warm the ball of cold putty in the middle of my chest. Every sound that came up from downstairs had my ears on end. Talk about a little Kafka animal sweating down its hole! Once I thought I heard her singing as she worked. I downed the drink in a few gulps, and quickly, before she could get back up the lift and prevent me with some female notion of what was good for me, wheeled over to the refrigerator and sloshed another couple of ounces onto the ice in my glass and wheeled back. I was waiting there with an empty glass, my chair turned so that I could look out the window and watch night come on, when she came upstairs with a tray.

"Tell me about your book," she said while I sat eating the soup and sandwiches and fruit and milk she had brought. She herself was walking restlessly around the room, stocking-footed again, a drink in her hand. She seemed to dislike the sound of her heels on the bare floors —very different from her son. "What do you call it?"

"I don't know yet. I was thinking of calling it *Angle of Repose*."

Her sliding and pacing stopped; she considered what I had said. "Is that a very good title? Will it sell? It sounds kind of . . . inert."

"How do you like *The Doppler Effect*? Is that any better?"

"The Doppler Effect? What's that?"

"Forget it. It doesn't matter. The title's the least of it. I might call it *Inside the Bendix*. It isn't a book anyway, it's just a kind of investigation into a life."

"Your grandmother's."

"Yes."

"Why she wasn't happy."

"That's not what I'm investigating. I know why she wasn't happy."

She stopped halfway across the floor, her drink in her hand, her eyes bent down into the glass as if Excalibur, or a water baby, or a djinn, or something, might rise out of it.

"Why wasn't she?"

I set my half-eaten sandwich down on the tray that boxed me into the chair, and took one shaking hand in the other, and cried, "You want to know why? You don't know? Because she considered that she'd been unfaithful to my grandfather, in thought or act or both. Because she blamed herself for the drowning of her daughter, the one Grandfather made the rose for. Because she was responsible for the suicide of her lover—if he *was* her lover. Because she'd lost the trust of her husband and son. Does that answer your question?"

Her lowered head had come up, her half-shuttered eyes widened and stared. She looked ready to run. I had reached her, all right. That air of self-confidence was a mask, that insouciant way of sliding with arched foot around my rubbed plank floors was an act. Underneath, she was as panicky as I was. For a good second her deep eyes were fixed on mine, her face was tense and set. Then she lowered her head, dropped

548

her lashes, backed away from the attack I had thrown at her unaware, arched her foot and slid it experimentally along a crack in the planks. As if indifferently, speaking to the floor, she said, "And this happened . . . when?"

"1890."

"But they went on living together."

"No they didn't!" I said. "Oh, no! He left, pulled out. Then she left too, but she came back. She lived in Boise alone for nearly two years, while he was working in Mexico. Then his brother-in-law Conrad Prager, one of the owners of the Zodiac, brought him up here to devise pumps that would keep the lower levels from flooding. Prager and his wife, Grandfather's sister, worked on him, and eventually got him to write my grandmother, and she came down. My father all this time was in school in the East—he never came home. He never came home, in fact, for years—Grandmother and Grandfather had been back together seven or eight years before Father ever showed his face here."

Large and dark, looking black in that light, her eyes rested on me. She said nothing, but her mouth twitched, the sort of twitch that is extracted by a stomach cramp.

"So they lived happily-unhappily ever after," I said. "Year after irrelevant year, half a century almost, through one world war and through the Jazz Age and through the Depression and the New Deal and all that; through Prohibition and Women's Rights, through the automobile and radio and television and into the second world war. Through all those changes, and not a change in them."

"That's what you told your secretary, What's-her-name, you weren't interested in."

"Exactly. It's all over in 1890."

"When they broke up."

"Exactly."

For a while she was silent, sliding her silken big toe down the crack between two planks, taking a step to follow it, sliding it again. Her head came up, the whites of her eyes flashed at me. "What do you mean, 'Angle of Repose'?"

"I don't know what it meant for her. I've been trying to make out. She said it was too good a phrase for mere dirt. But I know what it means for me."

549

"He was a warm and decent man," I said. I stared in hatred at her thin narrow back, I felt my voice rising and could not keep it down. "He was as decent a man as ever lived!" I said furiously. "He was the kindest, most trusting, easiest-to-get-on-with man I ever knew. My father always made me uneasy, but my grandfather made me feel *safe*. All he had to do was take hold of my hand and I was in the King's X place."

Even yet she did not turn, though she must have heard the edge of hysteria cracking in my voice. Dully she said to the bowie and horse pistol and spurs, "But you were fond of her too."

"I loved her. She was a lady."

"A lady who made a terrible mistake."

"And recognized it," I said. "Admitted it, repented it, accepted the consequences, did her best to live it down. Her real mistake was that she never appreciated him enough until it was too late."

The still, thin, bowed back never moved; she seemed hypnotized by the belted weapons on the wall. Her voice was small when it came. "What makes you think . . ."

I moved the tray aside, tipping over half a glass of milk, and set it on the table by the window. The very way she stood, facing away from me, submissive but reproachful, made me mad. I hit the power button, I rolled over behind her. It was all I could do to keep from raising my hands and hitting her on her frail shoulderblades. I wanted to slap her until she turned around and cowered and listened, really listened. I heard my voice let go in shouting, my stump flopped around my lap.

"But he never forgave her," I said. "She broke something she couldn't mend. In all the years I lived with them I never saw them kiss, I never saw them put their arms around each other, I never saw them touch!"

I was strangling on my words, my tongue was three times too big for my mouth. Weeping, I wheeled into the bathroom and slammed the door.

For a long time I heard nothing. I sat in the bathroom's reflective dazzle of light and glared at the one-legged poltroon—from Italian *poltrona*, a large chair—in the mirror above the washbowl. Stains of tears on the face, a gritting impotent anguish around the mouth, eyes that burned, hair that was gray, thin, and mussed. Napkin still spread in his lap from his invalid's tray, and under the napkin a jerky, spasmodic twitching, as if a monstrous phallus were being moved by fitful satyriasis in its sleep.

I saw him grow alert, not by cocking his head as an ordinary man might do, but by swinging the chair a little way around. He left contemplating himself in the mirror and rolled silently, a wheel's turn across the tiles, to listen at the door.

"Where is he?" I heard Shelly's deep voice say.

"In the bathroom," said the other voice. "How's your mother?"

"All right, I guess. They've given her digitalis."

"Her heart, is it?"

"I guess. A lot of pain in her chest and down her arm, and her pulse all irregular, way up and racing one second, and the next so faint you could hardly feel it. Arrhythmia, they call it. It isn't necessarily so serious, but it's scary. She really had us panicked."

Careful female voices, a dark and a light, carefully friendly, carefully open. They came on invisible waves through the hollow-core door to the rigid head, the listening ear. The light one said, "It must have been frightening. You shouldn't have tried to come over here."

"Oh, no trouble," said the dark one. "She's all right now. But she was worried about Mr. Ward. Has he had anything to eat?"

"I fixed him a tray."

"Oh. How about his bath?"

"His bath?"

"He has to have a hot bath every night, to soak out the pain so he can sleep."

"Yes. Well, I'll see that he takes it."

"He can't *take* it. He has to be given it. He can't climb in and out of a bath tub with one leg."

"All right, then I'll give it to him."

"I'd better do it. I know the routines."

I could not see the face of the man in the chair, listening behind the door, but I could feel the sweat that had been greasy on his skin ever since the woman arrived on the porch. The politeness was still there in the women's voices, but it was under a strain, it could crack any minute.

"Have you . . . given him his bath before?" said Light.

"Not usually. Mom does it," said Dark.

"Ever?" said Light.

"What does it matter?" said Dark. "I know how it's done, you don't."

Pause. Finally Light said, "Since you haven't given it to him before, I think I could do it quite as well, and a little more appropriately. There's really no need of your staying, Miss . . ."

"Rasmussen," said Dark. "Mrs. And I don't know about that appropriateness. Where have you been all summer, while we've been taking care of him? If he didn't want us to take care of him he wouldn't have hired us."

But he didn't! said the man listening ratlike behind the door.

"I understood that he had hired you as a secretary," said Light.

That's right! said the man behind the door. Your mother ran you out the one time you tried to come in! You stay out of here!

To his horror the door burst open, she came in, rolling him back. She seemed to have grown two feet, she was huge and broad-shouldered in a turtle-necked jersey within which her unconfined breasts bulged like eggplants, like melons. The man in the chair tried to dart past her out into the studio, but she blocked his way, shut the door, and put it on the chain.

"All right," she said cheerfully. "No tricks, now."

Like a bug trapped in a matchbox he darted from corner to corner. The door opened an inch, all the chain would allow, and he saw Ellen Ward's face peering in. She was pounding angrily on the door with her fists. The bathroom was as hollow as a drum.

"Now," said Shelly Rasmussen, turning on the hot water. Steam billowed up, half concealing her. Stooping to flop a hand in the rising water, she had to turn her face. Her hand clawed back her wet hair. With an impatient grunt she sat back from the tub and hauled the jersey over her head and threw it aside and bent back in, testing. Her great breasts hung into the tub, steam rose around her. Terribly smiling, nine feet tall, she stood up in the cloud of steam and put her fists on her hips. The eyes of her breasts looked at him insolently. As if amused by his fascinated, terrified, hypnotized gaze, she did a little bump and grind.

"Come on!" she cried. "Let's have a look at you. Off with those clothes."

She approached, he retreated, darted, got his hand on the chain, had to let go as she lunged. Ellen was pounding on the outside of the door, the tub was filling, the room was white with steam. For a wild instant his face raced across the mirror, a smear of terror, and then she had him. Her hands were at his fly, unzipping, tugging—the pants were gone. He clung to his shirt until it was torn from his back. He sat exposed in his underwear, his urine bottle strapped to his leg, its tube disappearing inside the slit of his shorts.

"Ah-ha!" cried Shelly Rasmussen. "You old dickens! Come on now, no secrets from me!"

Leaning over his chair, her great breasts hanging like water-filled balloons inches from his nose, she tried to tear his protecting hands away. He fought her off but she was back at once. He fought her off again, and she got hold of the tube and pulled, so that he had to spread his hands to cover his emerging organ, yanked like a fish out of water. "Ha ha!" she said. "You old dickens, look at that!"

To his horror, he felt the stump of his leg begin to swell and lift, filling with pleasurable warmth. It rose until it lifted clear out of his lap like a fireplace log, its stitched and cicatriced end red and swollen. He saw Shelly Rasmussen's admiration. She laughed, softly and hoarsely, and reached again.

"No!" he cried. "No!"

Weakly he pissed down the tube, and at once the great stump subsided, sank, went flabby, collapsed into his lap. Shelly Rasmussen took one disgusted look and grabbed up her turtleneck and left. She didn't bother to shut the door, and now Ellen Ward stood above him looking down. Her eyes were dark, and their edges were red with crying; she touched the deflated stump with tenderness. "You see?" she said. "It wasn't right to let *her*. It's my job."

Her face was close to his, so close that he could see the mottled coloring of the irises and the smudged skin under the tight curly hair of her brows where she had darkened them. She bent closer still, her mouth tender, her eyes sad. The eyes grew enormous, widened until they filled the whole field of his vision, shutting out the glare of light on white tile, the aseptic porcelain, the blank mirror. Closer and larger grew her eyes until, blurred by proximity, inches from his own, they were the eyes that a lover or a strangler would have seen, bending to his work.

That was the dream I woke from half an hour ago, my pajamas soaked with sweat, my bottle full—it was a piss-the-bed dream if I ever had one, but confusingly like a wet dream of adolescence too. It took me, in fact, all of five minutes to persuade myself that it *was* all a dream, that I had really pissed the bottle full instead of having an emission, that none of those women had been there, that Ada had had no heart attack, that Shelly had not come in brawling like a drunken logger to rape me in my bath. It made me think, I tell you. I am not so silly as to believe that what I dream about other people represents some sort of veiled or occult truth about them, but neither am I so stupid as to reject the fact that it represents some occult truth about *me*.

For a while I lay here feeling pretty bleak—old, washed-up, helpless, and alone. It was as black as a coalmine, there was no sound through the open window, not the slightest threshing or singing of the pines. Then I heard a diesel coming on the freeway, taking a full-tilt run at the hill. In my mind I could see it charging up that empty highway like Malory's Blatant Beast, its engine snorting and bellowing, its lights glaring off into dark trees and picking up the curve of white lines, a blue cone of flame riding six inches above its exhaust stack, its song full of exultant power. I listened to it and felt the little hairs rise on the back of my neck, tickling me where my head met the pillow.

Then the inevitable. The song of power weakened by an almost imperceptible amount, and no sooner had that sound of effort come into it than the tone changed, went down a full third, as the driver shifted. Still powerful, still resistless, the thing came bellowing on, and then its tone dropped again, and almost immediately a third time. Something was out of it already; confidence was out of it. I could imagine the driver, a midget up in the dim cab, intent over his web of gears, three sticks of them, watching the speedometer and the steepening road and the cone of fire above his stack, and tilting his ear to the moment when the triumphant howl of his beast began to waver or shrink. Then the foot, the hand, and for a few seconds, a half minute, the confident song of power again, but lower, deeper, less excited and more determined. Down again where the grade stiffened past Grass Valley, and then down, down, down, three different tones, and finally there it was at the dutiful bass growl that would take it all the way over the range, and even that receding, losing itself among the pines.

I reached the microphone off the bed table and told my dream onto tape, for whatever it may be worth, and now I lie here on my back, wide awake, cold from my sweating, the plastic microphone lying against my upper lip and my thumb on the switch, and wonder if there is anything I want to say to myself.

"What do you mean, 'Angle of Repose'?" she asked me when I dreamed we were talking about Grandmother's life, and I said it was the angle at which a man or woman finally lies down. I suppose it is; and yet it was not that that I hoped to find when I began to pry around in Grandmother's life. I thought when I began, and still think, that there was another angle in all those years when she was growing old and older and very old, and Grandfather was matching her year for year, a separate line that did not intersect with hers. They were vertical people, they lived by pride, and it is only by the ocular illusion of perspective that they can be said to have met. But he had not been dead two months when she lay down and died too, and that may indicate that at that absolute vanishing point they did intersect. They had intersected for years, for more than he especially would ever admit.

There must be some other possibility than death or lifelong penance, said the Ellen Ward of my dream, that woman I hate and fear. I am sure she meant some meeting, some intersection of lines; and some cowardly, hopeful geometer in my brain tells me it is the angle at which two lines prop each other up, the leaning-together from the vertical which produces the false arch. For lack of a keystone, the false arch may be as much as one can expect in this life. Only the very lucky discover the keystone.

It will do to think about. For though Ellen Ward was not here this afternoon and evening, I am sure she will be here, or her representatives will be here, sooner or later. If she does not come of her own volition, or at Rodman's urging, I can even conceive, in this slack hour, that I might send for her. Could I? Would I?

Wisdom, I said oh so glibly the other day when I was pontificating on Shelly's confusions, is knowing what you have to accept. In this not-quite-quiet darkness, while the diesel breaks its heart more and more faintly on the mountain grade, I lie wondering if I am man enough to be a bigger man than my grandfather.

RECAPITULATION
Bruce Mason returns to Salt Lake City not to perform the perfunctory arrangements for his aunt's funeral but to exorcise the ghosts of his past.
ISBN 0-14-026673-9

REMEMBERING LAUGHTER
In the novel that marked his literary debut, Stegner depicts the dramatic, moving story of an Iowa farm wife whose spirit is tested by a series of events as cruel and inevitable as the endless prairie winters.
ISBN 0-14-025240-1

A SHOOTING STAR
Sabrina Castro follows a downward spiral of moral disintegration as she wallows in regret over her dissatisfaction with her older and successful husband.
ISBN 0-14-025241-X

THE SOUND OF MOUNTAIN WATER
Essays, memoirs, letters, and speeches, written over a period of twenty-five years, which expound upon the rapid changes in the West's cultural and natural heritage.
ISBN 0-14-026674-7

THE SPECTATOR BIRD
Stegner's National Book Award–winning novel portrays retired literary agent Joe Allston, who passes through life as a spectator—until he rediscovers the journals of a trip he took to his mother's birthplace years before.
ISBN 0-14-013940-0

WHERE THE BLUEBIRD SINGS TO THE LEMONADE SPRINGS
Living and Writing in the West
Sixteen brilliant essays about the people, the land, and the art of the American West.
ISBN 0-14-017402-8

WOLF WILLOW
A History, a Story, and a Memory of the Last Plains Frontier
Introduction by Page Stegner
In a recollection of his boyhood in southern Saskatchewan, Stegner creates a wise and enduring portrait of a pioneer community existing on the verge of the modern world.
ISBN 0-14-118501-5

FOR THE BEST IN PAPERBACKS, LOOK FOR THE

In every corner of the world, on every subject under the sun, Penguin represents quality and variety—the very best in publishing today.

For complete information about books available from Penguin—including Penguin Classics, Penguin Compass, and Puffins—and how to order them, write to us at the appropriate address below. Please note that for copyright reasons the selection of books varies from country to country.

In the United States: Please write to *Penguin Group (USA), P.O. Box 12289 Dept. B, Newark, New Jersey 07101-5289* or call 1-800-788-6262.

In the United Kingdom: Please write to *Dept. EP, Penguin Books Ltd, Bath Road, Harmondsworth, West Drayton, Middlesex UB7 0DA.*

In Canada: Please write to *Penguin Books Canada Ltd, 10 Alcorn Avenue, Suite 300, Toronto, Ontario M4V 3B2.*

In Australia: Please write to *Penguin Books Australia Ltd, P.O. Box 257, Ringwood, Victoria 3134.*

In New Zealand: Please write to *Penguin Books (NZ) Ltd, Private Bag 102902, North Shore Mail Centre, Auckland 10.*

In India: Please write to *Penguin Books India Pvt Ltd, 11 Panchsheel Shopping Centre, Panchsheel Park, New Delhi 110 017.*

In the Netherlands: Please write to *Penguin Books Netherlands bv, Postbus 3507, NL-1001 AH Amsterdam.*

In Germany: Please write to *Penguin Books Deutschland GmbH, Metzlerstrasse 26, 60594 Frankfurt am Main.*

In Spain: Please write to *Penguin Books S. A., Bravo Murillo 19, 1° B, 28015 Madrid.*

In Italy: Please write to *Penguin Italia s.r.l., Via Benedetto Croce 2, 20094 Corsico, Milano.*

In France: Please write to *Penguin France, Le Carré Wilson, 62 rue Benjamin Baillaud, 31500 Toulouse.*

In Japan: Please write to *Penguin Books Japan Ltd, Kaneko Building, 2-3-25 Koraku, Bunkyo-Ku, Tokyo 112.*

In South Africa: Please write to *Penguin Books South Africa (Pty) Ltd, Private Bag X14, Parkview, 2122 Johannesburg.*

Praise for Katharine Weber's
TRUE CONFECTIONS

"Besides being a vividly imagined story about love, obsession, and betrayal, Weber's *True Confections* is a lively pocket history of the American candy industry. It's an irresistible combination."
—*Boston Globe*

"*True Confections* is her most delectable novel yet, a book that interweaves a history of candy, chocolate in particular, with a sweeping story of America's immigrants, race relations, and religion from before World War II to the present day. . . . *True Confections* has plenty to digest. The last line is delicious."
—*Los Angeles Times*

"With her fifth novel, *True Confections*, Katharine Weber has concocted a sly and playful book . . . a hoot, but a hoot with an edge."
—*Cleveland Plain Dealer*

"Weber has studded her narrative with tasty facts about the history of the candy business in America."
—*New York Times*

"A novel should give us 'that unique blend of sweetness and pleasure and something else, a deep note of something rich and exotic and familiar' that a bite of good chocolate does. *True Confections* certainly delivers that delectability."
—*Washington Post Book World*

"In Katharine Weber's tricky, treat-filled new novel . . . what you get is more than you might expect. *True Confections* is a layered and revelatory novel."
—*Hartford Courant*

"This novel is like *Charlie and the Chocolate Factory* for grown-ups."

—*More.com*

"A sweet confection of love, candy, and a family's troubled past."
—*The Daily Beast*

"Brilliant . . . In an age characterized by artificial sweeteners and cheap fillers, Katharine Weber's book feels like a gift—a novel filled with characters so real they come off the page and into your life."

—RICH COHEN, author of *Sweet and Low*

"Wickedly funny . . . The narrative delves lovingly into the history of a venerable immigrant industry and brings to mind the elegiac mid-career novels of Philip Roth. Unlike Roth, however, Weber manages to celebrate the past without ever lapsing into sentimentality. Crisp and delicious, her novel is a true confection indeed."

—National Public Radio

"*True Confections* is as slyly ambitious as it is funny, tackling themes such as greed, intergenerational strife, betrayal, and the decline of the small manufacturer. . . . It's a real treat."

—*Historical Novels Review*

"Weber writes knowingly and stylishly, with much humor, about the complications of family love."

—*Jewish Woman*

"Entertaining and fresh-voiced . . . Readers will find themselves eagerly flipping pages as they puzzle over what's the truth and what's, well . . . just Alice."

—*Tattered Cover*

"A wry, sly, sassy tale."

—*Barnes & Noble Review*

"Darkly funny . . . Who ever knew that candy could cause so much drama?"

—*BookPage*

"[A] winning, offbeat tale . . . A story of love, life, and sweets is a genuine treat."

—*Publishers Weekly*

"Weber unleashes a wacky comic sensibility. . . . Filled with candy lore, impassioned critiques of chocolate, and Alice's one-of-a-kind takes on marriage and family, this is sweet reading for fans of the offbeat."

—*Booklist*

"Mixing humor with sweets, Weber's (*The Music Lesson; Triangle*) latest novel is a nicely crafted literary tale about an enterprising Jewish family and the woman who becomes an integral part of their lives and business."

—*Library Journal*

"Weber's is a smart, wry satire, whose serious agenda—to remind us that appearances are almost always deceiving—is explored through crunchy bites of drama and humor . . . a scrumptious satire."

—*Haaretz Daily Newspaper*

"One of America's finest writers on Jewish themes . . . Weber uses the notion of ambiguous identity to write in a textured and thoughtful way about the nature of identity and family."

—*Jewish Daily Forward*

"Frank, funny, comfortably outrageous."

—*Globe and Mail (Toronto)*

ALSO BY KATHARINE WEBER

Triangle

The Little Women

The Music Lesson

*Objects in Mirror Are Closer
Than They Appear*

TRUE CONFECTIONS

A Novel

KATHARINE WEBER

BROADWAY PAPERBACKS
NEW YORK

For Barbara Findeisen, Bright Star!

I'm an empress.

I wear an apron.

My typewriter writes.

It didn't break the way it warned.

Even crazy, I'm as nice

as a chocolate bar.

—Anne Sexton, "Live"

TRUE CONFECTIONS

AFFIDAVIT

I, Alice Tatnall Ziplinsky, a resident of New Haven, County of New Haven, State of Connecticut, do hereby certify, swear or affirm, and declare that I am competent to give the following declarations concerning the history of Zip's Candies of New Haven, Connecticut, based on my expertise and personal experience derived from thirty-three years of dedicated employment, and as a shareholder in the Ziplinsky Family Limited Partnership, as well as my personal history as it pertains to the Ziplinsky family and Ziplinsky family business practices, before, during, and after my thirty-three years of marriage to Howard Ziplinsky, as the mother of Jacob Ziplinsky and Julie Ziplinsky, as the former sister-in-law of Irene Ziplinsky Weiss, and as the daughter-in-law of the late Samuel Ziplinsky and the late Frieda Ziplinsky, and I do hereby certify, swear or affirm, and declare that all of my information is based on my personal knowledge and experience, unless otherwise stated, and that the following matters, facts, and things are true and correct to the best of my knowledge:

1

On my first day of work at Zip's Candies, it took five minutes for me to learn the two-handed method for separating and straightening the Tigermelts as they were extruded eight at a time onto the belt that carried them toward the finishing chocolate-striping applicator tunnel. The necessary reach-shuffle-reach-shuffle Tigermelt-straightening gesture was demonstrated for me with condescending efficiency, with the belt running at half speed, by the irritable Frieda Ziplinsky, whose husband, Sam, had just hired me that morning, an impulsive act on his part that she would regret audibly every few weeks for the next thirty-three years. In the sixth minute, I had my first glimpse of my future ex-husband.

Across the whirring, clanking, chugging, sugar-caked Zip's Candies factory floor, there appeared Howard Ziplinsky, emerging feetfirst from the large, rotating drum used to tumble the Little Sammies in the thin hard-shell chocolate coating, just a little more brittle than a Raisinet's, that gave them their signature sheen.

That Little Sammies panning drum was one of the original machines still running on the Zip's lines that hot summer of 1975. It finally wore out beyond repair six years later, in late August 1981, an unforgettable time for me personally as well as a notable event in the history of Zip's Candies. I had just begun to be plagued with morning sickness, but Howard and I hadn't yet revealed to anyone that I was pregnant with our first child,

Jacob. I was working long, exhausting, split-shift days that summer, supervising the first and third shifts to meet Halloween orders, when the Little Sammies panning drum seized up for the last time. We had shut down the line twice that week because of fruit-fly infestations (the eggs probably came in with a contaminated batch of peanuts for the Tigermelts), which had required cleaning every piece of equipment on the line, including internal mechanisms. The gear shaft on the drum motor was probably insufficiently relubricated when the line started up yet again, and it broke down irreparably on that last Thursday night of August, just as the third shift was starting, causing the disastrous Little Sammies shortage of Halloween 1981.

Replacement parts for that panning drum had been fabricated as needed for thirty years, but by 1981, the very last known functioning machine capable of making those parts had become obsolete and worn out as well. The fabricator—Bud Becker, an elderly retired machinist who operated out of his Hamden basement (by then he was the last living member of the original start-up crew on the Zip's lines when Eli Czaplinsky opened his doors in 1924)—had thrown in the towel when he couldn't get the parts for his machine that made the parts for our machine. He was eighty-three, and for fourteen years Zip's had been his only customer.

A new panning drum, the one that still runs on the Little Sammies line today, was rush-ordered from Holland, making it the first-ever custom-built mechanism to grace the Zip's floor. (It would remain the most expensive single production-line element for several years, until the cost was surpassed by the overdue replacement of the entire Tigermelt line, from batch tables to wrapping machines, with some slightly newer used equipment, in 1989.) Those lost seven weeks before the new Little Sammies panning drum was installed on the line were a disaster.

We even tried hand-dipping on jury-rigged enrobing frames in finishing trays, the way Little Sammies were manufactured at the very beginning, in 1924, in those first months when Eli was still developing and refining his cherished candy inventions, well before Little Sammies were distributed beyond New Haven. But there was no chance we could duplicate the finish and gloss of the panned Little Sammies, and all we did was waste product and man-hours, because it is, of course, impossible to get that thin, hard, chocolate-shell coating onto Little Sammies any other way.

Imagine trying to finish M&M's or Reese's Pieces by hand. What we produced was perfectly good candy, but they were just little fudgy chocolate-covered figures, probably a lot like the earliest versions of Zip's signature candy. So it was useless. They weren't remotely like what people expect when they open a pack of Little Sammies.

I don't know if it is obvious even now just how catastrophic this was for Zip's at the time. Little Sammies sales have carried more than half of Zip's annual gross for decades, and almost three quarters of annual Little Sammies sales occur in that all-important zenith of candy-selling seasons, from back-to-school through Halloween. It was only the advent of the protein-bar contract work that changed Zip's dependence on Little Sammies. The Detox bar and Index bar lines have grown ever more significant for us in recent years. Every time I look at our balanced books I thank God for our nation's ongoing glycemic-index obsession.

That interruption on the Little Sammies line was a true crisis. Howard and I had been married for six years by then, and I had never before seen him cry, not even when his grandmother died just ten days before our wedding. We got through it, and I thought at the time that if we could survive the Little Sammies

Halloween shortage of 1981, we could survive anything, but I was wrong.

I HAVE BEEN instructed by Charlie Cooper, my attorney, to tell my story in as clear and detailed a way as possible, from the beginning, though what a lawyer means by "clear and detailed" and "from the beginning" is probably very different from what I prefer to make of those requirements for this account. So my recollection of events begins on the humid summer day that was the twelfth of July, 1975, when I applied for the job at Zip's out of the blue.

I say "out of the blue" because it really was just that, the consequence of picking up a discarded section of the *New Haven Register* to leaf through while I dawdled over my toasted corn muffin and coffee at the counter at Clark's Dairy, on Whitney Avenue, where I had taken to lingering each morning after I fled my family's house, my hair still wet from the shower. A classified ad with the heading "Dat's Tasty!" in the "Help Wanted" pages jumped out at me.

I had just been graduated from Wilbur Cross High School, where Miss Grace Solomon, my favorite English teacher, had instructed me in correct usage, which is why I just wrote "been graduated" instead of "graduated." Because whether or not I have a college degree, I consider myself to be a perfectly well-read and educated person with as good a command of language as any college graduate I know, including a certain member of the Ziplinsky family who considers herself to be quite educated indeed after those four years in Providence at that university named for those slave-trading Brown brothers.

It is a deeply ingrained Ziplinsky family trait to place a little too much confidence in what it says on the label without full regard for quality control. Trust me, no Ivy League diploma on the wall confers an automatic ability to discern the correct uses of the words *lay* and *lie,* nor is it an antidote to chronic split infinitives and dangling modifiers. Let us not dwell too long on the habitual incorrect deployment of the word *myself,* the use of which is apparently believed to connote superiority and classiness. Out of that smug Ziplinsky mouth often comes the cringeworthy phrase, "On behalf of myself," revealing, with those four inapt words, the truth of the matter to all literate people, whether or not they possess an Ivy League degree. I consider myself to be an autodidact. One definition of an autodidact is someone who knows what *autodidact* means.

I WAS IN the top tenth percentile of my class at Wilbur Cross, I was the winner of the Senior English Prize, and I had already picked my courses for my first semester at Middlebury College, which had been my first choice. But I had screwed up so badly a few weeks before my first day at Zip's Candies that I wasn't going to be heading off to college after all, though Middlebury was willing to consider deferring my admission to the following year, their inevitable letter rescinding my admission concluded (with a certain calculated and smug coldness that was meant to discourage me from pursuing the option while simultaneously conveying a superficial gesture in the direction of fairness), with my deferred admission depending on a demonstration of "sufficient growth of character in the interim, given the circumstances."

I already had a summer job, so there was no reason for me to be reading the classifieds section of the *Register.* But there was nothing else left to read in that particular lone, abandoned newspaper section after the horoscopes and advice columns and used-car ads, all of which I studied with a deep and pointless concentration each morning. (Plus, I had always enjoyed reading the want ads, starting in about third grade, when I would read them aloud to my mother while she made dinner, and together we would create stories about the people who applied for those jobs.)

I was at the end of my third week scooping cones at Helen's Double Dip out on the Boston Post Road in Milford, and I had come to dread putting on the claustrophobic, short, lime-green polyester uniform with its lumpy zipper and attached apron. I washed and dried my uniform every night, and it had already begun to pill. I dreaded everything about Helen's Double Dip. I dreaded the sugary slime of curdled cream underfoot, which had impregnated the soles of my bright new JCPenney sneakers. I dreaded the daily din of bratty children whining at their irritably indulgent parents, who rarely thought to tip as I labored to fill their orders while enduring a twinge in my elbow that was a direct consequence of scooping nut-infested flavors at an awkward angle with a bad scoop.

I took the job at Helen's Double Dip after three humiliating interviews for much nicer jobs had left me feeling that I would never do better and probably deserved exactly this punishment for everything that had happened. I had aimed much higher at first, when I applied for an entry-level editorial assistant position at Yale University Press. But when I sat down with an editor (a balding, middle-aged man with a stammer, whose scrawny polka-dotted bow tie heralded a vast collection of variously patterned bow ties, one of which he no doubt wore each and every day) and he leaned back in his chair and cocked one seersuckered leg over the other (exposing some hairless shin above a droopy sock) and asked me in a falsely avuncular fashion why I wasn't going to college in the fall, given that I had just finished high school, and I started to explain about the fire and the sentence and my family's money issues, he closed the file folder and stood up abruptly, even though I had been there only a few minutes and we hadn't yet discussed anything at all about the job.

My next interview was for a receptionist position at a big law firm on Church Street, but when I met with the human resources lady, before I could say a word about which job I was applying for, she took one look at me and shook her head, and then she quickly told me the job had been filled and then she started typing really fast and didn't look at me again. I stood on the sidewalk in front of the building in my dowdy interview outfit feeling waves of shame as office workers on their lunch hour brushed by me. I had just been intercepted attempting to pass myself off as a regular person.

I applied for a job at the bookstore on Whitney Avenue where my family had bought books my entire life, but the formerly friendly owner was abrupt with me and vague about actually needing anyone after all, even though there was a hand-lettered sign on the glass door advertising his need for part-time help. As I turned away I caught him rolling his eyes at one of his employees, a soft-spoken retired music teacher who had always been nice to me and who shared my mother's passion for Angela Thirkell novels. In the glass of the door, I could see her reflection, shrugging and grimacing in response as I made my way out.

At Helen's Double Dip out in deepest Milford, nobody asked me anything about whether or not I was going to college, and more significantly nobody seemed to notice or care that they were hiring a renowned pariah with a criminal record to work a daily shift from nine to six. All Freddie, the manager (with his Don Ameche mustache and his terrible acne scars), seemed to care about was my comprehension of the rules, which mandated showing up on time, thorough hand-washing, correct scooping technique, and the strict limit of three free samples per customer, no exceptions, not even for friends. I assured him I had no friends.

THAT MORNING, SITTING at the counter at Clark's Dairy, I was drawn to the quaintness of the little "Dat's Tasty!" ad declaring that Zip's Candies was seeking a "hardworking and honest individual willing to be dedicated to learning old-fashioned techniques at a world-renowned candy factory." Like the Clark's counter itself, the ad seemed to me like something from another era, an era so much simpler and nicer than my own. I wished I could make up a story about the person who applied for this job, to tell my mother while she made our dinner, but my mother wasn't speaking to me in those grim days, and it wasn't clear that she would resume speaking to me anytime soon.

Moments later, instead of driving a few exits south on traffic-clogged I-95 and going straight to work, I found myself driving under the highway ramp and navigating the desolate Krazy Kat landscape of the old industrial waterfront of New Haven on the other side of the train tracks, at the edge of the Quinnipiac River. I had gone once with my father to this part of town, years before, to buy a replacement part for the old-fashioned crank-out awning that shaded our backyard patio. Yes, we have no bananas, he would always sing as he cranked, deploying the green-and-white-striped awning to shade the table and chairs on our back terrace. In my memory, voyaging to the awning factory on River Street had been an expedition, far more of an adventure than the five minutes' drive from downtown that took me to the corner of River and James streets.

Though I had intended, out of pure idle curiosity, only to

take a quick look and keep driving, when I spotted the big, faded "Dat's Tasty!" ghost lettering embedded in the worn bricks up so high near the roof that you wouldn't notice them once you got closer, I stopped, and then I parked my car in front of the nondescript three-story factory building with the number on the door corresponding to the address in the ad. Were it not for that "Dat's Tasty!" declaration in old-fashioned italic lettering, which already felt oddly familiar to me as I gazed at it, I wouldn't have been at all certain I was in the right place. Was this worn brick building surrounded by boarded-up husks of long-gone industry at the baked edge of nothing really the home of a world-renowned candy factory?

I was not specifically interested in the candies themselves at this point in my life. Sure, I was always happy enough to find Little Sammies or a Tigermelt in my Halloween candy, who wouldn't be? Mumbo Jumbos were more problematic, as I was rather ambivalent toward licorice in those years, and I was always willing to trade away Mumbo Jumbos for something with chocolate (although my father liked them, so sometimes I would save them for him). And there was a family vacation on the Cape one rainy summer when my father used Mumbo Jumbos to replace some missing backgammon pieces in the set we found in a closet of the rental house.

But I had never gone out of my way to buy any Zip's candy with my allowance money in my earlier candy-buying years, when I would ride my bike to the newsstand on Whitney Avenue on Saturday afternoons. With my fifty cents I could buy three comic books, a pack of gum, and a candy bar. Frankly, I tended to favor Baby Ruths. I suppose I had a vague awareness that Zip's Candies was located somewhere in Connecticut, but I had no deep affection for boring and familiar New Haven, and my family was never one of those Chamber of Commerce, hometown pride kind of families. It certainly never occurred to me that I was destined to spend my life here.

There was a reason for the anonymity of the building, I would learn. Zip's had deliberately kept a low profile for a while at that point, although years earlier, especially in the 1950s, there had been a great deal of effort put into maintaining a very visible hometown identity, with local radio and television spots, sponsored parade floats, and lots of giveaways (rare Zip's memorabilia is avidly sought by collectors, especially the Zip's green umbrellas from the early fifties, a prize awarded to those willing to amass immense qualifying quantities of Zip's wrappers and mail them in, with a dollar for postage and handling; these occasionally show up on eBay for ridiculous sums).

Factory visits had never been permitted by Zip's, for reasons having to do partly with hygiene but mostly with keeping secret the specific manufacturing techniques for each line because of a not-unreasonable family paranoia about the potential loss of trade secrets. Plus, Frieda just never wanted to deal with groups of children. That woman didn't like people in general, and she really didn't like children, preferring to keep her distance unless she had a specific reason (like, if they were her own grandchildren) to tolerate them.

So, in my school years, I had experienced no class trips to the Zip's factory to see Little Sammies and Tigermelts and Mumbo Jumbos whizzing along the lines on their journey from raw ingredients to finished candies to wrapped products tightly packed into boxes for shipping. This is in distinct contrast to the way I had been marched through Lender's Bagels on three occasions by the time I was in sixth grade. In 1975, Zip's Candies was so low profile that there wasn't even an air of mystery about Zip's, unlike the fog of rumor and innuendo that has surrounded the legendary fortress that is the PEZ factory in

Orange, which no civilians have been permitted to penetrate since PEZ began American operations there in 1973. I fail to comprehend the allure of PEZ, I have to say. Even as a child, I was PEZ-resistant, more interested in the PEZ logo and the word itself, *PEZ* being a sort of Austrian shorthand for the word *Pfefferminze,* than I was in the cheesy dispensers or the actual candy (where's the charm in a stack of compressed, toothpastey chalk bricks?). How many PEZ bricks in the PEZ logo? Forty-four.

The Zip's building had no sign. The original sign was in storage, I would discover later that summer when I was taking a smoke break out back by the loading area and spotted it beside a bin of old wooden shipping pallets. Not that the official company history would tell you this, but the truth, according to Pete Zagorski, the old-timer on the loading dock, was that it had been removed in 1969, in haste (by Pete Zagorski himself, who had been rousted out of a deep sleep before the sun was up by a call from Sam, asking him to hustle down to James Street and take down the sign, which is why he was so authoritative on the subject), on the first of May, because of a tip-off by a friendly detective with the New Haven Police Department. He'd heard a rumor that the charged-up mob on the Green protesting the Black Panther trial in the Elm Street courthouse was planning a march across town to the Zip's Candies factory, to protest a certain candy inspired by Little Black Sambo, even if the company had for a while tried to revise history with statements about how in fact the myth that Little Sammies were named for Little Black Sambo is just one of those erroneous beliefs that circulate, because the truth is that the candy was really inspired by the birth of the owner's son, Little Sammy Ziplinsky, born the same year Zip's Candies started production.

In 1921, the Curtiss Candy Company in Chicago changed

their Kandy Kake bar into the Baby Ruth, claiming former president Grover Cleveland's dead daughter Ruth had somehow
inspired the name. This was implausible at best, and it is most
likely that the Baby Ruth bar was an unauthorized attempt to
cash in on the popularity of baseball great Babe Ruth. It hardly
seems fair that in 1931 Curtiss won their case to shut down Babe
Ruth's own licensed candy bar on grounds that it was too close to
their bestselling product.

Nothing happened to Zip's Candies during the Black Panther trial. There was no angry march from the New Haven
Green across the railroad tracks, even in that season of turmoil
when anything was possible. The whole city of New Haven
seemed to be one spark away from a great big Black Panther
conflagration. It was a potentially threatening time for a company known for making small, chewy, Negroid candies, no matter what the explanation for the name might be, no question. All
it meant to me at the time, a couple of miles up leafy Whitney
Avenue (named for that other ambitious and inventive Eli,
whose ingenuity gave the world the cotton gin, which led to a
vast expansion of cotton production in the American south,
which of course increased the demand for the slave labor necessary to pick all that cotton), was that my parents watched the
news on television compulsively and I wasn't allowed to leave
our block on my bicycle.

I COULD SEE through the big mullioned windows on the first
two floors that the factory lights were on. I turned off my Subaru
before the engine could overheat, which it tended to do, which
was why my mother was driving her new Volkswagen and I was
driving this old wreck, and I sat there. I knew I needed to back-
track to the highway entrance I had passed on my way. I could

get to work on time if I left now. Something kept me sitting there in the still car. I don't know what, beyond a general reluctance to face the day, to face the rest of the summer, and after that, to face the rest of my doomed life stretching out in front of me.

I harbored a hopeless vision of spending all eternity at Helen's Double Dip, where I would turn into an aging spinster furiously scooping triple Nutty Buddy cones with my by-then crippled arm while life passed me by. There's poor old Alice, people would say. The sad one, with the mustache. (I would have let myself go completely. Doomed felons don't pluck.) They say she's worked at Helen's Double Dip all her life.

The truth is, that summer, that day, that moment, I had come to the end of something. I had lost my place.

Sweat trickled down my neck in the suddenly stifling car. I opened my window. A certain burnt sugar and chocolate aroma hung in the air, that marvelous, inevitable, ineffable, just-right aura of Zip's Candies, that unique blend of sweetness and pleasure and something else, a deep note of something rich and exotic and familiar that makes you nostalgic for its flavor even though you may never have tasted it before. I have loved that smell every day of my life from then to now. Some days, I go to work for that smell. When I travel, I miss it, I long for it. On Mumbo Jumbo days there is an added spice in the air, a dark hint of cherry and anise that adds a top note of danger. In retrospect, I believe this was a Mumbo Jumbo day. The aroma wafting through my car told me what I already knew I had to do. I went in and applied for the job.

MY FUTURE FATHER-IN-LAW, Sam Ziplinsky, appraised me with a sidelong glance from behind his messy desk, never taking the unlit, moist stub of a cigar out of his mouth (he couldn't smoke on the premises, so he nursed a disgusting half-smoked cigar all day long instead) while barraging me with questions about my education, about my experience, about my family, about where I lived and what I wanted to do with my life.

He didn't seem to hear my hesitant, evasive, contradictory answers at all as he rooted through untidy heaps of papers and threw out more questions, one on top of the next—Why did I think I deserved to work here, did I know it was like joining a family, am I someone who gets sick a lot, am I reliable, where do I live, am I good with my hands, am I in college, why not, do I want to marry and have children, am I a team player, do I like licorice? Red and black, or did I prefer red and hate black? Which do I like better, Little Sammies or Tigermelts? Until finally he interrupted me to exclaim in triumph, Found the sucker! as he extracted a ledger book from beneath a pile of folders.

I stopped trying to cook up plausible and attractive answers to each question, in order, since I was about three questions behind and I seemed to be talking to myself anyway, so finally I just stopped speaking altogether and waited to see what would come next. Was he listening at all to my replies? Was this a conversation, or a job interview, or what was it? I was now late for my shift at Helen's Double Dip. Freddie would be seriously disturbed that I was not there to start the morning flavor batches of the day and complete the daily inventory checklist before the lines started to form. Was I reliable?

Sam sat back in his creaking desk chair, holding the formerly misplaced ledger book in his lap, and then he looked me in the face for the first time, for a long moment. There was a metal bowl of deformed, uncoated Little Sammies on his desk, some of them undersized and missing parts, some of them all stuck together in a blob of limbs and torsos. He ate a clump absent-mindedly while looking at me, and then he held out the bowl and I took a three-headed triplet cluster and nibbled on their heads while waiting for whatever came next. At last he said, with a wry smile, all at once, not pausing for my replies, the cigar still firmly planted in the corner of his mouth, You want to work here, kid? You're what, sixteen? Eighteen? You want a job at Zip's? You want to work? You a hard worker? Sister, this isn't just a summer job. It's hard work. You like candy, kiddo? What we make here are three great candy lines, true confections, that's what my father, Eli—he founded the company—that's what he called them, true confections. You like Little Sammies? That's me, you're looking at him, I'm the original Little Sammy. I used to be little, now I'm not so little. So what do you think? You know what? You're hired. I got a good feeling.

MY FUTURE MOTHER-IN-LAW gave no indication of having any kind of good feeling about me whatsoever. Pearl Anastasio, Sam's secretary, a Zip's stalwart who had started at Zip's as a Little Sammies summer wrapper when she was in high school and Eli ran the place (in the era before he rigged up the first wrapping machine on the Little Sammies line), someone who would turn out to be a true friend to me as the years passed, though I hardly made eye contact with her that day, led me down a corridor. We reached a windowless office, where Frieda Ziplinsky sat at a desk piled high with stacks of envelopes she was stuffing with what looked like order forms. She would stuff a dozen, then seal a dozen. Stuff, seal, stuff, seal. Her hands were a blur. We stood in the doorway waiting for her to stop and look up, but she didn't stop and she didn't look up. She was a stuffing and sealing pro, a stuffing and sealing maniac. Finally

Pearl announced loudly, Hey, Mrs. Z. Mr. Z said to say to you we've got our new hire. Okay, Mrs. Z.? Frieda finally glanced up and gave me a sour look. Pearl abandoned me with a friendly pat on the shoulder that was combined with a little push so I would step into that room.

You're not twenty-three, you look fourteen! You ever even worked on a line? You got line experience? You got another job? Frieda asked me, eyeing my absurd and too-short lime-green Helen's Double Dip uniform. I shrugged and shook my head apologetically, furtively yanked on my hem with one hand, and mumbled No, I had no line experience, and No, I was through with Helen's Double Dip, and today was my last day. She scowled. Not the racker and stacker from Entenmann's, from West Haven? I thought that girl was supposed to come in this morning first thing. I thought that was you. Sam maybe thought so too. He hired you? You have any idea what the job is? He say what the pay is? You know this isn't a summer job? You ready to train right now, while I have the time?

I shook my head again, and then again, and then I nodded, feeling as if anything I said or did would further the degree to which I had inadvertently taken Sam's side in an ongoing argument and was now allied with him against her forever. Which was true.

Sighing heavily, clearly having already reached the conclusion that asking me any more questions would be useless, Frieda got up, went over to a white metal cabinet, and rummaged around on the shelves, and without looking in my direction she handed me a hairnet, which I put on, and then a white factory coat, which I also put on. As I buttoned it, she gave me a look that suggested that covering myself more modestly from now on would be a good idea in general, regardless of hygiene requirements. The lightweight white coat was a foot longer than the hem of the uniform I would never wear again after this day. I stepped out of my sneakers and pulled on, over my little pom-pom tennis socks, the pair of too-big, white, galoshy go-go boots apparently required before a civilian could set foot on the Zip's Candies factory floor, as Frieda wordlessly handed them to me, first one, then the other, with a look on her face as if I was putting them on incorrectly. She herself wore Keds.

She walked out of the room, and I waded down the hallway behind her, sloshing along in the boots, mimicking her when she paused to glove up with latex gloves from the wall dispenser by the big swinging double doors to the factory floor which have always made me feel as if I am about to enter an operating room, and then I followed her into the chaotic din and clatter of the sweet mechanical ballet of the Zip's Candies factory for the first time.

Even before my Tigermelt-handling indoctrination, I already knew I belonged at Zip's Candies. I knew it out on the sidewalk when I breathed in that burnt sugar and chocolate aroma. I knew that being here—hairnet, white coat, rubber boots, and all, forfeiting my job at Helen's Double Dip (along with my second and final paycheck, which I never had the nerve to go pick up), even as I was scornfully instructed on the nuances of straightening Tigermelts as they dropped onto the belt—was deeply, essentially right. Perhaps some people would call this destiny. Zip's Candies needed me, and I needed Zip's Candies. An inexplicable joy welled up in me as I realized that I knew that my life could start again from here, from this moment.

THAT FIRST TIME I saw Howard, thin and dark, handsome like a foreign doctor in his white lab coat (despite the stray, uncoated Little Sammies clinging to a sleeve), his face and eyebrows were freckled with a fine spray of chocolate droplets. This was the thin, glossy chocolate used to apply the final coat to Little Sammies in the panning drum from which he had just emerged, having reamed a clogged nozzle with a pipe cleaner. He had been working on the Mumbo Jumbos blending unit just before that (it was one of those days when the summer humidity soaked into everything, despite the chugging air-conditioning system; it was overdue for upgrading, but Frieda didn't want to spend the money, which was foolish, as the humidity affected every piece of antiquated equipment on the floor), and he was already dusted with the powdered sugar that had caked and clogged the feed tubes on the big licorice-blending pot. I thought he looked confectionary, like a sugared angel, and I could feel Frieda glaring at me, wanting to keep her beautiful son all to herself. And so we met.

Howdy, he said, coming toward me, not in greeting but introducing himself, because that's what he was called, Howdy Ziplinsky, and this confused me for a moment, as I sensed that nobody in the Ziplinsky family was likely to be from someplace where people said "Howdy" to one another, so I thought perhaps this was a Yiddish word I couldn't quite hear over the factory din, but at the same moment, through my confusion, I felt something completely new and profound stir in me, and I had to resist my unexpected impulse, as we shook hands for the first time, to lick him.

2

I DIDN'T MEAN TO burn down Debbie Livingston's house. Despite all the ridiculous stories that most people believed, the way people love to believe ridiculous stories, it is important to recognize that the events of that night were never fairly represented by the newspapers or the local television stations. At least the Internet didn't exist in those days. That fire took place long ago, on May 7, 1975, to be precise, and the facts of that case obviously have no specific bearing on the current matters at hand, but establishing the truth is important to me. Howard has told me more than once that I am obsessed with the truth. He himself could have a little more respect for it. But Dr. Gibraltar, my psychoanalyst, always said that the truth is overrated. Dr. Gibraltar never did say much in all the years of my analysis, but when he spoke, it was usually to utter a little kōan like that.

Ellie Quest-Greenspan, my other therapist, who was supposed to be Howard's and my marriage counselor, talked a great deal, and often spoke about how I was on a quest toward finding my truth and how I was always learning how to stand in my truth. And Charlie Cooper has more than once advised me, as we walk through the door for this or that deposition or hearing, that answering questions truthfully isn't the same thing as saying everything I know. In other words, speak the truth in as few words as possible (which, apologies to Charlie, is not really my style). Apparently everybody is obsessed with the truth, one way or another. Anyway, given that my qualifications to provide information about the business of Zip's Candies are being called into question by a certain greedy member of the Ziplinsky family who has no idea what she is talking about, it seems important to explain about that fire now.

I know that many people in the Greater New Haven area believe things about me that are untrue. Some of them will always think of me as Arson Girl. I am bitter about that. Why wouldn't I be? I didn't mean to burn down that house. It isn't arson if there is no intent. It's just an accidental fire. Call me Accidental Fire Girl.

My one-year sentence for third-degree arson was suspended and I was given two years' probation. I didn't realize that when I agreed to a guilty plea (which I did because I was a distraught teenager, and also because I caused the fire), I was agreeing to a charge of arson. That was a mistake.

My parents had to pay the Livingstons a huge amount of money as part of the deal. This bankrupted my family, and my father had to close his real-estate business, because he had not incorporated, and so his personal liabilities sank Tatnall Realty. Plus, being the father of Arson Girl probably wasn't exactly good for business. By the end of the year, my father had gone to work for the Martha Rivers Agency, headed by the calculating and rapacious Martha Rivers (whom he had always mocked), the most underhanded and manipulative high-pressure real-estate agent in town. Martha was the only one who made him an offer, and that may well have been prompted by a perverse attraction to our pariah status, given how loathed she herself was by so many people in the community. She represented everything my father hated in the business, and now he was her employee, and it was my fault.

My mother went back to substitute teaching in the New Haven and Hamden public school systems the following autumn. My parents stopped talking about their dreams of certain trips or their wish to build a vacation house in Vermont. Both my parents pretty much stopped talking to me altogether that summer, without admitting that they weren't talking to me, and the pretense that they were talking to me was much worse than out-and-out silence. I was an only child, there were no cousins for hundreds of miles, and I was really marooned. Only when Jacob was born was there anything like a thaw, and even then, they never really opened their hearts to me again. I don't know how you turn away from your child the way they turned away from me. But it's something people do.

When Howard and I were married in early October, only three months after we met, my parents never questioned our plan, having little curiosity about this huge, possibly disastrous, and certainly reckless leap I was making just a few weeks before my nineteenth birthday. Working at Zip's Candies and then falling in love with Howard, a Jewish man ten years my senior, were for them just the latest two things I had gotten myself into. I like to think they were preoccupied with their bankruptcy. Under other circumstances, perhaps they might have been more concerned about me. But the fire changed them as much as it changed me, and I will never know what it would have been like to have parents who would question my choices instead of just being relieved that whatever I might do next, now it wouldn't be their problem.

At our wedding, they acted like guests, or remote relatives, the sort of people who tell you they remember when you were a baby because they have nothing else to say. We were married in the backyard of Frieda and Sam's house on Marvel Road on a beautiful Sunday afternoon by a groovy rabbi known throughout the tristate area for marrying couples like us.

I had grown up attending the First Unitarian Universalist Society on Whitney Avenue a few times a year; it was a compromise place of not quite worship chosen by my Episcopal mother to mollify my atheist father (he was raised a nominal Congregationalist). It was important to my mother that we belong to a church of some kind, with services in at least a vaguely Christian format, and this was the best she could do with my father, this church for atheists. I am sure my mother was drawn to the Unitarian philosophy offering a free and responsible search for truth and meaning, which allows each person an opportunity to find an individual path. She was always really big on individual paths.

When I was about ten, my mother took up a sort of spiritual meditation habit she called "discerning," and although she never instructed me about anything remotely religious, sometimes she offered to let me sit with her in silence so we could discern together. But it made me itchy to sit with her like that, and it felt like something too private, and I didn't believe she really wanted me right there next to her when she was doing it. Sometimes she and my father discerned together, and I would walk into their room and they would be sitting in silence and I would feel as if I had walked in on something so intimate the door should have been bolted to save us all from my embarrassing intrusion.

When we did go to church, services were led by members of the congregation, and as a child I couldn't differentiate those services from the earnest political meetings that took place in the same rows of chairs at other times of the day.

Jacob and Julie attended the progressive, cooperative preschool located in the carriage house behind the Unitarian Society, a pleasant continuity for me, though by the time they went to preschool there I hadn't set foot inside the church (really just a house) since high school. The preschool didn't exist when I was a child. I didn't go to nursery school at all, though I think it probably would have been a good idea if I had spent more time with children when I was little, as I was a solitary only child who was always more comfortable around adults than I was around other children. But my parents didn't think I "needed" to go, as if nursery school was some sort of remedial treatment.

When I got to kindergarten, instead of rushing to play with the other children, I preferred to spend recess chatting with the teacher, if she would let me. And if she gently suggested that I go play with the other children, that always made me feel such shame, because I was exposed for having wanted something from her—adult friendship—which she certainly wasn't going to provide, no matter how much of a serious little savant I made myself.

When I was invited to play at someone's house after school, my playmate would become irritable when I lingered at the kitchen table long after the snack had been consumed, deep in conversation with an impressed mother. I was that child your mother always suggested for playdates until you explained to her that she liked me better than you did.

I don't really know why it never occurred to me at the height of the fire crisis to seek solace or wise counsel from anyone connected to the Unitarians, but I didn't, and as far as I know neither of my parents turned to anyone in the church either, possibly out of embarrassment. At certain times in my life I have wished with all my heart that I had a rabbi or a priest to whom I could have turned. I truly envy those with genuine faith. Their lives must be so much easier to bear.

I have chosen instead to worship in the house of psychoanalysis, which offers little solace in any immediate sense, and which in fact holds the possibility of a great deal of shame for anyone who voices a wish to be held and comforted and soothed.

You can only analyze your desire to be held and comforted and soothed, and you can discuss why it wouldn't be appropriate for that ever to take place in this room with this person you employ to listen to you talk to yourself, and you can feel waves of shame that you are in the grip of the transference neurosis that drives this attachment to the doctor, to whom you pay enormous sums of money.

This is how I started seeing Ellie Quest-Greenspan on the side. Howard and I went to her just four times, at the recommendation of my dentist, who told me that her imperiled marriage had been saved by Ellie. Perhaps that sounds silly. I thought we did good work, as they say, in those appointments, but Howard was really only showing up to humor me. It was the least he could do, he said, with that door-opening, chair-pulling-out, walk-on-the-street-side-of-a-lady, superficial gallantry of his. Nothing that was said in those sessions (though he acknowledged that he knew he was breaking my heart, which was better than if he had no idea, I suppose) was going to change his plan to leave me and go to Madagascar, where he could finally truly inhabit his other life, his real life.

Howard walked out of the appointment halfway through that fourth and final meeting, saying he would get more satisfaction out of hitting a bucket of balls, and that was it. Ellie simply held me and rocked me while I cried for the remainder of the appointment. She asked if I wanted to come back, and I said I did, and I kept seeing her, with appointments every other week, while I was at the same time still seeing Dr. Gibraltar three or four times each week.

I would like to point out that I was never a big spender of the Ziplinsky millions in any way other than this, the tens of thousands of dollars in checks I wrote to Dr. Gibraltar over those twenty-five years of psychoanalysis. For all those prosperous years with Howard, in that era when everyone around us was so frantically getting and spending, I lived modestly. For twelve years I was comfortable driving a sturdy Saab acquired when Julie was in preschool, though Howard, a car nut, was always urging me to get a fancy German sedan. (He was disappointed when the Saab finally died and I switched to a Jeep.) Unlike ordinary women (according to the magazines I read in the checkout line at the supermarket), I have no desire to own more than just one handbag, a nice one, a Coach bag in red leather, and I have only a few pairs of shoes. I have certainly never bought myself fancy jewelry or designer clothing. I have never gone to a spa to have processes applied to my body, and I have never taken vacations in the Caribbean or gone on a cruise. Wouldn't most women in my position have felt utterly entitled to do all of those things routinely?

The most money I have ever spent on myself was when I bought an original Harriet Rose photograph, a charming picture of a cat sleeping in the window of a pharmacy, for my fiftieth birthday. I have modest needs and desires.

I resent, therefore, the statements that I have recklessly squandered Ziplinsky money on neurotic quantities of psychotherapy hours. (a) My medical expenses that are not covered by the insurance provided by Zip's Candies are in no way relevant to the matters in dispute, (b) nothing about my psychotherapy has any relevance to my competence as an employee or an administrator at Zip's Candies, (c) I concede that the gasoline in my Saab was paid for with a Zip's Corporate ExxonMobil Speedpass account, though records have never been kept concerning personal mileage of Zip's employees, and this is an irrelevancy, and (d) I am angry that in the name of family loyalty Howard has apparently chosen to disclose details of my private life to his sister.

❋ ❋

DR. GIBRALTAR DIDN'T know about those continuing appointments with Ellie Quest-Greenspan. I didn't want to tell him I was still seeing her, without Howard, because I had felt his skepticism hovering like a cloud in the air behind my head as I lay on the couch reporting to him about our first appointment with Ellie. When I described her credentials (surely not everyone with a degree from an alternative modality institute in Colorado is a kook) he shifted uneasily in his chair. When you've been in analysis a long time, you know how to read things like this, and he might as well have leaned over and smacked me in the face. Despite his obvious disapproval, I went into the details of the role-playing and nondominant hand, silent finger-painting dialogues that had taken place in that first fruitless appointment with Howard, and Dr. Gibraltar withdrew his attention and stopped taking notes (his scratching pen went silent). I knew he was punishing me, waiting for me to get to more reasonable material before he was willing to engage with me again.

After Howard and I met with Ellie the second time, when I told Dr. Gibraltar that she had been concerned about my cough and at the end of the hour had given me a CD of James Galway playing that ubiquitous *Echinacea Serenade* you hear in every massage therapist's office, and that I had listened to it over the weekend and I thought it had really helped me get over my bad head cold, he made a doubtful sound in his throat, and I could hear his pen fall onto the rug, where he had dropped it in disgust.

I didn't tell him that Howard had walked out of that fourth appointment, because I knew Dr. Gibraltar would have admired him for doing so, and if he took Howard's side I would have been devastated. It was bad enough that I would have been expected to analyze why I thought he had taken Howard's side, while being stonewalled with the usual "I am a tabula rasa"–inflected interventions such as "How does that make you feel?" and "Where's that coming from?" (It makes me feel that your countertransference is showing again, Doctor, which is always thrilling, but also it makes me feel like crap, and surely you're the one who should know where it's coming from, just check the tags on your own psychodynamic baggage!)

Meanwhile, something I said to Ellie a few weeks into our work together about missing analysis made her think I had terminated my treatment, though Dr. Gibraltar was in fact only away for the month of August (every year he went to Wellfleet with all the other psychoanalysts). I didn't correct her impression at that moment, as I had only been taking a break before getting in touch with my anger at my unavailable father by doing some more screaming and hitting a pillow with a plastic bat, and I didn't want to lose my emotional momentum.

No, that's untrue. I didn't want to admit to her that I was still on Dr. Gibraltar's couch, still working away at the glacially slow process he once called "turning ghosts into ancestors." When we had our first (I thought), hopeful marriage counseling appointment with Ellie, and I made reference to my long and ongoing experience with psychoanalysis, she had gotten a look on her face that was like the expression of a tolerant vegetarian friend to whom you have just mentioned a fantastic steak dinner. So I didn't want to admit to her that I was still seeing him almost every day. Consequently, each of them thought I had come to my senses and stopped seeing the other.

I was committing therapist adultery. But what of it? I could afford it. I had the time. It helped me, and it made me feel more in control during the appointments. It pleased me especially when I was lying on the couch in that beige room with the

annoying wrinkled Escher poster that attracted my gaze even
when I didn't want to look at it (I get it, we cannot trust our distorted perceptions!) and I would parrot a bit of Ellie's wisdom,
and I could feel Dr. Gibraltar's glowing approval of my progress
as evidenced by this analytic insight, which was manifest in the
way he made his little approval noise, sort of a satisfied chirp,
and the way I could hear his pen scratching as he jotted process
notes. It was the same set of approval sounds I loved to hear
when I rambled through an especially successful interpretation
of one of my fabricated dreams. Dr. Gibraltar was obsessed with
my dreams. What harm did it do, paying the dream extortionist
with counterfeit dreams that delighted us both?

Similarly, when working with Ellie in a feeling session, I
would appropriate some of Dr. Gibraltar's interpretations of my
personality, blurting them out as if they were my own sudden
associative insights in the middle of a process, and Ellie would
always tell me she was proud of me and hold me in a particularly
loving maternal hug that meant the world to me.

I liked the way this worked. I really miss all that therapy, now
that Ellie has moved to Big Sur and Dr. Gibraltar has died. He
broke his neck diving into the surf last August, in Wellfleet. I read
about it in the *New York Times*. He hit a sandbar. He was seventy-
three, and his wife is a social worker who was born in Santiago,
Chile, and there were two married daughters and five grandchildren. A secretary called me a week after that to tell me the
news and cancel our scheduled post–Labor Day sessions. She said
she was a secretary but I knew she was actually one of his daughters. I could hear it in her voice. I let her tell me the sad news in a
sensitive, caring way, and I pretended that I didn't already know,
because it was the only conversation I was ever going to have with
anyone about Dr. Gibraltar's death. I had nobody to tell.

So I miss all that therapy, but also, I do miss that funny private dynamic. My only consolation is a secret little minor habit I have recently developed. Although I have the sturdy Tatnall teeth and gums and I floss regularly, and all of my dental check-ups are quite routine, I have become a patient at three different dental practices, rotating my cleaning appointments among them on a regular schedule. Whenever I go for a cleaning, each of my dental hygienists praises me for my extraordinarily pristine oral hygiene. I like this. And for someone in the candy business, I do have exceptionally good teeth.

STRANGE AS IT seems, when we met to discuss our wedding plans, Rabbi Matt didn't care that I hadn't formally converted, though in those days, when I was under a sweet spell of Ziplinsky enchantment, and grateful to have found this new and better family, I would certainly have done it, gladly and willingly. But Frieda insisted, perversely, that I shouldn't, that it wasn't at all necessary. In retrospect, it was just one more way she tried to keep me out. If I had converted, she wouldn't have been able to hold it against me that I was a Gentile; she wouldn't have been able to be such a martyr to her son's mixed marriage.

My mother chose not to walk down the aisle formed between the few rows of folding chairs on the grass. Howard's best man, Ted Thorntel (his Yale roommate), played Bach's "Bourrée in E Minor" on his guitar as my father walked me stiffly to the front. He left me there with the intimacy of a man dropping a letter in a mailbox, and then he went to sit with my mother somewhere near the back. The ceremony was more bizarre than I realized at the time, as this was my first Jewish wedding, and it wasn't until I accumulated some experience of ordinary Jewish weddings over the years that I realized retrospectively just how flaky and altogether nonstandard ours had been.

When Rabbi Matt pronounced us man and wife, we kissed a little self-consciously, and then Howard stomped on a glass wrapped in a linen napkin. We had debated skipping this ritual, but the rabbi had persuaded us a few hours earlier that it didn't represent the consummation of the marriage so much as it symbolized the unchangeable transformation of the two of us, who would be as permanently altered by the state of marriage as the broken glass would be forever beyond reconstitution. Rabbi Matt, swaying slightly as he stood before us in his off-clean embroidered shirt, offered a final admonition as we faced him. Both of us were trembling and tearful as he told us that our love would be everlasting if we remembered each day to "Sprinkle, sparkle, and do art!"

Howard squeezed my hand tightly and I caught his eye and damp sobs of laughter erupted from both of us at once. Ted picked up his guitar and began to play the recessional music we had chosen, Gershwin's "Love Is Here to Stay." I felt incredible happiness at that moment, as we turned and walked the few yards across the grass between the rows of smiling people, and there it was, like a déjà vu of a déjà vu, the faint lingering notes of a lovely and familiar tune that cannot quite be identified. It was the echo of the burst of inexplicable joy I had felt on that first day at Zip's Candies.

My parents were barely present that afternoon, at the margins of the gathering of perhaps fifty people. Neither of them met or talked with anyone they didn't already know, except when absolutely cornered. Many of the guests on the Ziplinsky side (and most of the guests were on the Ziplinsky side) didn't realize my parents were even there that day. I was Arson Girl friendless; neither of my parents had close family, and they had declined to invite as many guests as they had been offered to by Frieda, who was, to her credit, very gracious about hosting the wedding, even though the family of the groom has no such obligation. It suited her; it gave her the advantage.

There were three black people among the guests. One of them was Minnie, the bright shining light of my childhood, maker of perfect tuna sandwiches, affectionate possessor of the only bosom, and an ample one it was, that I had ever been completely comfortable snuggling against. I hadn't seen her since her retirement a couple of years before. I had glimpsed her wiping her eyes with a big handkerchief as Howard and I walked up the makeshift aisle. I didn't know the others, a well-dressed couple in their early thirties, who had come in during the ceremony and were standing at the back, near my parents. I am ashamed to say I assumed they were Ziplinsky family past or present household employees, since they weren't familiar faces. (Zip's did have several black employees by 1975, but only a few select front-office people had been invited that day.)

As the curiously vile refreshments circulated (a troll in a white uniform kept breaking into groups and thrusting trays of hors d'oeuvres up from below drink level while braying, "Corned beef twist? Miniature knish? The lox on the blinis is very moist!"—I think it's pretty safe to assume my parents ate nothing that day), the distinguished black couple headed purposefully toward us. I felt Howard stiffen, and then he said quietly, "I'll be dipped. Darwin and Miriam are here. I didn't see them. I'm sure my mother didn't think they were coming."

I shouldn't have been so surprised by their skin color. (But then, in retrospect, there is a great deal about which I should have been more observant. *Had I But Known,* the story of my life.) At this time I had heard only a few references, mostly from Sam, about his uncle Julius, Eli's younger brother, the one who stayed behind in Budapest when Eli and the oldest brother, Morris, came to America. Julius was the one who went to Madagascar during World War II and then never left. He had an unlikely and prosperous life there, presiding over his cacao and vanilla plantations until a malaria epidemic killed him, a couple of years before Howard was born. Remember, I had only known the family for three months at this point, and all I knew was what I had gleaned in passing, in fragments. Nobody ever tells you the story of a family in a coherent sequence.

I had heard a few stories about how Howard had spent many summers staying with the Madagascar cousins, mostly weeding around cacao trees and performing menial tasks in the pollination and harvesting of vanilla seed pods. Irene had gone just once and never went back, finding the accommodations too primitive and the work too hard, but it was a really important part of Howard's life growing up. The way this had been described to me in passing made it sound like some sort of fragrant family kibbutz floating out there on that unlikely island in the Indian Ocean.

I gathered that Julius had children, but not until he got to Madagascar, which was why Darwin, his son, was Howard's contemporary, though Darwin was Sam's first cousin. I knew the plantations were still in the family, and that Howard had been on Madagascar in the spring of that same year, just three months before we met, though he said more than once that he should have known better than to go in monsoon season. I wasn't even sure where Madagascar was until Howard told me he had family there, a few weeks into our romance, which prompted me to look it up in the world atlas in my bookshelf at home, where I was still technically living that summer. But until this moment at our wedding, I had simply not considered what these cousins might look like. And so I met Darwin Czaplinsky and his wife, Miriam.

Howard was clearly nonplussed by the sight of them, as their inclusion on the guest list had really been meant only as a gesture, and nobody had expected any of the Madagascar branch of the family to come on such short notice, especially since none of them had replied to the invitation. Darwin was fierce and uncanny-looking, with dark brown skin and deep-set midnight-blue eyes. Miriam was a true Malagasy, exquisitely beautiful in an unidentifiably exotic sense, with a bearing like one of Gauguin's Tahitian women. I would learn later that she was from the Merina people, from the highlands, where Julius had settled among his vast estates.

They were dressed perfectly, better than anyone else there, like diplomats among the native peoples at a rural village festival. As they bore down on us, they both arranged their mouths to reveal their beautiful teeth, and they each looked me hard in the eye as we were introduced. After a moment's hesitation, they each kissed me on both cheeks, French-style. Then they surrounded Howard, pulling him away from me, and I heard Darwin say in his low, precise, accented voice, "Howdy, what have you done?"

Miriam looked at me over Howard's shoulder and said, "You may have the use of him, my dear, but you must never, ever forget that Howdy is ours." She showed me her beautiful teeth again. It wasn't a smile. The bad fairies had come to the wedding party. In a fairy tale, there are warning signs: the sun suddenly goes behind a dark cloud, a chill wind gusts through, frolicking gnomes run away and hide, the tranquil cat puffs herself up and hisses. But this was not a fairy tale, so I didn't recognize the signs, though I do believe I felt a distinct chill.

ONCE HOWARD AND I were married, my parents evidently stopped feeling at risk for further liability consequent to whatever disastrous thing I might do next, which made them much nicer, though there was never more between us than an occasional tiny flicker of fondness. As the years passed my father grew very deaf, and my mother's arthritis worsened, and then when Jacob and Julie were still in grade school my parents retired and moved to a well-regarded continuing-care community in Chapel Hill, south of snowy winters. It was a sensible alternative to Florida, of which they shared an unreasonable horror.

We made a few awkward visits so Julie and Jacob would continue to know their other grandparents, but then came my father's stroke, and then my mother had a heart attack, and they ended up spending their final years in separate wings of the nursing facility at Woodfield Farms, each of them unwilling to make any further effort to deal with the other. According to the social worker there, this turn of events is not entirely uncommon.

And then they died, a few months apart, nine years ago. They left their modest estate to my kids, their grandchildren, in equal shares, which was as it should be, but I have to say I would have liked to have been left some specific personal object by either one of them. When I went through their few and tidy papers, I hoped to find a letter addressed to me. Something, anything, personal. But there was nothing like that, just all the very impersonal and efficient legal documents. The year they both died, people who heard my news would try to comfort me with the trite observation that so often in the case of couples who have been married for so many years, when one dies, the other one loses the will to keep living on alone. Usually, I didn't have the heart to disagree. So that's my *mishpochah* of origin, as the Tatnalls never used to say.

It's not the meek who shall inherit the earth. It's the ambitious, the passionate! How much love could I be expected to feel for these ungenerous people as the years went by? I don't believe it's just my life among the door-slamming, bellowing Ziplinskys that led me to hope for more, more of anything, from those chilly, murmuring WASPs. Dr. Gibraltar told me I had displaced my unfulfilled desire for their approval (even before they were dead, but especially since their deaths, as after that it was concretely too late for them to come through), onto the living, breathing Ziplinsky family. Is that really what I wanted most of all, Ziplinsky approval? Good luck to me.

MISTAKES WERE MADE, as Nixon would say. Starting with my guilty plea to the felony arson charge. This was all consequent to the biggest mistake of all, which was my having been represented by Lou Popkin in the first place. Lou was the attorney who handled closings for my father. He had no experience with criminal cases, or much of anything else that didn't have to do with real estate, and had hardly ever appeared in front of a judge. He told me the only way I could stay out of jail for having burned down Debbie Livingston's house was if I just said yes to everything the judge asked me, and he would take care of everything else and not to worry, it was all set, I should just say yes. So that's what I did, I said Yes, and Yes, and Yes, Your Honor, and the next thing I knew I had agreed that I understood the charges, I had admitted to arson, and I had asserted that I felt extreme remorse. Moments later, I was found guilty of third-degree arson, with a suspended sentence and probation. I was a convicted felon. I was Arson Girl. And so I want to take this opportunity to set the record straight about that first fire, before I refute the allegation against me concerning the Zip's fire.

Once again I am involved in an accidental fire. People are so unimaginative. Inevitably, everyone smirks and says, Uh-huh, okay, we see, another fire, another accidental fire like the one that burned down Debbie Livingston's house, what an interesting coincidence, *Arson Girl*. Because only in novels do people accept wild coincidences without comment, let alone skepticism. Maybe it's the fault of all those plotlines on television and in movies (the same ones with music sound tracks that tell you how you're supposed to feel) that depend on coincidences always having a huge amount of meaning, and this makes the audience feel smart and insightful. The truth nobody likes to accept, out of a fear of missing something and being exposed as naive, is that sometimes a coincidence is only one of life's strange repetitions, only a coincidence. It's a funny thing about human nature, the way we resist genuine patterns and meanings, but when events form random patterns, we insist on seeing relationships and adding meanings that aren't really there at all.

THE FIRE THAT burned down Debbie Livingston's house in 1975 is not just old news, it's also new news, and not just because of the Zip's fire last month, but also because two years ago those television news clips were dredged up and aired, when Zip's made the news in the middle of June 2007. That was when Guadalupe and Hilaria Diaz, two Guatemalan sisters on our night cleaning crew (we have found Guatemalans to be very dependable workers in various capacities at Zip's, though when each was hired in the last few years we did not anticipate the collective impact of their religious devotion, which around certain obscure saints' days has required us to plan ahead so as not to disrupt our production schedules, as we were far more focused on issues of counterfeit green cards and false Social Security numbers, and we had to define a benevolent "Don't ask, don't tell" hiring policy for Zip's), attracted a lot of attention when they perceived the Virgin Mary in a concretion of hardened chocolate drippings that had formed under one of the Tigermelt striping nozzles after the line had been shut down for the night.

First Guadalupe sees a dazzling, bright ray of light beaming down on this inexplicable dark object on the belt that she immediately knows in her heart is the Blessed Virgin Mother, and then Hilaria swears on her sainted grandmother's soul that she sees it move, and then they both see a blob of chocolate drip from the nozzle and land perfectly on the Virgin Mary's head, like a halo, which is, of course, a clear sign. (Indeed—a clear sign that someone hasn't emptied and cleaned the striping applicator tank and nozzles per standard operating procedure when the line was shut down for the night. And that celestial ray? Probably a flaring high-intensity ceiling-fixture bulb in the security night-lighting system on the verge of burning out.)

Channel 3 ran the story the next day, a perfectly charming little human-interest segment to cap their six o'clock local news broadcast, the final feature before the local station switches over to the network national newscast, which was certainly a solid hit for Zip's public relations at the community level. We couldn't run the Tigermelt line for three days, not until the Blessed Chocolate Virgin (who looked to me more like a six-inch, poorly tempered chocolate version of the Incredible Hulk than like a divine manifestation, but I did not grow up in a culture that conditioned me to see images of Our Lord Jesus or the Blessed Virgin in every burnt taco or chocolate stalagmite) had hardened sufficiently so she could be carefully sliced off the Tigermelt enrobing belt and moved to a suitable place for preservation and worship. This was done two days later, with much ceremony, under the supervision of Father Carlos Asturias, the elderly priest from the church in Bridgeport to which the Diaz family belongs.

Jacob used a cutting wire to slice the Blessed Chocolate Virgin off the belt cleanly, and I was proud of him and the way he was suitably serious and professional throughout the procedure, maintaining a steady hand and a respectful mien that his father would probably not have been able to muster without cracking wise or smirking in my direction.

For more than thirty years, when things were good between us, I had a huge tolerance for Howard's unwillingness, or constitutional inability, whichever it was, to play the part of a grown-up without breaking character. I don't think Howard has ever appreciated the degree to which the way he behaves has so often undercut his authority at Zip's. I knew this about him before I married him, but I suppose I hoped he would outgrow it. He has that particular form of arrogance that can afflict those who have had all their good fortune handed to them. In inverse proportion to actual achievement, people like Howard crave credit and admiration for having reached the summit. It's definitely caused resentment among some of the most loyal employees over the years. Why would they enjoy taking orders from an idiot prince?

For years, I would have reminded myself at such a moment that Howard was essentially a good man with a good heart, and I would have had myself convinced that his clowning bid for my attention was a harmless signal in our secret code, a symptom of our closeness as a married couple, in the Mrs. Miniver sense of there being always an eye to catch.

But Howard wasn't there that June day two years ago on the floor at Zip's to swagger around his candy kingdom before deftly and casually slicing the Blessed Chocolate Virgin off the Tigermelt belt with his unique blend of competence and irresponsible insouciance, while cracking some joke about how he was just the right man for this job because innate skills for slicing halvah and lox were in his blood. Instead, Zip's was in a secret management crisis, Howard having been in Madagascar for two months at that point, living his true authentic life while a lot of urgent issues gathered like storm clouds over the business. I did all I could, with Jacob shouldering a lot of responsibility, to carry on the day-to-day business without letting anyone know how long Howard had been gone or how unclear it was when, if ever, he would be back. Instead, Jacob, dignified and authoritative at twenty-five, stepped up that day.

I was immensely proud of our son, proud of the way he presided over the situation with an appropriately respectful grace and authority that would have completely eluded Howard. Seeing Jacob take over at that moment, seeing his tender gallantry with the devout Diaz sisters, who hovered anxiously over the operation, I had a sudden revelation about just how corrosive Howard's behavior had been for Zip's. His perpetual undermining wisecracking, which I had tolerated and excused for so long, was demoralizing for everyone. I realized that I was glad Howard wasn't there, and at that moment I knew Zip's Candies would survive, that the business would be okay, better than okay, without him.

We had sufficient Tigermelt stock on hand. Let's face it, Tigermelts are a very small and stable line, which at Zip's is code for stagnant, with an ever-dwindling market share. Because of that one catastrophic new product failure at Zip's, Howard has been especially reluctant to mess with the Tigermelt line in any significant way for years now, even though he knows perfectly well that the only way Zip's can hope to hold our place in our little niche (since we can't possibly compete with the big companies and their multimillion-dollar advertising budgets and endlessly deep pockets for slotting fees) would be with modest forays into brand extensions. And of course, while we hardly like to admit it, and don't reveal this publicly as a matter of both corporate pride and industry confidentiality, it is the contract manufacturing of those two energy bars that has kept our lights burning these past few years.

So the briefly suspended Tigermelt line didn't hurt us. It would have been a very different story if this had occurred in the run-up to Halloween, but June isn't a big candy season, though God knows we need a few more occasions and holidays in the year that trigger candy consumption the way Halloween and Easter do. I am convinced there has got to be some way to penetrate the Fourth of July market much more deeply, for example. Consider what you buy at the grocery store for the Fourth of July: hot dogs and hamburgers, buns, ketchup, mustard, pickles, chips, soda and beer, ice cream and cookies, maybe watermelon—but where's the candy? There's no specific tradition for it. So that's a lost opportunity. There is an enviable reflex to reach for a Hershey's bar when you buy s'mores ingredients, but that's about it. Tootsie Roll, among others, does a Fourth of July wrapper, but I'm not sure that in itself is sufficient to create an association for the consumer.

We do well enough with theater box sales for summer movies, but it's diffuse, not pegged to a specific holiday. Oddly enough, we also do really well with the back-to-school season, especially if the heat of summer doesn't linger. Something about autumn leaves and crisp new notebooks and sharpened pencils seems to inspire the purchasing of Tigermelts and Little Sammies. Possibly it is a strong season for all the older brands, like ours, like Mary Jane, like Baby Ruth, because of a semiconscious nostalgia for their own childhood experiences on the part of parents. Or perhaps candy sweetens the loss of summer's freedom. In any case, it didn't hurt us to shut down the Tigermelt line for a few days.

Who knows, the Blessed Chocolate Virgin could have been the trigger for a whole new market for Tigermelts among the Central American immigrant population, if the company had ever been willing to spend more than a few begrudging nickels on promotions of any kind (you have to go back to the 1960s to see good Zip's merchandising), let alone creative marketing. "Strike while the iron is hot" are words that might as well be in Esperanto when it comes to our small-minded distributors, who are both satisfied with the status quo for accounts like ours and at the same time have bigger fish to fry, so to speak.

That reminds me of how desirable I have long thought it would be if we could find a way to inspire, to incentivize (as we say in the business, with apologies to Miss Solomon, who hated vulgar words like *finalize* and *incentivize*) country fairs and carnivals to feature fried Tigermelts along with all those fried Milky Way and Three Musketeers bars. I've done a little testing with Tigermelts, and as is true for Milky Way and Three Musketeers, the bars have to go into the batter frozen, and then they should be fried for no longer than two and a half minutes or you end up with fried goo. In Scotland the big thing is fried Mars bars, sometimes offered in chip shops, dessert to go with your fish and chips, and I am certain they freeze them as well, given that nougat and caramel core.

None of our distributors is willing to think through any of the possibilities for increasing the numbers on Little Sammies, Mumbo Jumbos, and Tigermelts with imaginative promotions. If I could clone myself, this was one of the times I would have worked the phones, to make the most of the Blessed Chocolate Virgin, and if I had felt more comfortable in my de facto role as head of the business at that time, I might have tried to get going with a fast production of a Limited-Edition Zip's Blessed Chocolate Virgin, using the Little Sammies production line, with a molded figure replicating that holy object sent by God to Zip's Candies, here on Earth, in New Haven, Connecticut, at the edge of the Quinnipiac River, to blorp out of that striping nozzle onto the Tigermelt belt.

We are long overdue, to the point of real negligence, to find some room in the budget for a Spanish-language campaign with print ads, bus cards, urban street-level billboards—and this would have been our golden opportunity. But we were just treading water as it was at that time, and that was before Channel 8's ambush, so there was really no chance for Zip's to cash in on the Blessed Chocolate Virgin.

And so, Zip's being Zip's, the whole Blessed Chocolate Virgin moment was only good for some meaningless local color news coverage and temporary fodder for those lunatics who apparently sit at their computers all day long and post constantly in the comments area on the strange fan blog devoted to Little Sammies that Julie monitors (she tells me the bloggers call themselves a community), and we got no bump, not even a discernable blip, on our Tigermelt numbers for that quarter.

And we probably lost any chance we had for Tigermelt traction from the Chocolate Blessed Virgin not just because of our trademark inertia (there's an idea—we really should make a Zip's Inertia bar, a glucose-saturated bar guaranteed to zap your glycemic index and keep you sedentary, unproductive, and ambition-free, and market it to the burnt-out middle management worker), but also because of what happened with Frieda when the busload of Guatemalan nuns from Queens arrived to see the Blessed Chocolate Virgin.

I was supervising the floor, with two lines running, and Jacob was trying to cover both the front office and Receiving. Jacob was on the loading dock arguing with the delivery guy for our sugar supplier about some ripped bags and consequent moisture damage and waste in the previous delivery. Julie had called in to say she was working from her apartment, which is code for too depressed and disorganized to get up and get dressed, I am sorry to say.

It was one of Frieda's good days, so instead of being at home expressing her contempt for one of the extraordinarily patient home health aides we employed in thankless eight-hour shifts to keep her out of trouble and to make it possible for her to keep living in the house she and Sam shared for the last forty years of their fifty-two years together, she was on the premises, in the old, little-used bookkeeper's office down at the end near the factory door. There she could spend an hour or two zealously date-stamping stacks of old, now-meaningless invoices from the 1980s in a kinetic parody of the actual work she did at Zip's for so many decades before that well-tempered mind grew softer and duller, losing its snap and gloss. I have a mental picture of what happened to Frieda's brain as it gradually lost its deep crenellations and became smoother and smoother and duller and duller, like what happens to the Tigermelts when there's a pileup on the belt running through the enrober and some bars get stalled under the nozzles and become heavily overcoated.

Five years ago, Frieda's loosening grasp of reality forced us to maneuver her gradual withdrawal from any genuine responsibilities at Zip's. Irene knew about this shift, and she certainly knew about her mother's faltering mental state, so it is hardly legitimate for her now to characterize the way her mother was treated as a power grab on my part. Irene knew what we were dealing with. It was very clear at the time that the only interest she had in the management issues at Zip's was her uninterrupted income. Those who did all the work continued to do all the work. Those who sat back and cashed checks continued to sit back and cash checks.

We carefully eased Frieda out of the daily workings of the business inch by inch. It helped with the transition to set her up on her good days with something familiar to do, though the tasks grew smaller and smaller until they were only gestures, and then finally they had no meaning at all. At times it took a lot of effort to make her feel useful, but it was the right thing to do. Even with Howard AWOL, I wanted to do everything I could to see to it that she was welcome to come in when she was up to it, no matter how much energy it took to accommodate her, until the incident with the nuns. Are these the actions of a gold digger?

On those good days, after checking in with her keeper to see what kind of night it had been, Jake would go pick her up at her house in Westville (he carried a milk crate in the back of his Jeep so she could step up to climb into the seat), drive her to Zip's, park in the visitor's lot, and walk her in the front entrance (instead of parking out back and going in through the loading dock area as he would otherwise begin his workday). Then he and I would arrange everything for her, the way you would organize a busywork activity to harness the energies of a competent toddler visiting an office, with a few tall stacks of old useless paperwork that had been set aside for recycling and the big, heavy chrome date stamp we used to use for logging invoices, and she would go to work.

THE NUNS WERE just two hours too late. Renee Cohen, the front-office manager (she's my age and has been with us seventeen years, and for just one small example of the way we treat our employees like family, I'll mention that in 1996 Zip's helped her with a low-interest loan for the down payment on her little Cape in Short Beach), politely told them they had missed it, and explained that the Blessed Chocolate Virgin had left with Father Asturias and was by now presumably ensconced in the church in Bridgeport, where they could go see it. The nuns just milled around uncomprehendingly in our dingy reception area, though the ones with sufficient English were tearful. You would think that the Blessed Chocolate Virgin had been scraped into the trash instead of transported to Bridgeport to be worshipped and venerated, but apparently they had their hearts set on seeing the miracle in the place where it had occurred.

Renee had wisely paged me off the floor, and I had just invited them into the factory for a quick, consoling glimpse of the actual Tigermelt striping apparatus from which the holy object had been extruded, when Frieda, having either completed or lost interest in her morning's task, came shuffling down the hall. She got one look at the nuns and began shouting that they couldn't set foot in her factory, it would violate hygiene regulations, those dirty habits could catch on the machinery or spread germs, she would call the health department herself, they all had to leave, no tours, no tours, no exceptions, get out of here, all of you, go in your *schvartze shmattas,* vamoose!

As I signaled to them to disregard her and keep following me, she became agitated and yelled at them, Ignore her! That woman is not family! She has no authority here; she is just summer help! Then she ran out of steam and just stood there in the doorway to Howard's office, panting and looking pitiful, trying to catch her breath after her strenuous shouting. Sam, where is Sam? Sam? Howdy? Where's Dad? Howdy! She kept calling out, looking around in a new kind of panicky confusion that was the herald of further deterioration. This was the last day we ever had her come in to "work" at Zip's.

Frieda wouldn't let me touch her, let alone steer her to a chair, and fortunately her beloved Jakie arrived on the scene at this point. I tried to coax the nuns past her and down the hall to the factory doors while he strong-armed his grandmother into Howard's office, but they were frightened and confused, and clearly troubled by her indignant muffled cries, so they fled in the opposite direction, to the sidewalk out front. I followed them to their bus and gave their driver directions to the church in Bridgeport, and the driver waited while I ran back in so I could fill a bag with Tigermelts, Mumbo Jumbos, and Little Sammies to sweeten their disappointment.

ALL OF THIS is to say that the Zip's Blessed Chocolate Virgin story would have played out quickly, if not for that damned producer at Channel 8, who apparently had a mother who recognized me—Arson Girl!—in the Channel 3 report for which I was taped out in front of Zip's (we don't allow photographs of anything on the floor, because, no joke, this is how the competition can figure out how you do what you do), unwrapping a Tigermelt and explaining to that idiot reporter, whatever her name is, the one who looks like a guppy and dresses like a flight attendant, who kept calling me Alice Zip instead of Alice Ziplinsky and then she overcorrected and referred to Ziplinsky's Candies instead of Zip's as she ended the interview, so they had to do the whole segment over again, twice, which was surely not my fault (she got very irritable with me), and I had to unwrap two more Tigermelts while explaining each time in the same way how a combination bar is made and how the Tigermelt bar gets that final signature dark-chocolate tiger stripe from the nozzles from which dripped the little chocolate miracle.

The producer's mother had lived on that same block on

Canner Street and had been friendly with Mrs. Livingston. And so, when Channel 8 ran their catch-up story the next evening, featuring Father Asturias entering his Bridgeport church in a solemn procession with the Blessed Chocolate Virgin carried aloft behind him, it was heralded by a teaser promising an exclusive shocking surprise revelation about how a member of the prominent (in New Haven, maybe) Zip's Candies family, Alice Tatnall Ziplinsky, had a dark history (those were the words, *dark history,* which sound now, as I write them, almost pleasingly bitter, like dark chocolate) and a criminal record.

And then, not that it had anything whatsoever to do with the Blessed Chocolate Virgin story, after maybe only ten seconds (at most, for all that fuss and bother) of me squinting into the camera and unwrapping a Tigermelt and explaining the dark-chocolate tiger stripe all over again for the Channel 8 reporter the way I had done it for Channel 3, there was footage of the 1975 fire that burned down the Livingston residence on Canner Street, and guess what? Arson Girl, so called because she pleaded guilty to this terrible crime of arson and yet she never served a day in jail, what about that? She grew up to be a member of the prominent Zip's Candies family! Are your children consuming candy made by a convicted criminal? Several people interviewed on the street expressed their determination not to buy candy made by felons. And now, in other news.

The shock of that unexpected exposure gave me a sick, punched feeling in my gut. Just remembering it now, I am feeling waves of nausea all over again. (I have never liked the word *prominent*. It always means more than it means.) I have felt that kind of panicky free-fall horror only a few times in my life. The day of the fire, the day of the sentencing, the day I got the letter from Middlebury telling me to never mind. Life has been much kinder to me for a long while, with many joyful experiences, and it was not until the dawning of the whole truth about Howard's other life in Madagascar that I felt such blackness again.

I certainly had a doomy feeling the day I first saw Frieda exhibit symptoms of dementia and had to admit to myself what I had known for a while, that she was losing it, but I suppose that was a different shade of black, in the pantheon of my darkest moments. Our relationship was always tricky, and she made it hard for me to love her, but there was something really admirable in her toughness and her loyalty to the family, and to the business, even though she was pretty hard on me over the years. She did soften a little toward me after Jacob and Julie were born (I once overheard her telling one of her Hadassah cronies that the problem with me was that I was a dumb goy with two smart Jewish children). Given that my purpose in these pages is to say everything I can about Zip's Candies and to give history and background to establish my knowledge of the facts about the current issues, and given that every piece of Ziplinsky family history is also Zip's Candies history, and also given that I have just described an instance of Frieda's dementia that was potentially harmful to the business, I might as well describe that first incident now, given that Frieda's behavior in her final years could have exposed Zip's to very damaging liabilities, for which I could have been blamed.

I documented this incident at the time, seven years ago. I was helping with a pour and blend for a big batch of Tigermelt nougat. People are amazed at how much is still done by hand at Zip's. Creating the necessary machinery to automate some of these functions on the line would cost a fortune, and our batches are so small, it just wouldn't pay to automate each of these steps unless it was part of a bigger plan to increase production and distribution in a substantial way. And it could be surprisingly difficult to get it right, to create efficient machines that would duplicate precisely every step of the unique processes that are integral to production on our three lines.

Ironically enough, Tigermelts contain no butter. We all know what happened to the competitive tigers in *Little Black Sambo*— "they all just melted away, and there was nothing left but a great big pool of melted butter . . . round the foot of the tree." For the Tigermelt centers, when the marshmallow nougat (a proprietary blend of egg whites, sucrose, and corn syrup) and the caramel (dried milk solids, sucrose, molasses, and vanilla) are cooled to just the right temperatures in their blending pots, they are then poured and swirled together in a partial blend, not a fifty-fifty blend, more like seventy-thirty, with more nougat than caramel, and then the hot fried peanuts are stirred in. This all takes both physical strength and coordination and also really specific timing, so it requires teamwork. You are rushing to beat the clock as you blend this beige goop just a certain amount in a very precise way, on a big, sinklike batch table.

Time and temperature are two key ingredients in every candy line. Time and temperature, Sam used to say, they're your friend, or they're your enemy. If you don't control the time and the temperature, you will have no quality control, you may ruin your product, and you will never have a smooth-running line. You have to own the time and the temperature, or the time and the temperature will own you. Eli cared about tempering, and it was a point of pride for Sam that Zip's Candies has always had a high standard for well-tempered chocolate, and it is a feature of the Tigermelt coating. Tempering is chocolate alchemy, mechanical manipulation plus precise heat in order to force chocolate into the desirable crystalline form so that when it is properly cooled it forms a stable solid with a smooth and shiny surface.

When the Tigermelt center mixture is sufficiently blended

and cooled, you have only about a seven-minute window to stir in the hot fried peanuts. It has to happen at just the right time as the temperature of the mixture cools, so the peanuts are blended all the way through the nougat, so they get mixed in with the caramel swirls instead of sinking too quickly or failing to penetrate and getting stuck all bunched together on the surface, which creates enrobing problems and leads to misshapen bars. (It's like baking *shmura* matzo; to prevent inadvertent leavening, within eighteen minutes the flour and water have to be mixed, the dough has to be kneaded and rolled, and the matzo has to go into the oven.) The average number of peanuts in a Tigermelt is twenty-eight. Other than Baby Ruth, I defy you to name another combination bar with national distribution that has such a high proportion of whole peanuts. (Not peanut halves or pieces, whole peanuts.)

It's simple enough, but if the blending isn't done correctly it throws off the texture and the consistency of the Tigermelt bar. Most popular combination bars are made of these same ingredients and the same inclusions, more or less, in varying proportions and consistencies. What gives each bar its unique flavor and texture are the recipes—the established proportions and protocols that guarantee predictable results and uniformity, batch to batch. When you take a bite of an Oh Henry!, a Baby Ruth, or a Tigermelt, you know what to expect. That's what makes you take your favorite candy bar off the rack at the supermarket checkout and put it on the belt with your grocery order week after week, even though you would never write it on your shopping list.

Your mouth and taste buds have their own kind of sense memory. You have a deep, semiconscious anticipation and desire based on experience for what's going to hit your tongue and your teeth first, and then what happens after that, how it's going to blend when you bite down and start to chew and the flavor hits the roof of your mouth and then the back of your throat as you begin to swallow. If there is no consistency to the consistency, then there is nothing on which to build loyalty. And loyalty is a fundamental key to success in selling candy bars, along with creating in you, the consumer, certain deep feelings of desire, cravings that can be reinforced and triggered in calculated ways by branding and advertising.

Loyalty is the key. The successful candy bar is supported by a consumer belief that he or she is honoring family traditions, so that loyalty is all bound up with nostalgia for childhood experiences either actual or longed-for. Ideally, too, the consumer has a sense of entitlement to self-indulgence driven by an ambivalence toward guilty pleasure. I mention all these things because my knowledge and experience in the candy manufacturing business in general, and with Zip's Candies in particular, should be above question, but they have been questioned, so it seems necessary for me to provide ample evidence that will establish my credibility in these matters.

To give one more example of my role in the business over the years, Sam told me many times that I was a smart cookie for advising him long ago that Zip's could do better at Easter, a holiday with which I had personal experience. Consequently, Zip's Candies ended up in more Easter promotions and in more Easter baskets. I loved being able to provide that valuable insight. I love the candy business.

So, THE MOMENT: Frieda, who was kibitzing as usual, telling everyone to hurry up or be careful or slow down and then hurry up, the way she always did, suddenly went quiet, which was, for her, unusual. We finished the pours, without her customary admonition about squeezing out the last caramel sludge from inside the nozzle so as not to be wasteful, and then I looked across at her in time to glimpse an expression of confusion sweep across her face, as if she didn't quite know where she was, as she backed away from the batch table. She immediately bumped against a rolling rack that holds the wooden mogul trays for Mumbo Jumbos, but the rack, being empty, this not being a Mumbo Jumbo day, wasn't chocked, so it rolled back, causing her to lose her balance a little. Then Frieda took another step back, and now she was at the edge of a worktable against the wall. All this happened in just an instant, a few seconds, and it was really nothing, but some tiny sense that there was something wrong kept me watching her. Sally Fernstein, one of the steadiest line workers at Zip's, passed just then, pushing a stack of Tigermelt wrapper boxes on a dolly, and she eyed Frieda quizzically, also sensing something awry, then looked over at me with a raised eyebrow.

On the worktable behind Frieda was a coffee can (Maxwell House, I can see the blue can with that tilted cup in my mind's eye even now) filled with small pliers and wrenches, greasy bolts and brads, pins and washers and screws, and stubs of little pencils, along with some pushpins and a couple of rolls of electrical tape and little springs and hinges and coils of wire and who knows what else. That can of essentials was part of our arsenal for keeping the ancient equipment chugging along for one more day (and of course it shouldn't have been anywhere near an active production line, but hardly a day passes when something isn't being tightened up or readjusted, if not flat-out jury-rigged, at some point in the shift).

Just as Petey Leventhal (who came to Zip's in 1978, when Cadbury took over Peter Paul in Naugatuck) returned on cue, lugging the ten-gallon stainless-steel pail of hot fried peanuts and calling out, "Hot soup! Hot soup!" over the factory din the way he always did to clear his path to the batch table from our medieval-looking peanut fryer (it's a repurposed vat originally designed for use in a poultry processing plant, when freshly electrocuted chickens are dipped briefly into boiling water to loosen the feathers before being processed through the plucking machine), I saw Frieda pick up the coffee can and peer blankly at the contents.

As Petey poured the peanuts into the mixture and I began stirring with a big wooden mixing paddle that looks like a small rowboat oar, and then Petey set down the empty pail and picked up his paddle and began stirring even more vigorously, Frieda (who should have been dabbing at the mixture by now as well with the third paddle), as if mimicking his gesture of pouring out the peanuts a moment before, emptied the contents of the coffee can into the mix in one big sweeping motion. Out of this cornucopia of hardware remnants came a cascade of nuts and bolts and screws and springs and cogs, all instantly deployed in a perfect parabolic wave across the surface of the peanut-studded Tigermelt nougat and caramel mixture. The metal pieces sank down and were instantly and inextricably bound into the cooling sweet and chewy, salty (we salt the fried peanuts) and crunchy secret blend that gives Tigermelts their irresistibly delicious Tigermelt taste. Most people can taste this core of the bar and recognize the Tigermelt identity instantly, even before the two applications of enrobing milk chocolate and the final dark-chocolate signature tiger stripe have been applied.

Why on earth did I do that? Frieda murmured under her breath before walking away from the batch table, still holding the empty coffee can. Petey and I just stood there for a moment and watched the shrapnel glistening in the blend, stupefied. Both of us had kept stirring for one more moment, as if keeping on with our routine could in some way override the reality of what had just happened. We had to shut down and throw away that entire batch, of course, and sterilize the batch table. When I told Howard what Frieda had done (he had been out on the Yale golf course with a grocery-chain buyer from New Jersey most of that afternoon), he laughed it off, and went around the rest of the day singing an adaptation of that pernicious and effective Peter Paul jingle, so his version was about how sometimes you feel like a nut, sometimes a bolt. But we both knew it was a turning point, even if no one ever said another word about that incident.

AND TO FINISH about that ambush of a Channel 8 evening news report on the Blessed Chocolate Virgin story two years ago, by the time the eleven o'clock report rolled around, they had expanded their coverage. Having broadcast teasers for the story in the little newsbreaks between commercials all during prime time, they led off with a breathless intro about a developing story uncovered by their team of investigative reporters. I kept expecting my phone to ring at any moment with a call from a friend, a family member, an employee, but either nobody had caught it or everyone had.

The piece began with the Zip's Blessed Chocolate Virgin story recap, with a good exterior shot of Zip's and a few words from the generally incoherent Diaz sisters, then there I was with the Tigermelt, followed by a nice little sidewalk interview with Jacob about the history of the family business, and then came some footage of the procession into the church, led by Father Asturias, with the Blessed Chocolate Virgin on a platter, held aloft by a throng of worshippers. This was followed by a dramatic candlelit glimpse of the Blessed Chocolate Virgin safely ensconced in a place of honor inside Saint Thomas's, on her own blue velvet altar. Then the story shifted back to 1975 and there were dramatic captions and dramatic scenes of the blazing Livingston house, ornamented by useless streams of water pouring from the firemen's hoses into the smoke and flames.

They cut to overexposed daytime courthouse exterior footage, and there I am, a zombie of a teenager in a peasant blouse and a denim skirt, my tear-blotched face masked by a huge pair of sunglasses that aren't mine, my unruly hair bunched into an indifferent ponytail, shuffling in Dr. Scholl's wooden sandals into the courthouse under a harsh glare that is probably a combination of relentless summer sunshine and the bright lights of the news cameras. I am flanked by my grim, squinting parents (they are willing to appear supportive in public) and our lawyer, the hapless Lou Popkin, with those sideburns, sweltering in his regrettable orange corduroy suit with the pointy lapels (he will commit suicide a couple of years later, for no apparent cause), and suddenly this stupid thing I did by accident a lifetime ago, when I was a child, something having nothing whatsoever to do with Zip's Candies or the Blessed Chocolate Virgin, this rancid and bitter piece of the past, becomes inexorably blended into the present.

I KNOW I will never be able to clear my name completely. I will always be Arson Girl, and nothing can be done about that. I am especially sorry that Julie and Jacob have to live with it. I can only say once again that while my actions did cause that house to burn down, I was a foolish high school kid, and it was an unpremeditated, freakish accident for which I was then and am now truly sorry. (I am not entirely sorry about the Zip's fire, which I know I probably shouldn't admit, but my willingness to admit that I am not entirely sorry should be in my favor, because of what it says about my willingness to be completely truthful and honest about my statements pertaining to Zip's Candies.)

How was I to know that water pistol had charcoal lighter fluid in it? How was I to know Beth Crabtree's father always lit their barbecue that way? That's really stupid and dangerous, when you think about it. Yet he was never charged with reckless endangerment or whatever. I only took the water gun for a joke.

State of mind is important in the eyes of the law. I recall with perfect clarity my state of mind. When I saw the transparent red plastic Luger lying on the windowsill in the Crabtrees' kitchen, as I waited by the back door while Beth lied to her mother about what movie we were going to see, I picked it up, and feeling that it was loaded—what else but water should it have been filled with, I ask you?—I slid it into my fringed, patchwork shoulder bag, which I had bought on Eighth Street on a day trip to New York's Greenwich Village with a group of girls from my class a few months before. It was a spontaneous gesture, with no more than a second of premeditation before I took it, if that. (And no, I did not smell the lighter fluid, hard as that may be to believe.)

Why did I take it? I can never answer this question satisfactorily enough. Just on an impulse, to be silly, to whip it out at some point later that night as a joke. My mother used an old water pistol to discourage a neighbor's cat who liked to dig in our flower beds and shit all over her penstemon. If I had really planned only to use a water gun as a joke, the assistant district attorney, Kevin what'shisname, kept asking triumphantly, why hadn't I taken that water gun from my home? Which only proves that this was a spontaneous act, my taking the loaded water gun off the Crabtrees' windowsill, wouldn't you think? I had no plan!

What did I have in mind? Absolutely nothing. Yes, it is true that at Debbie Livingston's party I anticipated that I was likely to encounter Andy Ottenberg, who had developed a nasty habit of mocking me cruelly when I was at my most heartfelt and impassioned. He had done this all through our senior year at every opportunity. He was the managing editor of the school paper, for which I wrote an excruciatingly pretentious advice column called "Go Ask Alice." But I had no plan. And it really didn't feel like theft of a potentially lethal weapon. It was just a plastic water pistol.

After Beth's mother told us to have fun at our movie (we told her we were going to see *Dog Day Afternoon*), we headed over to Debbie Livingston's house, where there were no parents, because Mr. and Mrs. Livingston thought their little darling was still the sweet innocent who not so long ago dressed as a bumblebee three Halloweens in a row. They had no idea that these days she was famous not for her imaginative costume skills but for her imaginative and dexterous approach to certain skills of sexual manipulation, which she provided willingly to a select group of the most popular senior boys, and her parents had definitely never heard her personal motto, "It isn't a sin if you don't put it in." Mr. and Mrs. Livingston thought they had no worries at all that night, since Debbie had told them she would do homework and feed the cat, and maybe her best friend, Mara, would sleep over and they might watch some television before bedtime; meanwhile her parents should have a super great time in the city. So off they went to New York, for dinner and a musical and then an overnight stay at the Plaza Hotel. It was their wedding anniversary.

I FINALLY SAW *Dog Day Afternoon* on television one night when I was up late with Julie, who was a colicky infant who frequently needed to be held and rocked and soothed. Howard had gone to bed because he had work in the morning. (I took six months maternity leave for Jacob, and for Julie, but in fact both times I was back at Zip's before that, working a few hours a week, wearing my baby in a sling.) Watching Al Pacino grow more and more frantic as he realizes he has no good way out of the bank he is trying to rob, I found myself growing more and more regretful that Beth Crabtree and I hadn't just gone to see the movie to which we claimed to be headed, out by the mall. We would have shared a giant tub of popcorn, watched the movie, and gone home. I would have spent four years at Middlebury College, and today I would be a college graduate with many friends doing who knows what, living who knows where, and if I were to attend my Middlebury reunions nobody would call me Arson Girl.

Perhaps Beth Crabtree and I might have remained good friends over all these years. But we never spoke again after that night. If we had gone to the movie we said we were going to see, the Livingstons would have come home from New York the following day to find their spacious, five-bedroom, neo-Colonial house with its attached two-car garage and its overgrown rhododendrons pretty much as they left it, with no discernable trace of yet another of Debbie's very popular, unauthorized, parent-free parties. The Livingstons would not have returned to the Plaza after their show in a festive mood (they had a pretheater dinner at Mamma Leone's and saw *Chicago,* I read in their statements) to find four urgent messages from the New Haven Police Department, and they would not have driven back to New Haven at top speed in a panic after midnight, and they would not have returned to Canner Street to find a smoldering, blackened, three-story neo-Colonial husk surrounded by blackened rhododendron skeletons, with three fire engines still churning, police cruisers with flashing lights parked all over the street, barricades at both ends of their block, and disembodied radio-dispatcher voices squawking occasionally from the dashboards into the hot, smoky night air. I saw them arrive. I was in the back seat of one of the police cruisers, although I had not yet been arrested.

If Beth Crabtree and I had gone to see *Dog Day Afternoon* that night, then poor old Homer, Debbie Livingston's ancient orange cat, would not have been found dead three days later, wedged up high in a tree in a neighbor's yard, his severely charred tail tangled in the branches. Accidental incineration of a beloved pet is not a crime in the state of Connecticut, but it is a terrible, terrible crime. If I were Debbie Livingston, I wouldn't have forgiven me either.

THAT NIGHT IN the Livingstons' backyard, when he saw me come through the gate with Beth, Andy Ottenberg said something to the group of his friends with whom he was standing around a rusty and tilted three-legged barbecue grill, which was very close to the side of the house, right by the back steps that led up to the kitchen door. I know this sounds middle-aged and suburban and unlikely for a bunch of high school kids, but that is what they were doing. I have a very clear recollection of the way the grill surface was entirely covered with sizzling hot dogs, and there were several washtubs of ice beside the grill, filled with beer and soda cans, with more packages of hot dogs piled on top, and there were packages of buns on a card table, next to big bowls of potato chips and a stack of paper plates and napkins. I absolutely love hot dogs, and I remember distinctly feeling too self-conscious to be observed eating one at that party, although I was instantly hungry after my first whiff of that alluring, greasy smoke.

The boys around the grill all snickered and turned to look at me and I heard somebody say the words *tits* and *bitch* as Beth and I approached. If Andy had ever sincerely liked me, the feelings had curdled and gone rancid long before this night, and his merciless teasing had become painfully personal and barbed, it is true. I have never denied that.

"What did you just say?" I demanded of Andy, who was leaning one-handed with a studied casual air against the side of the Livingstons' house, chugging beer from a bottle. Maybe he was a little drunk. Maybe they all were. I was so self-righteous! Why did I care so much? Possibly I was already resenting my self-imposed hot dog deprivation. "What were you saying about me?"

"I said everybody knows you're a bitch because you're sexually frustrated," Andy said with a smirk, putting his beer down on the ground so he could thrust the curved end of the barbecue tongs up and down through circled fingers in a lewd and monkeyish gesture. His friends erupted in knowing laughter again. "You want some of this, tat for tits?" he added. (And you question why I took the name Ziplinsky gladly and willingly, so happy was I to be done with my tainted Tatnall name.)

And that's when it happened, in an instant. I lost my temper. I had turned away, but then I turned back toward Andy and took a step forward, swinging my shoulder bag at him in frustration and anger, and some embarrassment. He ducked, and I missed, but my bag, which was weighted with makeup; a thick, dog-eared paperback of *The Moonstone* by Wilkie Collins; my wallet and keys; the loaded water pistol; and a hardcover copy of *Slaughterhouse-Five* (from the New Haven Public Library, which many months later began to send me a series of importuning letters about this overdue book until finally, without telling me, Howard very gallantly went there one autumn day and paid for the lost book in order to stop the letters), flew off my shoulder and out of my grasp. It hit the barbecue grill, which tipped over in a shower of sparks, scattering white-hot coals and all those hot dogs on the flagstones, and then there was an enormous *whomp* of an explosion.

In an instant, the side of the Livingstons' house was a blue sheet of flames. Was this a nightmare? Time stopped and started again, and then everyone was shouting in the yard, and someone started screaming inside the house, and the sheet of flame grew and spread, the front line of inexorable flame advancing on a tide of curling, blackening, burning, melting vinyl siding. Wisps of lacy black smoke leaked along the edges of the siding in lengthening tendrils that curled together and knotted the air with a thickening haze. Now billows of poisonous black smoke poured from behind the siding, sifting through the seams, as another and another segment softened and smeared and then melted.

Smudgy plumes leaked around the edges of the kitchen window frame for a long moment before that, too, burst into flames as it was engulfed in the upward melting tide that advanced up the side of the house in a sheet of thin blue flame. Acrid black smoke was now pouring thickly from several places at once as the fire spread across the wall of the house and ate its way up toward the roof.

Everyone was screaming and shouting, and kids came pouring out of the house coughing and gagging and crying as the house filled with clouds of choking black smoke, and the flames spread unbelievably fast. And then the inside of the house was completely on fire, and windows were breaking, and the sound of the fire was ferocious as it roared and consumed everything; now the roof was on fire, and the scorching heat coming off the house was like an invisible wall that kept pushing everyone back, back, back.

Big black flakes wafted through the air, hideous confetti, some still glowing with a rill of toxic flame at their edges, and they floated up and down and up and down on the weirdly billowing hot air that surrounded us, before landing in the trees and on the parked cars with a festive glow, leaving faint scorch marks. Everyone standing there gaping and screaming and crying and shouting had to dodge and dance out of the way as these enormous glowing flakes of bitter ash rained down.

The police and the fire trucks arrived after what seemed like hours but was in fact nine and a half minutes from the first 911 call (not a great response time, really, now that I think about it as a tax-paying home owner), and I stood across the street with everyone watching the house burn while Beth Crabtree stared at me in horror, saying again and again, "Oh my God! What did you do? Oh my God, Alice! Your life is over! Oh my God!" until I told her to shut up, could she please just shut up, and she did. She left me and went to stand with the other kids, and then some parents began to arrive, and I was alone, and I could feel everyone looking at me.

3

FRIEDA OBVIOUSLY THOUGHT I was trouble from that very first day I walked in the door at Zip's Candies. She couldn't keep her beautiful son away from me; she couldn't even keep her unbeautiful husband from being charmed and amused by me right from the start. She recognized these defeats, but she never let me win her over completely, though she permitted numerous temporary small victories, which was, in its own subtle way, deceptive and controlling.

When Howard told his parents we wanted to get married at the end of that summer, they were having dinner at Kaysey's, their downtown favorite in those days (Frieda loved the big, high, red leatherette booths, which reminded her of sophisticated New York places like Sardi's, and Sam loved the potato pancakes with applesauce). Howard told me that Sam was elated, which irked Frieda considerably. "If you don't marry that girl, I will!" was probably not a good thing to say in Frieda's earshot, even if he didn't mean it literally.

Howard reported to me that his mother had sighed heavily and would only say she knew this was coming, knew it from her first glimpse of me in that ridiculous ice cream *shmatta,* when she should have recognized me as that scheming Arson Girl from the newspapers, a part of my résumé that I had failed to disclose to Sam, and perhaps I could fool everyone else, but not Frieda. She knew trouble when she saw it.

Although Frieda didn't want me to convert, as I have already mentioned (and how deeply strange is that, seriously?), I really tried to embrace the Ziplinskys and their beliefs. Which turned out to be my beliefs about their beliefs. I studied all aspects of the Jewish religion, all the rules and meanings. The more I learned, the more confusing it was, because nothing I could find in a book ever precisely matched the Ziplinsky methods for observing Jewish tradition. Were they Reform? Were they Reconstructionists? Howard was useless, because though he found my efforts touching, he would just laugh at my questions and say, "How the hell should I know?" even though he'd had a bar mitzvah, to please both his grandmothers.

Howard was much better versed in the quirky Malagasy *fady* taboos in some of the small villages on Madagascar, especially in the south. Even more nuanced than the Ziplinsky family definitions of kosher law, the *fady* beliefs varied from one village to the next. Here, it might be *fady* to touch chameleons, which could bring misfortune, there, it is *fady* to mention crocodiles. The prohibition of wearing red clothing was a common *fady*. All over the island there are certain *fady* rivers and streams in which one must never swim because they harbor evil spirits. There are *fady* days of the week on which one must never, ever, work, but those, too, varied from one village to the next. A deeply entrenched *fady* tradition the Madagascar government has been working to prohibit is the abandonment or separation of twins. When, during one of Howard's idyllic summers, the cat belonging to one of the kitchen workers on the vanilla plantation gave birth to just two perfectly matched kittens, one of them was killed instantly.

Howard admitted to me that he was such an indifferent Torah student that his bar mitzvah preparation was the quick and dirty kind, featuring a phonetic, easily retained Torah portion that would allow him to "read" while dragging the Torah pointer over random text. At his bar mitzvah, as Howard parroted his memorized Hebrew and performed this pantomime reading from the Torah, the crotchety rabbi had repeatedly grabbed the end of the pointer and slammed it down on the proper words on the scroll.

So Howard wasn't much of a Jew. I tried so hard, oh my God, for decades I tried to act like a good Jew myself. I was a parody of a good little Jewish wife, especially in those first years, when I went crazy memorizing all the rules, like the thirty-nine *melachot,* the categories of forbidden Sabbath activities. Do you know how hard it is for someone with my background even to pronounce a word like that? The "aacccchhh" does not come naturally to a Tatnall throat.

I probably did break many of the thirty-nine each Saturday, just the same (igniting a fire, extinguishing a fire, writing two or more letters, erasing, tying, untying, making two loops, transferring between domains), but as a member of the Ziplinsky tribe, I foolishly thought it was important to know the rules I was breaking. My favorite *melachot* among the thirty-nine? "Applying the finishing touch."

And the holidays! Ask me about Shavuot! Or how about that Tu Bishvat! I've got the scoop on Purim, the word on Haman and his tricorner hat, represented in those lead sinker cookies, hamantaschen, which I whip up in the Cuisinart, thanks to a Martha Stewart recipe.

Take Sukkot. There's a holiday. Ask me about the Lulav and the Etrog! The plural of Etrog, I happen to know, is Etrogim, not that I have ever been able to work that into a conversation, because you only need the one each year. *These Etrogim are so lovely it is hard for me to choose just one Etrog. Look, those Etrogim over there are even nicer.* I am sure Irene wouldn't know a Lulav from an Etrog from a Halloween pumpkin, but of course, that is what makes her a real Ziplinsky, her entitlement to her own indifference, the privilege of not noticing her own privilege.

THE FIRST TIME I hosted the Seder at our house was the year Sam died, when Passover was just a couple of weeks later. For some reason we thought it was too much for Frieda to manage the whole thing at her house so soon after Sam's death, so we decided to move the Seder to our house on Everit Street instead. Frieda resented this plan, but her resentment was in itself an activity that was very fulfilling for her. Logically, we should have gone to her that year, as always. She had that big, seldom-used dining room, and she had all that Waterford crystal she obsessed over (my failure to covet her damned crystal was yet another bone of contention between us), and she had those heirloom, gold-rimmed Pesach dishes that had once belonged to her aunt Pep in the Bronx. Frieda also maintained a fourth set of dishes, beyond the usual three for meat, dairy, and Pesach. This was a shelf of miscellaneous plates that were known as the trayfe dishes, which were reserved for pizza and other technically forbidden foods, a necessary accommodation when Irene and Howard were in high school.

I come from a family that believed one would never *buy* silver, because one simply *has* silver. My mother's second cousin Molly in Wilmington lays the table with her grandmother's service for twelve, which, she recalls fondly and frequently, was salvaged when Daddy's yacht sank off Nantucket in a squall in 1924. The loyal butler, Cope, had very nearly gone down with the ship. Family lore has it that he was thought to have drowned until he was seen staggering out of the surf, embracing the carved wooden chest containing this famous family silver. The family story does not include his first name, though the silver pattern, Sulgrave, is usually mentioned.

Frieda loved to cook and bake and freeze. How many times did she confound my kids by inviting them over with a promise that she was baking her delicious walnut cookies, only to offer them semithawed, dried-out walnut cookies from the freezer? These they were expected to enjoy while sitting at the kitchen table breathing in the wafting aroma that lingered from the day's baking, while racks of soft, warm, fragrant walnut cookies cooled all over the kitchen in preparation for layering in wax paper and entombment in those plastic freezer boxes she cherished, as if they too were her legacy from Aunt Pep.

Frieda had three freezers in her basement. For most of the years I knew her, even when she was still working admirably long days at Zip's at a point when she would have been entitled to cut back her hours at the factory, she cooked and baked large quantities of food several times a week, preferring to freeze each sour-cream Bundt, each batch of mushroom soup, in appropriately segregated and labeled containers in these freezers, with meat in one, dairy in another, and whatever Seder foods she could prepare in advance, stashed in her Pesach Tupperware (I'm not kidding), in her Pesach freezer. What's especially impressive and odd about this was that she didn't exactly keep a kosher home, though she made a lot of inconsistent gestures in that direction. (The Ziplinsky style of kosherness was like some encrypted dress code so difficult to understand that it would make you yearn for uniforms.) Because she did so much cooking in advance, one of the hallmarks of big family meals at her house was the eerie spotlessness of her kitchen.

Three-Freezer Frieda (as Howard secretly called her at times) vowed to give me all her Seder recipes. The day had come, after twenty-two years. She told me she knew it was her duty as a good Jewish woman to provide me, her only daughter-in-law, with all the knowledge she had about how to make a Seder, so that I could make a proper Jewish home for her son and for her grandchildren. Though of course I could only fail, she didn't say out loud, because a proper Jewish home for her son and her grandchildren would not have had me in it.

She made a big production out of this, the handing over of The Book of Frieda, as she dictated every single thing she could think to tell me about this annual event that went by three interchangeable names so I always worried I was using the wrong word, no matter which one it was: Seder, Pesach, Passover. (I have come to believe that I can never get it right, because it is like growing up a native French speaker, with the masculine and feminine identity attached to each word as you learn it, so you have a natural knowledge of gender, while the rest of the world can never get it quite right. Intuition is insufficient for French, a language in which a word for *penis* is feminine.) I wrote it all down, word for word, in the same notebook I had last used just a few weeks earlier for what turned out to be my final lunch at Clark's with Sam, when he could barely eat a little soup and I had to drive him there and help him into and out of the car, and he nearly fell stepping off the curb when we were getting back into the car after lunch. The last thing he said that I wrote down was this: "A good person never falls into the trap of loving things and using people—people should be loved, and things should be used."

Now here it was just two weeks after Sam's death, and we sat at Frieda's kitchen table, surrounded by the remains of various eastern European carbohydrates of mourning that had been brought by family, friends, and business associates calling on Frieda. She would soon banish them all, all the coffee cakes and strudels and rugelachs and kugels of sadness, even though the Seder would not be taking place in her house this year, in her great annual pre-Passover cleansing of the forbidden chometz. Paradoxically enough, Frieda's solution lay in giving them all to me in a few shopping bags when I left that day with my Pesach marching orders.

"Offer them to the employees, take them home, suit yourself," she said to me. This dovetailed nicely with her ongoing secret plan to tempt me at all times to eat calorie-laden foods so I would get fat. Also it was sending extra chometz into my house so as to sabotage any possibility that my Passover Seder could possibly be legitimate. And it was her way of handing off her chometz to a goy, part of her ritual that she thought I didn't understand, but I understood her perfectly.

And so I took a bite of a gummy raspberry rugelach I certainly didn't need, and I turned to a fresh page, and I wrote while Frieda dictated with great precision all of her extremely detailed bits of advice concerning the tiniest aspects of each recipe.

We began with the precious Ziplinsky family charoset recipe, which went well, though her charoset, an apple and walnut Ashkenazic formula, as she called it, was, in my annual experience, plausibly derived from the actual mortar used to build the pyramids when we were slaves to Pharaoh in Egypt. Year after year at the Ziplinsky family Seders, with various Bridgeport cousins and a couple of old Legion Avenue quasi relatives of Frieda's in attendance, as we got to that part of the group recitations, I would feel all the eyes around the table swivel my way in anticipation. Look, the shiksa wife is going to say it! Here it comes! There she goes! *When we were slaves to*

Pharaoh in Egypt . . ." If I do say so, my own charoset, featuring raisins, dates, ginger, dried pears, walnuts, pignolis, and almonds, is far superior. Also? Forget the Manischewitz. A good grapey pinot noir is best.

For her matzo balls, Frieda revealed that the secret to their being so light and fluffy (and truly, they really were—that woman was a very competent cook at certain moments) was that she used seltzer in the dough. The little seltzer bubbles aerated the matzo balls, she said, before adding sharply that I shouldn't think of using Perrier; it had to be true seltzer water, from a siphon, like for an egg cream. (Do I look like someone who would put Perrier in matzo balls?) Our household, like hers, had a weekly seltzer delivery, a Ziplinsky family necessity, so I didn't even keep Perrier in the house, as she well knew, since Zip's Candies paid all the Castle Seltzer bills for all those years. Then she got to the ingredients and instructions for the chicken broth for the matzo ball soup.

"Take boneless chicken breasts," she said.

"How many?" I asked.

"Oh, whatever you think you need," she replied with uncharacteristic vagueness, which should have been the tip-off. "Five, or six, maybe."

"Boneless chicken breasts? Skinless?"

"It doesn't matter," she said. Let me repeat. She said, *It doesn't matter*. Those were her words.

"Are you sure?" I asked, pen poised on the page. "Boneless, skinless chicken breasts?"

"Do you think I wasn't making chicken soup for the Seder every year since I was a little girl growing up on Legion Avenue and my mother taught me her recipe, and now all of a sudden I don't know what I'm talking about?" she said tartly. "Okay, fine, you know better, you do whatever you think."

I wrote down the remaining ingredients for the soup as she enumerated them, the carrots, the onions, the garlic cloves, the celery stalk, the bay leaf, and we went on to other elements of the meal until I had everything she thought I needed to make the Seder.

She had the family Haggadahs stacked up on the table for me to take. She would bring along the gefilte fish and the freshly grated horseradish, because it was impossible for me to learn to make either of these things, Frieda had decided. Irene would be bringing fruit. Knock yourself out, Irene. When I was leaving, as I bent to take from her the last shopping bag of coffee cakes, to carry all the chometz out of her house and into mine, there on her doorstep, Frieda leaned over and kissed me on the forehead. This was uncharacteristically warm, but it was probably fueled by her ebullience over the chicken soup recipe she had just foisted on me.

Howard thought I should invite my parents up from Chapel Hill. He liked them, and didn't quite believe me that they were as cold and distant as I said they were. If you have had Frieda and Sam Ziplinsky for parents, you probably just cannot imagine the true coldness of Kay and Edwin Tatnall. You think you see something that isn't there. As a consequence of being loved sufficiently by your parents, you normalize, you fill in the blanks. For Howard, my parents were so Other that he mistook one kind of Other for another kind of Other. In his own way, feeling fond and unconflicted about my parents as he did, Howard has always denied me the right to my outrage at them for their minimal devotion to me.

I was dubious that Kay and Edwin Tatnall could possibly see themselves attending a Seder, even one populated by their only child and their only grandchildren, given their reluctance to attend any sort of family get-together. They were remarkably uninterested in Howard's family, and in fact I knew it wouldn't have occurred to either of them to write Frieda a condolence letter if I hadn't prompted them. It had been impossible to entice them to consider flying up for Grandparents' Day at the kids' school the previous autumn. Sam and Frieda, aka Grampa Sam and Nana, had been delighted to attend. (My mother never wanted our kids to call her anything but Kay.) I was relieved when they declined the invitation because it conflicted with an important bridge tournament.

"Would Daddy have to wear a *yar-nol-kee* on his head?" my mother had asked anxiously when I phoned with the invitation (phoning them like that was a deliberate ambush on my part), hedging her reply even before she remembered with obvious relief the conflicting bridge tournament schedule. I wondered if she would deny ever having told me, when I was about ten, that the reason Jews have big noses is because air is free. People are usually themselves, it turns out.

TWO DAYS BEFORE the Seder, I phoned Frieda to report that the big pot of chicken broth bubbling on my stove was sort of tasteless, nowhere near as good as hers, what was I doing wrong? Any suggestions? And she said, Tell me what you did, step-by-step, what did you do? So I read the ingredients to her—the bay leaf, the carrots, the flat parsley (not curly), the quartered onions, the whole onion studded with eight cloves, the celery stalk with leaves, the cloves of garlic smashed but not chopped, the boneless, skinless chicken breasts. And she said, "Oh, you used boneless chicken breasts? Skinless too? They don't have so much flavor."

And I said, "But Frieda, you told me to use boneless, skinless chicken breasts. I have it written right here."

And she said, "Well, I suppose if that's what you want to use, you can. But it's not as flavorful."

And I said, "You told me to use boneless, skinless chicken breasts."

And she said, "If that's what you want, I'm sure it will be good enough. You didn't know better."

"But Frieda, it's not good enough; this chicken soup is watery and insipid, nothing like yours."

"Ah! Why would it be? What do you expect when you used the boneless, skinless chicken breasts, dear? Without bones and skin, and flavorful dark meat, you don't get so much taste. Now you know. I always use a whole fowl. You have to skim, but there's much more flavor that way. A kosher butcher would tell you what to do. But I'm sure your soup will be fine. You can't expect to make such good chicken soup from scratch when it's not in your blood."

THERE WAS A wild current of attraction between Howard and me from that first moment. I am certain Frieda could feel it too—it was in the air—and she knew I was going to take her golden boy, her beautiful Howdy, the only one she had left. She knew I would take him away from her, and there was nothing she could do to stop it. She didn't know it quite yet, but I was the answer to her prayers. I would keep him from leaving, but she had to let me have him.

On my third day at work, at the end of that first week, Sam came and watched me on the Tigermelt line for a moment. I reached, shuffled, reached, shuffled those Tigermelts like a pro, as if I was a career Tigermelt-straightener, never missing a single bar, and as the expertly aligned bars clanked past us on their journey to the cooling tunnel and the wrapping machine,

Sam told me I was doing a very good job, and his son Howdy would presently give me a thorough walk-through on all three lines at Zip's, because I obviously had a good head on my shoulders, and cool hands, which was important, because hot hands smudged the finish on the chocolate, which was why women were traditionally employed on candy lines in positions requiring touching the pieces, because women have cooler hands than men. They should use me for more complex work than this, Sam said, and then he said to me, Kiddo, you're going to be good for Zip's, and Zip's is going to be good for you.

When the first lunch break came, during which time skeleton crews ran the lines slowly, in shifts (if they shut down completely something could harden, cool, or clog, so a few people on staggered shifts kept the tanks swirling, the belts moving, the panners tumbling), Howard beckoned to me, and I followed him. We had scarcely exchanged a word since our first meeting, but since then, several times while I was working I would feel his gaze on me, and I would look up and there he would be, somewhere on the floor, watching me, frankly staring.

Each time, when our eyes met, he would smile without looking away, and one of those times, when he was leaning over a railing up on a catwalk above the chocolate coating tanks, he had leaned over and pointed at me and mouthed, "You." I didn't know who the hell he thought he was. Gene Kelly in some cheesy musical number? Or who the hell he thought *I* was. The indifferent ingénue in her first role? I didn't know whether to be flattered or irritated.

The ten-year age difference between Howard and me has vanished with time, but it did signify then, I suppose, especially to some of his friends. At eighteen, I was still a teenager. Howard and I had grown up in slightly different times as well as worlds. When we first started spending time together, there were all sorts of gaps. I didn't know how to play golf and had never imagined that I would want to learn, any more than I would want to learn how to play bridge. Howard had never smoked pot, preferring beer or Dewar's White Label, the official beverages of DKE House, while I had never been drunk, but I had inhaled passed joints at a few concerts and parties, not that it ever did much for me. I listened to the Beatles; the Everly Brothers's "Wake Up, Little Susie" was Howard's favorite song.

Howard often referred to various girlfriends he had dated in high school and college. Until we met, I had only hung out in groups, but had never gone out with one specific person on an actual date. I had only ever kissed a boy during party games. The merciless teasing from Andy Ottenberg my senior year was the most attention I'd ever had from anyone, but it's hard to look back on his cruelty and see it as a flirtation, though maybe it was, for him. The truth is, when I met Howard, though I let him think otherwise when he made a remark about my previous high school boyfriends, I had only ever been with one man, and that wasn't a date.

Eric Honig wrote to me two days after the fire. I had no idea how old he was, or where he lived, or why he was writing to me. My parents simply weren't curious about what came through the mail slot in our front door, beyond their anxiety about legal papers and money. Arson Girl received quite a number of hate letters in those days, which my mother left for me on the front hall table next to the bowl of keys and loose change. A lot of strangers were compelled to tell me they thought I should go to jail, starting the day after the fire, when there were so many crank phone calls we finally had to leave the phone off the hook.

The day Eric Honig's first letter came, there were several

other letters, including a really nasty one from someone who called herself "The Cat Lady of East Haven," telling me I deserved to die for what I had done to Debbie Livingston's cat. I felt horrible enough about poor old Homer as it was, and her letter had made me cry. I was grateful to read Eric's letter, because it wasn't like the others. It was a fan letter. His note was friendly and encouraging. He said I had a nice smile and he hoped I was getting some sleep because I looked tired.

After that, just about every day, right up to my last court appearance, I received a greeting card from Eric containing the most recent newspaper story on my case, clipped with pinking shears from the *New Haven Register* and festooned with his ballpoint-pen remarks, punctuated by multiple exclamation points cascading down the margins, about how unfair to me their coverage was. He mixed upper- and lowercase with abandon, and he drew smiley faces with word balloons saying things like, "ChEEr UP, SweET AliCe! YoUR're GReaT!"

There was never a return address on anything he mailed to me, so I had no way to reply, but as the days passed, his little notes and cards grew more intense and personal, as if we were corresponding. I looked him up in the New Haven phone book, but there was no Eric Honig listed, though his envelopes were all postmarked locally. He sent a greeting card with bluebirds sitting together in a nest, on the back of which he had scribbled "CAn'T WAiT Till Our SPECIAL Day!!!" The next week, though it was late June, a Valentine with lace trim arrived, signed, "Love you always, my sweetheart. Eric."

I never mentioned Eric Honig to my parents. Perhaps it sounds pathetic, but I was lonely, and whoever Eric Honig was, he was my friend, which was more than I could say for my former actual friends. (I never heard from any of my teachers, either, not even Miss Solomon.) The weekend after my regrettable guilty plea and sentence, on a hot, still Sunday afternoon, when I was home alone in front of the television, my parents having gone into New York for a bridge tournament, Eric Honig came to the door. I know I shouldn't have let him in, but it was hard not to, once he said he was Eric Honig. My first thought when I saw him was that he wanted to use our telephone because he had a flat tire. My second thought, when he said his name, was that I had been expecting just this moment, and I knew he had watched my parents drive away and leave me alone.

The next thing he said to me after identifying himself was that I was more beautiful in person than he had imagined, though I hadn't washed my hair in days and I was squinting through the screen door at him and wearing a frayed, blue button-down oxford shirt of my father's and cut-off jeans with denim shreds hanging down one leg, and I had a jar of Nutella in one hand and a spoon in the other.

As I opened the door, I realized that I was afraid of him (I wasn't an idiot), but how could I refuse him? This was Eric Honig, who liked me. And now he was inside the house, in the gloom of our front hall, and then we were on the couch together, while the 4:30 movie with which I had been wasting the afternoon, *Gidget Gets Married,* continued to flicker soundlessly on the television across the room, and then he was kissing me and telling me over and over how beautiful I was.

I can't remember what he looked like, other than in a general way. He was an ordinary middle-aged man. He wore a short-sleeved yellow shirt and khaki pants, and he had on bright new running shoes. I think his hair was wet. He smelled of cloves. He took a red and white tin of cloves from his pants pocket, and he put it on the coffee table in front of us as he sat down beside me, explaining that he was trying to quit smoking, and the strong taste of cloves helped him fight his cravings. He offered me a clove but I didn't want one, and then he started kissing me, and the clove taste on his thrusting tongue was as strange and inevitable as everything else about this moment.

He unbuttoned my shirt and rummaged for my breasts with one hand, while seizing my wrist with the other hand and pressing my palm down on the lengthening hardness trapped in his pants, sliding my hand rhythmically up and down on the hot lump under the thin khaki for a moment before shifting to unzip his pants while murmuring into my mouth, Oh yes, oh yes, babydoll, you light my fire, yes you do.

He really said that.

It wasn't rape, because I never asked him to stop. I never spoke at all. The clovey smell, the way he looked at me and spoke to me and touched me, the way he seemed to be reaching through me and speaking past me, that is what has lingered in my mind all these years, if I think about it at all, not the actual sensations, not what his face or his body looked like. (A week later, I wouldn't have known him on the street.) It must have hurt, but I have no memory of that either, though I spent half an hour scrubbing the bloodstain from the cushion of our faded chintz couch so when my parents returned they would notice nothing. The faint maroon wisp of the stain, twined through the vines and leaves of the pale green and pink floral pattern, was visible only to me, and then only when I looked for it, which I did from time to time when I was in need of a reality check.

What has stayed with me is the pounding, insistent weight of him as I sank into the soft, familiar cushions, pinned under his frenzied thrusting, my shorts bunched at my ankles. I grew more and more transparent until I was entirely invisible, doing everything I could to remove myself so he could penetrate to the core the exquisite object of his desire, which had nothing at all to do with me. It was over in a few minutes. He left in a hurry, his 1.25-ounce tin of Schilling whole cloves, packed in Baltimore, MD, USA, forgotten. I kept that tin in the back of my underwear drawer for years, until the contents were nothing more than a jumble of tiny, knotted twigs with no discernable aroma. He never wrote to me again.

The lesson of the story? Have sex with your stalker if you want him to leave you alone forever.

So here I was, not quite a month later, the once and future Arson Girl, grateful to be dwelling in the new, sweet, fragrant world of Zip's Candies, with Howard Ziplinsky walking me through the lines, machine by machine. I was perplexed by how powerfully attracted to Howard I was. On the face of it, he wasn't my type, if someone in my circumstances could be said to have a type. There was something a little too polished yet incomplete about him, even then, when he was still quite lean and had not yet developed that pampered, slumpy, too-tanned, executive-on-the-golf-course softness of recent years.

As I followed Howard across the factory floor, I stopped to glove up at the first dispenser we passed, and he waved in my direction impatiently for me to catch up. I noticed his beautiful hands for the first time. Howard's wrists are graceful and perfectly proportioned. For years, before he started wearing that ridiculous fancy watch the size of a Reese's peanut butter cup, every glimpse of his wrists made me inexplicably happy. Howard has always possessed an astonishing number of magnificent shirts, more than Gatsby, and I was attracted to that, too (my father wore only blue or white oxford cloth button-downs), to Howard's confidence and pleasure in having those shirts to choose from every morning. On that third day of my Zip's employment, the sight of his blue-and-white-striped shirt cuffs grazing the thick dark hair sprouting from those elegant wrists was almost embarrassingly thrilling, like a foreshadowing glimpse of his naked torso under a bedsheet. He was utterly unself-conscious as I followed those beautiful hands. I was mesmerized by each gesture as he pointed at the various Tigermelt wrapping machinery components and explained their functions.

As we approached the Mumbo Jumbo line, Howard put a hand on my arm to steer me across a treacherous spill of red licorice goo, and then he left it there as we stood at the side of the churning machinery watching rows of fragrant red discs tumble out, slide down the sorting chute, and land one by one by one before chugging by on the belt. The heat of his hand was shockingly intimate through the thin sleeve of the simple white cotton button-down shirt I was wearing over loose white cotton pants, an outfit that met the requirements of the factory floor for summer so I didn't have to wear a hot factory coat. I admit I knew my shirt was very snug and contrasted nicely with my tan, plus I never wore a bra in those days.

I asked as many questions as I could think to ask, as we stood there, but I wasn't listening to Howard's answers about the moguls and the cornstarch molds and the politics of red food coloring (Zip's had recently switched from cochineal extract, which is made from crushed insect carcasses, to Red Number Three, erythrosine, which enhanced shelf stability, plus was not made from insects), and from there he went into an exegesis on the history of the balky molding machine. I was leaning into the pleasant buzz of his voice over the clacking, chugging, and clanking all around us, all the while acutely aware of the radiating warmth of that hand.

"So are the red ones Mumbos and the black ones Jumbos, or are the black ones Mumbos and the red ones Jumbos, or are they red Mumbo Jumbos and black Mumbo Jumbos?" I babbled, truly curious about the answer, but also wanting to prolong the moment, feeling semimesmerized by the ceaseless flow of candy, candy, candy all around me; I had yet to develop immunity to the chronic thrillingness of that. An infinity of jittering red Mumbo Jumbos slid by. Or were they Mumbos? Or Jumbos? I wasn't listening. I felt light-headed, having left the house without breakfast. Nobody was near us, and we were momentarily alone in the middle of this candy hive.

Wordlessly, Howard steered me toward the Little Sammies panning area, and we stood over a deep bin filled with penultimate, uncoated Little Sammies awaiting their shiny hard-shell chocolate bath. He leaned over and reached into the bin with both hands and lifted them, letting the Little Sammies sift through his fingers back into the bin (I knew this was not in accord with Zip's sanitary standards) as he continued to explain the principles of each stage along the line to me. I asked some detailed questions about various mechanisms and adjustment controls, even though I could hardly hear Howard's answers over the din of the incessant sugary clacking. He had stopped talking, and now he was leaning close and brushing my hair aside to speak into my ear. Any more questions? What? Questions! Sorry, I wasn't listening! You weren't what? Listening! His hot breath in my ear was suddenly intimate.

He reached out to touch my chin, to turn my face so he could wipe off the smallest drop of Little Sammies coating chocolate. Like a first raindrop, a single stray chocolate droplet had landed on my cheek, and he dabbed this driblet with his fingertip, and then he put his finger in his mouth, onto the tip of his tongue, without speaking. He just did this and looked at me.

We looked at each other, and we just stood there, so close between the machines. I shivered. I could feel my nipples tingle and harden under my white shirt, and although he didn't take his eyes from mine, I could see in his face that he noticed. Why did the man yell "Fire!" when he fell into the chocolate? Howard asked me suddenly. What? Why? Howard leaned in close, his hot breath in my ear again, changing solids to liquids, tempering something deep inside of me, and murmured, Because nobody would come if he yelled "Chocolate!"

Several line workers were drifting back from their brief lunch breaks, and I turned away from him then, feigning curiosity in all the wrapping machines, trying to recover from this vertiginous moment. Howard followed behind me, and a moment later I had accidentally led us into a sort of blind alley formed by a stack of palleted wrapping materials and the back end of the Tigermelt wrapping machine. It was very loud, making a *chug-chug-chug-chug-chug-chug-CHUNK, chug-chug-chug-chug-chug-chug-CHUNK* sound that corresponded to six finished Tigermelt bars at a time reaching the end of the line, where they were each sledded onto a cardboard tray and then sleeved in a wrapper, which was then heat-sealed at both ends.

Howard stood right behind me, close, close but not touching, and he explained into my ear the steps required by the Tigermelt wrapping process, which was fully automated, unlike the semi-automated Little Sammies wrapping process, which required certain manual stages (because there was not yet a machine on the line that could efficiently pack the three Little Sammies together onto the cardboard sleeve all heads up, faceup, with any reliability), while I asked nonsensical questions, all of which he answered very thoroughly. Howard was extremely knowledgeable about the quirks and twists of every machine on the floor.

He was dedicated in those days. I would never say otherwise. For many years, Howard Ziplinsky was as dedicated and loyal to the family business as could be. Everyone saw in him the ideal heir, the future of Zip's Candies. I didn't know then that he had not been born to this role, but when his older brother, Lewis, died in childhood, everything shifted, and Howard, not the heir but the spare, had been moved up the line of succession. The future of the family business had weighed on him from the day Lewis died at fourteen, when Howard was twelve.

Finally I ran out of questions, and I felt Howard moving closer to me, and then, standing right behind me, he put his hands on my breasts, very lightly. Something like an electrical current ran through me, from here to there, and I felt as if parts of me were lighting up. Does that sound completely absurd? It was the single most erotic experience of my life to that moment. Perhaps even to this moment. What does *this* button do, he murmured softly in my ear, mimicking my earlier stream of questions, but not unkindly, touching me gently, so gently.

I rinsed his faint chocolate handprints from my shirt when I saw them in my reflection over the sink in the women's bathroom a little while later. I had finally detached myself from that intoxicating fermata, thinking I should make some kind of an effort to pull myself together. Had anyone noticed the smudges on my shirt as I emerged from behind the Tigermelt wrapping machine and skibbled to the ladies' room? My dabbing at the handprints left big wet circular splotches that rendered my shirt almost transparent, so I put a white factory coat on over it until it dried, which it soon did, but with chocolate tide marks bordering the former wet spots. This gave Frieda something to comment on at the end of the day as I clocked out, when she reminded me sourly that I needed to pay stricter attention to the hygiene guidelines for wearing a clean white shirt onto the floor if I wanted to keep my job at Zip's Candies.

What else can I say about Howard? I am trying to be fair. He was, when I look back now through the *Had I But Known* lens, a bit too pretty (prettier than me), maybe a bit too casual, certainly careless (careless with me). He was reckless. Howard was, after all, not only ten years older than I was, he was also, in effect, my employer. What about him was so enticing to me? Everything. I had never met anyone remotely like him before. Howard enjoyed privilege, he enjoyed having money, and he radiated a kind of entitlement, an entitlement to do anything, including this, this homing in on me. But his was a generous entitlement, one that invited me along. He made me feel that anything was possible.

At the same time, there was something a little smirky about Howard, something of the obnoxious frat boy. When his DKE brother George W. Bush was elected president in 2000 (if you can call that an election), Howard wanted to send him a case of Little Sammies to celebrate the inauguration, but I objected. Howard insisted that George had been a good guy at college, a lively presence in DKE House on Lake Place, a true friend, all of which seemed like somewhat revised history, a Howard specialty.

"Seriously, Howard?" I was skeptical. Howard had told me about some of the casual nastiness and racism he had witnessed, if not experienced, at Yale. "W. wasn't one of the anti-Semites you told me about?"

Howard got a look on his face that I know well, a defensive sheepishness, as he tried to find the words to explain what he meant. He was especially proud of his DKE affiliation, and I had heard more than once that the DKE man was in equal proportions the scholar, the gentleman, and the jolly good fellow. "It depends on how you take his sense of humor," he said, finally. "Once there was a group of us hanging out at Bulldog Pizza after a hockey game, and someone was complaining about this annoying guy we all knew who never put enough money on the table for his share of our beers when the check came, and George said, 'What do you expect from a Jew?' So I said 'Hey, asshole,

I'm a Jew too,' and W. said, 'Howdy, you're different—you're a white Jew.'"

Howard thought this was funny. I didn't. I had no sense of humor at all about the election—in fact I was sick about it—and I probably focused all my wrath and disappointment on at least keeping those Little Sammies out of the White House. I really insisted that he not send them. I was belligerent and relentless about it. Finally, Howard agreed that he wouldn't send them, and the subject was dropped. But then about a month later an envelope from the White House arrived in the mail for Howard. It contained a glossy color photograph of George W. Bush smirking at his desk in the Oval Office, and it was signed in black Sharpie with a scrawled "Thanks, Howdy—Say, Dat's Tasty! GWB." That photograph is framed and hanging on the wall in Howard's office (which is now my office) at this moment. I keep meaning to take it down. I know it's petty of me, and insignificant in the larger scheme of things, but every time it catches my eye, I am indignant all over again. How could he?

DESPITE HOWARD'S EXTRAORDINARY self-regard and sense of entitlement, which has always made him capable of behaving so badly, there was for so many years something very gentle and loving about him that always redeemed him in my eyes. Something genuinely sweet, too. I thought I saw in him more Sam's son than Frieda's. More kindness. I was mistaken. Like everyone else in this story, I have always seen only what I wanted to see. In 1975, our thrilling mutual attraction felt like a surprising yet inevitable part of my sudden immersion in Zip's Candies, my pleasurable slide into that warm chocolate vat.

We spent almost every night of the rest of that hot summer

together, and it was an exceptionally hot summer. Every evening after work we would drive around in Howard's old chocolate-brown Fiat Spider, making out at red lights, going for fried clams and lobster rolls at the beach in Madison. Top down, radio up! Sometimes we would cruise the Wooster Square neighborhood for a parking place so we could get a white clam pizza at Sally's. Often we would go to the last showing of a movie, it didn't matter what, for the air-conditioning. I loved freezing myself at the movies after baking myself at the beach.

Howard always lingered at the refreshment counter, scrutinizing the candy assortment with an appraising professional eye. He was genuinely annoyed with my fondness for Milk Duds to the point where I didn't dare choose them, opting instead for the safety of off-brand malted milk balls, even though they were inevitably stale, which pleased Howard. He would murmur a stream of candy talk in my ear while I chomped my way through the box as we waited for the lights to go down, feeling the heat of my sunburned skin glowing in the frigid air, my sunburned legs soothed by the worn velvet of the theater seats, knowing we would go back to his apartment and make love with all that frantic urgency we had for each other. It was a sweet time.

Whoppers, I learned, avid student that I was, started out being sold individually, two for a penny, but they were bigger than standard malted milk balls today, real gobstoppers, and when cellophane wrapping machines were introduced, a smaller-sized Whopper was packaged in "fivesomes," which sold for a penny a pack. I loved the way Howard cared so much about all this.

And it's a worthy passion, one the family has perpetuated. When the kids were growing up, we could talk all through dinner about candy bars of the past, and it was always fun to get

Howard started on candy-bar trivia. We would name any letter of the alphabet or any state in the country and Howard could name an obscure bar that started with that letter or was manufactured in that state, or he could bluff persuasively. The weirder the bar, the more certain we were that he was bluffing, but usually, such a bar had actually once existed and Howard not only knew its name, but he also knew the slogan for it and the makeup of the bar. When Jacob saw *Rain Man,* Dustin Hoffman's Raymond reminded him of Howard's encyclopedic candy-bar knowledge, and for a while that's what he called his father, Rain Man, whenever Howard started talking candy.

Jacob and Julie never tired of hearing about the Chicken Dinner bar (a pioneering concept, since it was in some ways one of the first protein bars, the succulent roast chicken on the wrapper suggesting as it did that one could have something equal to a nourishing dinner for a nickel, though it was an ordinary candy bar, and chicken was not an ingredient). First introduced in the 1920s by the Sperry Candy Company, possibly inspired by President Hoover's campaign promise of a chicken in every pot, the bar grew in popularity during the Depression, when many people couldn't afford a real chicken dinner.

Prohibition, which began in 1920 and ended thirteen years later, was great for the candy business, and it is not a coincidence that those dry years were the heyday for candy bars, a convenient and cheap replacement for a quick pick-me-up. Never before had candy been consumed in such quantities. Never before was candy so conveniently packaged and available, the candy bar offering an experience distinctly different from selecting a single morsel from a gift box of bonbons.

Candy bars were a playful gratification that could be enjoyed by men, women, and children equally. In 1927, Lucky Strike cigarettes aimed a daring campaign at women, encouraging them to smoke. Eating a lot of candy bars could lead to weight gain, and here was a healthful alternative: "Reach for a Lucky instead of a sweet." Sugar and nicotine were legal stimulating habits when alcohol wasn't, and even after the Volstead Act was repealed in 1933, America continued to smoke and eat candy as never before, though some of the stranger bars that had flourished in those golden years didn't survive past World War II.

Julie and Jacob could never hear enough about those ghostly candy bars such as Old Nick, Fat Emma, Whiz, Candy Salad, Chump, Big Dearo, Denver Sandwich, Zep, Vegetable Sandwich, Lindy, Roasty Toasty, Vanilla Jitney, Doctor's Orders, Baffle, Coconut Grove, Cherry Hump (tragically discontinued in the 1980s because of a chronic leakage problem), Pierce Arrow, Poor Prune, the Bolster bar, and let's not forget the Amos 'n' Andy bar, which had the slogan "Um-Um! Ain't Dat Sumpin!"

This bar came out several years after Little Sammies, and Zip's Candies actually contemplated legal action against the Williamson Candy Company over that slogan. Eli engaged in correspondence with a Philadelphia law firm specializing in copyrights and patents, which advised him that although he had several valid points, and they were sympathetic to his situation, they couldn't agree that he could prove a sufficient influence, given that the Amos 'n' Andy bar was a chocolate-covered, crisp-honeycomb-centered, two-piece product, and in any case they didn't think a court would find merit in Zip's Candies proprietary claim on the word "Dat" in a candy-bar slogan.

Jacob and Julie would make up bars, too, the sillier the better: the Mint Chipmunk Chunk bar ("Save One for Winter!"), the Thunder Thigh bar ("From Your Lips to Your Hips!"), and let us not forget their answer to the Mars bar, the Uranus bar ("The Protein Bar for Colonic Health!").

❀ ❀

THAT FIRST SUMMER, sometimes I didn't get home for three or four days at a time, spending most nights at Howard's Chapel Street apartment over the head shop called Group W Bench. The back stairs of the building always had a faint but persistent patchouli and marijuana vapor that seemed to float up from the shop, which was nicer than the building's top notes of litter box and frying.

Although Howard was twenty-eight when we met, and I was, in his words, barely legal (which definitely seemed to appeal to him), Sam told me years later that he had told Howard, soon after it had become evident that we were together (and in retrospect I am embarrassed at how transparent we must have been, rutting around the factory floor), that I might be the one who was too old. Sam observed a few times over the years that I had an old soul, which I took as a compliment, and I am inclined to agree. That's a perfect example of the kind of thing a Ziplinsky might say to you that no Tatnall would ever think to mention.

My parents had nothing to say to me about my new life, no questions, no opinions, though they must have noticed how absent I was that summer, and, when our paths did happen to cross, how inexplicably happy I must have seemed. Though it was my habit to feign indifference around them, if they were paying any kind of attention, you would think they might have wanted to check in with me. Also, my mother might have thought to offer a little chat about birth control. But she probably assumed I had taken care of all that on my own. (This was correct; my first experience at the Planned Parenthood clinic on Whitney Avenue, soon after I started working at Zip's Candies and long before I was to serve on the state board, was as a patient whose chart had a "Do Not Contact" sticker at the top.) It would have been a radical departure for her to get that personal. I might as well wish for her to have been more interested in my lonely independent life all along, more than she was interested in, say, her collection of vintage Nantucket Lightship Basket handbags. It wasn't in Kay's and Edwin Tatnall's natures to feel anything but relief that I was going, going, gone.

ONE DESULTORY SUNDAY afternoon that summer, on our way to dinner at Frieda and Sam's, perhaps the third time I had been there, Howard took me to the Jewish Home to meet his grandmother, Sam's mother, the legendary Lillian. For the first few weeks, even when I had begun to sort out the Ziplinsky family history a little bit, I hadn't realized she was still alive, because she had only been spoken of in the past tense whenever anyone mentioned her at Zip's.

But there she was, cheerfully demented and quite frail, and though she was only seventy-two, she seemed to me like someone in her nineties. (As it turned out, this was to be the only time I ever met her, because she died soon after that, on the last day of summer, in her sleep.) When we got to Lillian's room, she wasn't in it, but Howard knew where to look, and we found her down the corridor, in a wheelchair parked beside the piano in the dayroom, where a volunteer was earnestly plinking out "Willow, Weep for Me." The sour old spinet was missing some of the ivory veneers on certain keys and had a number of bad strings. There is a piano like this in every nursing-home dayroom.

Lillian smiled at us both in a warm and familiar way. Howard introduced me as if she could understand what he was saying. I loved how respectful and devoted he was to his grandmother. He said I was his girlfriend. Of course this is what I was by that time, but it hadn't ever been said before. She seemed delighted to hear it, and delighted to shake my hand, though she didn't speak, and then she seemed equally delighted to shake Howard's hand next, though he had called her Nana and told her he was Howdy as he kissed her hello only a minute earlier.

Howard told me that he was the only one in the family who still went to see her with any regularity, because it pained Sam too much that she no longer recognized him. Howard's sister, Irene, whom I had met only once at that point, was too busy to get there very often, though when she did show up, she tormented the staff by lecturing them on nutrition and the elderly, and she had apparently seriously offended the food service staff by demanding that they remove all aluminum pots from their kitchen. Frieda and Lillian had never really gotten along, each feeling crowded by the other for so many years. Howard told me that his mother's last visit, a definite disincentive for future visits, had concluded with Lillian's looking at Frieda with a sudden glimmer of recognition before she exclaimed, "Oh it's you! When did you get so fat?"

"The one thing Nana always seems to recognize is the Little Sammies jingle," Howard whispered to me, after I whispered to him about her obvious love of the labored piano music that was holding us captive. "You know the jingle? You must know it!" Howard was certain I knew it. How could anyone not know the Little Sammies jingle? He shook his head in mock exasperation. This was an example of the vast cultural gulf those ten years between us could suddenly open up at certain moments.

I didn't think I knew it at all, but I nodded that I did, feigning a sudden recollection, Oh yes, of course. Maybe it was one of those little riffs like "I'll fly to the moon for a Lorna Doone." In fact, when Howard sang it for Lillian (once the volunteer had finally concluded her self-important, community service–inflected performance and gotten up from the piano, releasing us from our respectful audience mode), it was familiar.

I had a fleeting recollection of the cartoony line drawings that went with the jingle for the television commercial for Little Sammies I must have seen in my earliest childhood, when the commercial was still running. Zip's sponsored a local children's television program on Saturday mornings from 1958 to 1962, so I would have been four, at most, when I saw it.

As Howard sang it again, and Lillian beamed and conducted with an age-spotted claw, I had a sudden, vivid, kinetic memory of sitting on the living room floor in front of our big console television, watching Larry, Barry, and Harry, three clown brothers who starred in the weird and creepy *Happy Playtime!* ("What time is it, kids? It's Happy Playtime! And who's here to play with you? Larry, Barry, and Harry! And what do they want Mom to give you for a treat? Their favorite Little Sammies! Be sure to ask Mom to get you some!")

So I hadn't told a lie after all. As Howard sang it a third time, I joined him, but I had only gotten to "One, two, three!" when Lillian cocked her head to one side with a troubled look, not sure she liked my harmony at all. She waved her hand in a correcting gesture in my direction, and I stopped, leaving Howard to finish, solo.

Little Sammies hit the spot
Just a nickel buys a lot!
They're the greatest, you'll agree,
You will eat them one, two, three!

Little Sammies are for you
Fudgy goodness through and through,
Don't be hasty, have another,

Don't be hasty, have another,
Don't be hasty, have another—

Say, Dat's Tasty!

Howard has a nice baritone. He sang the "Don't be hasty" lines in an increasingly sped-up and admirably unself-conscious sort of Mighty Mouse voice, before dropping down into a stagy basso profundo for the interrupting "Say, Dat's Tasty!" tagline.

"You know Jimmy Ray in shipping?" Howard asked me as we were pulling out of the Jewish Home parking lot. Lillian had been rolled into the dining room for her five o'clock evening meal, and though she accepted our hugs and kisses warmly, our departure had been of no consequence to her.

"Is he the old guy, the bald one who whistles?"

"That's Eddie Sohovik. No, Jimmy Ray, the black guy."

"Okay—"

"That was his voice. He's the 'Say, Dat's Tasty' guy," Howard said, blatantly running a red light at the corner of Winthrop Avenue as we traversed that desolate stretch of the abandoned urban renewal project that still bisects New Haven. This was the site of the old Jewish neighborhood, where Frieda grew up (though I didn't know it that day); it was destroyed in the early 1960s to make way for a new city plan that never materialized when funding vanished. The pointless destruction of their Legion Avenue home and the loss of that community was a bitter subject for Frieda in those years when I first knew her. The forced Oak Street diaspora had taken place the decade before, but she never got over her resentment, even though Sam told me her childhood block was in the heart of a slum that wasn't quite as golden as she now recalled it to have been, with rats the size of cats darting between parked cars on hot summer nights.

❊ ❊

THE SCATTERED LIEBASHEVSKYS have kept that proprietary blend of nostalgia and resentment simmering to this day. At Frieda's funeral, I overheard some of her cousins from Valley Stream and Great Neck criticizing the pastries from the Westville Bakery that I had obtained at the last minute for the post-funeral gathering, because Irene had promised to help with the food and then had changed her mind the night before. She had agreed only because she was under too much stress to refuse when we spoke about it, she told me, and her new therapist in Telluride had helped her to see that it was time she learned to stand in her Wise Adult and say No! to me, the competitive sister-in-law who has no right to steal her power, and so she stood in her Wise Adult and took her power back. The night before the funeral she phoned me just before midnight from Frieda's house, where she was presumably sifting through all the family treasures she was worried I might try to claim, to say, No, Alice! No! I cannot and will not help you with that! Furthermore, this was going to be her answer from now on whenever I tried to control her or place unfair demands on her. Listen, America! Irene Ziplinsky Weiss has hereby declared that she will no longer accommodate the needs of others at the expense of her own integrity! So I had to get the damned pastries myself.

The Liebashevsky cousins were like-minded about the Westville Bakery schnecken; both the raspberry and the apricot were very ordinary, nothing to write home about. (But what do you expect, from *her*? Julie told me she heard one of the Great Neck gargoyles say, pointing at me while helping herself to another of the offending pastries.) But then they began arguing with bitter urgency about which had been the best in the old Legion Avenue neighborhood, the transcendent strudel from

Rosenberg's Bakery or the miraculous poppy-seed cake from Cohen's Bakery or the astonishing babka from Ticotsky's Bakery, as if a determination had to be made here and now, though all three of these establishments vanished some fifty years ago.

"What do you mean, that's his voice?" I asked Howard as we headed toward his parents' Westville neighborhood. Three ghetto kids on raggedy banana-seat bikes cut in front of us repeatedly, zigzagging for sport while we kept pace behind them for two blocks, before Howard gunned the motor to show he meant business and nosed past them.

"I mean my mom sang it for the commercial, and he went with her and sang that last line."

"Wait, you're kidding. Frieda sang it? That was *her* voice I heard in the commercial when I was little?"

"She wrote it, she played the piano, and she sang it."

"Wow." A whole side of Frieda I had not yet glimpsed, her glam secret inner Kitty Carlisle.

"Yeah, she was inspired by the Chock full o'Nuts lady, whose husband owned the company. So first Mom talked Dad into running a radio commercial, and when he agreed to that, she worked out a deal for Little Sammies to sponsor baseball games on local AM radio for a season. Then she wrote the jingle, and then she went to the radio station in Bridgeport to record it."

"And how did Jimmy Ray get involved?"

"There was this other black guy at Zip's when I was little, Dave Washington. He and Jimmy used to work together in shipping—maybe they were cousins or something—and I think my mom overheard them singing doo-wop harmonies together while they stacked boxes. When I was a kid, I thought they were the coolest guys in the world. Whenever I went to the factory, those guys were so happy back there, singing and jiving. Dad always ignored their craps games, because they got their jobs done. Jimmy Ray got a hundred dollars and he got the whole day off, too."

I wondered even then if Howard knew how he sounded when he said things like this, or if he really had no clue that there was a hint of Massa on the plantation loving the sound of the happy darkies singing their charming spirituals while totin' dat barge and liftin' dat bale.

DINNER THAT NIGHT with Frieda and Sam was startlingly lively. Frieda's cooking was downright exotic compared to my mother's, plus these Ziplinskys talked avidly about everything they ate, which was somehow just not done in my family. I loved gossiping about the delicious food, I loved the jokey conversation, and I loved them, even if Frieda was determined to remain uncharmed by me. (I even kind of loved that, when it was still new, still a challenge I thought I could meet.) After dinner we watched *Maude* on television (Frieda was excited that Maude was so clearly Jewish) while Sam nodded off in his chair and Frieda kept jumping up during commercials to wash dishes.

Howard and I went back to his airless apartment on Chapel Street, where we lay naked in his bed and talked and laughed until very late, listening to the obscene shouts of the transvestite prostitutes who used to frequent his corner, clustering every night in their bulging hot pants in front of the regrettably named Gag Junior's Lunchette, until it got so late that even they finally gave up and went home, as the sky was graying with dawn.

We fell silent. Something shifted. We turned to face each other and lay there under the tangled sheet, not speaking, just tracing each other's bodies with a light fingertip. Howard's touch made me feel safe. We looked into each other's eyes in the dim light from the window and then we each leaned toward the other until our foreheads just touched, as if this were a familiar ritual of intimacy. He looked into my eyes, and I felt so deeply seen and known. I will never be that seen and known again. I roamed freely over the hills and valleys of Howard's clavicle with grazing fingers, walking an itsy-bitsy spider across his furry obliques, and everything else was still, stiller, stillest, until suddenly he laughed and rolled on top of me. We were so tender with each other, everything was so clear and present, and we made love for what was then only the eighth time, and it was the first time Howard told me he loved me.

You see? I remember everything.

Say, Dat's Tasty!

Words and Music by
Frieda Ziplinsky

4

THE DAY I FIRST walked through those factory doors, about half the Little Sammies line and the entire Tigermelt line still ran on the original machinery Sam's father, Eli, had cobbled together to start his candy factory in 1924. Establishing Zip's Candies in New Haven was the fruition of Eli's American dream, the Zip's literature will tell you. He had a brainstorm and then he followed his passion to manufacture the three candies he was inspired to create after he happened to pick up a copy of *Little Black Sambo* that had been left on a table at the Ottendorfer Branch of the New York Public Library on Second Avenue.

And so the fate of Zip's Candies has twice depended on someone's happening to pick up and read something discarded by another. Of course, the influence of *Little Black Sambo* on our product line has been in, then out of, and is now back in the official Zip's Candies history. These days, the political incorrectness of Little Black Sambo, that huge headache in the sixties, has been trumped by the appeal of Little Sammies to nostalgic baby boomers who, like their parents, grew up with them. What is even more of a market for us these days is the next generation of ironic hipsters, who have discovered for themselves the retro coolness of Little Sammies.

"Say, Dat's Tasty!," dropped from the Little Sammies wrapper for twenty years, was added back in 1999 for what was intended only to be the seventy-fifth anniversary limited-edition wrapper, but then we kept that wrapper, minus the seventy-fifth anniversary designation, when "Say, Dat's Tasty!" became a hip catchphrase first used by the rapper Krazy Koon, along with his famous signature gesture, that one extended index finger twirled comically against his cheek. The phrase and gesture were perpetuated all over the place, on radio and on television talk shows (thank you, thank you, David Letterman), and then high school kids everywhere started using the phrase and gesture sarcastically. William Safire wrote a column about the etymology of the phrase "dat's tasty," with citations from minstrel shows and a particular radio episode of *Amos 'n' Andy* during which the Kingfish exclaims, "Mm, ain't dat tasty!" over a succulent piece of fried chicken. Now of course it's all over the Internet; there are countless "Dat's Tasty!" and "Say, Dat's Tasty!" tagged videos on YouTube, and those words pop up on all sorts of other blogs and websites (my daughter, Julie, who has the self-conferred title of Zip's Web mistress, keeps track of these things). Just now, when I Googled "Dat's Tasty!" it produced 547,862 results. Some of these are vulgar and therefore extremely problematic references, but Julie and Jacob have persuaded me that it's all good, as they say.

THE COMPANY IS proud to tell you that Eli Czaplinsky, a Hungarian Jew, an orphan who arrived at sixteen with his older brother, Morris, at Ellis Island in 1920, was a pushcart peddler with ambitions to do better with the rest of his life than sell caramels and boiled sweets on Orchard Street in all kinds of weather for two or three dollars a day. The company history certainly doesn't mention the third and youngest brother, Julius, left behind with cousins in Budapest at the last moment when the two older brothers realized they wouldn't have enough money for the three of them to travel to Danzig, book passage, and procure enough food to survive the ocean crossing in steerage on the SS *Karpinski,* the dilapidated vessel that brought them to America.

The company history doesn't explain that Eli liked to go to the Ottendorfer branch library near the rooming house on East Seventh Street where he and Morris shared a room (and a bed) quite often—in fact, nearly every day—not because of his love of books, but because it had a nice toilet in a warm room in the basement, which he preferred to the foul communal toilet in a shack in the courtyard behind their tenement. Owing to a peculiarity of its endowment, half of the library's collection was in German. Eli would from time to time take a book from the shelves and struggle through a few pages, trying to make the most of German's proximity to Yiddish. More appealing to him were the three Yiddish newspapers to which this library branch carried subscriptions. These were much nicer to read than all the German books with their formal language that had nothing to do with everyday New York life. Eli would visit the public library, the official story goes, to read these newspapers in a familiar language, and to take home a new children's book each week in order to teach himself better English so he could get ahead in America. (It was his casual perusal of *The Tale of Tom Kitten* that led to his lifelong use of the surprising phrase "I am affronted" if something offended him.)

Also not in the official Zip's Candies history are any details about what happened to Eli after Morris died in the diphtheria epidemic that swept New York in 1921 and Eli was left alone in the world to fend for himself at age seventeen. He became a tough street kid, still roving the Lower East Side hawking caramels, bull's-eyes, blackjacks, and root-beer barrels from his pushcart, but now also running errands for a bootlegger called

Little Augie. Eli was one of the Little Augies, as the street gang was called.

It was a way to be safe and to make some extra money, and nobody was suspicious of the sweet boy with the big smile selling candy from his pushcart, which made him a very useful errand boy, and who can say what else might have been in the bottom of that pushcart? Eli transported guns from here to there, and more often than not there were hefty bundles of cash as he made his rounds peddling sweets, collecting from Little Augie's customers along his route. Sam would tell me about these things, but then he would half take them back, always concluding with a remark to the effect that nobody really knew for sure what Eli did for Little Augie, and maybe he just left New York to get a fresh start and everything about the money and the guns was an exaggeration, and anyway, it was all a long time ago. I note with interest the relationship between the names "Little Sammies" and "Little Augies."

WHENEVER WE TALKED about Eli—Sam and I—he would always say the same thing, in the same way, with a rueful shake of his head: that Eli rarely told him any significant details about whatever it was he did to get by in New York. Once, though, Eli described to Sam how he bought his first good shirt at Wanamaker's department store, the kind of shirt a gentleman would wear, with money he and Morris had made all in one day, when they had the idea of hawking sweets in Union Square at a union rally commemorating the tenth anniversary of the Triangle Waist Company factory fire. Eli and Morris circulated through the crowd shouting out, Remember the victims! Buy a Triangle Toffee! Which perhaps misleadingly suggested that their proceeds would benefit a union fund of some kind.

It was a cold and blustery March afternoon, and Morris had a bad headache and a sore throat. By the end of the day, he was too hoarse to speak at all. The next morning, Morris was feverish and couldn't get out of bed, and within a week he was dead and Eli was wearing his new shirt from Wanamaker's to stand at his brother's grave and say a Kaddish. Sam said that Eli always wondered if Morris had caught the diphtheria germ in the Union Square crowd, or if he was already infected and had perhaps spread his germs among all those people, including the many children for whom their toffees had been purchased.

What is established fact, if not the sort of detail Zip's Candies has featured prominently in its literature over the years, is that Eli left New York in great haste at the end of August 1923, because he witnessed the murder, in front of the Essex Market Courthouse, of a gangster called Kid Dropper Kaplan, who was at the time in police custody. The Little Augies were implicated in the killing, and let's just say there is reason to assume that Eli may have been more than a witness and it was a good time to disappear. All the rest of his father's life, Sam told me, even long after Augie Orgen and Louis Kushner and Lepke Buchalter and all the rest of them were locked up in jail or safely dead and buried, Eli got nervous and changed the subject abruptly whenever anything about this time in his life before New Haven came up.

That August day in 1923, the day Kid Dropper was himself dropped by a bullet in the back, Eli went straight to Grand Central Terminal. Sam told me this story many times over the years, often over lunch at Clark's, where we would go for a quick grilled cheese and a shared order of French fries, just the two of us, to take a break from the din and tumult of the Zip's floor and, no question, to have a relaxed conversation unsupervised by Frieda. Sometimes we shared a chocolate milk shake, too.

Write this down! he would command me. You're the only smart one who's got an interest, kiddo, so you're the only one I'm telling this to. Am I telling it too fast? he would ask, without slowing down, as he recounted yet another bit of weird Ziplinsky family lore, or as he expounded on his philosophies of the candy business, or as he theorized about some nuance of nougatmaking. And I would, I would write it all down, in one of the notebooks I always carried for just this purpose. I have those notebooks, all twenty-two of them, dated and numbered, on a shelf at home. We had lunch at Clark's once or twice a week for twenty-three years, until just before Sam died, when he wasn't really able to eat the kind of food they serve at Clark's, except for maybe a cup of soup. Their avgolemono soup is outstanding.

Sam loved his soup. He loved a lot of things. He loved life. I really miss that man. I have always had to deal with the way Frieda bore me so much inexplicable animus over the years, long before she had any specific reasons to dislike me. But her coldness was tempered for me by the genuine and deep connection I had with Sam, from that first day. Our mutual love really had nothing to do with Howard, strange as that sounds. Of course Sam was soon enough my father-in-law, and then my children's grandfather, but I really loved him for himself. And I know he loved me. And we all know there is concrete proof of this. He was of perfectly sound mind when he made his final decisions. He was an astute businessman and an astute judge of character, and so he anticipated the need to protect me as he did. He's been gone eleven years now, and I miss him every day.

SAM ALWAYS USED the same words, telling the story of Eli's flight from New York. Straight to Grand Central Terminal, straight from Essex Street, Sam would say, and then, invariably, he would pause to add, You know, kiddo, the right name for the train station is Terminal? You got that straight? Because Grand Central Station is a post office branch and all you could buy there for yourself is stamps, not a train ticket.

So Eli took himself from the Essex Market Courthouse straight to Grand Central Terminal, leaving his pushcart on the street, right there at the bottom of the courthouse steps, without even stopping at his rooming house to collect his few possessions, his habitual library book still in his jacket pocket, never to be returned. Straight from Essex and Delancey to Grand Central Terminal he went on a nickel train ride on the Brooklyn–Manhattan line, and there Eli bought a ticket for the last stop on the very next train to leave the station, and on the train he read and reread that little book he happened to have in his pocket, to pass the time, and to calm himself. It was a copy of Helen Bannerman's *Little Black Sambo,* which is how he got to the end of the line, New Haven, with an idea.

I AM PERFECTLY aware that a lot of this information about Zip's Candies and Ziplinsky family history and Eli Czaplinksy's flight from New York is not in dispute, and therefore some of this history could appear to be irrelevant to the matters that *are* in dispute, but in order to provide all the facts, I prefer to give the most complete context possible. The Ziplinsky family has tried to control the story of their business and their family history over all these years, which has made it especially necessary to tell this counterstory, to note the elements in the Zip's time lines and glossy official histories that have been shaded or obscured. Just as chocolate is tempered in order to achieve maximum gloss and snap, so has the Zip's Candies history been tempered. I have begun as I mean to go on; it is extremely important to me that these pages lay out with complete clarity every aspect of my knowledge and beliefs and experience with Zip's Candies and the Ziplinsky family. So this is a warning to any party reading this affidavit. If you get impatient and start to skim, believing either that you already know everything and there is nothing new here, or that the details I hereby provide so meticulously have no significance, you just might miss what is most interesting and important.

WHEN THE CURTAIN rises on Eli's next act, according to the official Zip's Candies time line, it is springtime of 1924, and he has been working in New Haven for Armenian cousins who make chocolate-covered coconut bars overnight in their basement kitchen when the air is cool so they can sell them door-to-door each morning before the day warms up and the Choclettos and Coconettos melt. So here is Eli once again walking the streets, selling candy from a pushcart, working for whatever he can make in a day. Is he restless? Is he convinced that he can do better? Of course he is. He is a married man now, with a pregnant bride, the former Lillian Rosenfeld, a pretty girl in her photos (though she thickened and aged very rapidly after the death of her second son). Lillian is a highly skilled dipper whose departure from the coconut bar line was a blow to the Armenians. She will soon give birth to their firstborn child, their son Sam, a robust eight-pound baby who will be born "two months premature."

Lillian had been their prize dipper, quick and precise, efficient and tidy. One day as Eli waited for his stock, she caught his eye. He was mesmerized by her quicksilver hands, enticed by her deft way with the lumps of shredded coconut, intoxicated by her speed and composure. He asked her to show him how she dipped the Coconettos so quickly and neatly. She giggled and showed him. He tried to imitate her movements, but he dripped melted chocolate all over the dipping table and down his shirt. Soon they were keeping company.

When Peter Paul Halajian and his brother-in-law Calvin Kazanjian, with backing from Shamlian, Hagopian, Kazanjian, and Chouljian cousins, decide to expand their operations and open a factory in Naugatuck (where they name the company after Halajian, and place their faith in their Mounds coconut bars), Eli is invited to stay with the business and move with them, but he sees a bargain and buys the old equipment from the Armenians for a few dollars. And with enough money to buy a building, money that may have something to do with his hasty exile from New York (who can say if he managed to take one of those bundles of money from his pushcart with him when he ran away from the Essex Street Courthouse? It was a long time ago, does it really matter? This is how Sam would always tell the story), he waves his hand in the air so frantically that nobody wants to bid against him and so he places the winning bid for the River Street building and its contents in the bankruptcy auction of a small machine shop.

The building has most recently been home to Peet Engineering, a young business driven into the ground by its hapless proprietors in less than two years. The Peet brothers are hell-bent on producing their single-minded invention, the One-Lock Adjustable Reamer, but they give no thought whatsoever to marketing and distribution. Milo and Alvy Peet pour all their funds into pursuing this dream, the perfection of the One-Lock Adjustable Reamer, but nobody knows about it, and so of course nobody buys it, and the day comes when they have no money left in the bank, no way to pay their workers or their creditors, and the bank won't give them any more credit, and that's that.

Perhaps even with brilliant marketing there would never have been sufficient demand for this innovative product to keep a factory going, but who can say? They didn't plan ahead, Sam would tell me his father would always say, with a rueful shake of the head. They had only one product, and they were undercapitalized, they didn't have the cash to get off the ground and stay off the ground long enough to find out if it was a good thing people would want. Bad break for them, lucky break for the Ziplinskys. Eli gets the building cheap.

There is a candy factory to be assembled from the welter of mechanical creations left behind by this failed venture, a cautionary tale in itself. Motor-driven assembly lines snake through a series of workstations, tool benches, lathes, packing tables. Wrenches lie where they were laid down on workbenches holding half-finished machined objects, blueprints beside them, by workers at the end of their shift who did not know when the whistle blew that they would never hear it again, that the doors would be padlocked by the bank before morning.

The assembly lines are adaptable, and Eli is an adapter. He makes a candy factory. He is a man with a plan. The factory itself is not hexed. He will not rely on just one product. Zip's Candies will diversify before it begins, and risk will be spread among Eli's three *Little Black Sambo*-inspired candy products.

Workers are hired. Factory machinists with experience and nerve and nothing to lose are employed to repurpose and retrofit and solve the giant puzzle of how to make the three candies Eli has in mind out of these machines and the wagonload of candy-making equipment the Armenians left behind when they decamped to Naugatuck to build their own factory. While Eli makes do with their castoffs, Peter Paul would churn out Mounds and Almond Joys (and, less successfully, Dream, Main Show, Almond Clusters, and the especially lamented Caravelle; when they acquired the York Cone Company, they made York Peppermint Patties, too) in their modern, streamlined factory, until the bleak November day in 2007 when the factory would go dark, the brand having been sold to Cadbury, which after a few years licensed it to Hershey's, who decided despite earlier assurances to the contrary to consolidate manufacturing operations by moving the Mounds and Almond Joy production to Virginia, putting two hundred and twenty loyal workers out of their jobs.

As a completist, I note in passing that Naugatuck has also been abandoned by the United States Rubber Company (as it was known until 1961, when it became Uniroyal), maker of automobile tires and the nearly eponymous Naugahyde, and Keds. Poor postindustrial Naugatuck, once proud home to so many industries churning out all-American products, but now just another very quiet, old-fashioned town built on an obsolete foundation, with only a few desultory small-town businesses dotting Rubber Avenue.

I don't know why, exactly, but Frieda used to characterize with her most withering disdain people or things that did not meet her standards as being "strictly from Naugatuck." Possibly this had to do in some way with her barely concealed jealousy about the immense success of Peter Paul compared to Zip's, which has always had a niche and held on to it, but certainly has never achieved a fraction of the market share of those ambitious Armenians and their coconut candies.

THE TIGERMELT IS a straightforward bar, distinguished by the tiger stripes of dark chocolate over the milk-chocolate coating, which enrobes a classic nougat and caramel peanut bar. It is inspired by the tigers in *Little Black Sambo*, who take all of Little Black Sambo's fine clothing, from his red coat to his blue trousers and his beautiful little purple shoes "with Crimson Soles and Crimson Linings"—they even take his beautiful green umbrella—only to get into an angry dispute about which of them is the grandest in his fine clothing.

"And at last they all got so angry that they jumped up and took off all the fine clothes, and began to tear each other with their claws, and bite each other with their great big white teeth . . . And they came, rolling and tumbling right to the foot of the very tree where Little Black Sambo was hiding, but he jumped quickly in behind the umbrella. And the Tigers all caught hold of each other's tails, as they wrangled and scrambled, and so they found themselves in a ring round the tree . . . And the Tigers were very, very angry, but still they would not let go of each other's tails. And they were so angry, that they ran round the tree, trying to eat each other up, and they ran faster and faster, till they were whirling round so fast that you couldn't see their legs at all. And they still ran faster and faster and faster, till they all just melted away, and there was nothing left but a great big pool of melted butter round the foot of the tree."

Mumbo Jumbos are two ridged discs of licorice candy, one black, one red, which fit together with a satisfying, yin-yang click, like two stacked contrasting checkers. They are named for Little Black Sambo's devoted parents, his mother, Black Mumbo, and his father, Black Jumbo. Mumbo Jumbos don't melt very easily. Every chocolate candy company should have a nonchocolate, warm temperature–stable candy option, like a seafood restaurant's having steak on the menu for that one person at the table who hates fish. It's smart business.

LITTLE SAMMIES, IN fact named for Little Black Sambo himself, are clearly the single confection to which Eli is most dedicated, having been profoundly influenced by his first American sweet, a Tootsie Roll given him by a kind guard while he waited for his medical inspection the day he arrived at Ellis Island. By the time Eli passed his trachoma inspection (the man in front of him, who was also from the Pest side of Budapest and had boasted to Eli and Morris about his cousin in Brooklyn who delivered ice and had a job waiting for him and said maybe he would help the Czaplinsky boys find work, failed the trachoma test, and his coat was chalked on the back with a humiliating X before he was led away), he was savoring on his tongue the last lingering, sweet morsel of that inaugural Tootsie Roll.

Little Sammies are by far the most complex of Zip's three products to fabricate. The inch-long chewy chocolate-toffee figures require precise molding, cooling, and coating. Hand-dipping is not entirely satisfactory for achieving the glossy chocolate coating shell Eli strives for, because in his mind's eye Little Sammie should shine, though the earliest Little Sammies are out of necessity hand-dipped, and soon enough the giant rotating kettle that had been used to hold the annealing bath for machined cogs and screws is converted into the Little Sammies panning drum and then, say, don't those Little Sammies shine as they tumble off the line!

ON NOVEMBER 12, 1924, a score of workers is poised. The power-supply lever is pulled, the first machines are switched on, and then the next machines are activated, all down the lines, and like new rides at a carnival, the mechanical contraptions that will make the three confections for which Zip's Candies will be known for decades to come, into the next century, all clank and whirr and hum to life. There is a photograph of this moment. We see a white-coated Eli, with a full head of dark hair, standing proudly with his hand on the lever like the captain at the helm of his ship, with his grinning paper-hatted crew at their places all along the lines. An unsmiling Lillian, in a flowered dress intended to conceal her postpregnancy bulk, can be seen off to the side, holding a swaddled bundle that is her infant son Sammy.

Moments after the photograph is taken, smoke pours out of the motor driving the head pulley on the Mumbo Jumbos belt, and it has to be shut down immediately. A month goes by before that line is running smoothly and true production of stock can commence, but the photograph reveals no herald of that temporary setback, and shows only the ignition of the Zip's Candies engine that would drive Eli just as Eli drove it, working perpetually to keep his dream of his beautiful sweet candies and the success and prosperity those candies bring moving forward, always moving forward. He kept the lines moving until the day he died at a regrettably young age of a massive heart attack only twenty-two years later, sitting alone in his office on a Friday night, reconciling order sheets to close out the week.

HERSHEY'S CHOCOLATE HAD contracts to supply the U.S. military with Ration D Bars and Tropical Bars, both created with an innovative formulation that kept them from melting, which made them stable in the North African desert, even if they did have the texture of chewy linoleum. In the course of the war, Hershey's produced more than three billion of these bars for consumption by American troops around the world. Eli admired the way Milton Hershey parlayed those contracts, because not only was this an extraordinary volume of business, but it also allowed Hershey's to expand production capabilities on the government's nickel. In 1939, Hershey's could produce a hundred thousand ration bars a day. By the time the war ended, Hershey's was cranking out twenty-four million ration bars a week. But Eli took more than a little satisfaction in the knowledge that even Milton Hershey was not immune to the stresses of war, which forced him to suspend production of Hershey's Kisses in 1942 because of a shortage of the foil used to wrap them (production would not resume until 1949).

Eli recognized a good marketing strategy when he saw one, and figuring that he had the advantage of offering his first line product, not some inferior-tasting, gritty, shelf-stable nutrition bar made to government specifications, he went after government contracts for Zip's, but his efforts failed. Instead, Eli went all out with significant Little Sammies donations to the Red Cross for food parcels in the final twelve months of the war and the first six months of occupation. It was a hardship, because commodities were expensive and unpredictably available. Lillian made numerous objections to giving their product away at a time like this. Perhaps he had gone too far. But Eli insisted, even though he was bitter about Milton Hershey's cleverness in finagling those contracts that eluded him. He recognized the genius that lay behind Hershey's investment in giving American soldiers a taste of home that would create a permanent atavistic association with America and the taste of Hershey's slightly sour milk chocolate.

By the end of 1946, the postwar sugar shortage had not quite ended, but the insatiable demand for Little Sammies by returning GIs was the payoff for all the Zip's Candies donations to the Red Cross. Sugar was very hard to come by from week to week. Milton Hershey had that angle covered as well, with his own Cuban sugar plantations, even his own railroad to carry the sugar across Cuba from his refineries to the port of Havana. Processed cacao supplies were irregular. Eli had taken to staying late at work in order to make call after call to chocolate processors and brokers who might have some new sources for him. There were rumors of small quantities of decent cacao beans coming out of Congo, Trinidad, Ghana. But now he had found the solution, a surprising source in Madagascar that would both ensure Zip's Candies a guaranteed supply of good cacao and also change the course of Ziplinsky family history. His body lay on the floor behind the desk, samples from the day's Mumbo Jumbos scattered around him, when young Sam, married just a few months to Frieda (who was by then pregnant with the first of their three children, the doomed Lewis), eager to claim his weekend off and irked by the disruption of his plan to take his pregnant bride to the movies (she adored Dana Andrews, and they were planning to see *The Best Years of Our Lives*), having been sent back to the factory by his mother that Friday evening when she became concerned that Eli hadn't come home for his dinner, found him.

THE TRADITIONAL MUMBO Jumbos pack has a very good reputation among licorice aficionados. The package is a graphic delight, one that has hardly changed from the original to the present moment. It features the Zip's green umbrella against a festival of contrasting stripes, which make reference to the colorful outfits worn by Little Black Sambo's mother and father.

The market for licorice has always been small but steady. Devotees are appreciative of a good, chewy, flavorful licorice disc, especially one modeled on the wheat-based Finnish licorice nibs Eli knew from his New York street peddling days, and not on the more elastic, corn-based products like those that had already been around for decades by then—Red Vines, made by the American Licorice Company in Chicago since 1914, and, even older, the various licorice candies made by Young & Smylie since 1845 (Young & Smylie became part of the National Licorice Company in 1902, which in turn renamed itself Y&S Candies in 1968), those red and black twisted vines that over the years mutated into the nearly plastic Twizzlers, which dominates the licorice market share today and which since 1977 has been owned by Hershey's (that insatiable devourer of small candy brands, from Good & Plenty to Heath Bars to Jolly Ranchers to Reese's to Dagoba to Scharffen Berger). I am partial to Red Vines, which are best eaten when slightly stale. They can be toughened up in a few hours by deliberate exposure to air.

TIGERMELTS DO WELL from the beginning, with plentiful orders—it's a familiar combination bar, the dark-chocolate tiger stripes are a pleasant gimmick, the wrapper features a row of tigers chasing one another in a circle, and there is a charming slogan on the original wrapper, too: "Plain Hungry? Or Tigermelt Hungry?" (We had to drop that slogan when we redesigned the wrapper to accommodate nutritional information, once that became a legal requirement.)

But it's the Little Sammies that are a tremendous success, once they are finally perfected by the middle of 1925 and are tumbling off the line with the glossy finish exactly right, exactly the way Eli dreamed up his Little Sammies, his true confections. The public loves them from the start. Originally, they are packaged in twos, in that waxy yellow wrapper with the Zip's signature green umbrella emblazoned with the words "Say, Dat's Tasty!" The innovation of adding the third Little Sammie comes in 1932 as a way to offer the penny-pinched consumer more value for the same nickel, and Little Sammies have stayed three to a pack ever since. (Because this is a bit crowded, Little Sammies may get stuck together in the package; we recommend that you open the package and expose them to the air before you eat them.)

Little Sammies have always been fresh, I would like to point out, unless you let them grow stale after purchase. We make them, we ship them, they sell. I can only laugh at the genius who dreamed up the Hershey's marketing campaign for "Fresh From the Factory" opportunities, one select line at a time, on their website. All of our candy is always fresh from the factory! It's true that any limited availability can create an artificial surge in demand for product, the same way a limited-edition brand extension does, whether it is a variation that swaps dark chocolate for milk, or uses almonds instead of peanuts, or adds a mint or a caramel option, to name the four most obvious limited-edition variations.

Last year Jacob and I sent away for some "Fresh From the Factory" Twizzlers in order to see firsthand what Hershey's was actually selling. The product was impressively fresh, to be sure. One of those F From the F Twizzlers will droop if held balanced on your index finger. In contrast, an off-the-rack Twizzler from the Stop & Shop is darker and so much stiffer that holding it in the same way is like balancing a pencil. The not-so-fresh Twizzler was also noticeably tougher, bite for bite. Jacob admitted that he preferred it to the droopy Twizzler, which was like an edible lanyard. Jacob can be perverse that way. If "Fresh From the Factory" is billed by Hershey's as the optimal, premium taste and texture experience, isn't that a rather risky strategy, cultivating in consumers an awareness of the staleness and inferiority of all the rest of your retail stock?

❊ ❊

THE FIRST LITTLE Sammies sell out in New Haven and then they sell out again; production is increased, and they sell out all over New York. Soon national retailers are clamoring to place orders, and then the New Haven Railroad wants to sell them on all the passenger trains that run through New Haven, and then the Boston & Maine Railroad wants Little Sammies as well, and three chains of movie theaters start stocking Little Sammies. Within months Little Sammies have slots in grocery stores and gas stations across America. And canny Eli requires that for every case of Little Sammies ordered, a certain number of boxes of Tigermelts and Mumbo Jumbos must be ordered as well, thereby ensuring growth and steady business for the other two Zip's lines.

And so former Little Augie errand boy with a pushcart Eli Czaplinsky becomes Eli Ziplinsky, the beloved, innovative, industrious, hardworking, visionary founder and proprietor of Zip's Candies, maker of one of America's most beloved childhood treats, Little Sammies. The lines are in perpetual motion forever after, these crazy aggregations of thriftily appropriated machinery mixing and blending and forming and extruding a never-ending flow of Tigermelts, Mumbo Jumbos, and Little Sammies.

5

Sam, obviously, felt that I was family. He chose to reward my loyalty and devotion to the family and the business. That is the only explanation for his decision to leave me, as he did, 25 percent ownership of the Ziplinsky Family Limited Partnership, which is to say, Zip's Candies. Whether or not all family members agree with his choices, whether or not all family members respect his choices, surely the time has come to accept them. For God's sake, it's been eleven years now. The last will and testament of Samuel Ziplinsky has been honored by every court. The estate is settled. The distributions have been made. The identities of the Ziplinsky Family Trust beneficiaries are in dispute, but there is really nothing left to haggle over in Sam's estate. As the only living child of Eli and Lillian Ziplinsky, Sam had total ownership of Zip's Candies, having inherited the business from his mother, Lillian (to whom ownership had passed when Eli died without a will in 1946), when she died in 1975, just a few weeks after I walked in the door at Zip's. I am glad I met Lillian that one time, as it connects me to every generation of the family business.

I should add here, in the interest of delineating every branch of this bonsai of a family tree, that Sam's younger brother, Milton, died just months before the end of World War II, in his first week of basic training, at age nineteen, when he was accidentally shot in the face on the rifle range at Camp Jackson. Fortunately, he had no children—none that have been identified, anyway. I should know better than to assume anything about the reproductive habits of the Ziplinskys, but if Milton's children exist, they have badly missed the boat on stepping forward with their hands out, and given how useful their existence could have been to swing the majority vote in order to force a sale of the business, and how nightmarish that revelation would have been for me, I am pretty sure any issue of the late Milton Ziplinsky would have been truffled out by now.

So Milton doesn't play any part in this history or the present set of conflicts, though as the unofficial family historian/counterhistorian, I note with interest that he does take his hallowed place among the missing in this peculiar family, Milton being his generation's golden boy who dies a tragic early death and leaves the family out of balance, with a cascade of shifting roles.

Howard and Irene's older brother, Lewis, is another piece of the strange pattern. Frieda's golden boy, Lewis—her firstborn, the clear heir apparent to the business even as a child, by all accounts a wonderful, charming, smart, handsome boy—died at age fourteen when he was struck by lightning in Madagascar. I know how outlandish that sounds, like a perverse joke. He and Howard were there together that summer. Howard was twelve. They had been working among the vanilla orchids, doing a lot of tedious hand pollinating, and then the two of them had skived off with Andry, a local boy apparently their age who was nominally in charge of them, for a swim in the river. (They had been warned to keep a watch for crocodiles, believe it or not. How could anyone have thought this was a safe place for these tender boys to spend their summers? Especially cautious Jews?)

Black thunderheads rolled in, the wind shifted, and fat drops of heavy rain were suddenly pelting down on them. Tropical rainstorms can be sudden, and they can end just as suddenly. As the boys horsed around in the water, the rain seemed to let up, but then it intensified all over again and there was a rumble of thunder. Andry and Lewis very responsibly swam to the water's edge and started to hoist themselves out onto the sandy riverbank. Howard was still bobbing around in the middle of the river, his head tilted back with his mouth wide open to catch the raindrops, when lightning struck the wet boys as they clambered out. Andry, who was touching Lewis's arm when the lightning strike occurred, was severely burned, but he lived, though today he walks with a limp and is thought to be a bit simple. (He is still employed by the Czaplinsky family, as a gardener with few genuine responsibilities.)

Lewis had been struck directly, and he died instantly. Howard told me this story when we went out to dinner that first time. He narrated in a careful and remote way, with little emotion beyond a small sad smile that wasn't really a smile, pulling his mouth down at one corner, and I really thought at first that he was making it up. He described these events to me the way he might have been telling me about a disturbing movie he had seen a long time ago. When I look back now on the way I fell into that inexplicably intense relationship with Howard, I believe Lewis is in the story. His tragic death, the way each Ziplinsky carried that sorrow—it attracted me. I know it did. I was moved by the unbearable sadness that surrounded the story of the short life of the older brother, which added meaning and context to Howard's glibness and clowning, but at the same time, Lewis's absence made me feel that there could be a place for me in this family.

MORRIS, MILTON, LEWIS: all those missing sons. Irene would tell you it is Kennedyesque, the way those first sons were struck down. This pattern has obviously been broken in the next generation, though I say that with just a little bit of a sense of whistling in the dark. My two kids are healthy, as is their cousin Ethan. But who can guarantee anything? (And of course there are the cousins in Madagascar. I know I brought them up, but Newton and Edison Czaplinsky don't come into the story quite yet, though of course they will have been there all along.)

I suppose you could count Irene's high school abortion as technically having fulfilled the peculiar Ziplinsky destiny of doom for the firstborn child. Please don't misunderstand me; I served two terms on the state board of Planned Parenthood of Connecticut twenty years ago, and I was tireless in my efforts to keep abortion safe and legal and available to girls like Irene. The offices were in those years located above the New Haven clinic on Whitney Avenue, and some afternoons, on my way out after committee meetings, I would see high school girls in the waiting room, many of them in the plaid skirt and green sweater that was the uniform of St. Mary's two blocks away. I was the youngest member of the board at that time, and I knew that many of the older board members were motivated by their fond dedication to a lifted-pinky and benevolent sort of eugenics. These dowagers in Lilly Pulitzer dresses and Mother's pearls worked like busy little bees providing birth control to the lower order, poor people and "minorities." Until 1965, all birth control was technically illegal in Connecticut. In its way, it was admirable if misguided work. Sometimes people do the right things for the wrong reasons.

Anyway, Irene had an abortion three years before *Roe v. Wade* made abortion legal in Connecticut. Howard only told me about his sister's abortion when she was pregnant with Ethan. She had just begun eleventh grade at the Day Prospect Hill School, and Howard was a sophomore at Yale. Apparently her boyfriend (or boyfriends, who knows) had no awareness of her pregnancy. Howard even paid for Irene's abortion. (I find that creepy, the way it suited her to have him take the responsibility as if he was the father.) He set it up with a doctor he found because one of his Yale freshman-year roommates had been through it with his Smith College girlfriend. Never let it be said that the chief benefit of a Yale degree is being a Yale alumnus. Those Ivy League educations really prepare you!

Howard drove Irene to Springfield on the appointed day. He left her off at a certain intersection, as instructed, and watched her get into the green Buick that pulled up a moment later, and then he waited on that corner six hours later for her to be dropped off. In the intervening time Howard took himself to a German restaurant festooned with hideous beer steins hanging down from the ceiling like Prussian stalactites. It was October, and they were having a game festival, with partridge and elk and bear on the menu, so he ordered a bear steak and a mug of sudsy lager, but a group of people at the bar were singing drinking songs in German, and when his food came, he couldn't eat it. Was he the only person in the restaurant who wasn't there for the monthly meeting of the Springfield branch of the Baader-Meinhof Gang?

With a great deal of time to kill, Howard then went to visit the site of the apparently historic first Indian Motorcycle factory. (He had always wanted to own an Indian 101 Scout, and when I bought him one, a beautiful, cherry red, restored 1930 101 Scout, for his thirty-fifth birthday, despite my very reasonable fears about head injuries, I did so with the hope that this would satisfy Howard's chronic adolescent need to flirt with danger.) It began to drizzle, and it got dark, and Howard sat with an unread history text in a donut shop near the appointed intersection, and there he waited and waited for Irene to reappear.

She was almost two hours late, and he had begun to imagine that she was dead and he would be blamed. How could he face Frieda and Sam and tell them they had lost another child because of the carelessness and stupidity of their only remaining child, the dumb one? Irene threw up in his car on the drive back to New Haven, Howard went to a party that night, where he drank until he passed out, and they never, ever spoke of that day again.

If Irene is outraged that I have just provided these private details in this account of family history, then I can only suggest that she review her own choices, which have led to the necessity for the whole truth of this document.

SAM TOLD ME more than once, usually in the context of memories of the family's anxious vigil when the draft lottery numbers were announced in those Vietnam years (Howard got lucky each time, with very high numbers in the years when he had no deferment), that he felt terribly guilty about his younger brother's death, which he always believed contributed to Eli's fatal heart attack not so long after. Sam had been ineligible for military service, being nearly entirely blind in one eye, a trait he inherited from Eli.

Howard did not have this familial refractive amblyopia, which would have kept him from military service even with a low draft number, but Irene did. She says this is why she has never worn eye makeup, because she can't see with her blind eye when her good eye is closed, so it's very difficult to apply makeup, but she has also said at other times that she never wears eye makeup because of animal testing, and there was a year at Brown when she was militantly opposed to makeup since it represented the tyranny of the male fantasy of woman as whore, because cosmetics are designed to enhance and exaggerate the secondary sex characteristics of the female, and lipstick in particular is used because it makes women's lips look labial. That was the same year she stopped shaving her legs and under her arms. All that ended when she started going out with Arthur. As is so often the case with Irene, who can say what the truth is?

IN ANY CASE, Sam was the only heir to the Zip's Candies empire. What he made of it was his legacy to the family. Given how he was forced to take on the huge responsibility of running the business when he was twenty-two, when his father died so unexpectedly, Sam's stewardship of Zip's Candies was almost not a second-generation passing of the torch so much as it was in many ways simply the continuation of everything Eli had started. There was much more of a next-generation feeling when Howard took over in 1998.

Running a candy company was probably not what Sam would have really wanted to do with his life had he not been born into it. But Sam never had a chance to have any other kind of vision for himself. His life's work was simply to do everything he could to honor his father's vision and ambition, and to support his mother. Keeping Zip's healthy, making Zip's bigger and better, little by little—that was the only thing he knew how to do, the only thing he could do, after Eli died.

I asked Sam once, over one of our hundreds of grilled cheese sandwiches, if he had ever thought of not going into the family business at all. After a moment's reflection he admitted that he would have loved teaching, and perhaps coaching high school baseball, but then he interrupted himself to declare that he really couldn't remember even imagining any other life. He was proud to have been so successful with Zip's that he could offer that freedom he never had to his children and grandchildren, whom he claimed were welcome to go anywhere and do anything they wanted to do, with his blessing.

That said, and said sincerely, and often, I do think he would have been devastated if in his lifetime there were no heirs apparent named Ziplinsky, whether by blood or by marriage. "Candy makes people happy," Sam used to say as a way of summing up and moving the conversation past a challenging moment, "and I make candy. So my business is to make people happy. Who could ask for anything better?"

Zip's Candies might make people happy, but it doesn't make the Ziplinskys happy. I take peculiar solace in finding myself part of a great American tradition of troubled candy families. At an awards dinner during a candy and snack show in Atlanta last year, an inebriated vendor told me fascinating details of two Mars family divorces, which make my situation seem like a piece of cake. And let us reflect for a moment on Hart Crane's suicidal leap into the sea from a ship sailing between Havana and Florida at age thirty-three, in 1932. His father, Clarence, had invented Life Savers candy twenty years before, inspired by the recent innovation of round floatation lifesaving rings on ships.

When he sold it in 1909, Clarence Crane's Ohio maple-sugar business was the largest maple-sugar producer in the world. He started the Queen Victoria Chocolate Company after that, and he went on to develop hard peppermint candies for the summer season, when business slowed because chocolate melted in the heat. Crane was inspired to create a new round shape for his peppermint candies by a glimpse of a hand-operated pill-making machine at the Cleveland pharmacy where he bought his flavoring extracts. He formed his round, flat peppermints on a machine adapted for the purpose. The finishing touch was a small hole punched in the middle of each one to create Crane's Pep-O-Mint Life Savers, packaged in cardboard tubes depicting a sailor tossing a life preserver to a pretty girl, "For That Stormy Breath."

But the Crane family hardly profited from this innovation, as the rights to Life Savers were soon sold for only $2,900 in 1913 (doesn't every family have at least one mythic lost family fortune?), and Clarence Crane went back to chocolate, which did not interest his poet son one bit.

As Hart Crane removed his topcoat and in his pajamas climbed over the railing of the SS *Orizaba,* "tilting there momently, shrill shirt ballooning," did he note the irony? He was last seen swimming toward the horizon. His body was never found.

IT's A GOOD thing Sam never lived to see the family at war this way. Though of course it was his death that set the crisis in motion. Howard must have known, if he thought it through, that everything would come to light sooner or later, but Howard has not exactly made a name for himself as the man who thinks things through.

I SHOULD EXPLAIN why I am the only member of the family who doesn't call Howard by his nickname, Howdy. Actually, I am the only person in his life who doesn't call him Howdy. It's like the way Beaver Cleaver's mother was the only one to call him Theodore. Everyone knows Howard as Howdy. It's printed on his Zip's Candies business cards. I have been Mrs. Howard Ziplinsky for more than thirty years now, but you wouldn't know it. If I identify myself that way when charging something, or phoning in an order, there is always a puzzled silence, followed by a correction: Oh, you mean *Howdy* Ziplinsky. Okay, thanks, Mrs. Ziplinsky! Have a nice day!

When Howard and his older brother, Lewis, were little, they loved to watch *Howdy Doody* on television on Saturday mornings, and Sam started calling them Buffalo Bob and Howdy Doody. I don't know if Lewis was called Buffalo Bob for very long, or if it was ever shortened to Buff, or Bob. I wonder now if Sam realized that he was assigning Lewis the part of the responsible adult while Howard was designated the unserious puppet. Nobody talks easily about Lewis. Because he died the way he did at fourteen, every memory of him seems to be encoded with that inevitability, as if he lived his short life hurtling toward his death, and so the fact of his death retrospectively colors every fact of his life.

In his childhood, Howard was called Howdy until it caused some bullying in seventh grade and he made everyone drop it. He signed his name with a very serious "Howard M. Ziplinsky" all through junior high and high school. But when Howard went to Yale and his DKE frat brother George W. Bush started calling him Howdy, though it may have been intended as a put-down, Howard went with it, and soon everyone, even his professors, was calling him Howdy.

It's a friendly name, I admit, an openhanded, slap-you-on-the-back, pleased-to-meet-ya! kind of name, but it doesn't work for me. I tried to call him Howdy when we met, but it's not really a very respectful name, and then, soon enough, it didn't feel like a very romantic or sexy name either, and I just never could say it and mean it. If I called him Howdy it came out with a forced casualness. (And as a name, it's a bizarre one for an adult Jewish man from New Haven, isn't it? Wouldn't you expect it to be the nickname for a broncobuster from Oklahoma, at least?) Long before Howard started being a little too eager to tell people that his nickname had been conferred at Yale by that incompetent who occupied the White House for those eight long years (which of course isn't quite true), I had ceased calling him anything but Howard.

"Howdy" suggests goofiness to me, jerkiness, clowning. And as a child, the few times I happened to see it in reruns, I was genuinely frightened by the *Howdy Doody* show. It seemed sinister to me, the idiotic Howdy puppet itself, with those cruel freckles, and the supporting cast was unspeakably creepy, from the Flub-a-Dub thing (which had a duck's bill, cat's whiskers, a giraffe's neck, and spaniel ears, on a dachshund's body, with seal's flippers, and a pig's tail, plus an elephant's memory), to that big-headed Princess Summerfall Winterspring. Clearly, the show's writers had a weird obsession with blending and hybridizing, and it gave me the willies. But then, I was a child who didn't want my vegetables touching on my plate. My mother used to be irritated with me when I told her I didn't like food with ingredients. I have never liked things that begin and end and begin again. I have always liked clearly defined borders and boundaries, lots of space between one thing and another thing. I hated the pushmi-pullyu in *Dr. Doolittle*. I traded with Beth Crabtree in seventh grade to avoid doing a report on the Minotaur, opting instead to take her far more manageable assigned topic, Daedalus and Icarus. Even now, I don't like ligatures in type, and I don't care for succotash. When Jacob went through a grade school Transformers obsession, I managed to tolerate them, but it was a huge relief when he lost interest and we could donate his collection to a homeless shelter.

But really, there was nothing to like about the *Howdy Doody* cast of characters. I hated them all: Clarabell the Clown, Chief

Thunderthud, Phineas T. Bluster, Dilly Dally, and let's not forget the obscure sister, Heidi Doody. (I admit that at times my secret nickname for Irene has been Heidi Doody.) And they all lived in Doodyville, which was a name that frankly embarrassed me, growing up as I did in a household where we didn't speak baby talk but called things done in the bathroom by their proper names, urination and defecation. (In elementary school I was horrified to discover all the pee pee poo poo talk that went on in my friends' households. Barbara Roth's family called it wizzy and push, for God's sake.) And another creepy thing about *Howdy Doody* was the frantic laughter from the Peanut Gallery, which was like the sound of a fever dream.

And so I have always called Howard, Howard, and I am the only one to do so. He even wanted Jacob and Julie to call him Howdy, instead of Dad, but both of them called him Daddy when they were little, and these days they call him Pop, or, when they are speaking to me, sometimes they simply refer to him as "my father," or "your ex-husband."

Therefore, Howard, his actual given name, is, in effect, my private nickname for him, since nobody else uses it. Dr. Gibraltar said that this impulse of mine, this refusal to call Howard by the name he wants me to use, my too-rigid insistence on addressing my husband with a formal adult name instead of a childlike nickname, was a way of avoiding my own id-driven desire to regress to that child I was who was so frightened by everything about the *Howdy Doody* show. Ellie Quest-Greenspan helped me see that I have spent all these years fruitlessly addressing Howard's inner adult in the hopes that he would respond as Howard the grown-up instead of Howdy the child. She said that when she looked at Howard she could clearly see his ungoverned and endlessly needy wounded inner child, the Howdy who was splashing in that river with his big brother that terrible day when he witnessed Lewis's death, a stuck, wise-cracking Peter Pan with car keys and a credit card and a fractured heart.

So MUCH HAS now changed in the family, in our situations and circumstances. But I want to be clear about something. I really had no clue for nearly thirty years that mine was not a happy and contented marriage with the mutual intention to grow old together, the best is yet to be. I didn't know that those were the best years of my life. And those years with Howard were happy years, with a comfortable intimacy between us, a good work relationship, and an endless variety of ordinary, pleasant family activities.

We took a family trip to Vermont every summer, just before Labor Day, staying at the same farm, where the kids could gather eggs and watch the milking and help roll out piecrusts with the farmer's wife (she used canned pie filling, but in its way, that, too, was part of the authentic experience). We spent happy days at the beach in the summer, we drove down to the Bronx to go to Yankees games, we went skiing at Butternut in the winter. Howard is a graceful skier, and he taught the kids to ski with infinite patience and humor. We laughed together all the time. For so many years, there was always that eye to catch at those moments of mutual recognition, especially in our shared pleasure in our children, as for example the time we were driving home from an entirely rainy and muddy Vermont trip and the whole family had become irritable, and then we overheard this from Julie and Jacob as they squabbled in the back seat:

"You're ovnoxious," said Julie self-righteously.

"It's not *ovnoxious,* it's *ibnoxious,*" Jacob retorted with all the superiority and confidence in the world.

❋ ❋

ZIP'S CANDIES HAS been in a state of flux for too long. It is only thanks to my loyalty and hard work that stability has been maintained while the internecine battles have raged. Not that I am waiting for anyone other than my own children to send any gratitude my way. But nobody in the family can claim to have been impoverished by the outcome of Howard's and my divorce settlement or the way the courts have denied the challenges to Sam's estate. Meanwhile, all the attorneys have certainly prospered.

I do resent the continuing insinuations about the nature of my relationship with Sam. He was my father-in-law. He was my children's grandfather. Our relationship was one of mutual love and respect. He recognized my aptitude for the business. He appreciated the spirit and energy I brought to Zip's. Surely my tireless efforts over the years to make Zip's Candies grow and prosper are not the usual hallmarks of a gold digger. Surely a gold digger would be first in line to cash out and would hardly go to so much trouble to preserve the family business. How could any reasonable person deem my actions "irresponsible" or "dangerous," let alone "duplicitous" and "manipulative"? (Not to mention the outrageous statement that I'm the one with the "vicious temper.") I have been a more loyal Ziplinsky than anyone.

It is inevitable, I suppose, in Irene Ziplinsky's world, when viewed through her lenses of jealousy and suspicion; a sexual connection between Sam and me would seem like the obvious explanation for his favoring me so generously. I suppose, too, it is a mark of my outsiderness that I see this assumption as perverted and offensive, insulting to me and insulting to the memory of Sam Ziplinsky, rather than logical. I have nothing more to say about these vile assertions.

No, actually, I do have one more thing to say about these vile assertions. Shame, shame, shame on you, Irene Ziplinsky Weiss, sitting there smugly in your $7 million log cabin in Telluride with your fond belief that you have, in your words, "stepped outside the economic factor" with your solar energy and your composting toilet, spouting your virtuous fair trade, sustainable, organic, free-range, antibiotic- and hormone-free, handwoven, sanctimonious crap. He always loved you like a daughter, because you *were* his daughter, as hostile and rejecting and critical as you were. Sam was a devoted father.

He loved both you and Howard, and he came to love me—his son's wife, his daughter-in-law—for good and honorable reasons. I don't know why this is so unbearable for you, but I recognize that it is, and I am sorry you feel so diminished and threatened by something that has never been about you at all. Sam's bequests weren't final report cards. It's time to stop acting as if I cheated and got an undeserved A, while you dutifully turned in all your homework on time yet somehow failed.

I AM CERTAIN that Sam's decisions were very considered. His longtime lawyer and adviser, Ben Gottesfeld, won't take my calls and hasn't been very helpful to any side in this situation, preferring to step back and leave all his options open. I'm disappointed in Ben, who used to be more of a mensch, and I do think Sam misjudged him. But I am certain that Ben wouldn't have let him make mistakes in the execution of his intentions. Especially given the way Sam and his mother were left to deal with the consequences of Eli's not having had a will, Sam was clearly focused on taking care of his family and seeing his legacy passed down just the way he wanted it.

By leaving 25 percent of the Ziplinsky Family Limited

Partnership (which owns Zip's Candies) to Howard, Sam obviously thought he was protecting the legacy of the family business, handing stewardship and prosperity down the line to the next generation. He often said to me, Blood is thicker than water, but business is business. I have certainly wondered if Sam was somehow assuming that Howard and I would stay together and our interests would therefore continue to be one and the same. He knew what Howard had done. I have proof of that, or I did, anyway, before the fire. Maybe Sam hoped, like Howard, that I wouldn't figure it out for a long, long time. Or maybe he intended to provide me with an independent source of wealth and security, come what may. After all, he could have simply left Howard half ownership of the Family Partnership. Or he could have named us as joint owners of a half interest, with right of survivorship. But he didn't do either of those things. He broke his agreement with Howard, to reward him with the business if he stayed long enough. Sam knew the score, and I believe this was his way of trying to offer me some compensation and balance. It was a gesture of gratitude.

Either way, in our divorce settlement, given community-property laws in Connecticut, and given our history, and given the terms of the divorce (Howard's position was *vacuus a crur subsisto in*, according to Charlie, in other words, without a leg to stand on), whether or not any portion of the business was already in my name had no bearing, and I was entitled to half of Howard's interest in Zip's.

Howard claimed at the time of Sam's death that his father had promised to leave him a controlling interest in the company. Howard said that he and Sam had a deal they had made at the time of our wedding. Whether or not this is true, and I have reason to believe that it is, though of course I never said a word about that during our divorce proceedings, it simply doesn't signify, since it wasn't in any of the provisions in Sam's or Frieda's estate. Apparently, Howard didn't know that his father had actually drawn up a contract for this agreement. Sam himself said to me more than once that a verbal agreement isn't worth the paper it's written on. It is certainly worth no more or less than a draft of an unsigned contract.

Owing to some tricky math of the kind they do in Superior Court, our settlement agreement when we divorced awarded me a little less than half of Howard's 25 percent of the business— as we all know, in addition to the house and an equitable portion of our other assets, I was given two fifths of his share of the partnership, in other words, 10 percent of Zip's. Which is why today I am the largest single shareholder of the Ziplinsky Family Limited Partnership.

I am really, truly not some destructive, power-hungry monster who has invaded the precious family in order to seize control of the business, notwithstanding Irene's hilarious remark to me outside the courtroom last time we appeared for a hearing, when she muttered at me, "Ours was a decent family before you entered it." I'll say it again: Sam chose to leave me 25 percent of the business. That's the way the cookie crumbles. I have only been a Ziplinsky for three fifths of my life, unlike all natural-born Ziplinskys, but now I own two fifths of the Ziplinsky Family Limited Partnership, which is to say two fifths of Zip's Candies, and unlike most natural-born Ziplinskys, I have earned it.

MAYBE I NEED to explain the outrageousness of Irene's claims more clearly. Sam left Irene a portfolio of stocks and bonds worth almost half the paper value of Zip's Candies, which was, as he made clear in very precise language, compensation for not giving her any ownership of the family business. However, her only child, Ethan, as a grandchild, has a share in the Ziplinsky Family Trust, which now, with Frieda's death, goes to the beneficiaries. The trust owns half of Zip's Candies. Under the terms of the trust, the CEO of Zip's Candies is one of the three trustees of the trust, and I maintain that with Howard's departure, I have been functioning in that capacity ever since, which means that I am, by definition, one of the three trustees of the Ziplinsky Family Trust.

Irene's son, Ethan, being a beneficiary of the trust, owns a share of the family business. And so despite the dispute about who exactly are the beneficiaries of the trust, which is at the heart of this mess, no matter what else Irene might claim, there is simply no validity to Irene's belief that she has been unfairly treated. And meanwhile, irony of ironies, all the discovery documents make evident that Irene is the richest of us all, despite her poor-mouth campaign. Why choose to be pathetic and victimy and undignified? Why the determination to be seen as someone who has been cheated and disinherited?

Frieda's death also ended the regrettable tradition at Zip's of distributing big, unearned quarterly checks to Howard and Irene equally. Not exactly the definition of sound management practice. Howard has always drawn a good salary with benefits, and there were all kinds of over- and under-the-table benefits, but until he left, he worked hard for the business. He put in his hours, and he was kind and fair to his employees; it could be said that those quarterly payments were a reasonable bonus.

But Irene was just a parasite with a no-show job on the so-called Zip's "board," which "met" once a year at Passover. You would think she would have some pride. She's fifty-six years old! Surely the time has come for her to stop thinking of Zip's Candies as her personal Xanadu, from which she has been inexplicably exiled.

Now she is an angry baby denied her bottle. No more having

our bookkeeper pay her credit-card bills, no more having our accountant do her tax returns for her, no more sending imperious holiday emailed lists to the office with names and addresses of people to whom we must send gift boxes of Zip's Candies "from" Irene. She has been tempered and molded and enrobed and drizzled and cooled and wrapped and extruded right off the end of the line. And I canceled her company ExxonMobil Speedpass, too.

IRENE'S ENTIRE OTIOSE connection to the business was really only ever about her own status and prosperity. She has used her money over the years to fund a wide variety of half-baked do-good, feel-good enterprises of the moment. The sad truth is that Irene could have done anything in the world if she'd had the motivation. But Irene never gets traction on anything for very long, and she has never had any singular abiding passion. She's never been hungry enough to succeed at anything that required persistence. I know I can be like a dog with a bone, but my God, she has the attention span of a gnat. She's too self-involved to be reliable in ordinary ways, which is why she has never had a real job, though she allegedly worked in the office at Zip's each summer while she was in high school, before I came along.

Irene has always been satisfied just coasting. In every part of her life, really. She got good grades at Brown, which she manages to mention very, very often, because it is one of her only achievements that wasn't entirely bought and paid for. She met Arthur Weiss in their junior year; they married right after graduation, and they divorced after eleven years together, when Ethan was five. Arthur is now a successful anesthesiologist (how often those two words go together!) living in Princeton with his second wife (his former office manager) and their children.

Irene has made a career out of discovering herself since the divorce. She is always totally obsessed with her projects of the moment, and even now when we are barely speaking I still get email bulletins about her sensitive responses to world disasters and her deep personal awareness of global warming and the need for worldwide sustainability. I find her very silly. I suspect Ethan does too.

It's a miracle he has turned out to be as decent as he is, with those parents. He was a monstrous child, "self-regulating," rather than disciplined in any way whatsoever, so he was always cranky and sleep-deprived, always whining, always eating sugary things right before meals, always having tantrums, always demanding the next thing and the next thing. And Irene's attempts to civilize him were always situational, with no underlying consistency or ethic.

"Stop smearing your cupcake on the sofa, Ethan, sweetie," she would say, only after I was clearly reaching the end of my tether, though under ordinary circumstances I was reasonably patient with most kids. "Your aunt Alice doesn't like it when you do that." I felt guilty disliking that child as much as I did. One shouldn't loathe toddlers, should one? But he was a disaster.

To his credit, Ethan would clearly prefer to stay the hell away from both of his parents as much as he possibly can these days, and he's turned into a reasonable adult. Neither of my kids is especially close to him, their one and only American first cousin.

This brings me to the Madagascar cousins. Darwin and Miriam have no children. Darwin's sister, Huxley, had a baby a few months after Howard and I were married. I remember hearing about it from Frieda, who mentioned it several times, in a rather conspicuous way, in retrospect. Was she testing me, to see what I knew? Newton (don't those Czaplinskys have the craziest names? Where's Copernicus Czaplinsky?) was an only child for a long while, until his younger brother, Edison, was born, soon after I had Jacob.

Because Newton was five years older, Jacob never really got to know him the way he became close to Edison during those summers they worked and played together on the plantations. Jacob and Edison, though both born in 1982, were not technically of the same generation, since Newton and Edison were actually Howard's second cousins, making them second cousins once removed to my kids.

I know that parsing who is a first cousin once removed as opposed to who is a second cousin is excruciating for most people, who couldn't care less. It's a particular skill you develop at an early age in a family like mine. To be a Tatnall is to have an anxious desire to have precise knowledge about your degree of relatedness to Benedict Arnold's wife. But it's important to understand these Ziplinsky relationships with clarity, given the situation we're in now. The obsessive scrutiny and analysis of the family tree with which I was raised turns out to be a somewhat more useful skill than, say, scrimshaw, after all.

I NEVER WENT to Madagascar. I always meant to, and most people who know a little bit about our family story—Eli's amazing reconnection with his long-lost brother, who settled in Madagascar during the war, the fortuitous way the families found each other just before Eli died because a cacao broker with whom they both did business happened to notice and comment on their similar names—assume quite naturally that I have been there. People who heard about the Madagascar family would tell me they envied me the exotic trips they assumed I had made, and I would usually gloss over it and change the subject, unless pressed, when I would have to say with some awkwardness that it had never worked out for me to go there, though everyone else in the family has spent time on the family cacao and vanilla plantations.

That's not quite true. It is more accurate (and painful) to admit now that I allowed myself to be kept away. The human heart has an amazing capacity to know and not know at the same time.

In the first years of our marriage, Howard would travel to Madagascar once or twice a year, often during the rainy season, which can be dangerous, with mudslides and flooding. It is certainly not a brilliant time for tourism, he pointed out on each occasion when the possibility of my accompanying him arose. He always told me I should go in another season, for sure, maybe in the fall, maybe in the spring, and we spoke of making such a trip together, but the years kept passing. His photographs were beautiful. The immense baobab trees lining the road leading to one of the cacao estates looked as if they grew in a Delvaux landscape.

Then I had babies, and they were too young to travel to a place like that, a malaria zone, and also too young to leave for more than a few days, not that there was anyone I would have trusted to take care of them. With whom would I have left Julie and Jacob when they were growing up? Irene? Frieda and Sam, so Frieda could brainwash my children to regard me, the one non–blood Ziplinsky, as an outsider the way she did? Now *that* would be evidence of irresponsibility! It might have been different if I'd ever had any close friends, the sort of people who very naturally love your children and are eager to take care of them so you can travel, but I have never cultivated or maintained friendships.

And then as the kids grew older there was always something urgent and unmissable of theirs on the schedule, and when Howard would go, it never seemed like the right time to leave our kids, or to leave Zip's, where I was very much a cog in the machinery, especially with Howard away. And it never felt right for me to consider making a trip on my own to go to this difficult, remote place to stay with these relatives I didn't know, beyond the one strange encounter at our wedding.

Over the years, Julie and Jacob and I enjoyed the times when Howard was in Madagascar, where he went every six or seven months. His absence was relaxing, because I had fewer domestic requirements for daily living without him. I suppose it is a cliché, the way I was a contented and unsuspicious wife who used to enjoy the luxury of my temporary solitude when Howard was on those Madagascar trips. I became indulgent about letting the kids stay up late on school nights, a secret violation of one of Howard's most serious theories of parenting. It was always clear to me anyway that his motives for maintaining strict bedtimes were based on his preference for the end of the evening to be unencumbered by the needs of children, not about any true philosophy of child development. It was a break for me when I didn't have to honor Howard's food preferences, which ordinarily had me preparing elaborate meals most nights of the week. When he was away, the three of us would depend on take-out Chinese food or pizza, in rotation with another Daddy's-away tradition of ours, which was what the kids happily called "breakfast-dinners."

On those nights we would have scrambled eggs and bacon, or French toast and sausages, or pancakes with sautéed apples and bananas swimming in maple syrup. Although Howard didn't manifestly endorse Frieda's belief that women who served their children scrambled eggs or French toast for dinner were all alcoholic Protestants, my doing this made him uneasy. What's more, the three of us would change into pajamas and robes and slippers before we ate our breakfast-dinner. This would not have suited Howard at all.

WHEN EDISON WAS twelve, he came to stay with us in Connecticut during a school break in the monsoon season. He was a beautiful boy, with an almost angelic look to him. I had never met his mother (and I never will—why would I want to meet the sperm embezzler who has taken away the life I deserved, the life I worked so hard for, the life I earned?), but I imagined her to look as fiercely exotic as her brother, Darwin. The fuzzy snapshot of her that Edison kept under his pillow (I found it when I made his bed) confirmed that. Those half-Czaplinsky, half-Malagasy offspring are remarkable genetic upgrades, I have to admit.

Edison was paler and more Caucasian in his features than I remembered his uncle Darwin being, but he had those startling blue eyes that run in the family, and that same fierce island look about him, like a young warrior who is coddled in his youth but will one day be challenged and hardened to face the responsibilities of manhood. He definitely didn't look Caucasian (I realize I am dwelling on his appearance), especially in February, in New Haven, Connecticut, where he seemed to glow with a tropical radiance against the New England grayness. He was amazed and horrified by the snow and ice, and he was miserable in the cold.

Edison was a sweet boy, polite, eager to pitch in, undemanding (though he didn't like a lot of our food and was happiest at any meal with a banana and a big bowl of rice), but he was very timid around me. He would always cast his eyes down when I spoke to him. I couldn't decide if this was a cultural imperative or something specific to his awkwardness around me. He was more relaxed around Jacob and Julie, whom he was meeting for the first time, since Jacob was also twelve and would make his first Madagascar trip the following summer, and Julie was then only ten.

It was difficult to get anywhere with him conversationally, because he was so shy with me. One morning while I watched him tuck into his banana and rice, I asked him if he had any brothers and sisters, and he replied, "Newton," in a whisper. That was the name of his older brother. Howard explained to me that Newton, who was some six years older than Edison, was beginning to take on some of the administrative tasks of the Czaplinsky cacao plantations, working for his uncle Darwin.

Edison was almost clingy with Howard, in a babyish way for his age, though what did I know about how a twelve-year-old Malagasy boy should comport himself? Whenever I tried to hug him he stiffened up and tolerated me politely, but it was like hugging a cooperative chicken. I wondered if it was considered unmanly to accept a woman's affection if she isn't your mother, let alone if she's a strange white woman, whether or not you have been told she is in your family. I asked Howard what his cousin Huxley was like, wondering if Newton and Edison's mother was very undemonstrative. I realized I had never heard a word about her in all these years. I cannot stress enough how out of focus the Madagascar family was always kept. Howard was very vague in his reply. Perhaps, too, there was residual resentment among the Czaplinskys over Julius's having been left behind? And about Eli's failure to find him over all those years in Budapest? I asked Howard about both of these issues more than once, but he told me dismissively that I was looking for trouble, and that most people don't carry grudges the way I think they do.

A few times in the course of those weeks, I heard Edison call Howard "Baba." When I asked Howard why, Howard told me it was just a nickname he had with the Czaplinsky boys, because when Newton was a baby, he hadn't been able to say "Howdy," and had used baby babble when he greeted Howard: "Babababa." And then it just stuck all these years, so it was natural for Edison to call him that as well, since that was what he grew up hearing Howard called by his older brother. While true, that was an incomplete answer.

And so the years passed, and Jacob began to go to Madagascar each summer. Julie never wanted to go that far away from us, plus she had developed a terrible fear of lightning on Madagascar, having heard the story of Lewis's death. Julie was an anxious child with a number of phobias, not only a fear of thunder and lightning (Astraphobia, murmured Dr. Gibraltar) but also a fear of lightning bugs and any other bioluminescent creatures that might light up anywhere near her; after his first Madagascar trip, Jacob had described seeing on the dock in Antsiranana harbor some bizarre glow-in-the-dark sea creatures from the deep that been inadvertently landed, entangled in a fisherman's nets.

Julie also had some significant allergies and easily triggered asthma, which at times made Howard impatient, because he thought she brought it on herself with her unnecessary anxieties. He felt that it would be unwise for her to go to that potentially difficult and primitive place, when something could go really wrong, as the family knew so well. And so the women in the family didn't go to Madagascar, just the men.

With Jacob on Madagascar for those two months each summer, having his independent time among his cousins, a summer visit for me became problematic, because, and Howard felt strongly about this, I would have been crowding Jacob. It would be unfair, a real Jewish mother thing, like something Mrs. Portnoy would do, for me to follow him there. Even Frieda had given Howard that freedom. The first time Jacob went to Madagascar, the summer he had just turned thirteen (having dropped out of Hebrew school after deciding against a bar mitzvah, a choice we let him make, which gave Frieda immense, grim satisfaction), Howard flew there with him and got him settled in, returning to Connecticut two weeks later, while Jacob stayed all through the summer and made the journey back on his own, just before school started, very pleased with his independence. After that, Jacob went on his own every summer as soon as he finished school, changing planes in Paris, returning over Labor Day weekend most years, until college, when his American life started looming larger, with friends, girlfriends, and internships breaking the pattern.

Was there a moment when I figured it out? There were so many moments, and yet I kept not knowing, and not knowing, over three decades. Did everyone in the family know the truth except for me? Did Irene know? She only went to Madagascar herself that one time when she was a kid. And she has always been remarkably uncurious about other people's lives unless they had a direct effect on her. Maybe she didn't. I can't believe she wouldn't have wanted to lord it over me in some way if she did. The Ziplinskys are notoriously bad at keeping secrets, though this was one Howard managed to hold on to for a very long time. Sam knew. Irene's argument that he didn't know, and so his intentions for the trust could not possibly have been meant to include Newton and Edison, is shamefully meretricious. Of course he knew. That's why he made the deal with Howard, promising him the business if he married me and stayed in New Haven and worked at Zip's. Ironically, given the lengths to which everyone went to conceal the truth from me at the time, I believe that had I known, I would have agreed to marry Howard just the same. I would have helped Frieda and Sam keep Howard. I would have been willing to go along with it. They didn't have to use me.

Frieda had to have known, maybe not in the beginning, but I am sure she figured it out or Sam told her at some point. She probably hated owing me for keeping her precious son tethered to the family and the business, but my being in the dark all those years must have given her huge satisfaction. Jacob knew for at least three years before I could stop denying the truth to myself. He told Julie a couple of years in, but he couldn't face confronting me with it.

And so Howard's betrayal effectively partitioned me off from the people in the world I loved and trusted the most—my kids, Sam. And I could always feel it, just below the surface, but I just wasn't ready to face the truth. Of course it was always there. Why was I in such denial? I could have dealt with it. I would have been reasonable about Newton. I know I would have been. It happened before Howard and I met. It's not even clear that he knew about Newton when we decided to get married.

But how am I to forgive Howard for Edison?

When I married Howard, I wrote a note in my journal, "I am being taken in by this wonderful family." How true was that?

Malagasy for "Thank you very much" is *Misaotra betsaka tompoko.*
Malagasy for "You are welcome" is *Tsy misy fisaorana.*
Malagasy for "I love you" is *Tiako ianao.*
Malagasy for "Daddy" is *Baba.*

Julie keeps her distance from Newton and Edison. She regards them as problematic strangers who have caused our family much unhappiness. But Jacob, having spent so much time on Madagascar, has a warm and close relationship with his half brothers, who are also his second cousins once removed. I try not to begrudge him it.

When Jacob came back from Madagascar at the end of the summer he was fifteen, he was transformed from a weedy teenage boy into something more masculine. He had turned into the man he is now, though I could still catch a glimpse of his baby face if I peeked in on him when he was sleeping. That autumn, he had a slightly different, somewhat pungent and very pleasant aroma about him for weeks after he returned. He would sense me sniffing his neck and say, Cut that out, Ma! and push me away, but I couldn't get enough of it.

Yes, I had missed him, but frankly I just loved this new smell. Vanilla, plus something earthy and raw. Was it an oil, a product, something in his diet? He had subsisted mostly on *mofo gasy*, a pancakey bread, and *koba akondro,* a sweet he would buy at the side of the road from old ladies with food stalls who spent their days wrapping a batter of ground peanuts, mashed bananas, honey, and corn flour in banana leaves, which they steamed until the batter formed a small cake. His other favorite from the roadside stalls was *caca pigeon*, literally, "pigeon droppings," a snack of deep-fried salted dough and steamed manioc over which they poured sweetened condensed milk.

When his Malagasy aroma started to fade, I tried to duplicate these dishes for Jacob in the secret hope that if he ate enough of these foods his spicy odor would return, but he was only slightly polite about my attempts to duplicate the food of rural Madagascar with ingredients from the Stop & Shop, and I gave up.

Jacob kept detailed journals during those summers before he

went to college, and while I would like to say he showed them to me (because I would like to think I am the kind of mother whose son would want to share all of his experiences), he didn't. But the journals weren't hidden, either. I never would have read them if he had hidden them out of sight. But Jacob kept them on the shelf over his desk, and so in the course of tidying his room I would always read his latest entries. I have such admiration for his vivid and sensitive writing skills. Reading his journals, I felt as if I had been there with him.

Jacob and Edison worked side by side through those summers, cutting cacao pods, pollinating vanilla orchids, preparing the fragrant and rare Porcelana cacao beans for drying in the sun. "Dancing the cocoa," they called it, the shuffling of the fermenting beans with their bare feet, turning the beans, kicking and dragging their feet in big sweeping circles. Jacob and Edison would exhaust themselves, slamming together in wild and athletic dances on the flat drying roofs of the cacao-bean sheds.

Now of course they are both involved in the production of the Zip's Bao-Bar, and that binds them in some new ways, but theirs is an incredibly complex connection, one they will be sorting out together for many years. Newton is also a partner with Jacob and Edison in the Bao-Bar venture, as is Zip's Candies (in a cashless exchange for the contract manufacturing on our premises; since the Bao-Bar runs on the Tigermelt line, Zip's has a 25 percent stake in the Madagascar Bao-Bar Company), and he is the main grower and supplier of the dried baobab pulp that makes this bar so different from all the other energy bars on the market. Dried baobab pulp, which is rich in fiber, has antioxidant properties to beat the band, is loaded with B1, B2, and C vitamins, and also has a stunning amount of calcium. And the

Bao-Bar is the only energy bar on the national market with Madagascar (or any other kind of) baobab.

One of the significant ingredients in the Bao-Bar is the tiny sprinkle of crushed cacao nibs in the core. These nibs are supplied to Zip's from the special Czaplinsky production of an exceptionally rare cacao, which otherwise is sold to just three chocolatiers, all of them in France, all of them willing to pay significantly more for these nibs, ounce for ounce, than the going rate for the finest Beluga caviar. Julius was cultivating this unusual cacao at the time of his death. (The time he spent under the mother trees in the humid, insect-infested, tropical environment required for cacao to pollinate and fruit exposed him to the mosquitoes carrying the malaria that killed him.) It's genetically related to the Porcelana and the Criollo cacao varieties. Julius's name for the variety in his notes (which he kept in Yiddish) was "Gewurzik Geshmak," which translates literally to Spicy Tasty. Edison honors this, and calls the cacao Gewurzik. Surely it is the only Yiddish appellation for any cacao production growing today in the fifteen countries in the equatorial belt around the world that grow 98 percent of the world's cacao. The Gewurzik is a slow-growing and unproductive variety, which limits the commercial possibilities, but the limited yield of cacao from the unusually small and rounded cacao pods is simply exquisite.

Jacob samples each small batch of roasted beans as it arrives, and his intensity gladdens my heart as he sits at his worktable, hunched over his bean guillotine making notes about nice fissuring and deep, even color. Every parent wants her child to find his passion. Not only is the flavor of the cacao nibs spicy and tasty indeed, but they also have an unusually sky-high level of flavonoids and other polyphenols, which have a proven antioxidant, anti-inflammatory effect on the human body, especially the heart. Further, the Gewurzik has loads of anandamide and tryptophan, both potent brain stimulators, and theobromine, which stimulates the nervous system.

There are lots of technical explanations for how these chemicals affect us, but the simplest way of talking about it is simply to say that the smallest nibble of Gewurzik cacao makes you feel really good. I am opposed to marketing the Bao-Bar as a "neutraceutical bar." I don't like the word. But my preference did not prevail, and I have to admit the success of the bar in these first months has been far beyond any of our most optimistic projections.

I know that Howard has taken charge of the Gewurzik project these days, even though it has never been acknowledged to me, with Jacob, Edison, and Newton running interference so I have no direct dealings with him. I hope it makes him happy. Maybe he imagines he is back in his boyhood, frolicking with his brother, Lewis, under the tangled canopy of the mother trees shading his precious cacao plantings. I am sure he is the Grandest Tiger in the Jungle, with his beautiful family at his side. Presumably he is taking his antimalaria medication.

Between the unusual texture from the dried baobab pulp and the presence of the Gewurzik nibs, the Bao-Bar is a pure and simple bar like no other. It is also chewy and delicious, with just a hint of Czaplinsky Pure Madagascar Vanilla, with neither the cardboardy, fiber-is-good-for-you texture nor the cloying virtuous sweetness of too many energy and protein bars.

Newton is impressively altruistic, a trait he surely inherited from his Malagasy grandmother, Julius's common-law wife, Lalao, and not from any Czaplinsky or Ziplinsky genes. His choices in life are truly admirable, and it isn't hard for me to say that. He is dedicated to running a baobab cooperative project in several remote villages on Madagascar, and he is keenly interested in helping the poorest Malagasy people learn how to utilize every part of the huge, ancient upside-down trees that have loomed over the dry deciduous forests for hundred of years.

The fresh fruit is sweet and chewy, while the white, powdery pulp of the fruit can be mixed into porridge. The leaves can be made into nourishing soups and stews, and the seeds can be pounded and pressed to yield a useful if odd-tasting cooking oil. Even the bark fibers can be woven into ropes and cloth. Jacob has shown me some of his literature, and it's impressively thoughtful. Utilizing the baobab trees in these ways offers an incentive to these tiny villages to preserve these trees and thus help maintain the soil structure and the whole fragile ecosystem instead of recklessly clear-cutting in order to plant transient cash crops, a chronic temptation. I'm actually quite proud to be associated with Newton, strange as that may sound.

THE FIRST PASSOVER after Jacob was born, I was so anxious to do everything right, to fit in with these people who had become my people, when we were all together around the table at Sam and Frieda's house on Marvel Road in Westville, the house where Howard and Irene grew up, the house where Howard and I were married. Ethan was born two years ahead of Jacob (and so he was at the table whining and threatening harm to Frieda's precious Pesach dishes), and I didn't like the way Irene was so triumphant about pointing that out repetitively, as if she had won a competition I didn't know we were having.

I was holding infant Jacob on my lap, and he was squirming and hungry, but I was worried that nursing him at the table, no matter how discreetly I did it, could be a conflict with the rules because it was a meat meal. I know this sounds really stupid, but at the time it was a serious worry for me. How was I to know how to make sense of these rules? Nobody could ever really explain any of the kosher laws to me very clearly, let alone how this family did and did not choose to follow them. There seemed to be no such thing as information, only interpretation. Three Ziplinskys, five opinions.

Whenever I asked questions at moments like this they would all start giving me conflicting answers, and then they would argue with one another, and then the disagreements and corrections would begin (I know this is a clichéd outsider's perception of Jews, but there it is) and there would be escalation until sometimes somebody would withdraw in aggrieved silence, or even storm out in a huff, and somebody else would have taken umbrage. For a while I believed *umbrage* must be a Yiddish word, having never heard it used before I met these umbrageous people. Meanwhile I could never get a straight answer to my questions about things like why shellfish is forbidden in the home but it is permissible to order Kung Pao shrimp at the House of Chao on Whalley Avenue, or the House of Chaos as we always call it, ever since Julie misread their sign when she was little and a precocious reader.

Sam was carving the standing rib roast Frieda had just brought to the table, but I couldn't catch Howard's eye to check with him about the breast-feeding question, because he was having a testy conversation with his mother about whether or not Princess Diana was an idiot. They both thought she was, so I have no idea what they found to argue about, but their perpetual mutual belligerence, their need to trump each other with superior credentials for holding shared opinions, this was a ritual of Ziplinsky family occasions as traditional as the lighting of the Sabbath candles.

The things Howard and Frieda found to agree about while arguing in this way! That evening alone, following the Princess Diana idiocy analysis, came the designated hitter rule and whether it did or did not ruin baseball (it did), the spelling of the word *ketchup* (they agreed that only the insane prefer *catsup*), the way most people don't use the term "hoi polloi" correctly (the hoi polloi themselves being the biggest abusers), and whether or not what John F. Kennedy said in 1962 when he was awarded his honorary degree—"It might be said now that I have the best of both worlds, a Harvard education and a Yale degree"—was a deliberate insult to Yale (it was, but in a good way).

The prayers, the narration about the symbols, and all the singing had occurred, and the Haggadahs had been put aside. Arthur, with whom I had a superficial sort of alliance in those early years simply because we were the two non–blood family members at the table, having silently watched the Ziplinskys being Ziplinskys with his slightly contemptuous gaze, leaned over and told me apropos of nothing that he had decided to specialize in anesthesiology because he preferred patients who were mostly unconscious so he would hardly ever have to talk to them. He was in a cardiology rotation at the time, which he complained about. He couldn't wait to get away from the needy patients who always wanted reassurance from him with each encounter.

"Then you might consider psychoanalysis, where you also would never speak and would be dealing mostly with the unconscious," I replied, and everyone around the table looked at me blankly. It was not the time to announce to the collective Ziplinskys that I had embarked on my analysis just a few months before, when I was pregnant with Jacob, although Dr. Gibraltar had warned me that it was a highly dubious time to begin an analysis, when the analysand is pregnant, and previously repressed female castration fantasies and phallic defenses might emerge. (He really talked like that, when he spoke at all. It was always very dry, but at the same time it made me feel like a respected colleague.)

It seemed to me like an outstanding time to begin analysis, if all that stuff might bubble up so easily, without my having to strain. Isn't that what analysis hopes for, previously repressed defenses emerging? I wanted to start right away, the sooner the better. I couldn't wait to throw myself down on his couch and begin the ambulatory brain surgery.

When not so long after that Irene found out about my analysis from Howard, who, typically, despite his promise, forgot to not tell anyone in his family about it, she was scornful ("Freudian?") and jealous ("You go four days a week? It costs how much?"), and soon enough she had embarked on her own short-lived analysis, with Andy Seckel, a very nonstandard practitioner with nonstandard credentials. He deemed the analytic couch infantilizing, and so they lay together on an inflatable mattress on the floor in his office over a grocery store on Orange Street. All the real analysts in town had their offices on Trumbull Street or Bradley Street, not to mention that they all sat in comfortable chairs as they presided over their couches with the requisite fresh paper towel laid out each hour for the next neurotic head.

I used to see Andy Seckel around New Haven long after Irene had divorced Arthur and moved to Telluride. Like so many New Haven analysts he had a white beard (I say this from personal observation, since for decades many of them, including Dr. Gibraltar, who had his own white beard, have congregated for their fifty-minute lunch hours at the Clark's Dairy counter, where there is an unspoken tradition that at lunchtime the doctors go to the right and the patients go to the left), but he often wore a pajama top and a cowboy hat, so he was easy to distinguish. When he died a couple of years ago, I read in the newspaper that he left his entire estate to Thunderbolt, a carved horse on the carousel at Lighthouse Point Park. Talk about estate nightmares.

On the rare occasions when we are forced together with the rebarbative Irene and her poor son, Ethan—the last time being at Frieda's funeral a year ago—the cousins have been able to be guardedly friendly with one another without acknowledging the family crisis. Not that it's relevant, but I think Ethan might be gay. Nature or nurture? Julie came out to us when she was in her junior year at Wesleyan, living in Womanist House, and at that point it didn't surprise me, but Howard was really thrown. He was more bothered and disappointed by this revelation than was reasonable, and I think he secretly blamed me for it, as if having a lesbian for a daughter was somehow a failure on my part.

Arthur Weiss doesn't seem like a man who would be thrilled to have a gay son. Well, I suppose not even the most enlightened man is overjoyed to have a homosexual son. I know Arthur has a successful practice and is well regarded, but there is something deeply wrong with that man. He's phlegmatic and bloodless, the opposite of Irene and her flighty enthusiasms. And why would any sane, normal man marry Irene? As Julie would say, what was up with that?

HOWARD HAS TOLD me for years that I could afford to cut Irene some slack. The hell with that! She has been cutting herself miles and miles of slack for years. She has been unstinting in her efforts to provide herself with every possible healing opportunity and alternative treatment, and since her move to Telluride she has become a real process junkie, always on her way to the next retreat or ashram, always flinging herself, checkbook in hand, at one or another guru of the moment.

Sam gave her enough. More than enough. Dayenu! To quote from that wonderful Passover song which everyone in the Ziplinsky family should probably have studied more carefully, because despite the rollicking annual renditions at Seder after Seder, there is no evidence that the meaning of the song has ever really been taken to heart.

As we all know, in his last will and testament, Sam created the Ziplinsky Family Trust, with Frieda as the sole lifetime beneficiary. The trust was funded with several million dollars in equities and bond funds, along with its biggest asset, half ownership of Zip's Candies. The trustees (Howard, as CEO of Zip's Candies, Ben Gottesfeld, and Carly August, a peppy banker who was always incredibly patient with Frieda, who made it very clear that she would never have the time of day for goyim), were given a lot of latitude to make distributions to Frieda, but the trust's interest in the business could not be sold or altered or deeded in any way. Sam's will named Howard to succeed him as CEO of Zip's Candies. These are all facts beyond dispute.

By making these plans and provisions as he did, Sam was of course ensuring family loyalty to the business into the next generation. But here is where it gets tricky. His intention regarding the generation after that, his grandchildren, should be just as clear, except that Irene insists it isn't clear at all.

And so here we are. At Frieda's death last year, the Ziplinsky Family Trust, in its entirety, with all those cannily invested millions (which have grown nicely despite the roller-coaster market, and despite the endless generous distributions), plus the half interest in Zip's Candies, became the property of the remainder Beneficiaries, per stirpes and not per capita, to be shared equally among them, with all administrative decisions concerning distributions of principle as well as income, up to and including the sale or division of any and all assets of the trust, including dissolution of the trust itself, to be determined by a simple majority vote among the beneficiaries. And in his will Sam identified the beneficiaries of the Ziplinsky Family Trust with this language: "my grandchildren who survive me, the issue of my son Howard and my daughter, Irene."

And there it is—that one simple, seemingly straightforward phrase that has put us in the soup.

6

As a naturalized Ziplinsky, I probably know and understand far more Ziplinsky family lore than anyone else alive. Unlike any natural-born Ziplinsky (my own two children excepted), I am completely interested in the inner workings and unique sensibilities of the family, and have been from that first hot afternoon when I crossed the threshold of Zip's Candies. I would also like to point out my clear and objective ability to put all of these facts into this narrative. I have been accused of exaggeration, of embellishment, of adding and subtracting meaning, but it should be abundantly clear that I am in fact a very reliable and coherent source of valuable insight. My memory is flawless.

I have always been a quick study, too. During my two-week home stay with a rural family in Burgundy, the summer I was fifteen, I picked up more French than anyone else in my group (we were assigned to families scattered throughout the village), despite, or perhaps because of, the unpleasantness of my host family, who were not at all interested in me, and were unabashed about being in the home stay student hosting business entirely for the money. Contrary to all the clichés about the French, *la famille* Lagache, who had a dry cleaning establishment in the village, were unattractively lumpen, unstylish, and very dependent on frozen food. I quickly learned how best to feign incomprehension while deciphering their mumbled, insulting, unkind observations about me (*Même le chien ne l'aime pas!*—Even the dog doesn't like her!) as we ate our depressingly identical portions of freezer-burned *dinde à la crème* in the flickering glow of Eurosport News.

Immersion in a culture helps you learn a language quickly, and I certainly had a Ziplinsky immersion that first summer working on the Tigermelt line, packing Little Sammies into boxes, cleaning the vibrator mechanism and the pre-extruder on the Tigermelt line, cleaning whatever else anybody told me to clean, simply learning by personal experience the intricate entropy of all three lines.

On that first afternoon, I pitched myself with headlong velocity into the Zip's machine, into a lonely exile from my own sad family. I was desperate to escape my Arson Girl fate, and I was captivated by every aspect of this stirring, sugary world of Zip's Candies and these lively, exotic Ziplinskys. I loved the roar and din of mechanical productivity. I inhaled that sugary, life-giving air with gratitude every morning when I walked through those factory doors, filling myself up with it, letting it sweeten and soothe every corner of my scorched, empty self.

I fell instantly into a rhythm with the routine at Zip's, and with my sense of having a place in that routine, my feeling of being a useful cog among many other cogs turning the gears of this vast machine devoted to simple pleasure, to the making of true confections. I was enthralled, utterly dazzled, to discover that every minute of every hour of every working day, the vast mechanism of Zip's Candies was chugging away, churning out row after row, box after box, stacked pallet after stacked pallet, hundreds and thousands of chewy, salty, sugary, nutty contributions to that quintessentially American privilege, the pursuit of happiness at the candy counter.

There was an old national distribution map of the forty-eight states, stuck with color-coded pushpins representing sales of Little Sammies, Tigermelts, and Mumbo Jumbos, which hung for many years on the side wall in Sam's office. This map was actually a bit grandiose, because until the resurgent interest in Little Sammies, sparked in 1999 with the "Say, Dat's Tasty!" phenomenon (and then bolstered by all the expanding sales opportunities with online candy sellers like OldTimeCandy .com, SweetNostalgia.com, CandyWarehouse.com, and Groovy Candies.com, to name just a few of our best vendors), Zip's penetration west of the Rockies was actually very small. Zip's has always really been a regional brand more than it could be called a true national brand, with most sales clustered on the East Coast, from Florida to Maine. But I have always loved the Zip's sales map and all the optimism it represented. The business of America is business! And the territory of Zip's is America! That map offered me an America that felt far more vivid and authentic than did the desiccated world of the Pilgrim Fathers and Original Signers and all those Patriots of the American Revolution from whom my family proudly descended on both sides.

Today, after all these years as a Ziplinsky, I feel quite disconnected from my family of origin, as Ellie Quest-Greenspan insisted on calling my parents whenever they came up, which was generally only when she brought them up. (Dr. Gibraltar brought up issues of billing and scheduling but otherwise initiated topics very rarely.) Yet of course I am not a *true* Ziplinsky, and so my Ziplinsky credential is deemed insufficient on the one hand and irrelevant on the other by those eager to discredit my standing. But I have pretty much left behind all my Tatnall and Dorr loyalties. So who am I?

"Family of origin" is such an odd sort of biological concept. "Origin" is a term used by the snobbiest of those self-important dark-chocolate connoisseurs, those irritating bean-to-bar obsessives for whom no dark chocolate is dark enough, the ones who carry their own little supplies for after-dinner duels of I'll see your 70 percent Ecuadorian Trinitario and raise you fifteen, as they deal out their precious little 85 percent, five-gram tasting squares of Indonesian Criollo, woody yet floral, with a heady nose and a long finish on the palate. Not that 'many of them would know in a blind test the difference between a decent Trinitario from Tobago and a square of that shoe polish Godiva calls chocolate.

The truth of the matter is, the percentage doesn't tell the whole story—what *does* ever tell the whole story?—and the question they usually don't know to ask is what percentage of cocoa butter and what percentage of chocolate liquor make up that precious little square. It's all about the balance and the mouthfeel, not just the straight numbers. Most of the boutique chocolatiers have started to cater to those so-called connoisseurs, forced to oblige them with ever higher numbers in order to stay competitive. But to preserve mouthfeel they are adding in more cocoa butter proportionately, otherwise the result of an 85 or 90 percent cacao chocolate would be about as appealing as dirt on your tongue. Seventy can be the perfect balance for a really good dark chocolate, and I see no reason to aim higher simply for the sake of number snobbery. But foodies (and my God, how much do I despise that twee term "chocoholic"?) love to follow trends, even as they love to deny that they do. Just ask the merlot people how they feel about the movie *Sideways*.

I think I have more than sufficiently explained how my years among the Ziplinskys have left me feeling untethered from the polite and chilly WASPy dynamic of my family of origin. Thirty years among door-slamming confrontational Jews will do that. Not that I am a door-slammer. I dwell in a kind of no-man's-land these days. Only my Jewish relatives think I am Protestant, and only my Protestant relatives think I am Jewish. I know the correct way to light the candles on the menorah for all the nights of Chanukah, and I know how to wrap a string of Christmas lights on a fragrant balsam fir in such a way as to get the lights to nestle deep in the innermost branches so the wires don't show and the lights aren't just flung haphazardly around the tips of the branches.

I am certainly the first Ziplinsky eligible for membership in the Daughters of the American Revolution. Julie is as well, given that she too has the requisite "direct lineal blood line descent from an ancestor who aided in achieving American independence." Though I can just imagine a chapter admissions committee casting its collective milky blue DAR gaze upon Julie Ziplinsky. At a glance, surely all they would see are the manifestations of those hardscrabble, entrepreneurial Ziplinsky and Liebashevsky genes. Next to the pale, prim, politely Episcopal, tiny-nosed Tatnalls and Dorrs, Ziplinskys look like gypsies. (The fur-selling Liebashevskys, who hail from Pinsk, tend toward potatohead shtetl faces; they all wear an invisible babushka. Let's just say they are also far from classic DAR material.)

Julie has her father's beaky nose and his dark, kinky hair (yes, all the clichés, but what should I do, pretend this is not so?), which she wears in what she persists in calling a Jewfro, just as she calls herself a Jewnitarian, while her girlfriend (her lover, her "primary dyadic partner," as they call each other, as if each is the other's case study for some ongoing anthropological research), the somewhat worrisome Kelly Harper, calls herself a Lesbyterian. They are affiliated with a group of people who call themselves "polyamory," and they claim to be comfortable having "multiple intimate, nonexclusive sexual and emotional relationships" (I'm quoting from the polyamory website they asked me to "visit," a term that in itself reveals such a disconnect between our generations, since they meant me to read some text on a screen while sitting at my own desk, and they were not actually inviting me to go anywhere).

It seems to me to be a rather limited and almost fetishistic way for them to define themselves, even though they claim their lives are more open and free than those of us monogamously inclined heterosexuals, who may be less open and free but who at least don't have to spend so much time codifying the nuances of our relationships with our various sexual partners. Frankly, when Julie and Kelly start explaining to me all over again about poly this and poly that, I just want to say to them, Polly put the kettle on, and we'll *all* have tea!

In other words, Julie is hardly living a life of DAR rectitude. And she does have all those facial piercings (and some others I don't want to know about), which always make me feel a little faint if I look at them too closely, though when I catch myself casting sidelong, sliding glances at Julie and Kelly, I feel guilty and inadequate and cowardly. Surely a mother should be able to gaze lovingly at her own child. What has become of my sweet little girl, who cried when I read *Are You My Mother?* to her at bedtime (it is, admittedly, a tearjerker), and later lovingly nurtured a pair of long-lived frogs (she named them Herbert and Cumulus), who dwelled in a tank in her room for eleven years? Julie used to be a kid for whom it seemed the world would be her oyster. She and Kelly are very devoted to each other, but I regret the way each seems to support the other's sense of being wronged by the world.

I am certain the ranks of the DAR have been filled over the years by numerous spinsters in Boston marriages, but nobody talked about it. Every time the Revolutionary War came up in my studies, my mother would stress with a certain pride that our heritage made us eligible for DAR membership, though to give my mother her due, and my father too, it should also be said that at our dinner table the DAR was mostly mocked and ridiculed and held up as the enemy, because they wouldn't let Marian Anderson sing at Constitution Hall in 1939. So we wouldn't have dreamed of joining, my mother and I, not in a million years—but we were eligible! The satisfaction in that! It was a bond of disdain that Frieda Ziplinsky surely would have understood.

The Ziplinsky family has an uneasy relationship with the heritage of ambition and success handed down not so long ago by that entrepreneurial goniff, Eli Czaplinsky. I think they should embrace it, the whole thing. The shadiest person in my family's history, the darkest sheep (until me), would be Margaret Shippen—Peggy, as we call her, as if she had been over for dinner just last week and not dead in her Tory grave since 1804—good old cousin Peggy, my first cousin six times removed, who married Benedict Arnold. Family lore has it that Peggy Shippen was poor, naive Benedict Arnold's downfall, her greed for status and her ceaseless desire for pretty things being what drove him to his treasonous betrayal. I suppose it is reckless of me to provide such obvious material about my background under these circumstances when questions of loyalty and betrayal are so prominent, but this is the fact of my heritage, which is not to say that sometimes the apple rolls quite far from the tree.

THE STORY OF Eli Czaplinsky coming to America and making his fortune is so much more real to me than the textbook history lessons that are my heritage. Everything about him has always intrigued me—his arrival at Ellis Island, the whispered connection to the murder of Kid Dropper Kaplan and his hasty exodus to New Haven, the touchingly naive if hugely misguided inspiration of *Little Black Sambo* for his three candy lines. But what about the undocumented interlude in Eli's life, when he first arrived in New Haven? How did he survive when he stepped off the train here in August 1923?

The official Zip's Candies history refers to his employment by the Armenians selling their chocolate-covered coconut patties. But before that he found work doing odd jobs for a pair of elderly spinster sisters, Emma and Dora Hodgson, who presided over a sweet shop on Chapel Street that was locally famous for chocolate-covered cherries and their unusual chunks of chewy nougat brittle, which they called Peanut Charms. They let Eli sleep in the back room for four months, and he learned from them all sorts of useful skills, from tempering chocolate to making fondant fillings for bonbons and mastering the alchemy required for cooking up delectable batches of caramel kisses from sugar, molasses, milk, butter, and salt.

All the Zip's Candies dead files have languished for years in a welter of sagging cardboard boxes in a corner of the factory basement. You can learn a lot, reading through the old files of a family business that has been documenting itself for better or worse since 1924. The Hodgson files, for example, had a folder devoted to a settlement agreement made in 1956, when Sam had to pay twenty thousand dollars to their only heir, the son of their brother who had married and moved to Ipswich. The Hodgson nephew, prompted by the growing success of Zip's Candies, had brought a suit alleging that the original formulation for the Tigermelt center was derived from the secret recipe stolen by Eli for those long-gone Hodgson Peanut Charms.

Sam told me about this claim over lunch one day so long ago the kids were still in elementary school and it would be years before they would have to decide if they wanted to work in the business. But he had brought it up, the question of the next generation, as he did from time to time. I never wanted to make

Jacob or Julie feel that they were expected to work for Zip's Candies, but from the time they could walk they both loved going to visit the factory, and as they grew older, they appreciated the social value of being in a candy-making family. For every school fund-raiser, for every auction benefit, New Haven Country Day could count on Zip's Candies for generous support. One year, we donated the top raffle prize, a Zip's Golden Ticket, which granted the winner free candy from Zip's every day for a year, up to ten pieces each day. Howard loved being admired for our support of all those school events. We were good citizens of New Haven Country Day, despite my many skirmishes over the years with various faculty and other parents over a range of small issues.

When the kids were little, I thought I might have a second chance in life to develop some friendships among the parents of their friends and classmates. But from nursery school on, I would feel drawn to people, their kids would get along well with my kids, we would start out with nice exchanges, playdates, outings, a few sleepovers, but then sooner or later the adult relationship would go off the tracks.

I have come to recognize that many people are both hypersensitive and judgmental. Apparently I can be too much for a lot of unimaginative people. I have always been very responsible for children in my care. But my altruism can be misunderstood, whether it takes the form of serving perfectly wholesome beef stew to a malnourished little second grader friend of Jacob's whose vegan parents were practically starving him, or giving a much-needed haircut to a kindergarten classmate of Julie's who was over for a playdate. That pixie cut really did improve the little girl's appearance. She had looked like Cousin Itt. I have no idea why her silly mother cried like that. It was just hair.

Howard usually shrugged off these minor dramas when he

heard about them, but he was quite irked with me when the kids were in the upper school and the parents association got involved with a Halloween campaign to post "No Candy Here" signs on the doors of known sex offenders living in New Haven neighborhoods conducive to trick-or-treating. Although I had certainly not volunteered for this, it was somehow assumed that as candy makers we would want to be involved in this ridiculous enterprise. I thought it was a terrible idea, one that seemed like harassment to me, and was possibly not even legal. And in any case, I didn't like the smugness of this virtuous shaming one bit.

The week before Halloween, I received in the mail a large envelope containing a list of fourteen names and a map of the Whitneyville section of New Haven, with fourteen marked addresses and fourteen "No Candy Here" signs to distribute accordingly. On Halloween night, children who were drawn to the "Candy Here" signs displayed at those fourteen addresses were rewarded with generous quantities of Little Sammies, Tigermelts, and Mumbo Jumbos. The signs were recognized, however, and later that night a group of perhaps a dozen indignant vigilante parents came to our door to pick a fight. Julie and Jacob weren't home yet, having been given permission to go to parties, it being a Saturday night (the second best night of the week for Halloween candy sales), and the trick-or-treating had subsided.

Howard answered the door with a bowl of Zip's candies, and instead of the almost-too-old final goblins of the night, he was confronted by this angry posse eager to tell him exactly what outrageous thing I had done with that list and those signs. People can be ridiculously judgmental and small-minded.

❊ ❊

WHEN SHE WAS in high school and had spent three summers working at Zip's, Julie told me I had hurt her feelings when I suggested, in response to a great seventh-grade report card, that with her powers of observation and her wonderful writing skills she might consider journalism. She admitted that for a long while after that she felt rejected by me, because this must have meant I didn't want her working at Zip's, that I was trying to keep her out with this diversionary suggestion, as if she was unsuitable for and unworthy of the family business. I was, of course, very sorry that I had given her that impression. As a parent I have always wanted my children to know how interested I am in their lives. It's what I wished for and never had. But of course each generation compensates for early deprivations by imposing new, different ones on our children.

THIS TALK WITH Sam about the next generation coming into Zip's Candies led to a chat about Eli's earliest days in New Haven, and the Hodgson sisters, and the subsequent claim. Sam told me where to look for the files on the settlement agreement if I was interested. Of course I was interested, as he knew I would be. This is why he told me things he never told anyone else. He also told me (I have my scribbled notes from that day right in front of me, in notebook #19, because I certainly did not burn my notebooks, and I can quote what he said) that while there was never any admission on the part of Zip's Candies when they paid off the nephew with this go-away money that bought a nondisclosure agreement, he believed that Eli did copy the recipe for those Peanut Charms.

"Eli was hungry," Sam said to me. "Hungry people don't always do the right thing. We're doing well, so we're not that hungry, so we can afford to do the right thing. The problem comes when people are well-fed for so long that they forget what hunger feels like, and then they also can start to forget what the right thing is. So the trick of it," he told me, picking up the check and studying it, having now eaten all our shared French fries while I was taking his words down in my notebook (I noted this too, in the margin—"S ate most of the ff again"), "the trick of it is to find the balance between being too hungry and not being hungry enough. And a rich man has to work very hard to find a way to make sure his children are just a little hungry."

He stopped my writing hand, wrapping it in his big knuckley paw, which was a strangely intimate gesture between us. Though he didn't smoke his cigar at Clark's, he always had that soggy, half-smoked unlit cigar in his mouth or in his hand, and so for the rest of that day my hand smelled strongly of his perpetual cigar, that corky odor I wasn't crazy about in his lifetime. Sam's office had a unique miasma, a blended aroma of the sweet candy-factory air and that sour cigar smoke, which I continued to taste for a long time whenever I had been in there for something. Sometimes it lasted into the evening hours, as if molecules of cigar smoke and chocolate and burnt sugar had lodged up my nose and in the back of my throat and on my soft palate.

Sam's own taste buds had been numbed by his years of cigar smoking, which sometimes led to arguments, especially when he sampled the Tigermelt center blends, since he always thought we needed to salt the fried peanuts more heavily. ("Everybody likes salt," he used to argue if he happened along as a batch of Tigermelt nougat filling was being blended. "Even if they say they don't. If two candies are very similar, and one tastes a little saltier, people will prefer that one. Always put in a little more salt.") Now that he is gone I miss that cigar smoke very much. I have more than once followed down the street a prosperous stranger puffing on a Macanudo, just to have a few stolen moments of breathing in that familiar aroma.

So I looked up when he stopped me from writing, and he said gently, "Alice, kiddo, you're the best thing to happen to this family. Howdy doesn't know how lucky he is. He thinks he makes his luck, but he has never been hungry enough to make his own luck. We gave him everything, after we lost his brother, and that was a mistake, because nothing was a struggle for him, everything came to him too easily. Frieda wouldn't hear me for many years, and I couldn't fight with her. She just wanted her Howdy to have what he wanted, when he wanted it. There was so much pain about Lewis. Howdy never learned how to make a plan to get what he wanted on his own, or how to do without. He never learned to wait, he never had to earn anything he got. He grew up believing that this was how life works, and he didn't realize that for other people there is much more struggle, much more conflict. Now maybe Frieda regrets this, because she sees what kind of man he is, but she doesn't say. He'll never be Lewis."

Sam was rarely disloyal to family members, unlike the subsequent generation, and though he seemed to be on the verge of saying something more to me after this soliloquy, he didn't. He still had my hand, as if to keep me from writing anything more (I made notes later, in my car before going back to work), so I closed the notebook. And then he said one more thing to me, which I also wrote down right away, so this is definitely accurate.

He said, "I'm not going to live forever, and I need to plan. One thing I didn't plan so well is that this family is small. If you want to keep a family business going, the smartest thing you can do is have a lot of brothers and sisters and a lot of children. That way you never have to scrape the barrel. You shouldn't have anyone doing a job in a family business if you wouldn't ever think of hiring that person if he wasn't family. In a big family, you find more qualified employees, you have family members who can find the right job in the business that suits them, and you can have good partnerships and plan your successions."

He looked at me then, and then he looked away and squeezed my hand very hard, and I could see him fighting tears. In retrospect this was probably as close as he could come to telling me what he knew and I didn't, but he breathed a long sigh instead, and then he just had one more thing to say:

"I'm counting on you to bring up Jakie and Julie so they know how to work for a living. It's the most important thing, and I know you won't let me down. It's up to you to keep our family going, even if things get complicated. If they know how to work for a living, they'll always land on their feet."

Mary the waitress came to clear our plates and drop the check on our table then. God, I miss everything about those lunches at Clark's with Sam. Ordering BLT's and grilled cheese sandwiches without a thought about cholesterol. The "plate of ice cream" on the menu. The creamy buzz of the milk-shake machines. Never once in all those years did Mary or Barbara ever ask us if we were "still working on that."

7

TELL PEOPLE YOUR FAMILY has a candy business, and soon enough *Charlie and the Chocolate Factory* comes into the conversation, the original Roald Dahl book and both movies based on the book, all of which are blended together in most people's minds as one delightful excursion to a fantasy chocolate factory, maybe one a lot like Zip's Candies.

Jacob and Julie each received multiple copies of the book when they were born, and subsequently not a birthday has ever passed without another copy turning up, as well as various videos or DVDs of both films over the years. We have probably had fifty copies of various editions of the book pass through this house. I can't throw them away fast enough. Sometimes I find mysterious copies of *Charlie and the Chocolate Factory* on a bookshelf, or a videotape of the 1971 movie, *Willy Wonka & the Chocolate Factory* (apparently the name "Charlie" had to be avoided in the Vietnam years because that was what we called the Vietcong, Victor Charlie) in with other old tapes. Twice, for no apparent reason, a DVD of the 2005 Johnny Depp film, *Charlie and the Chocolate Factory*, has arrived erroneously in our Netflix mailer. Sooner or later, no matter what I do, another version of *Charlie and the Chocolate Factory* will appear again somewhere in the house like a recurring fungus.

If Howard was more energetic and imaginative, I would suspect him of an elaborate plot to gaslight me. He always found my horror of all things *Charlie and the Chocolate Factory* amusing. He was not an attentive reader, and even when I elaborated on the reason for my loathing of this story, he always said it just didn't bother him. That in itself bothered me.

I regard each manifestation of *Charlie and the Chocolate Factory* with a white-hot, passionate hatred. I was given a copy of the book when it was first published in 1964, for my sixth birthday. My father read it aloud to me at bedtime, three nights in a row, until we reached the end. It was the only time he ever read to me, and I will never know how it was determined that this was the book for our one and only father-daughter bedtime bonding experience. I was utterly terrified, and hardly dared to go to sleep those nights, so fearful did the story make me.

Why did anyone think this was a suitable bedtime read for a child? (And why did my parents not take my terror seriously, instead of finding it funny?) The gratuitous cruelties, the violence, the casual viciousness—how did this book worm its way into our culture? How did it find its way so quickly to the beloved classics shelf, nestled between *Charlotte's Web* and *Little Women* in every children's library in the Western world? I hated it, and yet I couldn't resist it, and as I became a more proficient reader I would return to it again and again throughout my childhood and adolescence. I was like someone who despises black licorice but keeps coming back for just one more licorice allsort in order to savor her own disgust at the loathed flavor each time.

The world of *Charlie and the Chocolate Factory* is one in which all children are assumed to be greedy and obsessed with candy, while there is universal admiration for the sadomasochistic proprietor of the Wonka Candy Company. The cooked-up pathos of the poverty in which Charlie Bucket lives with his family as the book begins has always felt to me like a vicious mockery. Consider for comparison the genuinely wrenching penury of *A Little Princess* or *Oliver Twist*. Dahl is heartless. He is contemptuous of children; Veruca Salt's first name is the synonym for a kind of wart. There is an underlying contempt for all humanity, really, and an almost obsessive hatred for the innocent joys of childhood, as if all pleasure-seeking is a form of gluttony for which people must be shamed and punished. It's one big pleasure trap.

There is something obscene about the book, and I really mean that—this tasteless, horrible book feels to me much more like covert S and M pornography than children's literature. It is a wonder that I wasn't so scarred by my early exposure to this material that I didn't have an aversion to Zip's Candies, though when I got to this very issue in my analysis, Dr. Gibraltar suggested that my love for and attraction to a candy factory—and consequently, the way I have spent my life in the candy businesss—might well be a reaction formation. The blocking of desire by its opposite.

Meanwhile, everyone who has read *Charlie and the Chocolate Factory* or seen either movie version believes he knows something about the inner workings of a candy factory. Which brings me to the Oompa-Loompa problem. No, we do not have Oompa-Loompas working at Zip's Candies. And how very original of you to ask. How amusing is this notion of slave labor, this fun fantasy of workers who never leave the factory? What could be more pleasing than an army of small brown people who don't require wages working tirelessly in the production of cheap chocolate for the greedy public?

My copy of the book was the original first American edition. In it, the Oompa-Loompas are described as "black pygmies from the very deepest and darkest part of the African jungle, where no white man had been before." Later editions were revised in text and illustration, because of reactions to the blatant racism, so the Oompa-Loompas mutated into "dwarves" with "golden-brown hair" and "rosy white skin" who come from Loompa-land, a region of Loompa, a small isolated island in the Pacific Ocean. (In the 1971 movie, for which Dahl wrote an early version of the screenplay, they have orange skin and green hair, as if they have now mutated one step further into a tribe of enslaved laborers who match the Irish flag, surely another familiar and very British colonialist fantasy.)

But no matter how complected, we all know what Oompa-Loompas really are, don't we? Fun, guilt-free slaves! It's like diet candy, with zero calories! What cultural blindness makes it possible for people to cherish and adore Oompa-Loompas, while simultaneously recognizing the evils of child slavery in certain cacao-producing nations of Africa? How about if instead of a colony of pygmies dwelling in the chocolate factory, these tireless captive workers were diminutive Jews from a remote shtetl in deepest Siberia? Would that be just as charming and fun?

IRENE HAS NEVER shown any curiosity about the actual workings of Zip's, the day-to-day operations, how the raw materials are sourced, how the candy is manufactured and all we do for quality control, the concerns of marketing and sales, not to mention the issues of our hiring and benefit policies, which are so far removed from the employment practices of Willy Wonka. For years, her idea of involvement with the family business was the effort she put into generating an incessant barrage of newspaper clippings and sanctimonious emails.

These communications were always urgent, unrealistic demands related to the cause of the moment, usually a sudden inspiration that Zip's Candies should only use special biodegradable wrappers made of rice husks and printed with soy ink, or that we should immediately start using only organic ingredients, or that we should run our machines on used cooking oil instead of electricity, or that we should hire a bunch of displaced Katrina victims right away.

Then there was the unforgettable time she phoned me from her car, sounding desperate, asking me to meet her for coffee at Starbucks on Chapel Street right then, please! I postponed a meeting with a supplier and hopped in my car, worried that she had a health scare, or that there was some equivalently dire crisis that she needed to tell me about. Why me and not Howard? We had never met for coffee before.

I should have known. After I circled the block twice looking for a parking space, which were especially scarce because some recent heavy snows had left ugly scraped piles of dirty snow and ice along the narrow side streets around the Yale campus, I gave up and parked in a loading zone on Chapel Street (for which I got a parking ticket). Irene was at the front of the line, so I joined her and we gave our orders. I asked for a tall red-eye, and Irene ordered one of those narcissistic coffee drinks requiring modifications and extra shots of this and that, and the foam this way and not that way in relation to the caramel, and a venti cup for a grande drink. I could tell by the look on the face of the barista, a distracted high school girl who clearly hated everyone that afternoon as she listened to Irene's order, that she was going to give Irene real espresso despite the emphatic instruction about the three decaffeinated espresso shots.

When we had settled at a table, Irene pulled out a book from one of her many virtuous tote bags from do-good organizations and held it to her bosom before placing it reverently on the table between us. This system of understanding personalities would change everything at Zip's, she explained. It was the key to our future success. We needed to find out every employee's type right away so as to assign them to the tasks best suited to their personalities. We?

"You're a One, and I'm a Two," she said, "and this is why we haven't always gotten along very well." She seemed to think she was speaking rationally. I saw that the book was an introduction to Enneagrams. This was the emergency? "Twos are helpers," she explained. "Helpers are nurturers, focused on giving and receiving love."

I lost my temper, I admit. I told Irene that Zip's wasn't going to embark on a damned Enneagram management policy now or ever. And anyway, why not bring this to Howard if she thought it was so essential? Did she know I had canceled a meeting to rush here, because she had made it sound as if she had a personal emergency? What was *wrong* with her?

"Maybe you're not a One." She frowned, taking her book off the table and thrusting it protectively into a National Wildlife Federation tote. "Maybe you're an Eight. Ones are reformers and ideal-seekers, but maybe you're really more of an aggressive power-seeker than I had realized."

MOST URGENTLY, AND most repetitively and problematically, Irene was always badgering Howard and me with variations on the obviousness of the necessity for us to agree immediately to source all our chocolate from suppliers who guarantee that they only do business with cacao dealers who only do business with fair trade cacao buyers who only do business with organic cacao plantations. First of all, I think it is worth pointing out that the only thing the words "Fair Trade" on the label can ever really guarantee with certainty is that earnest crunchy people will pay a lot of money for any product so labeled. Fair trade is a nice idea, but the fact is that if you seek the best cacao beans and the best coffee beans, they are simply not going to be fair trade. And it's a system that has the potential to cheat farmers and workers, because it locks in buyer and seller relationships, but at the same time the prices can drop and the seller is closed out of the free market, while the buyer doesn't lose anything.

Second, organic shmorganic. I just don't see an adulteration problem with cacao and sugar, our two biggest ingredients. (But, by the way, do I get any credit at all for resisting the pressure from our brokers in recent years to buy cheap Chinese imports, from nuts to flavorings to condensed milk solids to enrobing chocolate? I have always had concerns about quality control, and I had several fights with Howard about this, the last one just a few weeks before the shocking news of melamine-tainted pet food broke. Only because of my caution did the worldwide melamine crisis of 2008 have no effect on us. Cadbury had to pull eleven different types of melamine-tainted chocolate made in their Beijing plant for the Hong Kong, Taiwan, and Australian markets. And tainted White Rabbit Creamy Candy from China was on shelves right here in Connecticut and across the country. But Zip's Candies were safe.)

I do worry a great deal about aflatoxins, which could be catastrophic in our peanut supplies, and so we really cannot risk sourcing organic peanuts. This means there is no point in sourcing any other organics at this time, because we wouldn't be able to capitalize on it; we wouldn't be able to put a designation on the label, since there is little value in a "Somewhat Organic" label, and if we can't profit from the extra expense by appealing to the crunchy upscale people, then it's a pure loss.

Anyway, lots of organic chocolate, perhaps most organic chocolate, has uneven quality control and can be unpleasantly musty, with a muddy mouthfeel and a moldy taste. That said, if Zip's Candies were to make a calculated decision to commit to fair trade and organic ingredients, we would have to charge north of three dollars for a pack of Little Sammies or a Tiger-melt bar, instead of a worrisome enough retail price that has finally gone over the one dollar line for the first time. That's not going to happen, especially not now, with the economy the way it is. This is no time to start making premium chocolates for the prosperous. Except for the Bao-Bar, the best strategy for Zip's Candies is to keep making cheap candy for working stiffs. I'm counting on this depression to create another golden era for the candy bar.

IRENE IS INCREDIBLY naive. I recognize that her heart is in the right place (about most things that aren't directly connected to me). I don't even disagree with her about these goals, in the best of all possible worlds. But one of the many differences between us is that unlike her, I was not born a princess, and I live in the real world. And meanwhile, since I have touched on fair trade and other problematic issues of cacao production, let us not forget that whole fiasco just six years ago, when Irene embarked on a campaign to end child slave labor on African cacao plantations, feeling, as she claimed, a personal responsibility, having "blood on her hands," she actually said more than once in interviews, because of her family's chocolate candy business.

I have always refrained from suggesting that there was any impropriety in Irene's relationship with Abu Nkongo, who was both younger than her own son, Ethan, and also extraordinarily attractive and charming in a very sensuous, almost animalistic way, in those months when she had him living with her and they did all that traveling around together. Perhaps others thought there was something going on between them. It's not my place to speculate.

Am I the only member of the family who has not forgotten about this episode, when Irene toured for months lecturing people on the shameful origins of their cheap chocolate? It was potentially very harmful to Zip's Candies, it was certainly embarrassing in candy-manufacturing circles, and it forced us to take a position. Julie, who was already remarkably adept at website management and all things Internet even then, created a page on our site for a bland statement about our views on the fair trade issue and our hopes for more future involvement, stating that meanwhile of course we support the efforts being made to improve the quality of life for all cacao workers in Africa. It's so much more complex than that, of course. But Irene pushed us to the wall. She forced us to say something about this so we would look good instead of bad, when we would have preferred to remain silent.

This issue of child slavery on cacao plantations in Africa became Irene's raison d'être. It ended in embarrassment, if not humiliation. The randomness of her lighting on this issue in the first place is actually funny. Irene didn't discover the plight of the African cacao workers because of her guilty conscience about living off a chocolate candy company. And she didn't discover her destiny as a spokesperson for the cacao slaves because of inner soul work with any of her rent-a-gurus, either. Hardly. It all came about only because she went to Paris for a meditation workshop she never even attended.

On her first morning there, Irene went out to do her daily requisite twenty-four Tai Chi forms in the little leafy park across from her Left Bank hotel. It was very early, and she was quite pleased with herself, being a fit American doing her Tai Chi in a park in Paris, feeling superior to the indolent, smoking Parisians, loving her own sophistication about being in Paris by herself, especially smug because she was staying in a cozy Left

Bank hotel instead of going back to the very grand Right Bank hotel where she stayed the only other time she had been in Paris, with Arthur, when they were first married. As she went into White Crane Spreading Its Wings, her favorite Tai Chi position, the one she most liked to catch a glimpse of herself doing in the mirror during her Tai Chi classes, she saw a huddled form shivering on a bench.

This was Abu Nkongo, a charming teenage boy who admitted to her, in answer to her questions, which she asked boldly and a little breathlessly while doing her stretches, using the bench on which he had spent the night for support, that he was hungry. She took him to a café for breakfast, feeling utterly thrilled and delighted with herself for doing this, and he told her his story, all about how he was from a small village in Côte d'Ivoire, how he had nothing, knew nobody in France, and had been sleeping in parks for many days, since arriving in the back of a vegetable truck full of tomatoes from Holland. How did he get into that truck? He sneaked aboard on a loading dock in Rotterdam. He had stowed away on a bulk container cargo ship in Abidjan three weeks earlier as it was loaded with cacao beans en route to a Dutch cocoa processor.

Droste? Irene wondered, naming the only Dutch chocolate company she knew, and Abu nodded. She was moved to tears by her sense of her own empathy welling in her chest for this sweet boy.

He was a Cameroonian citizen because his mother was from Cameroon, Abu explained to her as they walked back through the park, though his mother had arrived in Côte d'Ivoire before he was born, and so he had never seen Cameroon himself. Irene was able to get him a passport, working with a corrupt official at the Cameroonian embassy. I have no idea how, but apparently Irene, ditsy as she seems, knows how to find the people who know people who know how to make things happen (perhaps this skill is a by-product of her passing involvement in a druggy underworld), and she can certainly always come up with the cash.

Irene took Abu for photographs and had them delivered to the official, and then two days later she met the buyable Cameroonian embassy worker in a café, where they exchanged envelopes folded inside copies of *Libération*. He got up and walked away a moment later, and she sat there with her coffee for five more minutes, as instructed, peeking at Abu's new passport inside the folded newspaper. I am sure she thought she was Lillian Hellman in *Julia*.

Irene had meanwhile talked Howard into having Zip's Candies sponsor a work visa for Abu, some nonsense about cacao harvesting and consulting on chocolate candy manufacturing, and incredibly enough, after three dramatic weeks, during which time she fed him and paid for a hotel room for him, she was able to fly him back with her to New York. She brought him to New Haven for a week (they stayed with Frieda), where his consulting consisted of a tour of the factory and a prodigious consumption of Little Sammies and Tigermelts fresh off the lines. Howard took him along for a round of golf and lunch at his club, and reported afterward that Abu had been polite but quiet and had enjoyed driving the golf cart, and that if he was pushed off his set pieces, his fluency in English deteriorated markedly.

Julie and Jacob, who were both in college at the time (Julie had just started at Wesleyan, Jacob was in his last year at Kenyon), came home that weekend and found Abu strange and unlikeable. Julie thought there was something not quite right about him, but she couldn't really say why she got this vibe (she is a very good observer of people), and meanwhile, we were of course all contorting ourselves to find things to like about him and ways to make him feel welcome.

After it came apart, Julie accused the whole family of being naïve limousine liberals like the people in *Six Degrees of Separation*. We had been so eager to embrace Abu as this heroic victim who made us feel better about our own white privilege, she said. She had a point. Would Irene have taken him under her wing if he were white and homely instead of an exquisitely beautiful African boy?

Irene took Abu home with her to Telluride. She dressed him in a lot of Patagonia fleece, which he liked very much. She began to write letters to newspapers on the plight of the cacao child slaves in Africa. They were invited to speak at a Telluride school, at a church in Montrose, and then on a radio station in Durango, and then, with Irene growing more and more passionate about the issues, and more and more delighted with herself for her noblesse oblige, they embarked on a lecture tour together, which she bankrolled. She hired a publicist, who was able to get them invitations to speak at churches and schools mostly, and they got good press coverage wherever they went.

Over and over, for the next three months, Abu told his heartrending story about having run away from a brutal cacao plantation where young boys were held captive and forced to labor under the scorching sun, harvesting cacao pods fourteen hours a day in exchange for prisonlike accommodations and scant meals of corn paste and boiled bananas, at risk of being beaten by guards if they failed to work quickly or efficiently enough.

It was quite moving, their show (Julie and I saw them at Wesleyan, early in their East Coast run), with Irene working the PowerPoint, with photos and graphs and charts and bullet-pointed phrases, while Abu explained in his halting English that he has learned that it takes four hundred beans to make a pound of pure chocolate, and each pod contains some forty beans, and all of these beans are harvested by hungry, scrawny boys who have never tasted chocolate. Abu himself first tasted chocolate in Paris, when Irene bought him a *pain au chocolat* for breakfast in the café that first morning, and he thought it was the sweetest taste in his mouth, like something surely from heaven, not something from the earth, and he was amazed that those dirty, gritty beans could produce such richness.

Irene told me proudly that he would always stop to say this, always using those words. His already moved audiences were rapt as he went on to describe how the boys would labor every day on the plantation, with dangerous snakes underfoot and stinging insects circling their heads. The boys, wearing little more than shorts and flip-flops, would just work and work, lifting the heavy machetes high to cut the ripest heavy pods from the trees—the bosses would be angry when some of the cacao pods were useless because they were blackened with disease from rot or bird damage—and then with their machetes they would slice each pod all the way around and then pull the two halves apart to get the placenta, the gooey brainlike mass of precious beans in the core.

The boys would scoop out the beans and spread them on woven mats or on banana leaves, and cover them with more banana leaves so they would ferment properly. Every day they would cut the pods and split the pods and spread the wet beans on mats for fermenting, and each batch, after a few days, once the sweet milky fruit surrounding the beans had fermented and begun to dry on the beans, would then be uncovered and the beans would be dried in the sun for a few days, perhaps a week, depending on the weather. Once dry, the beans would be shoveled into large burlap bags, each bag weighing some sixty-eight kilos, and the boys would carry these big sacks of dried beans weighing nearly twice their own weight to a collection point, and there they would load the bags onto the trucks that came.

Abu said he had been lured to the plantation from a bus stop outside the town of Daloa, when he was traveling from his rural village to visit his grandmother. He had been promised money, $150 for a year's labor, and a new bicycle. He was sixteen at the time, and small for his age, and the man who approached him had thought he was younger. Many of the boys on the plantation were only nine or ten. Abu was taken hundreds of miles in a truck with some other boys who had also been picked up that day, to the plantation. He didn't really know where it was, this cacao plantation where he spent more than two years in captivity. Abu never found out the name of the townland and he never saw any nearby villages. He never got his money or his bicycle.

Details of Abu's escape were murky, and he would always hesitate and then drop his eyes and lower his voice and say he could not tell all the truth of the story because he could not name the people who helped him without endangering them even now, from the person who helped him climb in with the sacks of cacao beans as they were loaded into a truck, to the driver who smuggled him with the cacao as the sacks were loaded into the hold of a cargo ship that sailed from Abidjan. He felt responsible for the other two boys who had run away with him, Malik and Jumo, both younger than Abu, who died when the bulk container of cacao beans was fumigated a few days before the ship arrived in the Dutch port. Abu didn't die only because he had crawled out of the container in search of water, and was in another part of the ship's cargo area during the fumigation. He was found by a member of the crew, who heard his anguished cries when he returned to the container with water for his friends.

Although he was being held for the Dutch authorities, a sympathetic sailor who was supposed to be watching him (Abu thought the boat and crew were from Singapore) turned him loose on the dock, he said, before the police arrived. Abu would always emphasize that the details of his personal story were unimportant, and what mattered was that everyone should know about the boys who had not escaped, all the hundreds and perhaps thousands of children who were wielding those rusty machetes to cut the cacao pods, all those children who were captive to this labor, living on corn paste and boiled bananas, living in fear of the guards who could beat them or even kill them if they didn't work hard enough, so the world could have its chocolate.

THIS COMPELLING TALK was given probably thirty times in various locations, with Irene making all the arrangements and covering all travel expenses. They raised more than two hundred thousand dollars for Common Dreams and the International Labor Rights Foundation. I am sure everyone who heard one of these talks was shocked and moved and shamed by these revelations about where our chocolate comes from. Just as we are all shocked and moved and shamed each time we are reminded where our clothing comes from. It's always uncomfortable to stop and imagine for a moment exactly what the origins of the chocolate in your M&M's might be, and to consider who has labored in what way, under what conditions, in order to provide that sweet melting-in-your-mouth moment. It is also difficult to consider the life of the child in Bangladesh who was paid pennies to make your Old Navy T-shirt. So I want to say again, Irene's dedication was impressive, and even though the inspiration for her involvement turned out to be a fraud, that doesn't undo her accomplishments in getting attention and raising money for a worthy cause.

Irene was in talks with a literary agent about collaborating on a book about Abu's experiences when their interview on *All Things Considered* aired on National Public Radio. Within days of the broadcast, it all began to unravel. Numerous listeners phoned or wrote to say there were many details that didn't add up in Abu's story, starting with the way his accent was all wrong for Côte d'Ivoire. This was correct; Abu was actually from Cameroon. Everything else was wrong, too: dates, places, the story of the bulk container of cacao in the Dutch port and his two dead friends, his journey to Paris in a truckload of tomatoes. None of it added up.

Abu was, of course, a fraud. All the parts of his story that didn't add up were always right there in plain sight. His compelling story was true, in a sense. It just wasn't his story. It was a blend of several stories he had heard about or read in newspapers. An athletic boy from a family of cacao farmers on the edge of Mount Cameroon (his two younger brothers, Malik and Jumo, were alive and well), Abu, who did in fact spend time working on his family's small cacao farm, was the star of his school's soccer team. He had been recruited by a soccer scout to try out for the French national team. His family had given all their meager savings plus some borrowed money to pay his way for this opportunity.

And so Abu was brought to France, to the soccer training camp in Vichy, where he had been housed and fed, and he had drilled and played long hours every day with the French team for three weeks. But he wasn't good enough. Very few of the African recruits ever were, though they were useful practice fodder, and every now and then someone with star quality actually did make the team. And so at the end of the three-week tryout (that he had only ever been offered a three-week tryout was news to Abu), he had been put on a train to Paris with fifty euros. Ashamed and frightened, Abu didn't know what to do when he arrived at the Gare de Lyon.

A sympathetic Senegalese taxi driver gave him a free ride to the Cameroonian embassy in the sixteenth arrondissement, but there was a long line outside, and he was discouraged. Abu found a very cheap and not very clean hotel room near noisy train tracks in the Little Africa neighborhood the cabdriver had told him about, La Goutte d'Or in the eighteenth arrondissement, and in a café on rue Doudeauville he listened to two Cameroonians at an adjacent table talking about three men from Ghana who had been found dead in a container ship in New York City, poisoned by the fumigation of cacao beans in the container in which they had stowed away.

When he awoke the next morning, his money and his passport were gone. The man at the front desk shrugged and turned away. Abu found his way back to the Cameroonian embassy and got on the end of the line, but at noon everyone on the street was told that the embassy was only open a half day on Fridays and they should all come back on Monday. He spent the day walking aimlessly through the streets. The next morning, Abu woke from a fitful doze on a park bench to see a rich American in her black running tights and her red fleece and her puffy white sneakers going through her Tai Chi poses in front of him. He never dreamed that Irene would believe his story, he admitted in his official statement to the American immigration authorities (from which I have gathered all this information) before he was deported to Cameroon, and he had really only meant to get a free meal and maybe a little money from her.

Abu's story brought out the best in Irene. I have certainly never seen her happier. Was her compassion any less real, was the issue any less true, when it turned out he was a fraud? But the outrage over his deception and her unwitting part in it was hugely humiliating for her. She went into a depression. She didn't return calls from agents and editors clamoring for her to write a book about her experience with Abu, and after a while the calls stopped and everyone lost interest. The story got pushed down the page, and then finally it was off the page.

Irene had been so moved by her own virtue, by her compassion for Abu. As were all the people in their audiences who gave generously to help change the system of child labor on cacao plantations in Africa. Was harm done, in the end? (Other than the bruises to Irene's sense of her own certainties about the world?) The money they raised didn't enrich Abu; it went to agencies set up to assist the child slave workers on the cacao plantations in Africa. Abu lived well for a few months and dined out on his appropriated story for a while, but he ended up right back where he started, with a wardrobe of Patagonia fleece and polypropylene underwear he would never wear in Cameroon.

He hasn't been heard from since. I can't imagine why some enterprising editor hasn't tracked him down with an offer of a ghostwritten memoir deal. It wouldn't be the first time such a book has been published. Maybe Irene bought his silence. Maybe in his own way he has some dignity and integrity. Maybe he came to feel that *she* had taken advantage of *him*.

Do I believe Irene's repeated claims that she never suspected Abu of any deception, that she never once questioned his story at any point in those months, from their first conversation in the park in Paris to the unraveling that followed their Public Radio interview? She defended him in the beginning, when the holes in his story first came to light, but then once the irrefutable facts just couldn't be explained away, she never made any public statement reversing her belief in him. She just withdrew. She completely dropped all her involvements with the various organizations working to end child slavery in cacao production in Africa. When I asked her a few months after the whole Abu crisis had died down if she no longer felt concern about the child slaves in Côte d'Ivoire, she was irritated, and snapped something at me about how that issue had become toxic for her and she had refocused her positive energy on global warming instead.

Fortunately, Howard had listened to me at the outset, when I enumerated all the reasons Zip's Candies should make no official statement of any kind about Abu or about Irene's campaign, given all the obvious conflicts and problems that association could have ignited, so when it came apart we didn't have to do any embarrassing backtracking. We dodged a bullet, not that anyone thanked me for my judgment. The sad truth is, we use chocolate that has been made from processed cacao beans that have probably been harvested by children living in deplorable conditions. We use this chocolate every day to make our candy. We make Little Sammies and Tigermelts, and we make Mumbo Jumbos. We source the best ingredients we can, for the right price. Zip's Candies is a business. We are not the UN.

I DO BELIEVE Irene. Despite how irrationally suspicious Irene can be about people who don't match her distorted expectations—like me—I think she believed Abu's story with all her heart. As I said, it wouldn't be my place to suggest that sexual obsession blinded her to the truth. Perhaps she was made especially gullible by her desire to see herself in such a noble light.

Lady Bountiful solving the world's problems. Because sponsoring Abu, doing all she did to rescue him and help him tell his story, that worked for her. It suited her needs perfectly. In the end, that kind of naiveté is actually a form of entitled arrogance, isn't it?

8

I N 1920, ELI AND Morris left their little brother, Julius, in
Budapest with some cousins. There is nothing in any Zip's
Candies record or family story about what provisions, if any,
they made for him. Did they feel guilty about Julius, abandoned
at the last moment with the Fischer family, barely known second
cousins on their mother's side? Or did they put him out of their
minds completely as they sailed away, leaving him behind along
with everything else that was familiar? He was fourteen years
old. Their parents had died just a few months earlier in an
influenza epidemic (first one, then the other), and the brothers
had promised their mother they would stay together. Now his
two older brothers had foisted Julius on strangers who lived over
a shop in a strange, bustling city, nothing like the small village,
two days' walking distance from Budapest, where the Czaplinskys had been rooted for generations, selling live poultry in the
market square.

Did Eli and Morris miss him, as they began their new lives in
America? Did they think of him and wonder how he was managing, as they ate their meals, as they tried to get used to the
bland American flavors he might have enjoyed, or despised?
Did they wonder if that sour-looking aunt Borbála ever gave
their little Julesy any sweet treats, a kiss good night, if she ever
cracked that *ferbissenah punim* to give him so much as a smile?
Was he in school, or had the Fischers put him straight to work in
their dry goods business? Surely Eli and Morris had made

promises to send for him when they could. Did they try to write to Julius, to Aunt Borbála? Did they think of sending money?

If Morris hadn't died in the 1921 diphtheria epidemic that swept New York, perhaps the brothers would have saved up enough money for Julius's passage. What then? The joyful arrival of young Julius after those terrible but mercifully few years of separation, and after that, perhaps the three reunited brothers would have gone into business together. And who can say, Czaplinsky Brothers Candy might have been very successful, even without *Little Black Sambo* for inspiration, and their sweets could have been delightfully appealing to young and old, and their business might have flourished, not only rivaling the likes of the now-vanished D. Auerbach & Sons, Peaks Mason Mints, or W. P. Chase in those halcyon years of candy manufacturing in New York City, but perhaps even outlasting them, swallowing them up, growing bigger and bigger. Who can say if the synergistic energy of the three brothers might have made Czaplinsky a household name, maybe the third big name in American candy, after Hershey and Mars.

But of course, that never happened.

HERE'S WHAT I imagine did happen. Yes, these are my perceptions. These are necessarily my interpretations of events. Does anyone have a more authentic or plausible version of this story? If so, let's hear it!

Julius was grudgingly taken into the Fischer family, and as time passed he became more and more content with his life in Budapest, the so-called "Paris of the East," as his aunt Borbála liked to say as she unfurled an array of the latest yard goods from France across the worn wooden counter of Fischer's on

Dohány Street while persuading a prosperous customer that her social status required the more expensive Jacquard-loomed damask drapery materials favored in the most fashionable salons on La Rive Droite.

Julius finished school and went on to university, where he was a methodical but uninspired student, though he enjoyed the café life that surrounded the university. He wrote several letters to his brothers in America, but he could only address them to Morris and Eli Czaplinsky, care of General Delivery, New York City. He didn't know that Morris was dead or that Eli had moved to New Haven, Connecticut, where he had become a Ziplinsky. The name change made for simpler spelling and less confusion. Zip's Candies was such a good American brand name. And surely the change was also inspired by Eli's desire to make himself unfindable either by New York City detectives who could have wanted to discuss his presence at the Essex Market Courthouse the day Kid Dropper Kaplan was murdered, or by anyone nosing around on behalf of Little Augie, who no doubt wanted his money back, with interest.

Ziplinsky was, anyway, a little bit more of an American kind of name than Czaplinsky, Eli thought, and it was a nice zippy, peppy, zingy name at that. Changing it more would have signified shame about his heritage (he considered Zipple, but even with his beginner's English he recognized that it was an undignified name, too much like the word *nipple*), and he looked down on all those eastern European Jews who chopped their names, those Whites and Whitemans who used to be Wiedermans, the Breitkopfs who became Brodheads. (Perhaps he was unaware of a certain Saxe-Coburg und Gotha family who simply became Windsors not long before then, in 1917.) By the time Eli became an American citizen in 1928, he was proudly signing his name with a big, flourishing Z, with the bottom serif of the Z underlining the rest of the name, a habit he maintained to the end of his life.

Julius had no way of knowing that Eli had written to him five times from New York, the last time to tell him the sad news about their Morris having succumbed to diphtheria. The letters were intercepted by Aunt Borbála each time, who opened them when they arrived from America. Finding no money or specific promises about any, she hid the letters away in a desk drawer, feeling justified in keeping Julius from getting his hopes up. Maybe she would give him the letters some day, but not now. In the future, when he would thank her for keeping him grateful for what he had, for all that the Fischers had given him, instead of dreaming about America. Julius was better off if he didn't think his brothers were going to send for him. These useless letters would keep him from forgetting his brothers. He needed to stop moping around so much, as if he was always waiting for something.

If they did send money for Julius, she told herself, the first priority would be to pay her back for the expense and bother of having added Julius to her household. It was too bad about Morris, because now it was even less likely that any money would ever come. Eli was just a boy himself, and probably he would forget about Julius. Soon there were no more letters, which proved her right. Her father always said those Czaplinskys were good for nothing.

When Julius never heard from his brothers he began to think they might both be dead, and even though Aunt Borbála never said anything, he tried on his own to make himself stop hoping for a letter. He didn't even know with any certainty that they had ever reached America. He continued to work behind the counter at Fischer's for several years, until he left to go into business with his cousin Péter, the least gloomy and conceited of the

Fischers, whose apprenticeship to an elderly baker in the old Jewish Quarter had given him skills and ambitions to open his own shop.

Fischer & Czaplinsky, a bakery with an adjoining coffee-house on Kazinczy Street in the heart of the bustling Jewish Quarter (on the flat, Pest side of the Danube), thrived immediately, and within a couple of years there were five employees working alongside Julius and Péter to keep the customers satisfied with their good strong coffee and all their buttery little cookies and *kiffles*, their *rigó jancsi*, their flakey strudels, and especially their signature *kürtöskalácsus*, a yeasty sweet dough wound around cylinders that slowly rotated over hot coals until the pastry was browned.

Julius, now a handsome and prosperous citizen of the neighborhood, had become something of a ladies' man, with a series of girlfriends, each one believing that she would be the one to claim this attractive and slightly melancholy loner, that she would be the one with whom he would want to settle down and raise a family. But sooner or later, each one would discover evidence of a growing indifference combined with hints of a new woman in his life. Each one would withdraw, defeated, with a slightly broken heart, to be replaced by the next one, and the next.

Then Szilvia Weisz came to work in the bakery at Fischer & Czaplinsky. She was a quiet little worker with a refulgent smile and the nimblest fingers when it came to wrapping the dough for the *kürtöskalácsus*, not too loose or it would fall onto the coals, but not too tight or it would crack apart as it sizzled and browned. Something shifted inside of Julius, some corner of his brittle heart began to soften whenever he saw her, but each time he asked her to go out with him, she told him she would not go out with a playboy, no matter how handsome or charming.

For six months she refused his advances until finally, when

he told her he loved her and had not been with another woman in all that time (which was very nearly the truth), she agreed to go to a chamber music concert with him. A few nights later they went to dinner, and shortly after that they were keeping company every evening, and then they were engaged to be married, and then they were married. The Weisz family, all of them hardworking diamond buyers and cutters, welcomed Julius, and made him feel truly part of a family for the first time since he was a child. Soon there was a baby girl, Matild, born in 1937, and after that a boy, Geza, born in early 1939.

The First Jewish Law, restricting to 20 percent the number of Jews who could have certain administrative positions or hold certain kinds of jobs, had been passed in 1938. Ten years before that, the entire extended Fischer family had converted en masse, all twenty-seven of them becoming churchgoing Lutherans at once, and so they did not think these laws applied to them. Two days after Geza was born, the Second Jewish Law reduced the "economic participation" of the Jews of Hungary to 5 percent, and soon after that the business dropped the Czaplinsky name.

Cash payments to certain officials who were friendly with other officials allowed the Fischer family to continue to avoid being named as Jews. While Julius kept working on the bakery side, he was no longer welcome in any Fischer home, and he was asked to refrain from claiming any blood connection to them. Restoring his name to the business was nothing to discuss at this time, perhaps in the future, if peace should ever break out.

More and more Jews were moving from all over the countryside to Pest, and Fischer's had never been busier. Julius and Péter added as many tables and chairs as they could cram in. Hungary's right-wing government was allied with Germany, and the quarter million Jews of Budapest, though increasingly constricted by the new rules in their daily lives, continued to go to work, conduct their business, marry, have babies, and raise their families, believing they were reasonably safe from further losses or restrictions. What more could happen?

SZILVIA'S YOUNGER SISTER, Ágnes, worked as a secretary at a prosperous law firm until she was forced to leave when the Second Jewish Law was passed. Her boss was very sorry to lose such a pleasant and efficient worker. She was really a very beautiful girl, nice to look at every day, and she had such a good knowledge of German and French. He really regretted that she had to go, especially for such a shameful reason (he himself had a Jewish grandmother, but thankfully nobody was aware of this blot on his record). When he encountered a government bureaucrat he had known since childhood when they both went out to smoke cigars during an intermission at the opera, he put in a good word for Ágnes and all of her desirable attributes.

Ágnes, who was fortunately possessed of blonde, wispy hair and dark blue eyes, was soon offered employment in the Budapest central government offices as a correspondence typist-translator, where her German skills were desperately needed. The job was hers provided that she promise to keep her mouth shut about her background.

It was an open secret that the employment laws were enforced haphazardly, though the increasing power of the right-wing Arrow Cross Party was making both the Jews and their sympathizers more paranoiac with every passing day. Szilvia was home with the children and no longer worked at the bakery, but Julius would often come in the door at night with upsetting reports about groups of Arrow Cross Party members swaggering into the coffeehouse and forcing Jewish customers to vacate the tables they wanted. One afternoon Péter quietly took Julius aside to warn him that he might not be able to keep working at Fischer's much longer, and it might be safer for them all if he were to try and find something else, for now.

On a hot August night, Ágnes came for dinner with Szilvia and Julius, and after the babies were asleep, she took off her shoe and unfolded some sheets of onionskin paper, illicit extra carbon copies of documents she had translated into Hungarian and typed that afternoon. There was a memo from the Reich Central Security Office in Berlin titled *Reichssicherheitshauptamt: Madagaskar Projekt*. The author of the memo was Obersturmbannführer Adolf Eichmann.

The Madagascar Plan called for the resettlement of all the Jews of Europe on Madagascar, a million a year, over a period of four years. This was so much more desirable and efficient than the piecemeal efforts at deportation of Jews into centralized holding centers as they were flushed out from every city and every town and every village of Europe. No Jews, none at all, would remain in Europe.

The accompanying memo by Franz Rademacher, the recently appointed head of the *Judenreferat III der Abteilung Deutschland* (the Jewish Department of the Ministry of Foreign Affairs), which Ágnes had also translated into Hungarian for distribution among the various government departments, included references to the stopping of construction of the Warsaw Ghetto and deportations of Jews into Poland, which had both been suspended on July 10. The Madagascar Plan would render unnecessary all that effort to transport Jews into Poland for temporary containment.

The Madagascar Plan memo went on to detail cost estimates for coordinating and commissioning sufficient fleets of seaworthy vessels for the massive transportation effort that would be necessary, which depended largely on strategies for using ships from the British fleet, the imminent availability of which was confidently anticipated. The SS would carry on the Jewish expulsion in Europe, before ultimately governing the Jewish settlement.

Madagascar would only be a Mandate; the Jews living there would not be entitled to German citizenship. Meanwhile, the Jews deported to Madagascar would lose their various European citizenships from the date of deportation. Having all the Jews of Europe residents of the Mandate of Madagascar would prevent the possible establishment by Jews in Palestine of a state of their own. It would also help prevent any opportunity for them to exploit the symbolic importance of Jerusalem. The Madagascar Plan would create a central European bank funded with seized Jewish assets; this money would pay for the evacuation and resettlement of all the Jews, and the bank would also play a permanent role as the only permitted institution for any transaction between the Jews on Madagascar and the outside world. Hermann Göring would oversee the administration of the plan's economics.

Most significantly, the Jews remaining under German control on Madagascar would function as a useful bargaining chip for the future good behavior of the members of their race in America. The generosity shown by Germany in permitting cultural, economic, administrative, and legal self-administration to the Jews on Madagascar would also be very useful for propaganda purposes. The administration and execution of the Madagascar Plan was assigned to various offices within the Third Reich: Foreign Minister Joachim von Ribbentrop's office would negotiate the French peace treaty necessary to the handing over of Madagascar to Germany, and it would help design any other treaties required to deal with Europe's Jews. The Information Department of the Foreign Affairs Ministry, along with

Joseph Goebbels in the Propaganda Ministry, would filter all worldwide information about the plan. Viktor Brack of the Führer Chancellory would oversee transportation. There was no mention of any consideration for the native population of Madagascar.

The three of them sat at the table studying the documents until after midnight, talking very little. Finally, Julius crumpled all the pages into a ball on a dinner plate and set them alight with his cigarette.

JULIUS LEFT FOR Madagascar three weeks later, with as many diamonds sewn into the linings of his coat and his best three-piece suit as he could safely carry without attracting attention. Péter had bought him out of the bakery and coffeehouse with cash, less than Julius thought was fair, but more than Péter had any obligation to provide, under the circumstances. Leaving only enough money for Szilvia to buy what she and the babies would need for a few months, all the rest of their savings had been converted to diamonds thanks to Szilvia's brother, who had gotten the highest possible prices for Szilvia's jewelry and her great-aunt Lena's upright piano, though the babies liked to hear Szilvia play it after dinner and Matild had cried when the men came to carry it down the stairs.

Julius promised Szilvia he would get word to her as quickly as he could. He vowed that he would be sending for them just as soon as possible, sooner than she could imagine. They would all be together again, and safe once and for all. Although he could hardly bear to leave his family, he set out, determined to find a way to make a new and better life for Szilvia, Matild, and little Geza. Ágnes, too, and the rest of the Weisz family. And Péter, if he had the sense to raise his hand as a Jew and leave with his family, early instead of late, rather than live in fear of discovery all the rest of his days in Jew-cleansed Budapest.

Did those stuck-up Fischers think they wouldn't be found out? With those noses? How much praying on those sturdy Fischer knees in a fashionable Lutheran church would it take to change Aunt Borbála into a gentile from Buda instead of the imperious Jewess from Pest she always had been? Did they really believe they would be able to keep their place in the world that was changing around them?

Julius's arduous journey to Madagascar took almost six months. It had been surprisingly easy to get a visa for Zanzibar, with the assistance of Ágnes's supervisor, who gladly swapped a furtive and efficient groping from Ágnes for rubber-stamped traveling papers for Julius that would allow him to cross borders as he worked his way south to the Greek coast. Julius took some trains, but mostly, he walked. From the Greek coast Julius sailed across to Egypt on a barge laden with barrels of olive oil. It was by then January 1941. Working his way down the east coast of Africa, Julius arrived in Madagascar on a freighter from Zanzibar.

OKAY, ACTUALLY I have no idea how Julius got from Budapest to Madagascar, or how long it took. I am at the limit of my imaginative ability for reconstructing the most likely scenarios. It doesn't matter. So let's just say that when we next see Julius, he has arrived in Madagascar from Zanzibar. It is the middle of March, the height of the hot, rainy season. Picture him in your mind's eye. We pick up the narrative thread here.

The Malagasy dockworkers think Julius Czaplinsky is a very funny sight indeed as he totters down the gangplank in his woolen three-piece suit, with his greatcoat folded over his arm, staggering slightly under the weight of his leather suitcase. As Julius traipses around the muddy, rutted lanes of the port town of Mahajanga, having spent most of the past month sweltering insanely in the heat so constantly that he thought he might die of heat suffocation, he finally feels it is safe enough to take off the jacket and vest of his suit and carry them over his arm with his overcoat. At last, he can wear his damp and grimy shirtsleeves rolled up to his elbows.

Julius has that Czaplinsky motivation and determination that has become so diluted in Howard. He has arrived in Madagascar to figure out the best claim to stake, and then he plans to stake it hard and deep, ahead of the four million Jews who will soon begin to pour out of ships at every port, each of them hoping (as displaced Jews always do) to find a toehold to start a new life in this alien place.

Julius is here to get established ahead of the competition. Should he buy buildings in towns, begin constructing simple housing on empty lots that he will be able to rent or sell at premium prices? Should he stake a strong position in shipping and import-export in one or more of the port towns? Should he buy arable land for agriculture? Where would it be most desirable for his family to live? In the central mountainous region or along one of the coasts? He has to find his way and think it all through, make the most of his advantage.

The Madagascar Plan had described the possibility of an all-Jewish administrative government that would be overseen by the SS. Perhaps he would qualify for consideration for some official position of authority, should that prove desirable, given his foresight about getting established early, without simply waiting to be one of four million souls rounded up and shipped to this strange island only 644 kilometers off the east coast of Africa, a world away from anything European Jews have ever known.

✳ ✳

THE MADAGASCAR THAT Julius discovered was sparsely inhabited by a few Frenchmen here and there, but otherwise he was intrigued by the curious specimens of humanity he encountered everywhere he went. They didn't look like any people he had ever seen before in his life. The Malagasy people had probably never seen anyone who looked like him, either. Julius had those piercing blue Czaplinsky eyes, that familial beak of a nose, and a gaunt but somehow forceful bearing, though he couldn't have stood more than five foot eight. His wild hair was jet black, and it radiated out from his receding hairline, emphasizing his great domed forehead. Though clean-shaven in Budapest, Julius had a long dark beard by the time he arrived in Mahajanga on the Zanzibar ferry (or whatever). His skin was of such a pale, pink, nearly alabaster hue that he burned terribly after even a few minutes in direct sun. In Madagascar, as the weeks passed, his face and neck burned repeatedly and darkened to a leathery brown, but Julius's body was otherwise still milky white, and any inadvertent exposure of his usually covered flesh was a fascination for the Malagasy who happened to catch such a glimpse. They called him *Vazaha,* white man, and they often gathered to watch him eat, wherever he went, laughing with glee each time he pulled his spoon out of his pocket to eat his *koba,* the pasty mash of rice, banana, and peanuts that he had decided he could live on safely (after a few disastrous encounters with wretched, gristly bits of meat prepared with a stewy rice mixture studded with muddy bits of vegetation). As he fed himself this mash each day with his daintily deployed spoon, instead of scooping it from the bowl with his fingers the way everyone else did, he would remind himself sometimes, to make his meal more palatable, that he was the same man who once sat in his high chair at the table with his family, being a good little boy, spooning his mother's Sunday goulash from his bowl.

JULIUS WAS CONFIDENT that he could figure out the best of his options, and he felt the urgency of his situation, but time seemed to tick by very, very slowly on Madagascar, and soon Julius fell into the rhythms of the island. He found a little hut where he could stay, in a crooked lane at the edge of Antananarivo where goats were tethered, and he paid some men to guard him while he slept, and to guard his things whenever he went out. The first few nights, he was awakened continually by the sounds of geckos scrabbling across the earthen floor, and by the strange chirring sounds of the ring-tailed lemurs who swung from the trees and scampered about the underbrush with strangely graceful leaps, like a little troupe of two-toned, monkey-faced Cossacks.

Orb weaver spiders the size of grapefruits erected elaborate webs across his doorway while he slept, and he was unsettled each time he brushed into one of those webs inadvertently and made contact with the fuzzy scuttling body of its weaver. The hissing cockroaches startled him every time he disturbed one in the night when his bladder forced him to stir from his restless slumber. Julius was reluctant to leave his secret diamond hoard for more than short periods of time, and he knew he had to convert his stones to local currency, but the energies of living each day seemed to soak up all the hours of daylight, and each crimson sunset found him hunkering down for the night once more with nothing accomplished.

Time passed.

He found a woman who would wash his clothes and prepare his food for him in a way that he could eat it. (It helped that she was very beautiful.) Mostly he lived on sweet potatoes, steamed manioc, and *mofo gasy*, a hearth-baked pancake made from sweetened rice flour. Night after night Julius dreamed of the sweet pastries he had served a thousand times in the coffeehouse, each one on a plate with the signature red-and-black-striped rim incorporating the beautiful streamlined logo for Fischer & Czaplinsky, plates they continued to use even after the Czaplinsky name was scraped from the red, black, and gold lettering on the windows and doors. He dreamed of the unsold, stale pastries he had thrown away or given to beggars at the back door of the bakery at closing time night after night. *Kürtöskalácus* unfurled in his dreams, flakey puffs of pastry unwinding from the baking cylinders, dropping in big, buttery curls that he couldn't quite catch before they blackened to ash on the glowing coals.

Months passed before Julius was able to make an approach to a French banker he had been observing in a café, a lonely alcoholic whose misbehavior involving certain accounting irregularities at his previous bank in Paris had led to his exile in this remote French colony. The banker was charmed by Julius, who had the prescience at their first meeting to make a gift of the small bottle of good Slivovitz he had tucked into his baggage and carried all this way and hoarded all this time.

Malagasy wine, which Julius had sampled, tasted like horse piss mixed with vinegar. Perhaps he should start a distillery. Did sufficient sugarcane grow on this or any other near enough soil? Would grapes on vines rot and mold in the humidity or could a vineyard be established, perhaps on the windward side of the island? For modest kickbacks of which Julius was unaware, the banker made introductions for Julius to the right people, who would give him the best prices converting his diamonds to Malagasy francs.

People are people, business is business, money is money. By

the end of 1942, a land broker had secured Julius's rights to some four thousand hectares in the central rain-forest region of the northern part of the island, in the Betsiboka region of the Mahajanga province, where the soil is rich and the humidity high. Half of his hilly lands were covered in a dense pine and eucalyptus forest, while the rest was a crazy quilt of nineteenth-century French plantations fallen into disuse, though they had once yielded rich annual harvests of cacao, coffee, banana, and vanilla.

In Budapest, Julius had struggled to achieve and maintain a modest, bourgeois status. In Madagascar, where the Malagasy people lived a subsistence life on the land, his diamonds had bought such an unimaginable number of Malagasy francs that even after investing in these holdings, he was still an immensely rich man, with more houses than he could count scattered across his four thousand hectares, with dozens of overseers on his various lands, and hundreds of employees grateful for the very small wage he would pay them in exchange for working his plantations or providing whatever services he could possibly want or need. Time slowed and stopped. Time stood still for Julius.

By the spring of 1943, Julius had become the monarch of a small kingdom. The rest of the world seemed very far away. His brilliant strategy had proven to be far more successful than he could have possibly imagined. He was the Founding Jew, the First Jew, the Only Jew of Madagascar! Julius was impatient for the first signs that the transports had begun. Each day he scanned the horizon. The unbroken sea was empty of ships, dotted only by a few of the small square-sailed primitive fishing vessels that went out early every morning to check their crayfish pots along the coastline. Surely they would arrive today, or tomorrow?

Julius didn't consider that in faraway Budapest, time had not stood still. On Kazinczy Street, time had marched along quite briskly.

EVERY DAY JULIUS envisioned himself in his new role as the wise pioneer whose helpful advice would be eagerly sought by his people. He could see himself greeting and providing comfort and wisdom to as many of the newcomers as he could accommodate as they tumbled off the ships by the thousands, day after day, week after week, sailing into every port on the island, from Toliara to Antsiranana, each of them dazed, frightened, staggering under the weight of the few precious worldly goods they would have managed to bring along on the voyage from the Old World to this very New World.

We will begin again! Julius insisted to himself as he sipped the muddy coffee made from his own Caturra beans prepared for him each morning now by his housemaid, and served to him on the veranda of his headquarters, a plantation house that overlooked five hundred acres planted in Trinitario and Criollo and Porcelana cacao. The openwork lace of the early morning mist floated through the tops of the banana canopy that soared over the hodge podge of the cacao trees. He longed for Szilvia, Matild, and Geza. And of course, Ágnes too. He would welcome with open arms any of the Weisz family who wanted to come live on his plantations.

He was deeply moved by his own anticipated generosity as he envisaged himself presiding over his grateful family, perhaps dozens of them, all thankful that he had given them such a wonderful fresh start. He would be the patriarch, providing plenty for all. They would all be safe. They would all be prosperous. They would all be together again.

But the horizon remained empty. The ships filled with the Jews of Europe eager to begin their new lives did not arrive.

Julius had written to Szilvia steadily since his arrival, though the centralized postal service from Antananarivo was erratic at best and a complete disaster at worst, so he hadn't been overly worried not to have heard back from her in the beginning. But now when his letters continued to go unanswered, he began to fret. One morning as he sipped his coffee and gazed out over the treetops of his plantation it suddenly dawned on him with horror that while time stood still in Madagascar, it rushed ahead furiously and tumultuously and disastrously in the wider world.

That day he sent a long letter to the alcoholic banker in Antananarivo by messenger, with specific and urgent instructions for a wire to a correspondent bank in Budapest where the banker had told him long ago he might still have a contact who might be willing to deliver the message to Szilvia, or if that was risky, then to Péter, at the coffeehouse, who would surely be willing to pass a message to Szilvia. Wouldn't any banker in Budapest know Fischer's bakery and coffeehouse, on Kazinczy Street?

The wire Julius sent was three pages of dense advice about obtaining a visa for Zanzibar, traveling on the same route he had followed (whatever that was, let's agree that it's unimportant to the story), using the same sympathetic official as before, Ágnes's supervisor, the man who had approved his traveling documents. Julius's wire enumerated all the contact information he had for every leg of the journey, concluding with the name of the shipping clerk to see at the harbor in Stone Town once they arrived on Zanzibar.

THE ENSUING SILENCE was ominous. Julius had heard nothing for too long. He felt a sudden spasm of terror, and he realized that he had been insanely complacent. Anything could have happened in all this time. He had to do something more, take some kind of action. He could no longer just sit and wait. He set out with one of his plantation managers in the most functional of his three rusting, patched-together Ford Model A trucks, but a summer monsoon had drenched the highlands for days, and after a day of fighting the mud that filled the narrow, winding track that led to his aerie, the truck was hopelessly mired, and they had gone only ten dozen kilometers. Julius had to make the journey to Antananarivo in the back of a zebu cart. The jolting, slow-motion trip took many days, and he arrived feeling quite sick from the rocking of the cart and from the fear that now clutched his heart. How could he have been so blithely unconcerned all these months, months that had turned to years? It was now July 1944.

The dissipated and habitually hungover banker arranged for Julius to use one of the few telephones on Madagascar that could connect him to Budapest, in the central government office across from the bank. Julius had developed a fluent Malagasy-inflected French, and he was able to make his needs understood well enough. It took nearly an hour to make the connection, but finally, miraculously, the series of operators was able to hold all the necessary connections to patch him through to Budapest.

He gave the number to the local operator there in Hungarian, his eyes filling with tears as he spoke the familiar numbers to another Hungarian speaker, but a moment later her faint voice in his ear told him through the echoing static that the number was no longer in service.

Ah, of course, Szilvia was economizing. He begged the operators not to disconnect the line and then he gave the next number that came into his head, for Fischer's. Surely Péter would be willing to relay his message to Szilvia. The call went through more quickly this time, and he could hear the familiar ringing tones echoing faintly down the line.

"*Bitte?*"

An unfamiliar voice, with the clatter of the coffeehouse in the background. Why answer the phone at Fischer's in German? A wrong number? A bad joke? Julius's mind was racing in slow motion, every thought slippery and ungraspable. In carefully enunciated Hungarian he asked if this was Fischer's and the man said, "*Ja, ja,*" impatiently, before demanding, "*Wen wollen Sie sprechen? Was wollen Sie?*"

Julius switched to his rudimentary German and asked for Péter. The German laughed, a short mirthless bark, and said Péter had gone for a little swim in the Danube, and then he hung up.

Julius didn't know that even while he was still making his way toward Madagascar, the transports of Jews from German territories into occupied Poland had resumed, as had work to complete the fortifications of the Warsaw Ghetto. Eichmann's beloved Madagascar Plan had stalled. Germany had not achieved a quick victory over Britain (the Battle of Britain had not gone as predicted so confidently by the Luftwaffe, despite their colorful maps and pins), and so the British fleet, crucial to the Madagascar Plan, would not be available to ship all the Jews to their island colony in the Indian Ocean after all. There was no alternative means of efficiently transporting four million Jews out of Europe.

In late August 1940, Rademacher begged Ribbentrop to hold a meeting at his ministry so they could revise the Madagascar Plan and put it in motion. Ribbentrop did nothing. Eichmann's Madagascar memo was never approved by Richard Heydrich, chair of the Wannsee Conference. From time to time, one or another official of the Third Reich would raise the question of a future plan for the ghetto colony on Madagascar for all the Jews of Europe, but by early December of that year, it had been abandoned entirely. The Madagascar Plan was stillborn, and the massive logistical quagmire of Jewish deportations would be solved in another, more efficient way. If the Jewish island colony in the Indian Ocean was a First Solution, then the answer to the vexing Jewish Question would be the Final Solution.

I HAVE TO admit the time line is way off here. Why is the sudden and successful British invasion of Madagascar in May 1942 not in this story? I suppose it's not really possible that Julius had no awareness of the stealth landing in Courrier Bay by the combined forces of the 13th Assault Flotilla. He had already been on Madagascar for more than a year at that point. So let's allow for the possibility that he welcomed the British forces. Perhaps he even played a small role, and had a secret involvement in the mysteriously deployed guiding beacons that enabled the invading, unlit British flotilla to glide past the dangers in the shoals of the harbor and land the troops safely in the darkness, while the Vichy slept. That would be good, if Julius did that. It improves the story. Let's say he did.

Soon after the British secured Madagascar, Free French Forces took over from the Vichy government. But looking at Julius's land acquisitions, I have to admit that a less nice version of this story has Julius doing business with the Vichy officials one way or another from the moment he arrives on the island in March 1941. The drunken banker is thick as thieves with them. The Vichy haven't got much to do, governing this godforsaken jungle in the middle of the Indian Ocean, and Julius is an amusement. They are willing to assist this pushy, ambitious Hungarian Jew with his coatful of diamonds in securing a position of power and authority in advance of the hordes. Why not? He will be useful to them.

Perhaps Julius is unhappy to see the corrupt Vichy officials replaced by the Free French officers who now govern the island, as it dawns on him that the chances of the Madagascar Plan's being executed as proposed are dwindling with every passing day. Surely the Third Reich wouldn't want to go to the trouble and expense of delivering the Jews of Europe to Madagascar only to see them pick up and take themselves wherever in the world they pleased after that. Even without knowledge of what has transpired in Europe, it is clear that without the Vichy in control of Madagascar, the plan collapses.

Perhaps Julius recognized then that he and he alone has escaped to Madagascar, while his family, everyone he has left behind, will be swallowed up by the incoming tide of history. Perhaps he never tried to reach them at all. Perhaps he did nothing but cultivate his holdings and wait. He is helpless. What can he do, from here, but hope for the best?

It is established fact that he spent the war years on Madagascar, where he was safe. But he died there, too, of malaria, soon after the end of the war, at the age of forty-two. Julius left behind his beautiful, young common-law wife, Lalao (she had been his housekeeper), and their two children, Darwin, who was two, and Huxley, who was an infant.

I don't really have a good way of telling this story seamlessly. While it is true that it is difficult to reconcile the time line completely, or really nail down the facts one way or the other, how important is that in the larger scheme of things? Can we just skip over these discrepancies? Let's say Julius was isolated on Madagascar from the moment he arrived, and in a way he was a prisoner of his circumstances. The larger truths of this story are what matters, and it would be pointless to get too distracted by details. In fact, a failure of imagination may be the most honorable choice here. Think of it this way: if for even a brief moment any of us could possess the full realization of all the horrors of human experience, how would it be possible to live?

JULIUS HAD NO way of knowing that Germany had occupied Hungary in 1944, when Hungary was on the verge of negotiating with the Allies after the German losses on the Eastern front. Nor did he know that tens of thousands of Hungarian Jews had already been killed in labor camps and deportations even before the occupation.

He would not have been able to imagine that the shul on Dohány Street had been turned into a small concentration camp. Adolf Eichmann himself had taken over the rabbi's office behind the beautiful rose window in the women's balcony. Eichmann organized a Budapest Jewish council to oversee the Jews who remained in Hungary, all two hundred thousand of them, now concentrated in Budapest, crammed into two thousand homes scattered through the city, each designated Jewish dwelling marked with a conspicuous yellow Star of David.

Julius did not know that nineteen people had been assigned to his apartment, and that for several miserable months Szilvia, Matild, and Geza had shared a narrow bed in what had been Matild's room, a room in which four strangers also slept.

Nor did he know that the Arrow Cross Party members had rampaged through the Jewish Quarter, shooting hundreds of Jews and throwing their bodies into the Danube, Péter's among them. Szilvia, Matild, and Geza were among the thousand who lay buried in the mass graves in the courtyard of the synagogue on Dohány Street, just up the street from where Fischer's dry goods shop once did business, before the Arrow Cross burned it to the ground with seven members of the Fischer family, who had refused to wear their yellow stars, locked inside.

Ágnes had been arrested and placed in the Kistarcsa transit camp for two months before she was marched with hundreds of other prisoners all the way to the Austrian border in freezing November sleet. On the third day of the march, when Ágnes was so weakened by a fever that she was unable to walk, she was shot and left at the side of the road.

By the end of 1944, here is what Julius Czaplinsky did know. He was thirty-eight years old. His wife and children were dead. He was rich beyond imagining. He was safe from the turmoil of war. And he was utterly alone. The other four million Jews of Europe weren't coming. There would never be one ship unloading its bewildered cargo of Jews. There would never be a single grateful recipient of all the wisdom and generosity Julius was so prepared to bestow upon his landsmen. The Madagascar Plan had brought only Julius Czaplinsky, the first, last, and only Jew on Madagascar.

9

I SHOULD NOT BE held accountable for the Bereavemints fiasco. Why bring this up now? That is simply an unfair piece of Zip's history to lay at my doorstep. And even if I was involved, it was nine years ago. I am perfectly willing to take responsibility for certain poor decisions in the history of Zip's Candies, with Little Susies at the top of that list, but not the Bereavemints. It is true that I headed the product development team at Zip's Candies, but that's just a designation on paper, a fancy way of captioning the management scheduling and availability of our workers and equipment. "Product development team" was really just a bookkeeping term. Who was on that team? Petey Leventhal, a couple of hourly line workers, and me.

And the product was certainly not my idea, let's be clear about that, if we have to talk about Bereavemints. It was Howard's. He should have been identified as part of the Zip's so-called product development team, because it was his product. I encouraged him when I should have been more honest. In truth, I never thought it was a good idea, but Howard was proud of the concept, which he dreamed up after eighteen holes on the Yale golf course with his high school friend Morty Rubin, whose family has run Rubin & Sons Memorial Chapel on George Street for fifty years. It has always struck me as peculiar that someone in Sidney Rubin's line of work would name his son Morton. Morty the mortician thought Bereavemints was a great idea.

Howard came home from his afternoon with Morty brimming with enthusiasm, and I didn't have the heart to tell him what I really thought, which was that this product was not only questionable in concept, but was also neither a good match for the Zip's Candies image nor for our production lines. I was walking on eggshells with Howard by then, and I didn't want to discourage him if something made him happy, even if it meant biting my tongue at moments.

I had counted on Frieda to throw cold water on the idea, but I had underestimated the blinding effect of a Jewish mother's obsessive love for her wunderkind, and though she was a canny businesswoman with a good nose for the candy business, Frieda was impervious to any possible flaws in a new piece that originated with her precious Howdy.

It was 2001, and Sam had been gone for two years. In his lifetime, no problematic product like the Bereavemint could ever have been deemed of sufficient quality or potential value to carry the Zip's Candies name and signature green umbrella on the wrapper. Few people realize that Eli made notes for a fourth line that was never put into production, a wafery, layered buttercookie center enrobed in vanilla icing that he called PanKakes, which was consistent with the *Little Black Sambo* inspiration for each of our lines. Why? "When Black Mumbo saw the melted butter, wasn't she pleased! 'Now,' said she, 'we'll all have pancakes for supper!'"

Bereavemints had no such continuity with our existing lines or potential for brand association. I repeat: it wasn't a good fit at all for Zip's. I would have much rather pursued development of those PanKakes. But Sam was dead and mine would have been the lone voice of dissent while everyone else was so enthusiastic. In retrospect, it isn't clear to me that even if I had made my misgivings known, that Howard would have been willing to slam the brakes on this runaway disaster, in part because the small test batches were fine. It was the one and only production batch that was catastrophic.

Zip's Bereavemints, small, gray, rectangular, molded, spiced peppermints in somber black waxed wrappers printed with discreet green umbrellas, were not envisioned as a retail product in their first production phase, but instead were meant for distribution chiefly to funeral homes, support groups, grief counselors, and religious organizations. The concept was sound enough—something to freshen the breath of funereal personnel and the bereaved alike; it is a regrettable fact that sorrow and halitosis often go together, what with all the coffee drinking, crying, inattention to personal hygiene during the stressful experience, and the ceaseless consumption of funereal carbohydrates.

It was a good idea, in concept, maybe, for some other company, one already running a line of cough lozenges, for example. Perhaps it was even a brilliant idea for a niche product for the right brand, one with a more herbal-supplement sort of profile, but it wasn't for us. I have an intense aversion to the flavor of cloves, which admittedly may have clouded my judgment about the viability of the product in the market, but that has absolutely nothing to do with what happened.

We had to do most of the blending and pouring by hand, using certain processing elements on the Mumbo Jumbo line. That's where we lost quality control. I was specifically concerned that I could not be a good judge of the flavor adjustments, and I had made my limitations known to Howard. He said it didn't matter, but in retrospect I should have insisted that someone else have ultimate responsibility for sampling the test batches more frequently.

Owing to a terrible and significant last-minute miscalculation during production (we used a basic sugar and corn syrup hard-candy recipe, with cinnamon, clove oil, and peppermint extract), the proportion of cinnamon, clove oil, and peppermint extract in that first test batch of Bereavemints was terribly, horribly concentrated. I don't know how it happened. I had tasted a sample of the batch at an earlier stage of the blending and had not thought it necessary to do so again. I know that two employees have stated they saw me taste the batch again just before the pour, and I may have given that impression, but I am certain that I did not actually taste the batch again.

We wrapped the mints by hand and boxed them by hand, and then we stickered the boxes by hand with a simple and tasteful black-and-white label set in Castine, the font often used on traditional headstones. I employed Julie and her friend Wendy to come to Zip's one afternoon right after school and spend a few hours with green Sharpies, drawing a simple umbrella on the lid of each box. The Zip's green umbrella, though originally inspired by Little Black Sambo's green umbrella, has long been an integral part of our brand identity.

We distributed these inaugural boxes of Zip's Bereavemints gratis to some forty funeral homes throughout Connecticut. Within ten days, Bereavemints had caused twenty-three episodes of choking or bronchial spasm, two of them severe graveside allergic reactions.

The consequent cascade of lawsuits was inevitable, given how disruptive the Bereavemints reactions had been to any number of funerals and memorial services. Death and the rituals surrounding death are occasions when people are already very sensitive. Therefore, as so many documents from so many different law firms throughout the state suggested, if injured grievously by an improperly manufactured hard candy at such a fragile time, they are especially susceptible to trauma, which can lead to anxiety, sleeplessness, loss of gainful livelihood, diminished capacity for enjoyment of life, and poor self-esteem.

All the settlement agreements (the file, which was incomplete, owing both to the pandemonium surrounding this time period and to Howard's habitual slapdash approach to paperwork, showed fourteen different agreements, but I believe there were closer to twenty) cost Zip's Candies something like half a million dollars. Rubin & Sons was among the litigants with whom Zip's settled.

Never again, declared Frieda, blaming me for the miscalculation with the clove and peppermint formulation, although it was never determined where the error occurred in the mixing of the overconcentrated production batch. Frieda then became weirdly triumphant about this disaster, conveniently forgetting that her precious bumblebee Howdy had anything to do with it, because it offered concrete proof that she was right and I was wrong about the risks of Zip's Candies venturing one inch beyond the familiar territory of Eli's original Little Sammies, Tigermelts, and Mumbo Jumbos.

Howard let her dictate company policy on this. Not only would Zip's never again venture into new product development, but also Zip's would never even consider any brand extensions within the lines. None whatsoever. We had been burned. We had learned our lesson. That was that. No more risk-taking. I should never have repeated to Howard one of his father's favorite remarks about business practice, "It's easier to stay out of trouble than to get out of trouble."

The way Howard wouldn't listen to reason on this subject (meaning he wouldn't listen to me and instead chose to honor his mother's arbitrary edict) created a paralysis that no ordinary board of directors of a small business would tolerate in any corporate plan; shareholders would be indignant. But Zip's has never had any checks and balances. This de facto zero-growth policy remained in place for the rest of Frieda's life, even at the point when she was no longer able to remember her own opinions or understand very much of what was going on around her, and if foot-long, tutti-frutti Tigermelts had been coming off the line it would have been fine with her. But even after her death, Howard continued to coast with this lazy approach, right up to the day he left for Madagascar.

Howard grew bored with Zip's over the past few years, and this restriction has suited his indifferent management style. I cannot emphasize enough just how severely damaging this artificial limitation has been on Zip's Candies' ability to innovate and expand in natural ways. And I am not just making this observation because I am angry and hurt that in this same time period it became more and more obvious that Howard also lost interest in me.

I don't mean that we need to develop entirely new products willy-nilly. Completely new products can be hideously costly for many reasons, especially if they are pieces that cannot be made with simple adaptation on our existing lines, the way Index and Detox, our contract energy bars, are run on the Tigermelt line ten days of the month with minimal retooling. (They are so similar in formulation to each other, there is little adjustment downtime needed between the two runs, which is very efficient for us. The Detox bar has ground flaxseeds and dried blueberries in the base, while the Index bar has acai and goji berries, but their proprietary ten-gram-protein base is identical.)

I am not, despite the insulting language in Irene's ridiculously long-winded and crazy affidavit, trying to run the company into a ditch, and I am not, despite her allegations, proposing the development of any entirely new lines that are not extensions of existing lines. Painful as it is to admit, I do concede that a while ago I was motivated to experiment with brand extensions partly in the hope that a brilliant and successful development might reengage Howard in the business of Zip's Candies. Maybe Howard would have come back to me if Dark Mint Tigermelt Fun Bites had gone into production and had really taken off; who can say? I'll never know.

Zip's Candies has neglected some very obvious brand extension opportunities for decades. Even with stagnating sales—especially with stagnating sales!—we are overdue for some growth in those areas. For example, because the consumer continues to be extremely willing to increase purchases when he sees a familiar piece in a new flavor, I predict that the best growth in nonchocolate and gummy candies will continue to be in the tropical flavor category. This is why we should be making Tropical Mumbo Jumbos (which we could also call Hawaiian Mumbo Jumbos; we would have to pick whichever one tested more positively), in flavors like pomegranate, pineapple, coconut, and mango. We wouldn't have to change anything on the line other than the flavoring and the coloring in the blend to make limited-edition Tropical Mumbo Jumbos, for example, in two different combinations of those four flavors, thereby retaining the familiar two-color, two-flavor pack that consumers know so well in the Mumbo Jumbos. We could do new label graphics like our present design but in tropical colors, with palm trees. Frankly, I can't see how we could fail if we tested Tropical Mumbo Jumbos in movie boxes.

Limited editions are a good way to test a market, because their limitedness makes people rush to buy them before they disappear, and at the same time, if the product is really successful, there is room to keep it going, or at least to bring it back seasonally if that's appropriate. There are so many possibilities for limited editions, too; a Dark Tigermelt, which would be a dark chocolate–coated Tigermelt with a milk-chocolate stripe, for example. Or a White Tigermelt, which would be, obviously, a white chocolate–coated Tigermelt with a dark-chocolate stripe. It would be ridiculously easy to produce Mint Tigermelts, or Almond Tigermelts, or Crispy Tigermelts, with sugar wafers or crisped rice in the mix (either will reduce calories); that's another potential growth area we are neglecting at our peril: the reduced calorie, "light" version of the familiar piece—which can be anything from one-hundred-calorie stick versions with the same formulation to going a half step away from the original piece while developing a related yet distinct new product, like, for example, Annabelle's Skinny Hunk extension from their Big Hunk.

Another option for a Zip's brand extension, though it would be an expensive undertaking (because even with the same ingredients and basic formulation, all the equipment would have to be changed over, as would the wrapping and packaging), would be to introduce different sizes of our existing lines. Historically, Zip's Candies has never had any interest in making Halloween snack sizes. Sam believed that selling snack sizes (or bite sizes, fun sizes, minis, to name some of the common terms) would only be undercutting our own business, offering our customers a chance to go smaller instead of bigger.

Perhaps that was once true, and there is certainly value in driving consumers away from total dependence on Halloween miniatures, or Mars wouldn't have developed their 2008 Halloween campaign featuring the brilliantly manipulative slogan "Really cool moms give full-size bars!" But actually, size change-up attracts consumers, with increased sales of classic pieces when they are offered both smaller and bigger than the original piece. I heard from someone who knows someone who works at Mars that their studies show that when they first tested their bite-size

Snickers, people ended up eating one and a half bars' worth, a bite at a time, even though their written responses immediately after the sampling estimated that they had eaten less than half a bar!

You would think that with all my ambition for change and innovation at Zip's, I might have considered experimenting on some brand extension with myself, changing my hairstyle, for example, or having my colors done, as Marie Smith, one of our bookkeepers, did a few years ago (as a consequence, having discovered she was a Summer, all Marie ever wore after that were outfits in pastel blue, pink, lavender, and red, and what's more her nail polish always matched those outfits). Perhaps I should have done something like that to try to keep Howard. If I had a close friend, maybe this is the sort of thing she would have advised me to do. But I don't have anyone in my life to advise me about things such as this, and I am just not the sort of woman who would make desperate changes to my appearance in an undignified attempt to keep my husband. If that's all it would have taken to save my marriage, what kind of man would Howard have been all along? I didn't want to risk finding out.

In any case, the changes I wanted to make were at Zip's Candies, and I know I am right about this. In this era of chronic dieting and a kind of pseudo health consciousness, people who wouldn't dream of buying a couple of full-size candy bars are willing to take home a bag of minis and work their way through the equivalent of four bars instead. And the truth is, the snack size, fun bite, healthy mini, whatever we would call them, has a bigger markup, piece for piece, ounce for ounce. Tigerbites! Baby Sammies! Mini Mumbo Jumbos! And at the same time, because America loves a bargain and people are willing to consume buckets of coffee and soda when they are offered the chance for a few pennies more than the reasonable-size option, we should be producing larger versions of each of our lines as well. Tiger Kings! Big Sammies! Mega Mumbo Jumbos! Zip's has absolutely got to do this, go small and big. That's where the money is.

The huge growth area in recent years, as we know, is in premium chocolate. Contrary to Irene's insistence that we should be producing an organic, fair trade premium bar, there is no way we can or should extend our brands in that direction. Zip's Candies doesn't make gourmet premium chocolate products. We know who we are. Our customers expect a certain kind of candy from Zip's. I believe it is a mistake to stray too far from our brand identity.

I don't understand why Mars wants to dilute the M&M's line to the extent that they have with those iridescent Premiums. (Which are delicious.) Why not expand the Dove line this way instead? There have been numerous successful M&M's brand extensions, from Almond, to Dark, to Minis, to some innovative limited editions like Mint Crisp and Wildly Cherry. In both cases, the limited-edition product was a great match for the brand for several reasons, one being the logical and pleasing color coordination. But the new M&M's Premiums taste like a Dove product and lack the classic M&M's shell. This, to me, is confusing, and challenges the very definition and identity of M&M's. Why do it?

It is possible to go too far with brand extensions, no question. I am by nature cautious, and I would propose an extension only with much thought and planning. There are some really pointless extensions out there, cautionary exemplars of what not to do, like the Milky Way 2 To Go, which is a king-size Milky Way simple divided into two pieces, making it, what, more portable? So it can be eaten "on the go" without the usual elaborate preparations and accoutrements ordinarily required for the consumption of an unwieldy ordinary one-piece Milky Way? Maybe there is a calculation here that I am underestimating, that people will buy and eat more candy if they tell themselves they deserve it because they are always "on the go," as if the reward for the virtue of busyness is this 460-calorie bar divided into two convenient pieces. Zip's Candies would never insult our customers that way.

But there are numerous good examples for us to consider, from the Sour Apple Abba-Zaba, the Abba-Zaba Chocolate Cream, and Abba-Zaba Mini Morsels, important extensions to consider when you think about how iconic and unchanged that piece has been for decades, to the exceptionally appealing White Kit Kat. (Kit Kat is a bar with spectacular success, especially in the UK, where forty-seven Kit Kats are consumed every second, if you can trust Nestlé Rowntree's statistic.)

And let us pause a moment to admire the outstanding Twix Java, one of the most successful brand extensions I have ever tasted. When will Mars bring that fabulous bar back? How could they be willing to go so far down the wrong road with M&M's, yet throw away the huge success of this Twix extension? In the three months it was on store shelves, more Twix Java bars were probably sold than the total number of pieces we sell in a year, all three lines combined. We live on that, but it's just crumbs off the table for Mars.

ZIP'S IS TOO small to have marketing research, or even marketing. We have no product development like Mars, no matter what the documentation concerning the Bereavemints episode might suggest. The big three have test kitchens ten times the size of our entire operation. We employ forty-seven souls when we're at full throttle. The big three will always have us outranked and outflanked and outspent, they will always command the best shelf real estate, with their endless capacity to pay hideous slot-ting fees, and they will always outsell us eight ways, with presell deals that really move the merch.

And yet, companies like Mars and Hershey's don't have all the answers. They make mistakes. And we have the advantage, in our smallness, or we should, that we can follow our hearts, we can turn on a dime, and we aren't at the mercy of the vast machinery of a marketing department. I know this sounds immodest, but after all these years at Zip's, I have perfect pitch for the candy business. I can go to a supermarket candy aisle and talk to people about their choices, and with my expertise and experience I can come away from an encounter like that with a useful impression of consumer thinking equal to a six-figure marketing report.

I mentioned the Abba-Zaba, a curious candy, not a personal favorite of mine, but perhaps if I had grown up on the West Coast, I would feel differently. Though maybe not, as I am really not a taffy aficionado at all, and unlike many in my cohort, I harbor no fond yearnings for Bonomo Turkish Taffy or Bit-O-Honey either. When I was six I lost one of my baby incisors in a Sugar Daddy, in the darkness of a movie theater, where I had been taken to see *Mary Poppins*. I will always associate that supremely irritating song about how a spoonful of sugar helps the medicine go down with the shocking sensation of that sudden, bloody void in my mouth.

Abba-Zaba is a strange piece, with a thin peanut-butter core surrounded by unusually chewy taffy, with a dedicated follow-ing; it's one of those candies people either love or hate. While today it is made by the Annabelle Candy Company, Abba-Zaba was first produced by the Cardinet Candy Company around the same time Eli was starting Zip's Candies. Cardinet also pro-duced the U-NO; Annabelle bought them in 1978 and now produces both, along with their flagship bar, Rocky Road, and their Big Hunk and Look! lines, acquired in 1972 when they bought Golden Nugget.

Abba-Zaba shares more than vintage with Little Sammies. It also had a problematic icon. The original wrapper featured a savage-looking, almost simian jungle baby with a bone through the topknot in his hair, in silhouette, hanging from a vine. The Abba-Zaba jungle baby has vanished from the official story. According to Julie, who looked into this for me, a couple of candy blogs mention this and report that the company will only say that the design of their Abba-Zaba wrapper hasn't changed since they started making Abba-Zabas. Which is perfectly true.

I like the spirit of the Annabelle Candy Company, which was founded by Sam Altshuler, who came to America in 1917 from Russia, and was next headed for years by his daughter, the eponymous Annabelle. It is now run by his granddaughter Susan Karl, an energetic former prosecutor who took over running the business from her brother a few years ago (she's something of a role model for me). I have wanted to raise the delicate subject of the original Abba-Zaba wrapper when we meet at conventions, but I haven't yet found the right moment.

It seems likely to me that the name of the candy itself, when Cardinet started selling it, was probably somebody's idea of made-up African lingo. Possibly it was the Abba-Zaba baby's own utterance in the early brand concept. But that's just a guess. Perhaps the creator of this image was influenced by Kipling's *Jungle Book,* or by the popularity of Josephine Baker's Cuban- and African-inflected repertoire of jungle songs and dances, some of which were rendered with scat syllables.

Which is not to say that America invented this particular sort of casual racism. The French embraced Josephine Baker, and they still exhibit an unabashed nostalgia for their colonialist relationship to Africa. Jean de Brunhoff's *The Travels of Babar*, published in 1932, featured some wild cannibals dwelling on a remote island who resemble the Abba-Zaba creature. On French supermarket shelves today, there are all sorts of food labels featuring black Africans, including the Y'a Bon Banania man, a grinning Senegalese soldier who has been featured on the label of the Banania chocolate and banana breakfast drink in various versions since 1915. ("*Y'a bon*" is meant to represent his pidgin French for "It's good.")

From Rastus on the Cream of Wheat label to Uncle Ben (Uncle Ben's rice is owned by Masterfood, which is to say, Mars) to Aunt Jemima (who has been around since 1890, and who bears an uncanny resemblance to Helen Bannerman's 1899 illustration of Little Black Sambo's mother, Black Mumbo), there is something in our white American culture that has long made us want to associate plain, comforting foods with the suggestion that they are being provided to us by jovial black people. Let's not forget the Oompa-Loompas, who love their work so much. (Question: Why weren't there any dark-skinned winners of Willy Wonka's golden tickets?) Privileged Caucasians seem to have an abiding fantasy that the dark-skinned people who prepare and serve our food to us are actually quite fond of us and love feeding us.

I can offer no excuses for our own Little Sammies, which had been in production at Zip's Candies for more than fifty years before I arrived. It is beyond question that by the mid-1960s, if Little Sammies hadn't already been established as a successful brand, there is no chance they could have possibly seemed like a good idea to anyone.

Is *Little Black Sambo* truly racist? I could argue for its being naive rather than truly racist. Sambo is an adventurous child who survives his encounter with the vain and rapacious tigers who compete with one another for grandeur in their bits of clothing stolen from Little Black Sambo. His doting parents, who have provided him with his colorful outfit (the entire family dresses in a stereotypically riotous mix of colors and patterns), also feed him lovingly, while taking smaller helpings for themselves. Black Jumbo brings home the pot of melted butter made from those whirling tigers, which is poured over the "huge big plate of most lovely pancakes" Black Mumbo prepares for the family. So they are industrious, and are certainly not clichéd lazy Negroes. The story, which has the timelessness and simplicity of a fable from start to finish, concludes with the three of them sitting down to supper. "And Black Mumbo ate Twenty-seven pancakes, and Black Jumbo ate Fifty-five but Little Black Sambo ate a Hundred and Sixty-nine, because he was so hungry."

Helen Bannerman, a devout member of the Free Church of Scotland who lived most of her life in India and believed that blacks and whites would meet in heaven, probably didn't think that people with black skin were intrinsically inferior to people with white skin so much as she held them in her imperial British gaze as less fortunate Others. Eli the immigrant (whom she also presumably would have regarded as an exotic, less fortunate Other), eager to get ahead in his new American life, read her little book over and over as the train carried him from New York City to New Haven, finding in those pages his inspiration to make sugary treats based on what he thought was a simple American folktale. He didn't understand what he was looking at any more than Helen Bannerman did with her white dissecting gaze that sliced and fixed the specimens under that confident and superior microscope. Yet each of them in their misguided way made something beloved and enduring.

❋ ❋

BEFORE I GO into detail about what happened with Little Susies, let me explain a few more things about brand extensions. One of the brand extension areas that has been quite successful for a lot of established lines is a white-chocolate version, from White Chocolate Kit Kats and White Chocolate Twix bars to Reese's White Chocolate peanut butter cups. I have always been ambivalent about white chocolate. It is so often really terrible and cheap, very sugary and often gritty or chalky, with a predominant lingering flat note, that harsh telltale artificial metallic vanillin aftertaste. It isn't "real" chocolate. That's what so many people say, which is correct, though in true white chocolate there is substantial cocoa butter, and it is the cocoa liquor (this is the paradoxical term for the crushed and ground chocolate mass) that is missing. Unless it has been adulterated with vegetable fat swapped for the cocoa butter (which is actually a common practice, and makes for what is technically candy, not chocolate), true chocolate has a melt temperature that is almost the same as our body temperature. This, I believe, is one of the reasons we love chocolate so much—it loves us back. It melts from the heat of our tongue. Of course it's sexy.

I have tasted my share of white chocolate over the years, but since I have mostly been unimpressed or disappointed, in recent times I have chosen to avoid it. As I have gotten older, I have learned from experience and I have a greater willingness to offend rather than suffer. Like dubious hollandaise sauce that's been sitting for hours on a brunch buffet, or any item on any menu that begins with the three words *twin baked stuffed,* white chocolate is usually just something you're probably better off not putting in your mouth.

But then at last year's All Candy Expo in Chicago, I had an epiphany. I was taking a break from our booth, wandering the aisles, sampling a little more than I had intended to (it's pretty hard to resist nibbling, even for those of us who work in candy factories; you become immune to your own lines, but that doesn't mean you don't succumb to all kinds of candy outside your own product range).

My weakness is always the gummy aisle, and I would do well to avoid it altogether at trade shows. It's true that Mumbo Jumbos are technically gummy, but I hardly ever eat them, and I have to admit that for years I have preferred the aroma that comes off the mixtures as they are being molded to the experience of putting a Mumbo Jumbo in my mouth. The vast Haribo space was especially alluring, and I lingered there awhile, admiring the jewel-like mounds of Gummi everything; I admit to an intense relationship with their red and black nonpareil raspberries.

I spent some quality time at the Goelitz candy corn display. Fresh candy corn is such a different experience from stale candy corn. While I wasn't tempted by Farley's & Sathers's Jujyfruits, Now And Laters, or Jolly Ranchers, I did have a few Lemonheads at the Ferrara Pan space before going for a visit with my good friends at Just Born, who make Mike and Ike and Teenee Beanees as well as Peeps.

I had worked my way through a lot more sugary sampling than is a good idea, and I suddenly realized I was feeling lightheaded and jittery. I suppose I should have been carrying an Index bar, but since our contract work is confidential, I wouldn't ever want to be seen in public with an Index bar or a Detox bar in my hand. It would be too risky, especially at a candy show, where people could put two and two together. I suppose it is widely known in candy circles who makes what for whom, but that is still a confidential agreement, and I am an honorable person who means to respect not only the letter of the law, but also the spirit of the law.

I knew my sugar rush would be followed by a crash, and I was feeling worse by the minute, so I headed to the meat snack area, where I usually never bother to set foot throughout the three days of All Candy. I helped myself to some venison jerky, which saved me. When a candy show includes other snacks (like nuts, chips, dried fruit, cookies, and meat snacks), the meat snack and chip areas are always a strange departure from the festive, carnival aesthetic of the rest of the show. In meat snacks, most of the vendors are men. And a lot of them are burly lumberjack types dressed like Paul Bunyan, which makes sense, since a candy and snack show is our one point of intersection, and the rest of their trade-show calendar consists of gun shows, boat shows, and camping and hunting shows.

Having reached the end of the fortuitous meat snack aisle, I cut across the chips and nuts area and was on my way back toward the Zip's Candies booth when I stopped at the Green & Black's booth to see what they had going on. There I talked with the guy who designs their bars, whose cards say "Head of Taste," which is a cute term for product development manager. I admire the way Cadbury has strategized this brand since they bought it in 2005, letting it be independent and focused on quality, in much the same way Hershey's has managed Scharffen Berger and Dagoba since it made those acquisitions in 2004 and 2006. (Most casual consumers have no idea that these three companies are no longer the artisanal start-ups they once were, which is no accident.)

The Green & Black's guy was passionate and persuasive about his products. He had samples attractively laid out, and he was cutting up bars as he talked to a couple of buyers and a journalist about how the company sources the entirely organic ingredients and how they balance the cocoa mass and the cocoa butter for best mouthfeel. Since I was standing there with them, it would have been rude for me to refuse the proffered samples, so I nibbled on each as we discussed their lines, planning a return to meat snacks for some teriyaki turkey jerky I had espied, to balance this latest sugar infusion.

Then we got to their white chocolate. He spoke of the clean and fragrant taste of the Madagascar vanilla they use exclusively. I said, No thanks, I don't like white chocolate, and he laughed at me, holding out a small square on the tip of his knife, which I took. I put it in my mouth. Ecstasy! Revelation! Incredible mouthfeel! Creamy vanilla pleasure flooded through me. The intense chocolateness of this ambrosial substance was hidden in plain sight. He laughed at me again, holding out another square on the tip of his knife.

EVEN THOUGH ZIP's Candies takes one of the smallest possible spaces at the expo, the expenses for us to show our three little candy lines at this annual event are horrendous, more than twenty thousand dollars, and so we usually bring along only a couple of employees, and we like to have a strong family presence in the booth. I notice that other family-owned candy companies do too, and sometimes you talk to a third- or fourth-generation family member who is attending law school or who lives across the country from the family business and isn't involved in the day-to-day operations at all but who shows up at times like this. It's good for the company image.

I had never done Chicago without Howard before, and even though I was of course very angry that he had left me and gone to Madagascar to live his authentic life, I missed him incessantly for those three days of the show. It was so different, being there without him. I had a hard time smiling and giving vague answers when people asked for him. Everyone expected to see that nice guy Howdy Ziplinsky at the Zip's Candies booth the way they always had. Howard loved this show. It's a schmooze-fest, and that's the part of the business at which he excelled. I had never appreciated how good for business it probably was that Howard had an uncanny ability to remember every name and every face (a skill he honed at Yale fulfilling his pledge require-ments at DKE, when he memorized the names of every frat brother).

It was even harder to carry on imperviously when people we've known for years at these shows—lots of buyers, but also some of the perennials from our tribe, the other small, family-owned candy companies (like the Sifers family, who make those quirky Valomilks in Kansas; or the Sioux City–based Palmers, who make Twin Bings (and even *they* have ventured into an extension with King Bings), or the Wagers, who make the Idaho Spud Bar, the Old Faithful Bar, and the Cherry Cocktail Bar)—didn't ask for Howard, because they had heard through the grapevine that he had left me. I am sure there was a buzz of speculation about the future of Zip's Candies as well. But isn't this always the question for every small family-owned candy business in its third or fourth generation, how long they will hold out before selling?

In 2003, when we were in Chicago and everyone was talking about Just Born having bought the fourth-generation Golden-berg Candy Company (makers of Peanut Chews in Philadelphia since 1890), I overheard Howard telling a buyer that he was hop-ing that one of these days Just Born or Annabelle would make him an offer he couldn't refuse. I didn't say anything until the show was over and we were at O'Hare and checked in for our flight to Hartford. When I finally confronted Howard about what I had heard him say, we had a fight, right there in the boarding area. Our seats were in different rows on the flight home; Howard had assured me he had booked our seats together, but he neglected to follow through on that, and neither of us attempted to swap with other passengers in order to sit together.

AFTER MY WHITE-CHOCOLATE epiphany in the Green & Black's booth, I asked Julie to scout out some other white-chocolate samples from around the show, and back at our hotel that first night, we spread them on a clean towel on the bedspread and sampled our way through them. You know these brands, all the usual suspects. Most of them were terrible. A few were barely acceptable. Nothing was good. I took out the Green & Black's white-chocolate bar I had helped myself to after that transcendent taste; we swigged some water to clear our palates, and then we each took a bite. What a significant contrast to everything we had just tasted. It was rich and creamy, and the vanilla was powerfully fragrant. It was the combination of the high-quality vanilla from Madagascar and the very pure cocoa butter from their high-quality organic Trinitario cacao beans, which are from Belize or the Dominican Republic.

"We could do this," Julie said, licking some crumbs off the wrapper. Between us we had devoured the entire hundred-gram bar. I asked her what she was thinking. "Couldn't we do something with white chocolate, like White Tigermelts?" Perhaps this was it, a white-chocolate product extension as the optimal first step for Zip's. We could do something with Little Sammies or Tigermelts and high-quality white chocolate, without losing our identity, without getting too fancy. I looked at the array of undistinguished white-chocolate brand extensions strewn on the towel, each one missing a sampled corner. They were each bitter, chalky, or harsh, with that chemical telltale aftertaste of vanillin, the cheap and artificial vanilla substitute that Zip's Candies has never used and never will. (Most months now we go through three fifty-gallon drums of Czaplinsky's Pure Madagascar Vanilla, which has always been an ingredient in both Tigermelts and Little Sammies, and is now a significant flavoring in our Bao-Bar as well.) In contrast to the creamy luxe taste and mouthfeel of the Green & Black's white bar, there was no comparison. This is how you figure out what not to do, sampling this way.

It was nice to have Julie at the show that year especially, and it was a rare moment for the two of us to share a hotel room and spend some time alone, since Julie and Kelly are very rarely apart. That was the same trip when Julie suggested to me that I should consider becoming a situational lesbian because I would have more options for finding a new partner after the divorce. I didn't and don't see it, but in a curious way her thinking about me this way was flattering, like an invitation to join an exclusive guild.

That night I had one of my Zip's dreams, as I often do when I am just falling asleep or am on the verge of waking up. I think there is something about the endless repetitive movements and sounds of the factory that penetrates my unconscious mind and manifests as complex and fantastical machinery that is often out of control, with switches I cannot reach, and dials and indicators I cannot read. There are weirdly intricate and clearly sexual images of things with apertures closing to slits and opening to quivering gaping orifices, and there are often strange cylindrical objects being thrust into slots and receptacles, over and over and over, with an urgent mechanical insistence; often, too, there are disturbing mucilaginous substances being extruded in menacing coils, or oozing out of or into places they shouldn't. Sometimes I don't recognize the viscid matter at all, but other times Little

Sammies are piling up uncontrollably, or enormous Mumbo Jumbos are rolling toward me like runaway wagon wheels. I start awake from these dreams tasting a faint note of chocolate, cherry, and anise in the back of my throat. Dr. Gibraltar once told me that my dreams like this are probably not really dreams, but are more likely hypnagogic or hypnopompic hallucinations. Whatever—they're vivid and exhausting. Mornings after those nights, I feel as if I've worked an overnight shift.

This was a Little Sammies dream, but the Little Sammies were white.

IT WASN'T VERY difficult to make Little Susies. The most challenging element was creating a new mold that had a little less volume than the Little Sammies, but was clearly a girl in a dress, with more feminine features. The figures are pretty blobby anyway, so the details of the head didn't matter as much as the shape of the body. The Halloween crisis of 1981 had taught me how to hand-dip Little Sammies, even though in the end that got us nowhere close to an approximation of the panned hard, shiny shell. But Little Susie, as I conceived of the product, our first brand extension, wouldn't be panned at all. Even if we could match the shell coating, it wouldn't have enough thickness to give a real white-chocolate flavor, and I didn't want just an appearance of white chocolate, I really wanted that flavor to come through. Little Susies would be dipped in white chocolate.

The slightly smaller interior core of the same fudgy mixture as the Little Sammies (the core ingredients for Little Sammies are sugar, corn syrup, molasses, partially hydrogenated soybean oil, condensed skim milk, cocoa solids, whey, soy lecithin, salt, and vanilla) would allow the finished piece to match the Little Sammies and fit in the packaging, because the balance of the thickness would be added with the pure white-chocolate enrobing.

Little Susies would offer a pleasing contrast to Little Sammies. Little Sammies are boys. They're shiny; they're fudgy. Little Susies would be girls, with creamy smooth white chocolate on the outside, but with the familiar Little Sammies recipe core. How could this not be a winner? It was innovative, but still familiar. I wished Howard could be a part of this, sharing with me the birth of Zip's Candies' new baby. If only I had thought of Little Susies sooner. I believe it would have been a bond between us.

I WORKED FOR the next couple of months with Jacob and two of my most loyal and experienced employees, Petey Leventhal and Sally Fernstein, developing the Little Susies slowly and carefully, troubleshooting batch by batch. We figured it out, and began our laborious production in earnest. In the last hour of each Little Sammies shift, we made cores for Little Susies, and then the four of us would do the white-chocolate enrobing dip, sixty at a time.

In this way we began to build some prototype stock in order to have samples for CandyCon at Javits, in September. It's the other big show we do, every fall. It's a little smaller than All Candy, but it's a bigger show for us—we take a bigger space and have more people on the floor, because we can truck everything down from New Haven instead of airfreighting our stock and worrying about Tigermelts melting and resolidifying out of temper along the way, and we don't have to rent as much furnishings for the booth, either.

It was now August. We hit our stride and were able to produce a consistent product, batch to batch. My plan had been to sample Little Susies at the Con and get enough orders to pay for a proper line setup, and to develop a design and print the new labels we would need. I had a vision of something that would mirror the Little Sammies wrapper, but in contrasting colors and with the words *white chocolate* on the green umbrella. Once they were in production, I could see running the Little Susies on the Little Sammies line every third or fourth day, and then, who knows, if sales were significant and sustained after the true roll-out, we would consider a dedicated line.

The white chocolate cost Zip's—well, a lot. More than I want to say right now. If there is going to be a forensic account-ant reviewing our books anyway, fine; let him hunt for that information if it's so important to Irene. It was a reasonable deci-sion. In the press of those hectic weeks, I made the choice to triage our energies and go with a sure thing, knowing that at a later stage we would have to develop our own white-chocolate enrobing recipe. We used Green & Black's white chocolate for our Little Susies prototypes. It tempered beautifully. Well-tempered chocolate is glossy, breaks with a clean, crisp snap, and has a molten mouthfeel. Badly tempered chocolate feels gritty and crumbly in your mouth. It is the taste of failure, disappoint-ment, and broken promises.

The Little Susies were perfect, if I do say so. It was a great combination, the soft fudgy core, identical to Little Sammies except, going for a contrast with Little Sammies, and also fol-lowing Sam's advice, with a slightly saltier formulation, which played beautifully off the nicely tempered white chocolate. The proportion was very good. Little Susies were a great innovation. Fantastic mouthfeel, tremendously appealing in alternating bites with Little Sammies. A brilliant product extension. This is undeniable.

❋ ❋

WE HIT A snag when we realized that we really didn't know how to put Little Susies in the hands of buyers at CandyCon in an advantageous way. They didn't look good enough to display on plates or in bowls—Little Sammies would also look like nothing much if displayed that way. The packaging is important. Who would want naked Idaho Spud Bars? Unwrapped, they look . . . well, I don't want to say how they look; it would be disrespectful. (Unwrap one yourself, if you're curious.) Anyway, if you think about it, out of the wrapper, all the bestselling bars are just five indistinguishable inches of lumpy brownness. Once the buyers walked away from the booth with some unwrapped Little Susies, what would they have? A one-page handout and some pathetic bare samples in a plastic bag? We would have to do better than that. We needed to launch Little Susies decisively.

In any case, although I had envisaged Little Susies being packaged three to a pack, just like Little Sammies, I was reluctant to give our precious handmade prototypes away three at a time, which is what we would have to do if they were packaged in a standard pack. What had we gotten ourselves into? We had already invested an insane amount of hand labor at each stage of production along the line in order to create a finished product that could pass as a manufactured candy already in production. Even if we had enough stock, we had a wrapping problem. I couldn't just put Little Susies into Little Sammies wrappers, and we didn't have a Little Susies wrapper. We weren't prepared. We had to think fast. The Con was now ten days away.

Jacob and I were dipping what would have to be the last batch of Little Susies on our own, and the third shift was leaving. We worked together without speaking, and then he said quietly, as we moved a completed tray of sixty Little Susies to the drying rack, "I have an idea." He cocked his head for me to follow him, and after the tray was locked in place, I did. He led me to a worktable where he had laid out a row of some thirty alternating Little Sammies and Little Susies. Jacob explained that he had just been fooling around at first, but now he wondered if this might be the answer. We could package Little Susies in with Little Sammies in specially marked packs as a promotional gimmick at the CandyCon.

Of course! It was perfect. I loved the way they looked lined up that way. Together, he and I created another row, and another, in reverse alternation so as to form a checkerboard pattern of Little Sammies and Little Susies. It was striking, and it would be perfect for our Little Susies display strategy in the Zip's booth at CandyCon. Jacob took a Little Sammies cardboard sleeve and placed two little Sammies on either side of a Little Susie. The three fit perfectly together. We could run these through the usual wrapping machine, and then get some rush-printed "Little Susies" stickers that we could slap onto those Little Sammies packs to distinguish them from the regular stock. The stickers would have the added ingredients of the white-chocolate enrobing in agate type running around the "Little Susies" lettering. We certainly weren't going to identify the source of the white chocolate, so we decided simply to list the ingredients (cane sugar, cocoa butter, milk powder, soy lecithin, vanilla extract), omitting the organic designation, since there is nothing organic about our products ordinarily, and that term, while true for the time being about the enrobing, wasn't our kind of word. So that's what we did.

WE DROVE DOWN to the show in a convoy of Zip's Candies trucks and vans, with our usual show stock and twenty boxes of the specially stickered Little Sammies/Little Susies packs, forty-eight to each box. We had almost a thousand Little Susie giveaway packs, and we had about fifty more Little Susies to display in a glass countertop flat case, which Jacob would set up with that striking checkerboard arrangement of Little Sammies and Little Susies.

Julie brought Kelly along, with a Zip's employee badge for her, which was slightly awkward because she was overwhelmed by all the candy and wasn't as helpful with our setting up as she could have been. Most people go into a Stendhal candy swoon the first time they attend a big trade show. It's understandable, but we needed all hands on deck, and I was annoyed that Julie didn't even try to reel her in, but seemed charmed every time Kelly staggered back into the booth with more booty from around the floor, giddy as a child having an ultra Halloween experience. I felt myself being quite irritated with the two of them giggling together and littering our booth with wrappers of other candy brands, which I kept picking up with exaggerated efficiency, but they were too entranced with each other to take my irritable tidying as personally as they should have. Kelly watches me closely when I am speaking to Julie, and I often feel that she is observing me in order to give Julie advice about how to handle her problematic mother.

Jacob has made the point to me that I would probably be more welcoming and flexible if he brought a girlfriend along as often as Julie brings Kelly. I know he's right, but it isn't likely that he would have a girlfriend with such a passive-aggressive vibe. Anyway, Jacob doesn't let me meet his girlfriends, a regrettable and unfair policy based on his erroneous belief that I am "intrusive" and "controlling" and "don't respect boundaries," which was perhaps somewhat true when he was younger and less mature, but it is not a fair characterization. I don't press him. I am optimistic that one day soon, when Jacob is ready, I will meet Becky, the girl he has been seeing for a while now. (A law student at Yale, a runner and a devotee of early music, she is very articulate and intelligent, and quite devoted to Jacob, based on the emails I read over a few months' time, before Jacob changed his password. He uses "jakezip" for so many of his passwords, though I have advised him repeatedly that diverse passwords are far more secure.)

CANDYCON WAS LIKE any candy show; it was hectic and crowded, and there were problems with the electrical supply and confusion over the rental delivery, but we got set up. Jacob had burned a CD from Howard's old Everly Brothers album, so we had "Wake Up, Little Susie" playing, we had organized our space according to our usual show planagram, and Jacob and Julie had done a great job with the displays. We had order sheets with our usual lines and a new space for Little Susies orders, with some special show discounts and deals for orders placed at the booth.

There was some Little Susies buzz even before the show doors officially opened; lots of nearby vendors had checked us out, drawn by our music, plus we had better real estate on the floor than ever before. Instead of being shunted off among the start-ups and really small companies like the nice Glee Gum people from Providence, or those ambitious Sweetriot women from New York, for once our space was in the middle of the action, across from Tootsie Roll, which may have suited us a little more than it suited them, since there is that slightly uneasy kinship between Little Sammies and that primal Ellis Island Tootsie Roll of Eli's. Call it the anxiety of influence. But they're enormous and we're small, and they've been in business since 1896 and we started in 1924, and they can afford to tolerate our existence.

The morning went well. There was a good, upbeat atmosphere at the show, and everyone was psyched for what felt like a strong back-to-school and Halloween season. A number of vendors greeted me with real warmth, and a few told me it was good to see me at this show, because they had heard that things were up in the air at Zip's. I knew they were speaking of Howard's departure from our marriage, which had fueled the inevitable speculation about the future of the business. All the more reason to have a strong presence, with a new product to showcase, to make it clear to everyone across the industry that Zip's Candies was doing just fine, better than ever.

In a momentary lull, I had an intriguing conversation with a reporter who was interested in the Little Susies, though she admitted she wasn't really there to cover the show, and was actually writing a novel about a candy company. She quizzed me rather insistently on my thoughts about Jewish family-owned candy companies. Why did I think so many had been founded by Jewish immigrants: Sam Born, who came to America in 1910; Sam Altshuler, who arrived in 1917; Eli Ziplinsky, who landed in 1920; Nathan Radutsky, who started Joyva halvah, who arrived in 1907; David Goldenberg, who invented Peanut Chews, who came in 1880; and so on.

I thought about what she was asking. Perhaps the candy business was one that offered opportunity to immigrants with few resources. What other product could be developed for a few pennies and made in a pot on a stove, or at a kitchen table, with everyone in the family helping to do something, stir the pot or wrap the finished pieces? They might have recipes from the old country that would appeal to people from the same background living in their neighborhood, and they could sell their product on the street with no overhead. I had never considered the pattern in quite this way before.

After lunch there was a flurry at our booth, with a lot of people specifically coming over to grab a Little Sammies/Little Susies pack. Because we didn't want to run out of stock on the first day, we had to be selective about giving them out. At any show you waste a certain amount of product on giveaways to other vendors, or to people with press passes who aren't going to be writing about your product, or to bloggers who might be planning to rave about your product or diss your product but who are also cruising for free samples they can then offer up in giveaway contests on their blogs. A certain amount of that is fine, and all of it is ordinary and expectable at a trade show like this. We tried to get selective and target the buyers without being rude to anyone who really wanted a Little Sammies / Little Susies pack. The booth was now weirdly mobbed, with a lot of younger people, a lot of journalists with blog and website credentials. Julie was looking unhappy and overwhelmed, trying to deal with people. Two of our new, young workers had not come back from lunch on time, and we were shorthanded, struggling to keep up with samples and questions. The hundredth repetition of the Everly Brothers singing "Wake Up, Little Susie" was getting on my nerves, and it was making me miss Howard, too, which also got on my nerves. I turned down the sound a little. Why were we getting slammed all of a sudden?

The reporter who was really a novelist was back. She semaphored urgently to me over the heads of the buyers and journalists thronging our little counter area, and I waved her to come around the side into the booth and talk to me. Did I know about the live blogging, she wanted to know. I didn't have a clue what she was talking about, but I thought Julie might, so I asked her to repeat her question to Julie, and a moment later Julie was sprinting off to the exhibitors' break room, where she could go online. When she returned, she looked stricken.

❊ ❊

To PUT IT bluntly, the white Little Susie snuggled in between the two brown Little Sammies apparently struck a certain snarky culture blogger with a devoted following as a representation not only of tawdry, three-way sex, but also of tawdry, three-way, mixed-race sex. Candy miscegenation. I pushed my way through the people standing expectantly around the Zip's Candies booth and reached into one of the open boxes under the counter for a pack of Little Sammies / Little Susies. I turned away and opened it, trying to look with the eyes of a stranger, to see how it would strike me if I had never laid eyes on them before. I was startled.

They were wedged together shoulder to shoulder, Little Sammie / Little Susie / Little Sammie. It did sort of look as if they were three in a bed. I tried to see it the way the blogger had apparently seen it, the innocent, creamy white Little Susie, lying there, flanked by glistening black savages. Was it obscene? Did it really seem like an erotic representation of what he was calling a "chocolate sandwich"? Another blogger was apparently analyzing the "Wake Up, Little Susie" lyrics line by line, to demonstrate our intentional erotic message.

I know I made a terrible mistake, not anticipating the error in our packaging presentation, but none of us had seen it. When you are overly focused on your product, you lose the ability to view it with fresh eyes, the way the public might see it. Two years ago, Mill Farm Gummi Lighthouses got a lot of unwanted candy blog attention because somebody noticed that if you turn them on their sides, each one looks like a colorful penis and testicles, which was presumably not something the Mill Farm people had ever considered or aspired to. But when you look at them now (on the Web), you can hardly believe they shipped them.

I realize our packaging decision seems utterly foolish in retrospect, but I can only say again that not one person who handled the packaging as we made those prototype handouts for CandyCon anticipated how a white Little Susie would look nestle between two brown Little Sammies. Let me be really clear about this: nobody who was aware of the time and energy and money that were poured into the Little Susies development could possibly think that I had anything but the best interests of the company at heart. I know it was a good brand extension. I know what my state of mind was, and it is deeply insulting to suggest that any action of mine was deliberately calculated to drive down the value of Zip's Candies just as it was under consideration by a serious buyer in ongoing negotiations with Howard's duplicitous lawyer. Since this possibility, the potential takeover of Zip's Candies, had been actively concealed from me, it is an outrageous suggestion, accusing me of having acted with that knowledge to sabotage a potential sale of the business. I am the betrayed, not the betrayer. I know what Sam would have said: your best teacher is your last mistake.

I TRIED TO remain calm. Surely this blog thing was not a major problem? Anyone who thought the sight of these candies lined up together was suggestive would presumably go into spasm over the incipient orgy in a tin of sardines. Was it possible the bloggers weren't serious at all, they were just having fun, doing what they do, riffing on the material? Candy bloggers can have a certain sardonic tone, as we well know. (I think Mumbo Jumbos deserve more than a 2.5 on the AndyCandy scale, for example.

And I think Sugarbomb was unnecessarily harsh about the occasional summer leakage problem in Tigermelts.)

Julie couldn't be calm with me. She was convinced that once something like this gets onto the Web, it is linked and repeated everywhere, and you don't know who is going to take it seriously as a deliberate statement on our part. After all, think of all the people who fall for stories in *The Onion*. Kelly, who had now rematerialized breathlessly, amped up on sugar and toting a bag spilling over with samples from all over the show, reported that Little Susies were being talked about everywhere she went on the floor. In a good way? I asked optimistically. She said she thought we were in deep shit. She's immensely irritating, but she was right.

Within the hour Julie reported that there were more than three hundred new posts on the Little Sammies forum, and her mailbox was flooded with questions and comments of one kind or another from our website form. Our website server crashed at some point later that day, the traffic was so intense. And we hadn't even had time to update the site with an image of Little Susies, though we had intended to, so the only mention was the teaser Julie had added a few weeks earlier, about how anyone attending CandyCon in New York would meet the newest member of the Ziplinsky Candy Family, come see us at the show! So people hoping to find a picture of this controversial candy artifact were frustrated, and they left a lot of angry and obscene comments.

It took only a few hours for the viral tsunami to hit. Of course it jumped from the blogosphere to television and print media, especially since everyone is always looking to cover a trade show like this with a new angle. They had found their story. What followed with the wire stories, all the press coverage, was a terrible déjà vu of the Blessed Chocolate Virgin coverage, which was of course among the first items anyone searching for references to Zip's Candies would find, which in turn led to yet another airing of the fire story from 1975, and how I was once known as Arson Girl (the way it might be said of someone that she was the Munger Potato Festival Queen of 1975). Add to that an endless exponential web of interconnected blog and Internet mentions that persist to this day.

You can find references to Little Susies and Little Sammies on websites devoted to preserving the purity of the white race; you can find references on numerous sites that also use the key-word *kike* (given the Ziplinsky heritage, I suppose that was inevitable). There is a website with lyrics for a version of the Little Sammies jingle that begin "Little Sammies are for you / If you are a hook-nosed Jew." Some of the white supremacy web-sites have put us on a list of companies whose products should be boycotted permanently. (Did anyone seriously believe that Zip's Candies was using this product launch to subversively put for-ward a positive image of mixed-race threesomes?)

There are some pornographic images on the Web, involving a sex-crazed Little Susie with two very well-endowed Little Sammies having their way with her. Julie tells me Little Susie threesomes will be on the Web until the end of time. They are horribly easy to find now, in any case. There are endless num-bers of obscene videos of crudely animated Little Sammies and Little Susies in motion, on YouTube and elsewhere, and there are thousands of images on the Web that all seem to follow the same format, with one white something between two dark somethings (kittens, shoes, cows in a field, wine bottles, cars, etc.), captioned with the implicitly suggestive punch line, "Say, Dat's Tasty!"

Some of the videos of animated figures remind me of the awk-ward Claymation of *Gumby* television shows of my childhood.

(Gumby's mother was Gumba, and his father was Gumbo.) If you soften Little Sammies briefly in the microwave, they become temporarily pliable, though the coating will lose its gloss when it cools. I imagine this is what was done for the porno Little Sammies; their fudgy genitals were sculpted out of parts of other Little Sammies and stuck on their bodies while they were still warm.

Loose Little Susies and unopened Little Susies–stickered Little Sammies packs that we gave away at the CandyCon were a hot eBay item for a while, and there were even, weirdly enough (think of the effort involved), some counterfeits.

The blogger who started the whole thing—Leonard Blatt is his actual name, but being an ironic hipster with literary pretensions, on his blog, Kretschmar's Lunch, he is known as Vivian Darkbloom—has made quite the name for himself with his particular brand of deadpan prudery. At the peak of the Little Susies nightmare, he wrote me an email to tell me that he had really enjoyed Little Susies, and was very sorry that his actions had contributed to their being unavailable indefinitely. He offered to begin a "Bring Back Little Susies!" blog campaign, but I emailed him back to tell him he had done enough.

10

She saw every relationship as a pair of intersecting circles. It would seem at first glance that the more they overlapped the better the relationship; but this is not so. Beyond a certain point the law of diminishing returns sets in, and there are not enough private resources left on either side to enrich the life that is shared. Probably perfection is reached when the area of the two outer crescents, added together, is exactly equal to that of the leaf-shaped piece in the middle. On paper there must be some neat mathematical formula for arriving at this; in life, none.

—JAN STRUTHER, *Mrs. Miniver*

WE DID NOT HAVE enough private resources, Howard and I, to enrich our shared life. I loved him with all my heart, such as it is, but he never loved me with all of his. Howard chose to reserve his most private and precious resources a world away, while I poured my heart and soul into Zip's Candies and the Ziplinsky family, thinking we were in it together, for life. The maintenance of an enduring marriage is a process sensitive to both time and temperature. You have to balance and maintain the heat over the years. Too much heat can melt even tigers, as we know. But we had a good, rich life, one that could have endured. Of course, over time, there are infinite adjustments to make, and make again. It always comes down to time and temperature. Good tempering is essential for durability. A badly tempered marriage becomes dull and brittle, and then it breaks.

HOWARD, HOWARD, HOWARD. The love of my life is a shmuck (who taught me the word *shmuck*). The love of my life turns out to be Carson McCullers's "most mediocre person," who can be the object of a love which is "wild, extravagant, and beautiful as the poison lilies of the swamp."

I AM SORRY about the Little Sammies I put in the gas tank of Howard's ridiculous Porsche Boxster in the Zip's Candies parking lot the week before he left. I take full responsibility for the expense involved in replacing all the engine parts that were clogged when the dissolved Little Sammies passed through the fuel injector as Howard was driving on the Wilbur Cross Parkway. However, I take no responsibility for the added inconvenience and expense of the car's breaking down inside the West Rock Tunnel, which would not have happened if he had followed my advice to avoid the parkway, especially in the late afternoon, and instead, when driving from East Rock to the Yale Golf Course, always to take Morse Street to Fitch Street to Fountain Street. How many times have I told him that this is the best route?

Also, I shouldn't have put Howard's Patek Philippe watch in the Cuisinart. I was frustrated, but it was wrong. I will pay for another if it is important to Howard that even if he no longer cares to know the day of the week, he has an insanely overpriced watch that offers "timeless aesthetic perfection," and is "not merely a method of telling time [but also] a silent statement about your values," a watch that has "the ability to create an emotional response." Instead of, you know, a Timex or something.

My willingness to accept responsibility for these two uncharacteristically destructive and immature actions, which I took at a moment of extreme emotional distress, should be considered further proof of my honesty and integrity.

The most fundamental business philosophy Sam ever told me to write down, "We'll cross that bridge when we come to it" and "There's no use crying over spilled milk," are useless beliefs when it comes to running Zip's Candies. Our philosophy must be: first cross every possible bridge in your imagination. And spilled milk is the only kind worth crying over.

HOWARD TOOK A little more than four hundred thousand dollars of company funds out of the business over the last four years. He tried to hide this theft and spread it around through various accounts, but after he left for Madagascar, the company books turned out to be a big, sugarcoated mess. After one meeting, I cut loose Howard's sleazy friend and accountant (and accomplice), the despicable Marty Shapiro, and hired a new accountant as part of my effort to pull Zip's Candies together.

Casper Weisswasser is probably a high-functioning autistic of some kind. He's a cross between Kaspar Hauser and Casper the Friendly Ghost. Large and pale and awkward, he seems surprised by ordinary clichés, as if he has never heard anyone say anything like "When it rains it pours" or "If you can't beat 'em, join 'em." He was amazed when I told him his name means "white water." He speaks in a slightly loud monotone, as if making announcements in a bus station through a PA system, and he identifies himself to me in full every time he phones, even if we have already spoken several times within the hour. Casper has that perfect accountant's obsessive ability to make order out of disorder. Order, disorder, counterorder. That's what Sam always said when a line broke down. That's how I live my life.

The money Howard took apparently seeped into his Madagascar bank accounts in increments, laundered through various Czaplinsky accounts, with padded billing and duplicate payments. I am not going to make any claims about the money now. I don't want to hurt the Bao-Bar venture, and the business relationship between Ziplinsky and Czaplinsky interests is too valuable to damage that way. The money signifies to me (the way a dagger in the heart signifies), because it tells me how long it has been since Howard had any intention of staying here, in his Connecticut life with me. I now realize that he left me long before he actually left.

The stolen money is spilled milk, a minor spill in the larger scheme of things, the kind worth shedding just a few tears over, to be sure, especially when I think about the ways I have juggled shifts to keep the lines running at maximum efficiency, and shaved expenditures all over the plant, and bargained with all of our suppliers so hard that Manny Feldman, who sells us our corn syrup and sugar complained to me a few months ago, "You really Jewed me down on that last order."

SAM SUGGESTED THAT I become a notary public, which I did, twenty years ago. It's a useful thing for any business, having an in-house notary. He also encouraged me to learn how to do his signature perfectly, which was useful for signing checks, or if anything else came up requiring authorization, when he and Frieda were in Deerfield Beach every February for so many years. You see how much he trusted me? It was our little secret.

❋ ❋

THE ZIP'S CANDIES fire occurred on a Sunday, when I knew I was unlikely to be detected, because I wanted to burn a large quantity of papers efficiently and discreetly. I used two of the three empty fifty-gallon drums that were on the loading dock. I didn't use the third one because it had a couple of inches of liquid in the bottom, which I assumed, erroneously as it turned out, was rainwater. It is beyond obvious that I was not in any way trying to cause damage to the premises of Zip's Candies, or I would not have set a fire out on the loading dock when I had full access to every corner of the building and could have in fact burned the place to the ground very efficiently if I so chose, by setting the fire in the basement.

When the third drum blew up, igniting everything on the loading dock, the only damage to the building was to the roof overhang on the loading dock, which was in terrible condition anyway, and had been patched and patched again over the years. A mess of framing and plywood with several layers of buckling tar-paper patches laid down haphazardly for quick rainwater leak prevention (Howard's management style, not mine), the roof got scorched when a stack of wooden pallets ignited.

I have had an intention for quite a while now to reroof our entire premises with standing seam metal, perhaps in a cheerful green to echo the Zip's umbrella, which is of course an echo of Little Black Sambo's green umbrella. The cost of new roofing would be approximately a hundred thousand dollars, however, and it is not in our budget at this time. We lost the original Zip's Candies "Say, Dat's Tasty!" sign, too, the only serious loss from the explosion. I do think the fire would have burned out on its own even if the fire department hadn't responded to a 911 call from someone who saw the black smoke rising and thought the empty Bigelow Boiler complex beside us was on fire.

The Zip's Candies building stands on ground with an ironic (to me) history. The corner of James Street and River Street lies at the edge of a filled swamp old maps call Grapevine Point. This very corner was the site of the administration building for Camp Terry, which was a compound of nine barracks erected to house Connecticut's two Colored Civil War Regiments, the 29th and the 30th, while they were trained for battle. (Today the parade ground is Criscuolo Park.) Governor William Alfred Buckingham brokered the sale of the land to the U.S. Army by Yale University, in order to avoid the risk of colored troops, armed with rifles, being drilled on the New Haven Green, where many other Connecticut regiments had been trained. After the war ended, the army disposed of the property, and the Bigelow Boiler complex of buildings was erected on the site. Thirty years later, the Peet brothers bought one of the smaller Bigelow buildings for their short-lived enterprise.

THOSE FIFTY-GALLON DRUMS had held Czaplinsky Pure Madagascar Vanilla, which is highly inflammable, being two-hundred-proof ethyl alcohol. The drums should not have been left on the loading dock like that, especially not unrinsed, and with one of them containing several inches of vanilla extract. It was an extraordinarily careless waste of one of the most expensive commodities we use, and I am conducting an investigation to find the person who deemed that drum empty. The stacked wooden shipping pallets should have been disposed of properly or recycled, not left to pile up like that on our loading dock. Also, the decaying roof on the loading dock should have been replaced with a standing seam metal overhang years ago, even if we weren't ready to reroof the entire building, but Howard kept deferring the expense.

That all these elements of danger were present on the loading dock demonstrates to me that I have failed to maintain the high management standards that should always govern Zip's Candies. It should have been perfectly safe for me to burn documents in those two drums, undetected, without mishap. The material safety data sheet on Czaplinsky's Pure Madagascar Vanilla says: "Pure vanilla has a flash point of 60 degrees Fahrenheit. The flammable limits are in the upper 19 percent. The product is highly flammable in the presence of open flames and sparks. The risks of explosions of the product are low. Containers should be grounded. Vanilla extract may burn with a near-invisible flame. Vapor may travel considerable distance to source of ignition and flashback."

Admittedly, I wasn't thinking about that when I lit fire to those papers. But I maintain that if all three drums had been empty and rinsed, the fire would have burned uneventfully, and my actions would have gone undetected. I take full responsibility for the fire getting out of control as it did. There are no bad soldiers, only bad officers.

NOT THAT ANYONE other than Julie and Jacob has asked, but I was not on the loading dock when the explosion occurred, because my BlackBerry signal was weak and I had jumped down into the parking lot to get more bars so I could look at my email while the papers burned. So I wasn't injured.

IF ANYONE IS going to be accused of acting with fraud and malice, it shouldn't be me. (And in memory of Miss Solomon and in honor of all that she taught me, I would like to point out that one doesn't act "with fraud and malice," one acts "fraudulently and with malice.") There is no extant evidence that I have done anything malicious or fraudulent. And despite the explosion, everything I wanted to destroy was in fact successfully incinerated. I could have spared myself all the ridiculous attention this fire has brought if I had only used our shredder. It would have taken me a few hours, and that would have been that. But there is no beauty in shredding, no grace.

WHAT I BURNED: all the documentation and correspondence I have described in this affidavit, and much more that I haven't described. All the significant files of Zip's Candies, going back to 1924. I'm not crazy. Nothing that affects day-to-day operations is gone. Copies of our tax returns and current personnel files have been retained. All the invoicing, all the billing, accounts receivable, everything to do with the ordinary business of the factory, that's all intact. All current contracts and documentation pertaining to the plant operations are untouched.

I burned every scrap of paper about the numerous lawsuits over the years, all the litigation, all the settlement agreements, all the correspondence about stolen recipes and agreements of nondisclosure with Hodgson relatives and a few others. I burned the stolen Peanut Charms recipe scribbled in pencil in Eli's slashy scrawl on a yellowed Hodgson Sweet Shoppe envelope. I burned all the drafts of wills, letters of intent, promissory notes, agreements about company loans to family members that were never repaid. I burned all the notes about the creation of the Ziplinsky Family Trust (a highly ironic name for a legal instrument, when you think about it).

I burned the agreement between Howard and Sam, promising Howard the business if he married me and stayed in New Haven until he was forty-five years old.

I burned all the blackmailing letters with pretty Madagascar stamps on the envelopes from Huxley to Sam, starting with infant photos of Newton in 1976, the ones from 1982 with photos of Edison, and the more recent ones as well, with photos of Howard and his sons and their mother, his second cousin Huxley, who claimed, in childish print on the back of the photo, to be the true love of his life. May I just say that even though it's not literally incest, surely this attraction is a little incestuous? Maybe if you're a Ziplinsky, nobody but family is ever really good enough.

I burned all the correspondence from 1946 concerning a planned agreement between Julius and Eli, granting each a 25 percent interest in the other's holdings. This was to be the first step in Eli's ambitious plan to follow the Hershey's model of ownership interest in suppliers. The Ziplinsky/Czaplinsky brothers would form a mutually beneficial alliance. If Milton Hershey found it worthwhile to grow sugarcane in Cuba, then Zip's Candies would have its own cacao and vanilla in Madagascar. Sam told me about this. He found both copies of this agreement on Eli's desk the day he found Eli dead in his office. Eli had just signed and dated the documents earlier that same day, a few minutes before closing time, on that Friday afternoon, with Rosalie Fleischer, his secretary in those years, domiciled at 266 Orange Street, New Haven, Connecticut, as his witness. Sam never sent Julius his executed copy, though Julius outlived Eli by two years.

Sam buried the contracts in the safe, and when Julius wrote in response to the news of Eli's death, inquiring about the agreement they had made, Sam took his time writing back, and when he did, he was deliberately vague, saying he didn't really know much about this matter but would look into it, and then he made sure to put inadequate postage on the letter, which he addressed with slightly wrong spellings. The delay in the correspondence bought several months. Julius wrote again, and Sam replied just as slowly and vaguely. He really hadn't decided what to do, Sam told me, he just hadn't yet come to any conclusion about whether or not it was in the best interest of Zip's Candies to honor the agreement, and so there were a few more such letters back and forth, and then Julius died.

Sam didn't destroy those contracts when he should have. And so I have done it for him. They're gone now. Everything is gone, everything on the loading dock burned to ash in that aromatic, white-hot blaze.

FIRE DESTROYS. BUT fire also can cleanse and purify. Fire is life, but fire also is damnation. We speak of fiery passions, fiery tempers, flaming arguments, flaming assholes, flaming homosexuals. Ellie Quest-Greenspan said that Jung saw fire as a symbol of transformation. Dr. Gibraltar told me that Freud believed fire symbolizes the libido. Well, duh. Freud thought that human beings were wired to piss on flames, only some of us end up being relegated to the domestic sphere because we can't. He wrote that it is "as though woman had been appointed guardian of the fire which was held captive on the domestic hearth, because her anatomy made it impossible for her to yield to the temptation of this desire."

LANGUAGE HAS THE ability to express and to conceal. The sentence is one of the great inventions we've got, as elemental as fire and the wheel. Sentences like the ones I have been using can enlighten and enhance meaning, or deny it and undermine it. Sentences such as the ones Irene has used to level all of her baseless, mendacious accusations tell her story, not mine. Irene calls my words wild. Are my words wild? I certainly hope so. Keynes said words ought to be a little wild, for they are the assaults of thoughts on the unthinking. Think! Think, Irene! This, *this* is my story.

I HAVE BURNED all the documents, the real ones and the ones I made up. Trust me, or don't trust me. Either way, they're all gone now. According to some sentences I have been reading, Alice Ziplinsky embellishes. She is unreliable and she makes things up. She has a distorted sense of the events that surround these conflicts, and she has acted with fraud and with malice. She was responsible for fiscal mismanagement over the past decade when in a position of unwarranted authority. Alice Ziplinsky is unwilling to turn over documents and threatens to destroy them. Her actions have caused the company to lose value at a sensitive time when potential buyers will be alienated, thereby precluding the completion of a preliminary agreement for an unnamed large corporation to make an offer to shareholders for the purchase agreement concerning Zip's Candies premises as well as full license to produce Little Sammies, Tigermelts, and Mumbo Jumbos.

If I am that Alice Ziplinsky, then perhaps there never were any documents such as the ones I have described. Who knows what I burned? Maybe I have made it all up. Maybe I'm losing it, like Frieda, and all I burned were old meaningless invoices and bills. Nothing of what I have described in all my many precise sentences is legally binding without documentation.

Where's the evidence? Am I reliable, as Sam asked me that

first day? Who has been more reliable over these years? Who, who has ever been more loyal to Zip's Candies and the Ziplinsky family?

Nobody will ever know which signatures of Sam's are really mine. Comparisons of everything he signed in the last twenty years of his life would be meaningless. Whose signatures match, his to his, mine to mine? The testamentary Ziplinsky Family Trust instrument has been accepted by the Probate Court of New Haven. The appeals were denied. What's done is done.

HOWARD OWNS 15 percent of Zip's Candies. I own 35 percent. The Ziplinsky Family Trust owns the other half of the business. Samuel Ziplinsky's grandchildren share equally in the Ziplinsky Family Trust. That is the letter of the law, but it is also the spirit of Sam's intentions. How many slices of this pie are there?

It's not three, Irene; it's five. Each grandchild—Newton, Ethan, Jacob, Edison, and Julie—owns 10 percent of Zip's Candies. Whether we agree in the end that Howard is the third trustee of the Ziplinsky Family Trust or I am, the five grandchildren are the beneficiaries, and in this Howard and I are in rare agreement. Did you believe, Irene, that you could count on my rage over Howard's betrayal to blind me to fairness? Did you think I would be as greedy on behalf of my two children as you have been on behalf of your son? That greed by proxy has no influence. Fortunately Ethan doesn't support your position. Nobody does. And beyond my sense of fairness, my clarity on this matter is that much sharper because of my unwillingness to agree with you, Irene, about anything at all, if I can possibly help it.

Newton and Edison are Howard's children, Howard's issue. The trust language could only have been clearer if Sam had named each of his grandchildren individually, but that's not relevant. There are five grandchildren, five living issue of Sam's two living children.

And as to your outrageous, faux-generous "offer"—can't you see it's not yours to offer, Irene?—that Newton and Edison could share a quarter interest in the trust? That's absolutely out of the question. Either they are Howard's issue, or they are not, and since they most certainly are (and your suggestion that we demand paternity testing is pathetic and mean and pointless; just look at them!), they are each entitled to full recognition as a grandchild of Sam Ziplinsky's, and an equal share in the Ziplinsky Family Trust, whether you like it or not. I would have thought you would be pleased to have two brown nephews. Apparently, when it gets personal, your greed trumps your sanctimonious virtue.

Sam recognized that giving Newton and Edison their fair share would be the best way to bind Howard to Zip's Candies, if not to me and to his life here. Ownership of Zip's Candies binds us all together, except for you, Irene, and you've been fully compensated. These were Sam's intentions for his family and for his business.

Can we move on now, with malice toward none, with charity for all? Can we strive to finish the work we are in, to do all which may achieve and cherish a just and lasting peace among ourselves, as Abraham Lincoln suggested so long ago in an admittedly different but certainly not ungermane context?

WHICH BRINGS ME to a significant Zip's Candies decision. And in case it isn't clear by now—we're not selling! With my 35 percent ownership plus Jacob and Julie's combined 20 percent, we three Ziplinskys control more than half ownership of the company. They don't want to sell. Not now. The Bao-Bar is a huge success, with exponentially increasing sales every month. It's not clear how much longer we will be able to keep up with orders at this rate, and the time is coming very soon to expand our production capabilities. As it is, we're running Tigermelt production on that line only two or three days at a time every fourth week. The Bao-Bar has become the tail wagging that cat. It's an exciting development for Zip's Candies, both because it's extremely profitable and because it's a completely new product developed by the fourth generation of the family, who are prepared to take Zip's Candies into the future and make it their own.

WHEN PRESIDENT OBAMA was sworn in, and I watched George W. Bush as he stood there during the ceremony, grimacing and smirking and shifting his weight like a child enduring church, I found myself thinking about Howard's unconscionable breaking of his word to me in 2000 that he wouldn't send his DKE brother those congratulatory Little Sammies. And as Julie and I watched the inaugural pageant on television over our reheated leftover vegetable chow fun, seeing those two little girls with their mother gazing adoringly at their father, feeling the weight of that historic moment, like so many of us who felt betrayed for so long by the policies and actions of our government, I was moved, and I was proud. Dignity and grace have been missing for too long.

Julie, well aware of the history of that inscribed photo of W. on the wall in my office, asked me if I was thinking of sending some candy to the White House to welcome the Obama family. We looked at each other for a long moment. How could I? And I came to a realization. I have been thinking about it ever since that January day. Now, seven months on, I am certain. The time has come to end production of Little Sammies.

Of course it has. I have discussed this with Julie and Jacob, who agree. It's become an embarrassment to pretend they're fine, to act as if those who perceive Little Sammies to be racist and vulgar should lighten up and not be so PC. For all these years as a Ziplinsky, and as a representative of Zip's Candies (Sam used to tell every employee and every family member that we should never forget that every day, in every way, we were each Zip's Candies ambassadors), I have taken the position that Little Sammies are amusing, they're retro, it was Eli's innocent misperception, of course we're not racists, so how can our candy be racist?

But Little Sammies are really not okay. "Say, Dat's Tasty!" is not an acceptable slogan any longer, and it hasn't been for years. It's time to put Little Sammies on the shelf next to Amos 'n' Andy and Al Jolson in blackface. We've had a good run, but it's over. We are better than that. We can do better than that.

We won't simply stop production of our most successful line. This is the perfect moment to introduce a new product. We won't have to start from scratch. We have almost everything we need to go into production very quickly, after announcing the end of Little Sammies, and before we do that, we should run a final production limited edition of a few hundred thousand, with a commemorative wrapper designation, 1924–2009, which will sell like hotcakes.

The farewell to Little Sammies will be an excellent platform for the launch of our new line, which we will be able to run on the Little Sammies equipment. If our wholesalers and retailers aren't smart enough to make big buys of our new line, we can scrounge up some slotting-fee money to get the product out there in key markets, and I am certain it will succeed. I have an

instinctive feel for these things. It shouldn't be difficult to generate excellent publicity for this transition, with Julie and Jacob
speaking for the company as the next generation. It becomes a
human interest story, a classic American success story. Eli's
great-grandchildren take Zip's Candies into the future. I will
announce my intention to step down within the next five years.
We will court the candy bloggers. Julie will know the best way
to do that.

Jacob will delegate some of the Bao-Bar production supervision in order to work with me on refining the manufacturing
recipe so we can go into production. There is no reason to jetti-
son the humanoid form. We can modify the Little Sammies
mogul molds to make something more modern and streamlined
in shape, genderless and featureless (a bit like the Academy
Award Oscar statuette, but plumper and smoother), but within
the same basic Little Sammies dimensions and specs.

What I envision will be a pair of pieces that will be packaged
together. The first one will have a solid white-chocolate core, a
white chocolate as good as we can make it, using pure Czaplinsky vanilla and high-quality cocoa butter. Frankly, I would want
to aim for something very equivalent to the Green & Black's
white chocolate, with as comparable a flavor and mouthfeel as
we can achieve. But, in memory of Sam, ours will be just a little
saltier. We will pan this piece with the Little Sammies coating, so
they will have that same familiar, shiny finish, but perhaps with
a darker chocolate, one with a lower sugar content in keeping
with contemporary taste.

The second piece will have the identical form, but the core
will be an increment smaller, and it will be made with our original, fudgy Little Sammies recipe, which will give this new line
the familiarity and continuity of a brand extension, and will
appease those aficionados who will mourn the end of Little Sam-

mies. (If only Peter Paul had offered something similarly compensatory to the Caravelle mourners!) We will coat this piece in white chocolate. In other words, we will use the Little Susies formulation, but the two pieces together will match, and will share this new, identical, genderless shape. We will package them as a pair, and by selling two instead of three in a pack, we can keep the unit pricing in the Little Sammies range, despite the higher-quality ingredients, which will cost us more, piece for piece. They will be delectable. This new line will be what Sam, and Eli before him, would have called a true confection.

Of course, in the most basic sense that matters most to the consumer, this new piece isn't exactly new, but has the appealing blend of familiarity and newness, since it is in some ways a reintroduced upgrade of Little Sammies. I am reminded of the brilliant Post Shreddies campaign that Ogilvy & Mather started a couple of years ago in Canada. Shreddies is a shredded-wheat square breakfast cereal that was cleverly relaunched with a tongue-in-cheek campaign promoting new Diamond Shreddies, which were simply the same old square Shreddies viewed from a different angle. (The Third Reich did precisely the same thing with the traditional swastika form by turning it forty-five degrees.) They even marketed boxes promising a "combo pack," with both square and diamond Shreddies in equal proportion. Sales, which had been stagnant, exploded.

For the new wrapper, I'd like to keep the continuity of a Zip's umbrella, but without color, with the name of the candy in white on a black umbrella, against a checkerboard background, all in black and white (a subtle tip of the hat to the Abba-Zaba checkerboard border, to be sure, but surely they can't copyright such a universal design as a checkerboard). I think the time is just right in our history, as a candy company and as a nation, if I may say that without sounding too grand, for a black-and-white contrasting piece such as this. And I mean black and white in every sense.

During the Little Susies crisis, Julie told me that the term "white chocolate" is ghetto slang for two things with opposite meanings. Intriguingly enough, the term can be used to deride a black person who acts white, and it can also be used to deride a white person who acts black. Surely this is an excellent moment for this paired candy piece with something to say, one white on the outside and brown on the inside, and the other brown on the outside but white on the inside.

I have been thinking long and hard about what to name this new line, and I believe I have come up with the perfect name, one that has a friendly and cheerful sensibility, yet sounds timeless and classic, like Oh Henry! Julie and Jacob have agreed to it, if Howard doesn't object. It will be in his best interest not to object. Who knows, he might even like it. We will call this new candy the Say Howdy!

WHEN I WAS pouring starter fluid on the papers, and when I struck the match, and as I fed the sheets to the flames, I found myself, college degree or not, thinking about not just the selflessness but also the literariness of my act. I did, after all, intend to major in English at Middlebury, and as these pages should have made abundantly evident to any reader, despite the turns my life has taken, I have educated myself. And I thought about how Thomas Carlyle's only copy of the manuscript for *The French Revolution,* which he had sent over to his friend John Stuart Mill, was thrown in the fire by Mill's maid. Carlyle rewrote it. So many other significant pages have gone up in smoke. Thomas Moore burned Byron's memoirs. Jane Austen's sister Cassandra burned her letters. Henry James burned . . . well, we don't really know what he burned.

Kafka wanted *The Trial* burned, but he was thwarted. If Nabokov was serious about wanting his last, unfinished novel to be destroyed, he should have done it himself. It is rare to find sufficient loyalty when it comes to honoring such a request. Miss Tita, though a fictional character, is an example to emulate, burning the Aspern letters one by one as she did, in order to honor her aunt's intentions. I believe that my burning of all the old files and documents at Zip's Candies was the best way I could honor Sam's intentions. And that's the truth.

"Truth is truth to the end of reckoning." That's Shakespeare, Irene, *Measure for Measure,* which I happen to know you have never read or probably even heard of because you haven't been curious about what you don't know for a very long time, not since college. And even then, when that expensive education was at your disposal, when you could have done anything, gone anywhere, studied anything, thought about anything, you didn't have time for Shakespeare, because you were too busy reading about gendered space in the workplace and the sociology of heterosexuality and feminist environmentalism.

HOWARD ZIPLINSKY MADE me a member of this family, and now he is living a world away, where he is the Grandest Tiger in the Jungle, even though he left most of his beautiful shirts behind. He believes he has changed himself into the person he was always meant to be by living that life. Maybe I have changed myself, too, by finally accepting that I am also living the life I was meant to live.

I will end my affidavit here. Leonardo (it is as erudite to call him by his first name as it is uneducated to call him "Da Vinci") said that art is never finished, only abandoned, and I can only add that most everything important in life is never finished, not just art. Julie and Jacob are coming over for dinner so we can work on the details of the Say Howdy! launch. Madagascar is eight hours ahead of us, so if we wait until midnight, when it is his morning, they can call Howard and talk to him about the name of our new candy line (if they can get through to their father on that primitive telephone connection). It will be just the three of us on our own, like old times, when Howard was in Madagascar, and I would let the children stay up until midnight in order to call him while he was having his breakfast, because we missed him. Surely it's a perfect night for a breakfast-dinner. I have flour and eggs and milk and butter. I will make a huge big plate of the most lovely pancakes, as yellow and brown as little Tigers.

WITNESS MY SIGNATURE THIS FIFTEENTH DAY OF
AUGUST, 2009
SIGNATURE OF DECLARANT:

READING GROUP GUIDE FOR
TRUE CONFECTIONS

ALICE TATNALL ZIPLINSKY's marriage into the Ziplinsky family has not been unanimously celebrated. Her greatest ambition is to belong, to feel truly entitled to the heritage she has tried so hard to earn. Which is why Zip's Candies is much more to her than just a candy factory, where she has worked for most of her life. In *True Confections*, Alice has her reasons for telling the multigenerational saga of the family-owned-and-operated candy company, now in crisis.

Nobody is more devoted than Alice to delving into the truth of Zip's history, starting with the rags-to-riches story of how Hungarian immigrant Eli Czaplinsky developed his famous candy lines, and how each of his candies, from Little Sammies to Mumbo Jumbos, was inspired by an element in a stolen library copy of *Little Black Sambo*, from which he taught himself English. Within Alice's vivid and persuasive account (is her unreliability a tactic or a condition?) are the stories of a runaway slave from the cacao plantations of Côte d'Ivoire and the Third Reich's failed plan to establish a colony on Madagascar for European Jews.

Questions for Discussion

1. How reliable a narrator is Alice? Do you trust her? She observes the hidden meanings and subtle inflections all around her, but is she equally aware of her own subtexts?

2. Can you identify moments in each chapter of *True Confections* in which Alice adds meaning to what she experiences or

describes? Can you also identify moments in which Alice seems to overlook or gloss over meanings in what she experiences or describes?

3. Are Little Sammies racist? What does it really mean to be racist? If you are aware that others may define something you have said or done as racist even if it was not your intention, is it still racist?

4. *True Confessions* is a novel in which there are many instances of lies and deceptions. Alice stakes a claim for her own veracity, starting with the title of the book. What is the truth about the history and meaning of Willy Wonka's lovable Oompa-Loompas? What is the truth about the runaway boy from the cacao plantation of Côte d'Ivoire? What is Howard's relationship with his relatives in Madagascar? What is the truth about Frieda Ziplinsky's chicken soup recipe? Is Alice entirely innocent of the arson charges that seem to be a pattern in her life?

5. Why do you think Alice cheats on her psychoanalyst by seeing another therapist on the side?

6. Why is Alice so eager to become part of the Ziplinsky family?

7. Why is Alice's relationship with Sam Ziplinsky so much more successful than her relationship with Frieda Ziplinsky?

8. The Madagascar Plan is a historically true though unrealized goal of the Third Reich during World War II. Were it not for Julius Czaplinsky's ambitions when he learned of it, which in turn led to establishing a Madagascar branch of the Ziplinsky family, what do you imagine Alice's marriage to Howard Ziplinsky would have been like?

9. Did reading *True Confessions* change the way you think of chocolate? Did it make you crave candy? Which kind? Did you succumb? Did you gain weight while reading *True Confessions*?

10. What would it be like to have Alice Tatnall Ziplinsky as a member of your book group?

About the Author

KATHARINE WEBER is the author of the novels *Triangle, The Little Women, The Music Lesson,* and *Objects in Mirror Are Closer Than They Appear.* She lives in Connecticut with her husband, the cultural historian Nicholas Fox Weber, and teaches in the graduate writing program at Columbia University.

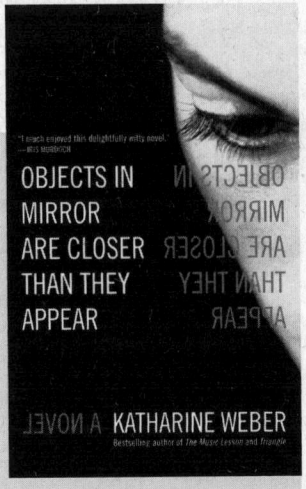